THE COMPLETE SERIES

EVA CHASE

Flirting with Monsters: The Complete Series

All rights reserved. This book or any portion thereof may not be reproduced or used in any manner without the express written permission of the author, except for the use of brief quotations in a book review.

This is a work of fiction. Any resemblance to actual persons, living or dead, or actual events is purely coincidental.

First Digital Edition, 2022

Copyright © 2022 Eva Chase

Cover design: Story Wrappers

Character illustration on interior cover: Alba Palacio

Ebook ISBN: 978-1-990338-44-1

Hardcover ISBN: 978-1-990338-45-8

SHADOW THIEF

FLIRTING WITH MONSTERS #1

ONE

Sorsha

The story of how I was going to end the world began not with a bang or a whimper but a kerplink.

The kerplink came from the latch of an arcanely ancient window lock hitting the sill as it disengaged. Adjusting my position on the ledge outside, I withdrew my equally ancient wedge and probe—gotta have tools that fit the job—from beneath the sash. At my tug, the window slid upward with a faint rasp.

Shadows draped the hallway on the other side even more densely than in the backyard below me, where the glow of the mansion's security lamps cut through the night. Less work for me. Dressed in black from head to toe, with my hands gloved to avoid fingerprints and my vibrant red hair tucked away under a knit hat, I blended in perfectly.

I slipped from the flutter of the warm summer breeze into the stillness of the hall and eased the window shut. The ceiling loomed high above. The tangy scent of wood polish tickled my nose. No doubt the floorboards that showed at the edges of the Persian rug gleamed like glass in daylight.

The thick rug handily absorbed my footsteps as I slunk along it, eyeing the doors. If I'd been able to get a good view from outside, I'd have snuck straight into the room I was aiming for, but with the coverings on the other windows, it'd been impossible to know whether I'd hit the jackpot or stumble onto inhabitants I wasn't looking to meet.

Looking around now, there were a couple of signs that this wasn't the home of your typical collector. Most of them kept the rest of their living space free of anything that would hint at their secret interests, a portrait of normality. Here, paintings of eerie, twisted forms with glowing eyes hung on the walls. Farther down, a patch of thicker darkness streaked across the pale paint of the ceiling as if it'd been scorched. What the heck had this dude gotten up to?

But then I spotted the door that had to lead to his collection room, and that question fell away behind a tingle of exhilaration.

I couldn't tell exactly what kind of security I was dealing with until I got right up close and flicked on the thinnest beam on my flashlight. The sight made me grimace. Son of a donkey's uncle.

In my experience, there were two kinds of collectors. Some went all in on traditionalism, preferring esoteric fixtures and devices of times past—the older the better—to match the nature of the creatures they'd stashed away. Others valued modern tech over keeping a consistent ambiance and secured their collection areas with the most up-to-date electronics.

I preferred the former. Forget fancy do-dads hacking digital codes—it was much more satisfying getting to tackle concrete objects hands-on, like a puzzle I was putting together... or, more often, pulling apart.

This guy clearly leaned that way too. Except he leaned it way too far. One look at the mass of interlocking metal around the door's handle told me my standard picks weren't getting anywhere with that lock. I didn't encounter many that required more forceful methods. Tonight's collector was awfully paranoid about protecting his treasures.

Or he had something in there that was so special it justified the lengths he'd gone to.

A prickle of apprehension quivered down my spine. You know the feeling when you realize that the thing you're in the middle of doing might actually be a horrible idea—but you're so committed already that stopping would feel even worse? Yeah. I lived there so often I might as well have made it my permanent address.

Which meant I shrugged off the uneasiness and reached into the cloth bag hanging from my belt. I had ways of defeating even a ridiculous lock like this, and I wasn't going to let some wannabe master of the macabre get the better of me. Once I set out on a mission, I saw it through. And so far I always *had* seen them through, no matter how tricky the situation got.

I broke a pea-sized bead off my lump of explosive putty and poked it into the deepest cranny in the center of the mechanism. "Beating you with some goo, eat your fill," I sang at a whisper to the tune of Duran Duran's "A View to a Kill." Mangling '80s song lyrics always put me in a better mood.

Hey, everyone needs a hobby.

Bracing myself, I aimed my lighter at the cranny and flicked on the flame. The putty burst with a crackle and a puff of smoke—and the tinkle of several antique fittings shattering apart. I held myself totally still for several seconds, my ears pricked for any indication that someone in the house had noticed the sound, but the hall stayed silent.

When I pressed on the handle, the lock creaked, balked, and then crunched with a harder jerk. At my push, the door swung open.

Holy mother of mackerels, this was a collection room all right. I'd seen a lot of them, but even so, I couldn't help gaping.

The "room" looked as if it had actually been three or four rooms with the walls taken down between them, stretching like some grand ballroom into the distance. Built-in wooden shelves stuffed with books, trinkets, and other objects lined the walls on either side of me from floor to vaulted ceiling. In front of those shelves at regular intervals, globe-like lights beamed down into glinting cages not so different from those you'd expect to house birds. Their vertical bars rose into domed tops, and their bases ranged from the size of my palm to the length of my arm.

I counted at least a dozen of them spread out down the vast space. It was rare to come across a collector who'd managed to get his hands on more than a few shadow creatures. This dude had been busy.

I tore my gaze away from the cages to skim the wall and note the thick velvet curtains that covered the room's narrow windows in the few gaps between the shelves. There were my possible escape routes.

Another, more massive velvet curtain hung across the entire width of the room at the far end. What in Pete's name lay past that?

A reddish blotch caught my eye in the middle of the blue-and-gold patterned rug. That maroon shade verging on brown—it was a bloodstain. One so big I could have lain down on it and not covered the whole thing.

A fresh twinge of nerves shot through my gut. It wasn't at all unusual for collectors to experiment with all kinds of supposed supernatural rituals, including blood-based spells, but this guy appeared to have gone all out and not made any attempt to clean up afterward. He'd left the evidence on display as if it were a valuable part of the exhibit.

There was creepy, and then there was "here's a fellow who might very well enjoy wearing other people's skin as a three-piece suit."

Before I returned my attention to the cages, I took a few moments to browse the shelves and pocket artifacts from the dude's non-living collection—whatever looked both valuable and not so distinctive it'd be easily recognized when I sold it on the black market. I settled on a gold bangle, a large ruby set in ebony, and a handful of antique coins.

That should cover at least a few month's room and board while I figured out my next heist. A gal's got to pay the rent somehow. It seemed fitting that the collectors indirectly funded my efforts to shut them down. Call me the Robin Hood of monster emancipation.

Because that was what lurked in those cages under their spotlights. At least, the collectors called them monsters. And to be fair, for the most part the creatures that slunk through rifts from the shadow realm into our mortal one did fit the standard criteria.

Those of us who both knew of the creatures' existence—and had bothered to speak at any length with the ones capable of talking—chose our terminology with a little more respect. "Shadowkind" came in all shapes, sizes, and inclinations, and most of them were a heck of a lot *less* monstrous than the worst human beings I'd tangled with.

It was difficult to tell what exactly this guy had caged in his extensive menagerie. Shadowkind could literally meld into our world's shadows and travel through them, hence the name, but they had to be able to reach those shadows first. The spotlights were positioned to fill each entire cage and the space beyond the bars with light, preventing that sort of escape.

Distressed by their incarceration and that constant glaring light, the creatures shrank in on themselves. I could only make out a blurred, flickering smudge of darkness in each: a glimpse of spines here, a flash of fangs there. When the collectors wanted to gloat over their prizes, they dimmed the lights just enough to coax their captives into showing themselves more clearly without allowing any full shadows to fall into range.

Silver and iron twined together to form the cages' bars and base—true to mythology, most otherworldly beings recoiled from one or both metals to some degree. Most creatures of this size weren't strong enough to leap into the shadows through the narrow spaces between those bars even if they'd had shadows to travel through. That meant freeing them was a multi-stage process.

I started with the nearest cage, drawing a dense black cloth from the larger bag on my belt and wrapping it around the light to blot out the illumination completely. Breaking the thing obviously would have done the trick faster, but even the lovers of antiquities often resorted to higher levels of tech when it came to ensuring their most valuable possessions didn't escape. Chances were high an alarm would go off if the flow of electricity were interrupted.

The same possibility existed for the cage doors. Instead of messing with the lock, I unhooked the juiced-up knife I kept at my hip, hit the button to flood the blade with heat, and applied it to the bars on the side.

The titanium tool had been enhanced not just by black-market skills but a sorcerer's supernatural efforts as well. Its blazing edge sliced through five of the bars in less than a minute. They bowed upward at a push with the flat of the blade.

The second I'd lowered the scorch-knife, the creature inside sprang through the gap. I got a clear look at it in that instant—a ball of raggedy gray fur from which six spindly legs and two bat-like wings protruded, a glitter of yellow eyes—and then it flitted off into the thicker shadows to enjoy its freedom far from here.

With a roll of my shoulders to loosen them up, I let out my breath.

One down, a hell of a lot more to go.

Using the same technique, I made my way down the room one cage at a time. It was only when I'd hacked through what turned out to be the thirteenth—what a fitting number—that I glanced up and realized I'd come to the end of the line. Well, almost. I'd reached that vast curtain.

Bracing myself, I nudged one edge of it aside—and froze. More spotlights gleamed off more silver-and-iron bars ahead of me, but the three cages that awaited me there... I'd never seen anything quite like them. Set back at the far end of the room, a good fifteen feet from where I was now standing, they loomed almost as high as the ceiling and wide enough that I couldn't have reached from one side to the other with my arms straight out.

My breath stayed locked in my lungs as I slipped past the curtain and walked toward them. What was this dude keeping in *there*? It'd have been hard enough keeping his collection of thirteen minor "monsters" properly fed and exercised so they didn't totally dwindle away. Any creatures big enough to require cages like these—they could have gobbled him up the second he made a wrong move, if they were so inclined. And it wouldn't take very long shut up in a cage to so incline them.

I'd already thought he was over-ambitious and possibly insane. Now I'd have to go with completely cuckoo, and not just for Cocoa Puffs.

As with the smaller shadowkind, the beings in the huge cages had contracted into blurry dark forms. I couldn't tell whether the cages' height was overkill or if all three were simply hunched down in that space, but they all looked like big balls of, well, shadow condensed in the lower third of the space. The ball on the left was about twice the width of the one in the middle, the one on the right somewhere in between. I caught a flicker of pale hair, a glimmer of neon-green eyes—

My foot landed on the smaller rug between me and the cages, and an electronic shriek pierced both my eardrums.

Shit! I scrambled back so quickly I could have given a professional tap dancer a run for their money, but the alarm continued blaring through the room and no doubt the whole of the mansion. A pressure sensor under the rug must have triggered it. I hadn't even thought—I probably *should* have considering the maniac I was obviously dealing with here—

No time to curse him out. No time to do anything except the bare minimum I'd come for. Whatever the hell was in those cages, they deserved their freedom just as much as the smaller beings I'd released did.

With the alarm already shrieking around me, I could throw caution to the wind. I sprinted to the first cage, chopped at the lock itself with my scorch-knife, and managed to sever it with several sawing motions. At my yank, that door flew open. To ease the captive's escape, I hurled my blackout cloth at the lamp overhead. It covered the light for only a moment before it slipped back down for me to catch it, but in that moment a presence hurtled past me so large and so close the hairs on the back of my neck stood on end.

No time to make any formal introductions. I dashed to the second cage, sliced through that lock a little faster than the first, flung my cloth, and raced to the third without stopping for a "How do you do?" No sounds of approaching doom reached my ears through the wail of the alarm, but it was practically deafening me, so that wasn't much comfort. It wasn't a question of *whether* the master of the house was charging toward the room, only how quickly he could get here—and how lethal the reinforcements he'd bring would be.

As I snatched back my blackout cloth for the third time, I was already digging my final gambit out of my bag. With a pop of the bottle's lid, I tossed a splash of kerosene across the traitorous rug. Then I whipped the flame of my lighter at it.

The damp patch caught fire with a whoosh of heat. I glanced around one last time to make sure no living things were left in the place—I hoped my signature farewell would destroy as much of his *inanimate* collection as possible, considering the uses he'd put it to—and realized that in my rush I'd nearly cut off my route to the nearest window.

Heat licked my face. I dodged to the side as the fire shot up higher. Smoke seared down my throat, and my pulse thrummed through my body with its own inner burn of adrenaline. If the flames would be kind enough to travel more to the right than to the left, attack those rows of books before it snatched at the window curtains…

Luck was on my side. The thought had barely crossed my mind when the flames flared with sharper intensity toward the bookshelves at the opposite side of the room, giving me a smidge of an opening. A shiver passed through my nerves at just how convenient that was, but who was I to argue? I dove around the growing wave of fire and whipped the curtain aside.

Without needing to think, my grappling hook was in my hand. I slammed it into the pane, and the glass burst with a rain of shards onto the patio below. As I leapt onto the ledge, I was already sighting the utility pole just beyond the nearest wall of the backyard. One swing of my arm sent the hook soaring to latch onto the fixture at the top of the pole.

A shout of rage reverberated through the room behind me. Adios, asshole. With my hands tight around the rope, I launched myself out into the much more temperate night air.

I aimed myself at the perfect angle to catch hold of one of the metal bars protruding farther down the utility pole. Piece of cake. A flick of my wrist detached the grappling hook overhead. I clicked it onto the back of my belt, dropped down onto the sidewalk, and vanished into the shadows as completely as the creatures I'd come to save had, all ties to the place behind me severed.

At least, that was how it'd always worked before.

Despite the weirdness I'd encountered on the mission, everything about my escape appeared to go perfectly smoothly. I arrived back at my apartment in the wee hours of the morning, showered the smoke stink out of my hair, and curled up in bed. When I woke up, the sun was beaming outside, the birds were chirping, and I had new treasures to sell sitting on my desk.

I poked at them, grinning at the thought of the cash they'd bring in and the collector who'd now hopefully be agonizing at least as much over his loss as his captives had in their cages, and headed down the hall to grab some breakfast singing, "How wrong, how wrong was that dinged-up dong. How wrong, how—"

My voice jarred in my throat. I jerked to a halt a few steps from my kitchen, which was currently inhabited by three inexcusably stunning —and unfamiliar—men.

TWO

Sorsha

To be clear, I was all for shockingly handsome men as a general principle. I enjoyed resting my eyes—and sometimes other parts—on them as the occasion presented itself. Just not when the occasion was them randomly appearing in my apartment without prior invitation or me having any idea who in the wide blue yonder they were.

These three had certainly made themselves at home. The brawniest of the bunch, a hulking dude with several scars marking his chiseled face and white-blond hair that grazed his considerable shoulders, had pulled out one of the chairs at the kitchen table. He sat there with his legs sprawled out and one of my dinner knives held to the light from the window.

Next to that window was a young man who could have been a sun god, all golden curls and radiant beauty. He'd perched his tall, slim form right on the counter, one knee drawn up and the other—bare—foot dangling. His long fingers curled around my last banana, now half-eaten.

Beside him, the last of the trio was poised by the sink, the sleeves of his collared shirt rolled up past his elbows and his well-toned arms submersed in the mountain of bubbles he'd stirred up under the running water. His eyebrows arched nearly all the way to the fringe of his messy chocolate-brown waves as he met my eyes.

"Have a good sleep?" he asked in a voice that was equally chocolatey: smooth, dark, and sweet.

They were all watching me now, the bubble enthusiast smirking, the sun god beaming like, well, the sun, and Mr. Brawn forming an expression as if he were trying very hard not to frown but his face wasn't quite sure how to do anything else.

My body had tensed with that good old fight-or-flight instinct, faced with uncertain and potentially dangerous circumstances. "What the hell are you—" I started. Then my gaze caught on a couple of details that threw my understanding of the situation for a loop.

Paler shapes, more caramel than chocolate, poked from amid the bubble guy's wavy hair. They were the curves of two small, pointed... horns, just above his ears. And the sunlight was glinting not just off my dinner knife in the hulk's hand but also off his knuckles, which had crystalline edges even harder than his face and a bluish white tint like ice.

You could still have called them men, yeah, but a substantial portion of the population would have also called them monsters. I had three of the higher shadowkind camped out in my kitchen.

Which still begged a whole lot of questions, but also meant a different level of caution. I backed up a step. "Just a second. Stay right there."

I hightailed it back to my bedroom and snatched up the undershirt I'd been wearing beneath my cat burglar outfit last night. The badge of silver and iron I wore over my heart was still pinned to it. I plucked it off and fixed it to my current T-shirt in the same spot.

The metals' effects wouldn't make me impervious to shadowkind powers, but the badge did deflect most attempts to manipulate human minds and emotions. While I believed in letting the shadowkind live freely, that didn't mean I trusted them to keep their voodoo to themselves. Some of them had *earned* the label "monster." And even the sweetest of shadow creatures often didn't understand kindness and consideration the way we mortals did.

My hasty preparations woke up Pickle where he'd been baking in the sun on my bedroom windowsill. The kitten-sized, dragon-shaped creature, whose scales were as green and bumpy as his namesake, blinked at me, stretched his wings, and scrambled up into a jumping position.

I hesitated and then leaned toward him. "All right. But you might not like what's out there." He wouldn't be much help if it came to a fight, but his response to their presence might tell me things my mortal senses didn't register.

Pickle leapt into the air with a clumsy flap of his wings and landed on my shoulder. He hooked his claws—gently, after a couple of years of trial and error—into the fabric of my shirt and nudged my jaw with his flared nose. Sometimes it was hard to tell whether he saw me more as a helpful companion or a steed.

He settled in happily with his cool cheek tucked against the crook of my neck until I'd reached the threshold of the kitchen. The three gorgeous men had stayed exactly where they'd been when I first saw them. At least they were capable of following direct instructions.

Pickle flinched and sprang away from me—and away from his much larger shadowkind brethren—with a squeak that released a puff of sparks. He landed on the shoulder of the mannequin that stood just inside the living room.

I'd emancipated that object from the long-abandoned store my apartment sat on top of, a place that used to offer fabric and clothing alterations. The headless, armless figure looked almost as unsettling in my apartment as it had amid the dust and darkness downstairs, but I'd decked it out in one of my shirts, unwashed to keep my scent, so that Pickle had somewhere to perch other than on me, which was where he'd have wanted to be every waking moment otherwise.

Apparently he preferred substitute-me to the real deal if it meant getting farther away from the beings in the kitchen. Once on the mannequin, he hunched his back, his beady black eyes fixed on them and another, fiercer squeak escaping him.

Okay, so he thought they were pretty scary dudes. Of course, that might have been more to do with the fact that they were about a hundred times bigger than he was than any horrifying powers he'd picked up on.

The men still hadn't moved, but Mr. Brawn's expression had shifted into total frown territory as he considered my pet dragon. The bubble enthusiast with the chocolate hair and voice appeared to focus on my protective badge for a moment before he caught my gaze again with another teasing arch of his brows.

I'd worn it on the outside of my clothes on purpose, so they'd know *I* knew what I was dealing with—and how to defend myself if I needed to.

I crossed my arms over my chest. "All right. What are you doing here?" They seemed tame enough so far, Mr. Brawn's scars aside, but with the higher shadowkind, you really couldn't go by appearances. They were capable of hiding their more monstrous forms beneath a nearly fully human veneer, only one tell-tale characteristic like those horns or those knuckles showing through. I could be dealing with any manner of demon, shapeshifter, fae, vamp, or the many rarer but equally caution-worthy types.

"You let us out," the slim sun god said in a bright, awed voice. "It was fantastic." He took another bite of the banana, and I realized he hadn't bothered to peel it. He was downing it skin and all.

His tongue flicked across his lips—was it *forked*?—and his smile turned swoony. "This is fantastic too. What did you say it's called?"

He glanced at the guy at the sink, who answered with obvious amusement. "A banana. While we're working on B-words, what do you think of these?" He lifted his hand and blew a stream of the dish-soap bubbles into the air. As they floated along with more airlift than I could have managed, the godly guy's eyes followed them. He reached out to touch one bubble's glossy surface and guffawed when it popped.

Mr. Brawn had set aside the dinner knife and gotten to his feet without any sign he'd noticed the others' chatter. He looked even bigger standing up—at least a foot taller than me, and I was no shrimp at five-foot-six. He bobbed his head, his expression as somber as before. His voice came out deep and gravelly.

"My name is Thorn, and my companions are Snap"—he indicated the sun god—"and Ruse"—the bubble enthusiast. "After the efforts you took and the repercussions you risked to ensure our freedom, we owe you a great debt. We'll repay it to the best of our ability, m'lady."

Had he really just referred to me as "m'lady" like some courtly knight? I might have questioned the title, but I was too distracted by the larger implications of what he'd said. Ensure their freedom—let them out—*oh*.

The pieces clicked together. The three huge cages in the collection room. The glimpse of pale hair I'd gotten—that could have been this Thorn guy's. The brilliant green eyes... Snap's were a more subdued mossy green, but in his more monstrous form they might very well take on that neon shine. Shadowkind tended toward extremes in their natural state.

I *had* freed these three. And then apparently they'd followed me home like a pack of lost puppies. Extremely hot lost puppies, but still. Pickle was enough trouble.

My arms relaxed a little, but I didn't move from my spot on the threshold. "You shouldn't have come after me. I wasn't looking for repayment. I let you and the lesser beings there out because you didn't deserve to be caged in the first place. You can go on back to the shadow realm now."

Ruse blew another waft of bubbles into the air. "No can do. You see, we lost our boss."

Snap's cheerful expression dimmed at that comment. He downed the last of the banana like it was a shot of tequila.

"Your boss?" I repeated, knitting my brow.

As far as I'd gathered, the shadow realm didn't operate with much social organization, let alone jobs and employers. There were higher shadowkind who'd come over to the mortal realm permanently and lived alongside humans with most of the trappings of mortal life, but this trio didn't fit that mold. From Snap's awe at the basic contents of my kitchen, I'd guess he'd spent very little time outside his own realm at all. Thorn's formal way of speaking and outfit of tunic and trousers suggested any significant time he'd spent here had been a few eras ago. Ruse might have fit in all right, though his fitted shirt and slacks were more clubwear than work uniform, but he'd said *our*.

"We were brought together for a specific cause by another of our kind who suspected treachery was being carried out by certain mortals," Thorn said. "The fate that befell him suggests he was right. On our third cross-over, he was ambushed by attackers well-prepared to combat our abilities. We were able to avoid the fray, but before we could track down him and them afterward, we were trapped by another party." His face darkened, his head dipping.

"I did tell you I had a bad feeling about that building," Ruse put in.

Thorn glowered over his shoulder at the other guy before turning back to me. "Techniques have changed since I last engaged much with mortals. They've become more... potent." He sat back down as if overburdened by that admission.

Snap gave a little shudder as if trying to shake off the tension of the moment and hopped off the counter. He reached into my fruit bowl on the table, the glow of curiosity coming back as he examined his finding. "What's this one called?"

"That's a peach," Ruse said dryly. "They're nice too."

Snap took a bite and hummed delightedly. I did my best not to ogle the pale curve of his neck and that heavenly face as he held the fruit up to let the juice drip into his mouth. I might not have invited these guests, but I could be polite enough not to openly leer.

"Omen brought us together," Thorn went on from his chair. He aimed his mournful glower at the dinner knife as if its dull blade offended him. "We can't return without him. And if he's right about the sort of people who captured him, many more of our kind are under grave threat."

An uneasy prickle ran down my spine. Collectors and the hunters who supplied them didn't normally deal in higher shadowkind. Too risky and too much effort required. If there was some kind of organized campaign underway to seize beings like these—if it was happening enough that some shadowkind were starting to realize... It didn't bode well that none of the people I worked with had noticed.

I shifted my weight from one foot to the other. "I can see why you'd feel that way. The last thing I'd want to do is get in the way of that mission. By all means, go off and search for him." And I'd check with my contacts to see if they had any idea about the bigger picture here.

"We will of course continue our search," Thorn said. "But we can see to it that you remain protected and aided in any way you require in the meantime."

Three unexpected, monstrous house guests—not what I'd signed up for. "That's really not necessary," I said, holding up my hands. "I'm sure I'll be fine. Don't worry about me."

"Oh, but we owe you," Ruse said in that smooth voice of his. I thought there might be a teasing note in it. "If it's simpler for you, we could sink into the shadows to stay out of your hair."

"Her hair," Snap murmured. He looked from the partly-devoured peach to me and sidled close enough to lift a ruddy lock that had fallen across my shoulder. His head cocked as he rubbed it between his lithe fingers.

My pulse stuttered despite myself. Thorn might be ruggedly handsome and Ruse devilishly stunning, but up close, Snap's divine face was literally breathtaking.

"It's almost the same color," he said, sounding pleased with his observation. He held the strands up to the peach's red skin. "And just as soft."

I managed to catch my breath, but the only sound that came out of me was, "Er." I should probably step away, but I couldn't quite convey that message to my legs.

Ruse chuckled. "I'll bet she tastes just as sweet too."

There was no mistaking the suggestiveness of that comment, but Snap's head jerked toward him with a flicker of horror. "You can't eat her!"

Thorn stirred at the table as if tuning in to his companions' asides for the first time. "No one should even be *thinking* about eating anyone around here," he commanded.

Ruse rolled his hooded eyes. "I'll have you know that in my entire existence, I've never eaten a person—not like that, anyway." He winked at me. "I apologize for my associates' inability to follow a metaphor."

I held up my hands, finally convincing my feet to back away from Snap. "Enough. Let me think."

No way in hell did I want these guys lurking around in the shadows, keeping an eye on me for my "protection" without me having any idea where exactly they were. I valued my privacy, thank you very much. At least while they were visible, I'd know when I was actually on my own.

As the entire conversation had demonstrated, shadowkind didn't have the same concepts humans did of social niceties… or basic legalities, for that matter. The fact that they had no right to occupy my apartment and that I might not *want* them hanging around "repaying" me meant zip. If they'd decided to temporarily adopt me, I wasn't sure there was anything I could do to convince them otherwise—not without provoking hostilities I wasn't prepared to contend with, anyway.

Because I'm nothing if not stubborn, I had to make one last attempt. "Can you really not believe that I'd rather you put all your energy into finding your 'boss' instead of looking out for me?"

Thorn blinked at me as if I'd said something completely preposterous. "It's not about *believing*. It's about what's right."

He said it with such solemn commitment that I barely held back a laugh. What was right, according to him: crashing the home of a woman they barely knew and insisting on watching over her despite her protests. Welcome to shadow logic.

Ruse and Snap looked equally disinclined to budge. I inhaled sharply and squared my shoulders. In that case, I'd just have to do what I could to get them moving on with their other responsibilities.

"Fine," I said. "There are some people I can meet up with tonight who might have information that'll help you track down this Omen guy. In the meantime, I'd prefer if you did your protecting from the kitchen."

I slipped into the room just long enough to grab a muffin out of the breadbox for my breakfast, waved Pickle onto my shoulder, and stalked back to my bedroom to figure out how to get myself unadopted ASAP.

THREE

Ruse

"Well, that went just spectacularly," I said, leaning back against our savior's kitchen counter.

"Really?" Snap looked toward me with that dopily hopeful expression of his.

Thorn shifted forward in his chair as if debating whether to spring into action right now. "I thought so."

Unfortunately, my current associates understood sarcasm about as well as they comprehended metaphors. I wiped the lingering bubbles off my hands. The lemony scent made my nose itch, but at least the stuff had entertained Snap for a little while. Not that he was all that difficult to impress.

"I was joking," I said. "She all but told us to take a hike. Repeatedly." Her noxious silver-and-iron brooch might have deflected most of my ability to read her emotions the way I generally could with mortals, but from the moment she'd retreated to put the thing on, her wariness about our presence should have been perfectly obvious to anyone with functioning eyes.

Anyone other than these two. Why had I let Omen rope me into this posse again? I hadn't taken into consideration the possibility of being snared and shut away in a cage for darkness only knew how long.

Longer than was good for my health, the more insistent itch in my chest suggested. The ravenous sensation I'd been fighting off for days was producing claws.

"She told us to stay," Thorn said, which was the most generous possible interpretation of the young woman's instruction for us to keep to the kitchen. "She even offered to help look for Omen, not that she should feel obliged."

I sighed. "I'd imagine she's counting on us leaving as soon as we've found him, and she'd like to hurry up the process."

Snap's eyes grew even rounder than usual. "We can't leave. What if the mortals that attacked us come after her because she freed us?"

"I get the feeling she'd prefer to take her chances with them more than us," I replied, but I couldn't help smiling as I said it. Our rescuer had plenty of spirit in her. I'd pass up a seduction or two for the chance to watch her face off against those asshole hunters.

At Snap's crestfallen look, I added, "It isn't your fault. She hasn't had the chance to see all we have to offer."

Our mortal-realm neophyte was easily reassured. He nodded with earnest determination and popped the rest of the peach into his mouth. The pit crunched between his teeth.

I didn't have the heart to tell him he was eating it wrong. His jaws could handle it. He was a devourer, after all.

Thorn's determination was much grimmer. "Whether she appreciates our company or not, we must ensure she doesn't suffer because of the immense favor she did for us." He paused. "But we must also come to Omen's aid as quickly as we can. The trail will have grown cold. It's been too long already."

The twist of his mouth showed how his opposing duties tore at him. Having a sense of loyalty was awfully troublesome, as far as I could tell. I was glad I'd never cultivated one.

I pushed myself off the counter to amble over, and a tremor ran down the back of my legs. I tensed them before I could visibly wobble. My jaw set.

Oh yes, *that* was a perfect reminder of why I'd agreed to join in on this operation—and why I wasn't going to shirk the duty I'd pledged to carry out even if the job had gotten much more complicated than expected. It wasn't loyalty; it was self-preservation.

Thorn could stick to our mandate out of higher principles, and Snap out of his desire to please or whatever exactly drove him, but for me, being able to slip between the realms was a matter of survival. Shadowkind like me relied on mortals to sustain us. I might not be capable of *dying* while I was in my native realm, but I wasn't sure that wasting away into a sliver of a shadow would be any better. It might be worse.

And any of us could die on this side of the divide.

I made sure my body had steadied and then stepped toward the table as I'd planned. The scrabbling of my hunger burrowed deeper between my ribs. No piece of fruit would satisfy it.

"The answer is perfectly clear," I said to Thorn. "The last time we went searching, our poking around got us caught. Neither of you is really prepared to navigate this realm without guidance, and I know you don't want to listen to my advice. Our host, reluctant or not, knows this world far better than any of us, Omen included."

"What are you suggesting, then?"

I shrugged. "She's offered to make inquiries. She's motivated to see us on our way. We should let her take the lead in the investigation, and we can see that no harm comes to her by following along behind. Two birds with one stone, as the mortals like to say."

"What do the birds want with a stone?" Snap asked.

"It's more what the stone wants with the birds." I reached over and spun the knife Thorn had left on the table. It rattled around to point its blade at him. "So? Can you agree that my approach makes sense even though it came from me?"

Thorn gave me one of his long-suffering glowers. I'd gotten plenty of practice at ignoring those. But it seemed he couldn't come up with any actual argument.

"Your proposal sounds reasonable," he said after a moment. "We'll see where her connections can take us."

"Excellent." I straightened up and sauntered past Snap toward the hall, alert for any new tremors in my muscles. The last thing I needed was Thorn picking up on my current weakness.

His gaze swiveled to track me. "Where are you going? She said to stay in the kitchen."

I smiled sweetly at him. "And as you well know, I'm not very good at following orders I never agreed to in the first place. I'll go see if I can't spin our dropping in on her home into a more welcome visit."

And if I could sate my vital appetites at the same time, we'd all win.

FOUR

Sorsha

EXPECTING MY NEW SHADOWKIND ENTOURAGE TO FOLLOW *ALL* MY instructions to the letter was obviously too much to hope for. I'd only just wolfed down my breakfast and opened my laptop to get down to business when a knock sounded on the door. Biting back a sigh, I got up to answer it. Was there the slightest chance they were stopping by just to tell me they'd reconsidered and would be taking off now?

Nope. I eased open the door to find just Ruse standing on the other side in a casual stance, his heavy-lidded eyes languid. Up close, I couldn't help noticing that the chocolate theme extended to his scent. A bittersweet smell like pure cacao mixed with caramel filled my nose —and made my mouth water despite myself.

He wasn't as tall as hulking Thorn, but he still had a good half a foot on me. As he gazed down at me, his lips quirked into a smile that cracked a dimple beneath one of those high cheekbones. I wouldn't be surprised to find out that grin had melted the panties off thousands of women around the world.

"I'm sorry our initial conversation went so poorly," he said in that smooth but slightly teasing tone. "If Thorn had been named 'Prick,' it would have been a lot more fitting. I thought I should make an attempt at a proper introduction. I can't believe we didn't even get *your* name. So—"

He made an elaborate flourish with one hand and dipped in a playful half bow. "Ruse of the shadow realm," he said when he'd straightened up again. "A pleasure to meet you. And you are?"

"Sorsha of the mortal realm," I said, bemused. I couldn't return the sentiment about it being a pleasure.

"Sorsha," he repeated, trying out the syllables as if they were a rare delicacy. The richness he gave to them sent a tingle down my spine. "I think you're the first with that name I've encountered."

I felt abruptly awkward and annoyed by that awkwardness. "It's from an old movie." My parents had apparently been as obsessed with '80s media as Luna had been. "Is that all you wanted—to get my name?"

"Well, no, I have to admit I have an ulterior motive." He shot me that smile again, even slyer this time, and damn it if *my* panties didn't melt just a tad.

Resting his hand on the doorframe, he leaned into the room as if to indicate that this part of the conversation wasn't meant for the ears of those down the hall. "I have a small predicament. Unfortunately, it means asking for your help when you've already gone above and beyond, but I can promise it'd be very enjoyable for you too."

I crossed my arms and raised my eyebrows at him the way he had at me when I'd first encountered the trio. "Oh, yeah? And what exactly is this favor?"

"The trouble is, our former jailor didn't offer the kind of food that can actually sustain me. I need a different sort of nourishment."

His warm hazel eyes took on a meaningful gleam, and I connected the dots.

"You're an incubus," I said, mentally kicking myself for not figuring it out sooner. The guy did ooze sensuality, after all. "You need to have sex to survive." Like a vampire needed blood. Fair enough. But why would he— Oh. "And you're propositioning *me*?"

His grin stretched even wider. "You are a sharp one, aren't you, Miss Blaze?" He reached out to gently tug a strand of my hair, which might have inspired the nickname as much as my farewell to the collection room had. "The feeding won't hurt you. We leave our intimate companions better off than when we found them, not worse."

His fingers nearly grazed my cheek. The closeness set off a much headier pulse of attraction than Snap's heavenly beauty had provoked.

I'd rather a love bite than one with fangs, and to be totally honest, I *had* wondered from time to time just how much a supernaturally sexual being could bring to the table. But all the same... "I'm flattered, but no thanks. We did only just meet. And that might complicate things even more than you just staying in my apartment out of the blue. I'm not going to stop you from heading out on the prowl, though. By all means." I motioned toward the apartment's front door beyond him.

Ruse's mouth pulled into something more like a grimace. "Given what my companions and I have already been through, I'd rather not risk taking my needs to the streets. Any potential lover I encounter out there is also a potential jailor. I know *you* have my best interests at heart."

I wasn't sure I'd put it exactly that way, but he did have a point. That didn't mean I had to go along with it, though. "You've toughed it out this long. You can't hang in there a little longer while we get this whole Omen situation sorted out?"

He shrugged, the twinkle coming back into his eyes. "I could, but I'd rather be at my full capacity, so I can properly contribute and all. Is the thought really so distasteful?"

He was definitely teasing now. I doubted he could sense much from me using his powers while I was wearing my badge, but certain parts of me *were* responding to his appeal. From the heat creeping up my neck, I suspected I had a flush coming on. Lord only knew how dilated my pupils might be right now, taking in that striking face.

I was only human, after all. And it'd been months since I'd last gotten it on with anything not battery-powered, let alone a master of the sensual arts.

That was exactly why I shouldn't give in to temptation, wasn't it? I couldn't be completely sure Ruse had *my* best interests at heart, and I wasn't sure how clear a head I'd keep in the heat of the moment.

At the very least, I should take a little time to think about it. He and his friends clearly weren't planning on going anywhere anytime soon.

Maybe someone at the Fund would have an idea of extra precautions to take with the cubi type of shadowkind.

Vivi would love to know what had provoked that line of questioning, wouldn't she? I was definitely going to have to keep this unexpected roommate situation on the down low when it came to my best friend. If the trio had gotten themselves caught up in something dangerous, which it sounded like they had, the last thing I wanted was to drag her into the mess too. She had no idea about any of my totally illegal nighttime crusades.

I opened my mouth to tell my attempted paramour that I needed a rain check until at least tomorrow, and my gaze snagged on the hand he'd set on the door frame. The hand that wasn't simply resting there now. A faint twitch of his fingers had caught my attention—a trembling he must have mastered by grasping the frame harder, because his hand had stilled, but his knuckles had whitened.

The second my gaze landed there, he jerked his hand away and tucked it behind his back in another flirty pose. But now that I was alert to the possibility, that stance looked a tad more rigid than fit his laissez-faire expression.

He'd talked as if he wasn't doing that badly, but how much was he downplaying his weakness? He was aiming to win me over with charm, not pity.

A sudden flicker of concern gnawed at my hesitations. I didn't enjoy seeing any being in pain. And it would make a hell of a lot more trouble for me if one of my new volunteer bodyguards collapsed on my watch. That was the main reason I was reconsidering: a totally practical consideration.

Oh, come on—would your resolve really be unshakeable in my position?

That didn't mean I was going to leap straight into bed with the dude, of course. I prodded his chest—ooh, he was packing some muscle under that silky shirt. "Maybe I'd be open to, let's say, making out a bit. Nothing too intense. I wouldn't want you using any voodoo on me. Can you feed while I've got this badge on?"

He cocked his head, considering the circle of twined silver and iron. "A little energy would seep through—more a light snack than a meal, but it'd help. And I can provide plenty of satisfaction without any extra-worldly influence necessary. All I ask is that you reconsider the whole protective amulet thing once I've proven that. If you don't want me affecting your emotions, I have no problem staying out."

He could say that all he wanted, but that didn't mean he'd stick to it. The thought of him meddling with my mind sent a cold jab of panic through me. I stifled it and the shiver that came with it. "Badge stays on. That's the limit of my trust right now. Keep in mind that you did barge into my apartment without an invitation or even asking."

He lowered his head in mock shame. "Point. The limits are yours to set. So…" He grinned at me again, making his face somehow twice as handsome than it'd already been. My pulse hiccupped. Maybe this wasn't such a great idea after all…

What the hell. I'd pretty much committed already. It'd make a great party story someday. *Did I ever tell you about the time I made out with an incubus?*

I stepped back from the door. "Come on in, then."

Ruse sauntered inside and kicked the door shut behind him. His eyes shimmered with a golden cast now—a little of his mortal façade fading away to reveal the shadowkind form underneath.

He brought his hand back to my face, letting his knuckles tease across the line of my jaw in a way that left my nerves shimmering too. He set his other hand on my waist. With our bodies just a few inches apart, the heat of his washed over mine, setting off a fresh flare of desire. I swallowed hard, resisting the urge to meld right into him, and he tilted my chin up to meet his first kiss.

Holy fucking cannoli. I'd thought I'd been kissed pretty skillfully in the past, but just the brush of Ruse's lips set all those past encounters into pale relief. My mouth tingled, more heat swelling in my chest, and he drew me closer. The perfect pressure turned the shimmer of my nerves into outright sparks.

Before I'd realized I was moving, my fingers had curled into the front of his shirt, holding him in place as if I had any reason to worry he might be going somewhere. I kissed him back, instinctively seeking even more, and he hummed encouragingly. With a small shift in angle and a stroke of his tongue, he coaxed my lips apart.

If he was feeding off the intimacy of this interlude already, I couldn't sense it. All I could feel was the blissful heat and the delicious curl of his tongue around mine. The hand on my side trailed higher until his thumb traced the curve of my breast.

More sparks shot through me at that touch. I swayed into it automatically.

He caressed my cheek once more and then tangled his fingers in my hair in a gesture that was somehow both confidently controlled and wild. The passion stirring inside me spread further, pooling between my legs with a growing need.

How could I give up everything he could offer now that we'd started? How could I possibly ask him to stop?

A fresh flash of cold broke through the haze of pleasure that'd been consuming me. Those questions were exactly why I needed to stop it—now.

I pulled myself back with agonizing effort. My face was definitely flushed now. As I pursed my lips, my mouth tingled with the aftereffects of the kissing. I gathered myself enough to say, "That's enough. We'll leave it there."

The incubus didn't make any move to persuade me otherwise. He simply studied me with an expression halfway between amusement and approval. A little more color had come into his previously pale skin—a sign that my contribution had given him enough of a "snack" to make a difference?

"For now?" he suggested, with an implied, *until later?*

I wet my lips without meaning to, sending a renewed quiver of bliss through my body. "We'll see," I said, ignoring all the parts of my body screaming, *Yes, pretty please, with multiple cherries on top! And also, let's see what you can do with those cherries...*

I'd enjoyed that little make-out session—hoo boy, understatement of the year—but I'd rather be sure I didn't come to regret the gamble before I rolled the dice again.

FIVE

Sorsha

MONSTER ADVOCACY WASN'T EXACTLY THE TYPE OF WORK YOU COULD openly advertise. Technically, the group where I did almost all of my socializing—along with picking up tips for new collectors to target—called themselves the Shadowkind Defense Fund. Outside of the four walls in which they held their twice-weekly meetings, we usually shortened that first word to "SK" or simply referred to the group as "the Fund."

Those four walls were contained in a discount movie theater that showed second-run films. Tonight, the warble of a recent Marvel soundtrack filtered in from the showing beside us, all epic orchestration punctuated by the occasional explosion. The small popcorn machine brought in for our private party filled the air with a salty buttery smell—and something spicy that tickled my nose.

Ellen, co-owner of the theater and unofficial co-president of the Fund alongside her wife, had a thing for experimenting with new popcorn flavors. We Fund members served as her guinea pigs. As I strolled around the rows of red-velvet-padded seats to check out her current attempt, a petite figure bounded to join me with a swish of her buoyant curls.

"Sorsha!" my best friend cried, catching me in a hug I returned with a laugh. From Vivi's enthusiasm every time I showed up, you'd have thought my attendance was a rare occurrence. The truth was, I rarely missed a meeting, since the people in the Fund were pretty much the only people I could talk to without having to lie about the vast majority of my life. And even with them, there was plenty I edited out.

When I'd first showed up at a Fund meeting as a much more hesitant and recently traumatized sixteen-year-old, Vivi had immediately swooped in and taken me under her wing. I'd even ended up living with her and her parents for a while. Two years older, she'd been the next youngest in the bunch, but she'd seemed awfully mature and worldly to me. Over the more-than-a-decade since, we'd come out on more equal footing, bonding over our unusual senses of humor and our mutual love for cheesy old movies and Thai food.

"It's chili pepper and brown sugar tonight," she said, nodding to the bags of popcorn already filled to the side of the machine. "It'll roast your tongue like a rack of honey ribs and then set the barbeque on fire."

I'd never met a lyric I couldn't mangle; Vivi had never met a simile she couldn't stretch to the breaking point.

I grinned back at her and swiped a Coke from the mini-fridge as well as my bag. "Thanks for the warning. I see you survived."

"Only barely," she said in a dramatic undertone, but her eyes still twinkled merrily. She struck a pose, one hand on her hip, the other in the air. "What do you think of the new get-up?"

Today's outfit consisted of a sleek white tank top with a pearly sheen and trim white capris. Vivi only wore white—"It's my calling card," she'd told me way back when—which to be fair did set off her smooth brown skin and dark features amazingly. She emphasized her eyes with thick liner and mascara, and her black hair ran tight along her scalp in braids before bursting into a gush of curls at the back. Perhaps most amazing was the fact that she somehow managed never to get a smudge or a stain on all that pale fabric.

"You look incredible," I said, "like you always do. Got something special happening later?"

"I'm supposed to meet this guy for drinks. We've talked a little online. I don't know. Hard to tell how you're going to feel about a person until you can see and, like, smell them, right?"

My mind tripped back to Ruse's bittersweet cacao scent, and a warmth I hadn't wanted to provoke flickered up from my chest. I tamped down on it in the same instant, but Vivi knew me pretty well.

"Huh," she said with a teasing tilt of her head. "What have *you* been up to, missy?"

I waved her off. "Nothing, nothing. Just thinking about times past and all." I didn't have to mention how recently past they were. Time for a subject change! "Hey, have you heard anything through the grapevine about hunters getting more organized or people trying to trap higher shadowkind as well as the little beasties?"

Vivi frowned. "I don't think so. Maybe someone else will have. Why, do you think something like that is happening?"

"Just seems like it could. Something to keep an eye out for." I scrambled for an excuse that wouldn't perk Vivi's curiosity too much. "It's coming up on the anniversary of Luna's death, and I guess that got me thinking."

My best friend's expression immediately softened with sympathy. She gave me a gentle tap of her elbow. "That's got to be tough. But it's been a long time and we haven't seen more incidents that were anything like that, so I don't think there's a pattern. Just a bunch of assholes who must have thought better of making that kind of move after things went wrong."

"True," I said. It could also be true that what had happened to the trio who'd crashed my apartment and their "boss" was an isolated incident, not part of a larger conspiracy, no matter what the guy in charge had believed.

"Can't hurt to ask, though, if it makes you feel better. Come on." She motioned for us to head back to the front of the room where several other Fund members were scattered across the folding seats, munching popcorn and chatting. The projection screen flashed briefly as Ellen and Huyen must have fiddled with their weekly visual report, which they would share once the meeting really got underway.

We'd only made it halfway down the aisle when one of the lounging figures yanked himself to his feet and ambled our way. My steps slowed. "Here comes the rain again," I murmured to Vivi, but my heart wasn't in the joke.

"Hey," Leland said as he reached us, his voice light but cool, his expression outright cold. The muscles in his stout frame, which a bodybuilder would have envied, flexed beneath his polo shirt. I forced myself to smile, but his gaze only rested on me for a second before flitting to Vivi and staying there.

Ever since we'd broken off our friends-with-benefits arrangement, emphasis on the benefits, months ago—or rather, since *I'd* broken it off after he'd started snapping at me for not doting on him like an actual girlfriend—he'd turned to ice around me. Somehow he couldn't stop making a point of shoving that ice in my face at least once a meeting. Did he think I was going to throw myself into his arms with sobs of regret because of his pointed demonstrations?

I wasn't, because honestly, I didn't miss even the casual relationship I'd lost all that much. I'd always found Leland easy on the eyes, that soft face and schoolboy haircut paired with his tough-guy physique, but in personality? We'd gotten along well enough when all we'd had to discuss was where we'd be hooking up on a given night. We hadn't had much to talk about otherwise. The fact that he'd apparently wanted more had thrown me for a loop.

But it still stung that I hadn't picked up on the signs soon enough to avoid his obvious hurt and that I'd managed to disappoint him so thoroughly even when we'd seemed to be on the same page... It wasn't the first time. No matter what kind of relationship I ended up in, it always turned out I wasn't giving enough.

I'd been doing my best to show *I* had no hard feelings and wanted to co-exist peacefully, so I ignored the intended snub with my smile still in place. "Hey. Looks like it's going to be a busy meeting tonight."

He responded with a noncommittal grunt, nodded to Vivi, and veered closer to the seats to pass us on her side. As he stepped by, his foot must have caught on the base of the nearest chair. I didn't see it happen, but one second he was striding along, and the next he was sprawling forward onto his hands and knees with an audible "Ooof!", ass in the air.

As Leland picked himself up, one of the old members who'd come over to the popcorn machine chuckled. "Watch yourself there, kid!"

Leland brushed himself off with a briskness that showed his embarrassment and hustled on giving the chairs a wide berth.

Vivi wrinkled her nose and leaned in to talk under her breath. "Maybe if he paid more attention to where he was walking than to giving you the cold shoulder…"

"At some point he's got to forgive and forget," I replied. I sure hoped so. For now, I could stick to giving him whatever space he felt he needed. It was a big room—plenty of chairs for everyone.

Shaking off the gloom of that exchange, I continued on to the other familiar—and much more welcoming—faces gathered near the screen. With Vivi looking on, I phrased my questions about new hunter behavior carefully, but all I got were shaken heads and doubtful expressions. If a larger than usual effort to confine the shadowkind was underway, word of it hadn't reached our group yet.

Which meant it either wasn't happening… or the people involved were covering their tracks incredibly well.

"All right, folks," Ellen called out as she and Huyen emerged from the projection booth. "Let's see what we can put in motion today. We had an incident earlier this week that should remind us all why none of the beings that cross over into our world deserve to be left in the hands of people who see them only as supernatural collectibles. A member of the Defense Fund in L.A. joined a group of mortal-side higher shadowkind who shut down a hunter ring, and this is what they encountered."

At the press of a button, a video started to play on the screen. It'd clearly been taken with a handheld camera, probably a phone, and the hand that held it was shaking.

The recording swiveled to take in a small, dim room. A couple dozen cages stood stacked against one wall. At the other, several furred or scaled forms sprawled on the steel table, bones protruding from their flesh like ghostly knobs.

"Oh my God," the video-taker mumbled with obvious horror.

My own stomach churned queasily at the sight. Some collectors were too nervous or fastidious to want to deal with living shadowkind. For them, the hunters carved up their haul to provide polished skeletons or taxidermy shells. Two sales for one catch. Some hunters even preferred those dealings.

There wasn't much we mortals could do to take down these hunter rings—or independent hunters and their clients—directly, especially a larger scale operation like in the video. They'd have at least one sorcerer on staff: one of the rare human beings who'd mastered the art of summoning shadowkind from their own realm and bending their powers to the sorcerer's will. Their magic would deflect any typical law enforcement we tried to sic on them.

Those of us in the Fund had all come to know about shadowkind in various, personal ways we couldn't have convinced the general public to believe. Maybe if the higher shadowkind had wanted to show off their powers and prove they existed, we could have made more headway... but understandably, they had much more of an advantage in keeping their true nature secret.

The best we could offer was to interfere with the hunting and collecting as well as we could in roundabout ways, gather money to buy and release caught creatures when we had the chance, and inform the higher shadowkind who'd taken up residence in our world of activities we'd uncovered so they could step in if they felt it worth the risk. At least this bunch had taken action before the people who ran the facility could torment any more unwitting beings.

A solemn mood had descended over the room when the video finished. Then a chart popped up on the screen showing our latest fundraising efforts—not a bad week, considering *we* had to keep secret what we were actually raising those funds for.

"One of the big old homes in Walnut Hill halfway burned down last night," someone piped up as the screen went dark. "We've seen signs that the owner was a collector. That's the third fire this year—do we still have no idea who to thank?"

I bit my tongue. I definitely had nothing at all to say about that.

If I wanted to continue my more vigilante-style interventions, it was best if no one else had any idea I was responsible. The other Fund members might joke about approving, but if they knew one of their own was committing the crimes, I'd be kicked out for "crossing too many lines" in two seconds flat. I'd seen it happen to a guy who'd leaned too far into vigilante territory not long after I'd first joined.

"If it's a higher shadowkind taking matters into their own hands, as we've discussed before, it's understandable that they're not advertising the fact," Huyen said.

A guy farther back clapped his hands. "I say we leave them to it. They can police what happens to their own in their own way."

Being raised by a higher shadowkind for thirteen or so years made me pretty much an honorary one, right? That was my story, and I was sticking to it. Auntie Luna hadn't deserved what the bastards had done to her, and I'd be damned if I let any other shadowkind suffer while I could prevent it by any means necessary.

Vivi glanced at me and must have caught something in my expression. "Still fretting?"

I shrugged. "It's okay. If no one's heard anything, then there's nothing to hear."

"We could always spread the net a little farther. I was thinking of stopping by Jade's on Friday night. Wanna come with? It's been a while since we let loose anyway."

Yes, Jade's would be the perfect spot to dig a little further—and hopefully solve my uninvited monster roommate difficulties. I smiled. "You're right—let's do it."

SIX

Sorsha

Popcorn was hardly enough to fill a gal up, scorch-your-tongue-off spicy or not. As I tramped up the stairs past the fabric shop to my apartment, my stomach grumbled about how long I'd delayed dinner time. It was definitely time to eat.

I fit my key into the lock, singing to myself: "When the meal's in sight, I'm gonna run all night, I'm gonna run to chew…"

I pushed open the door half expecting my new shadowkind roomies to be waiting on the threshold all but wagging their tails to see me home. Instead, the hall was vacant, the apartment totally silent, no movement even in what I could see of the kitchen.

For just a split second, my spirits lifted with the hope that the trio had changed their minds about the whole glomming-onto-Sorsha plan and gone off to pursue their rescue efforts on their own. Just a split second, because an instant later, three distinctive forms wavered out of the shadow cast by the front door like watercolor paints condensing into a sharpened image.

Pickle scampered out of my bedroom, saw the much larger shadowkind, and cringed before flinging himself the rest of the way toward me. I'd have been surprised he didn't flee right into the shadows, except he'd gotten so attached to me that he stuck to his physical form all the time these days. I wasn't sure he even remembered how to vanish into the darkness.

I scooped him up to set him on his preferred shoulder perch and eyed my obstinate guests. "You decided you'd rather lurk?"

Thorn was wearing the dour expression that seemed to come so naturally to his rugged face. He squared his broad shoulders as if his form wasn't intimidating enough up close. "It's much easier—and more discreet—for us to travel through the shadows."

Snap's moss-green eyes were lit with a neon sparkle. "Such a fascinating place," he said with an errant flick of his tongue that, yes, I was sure now was slightly forked at the tip. "So many chairs—and what is the purpose of them swinging up?"

Chairs that swung up...? My stance tensed, Pickle's claws jabbing my collarbone as he echoed my reaction. "You followed me to the theater?"

Thorn gave me a baleful look. "We could hardly ensure your protection if we stayed in the apartment when you've left it, m'lady."

I'd definitely heard him right that time. "*M'lady?*"

"Excuse the archaics," Ruse said with his typical amused smirk. "Our friend here hasn't spent much time mortal-side since the Middle Ages."

Thorn had said it so stiffly I got the impression he resented the honorific anyway, not that I'd required it. "Well, I'm not your *lady*," I said to him. "And I told you I don't need your protection. You can't go sneaking around after people without them even knowing—"

Except they could, because they were shadowkind, and that was how they worked. Even now, in the face of my irritation, Thorn and Snap only appeared to be various degrees of puzzled. I had the feeling Ruse understood my protest, but that didn't mean he sympathized. His smirk suggested the opposite.

"We didn't interfere with your activities," Thorn said. "I would like to know, though, what business that congregation of mortals has with the shadowkind."

"And how were those images put on that wall?" Snap put in. "So large and—moving!"

He drew in a breath as if to exclaim more, but Thorn cut his gaze toward the slimmer man with a firm glower. Snap shut his mouth with an apologetic dip of his divine head.

Suddenly I was twice as annoyed as before. Who'd put Mr. Brawn in charge of any of us? If their "boss" had brought all three of them on, then no doubt the apparent sun god here was just as capable as the others no matter how much the mortal realm amazed him. I'd rather answer Snap's awed questions than listen to Thorn's demands for information.

"You should have been able to figure that out if you'd been paying any attention," I said to the hulking guy, brushing past him on my way to the kitchen. They weren't going to stop me from grabbing the dinner I'd been looking forward to, even if my enthusiasm had dwindled. "The Fund is an organization of mortals who are aware of the shadowkind's existence and do what they can to help the creatures who've run into major trouble here. Whoever nabbed your boss, they'd be among the most likely to have heard something."

I snatched a frozen dinner from the freezer and shoved it into the microwave. I definitely wasn't in the mood for an extended cooking session right now.

The trio had followed me into the kitchen, Thorn in the lead. He folded his bulging arms over his chest. "It didn't sound as if they relayed any information that would direct us."

"They didn't," I agreed. "Because either your friend Omen got grabbed by some regular if particularly ambitious hunters and it's all a coincidence that he was talking conspiracy theories beforehand, or the conspirators are keeping their plotting incredibly quiet. I've got other people I can check with, though."

"You told the woman in white that you'd accompany her to a place called 'Jade'?"

Sweet jackrabbits and hares, how closely had he been eavesdropping? I gritted my teeth as I got my fork. The microwave dinged, not a moment too soon.

"Jade's," I said. "As in Jade's Fountain. It's a bar run by one of your kind, with other shadowkind as frequent clientele along with various mortals, most of whom have no idea. She doesn't like to get involved in inter-realm conflicts, but she'll pass on observations if she doesn't think it'll come back to bite her—or she might point me to someone else in the know."

Thorn didn't look convinced. "Are you sure this is the most fruitful avenue you could take? Talking hasn't resulted in any progress so far."

I resisted the urge to mash my newly heated container of pad thai into his face. Satisfying as it might briefly be, it'd be a waste of the food.

"It's the best strategy I can think of. If you want to keep busy in the meantime, how about tomorrow you show me the spot where Omen got ambushed and maybe we'll find something there?" Maybe I could move these three along before I even got to Jade's, and I could spend my time there chatting with Vivi instead of digging for clues.

"I highly doubt our attackers would have left obvious identifying ephemera behind," Thorn said, his glower deepening.

Of course he'd take offense to the slightest hint that he might have missed something. I shrugged. "Well, maybe I'll pick up on something you all wouldn't have. If you have other avenues you want to pursue, get to it. Now I'm going to go have dinner. Alone."

Since I wasn't likely to get privacy in the kitchen, I marched back down the hall. But my "protectors" couldn't take a hint. They trailed after me as if connected by a magnetic force.

I spun around when I reached my bedroom doorway, about to tell them off. Before I had the chance, Thorn barreled ahead with his interrogation.

"That young man you spoke to momentarily before the images on the wall started—he gave me the impression of hostility. Is there any chance he might have something against the shadowkind after all?"

Could I stab him with my fork? I did have plenty of those. Of course, who could say whether the guy's commitment to keeping me safe would hold firm in the wake of a direct assault. I settled for clenching the handle tighter and aiming my best death glare at him.

"Leland's hostility has nothing to do with his feelings about *you*, only about me. Believe me, if I'd thought he was relevant, I'd have mentioned him. There isn't *anything* else worth mentioning, so why don't you all go raid my kitchen again and give me a break?"

Thorn's face tightened, but he inclined his head. "If that is what you require. We will ensure your living space remains secure while you dine."

I couldn't help rolling my eyes, but he'd already turned his back. Snap slipped away too, still with a confused air that I couldn't help feeling a twinge of guilt over.

Ruse had eased back a step, but he lingered in the hall, his head cocked.

"You deserve much better than that dingus anyway, you know," he said. "He didn't have the slightest concern for *your* well-being or pleasure, only what he felt he was missing out on."

My hackles came up. "I told you to stay out of my—"

He held up his hands with a softer smile than usual. "I didn't need any mystic awareness to pick up on your discomfort," he said. "My regular senses work just fine. And you never said I shouldn't see what I could make of *other* people's emotions. His weren't subtle at all. I guarantee I could take you to heights he'd never even have bothered to attempt."

The seductive timbre of his voice sent a giddy shiver through me, stirring up the memory of our short interlude this morning. But he didn't stick around in any attempt to persuade me, just popped his dimple at me and turned to follow the others.

As the disdain he'd shown for Leland sank in, something clicked in my head. "You tripped him, didn't you? In the theater?" I said, remembering how Leland had gone sprawling out of nowhere. He'd never been particularly clumsy—and he'd been walking where the shadows of the chairs fell. It wouldn't have been hard for a shadowkind to extend just enough physicality to knock a mortal off his feet.

Ruse glanced back at me with a cheekier smile. "I figured he had it coming to him."

He'd acted on my behalf—because the way Leland had treated me and thought about me had actually bothered him? If it'd only been a ploy to win my affection, he'd have brought it up himself. I could easily have never realized.

The incubus was continuing on his way. "Wait," I said before he could reach the kitchen.

He stopped and turned all the way around, lifting an eyebrow in question. I didn't normally find myself speechless around the shadowkind or, well, anyone, but just this once, my mouth had gone dry. I scrambled to sort out the mess of emotions and impulses racing through me.

Ruse needed this. Maybe I did too. Why should I care what Leland or any guy before him had thought? If heights were being offered, I wouldn't mind going flying. I didn't know much about the incubus, but I was pretty sure at this point that, at the very least, he wasn't out to hurt me in any way.

And when would I get a chance like this again? Tomorrow they might find the lead they needed and give up the whole protection scheme.

"You think you can do so much better?" I said. "Let's see you try."

A pleased glint lit in Ruse's hazel eyes. He strolled back to me. At my gesture, Pickle leapt onto the bookcase just inside the bedroom and tucked himself away in the felt cave of a cat bed that sat on the top shelf, filled with rags he'd shredded. I raised my chin to meet the incubus's gaze in challenge.

"I'm so glad you've reconsidered," Ruse said, all smoothness and charm, but I thought I caught a hint of relief in his expression too. The earlier "snack" had only delayed his starvation a smidgeon. Of course, if I was going to give him anything more than that, we had a negotiation ahead of us.

I eased farther into the room so Ruse could come in after me and set my dinner down on the vanity. It could wait a little longer with this other hunger stirring inside me. I fingered the fabric of my blouse over the badge I'd returned to my undershirt. The incubus might not be able to see it, but the presence of those metals would prickle at his senses.

"It'll be even more enjoyable with the special effects," he said. "But if you're uncomfortable with me using any of my influence, I can hold back without your protective patch. My skills would hardly be worth bragging about if I didn't know how to ply my trade with the same parts any mortal can put to good use."

My hands dropped to the hem of the blouse. "You can feed, however exactly that works, but I don't want you peeking at anything inside my head—or heart—or creating feelings with your powers." A flicker of that icy panic passed through my chest. "Not even a tiny bit. Are we clear?"

"Crystal," Ruse said, with a grin that practically sparkled. "We can make this all about you, Miss Blaze. My most important need will be fulfilled perfectly by *your* fulfillment."

My body quivered in anticipation. The heat already rising through me overcame the chill of my worries. Why should I let events from decades ago dictate what I got to enjoy right now?

I grasped my blouse and tugged it up over my head. When I'd tossed it over the bed post, I reached for my undershirt, but Ruse touched my hand to still it.

"Allow me," he said, so low the words washed over me like a caress. I hesitated and then let my arms fall to my sides.

He leaned in, catching my mouth with his in the most delicate of kisses, like the brush of a butterfly wing. It shouldn't have affected me much, and yet it set off a sizzle through my lips and a pang of longing sharper than I could ever remember feeling before. At the same time, he drew the thin cotton of my undershirt up, skimming over my skin and grazing my nipples through my unpadded bra just firmly enough to provoke a jolt of pleasure through my chest.

He drew back for a second to flick the item aside, and despite my best efforts, a whimper of protest at the loss of contact spilled from my throat. Ruse smiled brilliantly as he gazed down at me.

"You're lovely," he said.

A giggle tumbled out of me. "I think we're past the point of you needing to seduce me."

"I'm simply making an honest observation."

He tucked his arm around me as he claimed another kiss. My head reeled with it, but I didn't intend to be the only one naked around here. As I drowned in the dark sweetness of his lips, I found the wherewithal to get to work on the buttons of his shirt. When I reached the collar, he shrugged it the rest of the way off for me without releasing my mouth.

Holy mother of miracles, his chest was as stunning as his face, all lean, sculpted muscle beneath creamy skin I couldn't resist running my fingers over. It felt as good as it looked, firm and smooth. The flames of desire kindling between us set off another flood of heat through my body.

Ruse kissed me again, this time so hard it left my head spinning. Then he tucked his face close to mine, nipping my earlobe and murmuring, "There is one other power you might appreciate me employing. If you'd like, I can make sure no sound travels out of this room while we're… occupied."

Um, yeah, that sounded like a good idea. "Be my guest," I managed to say over the eager thump of my heart.

He made a small motion with his hand and then brought that hand to the back of my bra. As the cups slipped from my breasts, he lowered his head to kiss my jaw and then my neck with careful attention.

His lips found every perfect point to spark bliss through my nerves. His hands stroked my breasts, his thumbs swiveling over both nipples at once, and a shuddering gasp tumbled out of me that made me abruptly glad he'd offered his soundproofing skill just now.

My hands settled on the incubus's head of their own accord. As he trailed his mouth down the slope of my chest, my fingers curled into the thick waves of his hair—and brushed against those small horns that protruded on either side. Their curved surface was as hard as bone and faintly textured to the touch, but warm as skin. I grasped them instinctively.

Ruse let out an encouraging growl and swept me off my feet. For a second, I really was soaring—in his arms, from the middle of the room to the middle of my bed.

The incubus bent over me, his gaze intent. His eyes flashed golden. The bright hue only stayed for a second before he blinked as if purposefully willing them back to their mortal-appropriate hazel.

I teased my fingers along his horns and back into his hair. "You don't have to hide it. I know what you are. Let out your regular form if you want."

Ruse smiled wryly at me. "Better not to when you aren't quite as swept up in sensation as I'd usually ensure. It's pretty… intense."

I studied him. "Do you normally need to magically sweep women away before they'll fall into bed with you?"

He dipped his head, teasing his mouth along the crook of my jaw, my earlobe, my cheek. "No," he murmured between the tantalizing kisses. "I happen to only pursue women who are whole-heartedly interested in the general experience. Shame and regret spoil the meal. But certain aspects are better accepted by the mortal mind when I can bring all my powers to bear."

I was about to argue that I could handle intense just fine without any voodoo, thank you, when he claimed my mouth again. The press of his lips was plenty intense on its own. Why argue when I could simply enjoy this?

He fondled my breasts as his tongue tangled with mine, alternately gentle and forceful at just the right moments. My skin was all but singing by the time he slid down to suck one nipple into his hot mouth, and then my nerves might as well have been performing a symphony. The only sound I managed to produce was a wordless moan.

His deft fingers made short work of the fastening on my jeans. As his lips and tongue drew every particle of bliss from my chest, the sensations flaring hotter and deeper with the graze of his teeth, he tugged my pants off me. One hand came back so he could work over both breasts at the same time to even greater effect, and the other drifted across my panties with a caress so light I couldn't stop my hips from arching up in a plea for more.

"Patience," Ruse drawled, the vibration of his voice bringing my nipple to an even stiffer peak. I clung to his hair. As he stretched out his torturously pleasurable attentions to my chest, I emitted all kinds of sounds I'd never have thought any man could drive me to produce. But this wasn't a man, not really.

Right then, I'd have said give me a shadowkind lover over a mortal one any day.

Just as I reached the verge of begging, the incubus eased even farther down my body, and I realized what he'd meant about this encounter being all about me. He hooked his fingers around my panties to drag them down, and then his breath was tingling deliciously over my core. Every inch of me quivered in anticipation. I barely held myself back from yanking his face to me.

He didn't extend the blissful torment too long. The tip of his tongue flicked over my clit at just the right angle. My hips jerked, and he held them while he brought his whole mouth down on me.

Lips and tongue and just the right hint of teeth, from that sensitive bud to my slit and back up again. The wave of pleasure that rolled through me shook a deeper moan from my lungs. Just like that, I was a goner. My head arched back, my eyes rolled up. I'd swear I saw shooting stars as I came.

Ruse wasn't done with me, though. He chuckled against my sex and lapped his tongue over me. I shuddered and whimpered, clutching his horns again, and he penetrated me with a skillful swipe. The ripples of the orgasmic aftershock swelled into a renewed surge, rushing through me higher and faster as he brought his hand to bear too. The pleasure built with each thrust of his fingers and press of his lips until I was bucking to meet him with abandon.

The second wave of release raced through me from toes to head and then crashed with a shower of ecstasy. I cried out with it, just shy of sobbing. I didn't know whether I deserved this bliss or whether I'd ruined myself for any regular man after this, but in that moment, I wouldn't have traded the experience for a million dollars.

Ruse lifted himself up over me. The flush in his cheeks and the satisfied gleam in his eyes told me he'd achieved everything he'd been looking for out of the encounter even if he hadn't gotten off. He leaned in to give me one last kiss on the cheek.

"That was perfect. I won't keep you from your dinner. Adieu, until tomorrow's adventures."

He stroked his fingers down my side in a final caress, pulled his shirt back on, and left with a soft click of the door closing behind him. My gaze lingered there for a moment longer.

Who would have thought? When all this was over, I might actually miss one of these intruders, just a little.

SEVEN

Sorsha

Even at midday with the summer sun beaming, we only passed a couple of dog walkers on the narrow path the trio led me down through the city's largest park. By the time Thorn came to a stop, we were completely alone in a denser stretch of trees. No sound reached us except the chirping of birds.

He motioned to where the path veered down a sharp slope ahead of us and passed beneath a broad concrete bridge. A vine clung to the rough cement surface. The drape of its leaves darkened the passage's opening even more.

"Welcome to the jungle," I muttered to myself. Despite the brightness of the day, this spot felt almost gloomy. "Is there a troll we should be paying a toll to?"

Ruse chuckled, but Thorn only frowned at me. "No trolls. Only enemy mortals, at least on certain occasions."

The guy had no sense of monster humor. I glanced around. "This is where the hunters—or whoever they were—grabbed your guy?"

He nodded, pressing one hand against the other palm. To cover his unusual knuckles while we were out where mortals not in the know could see him, he'd pulled on a pair of fingerless leather gloves, the same fawn-brown as his skin and thin enough not to draw too much attention on their own. Having his hands even slightly confined appeared to irritate him.

"Omen had noticed something unusual in this area. There's a rift between the realms not far from here, so shadowkind often pass through this area. We were… patrolling, searching for evidence. He told us to always remain in the shadows unless we needed to physically interact with an item. He slipped out for a moment just under the bridge—and they came at him from all sides in an instant."

"You hadn't noticed they were there?"

Ruse gestured to the trees on either side of the path. He was sporting a baseball cap to hide his horns, but somehow the sporty headwear didn't diminish his roguish good looks in the slightest. "We were farther back, spread out away from the path," he said. "I didn't even see what was happening until they were already on him. I'd guess they were waiting on top of the bridge, ducked down behind the wall."

Snap paused, his stance tensing as he eyed the structure. He'd seemed to take joy in just about everything he'd encountered in the mortal realm, but the attack here must have really shaken him.

"I could test the bridge," he said, his voice more subdued than usual too. "Over and under. Even with the time passed, if I'm thorough I might be able to taste something about them."

He walked on down the slope without waiting for our agreement. I glanced at Ruse. "Taste something?"

The incubus shot me a grin that set off a flicker of heat in my loins despite the situation. He'd disguised any weakness he'd been suffering from before well, but I'd definitely noticed more spring in his step since our encounter last night.

"You'll see," he said. "Come on. We did rush in after we heard the attack—let's see how much of the scene we can reconstruct."

"If we'd intervened in that first moment instead of holding back…" Thorn rumbled as the three of us followed Snap.

"We've been over this," Ruse said. "Even *you* held back because Omen specifically ordered us not to fight any battles we weren't sure we could win, and you could see that our chances were slim. Those jackasses were clearly prepared to fight—and capture—shadowkind, and there were at least twice as many of them as of us. They'd have taken us all, maybe to a worse fate than those ridiculous cages."

Thorn grimaced. "More than twice. There were ten. But in days past, I could have taken that many on my own. Perhaps I could have still. That's why Omen brought me on."

"You saw how quickly their methods subdued Omen—and he can put up a good fight when he needs to. I remind you again, you were following his orders." Ruse flashed another grin, this one at his beefier companion. "So really, if it's anyone's fault Omen got captured, it's his own."

Thorn made an inarticulate sound of derision, but he stopped arguing. Before he could grouse about anything else, I waved my hand toward the arch of the bridge. "What exactly did you see when you made it over here?"

Thorn tilted his head to the side as he considered the scene. His eyes, so dark I could barely make out the pupils within the irises, went distant as he drew up the memories. The breeze stirred his moonlight-pale hair.

When he wasn't talking or outright scowling, he really was something to look at. The scars that mottled his tan skin—one slicing across the bridge of his nose, another bisecting one of those hard cheekbones, various nicks dappling his brow and the edges of his jaw—only added to the valiant warrior vibe.

"There were the ten of them," he said. "All wearing a sort of plating of silver and iron over their entire torsos and like helmets on their heads. When Omen lashed out at them, it burned him. He still managed to take one down—slashed through his throat just under his chin—there." He pointed to a spot just beside the base of the bridge. No trace remained of the skirmish that I could see, but it'd been weeks, maybe months, and these people were obviously skilled at removing evidence.

"They didn't have just armor," Ruse put in. "Weapons too. Nets—not the dinky ones they use on the lesser creatures but like they were meant to haul in a boatload of fish, with silver and iron barbs all over. And these sort of whips that swung streams of light. I hadn't seen those before. They caught Omen up in the bindings before he had a chance to escape into the shadows."

Even powerful shadowkind had trouble using their powers if they were bound with iron and silver. As for the rest... As Thorn grunted in agreement with Ruse's account, a chill washed over my skin. *I'd* seen glowing whips in the past. A memory from much longer ago swam up: muttered commands, Auntie Luna's cry, and the arc of searing streams of light swinging at her to bind her in place.

That didn't necessarily mean anything. If there were new weapons that could disable higher shadowkind, anyone who set out to capture or kill them would be using them, with no connection to any other group implied. But I was about to press the men for more detail anyway when Snap leaned over the railing on the bridge above us.

"I think I've got something from that evening here," he said, and then, I swear on a unicorn's ass, he dipped his head lower and flicked his *tongue* across the concrete. It darted from between his lips farther than any human tongue could have, and he sucked in a breath with a snake-like hiss.

"Um," I said, momentarily lost for words.

Ruse was smirking now. "I told you that you'd see. Omen brought him on board for a reason too. One of his kind's primary talents is picking up impressions of the past from any object they encounter."

By "tasting"—right. I'd never heard of that talent among the shadowkind before. There mustn't be many like him.

The thought of licking that grubby cement made me wince, but it didn't appear to bother Snap any. "Yes," he said dreamily. "At least one of them was crouched here—she bumped her foot against this spot as they all vaulted over. A leather shoe, a little too tightly laced. Pushing fast."

"And probably no one else has touched that exact spot since then," Ruse said. "That's why Snap can still pick up something from that long ago. The most recent impressions end up overwhelming things from farther back."

Snap's gaze refocused on us. An apologetic note came into his voice. "That's all I've been able to find up here from the ambush. It doesn't seem as if it'd help us find Omen."

"The actual battle happened on the ground," Thorn said. "See if you can discover more beneath."

Snap leapt down to join us, landing on his feet more lightly than you'd expect from a guy that tall. He peered into the thicker gloom beneath the bridge. I found myself staring as his tongue flitted from between his lips to test one patch of wall and then another.

"He can't get sick from doing that, can he?" I asked Ruse. Lord only knew what microbes had taken up residence under there.

Ruse chuckled. "As offensive as it might look, he's not actually making contact, just tasting the energies clinging against the surface. As far as I know, *they* can't do anyone any harm."

That didn't sound so bad, but I couldn't have said I was entirely offended anyway. A certain amount of fascination was involved too. Especially when the dreamy tone came into Snap's voice again.

"One knocked his shoulder here in the struggle—a spot where the armor didn't cover his clothes. His shirt was torn. A piece falling. It might still be..."

He dragged his foot through the scattered leaves, twigs, and other natural debris that had collected along the edge of the passage. With a victorious exclamation, he fished out a small scrap of fabric. As he held it level with his face, his tongue flicked out again, not quite close enough to make the scrap stir with the motion. He inhaled deeply.

"Cotton. Blood from a cut underneath—Omen's claws. The one wearing it bought it—I can see the store—All Military Surplus."

I'd been in that place once or twice—a big warehouse type store on the industrial side of town. "That doesn't narrow things down much. There've got to be thousands of people in the city who've shopped there."

Snap's face fell. He looked so disheartened that I had to add, "It's amazing that you can tell all that in the first place, though."

"I can taste more when there's a stronger emotional association," he said. "He didn't care about this shirt very much."

"You're giving it your best shot," Ruse reassured him. "Anyway, that tidbit could end up being useful in some way we can't anticipate yet."

"I'll see if I can find more." Snap turned and ventured farther along the passage.

I turned to the others. "Can you remember anything else about the people who staged the ambush—any identifying details at all?"

The incubus spread his hands. "Unfortunately, my skills are fairly short range. I didn't get a detailed read on any of them—nothing beyond the expected aggression and fear."

Thorn studied our surroundings again as if searching for something to jog his memory. "Their faces were mostly covered. From their movements, they were thoroughly trained in combat. A few of them carried silver daggers as well, and one had—I'm not sure what to call it. Like a metal stick that shot electric sparks from one end."

"Some kind of taser."

"I don't know that word." His forehead furrowed. "It had some sort of symbol on it, didn't it? I only saw it for a second—it was mostly covered by the fighter's hand. But the swords in the design caught my attention."

Another, sharper chill prickled through me. "A symbol with swords?"

"Yes. Like a five-pointed star, but the two most horizontal points were drawn as the blades of a sword with a simple joint hilt in the center."

He picked up a stick from beside the path and dug its end into a clear patch of dirt. With several strokes, he sketched out an image so familiar it made my stomach flip over.

The star with the sword points. The hunters who'd come for Luna —I'd caught a glimpse of that symbol on one of the metallic bands they'd worn around their heads. And never found any reference to it since, even with all the searching I'd done in the first few years after her death.

I'd given up on getting justice for her, other than in the roundabout way of striking back against hunters and collectors in general. But the people who'd come for her hadn't just been a particularly vicious group of hunters after all. The symbol connected them to the trained fighters who'd come for the trio's boss as well, eleven years later.

They'd only captured Omen, not slaughtered him, as far as his companions knew. Maybe they hadn't been attempting to kill Luna either. What *were* they doing with the higher shadowkind—and what else had they been up to in the decade in between?

My three lost puppy dogs might be the key to getting answers, and to more questions than I'd even known to ask until now.

My heart had started thumping faster. "After they captured him, didn't you follow to see where they were taking him?"

Thorn let out a huff. "As far as we could. We can move quickly through the shadows, but not swiftly enough to keep pace with your mechanized vehicles."

"They drove off in a big truck," Ruse clarified. "No logos or anything useful there."

Snap emerged on the other side of the passage under the bridge. His tongue darted toward a spot at the corner, and he hummed to himself.

"One leaned back here briefly. Breathing hard. But he was pleased. Very pleased and a little relieved. They must have bound Omen by then." He paused with another flit of his tongue, and a faint smile crossed his face. "He said something—quietly, to a man next to him. 'Let's get it back to Merry Den.'"

Both of his companions stepped closer. "You could hear that?" Ruse said.

"Yes. The sound's blurry, but—he was so eager, the words stuck. Is that good?"

Thorn clapped Snap on the shoulder, so forceful in his enthusiasm that the slimmer guy both beamed and winced. "A name is excellent! The name of where they were taking him." He looked at me. "Do you know a 'Merry Den'?"

The bastards who'd come hunting didn't stand a chance now. I rubbed my hands together as a waft of elation filled my chest. "I don't, but you'd better believe I can find it."

EIGHT

Sorsha

Given that we had pretty much no idea who we were dealing with other than that they were formidable as fuck, discretion seemed wise. I held in all other questions until we returned to my apartment with the door shut and locked behind me.

"That symbol you saw on the one man's weapon," I said to Thorn. "The star with the sword points. Have you seen that anywhere else before? Any of you?" I cast my gaze to include the other two shadowkind.

Snap shook his head, a slight crease forming on his brow. Of course, from the way he responded to most things in the mortal realm, I didn't figure he'd seen much of anything on this side of the divide before this recent visit. Ruse contemplated the question for a few seconds longer before indicating no as well.

"I can't remember a time," Thorn said. "Why? Do you think it's especially significant, m'lady? Have *you* come across it before?" As he studied my expression, his near-black eyes darkened even more.

My chest tightened. I wasn't sure how much I wanted to tell them about that part of my life. I'd never gone into much detail with Vivi and the rest of the Fund members, even though they were the ones I'd run to—the ones Auntie Luna had told me to run to—after I'd lost her. My shadowkind guardian and I had kept so many secrets for so long, it was hard to break the habit.

But while I could hardly call these three friends, and they were by at least some definitions of the word monsters, they'd shared everything they could about their own catastrophe with me. I'd seen them at their most vulnerable, pinned by spotlights in giant cages. It wasn't as if sharing the story could hurt me other than the pain that came with remembering those times.

What I did know wasn't going to help us all that much on its own, though. Before I started making inquiries farther abroad, I should see if I could dredge up anything else from the past that might guide that search.

"I think so," I said. "Just once, a long time ago. But all I can tell you for sure about the people who had it is that they came after a higher shadowkind just like your bunch did. I don't know why or even what they meant to do with her. But maybe…"

I glanced at Snap. Ever since I'd seen his talent in action, the thought of other ways he might put it to use had been niggling at me. "Would you be okay with testing a few things I have here with your power and seeing what you can pick up from them?"

He brightened at the suggestion. "Of course," he said. I could see now how carefully he spoke so that his forked tongue barely showed. One of the first things all higher shadowkind seemed to learn was how to disguise their true nature among mortals. "What would you like me to examine?"

"I'll get the things. Why don't you sit down in the living room?" It'd be less cramped than my bedroom, especially since the other two would want to observe.

He tipped his head in agreement, his golden curls jostling against each other, and all but bounded through the doorway. You'd have thought I'd offered him a year's supply of ripe bananas, not asked to put him to work.

I ducked into my bedroom to dig into the back of my closet shelf. From what the trio had indicated, Snap's ability mainly picked up the most recent impressions. For there to be any real chance of him gleaning something about Luna's life, I'd need to give him objects I hadn't handled much in the past eleven years. I grabbed an Amazon delivery box I hadn't gotten around to tossing yet and plucked up a pair of sparkly sneakers and a purple scrunchie to set inside so that I didn't have to touch them too much now as I carried them over.

My attention stalled on a small, pearly box tucked in the corner of the shelf. There wasn't any practical reason to have Snap test that...

I wavered, a lump rising in my throat. Then, not letting myself second-guess the impulse, I wedged it into one of the hip pockets on my cargo pants. If I changed my mind in the moment, I didn't have to take it out at all.

In the living room, Snap had sat down on the plaid sofa, giving off definite eager puppy vibes. Ruse dropped into the not-at-all-matching polka-dot armchair that stood kitty-corner to the sofa; Thorn leaned against the wall by the doorway with his arms crossed. I set my box down on the wobbly coffee table in front of Snap and turned to the CD rack next to my little TV. I was pretty sure that at least one of these...

Ah ha, that one would be perfect. I slid the case out, touching as little of its surface as possible, and added it to the box.

"It doesn't matter what order you go in," I said. "Just see if you can pick up anything about someone who used them other than me. There might not be anything, but... it seems worth a try."

Snap set his godly face with such determination that his gorgeousness made my pulse flutter despite my nerves. "I'll do my best." He picked up the scrunchie first, giving it a curious look before raising it closer to his mouth.

Luna's devotion to '80s culture had included not just music but all forms of art and fashion. I'd rarely seen her without her light auburn waves pulled high in one of those contraptions. The purple one had been mixed up in my emergency-bag clothes—I'd only found it days after I'd fled. I didn't know how often she'd worn that one, but I'd never used it.

Snap's tongue flicked from his lips, and his moss-green eyes hazed. I stood beside the coffee table, trying to keep a relaxed stance, but my shoulders kept stiffening despite my best efforts.

I'd told him to look for impressions that didn't involve me, but that didn't mean he wouldn't still pick those up. When I'd pulled the thing out of my bag eleven years ago and realized what it was, I'd bawled for a good half hour.

The chance of him seeing that was worth the embarrassment if he also sensed anything that might tell us who'd been after my guardian—and what they'd meant to do to her.

Snap drew in a breath and paused. The corners of his mouth tightened. He shifted the scrunchie in his grasp and tasted its energies again. A restless itch crept under my skin.

Then his eyes widened. His voice came out as dreamy as it had at the bridge. "A shadowkind wore this. Yellowish-orange hair. A light sort of energy—she was fae. She fixed a flower into her hair with this once: an iris. *Purple goes with purple—I can coordinate at least that well.*"

His voice wasn't at all like Luna's high soprano, but he hit the melodic cadence just right. A shiver ran down my back, equal parts thrilled and pained. I hadn't expected to be offered an echo of the past quite that potent. What I wouldn't have given to really hear her voice—to have her still with me. What would she think of the woman I'd finished growing into?

Thorn stirred, his jaw flexing as if he wanted to say something, but he held himself in check while the other shadowkind continued his inspection. Finally, Snap set the scrunchie back down. When he looked at me, I saw more than just an apology in his gaze.

The lump in my throat came back. Everything else he'd gleaned must have had to do with me. Not surprising after all that time.

He might have been clueless about a lot of mortal things, but he was shrewd enough—and kind enough—to keep whatever private moments he'd uncovered to himself, no acknowledgment other than that hint of sympathetic sorrow. "I couldn't find anything else from her," he said. "She's the one you were hoping I'd reach?"

I nodded, not totally trusting my voice to stay steady. Thorn cleared his throat imperiously before Snap could reach for the next item. "Who *was* this fae? Do you believe she was captured by the same group that took Omen?"

I inhaled slowly, making sure I had a grip on myself, before I met his demanding gaze. Stick to the facts, keep it short, and there was no need to get emotional about it. All of this was more than a decade past anyway.

"My parents died when I was three," I said. "They were involved in the same kinds of activities the Fund is—helping the shadowkind. One of those was a fae woman named Luna. I don't remember much from back then, but I know they stayed close friends with her. She came by the house a lot, played with me... She was with me when my parents were attacked, and she got me away from there."

That day had become reduced to a few fragments in my memories: chasing fireflies in the backyard, their glow and the beat of their wings against my hands, a scream carrying through the back door, my mother's ragged voice crying, "Luna, go!" Luna's skinny arms around me as she'd leapt up with supernatural speed to carry me over the fence and away.

"Luna didn't like to talk about what happened, but from what I gathered, some hunters found out that my parents had interfered with their business and came after them in revenge. After that, she raised me. We moved around a lot because she was always nervous, but no one bothered us for a long time... When I was sixteen, she somehow knew people were coming—we grabbed the things we had packed to run for it—but they'd already reached the house."

"They captured her as they did Omen," Thorn filled in.

I shook my head. "I don't know what they were planning. At the time, I thought they were trying to kill her for being a shadowkind passing as human. They came at her with those whips of light like you said, and one of them had the star symbol on his clothing... They'd almost managed to bind her up when she must have decided she'd rather die on her own terms than theirs—and distract them so I'd have more chance to escape."

That knowledge came with a pang of guilt. I swallowed hard and managed to go on. "With her magic... She burst apart, like a firework."

It had been stunningly beautiful and horrifying at the same moment. I'd been so stunned myself that I'd frozen in place. Thankfully Luna's last act had also literally stunned her attackers, who'd stumbled around dazed for long enough that I'd remembered I needed to get the hell out of there if I'd wanted her sacrifice to mean anything at all.

"Maybe they were only going to capture her, though," I added. "If they were the same people who ambushed your boss. Hell, if they've been up to some kind of larger scale illicit dealings for even longer, it could have been their operations my parents disrupted—they could be the ones who murdered them too."

"Are you sure your parents *are* dead?" Ruse asked, his voice carefully gentle.

"Yeah. Luna wouldn't have kept me away from them. And, my dad at least... They cut off his head."

I had no visual memory of that moment anymore, only the fact of what I'd seen and the *thunk* of it hitting the ground after it'd been flung out the window. After I'd woken up nearly every night for weeks sobbing hysterically from nightmares of that moment, Luna had used some of her magic to wipe the image itself from my mind. *I don't want to take all of it*, she'd said. *You need to remember why it's important that we stay cautious. But the whole thing is too much.*

All three of my guests were silent in the wake of that comment. The weight of their hesitation filled the room. I motioned my hand vaguely as if I could wave their reaction away. "If it's the same people, then all the more reason I'll be happy to help you track them down. I just wanted to see if any impressions from Luna's things might be useful."

Snap took my cue to move along. "Let me try the others, then." He picked up the CD case and swiveled it in his hands.

Luna had indoctrinated me with a lot of her tastes, but I'd just never been able to get behind Def Leppard. Whenever she'd put that album on when I was a kid, I'd groan until she gave in and turned it off. I suspected *she* only liked them because of their name—she'd had a thing for big cats too.

Yet of course she'd kept it in the assortment of "essential music" that stayed in my emergency duffel bag. One of her top twenty, apparently.

Snap gave the case the same thorough examination as he had the scrunchie and frowned. "I hear a little laughter and the sense of her opening it on a couple of spots, but nothing more than that."

"That's okay. I knew not to get my hopes up."

He'd left the sneakers for last. I wasn't sure whether to have the most or the least hope for those.

Luna had adored them, called them her "fairy dust shoes"... but I'd also worn them for the most traumatic moment of my near-adult life.

Sixteen-year-old me, with typical teenage rebelliousness, hadn't left my shoes where I could easily snatch them up the night we had to flee. It'd started to seem so ridiculous that Luna insisted on so many precautions. Instead of waiting for me to search the piles of clothing around my bedroom, Luna had tossed that pair of hers at me on the way to the door.

They were too small for me by at least one size, maybe two. My recollection of the run away from the house she'd been renting was punctuated by the pinch of my constricted toes, sharper with each step.

No doubt Snap tasted that fraught impression first. He glanced at me again, his divine face haunted by a brief sadness, and then went on with his investigations. I resisted the urge to fidget.

"It's only fragments," he said after a while. "I think because it's been so long—I'm sorry. A lot of happiness when she wore them. And... I get a hint of missing someone they reminded her of, someone who was fae like her maybe? Did she have shadowkind friends? Someone else who might have been taken?"

"I don't know." I was a little ashamed that it'd never really occurred to me to wonder about Luna's social life or lack thereof. "Except when I was at school, she was always with me, and we never visited anyone. We never stayed in any city for more than a couple of years to make close friends."

But maybe there'd been someone she'd left behind in one of those cities—or way back in the shadow realm—that she'd never mentioned to me. Another sacrifice she'd made, one without my ever knowing.

"This line of investigation does not appear to be very fruitful," Thorn declared gruffly. He stalked over to the window to survey the street outside as if he felt he'd find more sense of direction there.

"It wasn't a bad idea," Ruse said more encouragingly. "When we've got this little to go on, can't leave any stone unturned." He flashed me a smile before getting up.

As the incubus slipped out of the room, Snap put away the shoes. He sighed, all this enthusiasm over contributing having faded away, and stood up. My stomach twisted, but if nothing else, he'd shown he could be respectful of my past traumas. Thorn didn't appear to be paying attention anyway—and what did I care what *he* thought, the big grouch?

I touched Snap's arm. "Wait. There's something else—not to do with Luna. Just, for me... It's even more of a longshot, but anything you pick up from it that doesn't involve me would be more than I've got now."

I pulled out the trinket box with its pearly shell casing. Snap took it from me with tentative fingers. He considered it and then my face.

"This wasn't the fae's," he ventured. "It belonged to your parents?"

"Yeah," I said. "It's—it's the only thing I have of theirs. They'd given it to Luna to keep for me, just in case."

There was a letter inside, one I'd pored over so many times I couldn't imagine it held any impressions that weren't of me. Telling me that if I was reading it, they were sorry they weren't there with me, but they hoped I was staying safe with Luna. That what was most important to them was me getting to live my life as fully as I could.

They'd known the hunters might retaliate. They'd been prepared. But I hadn't been. I remembered my mother's scream and the sound of my father meeting his death more clearly than anything else about them.

Snap dipped his head so low it was almost a bow. "I appreciate your trusting me with this. I'll handle it carefully."

He began his testing even more slowly than before, his tongue flitting here and there, his breath sucked in and expelled. I stuffed my hands in my pockets as I waited. Finally, he lowered the box.

"You're right," he said. "There isn't much. But they had a lot of feeling around this object, so a bit of it clung on even across that many years. They were very sad about the thought that you might need to receive this. Afraid of losing their time with you—but not of the course they'd taken. They were proud of that, of taking risks..." He took another taste as if to clarify that thought. "I get the sense they felt they wouldn't have had you in their lives at all if they hadn't taken those risks."

"Maybe they met through the Fund, through the shadowkind work they were doing," I said.

"That makes sense." He offered the box back to me. Our hands brushed as I took it, and he offered me a smile so soft but bright that I lost my breath like I had that first morning when he'd compared my hair to the peach. "The one thing I can tell for sure is they loved you more than anything else in all the realms."

I choked up abruptly. "Thank you. For all of this. I'll do whatever I can to find the people who took your boss."

"I know you will." He touched my hair again, just for a moment, still smiling. "I thought so when you broke into my cage, but I think it even more now. You're meant to do good things, Peach."

Then he ambled away, leaving me wondering why I felt as if I'd needed so very badly to hear someone tell me that.

NINE

Thorn

IF I WERE NOT BEHOLDEN TO OUR LIBERATOR'S EFFORTS ON OUR BEHALF, there were many things I could have complained about in regards to this mortal woman. The way she rattled the tines of her fork against the sides of one of the boxes our dinner had arrived in. The squeak of the kitchen chair's feet as she periodically tipped back her weight in it. The little laughs she made to herself while she prodded her "laptop" into producing information that apparently was more amusing than useful to our quest.

She made a lot of jokes, this one. Here in her home, out at the bridge, in that large room full of padded chairs where she'd met with the rest of her "Fund" friends. And always singing her silly songs too. As if Omen's life might not depend on how quickly we could decipher what had happened to him. As if so many other lives might not hang in the balance based on what we discovered.

But none of those things were worth putting into words, not when I knew that without her I'd have still been locked in a cage. I might not appreciate her attitude, but I'd ensure no harm came to her on my watch. If it itched at me that I wasn't out scouring the streets for our leader right now, I had only to remind myself that the mortal had uncovered far more connections in the past day than we'd managed in the many weeks before. The fact that most of those weeks had been spent in captivity only compounded that failure.

Omen had counted on us. He'd counted on *me*, specifically, to defend our group and subdue any enemies we encountered. It didn't matter what the incubus said—he was made to cajole and placate. I *had* failed, again, and if I didn't correct that failing quickly, it could turn into an even greater disaster than the time before.

"Ah ha!" the lady crowed, and waved her hand rather wildly at the glowing screen of her device. "There's a flea market in a town near here called Merry Den Market."

I couldn't imagine there being much of a demand among mortals to buy fleas, but she seemed satisfied with the discovery. I stirred in the chair I'd taken across from her. "You believe the people we're looking for could be keeping Omen there?"

"I don't know." A thin line formed on her pale brow as she tapped her fork against her lips. "It doesn't look like the kind of place hunters or anyone else dealing in shadowkind would operate out of… but you can't always tell by appearances. That could make it a perfect cover. It's closed now, but we can go check it out tomorrow. I won't be able to stop by Jade's until the evening anyway."

Ruse straightened up from where he'd been lounging against the doorframe. "A little road trip. I'm looking forward to it."

Since we'd finished our meal, Snap had been puttering around the mortal's living room asking the incubus about every object he encountered. Now, the devourer poked his head out, his eyes eagerly wide. "Road trip? Does that mean we'll take one of those… cars?"

The lady grimaced. "I don't have one. Not much need for it when you're living downtown—and you can make stealthier getaways on foot. I actually never even got my license." She looked vaguely embarrassed about this admission, as if there were any honor in burning gas through a metal shell to make wheels spin.

"I suppose it's too much to hope that there might be horses we can make use of?" I said.

Her mouth twitched, because apparently she found that remark amusing as well. "Sorry, but no. It looks like there's a bus that should drop us off right outside, though."

"Should we ever find ourselves with a car of some sort, I can manage to drive," Ruse offered. "I may even be able to help with the finding one part."

She shot him a skeptical glance, still smiling. "You mean you'd seduce someone into giving us theirs?"

He spread his hands with a smirk in return. "I'd rather think of it as reminding them of the potential generosity in their nature."

I shifted in my seat again, tamping down on my irritation. The incubus never took anything all that seriously either. His skill at reading and manipulating emotions *would* have come in handy if we'd gotten farther into our investigations with Omen, but he was no use at all in a battle.

"Let's see if I can turn up any other promising results, in case the flea market isn't what we're looking for," the lady said, returning her attention to the computer.

Snap was still peering into the kitchen. "What's a bus?" he asked.

Ruse motioned him back into the living room, following at his heels. "Let Sorsha do her computer magic. I'll explain."

"The computer runs on *magic*?"

The incubus chuckled before their voices faded out with the closing of the door. The lady's smile turned wry. "Sometimes it does seem that way. Including the unpredictable element. Oh, hey, Pickle."

She clucked her tongue, and the little green creature that appeared to follow her all around the apartment scrambled up to her lap and then her shoulder. She plucked one last morsel of sauced chicken out of the carton and offered it to him. He gulped it down with a bob of his long throat and a pleased thrum of his chest plates.

Watching, I found I couldn't quite hold my tongue about *that* gnawing complaint.

"You freed us and the lesser beings in that prison from our cages," I said. "Why do you keep this creature at your beck and call?"

She reached up to scratch the underside of the minor shadowkind's chin. "Beck and call? You haven't been paying attention if you think Pickle listens to me any more often than he wants to."

"He is confined here, is he not? You don't let him leave." I'd never seen him so much as dip into the shadows, though I couldn't see any evidence of how she might have forced his physical presence.

The mortal fixed her gaze on me more steadily then, with a puzzled blink. "He stays because he wants to. It's a pretty good gig—food and cuddles for doing a very half-assed job as a guard dragon."

Did she suppose that made her possession of him acceptable? "The 'collector' who imprisoned us fed us as well."

Her free hand balled where it was resting on the table. "You're comparing me to *those* pricks? Are you kidding me?"

Any trace of humor had left her voice. I'd clearly offended her. That seemed only fair, when the sight of her carting around her pet shadowkind offended me at least as much.

"You're welcome to educate me on exactly how it's different," I said.

Her jaw tensed. For a second, I thought I might see a flare of anger as scorching as that hair of hers. Then she appeared to master herself. She stroked the creature's flank.

"I don't need to justify myself to you," she said, her tone more cold than fiery. "*I'm* doing *you* all kinds of favors. But since you brought it up—Pickle can't survive on his own. The hunter who sold him or the collector who bought him had his wings clipped so he can barely fly, and he wasn't made to get around by walking—if you can even call that waddle 'walking.' Would anyone back in the shadow realm make sure he had all the food he needs and that he didn't go stumbling through a rift into a hunter's snare again?"

I had noticed the creature barely used those wings, but I had to admit I'd assumed it was laziness due to his captivity, not a disability. As to her question… I gritted my teeth before I answered, "No, I don't suppose there would be."

"Exactly. I wasn't looking to take on a pet, let alone one I'd have to hide from any regular person who comes around the apartment, but he was there in one of the houses I set fire to a couple years back, and he obviously couldn't look after himself, so I wasn't going to just abandon him."

She brandished her fork at me. "You should be glad I'm not in the habit of kicking shadowkind to the curb, or imagine where you could be. If you want to be mad at someone, make it the assholes who thought mangling Pickle's body was a reasonable way to treat another living being."

She was obviously mad at them. Her voice had stayed flat, but a tartness had crept into her tone, and the bright flash of her copper-brown eyes— I wasn't sure I'd envy any mortal being who went up against her. Imagine what she might do with a sword.

Perhaps, under the jokes and frivolity, she did care quite a bit.

"My apologies," I said, with a stiffness I couldn't smooth out. "I shouldn't have leapt to such a conclusion. You've been very generous with us—and it seems you are with your little green companion as well."

Sorsha eyed me for a moment longer as if confirming that I was being genuine. Then she relaxed in her chair. Now that I recognized the bond as one of protection rather than incarceration, it was impossible not to see the affection with which she tipped her cheek toward the creature to meet his nuzzle.

No, I hadn't been fair at all. I grappled with the twist of discomfort that acknowledgment brought and then leaned forward. If she could surprise me that much, I'd like to discover what else I might have missed.

"Tell me more about this 'flea market,' would you, m'lady?"

TEN

Sorsha

As we stepped off the bus by the flea market's gate, Thorn tugged at his fingerless gloves as if he'd like them better if he adjusted the fit for the one hundredth time. I checked Ruse's cap to make sure it was hiding all sign of his horns. Catching my examination, he tipped the brim to me in a jaunty salute.

"All monstrous features well hidden away," he said with a grin.

The four of us had gotten into a bit of an argument about them accompanying me at all. The trio had promised to keep their nature under wraps, but given Ruse's casual attitude and the others' inexperience with modern life, I wasn't convinced they'd keep it. I'd done my best to stress how ill-prepared most of my fellow twenty-first century mortals were to cope with the idea of supernatural beings in their midst.

I pointed a finger at him, just shy of waggling it. "I'll be watching you."

In some ways, Snap had both the easiest and the hardest time of it. Concealing his tongue didn't require any awkward fashion statements, but on the other hand, it also meant he had to rein in his enthusiasm at least a little—and refrain from using his power. From the way he gazed around us as we stepped under the awning that shaded the outer half of the market, he'd have liked to test a whole lot of the objects around us.

"Remember," I said quietly to the trio. "We're looking for any sign of shadowkind or that sword-star symbol. Try to stay focused."

Ruse gave me a thumbs-up. Thorn frowned as if he resented the reminder and strode on slightly ahead of the rest of us.

I had to give Snap a little nudge to get him moving again. He tilted his head at a curious angle, taking in a used electronics booth and a table stacked with scented candles. Farther along, pendulums swung on intricately carved wooden clocks. He couldn't seem to help stopping to follow the rhythm of one for a few seconds.

As I tugged him along the crowded aisle, he leaned close to me. His warm breath tickled my ear. "There are so many things here—and each array is so different from the others! Are they really all being sold? What were those objects with the numbers and the ticking?"

"Clocks," I said, scanning the shoppers and stalls around us. "They're for telling time. And yep, pretty much everything here is on offer—they'd probably even sell the tables if someone put up the cash."

"Telling time," Snap repeated in a puzzled tone.

"Like, how long it's been during the day. It took us an hour to get here on the bus."

"Ah! That *would* be good to keep track of." He peered back over his shoulder at the booth, so avidly I half expected him to bound back over there and grab one for himself. I guessed shadowkind didn't worry much about the passage of hours—or days or sometimes even years—while they went about their business in their own realm. From the way Auntie Luna had described it when I'd badgered her for information, things there didn't work in ways mortal senses understood.

The best I can describe it is that it's like a vast dark cave, one you'd never reach the walls or back of, she'd said. *You're aware of who and what's around you, but everything feels somewhat... flat. You could almost say it's like a dream, one interaction and another bleeding into each other without much logic to it.*

Do you miss it? I'd asked her, and she'd laughed and said, *Not while*

I can be here with you. But after what Snap had gleaned from her glittery shoes, I wasn't sure how true that was. No matter how flat and random the shadow realm was, how could you not miss the place where you came to be?

She would have loved this market. When I was a kid, she'd drag me off to garage sales and church bazaars and the like: anyplace where you never knew what you might stumble on that could be bought for not much money at all—not that she ever used real money when her illusionary magic could transform a few pieces of blank paper into a payment. She might even have gotten her fairy dust shoes at one of those places.

By the time I'd hit my teens, all I'd seen was a bunch of junk. I hadn't been to a market like this in years. So far, I hadn't spotted anything to make me think shadowkind other than the three who'd come with me had ever passed through.

Snap's slim fingers encircled my forearm with a gentle squeeze. "What are those for?" he murmured, his eyes almost round.

He was staring at a rack of bikes and—if you can believe it—unicycles in the corner of the market we'd just reached. The man behind the rack motioned to a kid I figured was his, who hopped up on a small unicycle and showed off her skills pedaling back and forth, her body swaying over the seat. Somehow Snap's eyes managed to grow even larger.

"Most people don't use those anymore," I said. "Not the things with one wheel, anyway. The two-wheeled ones are for getting around, like buses and cars, only they don't go as fast."

"Why use them, then?" Snap said as I ushered him onward.

"Well, speed isn't everything. You don't need any fuel to make them go, which saves money, and they're good exercise to keep your body in shape. And you don't need a license, so there's a lot less hassle and paperwork."

"Paperwork." His puzzled tone had come back.

I elbowed him playfully. "Believe me, you don't want to get into *that*. Come on, Thorn and Ruse are leaving us behind."

The other two had only made it about three booths ahead of us, but Snap took the warning with all seriousness. He darted between the other shoppers to reach them, faster than I could match. Then he stopped in his tracks, faced with a stall offering stacks of gleaming honey jars.

The woman behind the table held out a little plastic spoon. "Want a sample?"

Snap accepted the offering as if he wasn't quite sure how he'd gotten so lucky. He carefully dipped the spoon into his mouth so his forked tongue could stay hidden. Oh, boy.

If I'd thought I'd seen his face lit up with joy before, it was nothing compared to the expression I saw now. His eyes outright sparkled. He glanced over at me, not just reveling in the sweetness but wanting to share it, and my heart skipped a beat.

Oh, boy, indeed. That sensation wasn't just the awe I'd felt seeing his full beauty. Nope, the giddy tingle that had shot through me had at least as much carnal desire in it too. What would it be like to taste that honey off those godly lips? To experience his divine eagerness in all sorts of other ways?

I shook the giddiness and the questions off as quickly as they'd come. This wasn't the time for it. But when I dragged my gaze away from Snap, it caught Ruse's. He was watching me with a knowing smirk.

I gave him a light punch as I caught up with him. "Shut up."

"I didn't say anything," the incubus said, all innocence other than that damned smirk.

"You were thinking it very loudly."

Ruse tucked his arm around my waist as if we were some kind of couple. The slide of his hand across my back left me tingling all over again.

"It's nothing to be ashamed of," he said under his breath. "The boy's got something special. If I swung in that direction, I'd be angling to get him into my bed too."

I resisted the urge to kick him as a follow-up to the punch. "Did you miss the part about shutting up?" What if Snap overheard? Would he know what the hell we were talking about? I could only imagine trying to deal with *those* sorts of questions.

As far as I'd been able to determine, sex wasn't really a thing in the shadow realm. Shadowkind emerged from the ether, or whatever it was, rather than being born. The cubi kind had to venture into the mortal realm to sate their hunger. I'd never seen anything like a carnal longing in Snap's demeanor. He probably had no idea that kind of pleasure was even possible.

How ecstatic would he look when he discovered it?

Nope, nope, not chugging along with that train of thought right now. But I did let myself smile as Snap rejoined us, exclaiming over the spoonful of honey. His joyful sense of wonder might be catching.

Maybe places like this weren't all junk. I shouldn't let my former teenage cynicism color how I looked at it now. There was a sort of magic to the possible treasures you could stumble on—even more so when it was all brand new to you.

I spent most of my life dealing with paranormal creatures from an otherworldly realm. I had a pet miniature *dragon*, by all that was holy. I really ought to revel in that magic a little more myself, in between the difficult bits.

Thorn had marched deeper into the crowd. He doubled back just outside the doorway to the inner market.

"Did you spot something?" I asked.

His expression was slightly more grave than usual. I was learning to read the Thorn range of emotions, from vaguely discomforted (his happiest) through to "the apocalypse is nigh" (his most severe, I was assuming in the hopes of never seeing it).

"Not any sign that we were seeking," he said. "But I have a sense that a man several paces behind you has started following us."

I restrained myself from glancing back. Giving away that we'd noticed a potential tail was an amateur's mistake. "How sure are you? Everyone's kind of moving in the same direction along the stalls."

Thorn's frown deepened a tad more. "My instincts are well honed. I will observe more closely."

He headed off before I could say anything else. I glanced at Ruse. "Do you think we should get out of here?"

The incubus shrugged. "It's not as though anyone stalking us could have realized what we're looking for, since *we* haven't found any trace of it yet. I haven't picked up any ill intent toward us from anyone we've come near. And our disguises are firmly in place." He tweaked his cap. "I think we're fine. Let's keep going and see what they do next."

That sounded like a reasonable enough plan. Especially since while we'd been distracted, Snap had already wandered ahead into the sprawling building that contained the other half of the market. I hustled to reach him before he became so overwhelmed by amazement he forgot to tone it down to reasonably acceptable levels.

Somehow he managed to be equally fascinated by old leather jackets and the artwork on retro video game cases. But we kept him moving, studying the stalls as well as the walls and ceiling of the building around them. We'd made it up and down two of the four aisles when Thorn returned.

"Have you sufficiently defended our honor?" Ruse asked him.

Thorn glowered at him, but there wasn't much conviction to it. "The one I thought was following us went in a different direction and left."

"Ah. So either he's very bad at this whole following thing, or he wasn't interested in us in the first place."

"I might have misread the situation," Thorn admitted. "But I think it's equally likely someone else was monitoring us, and I simply attributed that awareness to the wrong target."

I scanned the crowd. "Do you feel like we're being tracked *now*?"

He paused, his gaze making a similar trajectory across the market. "I'm not sure. Not strongly enough to narrow down the source, in any case."

Ruse patted him on the arm. "That, my friend, is called 'paranoia.'"

The remark earned him a whole-hearted glower. Before they could get into a real squabble, I nudged them both. "Come on. We're going to lose Snap at this rate. Let's just get through the rest of the market."

My expectations had already been low. By the time we emerged from the market building's back door, they'd bottomed out. Even Snap's high spirits flagged as he took in our expressions.

"This wasn't the right place?" he said.

He was the one who'd given us the name. I couldn't bring myself to completely nix any usefulness he'd felt. "It could be that the sword-star bunch only used it the one time to pass Omen on to someone else or to get a different vehicle to transport him. It just doesn't look as if anyone with shadowkind connections has a regular presence here."

"I will—" Thorn started, and seemed to catch himself. He frowned, his gaze settling on me and jerking away again. "I'll endeavor to bring on a shadowkind or two willing to survey this location across the next few days to confirm that conclusion."

I suspected he'd been going to say that *he* would keep an eye on the market but then remembered his commitment to watch over me. It was hard to argue with him about that when he hadn't outright said it, though.

"You'd better let me do the smooth-talking," Ruse said. "That's *my* job here, after all. I'm sure I can find a willing candidate." As we meandered back toward the bus stop, he slipped his hand into his pocket. "And our expedition wasn't totally fruitless. For the lady."

He held out his hand to me with a little bow, his tone an obvious mockery of Thorn's formal courtesy. A gold chain with a pendant dangled from his fingers: a pendant in the shape of a curled dragon, its one visible eye a glinting ruby.

"Given your choice of pet, I thought you might appreciate it," he said, grinning.

It was a charming enough gesture that my chest fluttered—but also completely unacceptable. I admired the necklace for a moment longer and then tucked the pendant back into his palm. "You stole that, didn't you?"

"I liberated it from its display rack."

I rolled my eyes at him. "Stolen goods don't make a great gift, FYI. You can't go around just taking whatever you want." A decency you couldn't count on any shadowkind recognizing.

"You lifted some pretty trinkets from our collector," he pointed out.

I hadn't realized he'd noticed that. That didn't change my answer, though. "It's not the same thing. The collector had money coming out of his ass, and he was using it in horrible ways. The people who set up shop in that market—most of them are barely making ends meet. And even if they're doing all right, they don't deserve to be robbed. Take it back."

Ruse let out a little huff, but his eyes still gleamed with good humor. "As the lady requires." He stepped toward the trees beside the sidewalk and wisped away into the shadows to do so.

Snap had cocked his head. "Can mortals really produce money out of their—"

"Just an expression," I said quickly. "Don't worry about it." Especially when we had so many other things to worry about. I couldn't help studying the street around us in case Thorn's possibly imagined follower had trailed us out here.

No one I saw appeared to be paying any attention to us at all, other than a teenage girl who openly ogled both Thorn and Snap as she sauntered past. I could hardly blame her for that.

Well, our next course of action had already been decided. I exhaled, making a silent plea to the fates that today wouldn't be a total loss. "We've still got the bar tonight. Jade is a better bet than the market was anyway."

ELEVEN

Sorsha

I WOULDN'T HAVE CALLED JADE'S FOUNTAIN EXACTLY *POSH*, BUT IT DID have a vibe you needed to dress to match if you didn't want to stick out like a total rube. Inventive but sophisticated was probably the best description. I didn't get dolled up very often, but over the years I'd picked up a few suitable dresses for my nights on the town with Vivi.

For this evening, I pulled on the forest-green one that set off my hair—and my collarbone with its square neckline. The geometric element was repeated in the black buckle of the dress's wide belt and the cut-out pattern in the bottom few inches of the knee-length skirt. Flashes of my thighs in their silky black tights showed through those peepholes as I turned in front of my bedroom mirror.

Between the outfit and the makeup I'd carefully applied, toeing the line between striking and overboard, I looked a lot more sophisticated than I generally felt. Luna would have liked it, though, even if the colors weren't the bright ones she adored. I adjusted the cap sleeves, pepping myself up with a murmured lyric: "Neat seams are laid to please. Who am I to disagree?"

It wasn't just Jade's clientele this get-up would please, apparently. The moment I stepped out of the bedroom, Ruse let out an approving whistle from where he'd been hanging out by the living room doorway. "Not that I had any complaints before, but you *do* clean up nicely, Miss Blaze."

I pressed my hand to my chest in a mock swoon, although the appreciation in his voice had given me a quiver of pleasure too. "Be still my beating heart."

The incubus ambled closer. I could almost feel his eyes roving over me like a whisper of a caress. "I think it's much more fun to speed that pulse up. I hope you'll be down for some fun alongside all your hard work. You'll deserve it."

"Not at the bar," I reminded him with a jab of my finger. "You're staying put." I'd insisted that my entourage let me navigate this part of the investigation alone. They might be able to pass for mortal among people who weren't in the know, but there were bound to be at least a few shadowkind—including Jade herself, of course—enjoying a night out at the bar.

And Vivi. If she found out about my new roommates, I'd never keep her out of the perilous situation I'd stumbled into.

Ruse winked. "I'll just have to wait up for you then."

Thorn came out of the kitchen, where he seemed to have declared the one chair his official domain, to see what the fuss was about. His gaze skimmed over me and shifted to the incubus.

"She isn't going out to make merry or invite intimate relations," he chided. "This is about finding—and rescuing—Omen."

Ruse rolled his eyes. "Forgive me, my lord, for daring to distract the fine maiden from her quest. I'll just have to find another young lady to bestow my affections on." He sauntered back to the living room and swept Pickle's mannequin into his arms.

"You look absolutely exquisite tonight, my darling," he said. "No one could possibly compare. May I have this dance?"

I raised my hand to my mouth to cover a giggle. The incubus dipped the headless, armless figure low, filling his voice with exaggerated passion. "How can I resist you? And yet—how can I possibly kiss you when you have no mouth? My heart breaks!"

My giggle turned into a full-out laugh. Thorn's scowl deepened. "You're ridiculous," he informed Ruse, and turned back to me. "And you do look as if you've fashioned yourself to draw attention."

My amusement dampened. I folded my arms over my chest. "I don't see how what I'm wearing could be a problem, but maybe you should remember that I know a lot more about what I'm walking into than you do. This is how people dress at Jade's. People will trust me more if I look like I belong there instead of like I'm some clueless newbie."

Thorn let out a grunt that was barely conciliatory. He cut his gaze toward Ruse before returning it to me. "I suppose it's for the best that this one won't be along to divert you, then."

Something in his tone pricked at me. He hadn't said it in so many words, hadn't given any indication before now that he knew what Ruse and I had gotten up to in the privacy of my bedroom, but he knew what the incubus was. It wouldn't have been hard for him to guess. I was abruptly certain that I'd heard disapproval of our prior diversions under that statement.

As if there was something wrong with me getting a little enjoyment out of the company I'd been forced to accept. While I was running around the city and beyond it trying to solve their mystery for them, on top of that.

I let my lips curve into a smirk I intended to rival Ruse's. "Maybe I *should* bring you along. You could obviously use some practice in loosening up. Constantly going around like you've just put your best friend in the ground doesn't help us find your boss any faster, you know."

Now I was getting the full Thorn glower. "Do you have a problem with my comportment, m'lady?" he asked stiffly.

"Yeah, actually, I do. Considering all the favors you're asking of me, the least *you* could do is act like you're at least a little happy for the help."

"And what would 'happy' look like to you?"

I waved my arm in his general direction. "Allow a few words to come out of your mouth that aren't criticizing or ordering people around. Convince your face to appear somewhat less solemn than a gravestone. Just as a couple of options."

Thorn drew himself up even straighter, which with his considerable height meant that his head nearly brushed the top of the doorframe. Even Ruse, who'd set the mannequin back in place, tensed at the sight.

Snap peeked out of the living room and promptly ducked away to return to the TV he'd become enamored with.

"I haven't meant to disturb you," Thorn said, his voice even deeper and more gravelly than usual. He motioned to the living room. "I'm not one for chatter like these two. I say what I need to in order to see important matters through. And right now the matters we're facing give me no cause for happiness. The one who set me on this quest is lost, I was wrenched from my attempts to locate him for so long the trail has gone cold, and at any moment I might lose any of you as well—"

He stopped abruptly, his expression shuttering, as if he'd said more than he'd meant to. I'd definitely heard more than he'd actually said this time, but it hadn't been derision. The undercurrent of pain and fear had been palpable.

He blamed himself for what had happened to Omen. He felt responsible for his companions—and for me—and no doubt he would beat himself up all over again if we got hurt.

I could have told you those things already, as facts, but I hadn't grasped how deeply he felt that shame and commitment until just now. It wasn't simply an abstract idea of loyalty he was following to the letter. He was truly worried—about whether we'd find Omen, and also about what might happen to me at the bar tonight, to Ruse and Snap if we didn't unravel this mystery in time.

My own frustration simmered down. I still had the urge to give the guy a cheeky prodding and tease him into cracking a smile, but I could accept that it wasn't going to happen. And why should it? I hadn't felt like joking around or chatting or anything much besides lashing out when I'd first lost Luna.

"If you let yourself show a little more of *that* emotion from time to time, it'd be easier to take the grimness," I said, without any bite. "I admire your dedication. It's pretty impressive that you're working so hard to keep us all safe. Maybe we've all been a little on edge for good reasons."

His stance relaxed a smidgeon. "Perhaps."

"Well, then all I can say is that I've been figuring out how to keep myself safe for twenty-seven more years than you have, so I hope you can trust that I'm the authority on the subject. And I can handle asking a few questions around Jade's bar just fine like this." I gestured to my clothes and then couldn't resist arching an eyebrow. "I promise I won't stay out past curfew."

Ruse muffled what sounded like a snicker. Thorn sighed but inclined his head. And I reached for the front door with a sudden burst of nerves.

I'd been to Jade's dozens of times. I'd never run into any real trouble there. But somehow as I walked out to the stairwell, I couldn't shake the twist of anxiety that Thorn might be right to worry, and everything else might be about to go horribly wrong.

TWELVE

Sorsha

You've never seen a bar like Jade's, guaranteed. And not just because of the shadowkind clientele—or the human clientele, who were pretty unique beings in their own right.

Jade had taken the name "fountain" very seriously—and literally. Filtered water streamed in a waterfall across the entire back wall in front of granite bricks sparkling with mica. It was totally drinkable, and Jade encouraged customers to refill their cups there to hydrate between cocktails and shots. She'd also set up a little knee-deep pool in the center of the space, framed by matching granite tiles and curved limestone benches. People used it as both a wishing well and, when they'd had enough to drink, a wading spot.

Features like that attracted a pretty unusual bunch, but that worked in Jade's favor. It helped her and the inhuman customers, who had their own quirks no matter how well they'd adapted to mortal-side life, blend in with the rest.

Only about half of the limestone tables that stood at random intervals across the rest of the floor were taken when I stepped through the front door. The burble of the waterfall filtered through the upbeat chatter, and the sour tang of beer and spirits mixed perfectly with the mineral scent in the air. I dragged in a deep breath of it, letting it wash away the worst of my nerves. It was hard to feel all that stressed out at Jade's.

My gaze didn't catch on any explosion of tight curls or startlingly white outfit, so Vivi hadn't turned up yet. For all her fastidiousness about her clothes, she wasn't great at arriving on time.

That was okay. In fact, I'd been counting on it. I wanted a chance to chat with Jade one-on-one.

Jade might have owned the place, but she took a hands-on approach. Every night except Saturday, the busiest, she also served as the only bartender. Right now, she was ringing up the bill for a couple who must have stopped in for early drinks before heading on to other nightly exploits. Her dark green hair, almost the same hue as my dress, hung in neat coils halfway down her slim back.

Most people probably thought she'd picked the color to go with her name, but I suspected it was the other way around. If anyone ever asked, she gave credit to a special dye her stylist mixed for her, but I happened to know her hair grew in like that. It was the one shadowkind feature she couldn't hide away in her mortal form. In this company, no one batted an eye at it. The color complemented her smooth skin, the same rich brown shade as the tequila she was now pouring.

I sat down on the stool at the far end of the gleaming counter, which appeared to have been carved out of a single immense slab of quartz. That seat was a little removed from the others, and it had a splash of supernatural influence on it that would discourage any mortal not wearing a badge like mine from taking it. The understanding was that if you wanted to talk to Jade about shadowkind matters, you sat yourself down there and waited until she was ready.

It only took a few minutes before she moseyed over, giving me a crooked smile. "Sorsha. It's been a while. You're looking well. What's new in your part of the world?"

"Not a whole lot, but I was hoping to run something by you." I motioned to the rack of drinks on the wall behind her. "Jack and Coke, please." Only a cheapskate asked for info without offering their patronage first.

Jade mixed the drink with graceful efficiency and slid it across the counter to me. I took a sip and enjoyed the sweet-and-sour burn all the way down to my stomach. She never skimped on the quality of her ingredients, which was also part of what made this place popular.

She leaned her elbow onto the counter. "What's on your mind?"

Talking with her about Fund business or anything similar required a careful hand. Jade might have been shadowkind, and I was sure she cared at least a little about her people's well-being, but like most of the higher shadowkind I'd met who'd transitioned to living in the mortal realm, her own survival and that of her immediate friends was way higher on her list of priorities than any thought of the greater good. If she could lend me a hand without any consequences, she'd happily do so, but if the subject sounded at all risky, she was likely to clam up.

"I got a tip there might be something worth checking out at a place called 'Merry Den'," I said, pitching my voice low enough that the growing bar-room din would cover it. "That might be just a nickname, not something official. Any idea what that is or where I could find it?"

Jade's thin eyebrows drew together. She tapped the glass stir-stick she was holding against her lips. "That doesn't ring any bells," she said in a tone that sounded genuinely apologetic. "If it comes up, I can give the Fund a ring?"

"This is more of a private matter," I said. "Call me directly."

"Not a problem."

I sucked my lower lip under my teeth, trying to figure out how to phrase the next question in nonthreatening terms. "Has there been anything new in talk among the kind in general—about unusual behavior from hunters or anything like that?"

Her pale blue eyes went even more distant, and then she blinked, a flash of inspiration crossing her face. "You know, I have heard—and if anyone asks, it wasn't me who mentioned it—that there've been advertisements going out on the down low that offer collectors big bucks if they happen to have a particularly potent shadowkind in their stash. It sounded like some mega-collector trying to create the ultimate zoo." She gave a little shudder.

Huh. It was communications about a possible transaction to purchase shadowkind that had brought my attention to the guy who'd had my trio caged up. The way the pieces I'd seen had been worded, I'd assumed that collector was the buyer, but maybe he'd been considering selling one or more of his prizes. A higher shadowkind was about as "potent" as you could get. I might be able to get my black-market contacts to trace the other side of that conversation.

"Thanks," I said. "That could be just what I need."

"Just what you need for what?" The bright voice came with a skinny arm slung across my shoulders. Vivi leaned in beside me, shooting a grin at Jade. "Hey, Jade. Looks like you two are having a good chat. Anything interesting come up, Sorsh?"

I caught Jade's gaze for just a second with a twitch of my mouth I hoped she'd recognize as a plea to keep quiet about my inquiries. "Nothing major," I said. "But I'm glad I checked." I took a swig from my Jack and Coke. "What are you having? First one's on me."

"Well, now, that's an offer I can't refuse." My bestie laughed and drummed her hands on the counter. "One Cosmo, please, with extra lime."

As Jade went off to assemble the drink, Vivi tipped her head close to mine. "Come on now. It sounded like she said something you thought was worth pursuing. Is there a big bad hunter for us to sic the gangs on—if any of them will go for it? An illicit auction we could crash?"

I shook my head, shrugging her off as lightly as I could. I had to tell her something, but in a way that wouldn't invite her to join in. Going with a sliver of the truth seemed like the best tactic.

"It wasn't anything for the Fund," I said. "Just a bit of info that might help me find out a little more about Luna's life in general."

"Oh, hey! I've been dying to know more about her. Shadowkind woman takes in a mortal toddler and raises her for years—that's not your typical story."

My throat tightened. It was partly because of that attitude that I didn't feel totally comfortable getting into the details I did have about Luna with my best friend. To Vivi, it was a fantastic story. To me, it was the only life I'd known.

Vivi's childhood hadn't exactly been normal either, growing up with both parents already in the Fund and bringing her into that world, but she *had* two human parents still living—just enjoying a surprisingly ordinary retirement in Florida as of two years back—and never interacted with the higher shadowkind except for briefly.

In some ways, she probably hoped my weird history would bring some spice into her life the same way I'd been drawn to her relative normalcy.

"I'd like to look into this stuff on my own, at least to begin with," I said, as gently as I could manage. "It's pretty personal, and when I don't know exactly what I'll stumble on…"

"Oh, sure, of course." Vivi patted me on the shoulder as she grabbed her drink from Jade, but she didn't quite suppress her wince at my brush-off. Guilt twisted my stomach, knowing I was doing more than brushing her off—I was outright lying. Even if she couldn't totally understand where I came from, she was a good friend. And when I'd first come to the Fund, I'd needed that more than anything.

"How'd your date go?" I asked, switching to a safer topic.

Vivi pulled a face before sipping her drink. "Like watching paint dry while his grass grows. Why do they all turn out to be so *boring* when I actually get to know them?"

"Maybe because you've got a more unusual life than most people even know is possible?"

"I'm not asking that much." She sighed. "And it's not like the stuff we get up to is all that exciting most of the time. Fundraising and passing on anonymous tips—so thrilling! You know, my parents went busting up hunter clubhouses and all that when they were young."

The corner of my lips quirked up. "I'm pretty sure they only did that once—they just like telling the story an awful lot. I must have heard it about a hundred times while I was crashing at your place."

"Maybe so. But seriously. I'm going to be thirty in a few months, and I've never pulled off anything like that." She rested her elbow next to mine companionably. "You remember all the plans we dreamed up back then—epic rescue missions to free the shadowkind, sabotaging the hunters left and right?"

It'd be hard to forget those long-ago nights staying up in Vivi's room, chatting away until one of her parents had knocked on the door and told us to get to sleep already. She'd been the first real friend I'd had, the first person I'd talked openly about my life with other than Luna.

"What was it we were going to call ourselves?" I asked. "The Shadow Avengers?" We'd been too old to see the name as more than a joke, but the kernel of the idea, going out and literally fighting for justice—that eager rebelliousness from our teens resonated through me from the past.

I'd been seeing it through as well as I could, without her.

Vivi laughed. "Yeah. Like some kind of superheroes." Then her mood dampened. "We were going to track down the people who came for Luna too. You know, I'm really sorry the Fund never caught them. You'd think we'd be able to pull off at least that much."

The regret in her eyes made my throat tighten. Vivi might not totally understand what Luna had meant to me, but she knew how badly her loss had shaken me, and she'd truly wanted to make it right however she could. I hesitated against the urge to spill the beans after all—to at least tell her that I was probably on the track of those villains right now. It would be *nice* to share my hopes and worries with her.

While I grappled with the idea, a guy wearing a purple top hat bumped into Vivi as he passed her. She flinched toward the counter. "Hey, watch it with that drink!" she said, peering over her shoulder to make sure his beer hadn't stained her ivory jumpsuit, and my mouth stayed firmly shut.

If I told Vivi much of anything, she'd want to know everything—and could she handle getting into a *real* mess? These might be the same people who'd not only ambushed Omen and Luna but slaughtered my parents as well. If anything, it'd be selfish of me to involve her. This once, I could protect the person who meant the most to me.

I raised my glass, opting for distraction instead of a confession. "Enough about the past—drink up! It's time to hit the dance floor."

A few of the patrons were already swaying to the music in the open area next to the pool. When Vivi and I had downed our cocktails, I slid a twenty across the counter to Jade, told her to keep the change, and headed over to join them.

Vivi grasped my hand and swung me around with her, laughing. The broad legs of her jumpsuit swished around her calves. I focused half my attention on keeping up with her and the other half on scanning the bar-goers around us.

Jade wasn't the only being here who might have information they could share—and another shadowkind who wasn't as tied to this spot could be willing to say more. The tricky part was identifying the actual monsters amid the mortals who made themselves up like one.

I considered and then dismissed a guy with yellow cat's eyes—contacts, I was pretty sure—and a woman with a wolf's tail pinned to the back of her skirt that was obviously fake when I got a closer look. My gaze settled on an older woman with a dappling of shimmering scales across the back of her neck, only visible when her hair shifted with the motion of her head. She could have passed those off as a tattoo, but if they'd actually been one, I'd have expected her to show it off more.

Before I could think up an excuse to leave Vivi and sidle over to her table, four new figures marched through the bar's front door together. And by "marched," I mean they had the air of a military squadron.

An apprehensive prickle ran down my back as I watched the quartet in their business casual button-ups and slacks spread out through the bar. Each of them stopped by one of the nearby patrons, but from the other people's expressions, they didn't know these dudes. I got the impression the four were asking as many questions as I'd have liked to.

There was no reason to assume their arrival had anything to do with me. The clientele here could have been mixed up in all sorts of unusual dealings. But Thorn's warning that we'd been followed at the market came back to me with a nervous jitter. Any second now, one of those guys would come over this way and spot me. What would they do then?

It seemed wisest not to stick around and find out. At the very least, I could slip around to the front of the bar and watch them on my own terms—see if they focused in on someone else, and if they didn't, where they went after they'd finished their rounds.

I checked my phone, pretending I'd gotten a text, and wrinkled my nose at Vivi. "I've got to get going. Sorry to take off so early."

"Hey, we still had fun," Vivi said, but curiosity still shone in her eyes. "Need any help?"

"No, I'm good. Just going to duck out the back to avoid the crowd."

"Talk soon, then. And you know if you ever do need me, I'm all in." She made an air kiss at my cheek. "Ditto."

The corner of my lips quirked upward. "Ditto." We'd taken that as our way of saying, "Love ya!" ever since watching the movie *Ghost* together way back when.

I gave her a little wave and took off for the back door as fast as I could jet it without catching the preppy squadron's eyes.

THIRTEEN

Snap

THE PLACE SORSHA HAD CALLED A "BAR" DIDN'T LOOK ANYTHING LIKE THE long, straight pieces of metal I'd used that word for in the past. Even viewed from the shadows, the images slightly warbled and the sounds and scents faded, it was much more interesting. Interesting enough that I couldn't quite bring myself to ask Thorn whether it really was a good idea for us to be slinking through these shadows.

Sorsha had insisted it wasn't safe for us to come along. I'd have thought she should know, since she'd been here before and we hadn't. But Ruse knew a lot about the mortal realm and Thorn knew a lot about danger, and neither of them seemed concerned that we'd run into any trouble here. I could follow their lead.

Especially when it meant getting to take in so many new aspects of mortal-side life.

I slipped through a patch of darkness under an empty table to tip my head close to a glass that one of the mortals had left there, a trace of amber liquid ringing its base. I couldn't taste anything while remaining in the shadows, directly or with my deeper senses, but the sour smell tickled my nose.

"Why are they drinking these liquids?" I asked Ruse, a languid presence nearby. "They smell almost like plants gone to rot."

The incubus's chuckle came with a distant tone. "In some ways, that's what they are. It's called fermenting. It brings out some… interesting qualities that help mortals relax and find courage."

I peered at the people socializing in the room around us. "Are they bolstering themselves to head into some kind of battle?" Sorsha's world hadn't appeared to be the sort of place where masses of warriors took up swords against each other on a regular basis, regardless of the hints Thorn liked to drop about his past adventures in this realm.

Ruse laughed again. "Only battles with their own self-esteem and other people's opinions of them. Mortals come to establishments like this to enjoy themselves with friends and to pick up potential mates. Usually short-term ones, but for some reason many of them get much more anxious about that than looking for marriage material."

Mates. Like that couple over there, two men with their arms twined as they rocked with the music a few paces from where Sorsha and her friend were dancing. You could tell they were mates and Sorsha and her friend weren't because of the amount of closeness… and also a sort of energy around them that I could taste without even using my tongue.

Sometimes Ruse and Sorsha generated that kind of energy between them. But not always. I didn't fully understand what it accomplished other than that they seemed to enjoy something about it, which maybe was reason enough to want it. Like eating food I didn't need but that tasted so delicious.

Did they decide to create the energy or did it just happen? What did it feel like when you had it? I didn't think I'd ever encountered it in myself.

I might have asked, but as I turned in Ruse's direction, I spotted another shadowkind—not in the shadows like us but sitting at one of the stone tables with a drink of her own. A dappling of scales showed across her skin. From that along with her pose, I expected she was some sort of reptilian shifter.

"There are other kind here," I said, nodding toward her. "Should we avoid her?" We'd already known the being distributing drinks from behind the shiny counter was one of us, but she stayed on the other side of that large, carved crystal slab.

Thorn shifted closer to me, his presence looming as large in the shadows as it did on the physical plane. "Sorsha said our kind often come here. Why would any of them think it's strange that we're here too? It was an excuse to keep us away."

"She really should have known better than to assume we'd go along with that order," Ruse agreed with a teasing cluck of his tongue.

Why wouldn't she have wanted us to see the bar? Maybe I'd asked too many questions at the market earlier today. There were just so many things to experience that I didn't understand but wanted to.

Like the young man who was tossing coins into the circle of water to our left. I peered at him and then the coins, the metal discs glinting as they caught the tiny underwater lights. "That's money he's throwing away, isn't it? Why would they put it in the water? Is that how they pay for those relaxing courage drinks?"

"They pay for the drinks at the counter," Ruse said. "And mostly with paper bills or plastic cards. The coins don't buy much. They throw them into the water for fun and to pretend it'll give them the power to get whatever they want."

My gaze jerked back to the coins. "Does that work?" So far I hadn't met mortals who could work magic of any kind, let alone on that scale.

"Of course not. They just enjoy the pretending."

Mortals were rather strange about a lot of things. Before I could puzzle any longer about that, Thorn moved forward. I looked in the same direction.

Sorsha was stepping away from her friend with the swishy clothes and hair. She was smiling, but tension wound through her posture. A twinge shot through my gut. "Where's she going? Is something wrong?"

"She seems to think it is." I could feel more than see the flex of Thorn's considerable strength. "Four men came in together a minute ago. Their movements appear very purposeful. She may have had past dealings with them or seen some other warning sign."

"She's heading for the back door," Ruse pointed out. "We'd better keep up, don't you think?"

Thorn glanced toward the front of the room again, but then he turned to stride after Sorsha, leaping between shadows as need be. Ruse and I traveled along behind him. If any of the newcomers tried to harm her, we were between her and them now. It must have been a good thing we'd come along.

The incubus had been right about the door. Sorsha twisted the handle, murmuring a faint tune to herself, and pushed outside. We leapt after her into the thicker darkness of an alley.

A totally different combination of sensations washed over me: the faint chill of the night, the contrast between the dark, narrow space we'd come out into and the yellow glow of streetlamps at the opening a few buildings away, and a dank, definitely rotten smell seeping from the trash bin Sorsha darted around. It took me a moment to adjust—and to notice the figure that had already been out here in the alley.

The man looked so scruffy I might have taken him for a werewolf in mid-shift if everything else about him hadn't screamed *mortal*. He'd been standing farther down the alley, but at Sorsha's exit, he turned and headed toward her with steps that both lurched and swayed. A bottle of that sour-smelling liquid dangled from one of his hands. He didn't seem relaxed or brave to me, though, only unsteady. And intent on catching up with our rescuer.

"What's he do—" I started to ask, and sucked in the rest of the sentence and my breath at the gleam of a knife he'd pulled from his pocket.

He was going to hurt her. We had to stop him. Those thoughts blared through my mind clearer than anything—and my body went rigid. A sickly chill congealed in my stomach, so dense it erased even my memories of the treats I'd snacked on at the market and later at dinner.

I *could* stop him. I could—like that other time—but to do that again — Despite my urge to protect the woman who'd saved us, every particle in me flinched away from the thought with a smack of horror.

It was a good thing I wasn't the warrior among us. As I froze, Thorn hurled himself forward.

FOURTEEN

Sorsha

I PAUSED IN THE SHORT HALLWAY THAT LED TO THE BAR'S BACK DOOR JUST long enough to glance over my shoulder. None of the guys who'd set off my warning bells appeared to have clocked me as a target. As far as I could tell, they were still circulating through the front half of the bar, not yet looking or coming my way. Good.

In my bar-wear, I felt unnervingly vulnerable. The badge pinned to my bra might protect me from shadowkind powers, but it'd do nothing at all against human means of combat. After the mixed martial arts classes Luna had insisted I take in my early teens—*Because you never know if you might encounter some enemy that prefers brute force over hocus pocus,* she'd said—I could handle myself all right, but four against one wasn't great odds.

"Oh, girls just wanna have guh-uns," I sang under my breath as I slipped out into the back alley, not that I knew how to fire a gun anyway.

The alley was dark and dank, and a homeless dude was loitering outside the building next door, swigging from a bottle of vodka I could smell from seven feet away. Thankfully, it'd be just a short jog to the lights of the street. Once I was watching from outside where any searchers wouldn't expect to find me, I'd be much more in control of the situation.

I hurried toward the sidewalk, that sense of control already settling comfortably in my chest, and uneven footsteps scraped the pavement behind me. The drunk guy was heading this way too. I picked up my pace so I could keep well ahead of both him and his stink—and he lunged at me with a speed I hadn't expected.

The vodka bottle tumbled to the ground with a crackle of breaking glass. The second the guy's hand closed around my wrist—firmer and steadier than made any sense given his supposed inebriation—my fighting instincts kicked into gear. My body twisted, and my leg shot up for that most basic of self-defence maneuvers: a knee to the balls.

I'd say one good thing about him: he did have his private parts exactly where I needed them to be. My knee connected with his most sensitive appendage, and the air shot out of him with a pained grunt. He stumbled backward, flailing to keep his balance. A knife flashed through the air in his other hand.

Holy mother of mincemeat, what exactly had he been planning on doing to me with that thing? Drunk homeless dude, my ass. This guy had just put on a front while he waited for a target.

Had he been waiting for me specifically, or had I just gotten extra lucky tonight?

I didn't have the chance to ask him about it. I shifted my weight back, my fists coming up, ready to give him a lesson in why you don't attempt to knife random women, and the air between us split with a sizzling sound that raised the hairs on my arms. A huge, brawny form wavered into view in mid punch.

Thorn's fist slammed into my attacker's face just as the "drunk" guy had lurched back toward me. His crystalline knuckles raked through the flesh of the guy's cheek and nose down to a gleam of bone. A cry of pain had just started to break from the asshole's mouth when the shadowkind warrior *literally* broke his throat with a slash of his other hand. He gouged straight through the guy's neck, cutting off the cry into a gurgle and a spray of blood.

My attacker crumpled into a heap, blood puddling around him. Thorn stepped back with a satisfied swipe of his knuckles against his palm, and—holy mother of magnificence.

I stared, briefly distracted from the carnage. Specks of the guy's blood had spattered across the warrior's chest... His bare chest, with bulging muscles on full, glorious display. In fact, he was bare all the way down.

When shadowkind moved through their realm or through the shadows in ours, they dropped their physical forms, including any clothes they'd been wearing. It appeared Thorn had been too focused on leaping into the fray to remember to bring into being more than the essentials of his body, modesty be damned. And, wow, the equipment he was packing between *his* legs definitely lived up to the rest of his impressive form.

I jerked my gaze away after just a moment of gaping, but that was enough for Thorn to notice. He looked down at himself and let out a noise of consternation. At the edge of my gaze, I saw his typical tunic and trousers blink into being, covering all that deliciousness. It was almost a shame.

What was definitely a shame: the mangled body I was now staring at again, just a few feet away from me. My stomach flipped over. I sidestepped to avoid a rivulet of blood that trickled toward me. "What the hell was that?" I demanded, my heart thumping from the fight— and maybe a little from the eye candy I'd gotten right after, despite my revulsion at the rest of the scene.

Two other figures I should have realized would be along for the ride shifted in the darkness. Ruse tilted his head to one side as he regarded the dead man. He brought his hands together in a light clap. "Excellent smiting. A+ for technique. Maybe a little overboard in the nakedness department, but I'm really not one to criticize that."

Thorn glared at him with a twist of his mouth that might have been a little embarrassed. He turned to me. "My apologies that I didn't intervene sooner, m'lady. And for the... unfortunate oversight when I first arrived."

"I'm not complaining about *that* part," I said, and shot my own glare at Ruse when he smirked. "None of you should be here at all— you were supposed to stay at my apartment! And you—you massacred this guy." There really wasn't any better word for it.

"He was attempting to harm you," Thorn said, completely ignoring my first point. "He had a weapon. I was simply preventing him from using it." He frowned at me as if upset that I hadn't thanked him yet.

I supposed I did sort of owe him some gratitude. All the same... "Thanks, but I was handling it just fine by myself. You can't go around *killing* people left and right, even if they seem like real jerks. Unless someone's actually on the verge of killing me, you can stick to beating their ass and sending them running. Or rather, let *me* beat their ass and send them running."

Thorn's forehead furrowed. "I can hardly wait to see if an attacker will get to the point of a mortal blow. He was a miscreant of some sort. What does his death matter?"

I stared at him for several seconds while I tried to construct an answer his shadowkind worldview would understand. He clearly didn't subscribe to the idea that life was sacred regardless of what the living thing was doing with that life. Truthfully, I wasn't exactly *sad* that the asshole was dead, even if the sight of his battered body horrified me.

I'd never seen anyone die except Auntie Luna, and her departure had been more sparkly than bloody.

"On this side of the divide, we don't go around killing anyone who pisses us off," I said finally. "There are laws, and a certain mortal sense of morality... You might not agree with it, but it'll be easier for all of us if you try to respect it at least a little."

"I respect what keeps you and us alive," Thorn said. "That matters more than mortal laws or your qualms about our presence."

I resisted the urge to reiterate the fact that I probably would have been just fine even if he hadn't jumped to my rescue. One guy with a knife vs. my martial arts skills shouldn't have been a problem. Of course, who knew if my attacker had more than a knife? Bloody mess and all, I might find it in me to be a bit touched that Thorn was so dedicated to my safety.

They *all* were. Snap eased up beside Ruse and looked me over with a worried air. "You *are* all right, aren't you? He came at you very quickly."

"I'm totally fine." I brushed off my arms as if to demonstrate.

"If it makes you feel any better, this was no great loss." Ruse motioned to the bashed body. "I got a read on him before our fist-happy friend here took care of the matter. You aren't the first woman he's attacked—and if he'd had his way, you'd have been pinned up against the wall while he forced himself on you." He grimaced as he spoke those words as if it disgusted him to even voice that possibility out loud.

My skin crawled at that revelation. But the way the guy had gone after me, the pretense of being drunk and all, hadn't felt like some random rape attempt. "Is that all you picked up on?" I asked.

"I didn't have a whole lot of time to rummage around in his emotions and motivations before he and they ceased to be."

"Why did you come out through the back to begin with?" Thorn said. "Did you see a reason to be wary when you were inside?"

Oh, shit. I'd totally forgotten my original goal. "There were four men who came in—not part of Jade's usual crowd. I got the impression they were searching for someone. Considering what you three have gotten me mixed up in and your idea that we were followed this afternoon, I thought that someone might be me. I was going to double around and keep an eye on them from outside at the window."

I hesitated with a glance at the body and then hustled the rest of the way to the street. When I reached the front of the bar, I held myself to the side of the window and peeked inside.

I couldn't make out every corner of the place from here, but it only took a quick skim over the patrons to determine that none of the preppy guys I'd slipped out on were in view. Which meant they probably weren't in there at all anymore—it wasn't likely all four of them had squeezed into one of the nooks I couldn't see. My jaw clenched.

My shadowkind trio had gathered behind me. "It looks like they left while we were busy dealing with the jerk in the alley," I said. "Now there's no way of telling what they were up to." I might have been glad that my uninvited protectors had joined me if Ruse could have taken a read on *those* dudes. "I'm not sure they were looking for me—it just seemed better to be careful."

Snap peered past me into the bar. "Yes, that's why we came. To be careful with your safety."

It was hard to be mad at him when he put it like that with his sweetly melodic voice.

I headed back toward the alley with a sigh. "All right. We'll just all be extra careful until we find out how much attention we've already drawn. And if we want to make sure we don't stir up even more trouble, you'd better clean up the mess you left here." I shot a look at Thorn. "I hope you're as good at getting rid of dead bodies as you are at creating them."

FIFTEEN

Sorsha

By the time we made it back to my apartment, it was just shy of midnight. Normally after a night out with Vivi, I'd have returned pleasantly exhausted and ready to crash into bed. After this evening's events, uneasiness was still jittering through my veins. I couldn't imagine drifting off into dreamland anytime soon.

The clean-up itself hadn't been all that horrific. Living mortal beings couldn't travel into the shadows, but inanimate objects could, and my attacker had definitely been lacking in animation after Thorn's brutal defense. While the warrior had "given the body to the dark," whatever exactly that entailed, Ruse and Snap had spirited over a few buckets of water from somewhere or other. Based on the chlorine smell, I suspected it'd been a nearby public pool.

Splashing the water over the pavement had washed the remaining traces of blood down a storm drain. And voila! It was as if the dude had never set foot in the alley, let alone attempted to bring a knife to my throat there.

That didn't mean I was totally at ease with how callously Thorn had dispatched him in the first place… or with the attack and what had propelled me into the alley beforehand. Either I was simply having a very bad day topped with a sprinkling of some paranoia of my own, or someone had taken notice of the investigating we'd already been doing. I wasn't sure which was more likely, but the fact that the latter was even a possibility itched at me.

Luna would have said it was time to run. Hell, Luna would have been out the door with emergency bags grabbed the second these three had turned up in the kitchen. She was shadowkind, sure, but that meant her warnings about the rest of her kind had held even more weight. *Most of them won't see you as anything more than an inconvenience or dinner*, she'd told me. I *don't trust any of them I don't already know deserve it, so neither should you.*

But as questionable as I might find their methods, I thought the trio had proven that they did care about my well-being... and I didn't even have an emergency bag anymore. I hadn't needed one in the past eleven years—hadn't ever needed one except that night when the hunters came for Luna. As I meandered down the hall now, I found myself clutching my purse strap as if holding onto it would ensure everything was okay.

Snap leaned in to examine my face, his own divine visage so close that my skin flushed in spite of everything. The heat didn't reach my cheeks, apparently, because he knit his brow with concern. "You look a little pale. Should you eat something?"

Of course that would be his answer to the problem. I considered pointing out that there might not be anything to eat in my kitchen anymore, after the way the three of them—especially him—kept pillaging it, but I didn't want to make him feel guilty.

"No, it's not that." I flopped down on the sofa. "I'm just tense after... everything. If I put on some mindless TV and zone out for a bit, I'll start to unwind." At least, I hoped so.

Ruse hummed to himself as he sauntered into the room after us. "I think we can do a little better than *that* to raise your spirits." He ran his fingers over the shelves by the TV and plucked out a CD case. With deft fingers, he set the disc in the old boombox that sat on one of the end tables.

The buoyant beats of an '80s song careened from the speakers. Ruse came over to me and held out his hand to help me up. "You missed out on most of your dancing time—not that the bar was an ideal venue for it. This is more the music that'll liven you up, isn't it?"

I let him pull me to my feet, but I gave him a wary look. "Have you been peeking inside my head? I *told* you—"

He waved me off with a chuckle. "Miss Blaze, I don't need to read your mind to pick up on your taste in music. Your CD collection speaks for itself."

He had a point there. Considering CDs had been defunct for years now, I only had a few albums other than the ones from Luna's original essential stash. He'd picked the Top Dance Hits one—she'd owned every year from '80 to '89, but only '86 had made it into the emergency bag set. As the Bangles encouraged us all to "walk like an Egyptian," I had to admit she'd made the right choice.

"Okay, fair," I said, only grumbling a little.

He smirked at me. "Who has CDs anymore anyway? Are you as committed to the technology of times past as you are to the music?"

However much my spirits might have lifted with the beat, they sank again at that question. "They were my aunt's—I mean, they belonged to the shadowkind woman who raised me."

From the flicker of Ruse's eyes, he recognized that he'd stumbled onto delicate ground. He twined one hand around mine and tugged me into the middle of the room. His tone gentled but kept the same playful quality. "So that's where your obsession began. You honor her well by enjoying the era as much as she did."

I liked that way of looking at it. "I grew up listening to these songs," I said in my defense. "And they *are* catchier than a lot of newer stuff."

"I'm not going to argue. You're just lucky I even knew how to work that player." He gestured toward the boombox. "It's your good fortune that I happened to spend a decent amount of time in the mortal realm during the years those machines were popular."

He'd been passing over to seduce and feed at least a few decades ago. To look at him, I'd have placed him in his early thirties, but with shadowkind, that didn't mean much.

I gave him a sharp look. "Exactly how old *are* you?"

"A gentleman never tells." He winked. "Let's just say that on one of my first excursions across the divide, I shared pork rinds with Leonardo Da Vinci."

My eyebrows shot up of their own accord. "So, you've got several centuries on me, then. I never thought I'd be one to go for men quite that much older."

"I've made it worth your while, haven't I? Besides, age is more a mortal concern. In the shadow realm, we barely notice that time exists. If you calculated based on my visits into your world, it wouldn't add up to more than a few years."

I gave him a shove with my free hand. "In that case, I've been hooking up with a preschooler. *So* much better."

The next song was just starting. The incubus swayed my hand in time with its beat. "What does any of that matter? Humor me. You wouldn't want me to have to resort to dancing with the mannequin, would you?"

Actually, I'd have kind of liked to see that, but the rhythm was starting to work its way into my limbs. He'd waited awfully patiently. "I suppose I could give you this dance. Let's see what you've got."

Ruse grinned and spun me around, the motion taking my breath away for a moment. When he pulled me back to him, my free hand came to rest on his well-built chest. Gazing up into his roguishly handsome face with that dimple in his cheek made it hard for me to get my breath back.

I forced myself to step away from him, letting the beat carry my feet. It worked its way through me from toes to head. My arms lifted into the air, my waist twisted as I shimmied, and Ruse let out a little whoop of encouragement as he got down to boogie too.

We faced off against each other, sidled over to bump hips, and circled around each other as that song faded into the next. I was starting to work up a sweat, but the incubus didn't look the slightest bit affected by the exertion. He grasped my hand again to draw me closer and dipped me like he had the mannequin earlier in the evening. A laugh spilled out of me.

Snap had been watching from the sidelines, but something about that moment appeared to spur him to action. He stepped away from the doorway and started to sway with the music too, his golden curls glinting under the overhead light. He didn't know any dance moves

I'd ever seen, but his body caught the rhythm with such fluid motion that it was hard not to watch him. His sinuous style came to him naturally enough to look graceful rather than awkward.

Ruse pumped his fist. "Now it's a party!"

As if in agreement, Pickle scampered into the room. The little dragon hopped and flapped his clipped wings in a dance of his own as he darted around my feet. I scooped him up to set him on his favorite perch, keeping my hand by my shoulder to steady him as I twirled.

Thorn stood in the doorway as if on guard. His gaze followed us as we danced, but the typically grim set of his mouth suggested he didn't approve of this kind of frivolity. But it wasn't as if we had any leads we could be chasing down in the middle of the night, and frankly, I was a lot more likely to figure out this mystery if I wasn't all tangled up with tension. A gal had to let loose every now and then to stay sane.

I swiveled, dipped, and sashayed around Ruse again. Pickle bobbed his head in time with the rhythm. Ruse caught me by the waist for a moment, tipping his head to press a quick kiss to the other side of my neck, and heat shot through my body that had nothing to do with the workout.

He let me go, and I turned toward Snap, mimicking his motions as well as I could. I probably looked like an idiot next to his godly form, but what the hell. The heat kept flowing through me—along with a weird tingling that was seeping into my mind. I'd have blamed it on desire if it hadn't seemed to muddy my senses rather than heighten them.

I shook my head in an attempt to clear it, and a wave of dizziness washed over me. As my feet stumbled under me, Ruse caught me from behind. "Careful there," he said in that chocolate tone, but my pulse had hiccupped for reasons that had nothing to do with his sex appeal.

"I think—" My tongue was stumbling too. A chill prickled through me under the haze. Something was definitely not right.

The room was spinning now—or was that me? I pressed the heel of my hand to my head, but the dizziness kept washing through me, the fog closing in on my thoughts. My stomach listed as if I were standing in a boat on rough waters.

"I don't feel so good," I managed to say, and then I lurched right over to hit the floor on my hands and knees.

SIXTEEN

Sorsha

THE SMACK OF MY FALL RADIATED THROUGH MY HANDS AND LEGS. My stomach heaved, and I almost lost whatever remained of my Jack and Coke onto the living-room floorboards. My head drooped toward the ground.

Hands caught me before I could completely collapse. The music switched off. Ruse's voice reached me through the fog that had enveloped my mind. "Sorsha? What's going on?"

Then came Snap's softer but clear tone. "There's something in the air. I can't pick up any larger impressions from it, but I don't like the way it tastes. It's thicker over by—I think it's coming from the hall."

I couldn't find my tongue to offer any insight. Heavy steps I knew must be Thorn's thumped away.

Ruse stroked his hand over my hair soothingly. "Sorsha, something's affecting you—some kind of drug? I should be able to partly clear your mind so it doesn't knock you out completely, but I have to get in there first. Your little brooch blocks too much of my power for me to help all that effectively. Can you manage to take it off?"

A breath hitched out of me. My little brooch—my badge. He couldn't touch it himself—none of them could—at least not without it doing who knew what damage to them. The only way *he* could remove the badge would be by stripping my dress and bra right off.

I could do this, couldn't I? Just focus on that one thing. Move my hand off the floor to my chest. Under the fabric of my dress. Yank the badge off. Simple.

It should have been, but I wobbled when I lifted my hand. Even after Ruse steadied me, it took a few fumbles before my fingers caught on my neckline, and by then I'd half-forgotten why I was groping myself in the first place.

A metallic crash sounded from far away. Thorn's footsteps thumped back toward us. "There was a device at the door propelling some sort of gas underneath. I bashed it down the stairs. No sign of the person who placed it there—" He cut himself off. "Someone's coming."

"Watch for their shadowkind weapons," Ruse warned him. His grip tightened on my shoulder, maybe readying to get on with the stripping if I couldn't manage the task myself. "The brooch, Sorsha. You can do it."

Right. Right. I shoved my hand toward my bra. My fingers fumbled over the metal badge and snagged around its edges. There was a clip right... *there*.

It popped off the fabric cup with a click. I tossed it across the floor with a clumsy flick of my hand, and an instant later a warm tingling spread across my scalp. The sensation seeped through my skull and into my clouded mind.

Within seconds, the floor under me felt more solid, the sounds around me clearer. I raised my head, blinking. Ruse was crouched beside me, his gaze intent. Snap stood braced by the doorway, his eyes flicking between us and the hall, where I assumed Thorn was staked out by the front door.

The door slammed shut. "They're coming up," our warrior called back to us. "There are a lot of them—I can't tell what kind of weapons they have. I can take them on—"

"No," Ruse snapped, his voice gone ragged. I had enough awareness now to wonder how much the voodoo he'd worked on me had worn him out. That couldn't be a typical use of his cubi powers. "It's got to be the same people who came for Omen. You know they were prepared enough to take any of us down. And Sorsha's still out of it." His tone softened when he returned his attention to me. "Let's get you up."

He hadn't been able to drive all of the drug out of my system. My limbs still swayed as he helped me to my feet; my vision doubled for a moment before steadying again. My thoughts were clearer, but they jumbled every time I turned my head.

Something banged against the door so hard the hinges creaked. My pulse stuttered at the sound. Ruse gripped my arm tightly. "I don't think you're in any condition to stand and fight, Miss Blaze. Do we have any good routes out of here other than that door?"

I could think well enough to answer that question. "Fire escape. Outside my bedroom window."

"Got it. We're going to make a run for it."

He nodded to Snap, who slipped out ahead of us. I snatched the strap of my purse where I'd left it on the sofa. Pickle scuttled alongside me, his head weaving through the air anxiously.

In the hall, Thorn was braced in front of the door. It shuddered again, and his fists clenched where he'd raised them level with his chest. Determination shone in his dark eyes, but when he glanced toward us, taking in my near-stumble as Ruse helped me along, his expression shifted from severe to startled and back again in an instant.

"What have they done to her?" he demanded, and swung toward the door again as if he could pummel the attackers on the other side with the force of his glare alone.

"Some type of drug—meant to knock her out, I think. Either they figured it works on shadowkind too, or they didn't know we'd be here." Ruse hustled me to the bedroom. "Come on."

"If they don't know we're here, they might not have—"

"*Come,*" Ruse insisted. "We can't know either way. Is it worth risking us all ending up in cages again—or dead? Remember who was right the last time we got overwhelmed?"

Thorn let out an extended curse under his breath and swiveled toward us. At the same second, one final blow to the door burst the hinges if not the deadbolt. As it bowed into the hall, Ruse yanked me through the bedroom doorway.

"Open the window," he ordered Snap.

Snap shoved at the pane, which slid upward with a grating sound. My gaze caught on the curve of my backpack peeking from beneath the bed, and a cold shot of panic surged through me.

"There's evidence here—if they see it, they'll know for sure—I have to—"

My sentences broke with my colliding thoughts so many times I decided I was better off just acting rather than trying to explain myself. I grabbed the backpack, slung it over my shoulder, and then cast a frantic look around the room.

What else might I have lying around that would tell the invaders I was not just interested in Omen but had freed and destroyed the possessions of at least a dozen major collectors across the past few years? Shit, shit, shit.

If word got out that I was the sticky-fingered, monster-emancipating fire-starter, every hunter and collector in the state, possibly the country, would be looking to come at me the way they'd murdered my parents. I wouldn't be able to turn to the Fund either—they'd probably disown me.

The door clattered all the way to the floor, and shouts rang out from the hall. Thorn let out a wordless rumble, and there was an impact that sounded like his knuckles meeting flesh, but his own grunt of pain followed it. They had something that could hurt him.

There wasn't time to come up with a five-point plan of carefully considered action. My mind latched onto the strategy that had been my saving grace every other time I'd needed to cover my tracks.

As Ruse dragged me to the open window, a rush of warm summer air washing away the air-conditioned cool, I dug my bottle of kerosene and my lighter out of the backpack. My arm jerked, splattering the fluid in an arc across vanity, bookcase, and bed. "Thorn!" I yelled, and flicked on the lighter.

With a lurch of my heart, the flame seemed to leap from the tool I was clutching to my target before my hand had even reached the vanity. It licked across the polished surface with a waft of sharper heat and coursed along the trail of kerosene—over the floor, up my mussed sheets.

Ruse let out a hoarse chuckle. I snatched Pickle up, stuffed him into my purse as far as he'd go, and scrambled out the window after the incubus. Snap had already disappeared somewhere below.

More hollers, thuds, and grunts carried from behind us. The flames hissed, flaring higher—and then Thorn was charging through them, his fists bloody, a black mark slashed across his jaw where I guessed he was going to add another scar to his collection.

He spun just as he reached the window and exhaled a massive breath with the force of bellows at a forge. The flames whipped up all across the floor, crawling the walls toward the ceiling. A few figures I could only hazily make out through the flashes of light and the clotting smoke yanked themselves to a halt on the threshold. I tore my gaze away and dashed for the ladder.

The fire would only hold them off for so long. If they decided they couldn't charge through it, they'd race down to try to cut us off on the street.

A shout from below told me our attackers had been one step ahead. Someone had staked out the fire escape too. I wavered where I'd started down the rickety metal ladder, and Thorn burst through the window.

He sprang over me. Before I could so much as blink, he'd dropped from the second-floor platform to the ground with only a huff and a smack of his feet against the pavement.

Flesh mashed. Bone crunched. I fled down the ladder as fast as my limbs would allow, Ruse following just as speedily. Thorn let out a strangled noise, and there was a *thwack* that I would bet was a smaller body slamming into the wall below.

The second my feet touched down, the warrior grabbed my wrist and hauled me toward the street. He was limping—a jagged tear gaped open in his trousers just below his knee.

Shadowkind didn't bleed the way we did, as Thorn was demonstrating very vividly right now. Rather than liquid spurting, wisps of black smoke unfurled from the wound hidden by the fabric. The thicker darkness of the night swallowed them up.

I caught a glimpse of two bodies, one slumped by the wall spilling a lumpy mess of brains from its head, another sprawled nearby with its back wrenched to an angle that made my stomach churn. The smoke alarms were wailing above, gray billows streaming out the open window.

It wouldn't be only our attackers descending on this place soon. I ran with the shadowkind toward the street, thanking the heavens that I'd worn flats with this dress.

Get out of here—now, now, now. The urgent cry in my own head propelled me onward. Could I really outpace these hunters—or whatever they were—in my current state?

We sprinted down the street, my stomach roiling as much from the drug still in my system as the gruesome scene Thorn had left behind. My backpack battered my side. Then up ahead I spotted a veritable gift from the gods: a bike leaning against the fence outside a house on the other side of the street, not even chained.

I might not be licensed to drive, but I could sure as hell pedal with the best of them. I veered across the road, yanked it from the fence, and hopped on.

A startled yelp reached my ears—the bike's owner must have had it in view—but I was already flying along the sidewalk, the wheels whirring. My mind had narrowed down to one thing amid the lingering haze: get as far away from the attackers at my apartment as was humanly possible.

The buildings and streets whipped past me in a blur. My thighs burned, but I kept pumping my legs as fast as they could go, even as my balance wobbled. This late, hardly anyone was out and about. When a stream of traffic lights showed up ahead, I swerved down one side street and another until a perfectly timed green light gave me a chance to bolt across the busy road.

I'd lost all track of my supernatural companions, but at this hour, the city was more shadow than not. They might not be able to match a truck's speed, but I hoped they were keeping up with my bike by the means only they could use. Better they traveled in ways no mortals could see them anyway.

Every now and then, I shot down an alley or cut across a parking lot—taking routes no larger vehicle could use in case I'd picked up less welcome followers. After several of those and an ache that had expanded all through my legs, my panic eased off. I pedaled on for at least another ten minutes before I finally coasted to a stop at the corner of a block of low-rise apartment buildings.

The back of my dress clung to my skin, damp with sweat. The night air stung as I sucked it down my raw throat. My breaths and my pulse gradually evened out. In my purse, Pickle squirmed and let out a mournful-sounding squeak.

I still had him. I had my wallet and my phone and other purse essentials—I had my cat-burglar-esque equipment in my backpack. Everything else…

Three forms emerged from the shadows around me. As the last of the adrenaline drained away, the full impact of what I'd left behind —left behind in *flames*—hit me too hard for me to acknowledge the trio.

Luna's CD collection. Her fairy dust shoes and her scrunchie. I didn't give a shit about my own clothes—those I could replace—but the few fragments of her life I'd been able to hold onto…

The pearly box with my parents' letter. That realization came like a punch to the gut. I nearly doubled over as I clung to the handlebars.

I'd stuck the box back on the shelf in the closet. I hadn't even thought of it, I'd been in such a rush. The fire would have consumed everything in that room, if not the entire apartment. The one gift my parents had left for me was utterly gone, and I had no way of ever replacing it.

My guts felt as if they'd knotted into a solid mass of mourning. I hadn't been ready, not for any of this. More than a decade in the same city, three years in the same apartment—I'd gotten complacent. So fucking stupid. Luna had taught me better than that.

"Sorsha?" Snap said tentatively. He brushed a gentle hand over my shoulder.

I inhaled sharply and forced myself to straighten up. The ache in my weary legs was nothing compared to the stab of loss in my chest, but these three wouldn't understand why I cared so much about those things. I'd just have to swallow the grief down like I had Luna's death and the other losses since…

As I dismounted the bike, Thorn stepped closer. The tear remained in his trousers, but his calf had stopped leaking the smoke of his essence. That seemed like a good sign. Shadowkind did usually heal quickly.

"You should probably hold onto this," he said, holding out one of his brawny hands. "It seems rather... delicate. It didn't entirely survive the fighting I've already had to do—I apologize."

He was offering me the box I'd just been mourning. A crack ran through the pearly lid, and one of the corners was chipped, but it was *here*. Whole and unburned.

I snatched it from him much more hastily than was really polite and popped it open. The letter was still nestled inside, my mother's spiky handwriting scrawled across the notepaper. I snapped the box shut again with the irrational terror that a sudden wind might steal that treasure from me after all.

A lump filled my throat. I stared up at Thorn's face. "When did you take this?" And the bigger question: *Why?*

His rugged features revealed no more than his usual grimness. "I noticed it in your closet as I was coming into the bedroom. It appeared, before, that it was important to you. I thought you would want it saved from the flames."

I hadn't realized he'd been paying any attention when I'd talked to Snap about it, let alone that he'd recognized the depth of my connection to what must have looked to him like a fairly mundane object. He'd risked a few seconds in the battle to rescue it for me. That was worth a heck of a lot more than any heads he'd bashed in on my behalf.

"Thank you," I said, swallowing hard. "I would have hated to lose it. Honestly, I don't know how to thank you enough."

As I searched his face for the compassion he must have acted on, his expression tensed under my scrutiny.

"It was nothing," he said brusquely. "Certainly not compared to the debt I'm still repaying. We shouldn't linger out here in the open for much longer, should we?"

I winced inwardly at the curt dismissal. Maybe that was all he'd been thinking of—how he owed me for getting him and the others out of those cages. However he felt about me, he obviously didn't want to waste any time accepting my gratitude.

I slipped the box into a safe compartment of my backpack. "You're right. We've got to hole up somewhere for the night. I'm totally wiped —we can take stock and make bigger plans in the morning."

Ruse cocked his head toward the apartment buildings beside us. "It looks like we have an extensive spread of possible hideouts. Let's see which ones we can use."

SEVENTEEN

Sorsha

As we reached the apartment building, I started rummaging through my backpack for my lockpicking tools. Before I'd even set my hands on them, Ruse had slipped through the shadows into that of a potted plant on the other side of the lobby door. He opened it for us with a flourish. "Gentlemen, madam."

Right. Breaking and entering was a hell of a lot easier when you had supernatural powers on your side. For a second, my skills seemed to pale in comparison.

On the other hand, I couldn't be defeated by a spotlight and a few pieces of iron and silver, so maybe it was fairest to say we simply had different strengths.

Getting inside the building didn't solve all our problems. "We can't waltz into any old apartment," I whispered. "The current tenants aren't going to be as welcoming to uninvited guests as I was to you three."

"I can check to see which are unoccupied," Ruse said, and tipped his head to Snap. "If you take a taste of the doors for those, you might be able to tell how soon the residents were planning on coming back."

Snap nodded, eager as always to contribute to our plans.

As we checked out the hall of apartments that branched off from the dingy lobby, Thorn kept scanning ahead and behind, his stance tensed, as if expecting another attack. Based on the threadbare carpet and its faintly musty smell, this clearly wasn't a five-star residence—but that was better for us as far as security went. All the same, the atmosphere combined with the scene I'd just fled set my skin crawling.

With my next breath, I quietly sang a lyric I'd mangled into pure nonsense. "Til now, I always got pie on my own—I never really dared until I met brew." Ruse raised an eyebrow at me, and I grimaced back at him. "It makes me feel better. And I could use a whole lot of better right now."

"Whatever makes you happy, Miss Blaze," he said with a grin, and slipped through the shadows around the first door. He emerged seconds later shaking his head, and we moved on to the next.

"How many people know of your involvement with this 'Fund' and where you live?" Thorn asked, managing to keep his own voice quiet to fit our current stealth mode.

"No one outside of the Fund knows about the Fund," I said. "Well, other than some of the higher shadowkind who live mortal-side, like Jade—and the hunters and collectors are at least vaguely aware that we're around. I haven't had anyone over at my place since I adopted Pickle." I reached into my purse to scratch the dragon's back between his wings, and he let out a hum that was almost a purr. "Even the Fund people wouldn't really approve of me keeping him, despite the circumstances."

"But someone who'd visited you there before might have remembered."

"Possibly. That's still a very limited number of people—and no one I can think of would have given my address to a stranger." I sucked my lower lip under my teeth to worry at it as Ruse returned from the fifth apartment. He motioned to Snap, and we stopped while the godly shadowkind worked his powers.

"Whoever's decided they need to bring me in—or shut me up—wouldn't need to drag the information out of my friends anyway," I said. "If someone saw us at the bridge or the market, or realized I was at the bar asking questions, it wouldn't be hard for them to find out my name. Which is unfortunately a pretty distinctive name. Anyone who can orchestrate some kind of conspiracy against the higher shadowkind should be able to dig up my address from that no problem." My black market contacts did the same with collectors using less definitive information.

Snap drew back after several flicks of his tongue around the doorknob. "They expected to return in the morning," he said. We needed longer than that.

"The real question," Ruse said as we moved on, "is what made our enemies so sure you were going to cause trouble for them."

"They could be monitoring Fund activities—could know I've been involved with that. And then seeing me poking around at all made them nervous." Which made *me* even more glad that I'd kept Vivi out of this mess. If she'd come along on our earlier investigations, would they have stormed her apartment too? She wouldn't have had three shadowkind guards ready to jump in and protect her.

No, I couldn't let my best friend hear a peep about this, not while the assholes who'd come for me tonight were still on the loose.

"The sword-star people are very powerful," Thorn said darkly. "We can't know everything they're capable of finding out—or doing." He glanced over his shoulder again.

"There's no way they could predict we'd come *here*," I reminded him. "I don't even know where here is."

"We weren't truly prepared for them to launch an attack at your apartment. It could have gone much worse. I won't be caught off-guard again."

I wasn't going to argue with him there. As irritated as I'd been with my unexpected—and stubborn—houseguests, I was awfully grateful that they'd been around tonight.

"Next time," the warrior added, "if there's a chance that doesn't risk our escaping unscathed, I'll take one of the attackers for questioning. Ruse can persuade them to talk."

"You bring me the guy, and I'll work my magic," the incubus agreed as he wisped from the last first-floor apartment. "Looks like we're heading upstairs."

Uneasiness itched at my skin as we tramped up the steps, but after a few more unworkable apartments, Ruse found another that was currently empty. "There was a calendar on the fridge with the next week marked off as a vacation," he said. "We may have our jackpot! Snap, do the honors?"

Snap leaned in to sample the impressions that floated around the door. He straightened up with a brilliant smile. "They were imagining a plane ride and beaches on the other side. One of them asked the other if they'd remembered to have the mail held until they got back."

"Then they're not expecting anyone else to be dropping by either. Perfect." Ruse clapped his hands and vanished through the shadows again. A second later, he was opening the apartment door for us from the inside.

Crashing in some stranger's apartment had sounded like a sensible enough option when it'd only been in theory. Going to anyone I knew was way too risky, and I hadn't seen any hotels around here we could check in to. Stepping over the threshold into someone else's home, though, sent an uncomfortable prickle down my spine.

Everywhere I looked, my gaze caught on remnants of the people who lived here. A bright pink jacket with rabbit fur trim on the hood hung on one of the hooks in the front hall next to a scuffed-up leather duster. They must have eaten bacon for breakfast the morning before they'd left, because a hint of that salty, greasy scent lingered by the kitchen. The living room held an old record player and a stack of cardboard sleeves way more ancient than my CDs.

Standing in the living room doorway, the sense of mourning crept over me again. Those CDs were gone—melted in the fire, most likely. So were all my clothes except what I wore on my back. The pieces of furniture that might not have matched but that I'd picked out based on comfiness. My laptop, which had been lying on my unmade bed where I'd last been using it. The goofy hand-painted mug Vivi had given me several Christmases ago.

Everything I'd owned that I wasn't carrying, from the practical to the sentimental, had been burned away. Even if the fire hadn't reached every corner of the apartment, it'd be too dangerous to go back to scavenge. The thoroughness with which I'd thrown the life I'd built there away hit me at full force for the first time. I gripped the doorframe, riding out the wave of loss.

I'd picked up the pieces of my life before with nothing but a single duffel bag's worth of possessions and strength of will. I could do it again. And I couldn't say I regretted the actions that must have brought on tonight's attack. I'd rather get to the bottom of Luna's death than have all that *stuff*.

But still. It'd been *my* stuff. It'd been my home, the first one that had really felt totally mine after bouncing from one Fund member's house to another and then shacking up with the one serious boyfriend of my early twenties. I inhaled and exhaled, groping for my self-control, willing back the tears that had started to burn at the corners of my eyes.

Before my shadowkind trio could notice my momentary fragility—or at least, before they could ask any questions about it that might break open the floodgates—I pushed myself onward down the hall.

Mercifully, there were two bedrooms. The first one I peeked into, a small, windowless space that was probably meant to be a den, had just enough room for a double bed and a tiny birch table beside it, both of which might have come straight from Ikea.

I guessed that one served as a guest bedroom, because the master bedroom next door blared personality. A pink shag rug, flower decals all over the walls, lava lamp on the dresser, orange-and-pink patterned bedspread framed by velvet cushions—it was a '60s-style dream.

"Well, I can't possibly sleep in there," I said, grateful for the excuse. Slipping into a bed someone else had clearly made their own gave me even more creeps than simply entering their apartment. "My sensibilities are fully offended."

"It does have plenty of character," Ruse said, his tone amused.

Thorn shifted his weight on his feet. "I'm going to take a circuit of the neighborhood," he announced. "Ensure there are no additional dangers lurking that we should be aware of."

He strode off without waiting for a response. Snap had already bounded off into the kitchen, the cabinet doors squeaking as he opened each to ogle the contents. I should probably have felt guilty about the food that wasn't ours he was going to be chowing down on, but I couldn't quite bring myself to care in that moment. I'd just lost the majority of my worldly possessions. Mr. and Mrs. '60s fanatics could spare a little grub.

I crossed the hall to the other bedroom and set down my purse.

Pickle sprang out, shook himself with a huff, and trotted down the hall to join Snap, maybe pursuing a late dinner of his own.

Ruse had lingered at my side. When I turned to face him, his warm hazel eyes searched mine. "I expect you could use some rest. If you need anything, you know where to find us."

"Yeah," I said, and my throat tightened for a different reason. The incubus had worked awfully hard to lighten my spirits tonight—and then had his efforts ruined by that unexpected assault on the apartment. He hadn't needed to try to cheer me up.

All at once, I was sure that I didn't want to be alone right now. I wanted to be with someone who cared about my happiness.

He bobbed his head to press a light kiss to my forehead, his fingers grazing the side of my face with a trace of heat, and then he was swiveling on his heel to go. I caught his hand before he'd taken more than one step. He shot me a questioning look.

"There are a few things I wouldn't mind doing in that bed before I get to the resting part," I said.

Ruse offered me a crooked smile. "A generous offer, but there's no need. After our last interlude, I should be in tip-top shape for at least a few weeks."

Oh. Had the other night's encounter really been about nothing more than feeding for him? Embarrassment constricted my chest.

It'd been ridiculous for me to think anything else, hadn't it? He was an incubus—that was what sex meant to him. Just because he'd had fun setting up the impromptu dance party didn't mean he was interested in more intimate activities for nothing but the pleasure of it.

I dropped his hand, pulling back into the doorway. "Of course. If you don't want to—"

Something flickered in Ruse's eyes as he took in my expression, and then he was reaching for me, his hand teasing along my arm to grasp my elbow. His head bowed close to mine again. My pulse stuttered with desire I couldn't suppress, but maybe I didn't have to.

"I can't think of any way I'd rather spend my time more than sparking a different sort of fire with you, Miss Blaze," he said, his voice dropping low. "The only thing I don't want is for you to feel obligated."

All right then. I found myself grinning at him, maybe a little goofily, but really, can you blame me? It was about time I got a little good news.

I rested my hand on his firm chest. "You promised me the best sex I've ever had, and you delivered, and we haven't even really had sex yet. I promise you my proposition has exactly zilch to do with any sense of obligation."

"In that case..." He nudged me backward into the room, kicking the door shut behind us.

In the cramped space next to the bed, he cupped my face and dipped his to claim a proper kiss. The press of his mouth, hot and determined yet tender, woke up every inch of my body.

It'd been a long, hazardous night, but I definitely wasn't too tired to welcome this escape.

And I didn't want this time to be all about me. I intended to get the full incubus experience—well, emotional meddling aside.

As I kissed him back, my fingers sped down the front of his shirt to unbutton it. When the muscular planes were bared, I couldn't resist dropping my head to kiss him just below his shoulder, drinking in his bittersweet cocoa scent. Yum.

Ruse trailed his fingers over my hair. As soon as I eased back, he tilted my chin up to recapture my mouth. As his tongue twined with mine, he found the zipper at the back of my dress and slid it downward torturously slowly.

With each inch, his thumb stroked over the naked skin he'd uncovered. By the time he'd reached the bottom, a hair's breadth from my ass, my body was swaying toward his, wanting more: more closeness, more heat, more of that tantalizing touch.

"This looked exquisite on you," he murmured as the fabric slid down my thighs to pool at my feet, "but I think I like it even better off."

"I think I'd like everything *you're* wearing off," I informed him, tugging at his shirt.

He chuckled and shed it in a second. When he tipped me back on the bed, I reached for the fly of his slacks, and tonight he didn't stop me. He obviously understood that I was in this for the entire act now.

And he was clearly into it too. The length I encountered through the fabric of his underthings—an incubus wearing briefs; who'd have thought?—was rigidly erect. A pleased thrum emanated from Ruse's throat as I teased my fingers over it. He bent closer to jerk the cup of my bra down with his teeth, and gods above, I'd never seen anything hotter.

He sucked my nipple into his mouth, and for a few minutes, the pleasure he was conjuring in my breasts distracted me from my own mission. My head leaned back onto the pillow, a gasp slipping out of me. As he slicked his tongue around one stiffening peak and then tested his teeth against it, I dug my fingers into his hair, finding his horns.

Ruse rumbled again, low in his chest. He tossed my bra aside and turned his attentions to my other breast.

Every swivel of his tongue sent me soaring higher, but I didn't lose sight of my goals completely. When he traced his hand down my side to remove my panties, I sat up to make sure the rest of his clothes came off too. He drew back to slide out of his slacks and briefs, and then he knelt before me in all his leanly carved glory. His cock jutted so solidly aloft, I had the urge to down it like a shot at the bar.

One of the benefits of sex with the shadowkind—one I'd never needed to consider before—was that they didn't produce children. They simply sprang into being rather than being born, and there was no record of any human involvement resulting in pregnancy on either side. Which was a very good thing, because I hadn't exactly thought to pack condoms.

The mouth-watering visage I was taking in wasn't his *real* glory, though. This was only the human appearance he put on to blend in. I hauled my gaze from the parts I hoped to have penetrating me soon to his face.

"Like what you see?" he said with one of those typical smirks.

I ran my fingers down his chest, following the grooves of his muscles, until I reached his cock. I couldn't resist giving the silky skin that covered the rigid length an eager stroke, but I held his gaze.

"I do," I said. "But I'd like even more to see you as you really are."

Ruse tensed—just slightly, but his nudity made it hard to hide. He opened his mouth with an intake of breath that already sounded like a protest.

Before he could speak, I held up my hand to stop him. "I've seen a hell of a lot more than I'd bet any woman you've been with before had. If they could handle it while high on your seductive vibes, I'm pretty sure I can while sober. And I *am* totally sober now to make that call." Any lingering effects of the drug had dissipated during my frantic bike ride.

Ruse peered at me for a long moment. "Why?" he said finally.

I shrugged. "You can see me exactly as I am. It'll feel more equal if I can say the same about you. Besides, it'll make a much better story if I can say I got it on with a fully-fledged incubus rather than just a dude with horns." I knocked his hip with my knee playfully.

Something about my explanation appeared to make up his mind. His smile returned. "All right," he said. "Don't say I didn't warn you."

He closed his eyes, and a shimmer ran over his body. Ran over it—and stayed, a hazy golden glow emanating from his skin as if he were part firefly. His little horns lengthened, curving in a full loop and pointing toward the ceiling again. His cock curved too, his pubic bone protruding farther out at the same time. When he opened his eyes again, the pupils had dilated, but the irises had expanded as well, nearly filling the whites. They gleamed a gold as bright as if the brilliant summer sun were reflecting off them.

"Well?" he said, with a new smoky quality to his voice that seemed to wind around me in its own embrace.

Sweet shiny sugar-puffs, a story for the ages indeed. Had he really thought I'd run scared from *this*?

I raised my hand to touch his glowing cheek. "You were handsome before. Now you're fucking magnificent."

His smile stretched wider. He bowed his head to kiss me hard, the tingling heat of his lips spreading into mine and all through my body. "Let's get on with the fucking then," he murmured against my mouth.

He gave me a gentle shove to lie down, joining me as I did. Everywhere our skin touched, little shocks of bliss quivered into me. He wasn't even inside me yet, and the rush of my release was already building to a peak.

We kissed again and again, until the scorching pleasure of it blurred my thoughts together. His hand dipped between my legs, his thumb flicking over my clit, and just like that, I did come, with a shaky moan that had me thanking all that was good in the world for the existence of incubi and their soundproofing magic.

The sound had hardly finished leaving my lips when Ruse delved his fingers right inside me. With a few quick pulses, I was coming again on the heels of my first orgasm, my body trembling with the combined force. "Oh my God," I gasped out.

Ruse stole another kiss with a chuckle that vibrated into me. "I'd prefer you give me the credit."

I let out a laugh that turned into another moan as he rubbed the head of his cock over my slit and plunged inside. My fingers dug into his shoulders as if the ecstasy might wash me away if I didn't hold on tight. The next sound that leaked out of me was embarrassingly close to a whine of need.

"I've got you," Ruse murmured in the smoky tone that set me even more ablaze. He rocked deeper into me, and I discovered exactly what was so special about his official incubus equipment. The curve of his cock veered perfectly to press the hot button of bliss deep inside me. With each thrust, the bulge of his pubic bone stroked my clit. Pulses of a pleasure I'd never even imagined raced through me, faster and more searing by the moment.

I arched up to meet him, wanting to pay him back as well as I could with my more limited human means. Remembering how he'd reacted to the caressing of his horns before, I lifted my hands to his head. My fingers tangled in his hair and then found the enlarged points with their graceful spiral.

When I squeezed them, Ruse groaned and drove into me even harder. Another orgasm crashed through me, sending me flying and then dragging me down into depths like a blissful undertow. And once I started coming, I couldn't stop. Each thrust of his cock into me tossed me up and under all over again with just enough time to gasp for air. My entire existence became a gale of pleasure.

Through the storm of ecstasy, I had just enough awareness to realize that the incubus hadn't joined me, not with his own release. I managed to raise my jellified legs to his waist, welcoming him even deeper as I gripped one horn and ran my fingernails down the muscles of his back.

"Come," I mumbled. "Come with me."

Ruse's next groan shuddered as it fell from his lips. His mouth crashed into mine. With a roll of his hips, bliss tossed me up and over once more. A flood of tingling heat filled me as he followed.

As he eased to a stop over me, I couldn't help thinking that everything considered, this hadn't been such a bad night after all.

EIGHTEEN

Ruse

THERE WAS NOTHING QUITE AS GORGEOUS AS A WOMAN BASKING IN THE afterglow of ecstasy—an ecstasy *I'd* brought her to. Possibly it was even more satisfying seeing that release in Sorsha than any woman before. She was the first I'd taken to those heights while she was fully aware of what I was, and she'd welcomed everything I could offer all the same.

She sprawled out on the bed, her cheeks flushed with a rosy hue that might have been even more lovely than the waves of her red hair spread across the pillow. Her chest rose and fell where my arm lay just below her breasts. I stroked my fingers over her side just for the pleasure of touching that warm, smooth skin once more. Warm and smooth—and layered with toned muscle underneath. I appreciated a woman who could be both soft and strong. Her fiery sweet scent lingered in my nose, equally delicious.

My own skin still hummed with the aftermath of my orgasm. I'd drawn the glow back into it, returning to my more subtle mortal guise, since it wasn't wise for any of us to get used to walking around in this realm au naturel. I'd worn these trappings of humanity often enough that this false body felt more comfortable than my own in mortal-side air, other than when I was employing my powers.

I had enjoyed *my* release quite a lot. Watching Sorsha give herself over so completely to the act, hearing her beg me to join her just as completely, knowing she'd wanted this interlude as much as I had—I didn't think I'd ever come so hard.

But the moment was over, and I really ought to leave her to the rest her mortal body would be craving after the extended, chaotic night. I kissed one of those rosy cheeks and moved to push myself upright.

As I shifted on the bed, Sorsha's hand came up to touch my arm, as if she were beckoning me to stay. My gaze shot to her face, a quiver of uncertainty prickling through me—and before I had a chance to catch myself, I'd peeked into her mind.

The emotions at the forefront were easy to read once I let myself: a pleasantly drowsy haze and a longing to keep my warmth next to her as she drifted off.

I jerked my awareness back, a twinge fluttering through my chest. She really did get some sort of contentment from my presence even now that the act I was most skilled at was over. That knowledge sparked a little more contentment in *me* than I was comfortable with. And as I relaxed back down next to her, the twinge sharpened into a pang of guilt.

I'd promised her I wouldn't violate the privacy of her mind. She'd made it very clear that this one term was non-negotiable, no matter what physical intimacies we shared. If she knew I'd broken my word...

My first instinct—and, really, my second and third as well—was to dismiss that secret into the shadows where she never needed to find out. Why tell her something that would upset her if I didn't need to? But when she stirred and rolled onto her side, catching my gaze with a dreamy little smile, the pang stabbed too deeply for me to ignore.

She'd been genuine and open with me. She'd cared enough to let me feed despite her reservations—offered me more trust than apparently she should have. Hell, she'd literally rescued me from captivity and the slow starvation I'd faced there.

I was man enough to give her the respect she'd earned, wasn't I? Even if the consequences wouldn't work to my favor.

"Sorsha," I said carefully. "I—just now—I read your emotions. Only for a moment, only a few."

Before I could go on, she jerked back from me and sat up. Her hair spilled over her shoulders like rivulets of flame—or blood. From the look on her face, I might as well have cut her. "What?"

I sat up too, groping for an acceptable explanation. "I didn't intend to—it's second nature at this point, and I slipped, and as soon as I realized I pulled back. It won't happen again."

Her arms crossed over her chest, hiding the lovely slopes of her breasts. Her voice came out taut. "If you did it without meaning to, how can you be sure you won't accidentally trip into my head again?"

A reasonable question. "I'll be more on guard now. I'll—"

"No." She scooted farther away on the bed and motioned to the door. Her expression had tightened, shutting me out as fully as that brooch of hers once had. "I don't want to hear it. Just get out. I—" Her hand fumbled across the bedcovers for a second before clenching. Realizing she'd left the brooch and its protections behind in her burning apartment like she had so much else? Somehow that small gesture wrenched me more than anything before had.

I was already springing off the bed as I'd been planning to in the beginning, if more hastily than before. With a blink and an ounce of concentration, the clothes I'd shed in our encounter vanished from their disarray around the room and reassembled themselves on my body. I risked glancing at Sorsha one more time. "I'm sorry."

"Just go," she said, her voice firm but hollow, as if my confession had drained away all the pleasure I'd given her.

I winced, the guilt expanding like a vise around my lungs, but I went.

When the bedroom door was shut between her and me, I paused in the hall to catch my breath. Nicely done. Very smooth. I'd better hope I never needed her for more sustenance, because she sure as hell wasn't getting it on with me ever again.

She might not ever share another dance with me or laugh at my banter or, fuck, even smile at me.

None of those things should have mattered. I didn't require any of them to survive. As I slunk to the kitchen, I reminded myself of that over and over until I was almost convinced. Almost. Well, a little chatter with Snap might cheer me up.

It wasn't our naïve devourer I found in the kitchen, though, but Thorn, back from his patrol and looking about as grim as usual, which I assumed meant it was good news.

I dropped into the chair across from him at the stubby Formica island that protruded from the wall. "No sign of this sword-star crew?"

"Not so far," he said in a tone that suggested he expected they'd appear to wreak more havoc on our existence any minute now. You could hand this man a glass that was full nearly to the brim, and he'd still mutter about the smidge it was empty.

A little china bowl filled with hard candies sat in the middle of the island. I plucked one up and then simply turned it between my fingers, the cellophane crinkling. Physical food didn't do anything for me except perhaps offer a pleasant flavor, and I wasn't sure I was in the mood to actually stick anything in my mouth. Not after I'd already stuck my foot in there so badly with the woman down the hall.

Thorn glanced past me as if he knew where my thoughts had headed. His fathomless gaze came back to rest on my face.

Not for the first time, I wished I knew what in the realms *he* was. He'd never shown his full form where I could see it, and his presence in the shadows didn't offer any qualities distinctive enough for me to match him to other beings I'd encountered. The powers I knew of—his strength and alertness to aggression—could have belonged to any number of kind.

I'd never met a devourer before Snap, only heard rumors of them. Quite possibly Thorn was some rare creature that few of us ever encountered as well. Which meant I had no clue what other powers he might be hiding behind that scarred exterior.

Omen had wanted the best of the best, at least from the shadowkind willing to take up his cause. He'd trusted Thorn. I trusted Omen… about as much as I trusted anyone. Better to leave it at that than to worry.

"You've been getting rather close with the mortal one," Thorn said, with a tip of his head toward the hall.

I raised my eyebrows at him. "That *is* sort of my thing, as you well know. Have you got a problem with it?"

He stared right back at me, unshaken by my implied challenge. "I don't think such involvement will make it easier to protect her. If it affects your concentration, it may bring about the opposite result instead."

"My concentration is just fine. We cubi deal in bodily intimacies, not emotional connection—we make no secret about that."

"So, you have no interest in her beyond physical satisfaction."

He didn't say it like a question, but I felt the need to answer it anyway. "I like her well enough, but I'm hardly going to get attached in any way that would throw me off my game. Omen picked *me* for good reason too. Everything is under control."

And besides, it wasn't likely I'd have any more involvement with Sorsha at all after tonight, not that I wanted to mention that to Thorn. Not that, or the fact that Omen might not have picked me if he'd been aware of one particular past lapse.

No one needed to know about *that*. I knew better now.

"As long as it stays that way," Thorn said, getting up. He left me on my own in the kitchen, grappling with a rekindled uneasiness I couldn't quite shake.

NINETEEN

Sorsha

I'D NEVER FELT NERVOUS ABOUT HEADING INTO A FUND MEETING BEFORE. Never had any reason to believe the act of walking into a low-rent movie theater might be seen as suspicious. But now, given recent events, I was waiting in a dim alleyway four blocks away, shuffling my feet against the rain-damp concrete and praying that the clouds still clotted overhead didn't decide to open up again while I was out here. My umbrella: another casualty of last night's apartment fire.

The afternoon's rain had brought out a mildew-y scent that made my nose itch. Every time footsteps sounded on the sidewalk, I shrank back into the thicker darkness by the brick wall beside me. None of the people who passed through the evening looked like a possible threat to me, but then, I hadn't been prepared for a band of organized attackers to crash into my apartment either.

I'd been working with the Fund in this city for eleven years, and none of the members had ever even been so much as harassed, except maybe now and then by the mortal-side shadowkind who didn't appreciate our attempts to help. No one in this group had even known a member who'd been hurt in the line of duty. Only more proof that whoever had decided I needed to be eliminated from the equation, they obviously weren't your typical hunters.

Finally, Thorn wavered out of a dark patch in front of me. "I picked up on no sign of enemy presence nearby," he said. "I believe you can safely enter the building for your meeting. But I *will* be accompanying you through the shadows."

He'd already emphasized that point before we'd left our temporary new home. I nodded, gazing up into his rugged face for a few seconds. Searching for a hint of humanity in those coal-dark eyes and hardened features—something to reassure me that this was at least a little more than a cold transaction of favors owed.

There'd been passion in his voice, if a solemn kind, when he'd talked about defending me and his companions and finding his boss. He'd thought to rescue my one token from my parents for me. There had to be something other than steely chill behind all the brawn.

I couldn't pick it out right now, though. Well, at least steel was reliable. It'd turned out I couldn't say that for much else.

"All right," I said. "Off I go."

As I moved to stalk past him, he vanished, but I knew he was staying with me unseen. The evening was full of shadows for ease of travel.

The smell of buttered popcorn laced with mint and—was that *toffee*?—met me at the door to the Fund's private theater room. Only a few people had shown up so far, the Saturday meetings being less popular than the weekday ones, but Ellen and Huyen were over by the screen, and that was all I needed.

Unfortunately, Vivi had also turned up early. Before I could get one of our leaders' ears, my best friend had moseyed down the aisle to join me.

"Hey!" she said, and gave me a once-over. "I love that blouse. It's new, right? Where'd you get it?"

I tugged at the hem of the silky purple halter top self-consciously. It was new, but I hadn't been the one to get it. The entire outfit had been sitting outside my bedroom door when I'd gotten up this morning. Any of the trio could have realized that I couldn't wear my bar dress for days on end and swiped some clothes in the shadows of a shop, but from the hint of cacao smell that had lingered on them, I suspected they were an apology offering from Ruse.

Otherwise, he'd given me plenty of distance, which worked just fine for me. I couldn't remember any of the spectacular parts of our encounter last night without a flash of panic at the thought of him rummaging through my thoughts and feelings. How could I be sure he'd even admitted his full transgression, that he hadn't been using his powers on me the whole time?

It was going to take more than some pretty clothes to smooth things over, even if I did look pretty fantastic in them.

If I told Vivi it'd been a gift, she'd want to know who from, and I'd just tangle myself in a whole lot of bigger lies. So I stuck to a smaller one. "You know, I don't even remember. Somewhere at the mall."

"Well, it was a good choice." She bumped her shoulder against mine. "Good to see you got home all right after the bar. I was a little worried, the way you took off."

Ha. Yes, I'd gotten home all right. Getting *out* of the apartment had been much less okay. "It was no big deal," I said, feeling as if each new lie was adding to a heavy lump in my stomach. "I wish I could have stayed longer."

"No news on the tip Jade gave you?"

"Nope, I haven't had much chance to see what I can make of it yet."

Ellen left the conversation she and Huyen had been in with one of the older members and headed our way. I made an apologetic gesture to Vivi. "I've got to talk to the lady in charge. Grab me some of tonight's popcorn?"

Vivi hesitated for a second as if balking at the idea of missing what I'd say to Ellen, but then she shot me a smile and a thumbs-up. As she walked away, I hustled to meet Ellen.

Despite her love of flavors, our co-leader was thin as a rail, with frizzy, graying hair that was perpetually escaping from her loose buns. On meeting nights, stains on her fingertips often gave away her latest popcorn ingredients—today's greenish tint confirmed the mint.

I didn't have much time before my best friend would return and hear something that would make her even more curious what was going on with me. "Hey, Ellen," I said, cutting right to the chase. "Do you have a spare badge around? I seem to have misplaced mine." I wasn't giving Ruse any more chances to exercise his self-control—or not.

"Sure," the petite woman said, with a note of surprise. I'd managed not to misplace the first badge she'd given me in the past eleven years, but it could happen to any of us. She dug into her purse—of course Ellen the ever-prepared would have a little stash of those always on hand.

"Is everything else all right?" she asked as she handed it to me.

Maybe my general agitation was showing more than I'd meant it to. I pushed my mouth into a sheepish grin and pocketed the protective badge. "Yeah, I just seem to be having kind of a scattered week. I was also hoping—I wanted to get in touch with the group that monitors talk about the shadowkind for us online, but my computer's hard drive died." The whole thing had died a sad, fiery death. "Could I grab his contact info from you again? I knew better than to write it down somewhere not totally secure, but that means I'm out of luck."

I spread my hands in an attempt to look cluelessly innocent rather than like a lying liar who lied. From the weight in my gut, I might as well have swallowed a boulder. Ellen didn't appear fazed by the request, thank shimmering seal pups. She gave me a motherly pat on the shoulder.

"I'll send it to you by a secure link. You're still at the same email as before?"

"Yeah," I said with a rush of relief.

"FYI, they're looking for payment in organic kombucha these days—they take it by the crate."

Crates of kombucha it was, then.

As Ellen moved on, Vivi came up beside me. She handed me a bag of popcorn and cocked her head with a swish of her hair. "What'd I miss?"

I gave her a smile in thanks. "Nothing." One more lie to add to the pile.

My best friend's gaze turned unusually serious. She paused for a second and then said, "No matter what you find out, I'll be here if you need me. You'll remember that, right?"

The emphatic plea made my gut twist all over again. "Yeah," I said.

"Of course I'll remember." I just wouldn't be taking her up on the offer, not after I'd seen just how brutal my newfound enemies could be.

Maybe the love the apartment's true owners had for the '60s explained why they hadn't demanded the landlord replace their kitchen appliances, because the stove certainly behaved like it was several decades old. After an hour of slowly turning up the heat under the frozen stir fry I'd liberated from the freezer and watching the ice crystals barely melt, all at once half of the bits had burned to the pan.

I growled at the meal as if I could intimidate it into uncharring itself. Before I could decide whether to make the best of it or toss it and start over, the shiny new laptop my shadowkind friends had obtained for me chimed with an inbox alert.

Screw dinner. I plopped myself down at the kitchen island and let out a cry of victory. "We've got it!"

Thorn, who'd been skulking by the kitchen doorway in his usual glum way, stepped only a little closer, as if it would pain him to show any more enthusiasm than that. Snap, who last I'd seen had been sprawled on the master bedroom floor tipping the lava lamp this way and that with pure joy, came gliding over a second later.

"You have the information that'll tell us where to find Omen?" he asked, his eyes bright.

"Maybe," I cautioned. Pickle hopped onto my lap from where he'd been sitting on the other chair and peeked over the top of the island. I gave his chin a scratch as I considered the screen. "Jade said that someone's put a call out for 'potent' shadowkind, and that sounds like the M.O. of the bunch that ambushed him. Our contacts on the dark web are pretty good at digging up useful communications that were meant to be private."

Hunters and collectors had their own areas of the internet's black market where they operated, of course. As secure as they tried to keep those channels, the cabal of hackers who worked for the Fund for pay managed to crack their codes on a regular basis. Usually they could trace the usernames to the actual people behind the sales, purchases, and other posts.

As I opened the file my contact had sent me, Ruse slunk into the room too. He leaned against the counter at the farthest point in the kitchen from me, his stance casual but careful.

He was giving me distance for my sake, not his, I knew. Now and then he'd tossed out a joke or teasing comment, watching my reaction intently as if a laugh would tell him he was forgiven. If he thought he was going to win me over a second time that easily, he was kidding himself.

My hand rose to my chest of its own accord, taking a momentary comfort from brushing my fingertips over the edges of the new silver-and-iron badge pinned under my blouse. I leaned closer to the screen. My other forefinger skimmed over the touchpad as I scanned the list of names and summaries of what the hacker had found.

I almost scrolled right past it. My eyes slid over the letters, continued another half a screen down, and then recognition pinged in my head. Wait a second. I leapt back to that previous entry.

Looking at it, a chuckle slipped from my mouth. Son of a biscuit eater. We'd been barking up the altogether wrong tree, but I could see how the mistake had happened.

I pointed at the name that had caught my eye. "It's not Merry Den we're looking for, and it's not a place. It's a person. John Meriden. He's behind one of the aliases that's posted at least a couple of messages over the last few months, looking to confer with collectors about their shadowkind."

Snap's spirits visibly deflated. "I told you the wrong information."

I patted his arm reassuringly. Oh, the guy did pack plenty of compact muscle onto those slender limbs.

Focus, Sorsha.

"It was an easy mistake to make," I said. "You picked up on the sounds in a way that formed words you know. It could have happened to any of us. And hey, it still helped us find our man in the end."

Thorn loomed over me, scowling at the computer as if preparing to reach into the screen and grab our target by the throat through cyberspace. "Where is this 'John Meriden'?"

"Let's see what my contact found…" As I read through the entry, my own spirits sank a little. "He only made a small slip that allowed the hackers to find his real name, they don't say what exactly—

probably logging in somewhere he shouldn't have with the same IP address. But the address itself was some kind of front. They couldn't trace it back to an actual location that connects to the guy."

"With his name, it shouldn't be difficult to track down more details, should it?" Ruse put in. Pickle let out a chirp as if agreeing with the incubus.

"Yeah, I can ask them to investigate more about him specifically. They wouldn't have gone on a full-blown search for any of the names yet—this is more a summary…" I paused. "Except if he's connected to the same people who barged into my apartment last night, who knows how closely they're keeping an eye on anyone poking around in his business."

Ruse tsked. "You don't think your hackers can avoid getting noticed?"

"No, it's more that we can't be sure none of them are paid off by other parties too. They work for whoever fronts the moola—they don't have any specific loyalty to the Fund." I leaned back in my chair, rubbing the top of Pickle's head and frowning.

I'd given the cabal a general enough brief that it shouldn't have set off any major alarm bells. If the sword-star bunch sicced the same hackers on me, they could probably figure out where I was working from in five seconds flat. The black-market-savvy skills I'd picked up over the years were nothing compared to theirs.

"Let's see how much we can find out on our own without getting anyone else involved," I said. "It's safer that way. And if we can't find out anything ourselves, then we can take a gamble. We're definitely not finding Omen if the assholes who took him find us first, and they're better prepared than last time."

I opened up a regular search window and started my online game of hide and seek with Mr. John Meriden. Unfortunately, there seemed to be a few dudes with that name. Fortunately, only one of them turned up when I included the city name in my search.

The pickings were pretty sparse. Whoever the man was, he kept a very low internet profile. But I did manage to turn up a mention of a J. Meriden in connection to an address on the outskirts of the city. Checking the street view from the map, it looked like an office building

—but with no sign and no other features that would tell me what went on in there. How very suspicious.

"Should have known better than those deets to send," I sang in triumph. "Jackpot!"

"We've got him?" Thorn said with gruff enthusiasm.

"We're one step closer, anyway." I waved toward the online map. "Update your calendars—we've got plans for tomorrow."

TWENTY

Sorsha

If I'd hoped I might saunter into Meriden's office building and have a receptionist point me right to him, one up-close look at the current state of the place killed that dream. Obviously it would have been ridiculous to march right in demanding to speak to him anyway, but the dreary dimness that showed in gaps through the papered-over windows didn't inspire much confidence that we'd find anything at all.

Thorn had already patrolled several blocks around the place, watching for any hint of our previous attackers. Now, as the other two shadowkind and I waited in a coffee shop down the street after a brisk walk past, he'd gone to prowl through the building itself.

Ruse sipped the espresso he'd charmed the barista into giving him, not looking as though he was enjoying it very much. Even Snap was too restless to make more than a few half-hearted exclamations over the whipped-cream-topped hot chocolate the incubus had gotten for him.

I'd decided to forgo caffeine altogether, since I didn't need my nerves on any higher alert than they already were, but I was starting to regret leaving my hands empty. As I fidgeted with the napkin I'd pulled out of the dispenser, slowly tearing one corner, our hardened warrior stepped out of the shadows across the room as if he'd emerged from the bathroom rather than the darkness. I was pretty sure Ruse had coached him on that move.

"The way is clear," he said when he reached us, his voice low but formal as always. "There is an entrance at the back I believe it would be wisest for us to make use of. M'lady, my companions and I will travel unseen and meet you there."

I guessed that made sense. Still, I couldn't help feeling I had a target on my back as I ambled outside like I was just enjoying this lovely summer day. I'd committed plenty of crimes, snuck into plenty of buildings I wasn't meant to be in, but always with the cover of night. Under the blazing sun without my cat burglar get-up, I might as well have had a spotlight pointed at me.

If the place was empty anyway, there was no reason to poke around during the day. No employees to listen in on or even question if we'd dared. But we were here now. Thorn was even tenser about the situation than I was—if he thought we could go ahead, I was probably safer here than lounging on a beach in the Bahamas.

I just wouldn't think about the fact that he'd missed the hunters who'd shipped him off to that cage I'd rescued him from.

I strolled around the block and down the driveway beside the used furniture store next door. Cutting across the parking lot took me straight to a rather imposing steel door at the back of Meriden's apparently former workplace. Thank galloping gremlins that something about the process of melding iron into steel seemed to diffuse its repulsive effect on most shadowkind.

I glanced around to make sure no one was hanging out nearby to see me, pulled on my gloves, and tried the handle. It didn't budge.

Huh. I'd expected the trio to make it there before me. An uneasy quiver ran down through my gut. I looked around again, bracing myself to run—and the handle jerked over with a metallic crunching sound from the other side.

Before I could bolt, the door swung open to reveal Thorn's own imposing visage. The handle from the other side of the door, broken and twisted, dangled from his brawny hand.

"The place has some fancy-pants locks we couldn't manage to open without a certain amount of destruction," Ruse said with a baleful look toward the taller guy. "I *tried* to suggest to this lunk that we make sure you thought it was wise to literally break our way in before going ahead."

Thorn was already motioning me in with an urgent sweep of his arm. "We'd have drawn much more attention standing around outside discussing the matter—or leaving her out there wondering what had befallen us. She's in now."

Snap peered around the storage room I'd joined them in. "It doesn't look as if anyone's come by here in a long time."

The shelving units that filled the space were mostly empty, the few bedraggled cardboard boxes that remained holding nothing that revealed more than what type of printer paper the business had used. The date on a shipping label informed me that particular package had been delivered five years ago.

Had this place been empty that long? My hopes sank even further.

The storage room opened up to a hallway lined with interior windows. The rooms on the other side appeared to be labs with gleaming metal tables and fridges next to open spaces that held nothing more than scuffs on the floor suggesting there'd once been other equipment there. Only muted light filtered through the tiny, high outer windows set with frosted glass. A bitter chemical odor hung in the air.

Thorn got us into one of those rooms with a similar trick with the lock—if you could call brute strength a "trick." Inside, Snap crouched down by the scuff marks. The first flick of his tongue provoked a wince that echoed through his entire slim body.

"Silver and iron," he said, his voice gone tight. "There were cages here."

The kinds of cages that would only be used to hold shadowkind. The sword-star bunch had removed the obvious evidence, but they hadn't counted on a being with Snap's skills checking out the place.

"Can you pick up anything else about them—what sort of shadowkind they were keeping?" Ruse asked.

Snap took another tentative taste and shook his head with a shudder. He moved on, sampling the air over and around the table and then the fridge. His beautiful face tensed with a frown it was painful to see.

"I can't taste much about the people who used this room," he said quietly. "But they were doing something with—something *to*— shadowkind creatures. Something that hurt."

Thorn's hands clenched at his sides. My own fingers had curled into my palms. It wasn't as if we couldn't have guessed that whoever had taken their boss—and probably come for my Auntie Luna as well —had nefarious purposes, but if they'd operated out of this building, there was no doubting their intentions now.

We checked each of the lab rooms in turn, even though my stomach knotted at the growing strain that showed in Snap's demeanor. The impressions of whatever awful experiments he was having to glean became worth it when he straightened up from a cabinet in the last room with a brilliant grin.

"I saw it! Someone who opened this recently—however recently they were last working here—had that star symbol with the swords on the folder he was holding."

"We're definitely in the right place, then." I glanced at the pale walls around us with another shiver of uneasiness. "Meriden must be our guy." But so far we hadn't seen anything here that could lead us closer to him.

"The front of the building had more… debris," Thorn said. "Something there might give us a sense of where to continue our investigation."

I wasn't at all sorry to leave the vacant labs behind. We passed another steel door to reach the front half of the building, which opened up into a pretty typical office layout.

A maze of dividers wove across the floor, separating out a couple dozen cubicles other than where a few had toppled over. The plain steel desks remained, but weirdly none of the chairs. A water cooler without its jug stood next to a dust-coated coffee maker just outside a small kitchen area. Doors along the opposite wall led into private offices, but the name plaques had been removed from their brass holders.

Snap immediately set off to sample all the impressions he could find. I veered in another direction, picking through the crumpled papers, long-dried pens, and other garbage the employees had left behind in case any of it held an identifying clue that didn't require supernatural voodoo to discern.

Ruse followed the same course I did, inspecting the cubicles on the other side of the aisle. As Snap and Thorn drifted farther away, he glanced at me. I was bent over a desk, struggling to reach a paper that had fallen between it and the divider wall it appeared to be bolted to.

I half expected him to make a cheeky comment about my waving ass, but instead he blinked out of sight. The paper vanished into the shadows, and a second later the incubus was standing next to me, holding it out.

"Oh. Thank you." I couldn't stop my posture from stiffening a little at the warmth of his body right next to mine.

I took the paper, which turned out to have nothing but a couple of obscene dick doodles on it. Such amazing productivity.

Ruse stepped back, his mouth twisting into a grimace. His lips parted, and then he hesitated. "Sorsha," he said finally when I started to turn.

"What?" The word came out terser than I'd intended, but I hadn't been going for friendly either.

"I—" He let out a huff of breath, but from his expression, I got the sense he was frustrated with himself, not with me. "You can be angry with me forever if you want. I'm not telling you I didn't fuck up. But I do want you to know I didn't break your trust for kicks or to manipulate you in any way."

"No? Why did you, then?"

Despite my still-terse tone, he looked relieved that I'd even asked. "I know what value I generally bring to the table where mortals are concerned—or rather, to the bed. When the act is over, I haven't been in the habit of sticking around. No one's ever complained about my leaving. When it seemed as if you meant for me to stay with you, I wasn't sure whether I was only making assumptions or— I didn't like the idea of overstaying my welcome inadvertently. So I looked before I could catch the impulse, just to make sure that really was what you wanted."

The only thing I don't want is for you to feel obligated, he'd told me the other night when I'd invited him into my bed in the first place.

Remembering that and seeing the remorse that sat so awkwardly on his roguishly handsome face, some of the betrayal I'd been feeling crumbled away.

What must it feel like, being treated as if you had no worth other than your sexual prowess for centuries on end? Maybe it didn't matter to him as much as it might to a human being, but shadowkind could still experience loss and loneliness. To have all the pleasure but none of the closeness and connection of falling asleep in each other's arms afterward... Even the months when I'd been hooking up with Leland, the lack of actual intimacy had started to dull the fun parts of our agreement.

Ruse's skills might have knocked my socks off, almost literally, but I'd take the full experience of human intimacy over supernaturally powerful passion alone any day. If *I* ever got a chance to have that for real, that was.

"Okay," I said. "I can see why you might have slipped up. I still don't want you slipping *ever* again."

I looked down at my hands braced against the desk and decided that if he'd opened up, I could give him a little honesty in return. "Having my mind messed with is a particularly sore spot for me. There was this time—when I was seven, heading home one evening with Luna, another higher shadowkind spotted us together and started mocking her for taking care of a mortal. When we tried to simply walk away from him, he used his powers on me."

"He was an incubus?" Ruse asked softly, but his eyes flashed with a golden blaze of anger.

"I don't think so, but he had some kind of charm ability. He called out to me, told me to jump around and crawl on my hands and knees and would have ordered me to walk into traffic if Luna hadn't launched herself at him then."

A lump filled my throat with the memory. "It was awful, wanting to resist, terrified of what he was making me do, but being trapped in my body that was following his commands no matter how much I tried to stop it. I know that tormenting people isn't your thing, but the thought of anyone using their influence on my mind brings back that terror."

If I hadn't been completely sure of Ruse's remorse before, there would have been no mistaking it etched in his expression now. "I hate that I reminded you of that time—that you'd need to associate me at all with that dumpster fire of a being. If I can't manage to keep the promise of never slipping up again, you're welcome to light *me* on fire and cheer while I burn."

My lips couldn't help twitching upward at the vehemence with which he made that offer. "I think I can manage without burning anyone alive. Let's just see how it goes. And don't push your luck."

"Duly noted," the incubus said with a playful salute, though his eyes were still serious. I was just venturing onward to resume my search when a joyful voice rang out from the office kitchen. Of course Snap would have ended up in there sooner rather than later.

"I have something!" He loped out with his face beaming as bright as his curly hair. With one hand, he held up a mug that had a jagged shard missing from its side. "This cup belonged to Meriden. He brought it in from his house, and I can see the house in the impressions that've stuck to it."

Excitement raced through me. I hurried over. "Are you sure it's his?"

He tipped the mug to show us the base, looking so breathtakingly pleased with himself I had to restrain the urge to kiss him. "I can hear someone saying the name while he was holding it—and look. This is for John Meriden, isn't it?"

Marked on the mug's base in black sharpie were the initials J.M.

I laughed and settled for squeezing Snap's shoulder in a fragment of an embrace. "You did it. He'd better watch out now—we're coming for him where he lives."

TWENTY-ONE

Sorsha

Helpfully, the residents of the apartment we'd borrowed had left the keys to their vehicle in a bowl near the door. When Ruse pressed the unlock button in the parking lot at the back of the building, a shiny silver SUV beeped.

We'd treat it well, I told myself as we walked over. We'd even leave them with a full tank of gas as a thank you present.

Then I opened the passenger side door, and my eyebrows shot up. "Oh, for the love of sweet potato fries."

It'd looked like a perfectly normal SUV from the outside. The inside stunk of the '60s. Literally. A waft of musky, earthy patchouli washed over me. As I wrinkled my nose, I took in the bright pink mini shag rugs on the floor in front of each seat and the bejeweled peace sign glittering where it hung from the rear-view mirror.

Maybe walking would be better.

But no, given the house Snap had described from the impressions on Meriden's mug, we were heading out to the posh suburbs at the north end of town, and that was a hell of a hike even for me. So I clambered into the back of the car with Snap while Ruse took the driver's seat and Thorn stretched out his expansive legs next to the incubus.

I wasn't going to let this assault of decades past go unchallenged, though. Tapping at my phone's screen, I connected it to the SUV's sound system and started Tina Turner's *Private Dancer* album playing. Take that, flower children.

As the opening notes of "I Might Have Been Queen" spilled from the speakers, Ruse gave a knowing laugh. He backed the SUV out of its parking spot more smoothly than I'd have expected from a guy who'd probably only needed to use his driving skills about once a decade, and we were off.

We were looking for a big colonial style place: white walls, gable windows, and columns on either side of the double front door. A wide lawn with a tree that shaded the driveway. And, most importantly—because there were probably a thousand houses in the suburbs that fit the rest of the description—Snap had also caught a glimpse of a bronze statue of a rearing horse poised next to the front steps. We just had to hope it was still there after however many years it'd been since Meriden had last worked in the office building.

I opened up my map app. "Keep going north on this street until I tell you otherwise," I ordered Ruse. "We've got a ways to go."

"Navigate away, Miss Blaze!"

Receiving only a couple of honks—Ruse wasn't so smooth at the whole changing lanes thing—we made it around the edges of downtown and up into the wealthier district where I'd set more than one collector's home on fire. I got the incubus weaving up and down the streets while the rest of us scanned the houses beyond our windows.

After a couple of hours, my vision was starting to blur from staring so long. Snap made a soft hissing sound against his teeth. "I'm not seeing the same one—not the way I tasted it from the mug. I don't know for sure it was in this city."

"He might live farther out of town," I admitted with a grimace. It would take days to scour the entire greater metropolitan area—if even that got us what we wanted. Maybe I'd have to put our fates in the hands of a black-market hacker cabal after all.

"We're here now—might as well give it our best shot," Ruse said with good cheer. I guessed he enjoyed driving.

We continued on until my stomach started to grumble that it needed something more substantial than the bag of barbeque chips and mug of coffee I'd already downed as a sort of lunch. At a particularly loud gurgle, Thorn turned in his seat with a questioning look. With the final notes of *The Joshua Tree* fading from the speakers, I admitted defeat. We definitely still hadn't found what we were looking for.

"Let's head back and grab some dinner, and I'll try to figure out how to reach out to my internet associates in a way that won't get us killed."

"I approve of that plan," Ruse said. Even he was starting to sound a bit weary.

We cruised down one last residential street, heading south. Just as the houses started shrinking and the lawns were getting scruffier, Snap jerked toward his window.

"Stop! There, on that street we just passed. Turn around!"

We got five honks for Ruse's next maneuver, pulling a U-ey and then a left on the heels of his companion's urgent plea. Snap gestured to a house three from the corner: white walls gone a bit dingy, paint flaking from the columns on either side of the door, a rather bedraggled oak tree by the driveway. The late afternoon sunlight glinted off a tarnished statue of a rearing horse next to the front steps.

Ruse let out a low whistle. "Nice job."

He had enough sense of stealth to drive a little farther before parking outside a house on the other side of the street. I squinted at the building Snap had indicated, noting a key feature he hadn't picked up on from his vision.

"Meriden doesn't live in the whole place. It's divided into apartments. There are three different mailboxes beside the door."

Ruse motioned toward the driveway that ran alongside the house to a garage farther back. "And another around the side there." Another door stood atop a couple of concrete steps with its own mailbox, maybe a separate entrance to the basement or a back apartment.

"It seems we can be reasonably confident that the object of our interest resides somewhere in that place," Thorn said. He glanced at me. "We should investigate while you stay here, m'lady. We don't know how closely Meriden's home might be monitored. You can keep watch in case he leaves while we're conducting our search."

"I don't even know what he looks like," I protested. Like hell did I want to hang back in the car like a kid waiting for her parents to run an errand. Sure, the shadowkind could slink around unseen and I couldn't, but this guy had been working with—or on?—shadowkind for years. He might be able to detect them anyway. They shouldn't have to take all the risk, especially when investigating on our own had been my idea.

"Make note of any male who leaves the premises, then."

"But—"

Thorn's dark eyes turned hard as obsidian. "You're staying here. There's nothing you can do inside to help our investigation that we can't do ourselves."

That statement stung. I stiffened, groping for an argument in response that I thought he'd accept. "He's not likely to have left any obvious evidence of where he works just lying around, considering how careful the sword-star bunch are obviously being. I know the city —I know mortals. I might realize something is significant that you wouldn't."

"If we turn nothing up, then we'll consider it."

"He may be home," Ruse pointed out with an apologetic note in his voice. "You couldn't go waltzing into his apartment while he's there anyway."

I sighed. "Fine." As I sank back against the patchouli-scented seat, the reminder prompted a question I hadn't thought to ask before. I turned to Snap. "If Meriden is in there... can you test *him* and pick up impressions of other places he's gone, or—"

At the flinch that tightened the shadowkind's heavenly face, I cut myself off. His whole body had tensed, his green eyes going momentarily dark and distant, as if he was seeing something a long ways away that he wished he'd never had to see at all. Then he was looking to his companions, still rigid in his seat.

"No," he said, a quiver running through his clear voice. "I won't. Omen said— We agreed—"

"Hey," Ruse said in the same warm, gentle tone he'd used with me when I'd been reeling from the drugged air the other night. He reached over to grasp Snap's hand. "We're not asking anything like that of you. Don't worry about it. She was just curious—she didn't know."

I glanced between the two of them. "*What* don't I know?"

Snap's shoulders had come down at the incubus's reassurance, but he still looked haunted, as if a different sort of shadow had risen up through his usual brightness. He exhaled sharply and appeared to get a grip on whatever emotions my question had dredged up. "It's different with living things. It isn't something I would ever want to do."

I could hear an unspoken *again* in the resistance that wound through his voice and the way his gaze darted away from me. Something about his abilities… horrified him? Sweet harping Hades, how bad could it be for him to react like this?

Under all that joyful innocence, this god of sunshine had scars of his own. Scars and secrets.

I had the urge to touch him like Ruse had, to tell him that I knew what it was like to swallow down pain—that whatever haunted him, I wasn't going to judge him for it. But now wasn't the time for uncovering those secrets. We'd delayed here long enough.

I let myself give his arm a quick squeeze. "I'm sorry I brought it up. I had no idea. I'm sure you can dig up all kinds of useful dirt your regular way. You're the one who brought us here, after all."

Snap blinked at me, and a glimmer of his usual curious demeanor returned. He turned to Ruse. "Why would we want dirt?"

The incubus cracked a smile. "Another one of those silly mortal expressions. Come on. If we don't get moving soon, Thorn's likely to explode with his impatience."

"I'm hardly that limited in self-control," our warrior muttered, but he did vanish into the shadows around his seat awfully quickly after Ruse's remark. The other two slipped away a second later.

I refused to let myself slump. Although maybe it would have been a good tactic to avoid anyone wondering why I was sitting out here on my own. I settled for fiddling with my phone instead, as if I just *had* to finish this level of Whatever The Hot New Game Was before I could haul ass to wherever I was going.

Every few seconds, I glanced toward Meriden's house and all

around, but no one emerged from either door, and of course I couldn't see my shadowy friends. "Just a small town girl, living in a lonely world," I muttered to myself.

As if on cue, the phone in my hands vibrated. Vivi's number came up on the display. My throat tightened as I answered it, even though I should have welcomed the distraction.

"Hey!" I said with as much normal enthusiasm as I could feign. "What's up?"

"I was calling to ask you that, girl. You seem to be making all kinds of mysterious plans lately."

Her tone was teasing, but I winced inwardly all the same. "Not really. Honestly, all I'm doing right now is hanging out on my own." Not a lie! Somehow I couldn't feel all that victorious about it.

"No exciting news, then?"

"Still nothing. I promise, when I've got anything to tell, you'll be the first to know." I just wasn't going to tell anyone at all until I knew men with gas and guns wouldn't be coming for every person in the know.

Vivi laughed, which didn't really make sense—I hadn't told a joke. Something about the sound was a little forced. Apprehension pricked at me.

"We should get together for a proper hangout sometime," she said before I could go on. "Come over to my place, pick another movie off our watchlist, order in Thai. We could both use some time to unwind, don't you think?"

"Yeah," I said. "You know I'm always up for a movie-and-Thai night." I paused. "Is everything okay with you, Vivi?" The bastards hadn't harassed her in some way simply because they'd found out about our friendship, had they?

"What? Of course! Just missing that one-on-one time with my bestie. Hey, can you remind me how to get to that thrift shop on the east end you were telling me about? I was thinking of doing a little shopping after work tomorrow."

It wasn't an odd request, and I didn't see how it could have been prompted by nefarious villains, but her jump from one subject to the next still struck me as awkward. Was she grasping at straws to keep us talking? As I gave her the directions, I listened carefully for any hint of background noise that might reveal more than she was saying, but my ears didn't catch a thing.

"Okay, perfect," she said when I finished, and let out another giggle. "So, you're at home right now?"

I couldn't easily explain where I actually was, so… "Yep. Just finishing up dinner, actually, so I should get going." Save me from having to lie to my best friend even more. "Let's say Friday for movie night?" If my life was still precarious by then, I could always cancel.

"Sounds good to me. Is there anything else I can pitch in with in the meantime? You really shouldn't have to go it alone with, well, anything."

Her voice had taken on that concerned tone. I winced—but I wasn't actually alone in this mission, was I? "I know, Vivi. Thank you."

"Well, I guess I'll see you at the next meeting!"

She hung up without her usual "Ditto!" Of course, she didn't *always* say that when we were signing off, maybe not even half the time, so it didn't necessarily mean anything. Nothing about the conversation had been overtly weird. The tension of the past few days might simply be bleeding into all of my perceptions.

Still, a deeper restlessness gripped me as I returned my attention to Meriden's house. Had the guys found anything? Had we walked into a trap somehow? Why the hell was I sitting uselessly out here with no clue what was going on with anyone who mattered?

My hand came to rest on the door. I knew that walking over there was a bad idea, but—if they *had* gotten into some kind of trouble—

I was still wavering between common sense and impatience when the trio shimmered into being around me as if they'd never left. None of them looked exactly happy, but they appeared to have returned in one piece.

"Well?" I demanded before they'd had a chance to speak of their own accord.

"He's definitely living there," Ruse announced.

Thorn's mouth was set in its usual solemn line. "The back apartment. We have plenty of evidence of that, but nothing that points to where he might be spending his time otherwise—and he wasn't currently there."

Snap made a face as if that was his fault. "We do know what he looks like now. The impressions I picked up were mostly mornings and late at night. He might be wherever Omen is the rest of the time." He glanced toward the others as if to confirm.

Thorn nodded. "We'll come back tomorrow and see where he goes after he completes his morning routine. Then we'll discover where this Meriden is carrying out his wretched work now."

TWENTY-TWO

Sorsha

By the time we made it back to the apartment after picking up a drive-through dinner, night had fallen. The only light was the glow from the posts at the corners of the parking lot. The warm breeze carried a hint of smoke—from the flavor of it, it was a trash can fire. Great neighborhood we'd ended up in.

Since we had the pilfered keys now, I went in through the lobby as if I belonged in the building while the trio followed via the shadows. No point in drawing attention to ourselves with the guys' striking good looks and Thorn's nearly inhuman physique.

A middle-aged woman in turquoise scrubs was looking through a few envelopes by the mailboxes. She didn't even glance my way as I breezed past her to the stairs. I didn't think anything of her, or of the fact that she ended up ambling along several steps behind me. Only when she came out into the second floor after me did I realize I could have a problem. She might be familiar enough with her neighbors on the same floor to know I didn't belong in the apartment I was heading to.

It only took a small trick. I stopped and muttered a curse to myself as if I'd remembered something that frustrated me. Then I stepped closer to the wall to rummage through my purse. The woman walked by… and kept going all the way to the stairwell at the far end of the hall.

That was odd. Maybe she'd taken a longer route to her own floor to get some exercise? My skin prickled as I hustled the last short distance to the apartment door and ducked inside.

The guys took a few more seconds to appear, and when they did, it was in mid argument.

"How could they already know we're here?" Ruse was saying. "We only just got back from Meriden's house, and she was already in the lobby."

"They could have followed us from the office building," Thorn said, and spun toward me. "We have to leave. That woman who followed you—she stopped and watched to see which apartment you went into, and then she immediately took out her communication device. She must have been waiting for us. And if our enemies know we're in this building, the rest of them will be waiting nearby."

My pulse stuttered with a jolt of adrenaline. Fucking hell. Thankfully I'd brought my backpack along for the drive, so I had almost all of my things. But I couldn't take off without—

"Pickle!" I called, pitching my voice low but urgent. "Pickle, come, we've got to go."

The little dragon dashed out of the room I'd slept in, tufts of feathers clinging to his scales and floating into the air in his wake. He must have found a down pillow to nest in, damn it.

There wasn't time to make amends for our unwitting hosts' destroyed property. I bent down with my purse open and motioned for him to jump in. He balked for a second and then made the leap. My jerk of the zipper, closing it to hide him, was met with a snort of protest.

While I'd gathered him, Thorn had slipped away into the shadows again. He wavered back into the front hall with an expression even graver than before.

"They're just coming out from the stairs at both ends of the hall," he said. "More than a dozen of them—and this time they're fully equipped like the ones who took Omen."

I yanked the dangling strap of my backpack over my other

shoulder and held my purse close. "There's no fire escape this time. Do you think we have any chance of making it past them in the hall?"

"The three of us could take a shadow route, but you—" Thorn's head jerked to the side as if he'd heard something from the hall. His expression set with resolve. He swiveled on his feet. "The vehicles are... that way." Grabbing my wrist to tug me with him, he sprinted down the hall toward the bedrooms.

"What—?" I managed to get out as Ruse and Snap dashed with us. Before I could complete that question, Thorn had let go of me to charge straight through the bedroom door. It burst off its hinges with a crackle of splintering wood... and Thorn kept going, his fists rising in front of him, straight at the far wall.

He slammed into it arms first and drove straight through, plaster and plywood crumbling around him to rain down on the floor. As my feet jarred to a stop in the middle of the room, I gaped at the Thorn-sized passage he'd opened up between this apartment and the one next door. Oh my freaky stars, the guy didn't do things by halves, did he? We had a whole lot more than a pillow to apologize for now.

If I'd had any doubts about racing after him, they were resolved in an instant by the *boom* of our apartment door exploding open behind me. Yeah, we had *definitely* overstayed our welcome here. I hurled myself through the smashed opening after Thorn.

He'd already barreled right through the neighbor's apartment and out the other end, leaving another gaping hole in the kitchen wall. Shrieks spilled from the living room. As we ran by, I saw a young woman frantically hopping up and down where she'd jumped onto her couch, as if she thought she were dealing with a very large mouse that might come scurrying up her leg.

Add another person to the list of apology letters I was never going to send.

Shouts rang out behind us. I pushed myself faster, through the kitchen's hole and past an elderly couple sitting frozen in shock with their dinner forks halfway to their mouths. "Really sorry!" I managed to toss out to them as I raced by.

"Send the bill to the bunch coming after us," Ruse suggested with a breathless laugh.

A waft of outside air swept in from the hole in the couple's bedroom. Jagged edges of cinder block and brick protruded around it, framing the night and the parking lot lights. As I reached it, I gulped. I'd known Thorn was strong, but—fuck, he was a demolition machine. Was there anything he couldn't bash through?

I already knew the answer to that: silver or iron or both. Which the villains chasing after us would no doubt be carrying plenty of.

Thorn stood on the ground two stories down. He held out his arms. "Leap! I'll catch you."

He meant me, obviously. Snap disappeared into the shadows and emerged next to him a moment later. Ruse gave me an encouraging nudge.

"I've never seen him do this before, but I think you can count on him being *very* invested in making sure you don't go splat," he said with a wink, and then glanced behind us. "Unlike our tenacious fan club."

My sense of self-preservation was torn between fear of the twelve-foot drop and fear of the weapons the enemies charging after us might be carrying. At least, like Ruse had said, the guy below *wanted* me to survive. I sucked in a breath, clutched my purse to my chest, and sprang into the open air.

My stomach flew to my throat and my hair whipped up from my head. I had only a second for terror to burst through me before my body smacked into two incredibly strong arms.

Thorn caught me with just enough give that the impact left only a fleeting ache in my back. He didn't put me down, though, but sprinted with me toward the SUV. My head jostled against his expansive chest. The smell of him filled my nose, musky with a smoky edge like coals that had just stopped glowing: warmth and a warning wrapped together.

Ruse had whipped past us through the shadows and was starting the engine. Snap peered at us through the rear window from the back seat. Thorn wrenched open the door on the other side, tossed me in beside Snap with a slam behind me, and dove into the front passenger spot.

I landed in the middle of the seat, my hip jarring against one of the buckles, but I couldn't really complain about the warrior's haste. Yells and thumping footsteps carried from far too close behind us.

The second Thorn materialized inside the vehicle, Ruse hit the gas. The SUV tore backward and around. I tumbled farther to the side, bumping into Snap's slender frame. He grasped my arm to steady me as Ruse burned rubber, roaring down the drive and out into the streets.

"Sorry," I said to Snap, fumbling with my bags. I tucked my purse in the far corner on the floor's shag rug where I figured Pickle was least likely to get crushed.

"It's all right," Snap said softly. The light of the streetlamps passing by glinted off his eyes. As the roar of several other engines reached us, they opened wider. "Will they be able to catch us, do you think?"

Ruse let out a rough chuckle. "I swear on my libido, I'm going to do everything I can to make sure they don't."

"We can't stay in this vehicle," Thorn said. "They'll be familiar with it now. As soon as we can, we must abandon it and continue by other means."

"No kidding. I think I'd better lose the homicidal maniacs behind us first, though—don't you?"

Thorn gave a wordless mutter of assent, and Ruse jerked the wheel, spinning us in an abrupt ninety-degree turn—and then, an instant later, another. I still hadn't gotten the chance to fasten any of the seatbelts around me. The momentum threw me into Snap again, the second lurch landing me right on his lap.

I guessed I'd just have to resign myself to being a ping-pong ball for this ride. It beat whatever the sword-star bunch wanted to turn me into. "Sorry," I said to Snap again as his buffering arm came up to support me. He shook his head with a smile as if to say he didn't need any apology.

As the SUV jostled back and forth with more of Ruse's quick maneuvers, I swayed and gripped Snap's knee. The moment we stopped rocking around, I attempted to squirm off him to give him at least a little personal space. My shoulder knocked his chest, and all at once Snap's body went rigid against mine.

I held myself still, my gaze darting to him to check if I'd inadvertently hurt him. I'd never been quite this close to his divinely handsome face before, just inches between us. His chest hitched against my arm with a stuttered breath, and his moss-green eyes stared at me, as bewildered as if I'd suddenly transformed into a polka-dotted caribou.

Something was obviously not okay. I shifted my weight to get off him, and another swerve of the car sent me sliding back into his lap. My ass pressed into Snap's groin—into a solid form that was even more rigid than the rest of him.

Oh. *Oh.* My eyes caught his again, just as they flashed with a glimmer of brighter green, like that glimpse of neon I'd gotten in the collector's room. His hand braced against my thigh and then pulled back as if he wasn't sure where to put it. Heat seeped between us everywhere our bodies touched, which at this point was quite a lot of territory.

So he did have it in him to get turned on. From the uncertainty in his expression, he hadn't been any more aware of that fact than I'd been. But now that I'd noticed it, there was no mistaking the bulge of his erection.

His pupils had dilated slightly, his breath coming shallower and faster than usual. A tingle quivered through my lungs and down to the apex of my thighs in response. He'd gotten this turned on, probably for the first time in his existence, because of me. And every part of me was totally on board with that. I just couldn't tell how on board *he* was.

It wasn't as if we were in any position to explore the possibilities further. The awkward intensity of the moment broke with a screech of the tires. Ruse hauled the SUV in the other direction, and I flew off Snap onto my back, just barely catching myself before my head banged into the opposite door.

After one more burst of speed, the incubus slammed on the brake and cut the engine. "They're not going to find us here for at least a little while. Now we just have to figure out where we're taking off to next."

We'd stopped in a laneway so tight I could barely squeeze out of the SUV. Good thing the shadowkind, especially Thorn, didn't have to bother with the doors. The backs of brick buildings loomed on either side of us; the glint of streetlamps shone only faintly in the far distance. I had no idea where we'd ended up, but it definitely didn't look like an easy spot to stumble on.

"We'll want another vehicle." Thorn motioned to Ruse. "Why don't you slink around and see what you can turn up that couldn't be easily linked to us? I'll patrol the area to ensure our enemies haven't followed us too closely." He glanced at me and Snap. "You two get ready to flee if we need to, but stay here for now in case we don't find another vehicle in time. I won't be long. Ruse had better not be either."

"I can take a hint," the incubus said. They both slipped away into the darkness, leaving Snap and I in silence.

In the tight space that was as much as I could open the door, I picked my purse off the floor and gave Pickle a comforting pat through the fabric. He murmured his displeasure.

Snap flitted into the shadows and out again by the back of the SUV. I leaned against the trunk at the opposite end from him, giving him the space I hadn't been able to offer in the car. Snap gazed down the lane toward that distant haze of artificial light. In the dimness, I thought I could tell his cheeks had flushed, but a glance at his nether regions showed that he was no longer, er, standing at attention.

We stood there in silence for a few minutes. Then words spilled out of me before I could second-guess the impulse. "It doesn't have to be a big deal, you know. It's a totally natural reaction that anyone could have in close contact like that. Just a little friction, stirring things up."

His head swiveled with its serpentine grace to consider me. "Just a little friction," he repeated, in a tone I couldn't read. "Is that all it means to you?"

I opened my mouth and closed it again, abruptly unsure how to respond. "Not always," I said finally. "But I can look at it that way if that's what you'd prefer."

He looked away from me with a flick of his tongue over his lips. "I don't know. I—" He paused, apparently grappling with his words as much as I had. "It's not a sensation I'm used to. It was... unexpected. As it was happening, I wanted very much for it to be over with, but I also wanted more. I'm not sure which preference was stronger."

I found myself wetting my lips too. I sure as hell wasn't going to push him, but— "Well, if you end up deciding on more, just let me know."

He shifted against the trunk with an audible inhalation, but before either of us could say anything else, Ruse appeared in front of us. He jabbed his thumb toward the end of the lane. "I've got a cab waiting that-a-way, with a very agreeable driver who won't mark down the pick-up. Where's the lunk?"

"Right here." Thorn stepped out of the shadows just as the incubus finished speaking. "Our pursuers haven't made it this far yet, but we should move on with all haste. We can't shelter for the night in one of those taxis."

An idea clicked in my head, so fitting I could have laughed if tension hadn't still been knotted through my chest. "I know the perfect place for us to go."

TWENTY-THREE

Sorsha

Even though there was no denying Ruse's seductive charms, we had the taxi drop us off a five-minute walk from our actual destination. The incubus gave the driver a jaunty salute and said in a cajoling tone, "Thank you, my friend. You'll drive back downtown and forget you ever came out here."

As the cab pulled away, Thorn glanced at me. "What is this spot you wanted us to come to?"

I started walking, pointing to the glowing motel sign ahead of us, the letters distorted where half of the bulbs had burnt out. "This is a place people go to specifically when they don't want anyone to know where they've gone."

Every time Vivi had driven us to the outlet stores farther down this strip, we'd passed the motel with its weather-worn sign offering hourly rates. It'd become a running joke, making up stories about who would be so desperate for anonymity they'd take a room in a place that looked straight out of a slasher flick. A dude having an affair with his wife's sister—who was also his kid's teacher and his brother's girlfriend. A mafia foot-soldier on the run from both the mob and the cops after a catastrophic incident involving a thrown plate of cannelloni. And so on.

Now I was getting to experience that desperation firsthand. Lucky me.

The sign also declared that the management only accepted payment in cash, because they were just that classy. My hand settled on my purse as we approached the front office, but Ruse waved his hand at me dismissively. "I've got this."

In the last few days, my criminal activities had multiplied like rabbits. After yet another tight escape and looking up at the dingy shingles lining the motel's roof, I couldn't quite bring myself to care about this latest con. "Be my guest."

As we'd agreed in hushed discussion in the cab, Snap and Thorn lurked in the shadows while Ruse and I went in. I took one look at the sputtering fluorescent light mounted on the ceiling, the board of nails dangling tarnished keys with numbered fobs, and the faded floral curtains that must have been at least a few decades old, and swallowed a slightly hysterical giggle. I was standing in the middle of a real live cliché. The only thing missing was getting murdered in my sleep, but who knew—there was still time for that.

Ruse strolled up to the reception desk with its patchy varnish and shot one of his smooth grins at the woman there, who had bags under her eyes big enough to hold spare change. "Hello there, darling," he said in the same voice he'd used on the cab driver.

The woman gave us a look of utter boredom, but as Ruse drew out the companionable chitchat, a friendly warmth came into her eyes. By the time he asked her for "two rooms, side-by-side, with an adjoining door if you've got that," she was so happy to help that she handed him two keys off the wall without the slightest hint of skepticism about a young couple asking for completely separate rooms.

"We could have made do with one," I said to him after we'd stepped back outside. "It's not as if the three of you need beds."

Ruse clucked his tongue at me. "I was respecting your privacy. Besides, I need to get my fix of late night cable TV, and I wouldn't want to keep you up."

I rolled my eyes at him, but the truth was, I did feel better having a little space that the shadowkind weren't invading. And even if the incubus and I were on better terms now, I wasn't interested in doing anything *other* than sleeping tonight. As we reached our rooms, a yawn stretched my jaw.

"Let's have a look at them before I decide which is mine," I said.

There wasn't exactly much to choose between. Both boasted similar flower-print curtains that were more gray than any other color now, moth-bitten carpets, and bed covers dappled with faint stains bleach hadn't quite eliminated. A chlorine-y scent clung to them, but at least that meant they should be somewhat sanitary if not pretty to look at.

The first room had a slightly larger TV, so I left that one to Ruse and set my bags down on the bed in the other room. Thorn followed me in through the adjoining doorway. He closed the door and studied the knob.

"We should leave this unlocked on both sides," he said. "None of us will disturb you unless there's urgent need—but if we should have to escape in a rush…"

"No argument here." I sat down on the end of the bed and eased open my purse. Pickle sprang out with a distressed but ineffectual flapping of his clipped wings. He shot a steely glare at the purse, as if it were to blame for his troubles, and bounded into the bathroom to put as much distance between it and him as he could.

Thorn prowled through the room, eyeing every wall, corner, and piece of furniture for signs of danger, going as far as swatting at a spiderweb so tattered I suspected the spider had abandoned it months ago.

"I'm pretty sure there aren't any actual serial killers hiding under the bed," I teased, but that only prompted him to actually check under the bed just in case.

While he occupied himself with that, I slid the deadbolt on the outer door into place and went into the bathroom to fill up a glass of water for Pickle. The little dragon took a sip, allowed me to stroke his neck a few times, and then tugged one of the towels into the tub to make a fuzzy nest for himself.

When I came back out, Thorn was still there, now standing near the door between our rooms. As I flopped down where I'd been sitting before, he stayed in place, his pose oddly hesitant.

"M'lady," he said, and paused. When I lifted my head to meet his gaze, he cleared his throat and glanced briefly at the floor before continuing.

"When we first came to you, I intended to keep you out of danger. I didn't anticipate that our presence would propel you so much further into it. You have lost your home, most of your belongings, been drugged once and nearly captured twice in a span of three days…"

"I do remember all that," I said when he trailed off. "I was there."

He made a frustrated sound, his hands clenching. His voice came out even gruffer than usual. "I'm trying to say that I apologize for misjudging the threat—and that you may have been right to wish us gone in the beginning. I can't make up for what's already come to pass, but I can avoid dragging you into further peril. We're closing in on Omen's captors even as they attempt to close in on us. You've assisted us far beyond what I ever would have asked, so I can't possibly ask for more. When we continue on Meriden's trail tomorrow, you can go your own way, apart from us."

Understanding sunk in slowly and then hit me in its final burst like a slap to the face. "What?" I sputtered. "You're telling me to take off?"

Thorn grimaced. "We would see to it you have everything we can provide that you might need—Ruse should be able to supply you with money and perhaps other resources—and we would ensure that we draw our enemies' attention to us to give you time to make a clean escape. If that isn't enough—"

"It's not about whether it's *enough*." I pushed myself off the bed to face him on my feet, my hands balling into fists at my sides. "Are you fucking kidding me? I lost my apartment, yeah, and lied to my only friends and now have run all over this city with bad guys at my heels, and you think after all that I'm going to throw in the towel and say it was all for nothing?"

The warrior's expression turned puzzled. "You never intended to find yourself in such treacherous waters."

"Maybe I didn't expect exactly this, but I knew there were risks. I saw what happened to Luna because of these sword-star assholes. So what if things have gotten 'treacherous'? When exactly did I give you the impression that I'm the type to run off with my tail between my legs when the going gets hard?"

Thorn was silent for a moment. "You're offended," he said. "You're angry with me."

"Yes, I'm fucking angry." Was there anything nearby I could throw at his somberly stoic face? The lumpy pillow wouldn't be at all satisfying. "I committed to finding out what the hell is going on, and I'm going to see that through. It isn't just for you, you blockhead. It's because of these pricks that Luna is dead. They might have killed my parents too. Who knows how many other people and shadowkind they've hurt before then and since? And you really think I'd take the chance to shrug it off and walk away?"

I'd obviously rubbed him the wrong way now and then—it wasn't as if his attitude hadn't irritated me often enough too—but I would have thought that by this point he'd believe they could count on me just a little. I'd run when the hunters came for Luna, when it was too late to help her anyway, and it'd killed me doing that. No way in hell was I letting the bastards off the hook now that we had them in our sights.

But he'd really thought I'd accept his offer that I leave. Possibly even expected me to be *grateful* for it. My teeth gritted.

"That wasn't how I saw it," the warrior said stiffly. "I merely was concerned for your well-being and the strain we've put on it."

Since I couldn't throw anything at him, I set my hands on my hips instead. "Stuff your concern up your ass. I'm not looking the other way while someone's out there still sticking beings like you in cages and who knows what other horrors, so you can just forget about keeping me out of it. I *have* helped, and a lot, haven't I, as inconvenient as this mortal body might be to you all?"

"I would never deny that. We would not have accomplished anywhere near as much in our quest without your assistance."

"All right. Then assume I'm going to keep assisting, and keep your ideas about what kind of 'strain' I can handle to yourself unless I ask for your opinion. Agreed?"

Thorn bowed his head. When he raised it, his lips were twisted at a more pained angle than before. "M'lady," he said, and seemed to struggle before adding my name. "Sorsha. I apologize. I promise I didn't intend to insult you, although I see now how insulting my proposition was. I hope you will accept that my misstep was made out of lack of consideration and not contempt for your courage and resilience."

The flare of my anger simmered down, although I couldn't tell how much he meant those words and how much he was simply placating me. It was hard to read that ever-solemn voice.

"All right then," I said. "Apology accepted. And listen, I can promise you this—once we find Omen and whatever other shadowkind these assholes have trapped, I'm going to burn everything that belongs to *them* to the ground just like I did your collector's house. That's the least they'll deserve."

The corner of Thorn's mouth quirked up, just for a second, into what might have almost been a smile. "I look forward to that day," he said in the same sober tone. "I'll take my leave of you so you can rest and prepare for tomorrow's plans."

"You do that," I said, but my grumble was half-hearted. He stepped out, closing the door behind him with a click. I sank down on the bed, my heart suddenly heavy.

I was in this 'til the end. I hadn't the slightest doubt about that. The only question was how much of my life from before would end up in tatters before this mission was over—if I was left with any life at all.

TWENTY-FOUR

Snap

THORN CAME STRIDING INTO OUR ROOM FROM SORSHA'S LOOKING ODDLY irritated and invigorated at the same time. His jaw was tightly set, his eyes as dark as ever, but he moved with an almost eager purposefulness.

Ruse looked up from the sagging armchair where he was mashing buttons on the little box that controlled the bigger box of the TV and raised his eyebrows at our companion.

"Have a nice chat?" he asked, managing with the lilt of his voice to imply that they might have engaged in all sorts of intimacies other than talking. I supposed that was part of his particular talent. It made me want to squirm where I'd been sitting on the edge of the bed, even though he hadn't directed it at me.

Thorn glowered at him. "We did, actually. And *someone* had to confirm her room contained no hazards. We've brought enough woe down on her head already."

"But you have to admit she's handled herself just fine."

Thorn paused for a moment. "Yes. She has." He swiveled on his heel abruptly. "I'm going to keep up a patrol of the nearby streets until we can leave in the morning. Stay alert and ready to defend yourselves and the mortal one if need be. And *you*, figure out how we can safely follow Meriden without our former vehicle."

That last bit was clearly aimed at Ruse. If I'd had more experience with the mortal realm, perhaps I could have helped more with making plans, but as it was, I wouldn't be of much use to any of them until we were right at the scene.

That was all right. I'd contributed my share, just as Omen had expected I would. I hoped when we found him he was in well enough condition to be pleased with his choices.

It did mean that at the moment I was left with little to do but stew in my thoughts. After Ruse had given Thorn a coy wave good-bye, the incubus's gaze traveled to me. Another itch traveled over my skin. He was an expert in all things to do with bodily pleasure. Had he already picked up on a change in the energies between me and Sorsha?

I'd rather not give him time to notice if he hadn't yet. I got up from the bed, shaking out my limbs as if stiff from staying in place too long, and said, "I think I'll retire to the shadows."

Ruse shrugged. "Up to you, but you're about to miss some very excellent TV." He gestured at it. "Late at night is when you get to observe all the things mortals think no one will want to see but feel the need to put on the air anyway."

True or not, there was something I wanted to observe more. Or rather, someone. The strange vibe with which Thorn had left Sorsha's room niggled at me. He'd been hard on her before—he was hard in general. Had his spirits been lifted because this time he'd managed to affect her with his criticisms?

I slipped into the shadows that lay here and there across the room, but then I hesitated. I'd gotten more of an eyeful than I'd been looking for the last time I'd peeked in on our mortal companion. But I knew where my two colleagues were now. I could retreat in an instant if need be.

With a tingle through my being, I leapt from the foot of the bed to the darkness that framed the adjoining door. Then I was peering from that space into Sorsha's room, so much like ours.

She was lying on her back on the bed on top of the covers, one hand behind her head and the other resting on her stomach. Her coppery eyes were open, contemplating the ceiling with that haze I'd come to recognize meant a person was thinking of something farther away. She didn't look upset, at least, only thoughtful. A crease had formed between her eyebrows.

Nothing about her appearance had changed that I could pinpoint. I'd always found her enjoyable to take in with that ruddy hair against her creamy skin and the vibrant glint that so often lit in her eyes. Much more interesting than a peach, as delicious as the fruit might be. But now, ever since that unexpected development during our hasty getaway...

My gaze veered across her body, over the curves of her chest and hips that drew my attention much more intensely than they ever had before. She shifted up on one elbow, and I couldn't help following the sway of her breasts. Then the way her thighs slid against each other as she stirred again.

A strange, heated sensation unfurled through my being with the urge to find out if those parts beneath her clothes would be as soft to the touch as her hair was. To discover how her expression might change if I gave in to that urge.

I turned my awareness away, back to my own room. It was easier to master the emotions flowing through me when I couldn't see her. Beneath the heat of the impulse, a chill shivered through my nerves.

Somewhere in the longing I could taste the start of a headlong fall. Would I be able to pull back from it if I let myself tumble?

If I couldn't... The one time I'd careened past the point of control before...

My mind shuttered against the memories.

The new feelings hadn't emerged out of nowhere. They'd risen from the physical body that let me interact with this realm. If I understood why, how it all connected, what it *meant*, maybe it wouldn't be so unnerving.

Our bathroom door was already closed. I pulled myself out from the shadows there, the air settling more solidly around my form. Only a little city glow carried through the small window beside the sink, but I didn't want to turn on the light and make Ruse wonder what I was doing in here.

The appendage between my legs lay flaccid in my pants now. I let one hand drop to it, but it didn't stir at the contact. I hadn't thought much about that particular part since we'd first passed over to this realm with Omen, other than the occasions when I'd spent enough time outside the shadows that I needed to relieve myself using it—and during Thorn's initial, stern reminder that if we got into a physical fight, I should be careful not to take a blow there, or the pain would be temporarily disabling.

It had never become so taut before, or lifted the way it had in the car, even though Sorsha's bottom had been pressing down against it—

The memory of that firm yet pliant roundness, of my arm around her back and her hair grazing my cheek, rushed through my mind like the scent of her had filled my nose. And what a scent it was: sweet like the honey I'd sampled at the market but with a sharpness as biting as the flames she'd lit in the wake of our first escape. I wondered if I flicked my tongue against her cheek, not with any power but just to taste in the physical sense, would her flavor be as intoxicating?

And then that appendage, what I'd heard Ruse refer to as his "cock," had twitched and stiffened with a flood of pleasure totally different from any I'd felt before, hot and hungry and unsettlingly forceful.

Like it was stiffening against my hand right now in response to those memories. I swallowed hard and ran my fingers over it experimentally. Thinking back to Sorsha lying on the bed as I'd seen her just now...

It rose even higher, straining against the fly of my pants. With each brush of my fingertips, ripples of pleasure and the hunger that came with it radiated through the rest of my body. I closed my eyes, caught again between the longing for more and the terror that quivered up from deeper within me.

There had been a sort of pleasure in my first—and only— devouring. A cold, bottomless hunger that sucked in and shredded, and a tight, icy bliss as that hunger was satisfied bit by bit. The two together had driven me on and on...

Nausea coiled through my stomach at the memory.

That wasn't the worst of it, though. The devouring had been horrible and horrifying... and the part of me that had sunk in its ethereal jaws clamored to sate itself all over again.

My fingers had stilled over my erect member. With the thought of other acts, it was starting to wilt. I gave it another stroke, willing the distant past away.

This sensation wasn't the same kind of pleasure. It wasn't the same hunger. What I wanted when the heated tingles spread through my groin was not to satisfy myself so much as to create a pleasure that would satisfy her too.

She hadn't been disturbed by the idea. Recalling her offer that I should come to her if I decided to pursue my desire brought an eager flush into my chest and cheeks.

I wasn't sure I could control this sensation. I wasn't sure where tumbling into it would lead me. But it felt like a kindling rather than an obliterating. It was possible, wasn't it, that this unraveling could be different in that way too? That it might take us someplace good?

I could wait and see how things seemed by the light of day. Proceed with caution—until I couldn't be cautious anymore, if I took that route.

My thoughts slipped back to Sorsha: to the warmth she'd shown me, to her laugh, to her enduring strength through all the danger we'd faced. If I did dive in, it would be with her. I knew already there was no one else who'd make it worth the risk.

TWENTY-FIVE

Sorsha

"I SHOULD HAVE BROUGHT A PAIR OF BINOCULARS," I GRUMBLED, slouching against the leather seat with new-car smell prickling in my nose.

Ruse tsked teasingly at me from the driver's seat. "Patience, Miss Blaze. Our job is to be ready to drive when the Incredible Hulk gives the word."

He meant Thorn, who was stationed in the shadows somewhere down the road where he *could* make out what was going on at Meriden's house. Those of us keeping our physical bodies were staked out in a driveway a couple of blocks away. Ruse had even made a show of getting out of the car and walking around to the back of the house in case anyone was watching all the way over here and would have thought our arrival odd otherwise.

He'd slipped back through the shadows after, and the sedan's tinted windows ensured no one was going to be IDing me or my shadowkind friends through the glass. I appeared to have stumbled straight from a slasher flick into a spy caper.

It was a pretty posh car all around. I peered at Ruse from where I was still hunkered down in my seat. "Are you sure the salesman isn't going to snap out of your little charm spell and realize he's lost a major chunk of change, plus commission?"

"First off, I assure you there's nothing 'little' about any part of my prowess," Ruse said. "And yes, you can rest easy. He thinks *he* got the better end of the deal."

"But he didn't. Someone at the dealership is going to notice eventually."

"Your mortal conscience is so adorable." Ruse's smirk softened around the edges with a hint of affection. "If all goes well, we won't need to keep this lovely piece of machinery for more than a few days, and then I'll drop it off in the lot. No harm done!"

Other than the potential harm of whatever wear and tear we put it through, which considering how the past few days had gone might be a lot, but since the alternative had been sitting around in the horror-movie motel with my thumb up my ass, I shut up.

I suspected the only reason Thorn had agreed to my coming along at all, yesterday's apologies about misjudging my commitment aside, was because he'd be *more* worried leaving me on my own than having me where he could keep an eye on me. As annoying as his own commitment could be, he did take the whole protection racket very seriously.

Across from me, Snap turned his head, following the path of a gray minivan that was cruising by.

"Wrong direction for that to be Meriden," I said. "And much more the kind of car the white-picket-fence families around here would be driving than a conspiracy of shadowkind hunters."

He nodded as if taking my observations in stride. If last night's awkwardness was still affecting him, he hadn't let it show in any way I'd noticed so far. Maybe he'd decided pretending his momentary arousal had never happened and praying it never did again was the better course of action.

I was allowed to feel a *tad* disappointed about that, don't you think?

"Perhaps I don't understand because I haven't spent enough time in this realm," he said, "but I can't see what those people would want with us. With higher shadowkind in general. What are they *doing* with Omen and whoever else they've taken, and why?"

"The collector who had us felt awfully proud of the power he had over us, keeping us locked up," Ruse said. "Remember how often he'd come around to gloat? Mortals can be just as addicted to a sense of power as shadowkind can—maybe more so."

Snap hummed. "It didn't seem as if that building we searched before was for just holding and displaying the shadowkind they'd captured. They were going much farther than that."

"Everybody wants to rule the world," I said carelessly.

The godly shadowkind blinked at me. "Do they? I don't."

"No, it's just— It's words from a song. Never mind." I gave a vague wave of my hand. "Whoever these people are, they're probably power-hungry too, just for a different kind of power. The hunter M.O. has evolved before, right? From what I've heard, way back in the day, all they were interested in was tracking down and slaughtering any of you they could find. It took a while before they found out that they could actually make money from the hunt—mostly if they kept the beings they captured alive."

"There were always collectors," Ruse said. "Just like there were always sorcerers." He glanced at Snap. "Those are the mortals who've developed a system for manipulating shadowkind into using their powers for the sorcerer's benefit. But I remember hearing of collectors in my early days... There were only a few of them, and it was harder for them to arrange the purchases without the internet and all, I'd guess. And mortals in general were much more bloodthirsty about anything remotely supernatural back then."

"At least when the creatures are in cages, I can let them out again." I kicked the back of Thorn's vacant seat and scowled at the street outside. "These sword-star people are definitely something else, though. So many of them and so organized, plus they're trying to get shadowkind *from* the collectors instead of for them. And from what you said about the impressions you picked up in that lab, Snap—I don't like it; that's for sure."

The incubus opened his mouth as if he were going to add something else—and the gray minivan that had passed us just a few minutes ago drove back into view, turning toward Meriden's house at the intersection between him and us. I sat up straighter, studying it. Why would they have come back around?

The minivan slowed to a stop toward the end of the next block, and a figure hustled over to it from one of the driveways I could barely distinguish at this distance. I tensed even more. "Start the engine," I told Ruse on instinct, a second before Thorn flickered in and out of view in his signal to us to pick him up.

"Thorn's calling us!" Snap said.

Ruse peeled out of the driveway but rumbled on down the street at just a smidge over the speed limit, despite the urgency he must be feeling as much as I was. If we *looked* like we were chasing the minivan, we'd blow all the care we'd put into this cover.

I gripped the door, my heart thumping. A baby blue compact had pulled away from the curb behind us. Great, now we had two sets of spectators to worry about, not counting anyone who glanced out their house's windows.

The incubus didn't even slow down as we passed Thorn's post. The warrior must have sprung into the sedan from one shadow to another. With a blink, he was sitting in the passenger seat as if he'd never left.

He jabbed his hand toward the windshield. "Meriden got into that van. Don't lose it. But make sure they don't know we're tracking them."

"I remember the plan," Ruse said mildly. At a stop sign, he drummed his fingers against the steering wheel, the only outward sign of his own impatience. The minivan turned out of view up ahead, and I stifled a growl.

Now that the people in the van couldn't see us either, Ruse gunned the engine a little faster. When he took the same turn, the vehicle was still in view, the gunmetal-gray paint shining in the mid-morning sunlight a little more than a block ahead of us.

I let out my breath, and it snagged in my throat on my next inhale at a flash of color in the side mirror. Craning my neck, I spotted that baby blue compact taking the turn after us. Uneasiness itched at me. "I think someone might be tracking *us*."

Thorn glanced back, his lips slanting into a deeper frown. "It appears to be just a driver, no passengers. I could deal with them if need be."

I squinted at the figure, but between the light reflecting off the windshield and the pale hood pulled low over the driver's forehead, I couldn't even tell whether it was a man or a woman. "It only took one person to bring a whole squad down on us last night," I reminded him.

"Let's not jump to any conclusions yet," Ruse suggested. The minivan veered right, and several seconds later he copied the maneuver. I exhaled slowly—and here came that blue car, following us again.

The incubus's mouth twisted. "Okay, maybe we should start jumping now."

"We can't keep following the van with someone else following us," I said. "No one's seen who we are yet, but the more obvious it becomes what we're doing, the more likely they'll sound the alarm."

Ruse gave the wheel another beat of his fingers and made a pleased sound at the sight of the van's turn signal going on. We were coming up on a major throughway, four lanes with plenty of traffic as commuters headed to work. The incubus ignored the left turn lane the minivan had pulled into and drove straight ahead.

Thorn grunted in dismay. "What are you doing?"

"Just watch. Ah, here he comes."

The blue car stayed on our tail. Ruse sailed through the intersection and halfway down the next block, and then swerved with a jerk of the wheel into a gas station.

"Ooof." My chest jarred against the seatbelt I thankfully had on this time. Not that my ribs were thanking it.

I clutched the edge of the seat as Ruse tore through the gas station between the rows of pumps and out onto a different street. The engine roaring now, he careened into the next right, cut across the parking lot outside a print shop, and flung us around through a couple more hasty turns. Then, with one final squeak of the tires, we flew out onto the large street the minivan had turned onto.

And wouldn't you know it, there was the damned thing still only a block ahead.

Ruse chuckled. "Thank the dark for rush-hour traffic. Any sign of our hanger-on?"

I studied the view beyond the back window for several seconds as we cruised after the minivan. The baby blue sheen should have stood out in the sea of black and silver, but I didn't spot it. A weird choice for a stealth mission, really. Knitting my brow, I swiveled toward the front again.

"You lost them—but maybe they just happened to be taking the same route and weren't after us anyway. They didn't seem all that on the ball."

"Doesn't really matter as long as they're not behind us now. Let's see where Meriden is off to."

We skirted the edge of downtown, coming within ten blocks of the apartment building we'd crashed in—and then crashed through—not long ago. The minivan took a few more turns before ending up in the docklands, where aging factories loomed on either side of the streets and the smell of algae seeped into the air conditioning. The river that wove through the east end of town used to be a major shipping route before the manufacturing industries had started moving overseas.

With much less traffic on these streets, Ruse had dropped back to a couple of blocks behind the minivan. I stirred restlessly in my seat. How long a road trip were we on, exactly? And why hadn't I brought more snacks to—

The minivan jerked to a halt by the curb. A skinny figure topped with gleaming black hair scrambled out and darted out of sight between two of the buildings.

Thorn cursed. "Go! We have to see where he went."

The second the minivan had pulled away, Ruse hit the gas. We jolted back in our seats as he sped over. When he passed the last side-street before the drop-off spot, Thorn vanished, presumably rushing off through the shadows to track the man where the car couldn't follow.

"He might need me to test the area," Snap said, and wavered away an instant later.

As Ruse drove by the alley I thought Meriden had taken, I peered down it, but he'd disappeared as effectively as the shadowkind had. The incubus eased to a stop at the end of the block and idled there.

The minivan was long gone. As far as I could tell, there was no one around to make note of us. But I'd thought that before and been wrong.

I twisted to scan the street. "Do we just wait for Thorn and Snap? Should we be searching for Meriden too?"

Ruse appeared to make a quick deliberation. "Let's keep driving—it'll look less suspicious if anyone is monitoring the area, and maybe we'll spot our target somewhere around the block."

He circled around, and I leaned closer to the window, studying every doorway, window, and alley. The gloomy structures showed no sign of life at all, like giant, rotting carcasses of beasts slain long ago. An engine thrummed in the distance, but whatever vehicle the sound came from, we never saw it.

Ruse continued on a block farther, to where a rusty crane creaked in the wind over the river. He looped back around with a rough sigh. "Hopefully the Hulk had better luck."

We were just coming up on the street where we'd left Thorn and Snap when both of them slipped out of the shadows into their seats with a shudder through the air. Ruse eased over to the curb and cut the engine.

Thorn didn't wait to be asked. His voice came out taut with frustration. "We lost him. No trail to pick up. Snap couldn't tell where he passed by."

"If he didn't touch anything closely enough with his body, it wouldn't have left an impression I could connect to him," Snap said in a mournful tone. "Many shoes walked over that ground; I couldn't taste any that were definitely his."

"Quite the system this group has worked out," Ruse said. "I'd be impressed if it wasn't so irritating of them."

Thorn's shoulders tensed. "It's more than irritating. It's unacceptable. At every turn, they get the better of us, foil every measure we've taken. We fumble along while Omen faces who knows what torment—" He stiffened even more at the sound of footsteps outside.

An older man came into view, heading into our street from down by the river behind us. Not Meriden—his hair a mix of mouse-brown and silver, his shorter frame slightly slumped. But without a word, Thorn whipped open the door, sprang out of the car, and charged past my window.

A sound of protest burst from my throat. I jerked around to see the massive shadowkind barreling toward the man as if he meant to knock him right off his feet. For the love of little baby elephants, what was he thinking?

I hesitated for just a second, and then I leapt out after him.

The man had halted in mid-step at the sight of the colossus closing in on him, but Thorn didn't so much as slow down. He slammed his hand into the man's chest and yanked the front of his polo shirt up to his chin. The man swayed backward, scrambling on tippy-toe to keep his feet on the ground.

"What do you know about the man who got out here?" Thorn demanded.

"What?" his victim said in a reedy voice. "What man? When? I—I don't know what you mean."

"You must know *some*thing."

"I swear, I was only walking by—there's a shop down the street where they sell the only coffee my wife will drink." He jerked his hand, and the plastic bag dangling from it rustled. "Please. I'd help you if I could."

"Thorn!" I stopped on the sidewalk next to him, my throat constricting. "He's just some random guy walking by. He wasn't even near the drop-off spot."

"That's what they'd want us to think." Thorn shook the man. "Whatever you've seen, whatever you know, you'll tell me, *now*." His voice had gone hard and cold as a winter freeze.

The guy was trembling, his toes barely scraping the ground. He couldn't make anything more than a choked squeak now. I didn't think Thorn was trying to kill him—but he might with that incredible strength, if he was too distracted by his need for answers to notice the full effect he was having on that mortal body.

I wasn't completely sure the warrior wouldn't turn that strength on me if I crossed him in this moment, despite debts owed. The breath left my lungs, but I forced myself to grasp his arm.

"Thorn," I said, vaguely aware of the other two shadowkind reaching us. "He doesn't have any answers. I know you've been beating yourself up for not protecting Omen, for not finding him sooner, but this isn't going to make it right. It wasn't your fault anyway."

Finally, Thorn's gaze shifted to me. In that moment, the anguish in his eyes was so stark that my throat clenched up again for a different reason. It resonated through me, stirring up echoes of the guilt that had wrenched me so often in the first years after Luna's death—the unpredictable flashes back to the attack, the incessant attempts to piece together some way I could have saved her, as if it could have made a difference by then.

"How can you know that?" Thorn asked in a raw voice.

I made myself hold his gaze, even though the tension radiating off him set all my nerves jittering with alarm. I knew where that agonizing frustration came from. It wasn't aimed at me or even the man he was holding, not really. And I could tell him this with more certainty than I'd ever been able to absolve myself.

"Because I've seen just how far you'll go to keep the people under your watch safe, and it's *really* fucking far. I'd probably be dead at least twice over if it wasn't for you. We're going to figure this out. I know that much. Just... not this way. Please."

Gradually, the warrior's arm relaxed. The man's feet touched down. He sagged with a rasp for breath that brought Thorn's gaze jerking back to his victim. He took in the man's quivering form before glancing back at me, and a flicker of an expression that might have been distraught crossed the warrior's face.

Oh, there were feelings buried under that hardened exterior—plenty of them. The thought of the overwhelming loyalty that drove his guilt sent a shiver through me, one not entirely unpleasant.

"I only wanted to find out what he knew," he said.

I squeezed his arm where my hand still rested on it. "And now that's done."

Ruse sauntered over to the man and helped him gather himself with a grip of his elbow and a friendly pat to the back. "He's confused and terrified, and the confusion is real," the incubus said to us. "He really doesn't have any idea what this is about. And I think I'd better make sure he doesn't give it any more thought, hmm?"

He eased the man off to the side to talk to him in soothing, persuasive tones. I let my hand fall from Thorn's forearm. He watched it drop to my side as if he wasn't sure how it'd ended up on him in the first place.

"What do we do now?" Snap asked.

"Well…" I looked around. "We know where Meriden gets dropped off. They probably stick to a similar schedule every day—it'd get complicated constantly switching locations with no reason to."

Thorn picked up the thread of my thoughts. "We'll come straight here tomorrow morning. Be ready to follow him as soon as he gets out. Pick up the next part of the trail." He raised his head, his usual cool determination returning.

I found myself smiling at him—this brutally devoted monster. "Exactly. I'd call that a plan."

TWENTY-SIX

Sorsha

I could tell Pickle wasn't feeling so comfortable with our current situation from the massive nest-build he'd undertaken. The motel bathroom tub now held two bath towels, one hand towel, and at least four rolls worth of shredded toilet paper. He looked a little ridiculous curled up in one corner, his small green body taking up barely a tenth of the space, but I wasn't going to pick a fight with him over it. At least, not until I needed to take another shower.

"Sleep tight," I told him with a pat on the head. By the time I'd finished brushing my teeth, he was snoring with raspy little hiccups. I held back a laugh and shut the door to muffle the sound.

Like that, the intermittent rumble of passing traffic drowned him out. The yellow light of the parking lot security lamps streaked through the thin fabric of the curtains. I padded through the glow to the bed, sprayed the air with another puff of the lavender-scented freshener I'd bought, and settled down under the covers, hoping I was tired enough to tune out the lumps in the mattress. The padded surface did a pretty good imitation of the Sahara dunes.

I'd closed my eyes but not yet drifted off when a faint shift in the air made me suddenly certain I was no longer alone. One of my shadowkind friends had slipped into the room in their supernatural way. Ruse, I assumed, but as I started to roll over, it wasn't his languid voice that reached my ears.

"Sorsha?"

Snap was standing in front of the door between our rooms, as if trying to do the best approximation of having entered the normal way without actually having opened the door. In the dim light, his curls darkened from gold to bronze, but the smooth planes of his face still managed to catch a little glow.

As I sat up, he kept totally still. I couldn't tell whether that was because he wanted the distance or he thought I might.

My pulse stuttered. Had our enemies tracked us down yet again despite all our precautions? "What's going on? Is something wrong?"

"No. I mean, I don't think so." His tongue flitted over his lips. "You said, yesterday, that if I decided I wanted more, I should tell you."

His gaze dipped—just for a moment, but obviously enough that the warmth of his attention grazed my breasts through my undershirt. I'd only worn that and panties to bed, where the sheet was now pooled around my waist.

As his meaning sank in, the warmth drifted lower to settle between my legs. All at once, my whole body felt flushed.

"I did say that," I agreed. "So... you do?"

He hesitated, and then the smile that transformed him from handsome to heavenly spread across his face. "Yes. Very much."

I found I wasn't totally sure what to do next. With Ruse, it'd been easy. He'd known exactly what he wanted and what he could offer. Snap was clearly discovering all this for the first time. It was thrilling to think I'd been the one to stir up that sort of desire in him... but also a little intimidating.

I didn't have the best track record with men. Somehow I always seemed to end up disappointing them in the end. It'd be an awful shame if I inadvertently traumatized the guy so badly he fled back to the monk way of life.

We didn't have to rush into anything. I needed to figure out how far *I* wanted this to go. Obviously given who and what we were, it couldn't be anything more than a fling—like with Ruse, enjoying what we had in the moment—but it was hard to see taking any shadowkind as a lover as a totally casual act.

For now, we could simply explore the possibilities. I scooted over on the bed to make room. "Why don't you come here, then, and we'll see where the moment takes us?"

Snap crossed the floor as swiftly as he'd been still before and sank down next to me. As he gazed into my eyes, his lit with an eager shine. His hand came up to trace across my cheek and into the fall of my hair. His smile faded.

"I want you to know I'd never hurt you. My abilities—I have to focus to use them; it doesn't happen automatically. I wouldn't put you in any danger."

His voice held so much resolve that my heart wrenched. He really thought I might be afraid of him, of what he could do. Hell, I didn't even know what that *was*, and I still didn't have the slightest concern that he'd ever inflict it on me, not after the way he'd reacted the other day when we'd talked about using his powers on living things.

I reached up to wrap my hand around his with a gentle squeeze. "I know. I'm not worried."

"Good." His smile returned like the sun emerging from behind a passing cloud.

He leaned closer, his nose nearly brushing my temple. His breath painted heat down the side of my face. The scent that rose from his skin was fresh and bright as spring clover, with a darker mossy undertone like a reminder that there was more lurking beneath the surface.

"There's so much I want to do," he murmured. "I don't know where to start. I don't know what you'd like."

The desire that had settled low in my belly tightened into something sharper. At this point I suspected I'd be all for whatever he went with. "Why don't you start with what *you'd* like, and I'll let you know if we need a change in direction?"

He responded with a pleased hum that sent a tingle over my skin and dipped his head as he inhaled deeply. Drinking in *my* scent, I realized. Holy mother of pearl, he'd barely touched me and I was already soaking through my panties.

His hand drifted down to my neck, his fingers stroking across my collarbone. His lips pressed lightly against my cheek, charting a path across it to the crook of my jaw. At every point of contact, my body lit up with quivers of bliss. A shaky breath spilled out of me.

Snap paused. "Is this all right?"

"Oh, yes," I said. "That was a good sigh. You know, there is one thing most people find they like a lot…"

I'd meant to let him lead this exploration, but I couldn't help myself—so shoot me. I tipped the angle of his jaw and guided his mouth to mine.

His breath caught as our lips met, and then he was kissing me as if the understanding of how to perform that act were written into his soul. My fingers twined in the silky curls at the back of his head. The heat of his mouth was so hungry yet tender it drew a whimper from my throat.

With the parting of my lips, he deepened the kiss. His forked tongue teased over the seam of my mouth, sparking pleasure. Oh, yes, I'd like some more of that, please.

His hand had slipped farther down, following the curve of my breasts—and stopping with a flinch I could tell he'd tried to suppress, just shy of the protective badge I'd left pinned to my undershirt. Shit, I'd forgotten about that.

"Sorry," I mumbled against his mouth, and drew back just far enough to tug the undershirt off. I did trust him—enough to go without that small ward tonight.

Snap took in the sway of my breasts as I bared them, neon brilliance gleaming in his eyes. He cupped one, carefully but with more confidence than when he'd started, and seemed to study the shape of it, the point of my nipple, the way that nub pebbled with a tingle of pleasure at a swipe of his thumb over it.

His smile widened. He kept his hand there, caressing the curve of my breast and the peak at equal measures, and brought his mouth back to mine. I could have drowned in the sweetness of that kiss.

He lingered on my mouth before taking his kisses lower: past my jaw, down my neck, over my collarbone, setting me alight everywhere his lips touched. When he reached my chest, he raised my breast as if it were one of the mortal delicacies he so enjoyed savoring. As he sucked the peak into his mouth, I couldn't help gasping. The flick of his tongue over my nipple, the forked tips encircling it with a slight tug, brought an even headier rush of pleasure.

"I know what Ruse meant now," Snap murmured. "About how you'd taste. He was right. You're better than any peach."

"Considering how much you enjoyed the peach, that's a pretty high compliment."

He chuckled and pressed a peck to the curve of my breast. "He has tasted you—everywhere. Hasn't he?"

The heated flush that had taken me over deepened. "Why, has he been talking about it?"

"No. I only—" Snap pulled back so he could look me in the eyes, his expression turning slightly apologetic. "The first night, you told us to leave you alone, but Ruse didn't come away with us. After a little while, I went looking for him. I slipped into your bedroom in the shadows, and I saw— He was down here." His fingers glided down to my lap, and a flush colored his own cheeks. "I didn't mean to spy. I left right away."

At least he had some small sense of privacy. But the thought of him watching the incubus with me in the act, even for a moment, spurred on my desire.

"Ruse can be... very appealing," I said.

"It's in his nature to be." Snap eased down the sheet to uncover my thighs. "I saw how much you enjoyed what he was doing to you." He kissed my cheek and then my mouth again, long and harder than before. I'd almost lost the thread of our conversation, caught up in the press of his supple lips, when he slid them away to speak again.

"I want to make you feel as good as he did. I want to bring you that kind of pleasure. And even more."

Well, I certainly wouldn't complain about that. But I did feel the need to say— "You know, Ruse has centuries of experience perfecting his technique, plus powers and a form specifically designed for seduction. I'm not saying you shouldn't be ambitious, but maybe we should focus on one step at a—*oh.*"

His hand had skimmed over my panties, grazing my clit at the perfect angle to provoke another gasp. Snap gave me a grin that might have had a hint of the incubus's smirk to it and repeated the motion.

Then his long, lithe fingers dipped lower, and curiosity came back into his expression. "You're wet."

"Yeah," I said. "That means you're already doing an excellent job of making good on your ambitions."

He pressed between my legs more firmly, setting off a pulse of pleasure, and I bit my lip. I ran my hand down his chest to make my own exploration of his lean frame. This shirt definitely needed to go. As I pulled at it, he released me just long enough to help remove it.

With all that divinely toned muscle bared, Snap leaned toward me. He hummed happily at the sweep of my fingers over that terrain and returned his attention to my sex.

The unmistakable evidence of his own arousal showed in the bulge below the waist of his pants. There was the involuntary response that had started us down this unexpected path. It shouldn't go untended to.

I teased my fingers over the bulge, and this time it was Snap who sighed. His hips shifted nearer to me, seeking out that contact. I stroked him again, harder, and he burrowed his face into the crook of my neck. His teeth nicked the sensitive skin there with a shudder of breath.

"That sensation… makes it very hard to think," he said.

I laughed lightly. "The point of doing this isn't to think. It's to feel. And you can feel a hell of a lot more than this, if you'll let me show you."

He nodded into my hair and then raised his head to claim my mouth. The roughness of his kiss and the friction of his hand still fondling me through my panties left my head spinning. I managed to focus enough to curl my fingers around his erection through the fabric for a better grip.

He swayed into my hand with each pump up and down, chasing the pleasure I was paying him back with. At my nudge, he tipped with me so we lay on the bed next to each other. I squirmed even closer into his kiss and his touch.

Maybe it was best if we stuck to hands for this first spin around the block. Much simpler than navigating the mechanics of full-on sex, especially when Snap could hardly be prepared for the intensity of *those* sensations. I could already tell he'd get me off just fine like this. Hell, I wasn't sure how much longer I'd last as it was.

I found the wherewithal to jerk the zipper of his pants down and discovered Thorn wasn't the only one for whom dressing didn't come automatically. Snap hadn't bothered with any kind of underwear. He probably hadn't realized they were a standard part of a mortal outfit. How would a shadowkind know, after all, if no one had happened to mention it? It wasn't as if he'd had to consider clothes at all where he'd come from.

For now, it only made my intentions easier to carry out. I closed my fingers around his naked cock, reveling in the smoothness of the skin over his rigid member, and Snap let out a guttural sound. His tongue flicked right into my mouth to twine with mine, provoking a giddy shiver. I kissed him back just as enthusiastically as I swiped my thumb over the head of his erection and spread the precum forming there down its length.

Snap yanked at my panties and delved his hand beneath them. My chest hitched in delight at the stroke of his fingers right across my clit. The same instinct that must have guided his first kiss brought his touch down to my opening, testing the slickness there and then slipping inside me. He began a gentle pumping motion that became more blissfully forceful with each repetition.

I moaned, bucking toward him in pursuit of release. "That's good. So good."

He brought his other hand to the side of my face, watching me as the motions of his fingers built me up to that ecstatic shattering apart. Pleasure had flushed his face a deeper shade than before, and his breath came raggedly, but his attention never left me.

The swivel of his thumb over my clit and one final thrust inside me sent me reeling with the burst of my orgasm. My eyes rolled up, stars sparkling behind them while my body clenched around his fingers.

Snap caressed my cheek even as he rocked inside me through the aftershock. His voice came out soft and fierce at the same time. "My peach. My Sorsha. *Mine.*"

I wasn't in any state to argue that sentiment, if I'd even wanted to. It was all I could do to keep my hold on his cock and stroke him faster to bring him with me.

As the rest of my body sagged with satisfaction, he let his eyes haze, giving himself over to the pleasure now that he'd fulfilled my end. A groan reverberated from his chest. His hips jerked.

He tugged me to him suddenly, his mouth crashing into mine. A tremor raced through his body as the hot gush of his release spurted across my hand.

"Oh," he mumbled. "That—"

He cut himself off with a breathless laugh and kissed me once more. This one lit me up from head to toes even in my sated state. I nestled closer to him instinctively, resting my hands against the warmth of his chest.

When the kiss ended, I glanced at him coyly through my eyelashes. "So, was 'more' the right choice?"

"Yes. Yes. And for you too."

Apparently my enjoyment had been so clearly on display that he didn't feel the need to ask. I was okay with that.

As I tipped my head to rest it on the pillow, Snap gazed down at me. A hint of uncertainty crossed his face. "What usually happens now?"

Ah. Yeah, I guessed in some ways that was a trickier subject than the sex act itself.

I skimmed my fingers up and down the taut planes of his stomach. "Sometimes people like to consider it done and leave. Sometimes they'd rather be close for a while longer, so they stay together while they sleep."

"Then I will stay," Snap said decidedly. He wrapped one arm around my shoulders and lay his cheek down by me on the pillow, tucking my head under his chin. His mix of bright and dark scents enveloped me. I relaxed into his embrace with only a small pang of regret that for all I knew, this might be the only interlude we'd get before our lives went even more to hell.

TWENTY-SEVEN

Sorsha

THE COMPUTERIZED INTERFACE IN RUSE'S SNAZZY CAR WAS SO complicated I couldn't figure out how to connect my phone, so I settled for making my own soundtrack. "Don't stop deceivin'," I sang as the four of us cruised into the docklands, hidden behind our tinted windows. "Hold on, send 'em reeling."

Ruse shot me an amused smile as he took a turn. "You're lucky you don't get arrested, messing with the words that badly."

I stuck my tongue out at him, because I was just that mature, and leaned my arm against the window ledge. The faded factories along the river looked even drearier today with a haze of clouds graying the sky. There was no rush hour out in this part of town. The growl of our engine was the only sound on the street.

Of course, that'd be exactly how Meriden and his co-conspirators liked it.

We'd already decided that parking right by the drop-off spot was too risky. Ruse drove a few blocks farther and pulled up to the curb around a corner. The plan was that Thorn would lurk in the shadows where Meriden had gotten out yesterday, and Snap would linger close to our corner. When the minivan arrived, Snap would alert us and

Thorn would give chase on foot. We were hoping either he'd discover a building here where Meriden was conducting his current work, or we'd be able to close in on whatever other vehicle picked the guy up in the area, if one had.

At the very least, we'd figure out more about his route than we'd been able to last time.

Thorn swiveled in his seat to beckon to Snap. "It's an hour earlier than yesterday's drop-off. We've got time to patrol the wider area first. Come on."

Snap balked, his gaze sliding to me for a second before he met Thorn's eyes. "I'd rather stay close to the car. Isn't Sorsha's safety the most important thing?"

"We'll be ensuring her safety by confirming none of our enemies are staked out nearby," the warrior said. "You can test the surroundings for signs of where they might have been here before as well."

"And, y'know, *I'll* be right here in the car with her," Ruse said. "You're not leaving her unprotected. Not that she's defenseless on her own either."

"Of course she's not," Snap said insistently. "But we've seen how aggressive these people are. You're the only one who doesn't have any kind of power that's meant for combat." His hand crept across the seat to give mine a quick squeeze, his chin lifting. Apparently last night's interlude had stirred up a brand-new possessive instinct. I hadn't anticipated that.

Ruse rolled his eyes. "Are you referring to that dangerous skill of yours that gives you the shakes when you even think about using it? How many attackers could you take down at one time anyway—two? Three? I could charm them into not wanting to attack us at all."

"I don't remember that strategy getting us out of the last few attacks."

"All right, all right." I held up my hands in a time-out gesture. "I appreciate everyone's intense concern for my well-being, but for all we know, an entire militia is descending on us while you all argue about it. If anyone comes at Ruse and me, he can simply *drive away*, which so far has been the most useful power of all." I gave Snap's hand a reassuring pat in return. "I'll be fine. Go see what you can find out there. Without your other powers, we wouldn't have gotten even this far."

My touch and the reminder of his past contributions appeared to mollify my new lover. His posture loosened. He nodded in agreement and then, so suddenly I didn't see it coming, leaned in to give me a swift kiss.

His lips pressed warm against mine for all of a second. I barely had a chance to return the gesture before he'd slipped away into the shadows. Thorn let out a wordless mutter of what sounded like consternation and vanished too.

Ruse shifted in his seat to lounge sideways where he could look back at me. There was nothing surprising about his smirk or the raise of his eyebrows. "Well, *that* was certainly interesting."

"Shut up," I said, because that had worked so well before.

"I did notice that Snap wandered off for quite a while last night. Now I'm getting an inkling where he might have gone."

"Which part are you having trouble with: the shutting or the upping?"

"Who said I was criticizing?" A sly glint had lit in his eyes. "I'm impressed. I didn't know he had it in him, but you obviously woke up a sleeping dragon."

I folded my arms over my chest. "Is it going to be a problem? I *really* don't need you two arguing like that all day long."

The incubus laughed. "I'm hardly one to push for monogamy, Miss Blaze. As far as I'm concerned, you should take your pleasure wherever and from whoever suits your fancy. I'd just like to stay in the mix if that's an option." His gaze turned more heated.

I couldn't say that I wasn't imagining a repeat of our past encounter when he looked at me like that. "We'll see."

"Making me work for it. That just turns me on even more." He winked. "I could teach the newbie a few things, you know, if you ever wanted to invite me along for the ride. How to get you off, how to heighten that enjoyment…" He extended his arm to trail a finger down my leg from knee to shin. Sparks coursed from me from that line of heat.

Ruse and Snap attending to me in unison? What gods had I

sacrificed goats to in some past life to be worthy of that bliss? It'd depend on Snap being okay with the idea, though…

Ruse's smirk grew. "I can see you're thinking the possibilities through."

I huffed and nudged his hand away with a playful kick. The incubus just chuckled as he withdrew. "The offer will stay on the table as long as you'd like. Or if you'd really like, we could put *you* on a table. What a lovely platter to feast on."

If he kept going, I might melt into a hot, horny puddle right here on the seat. "Maybe we should be focusing on the whole saving your boss problem right now?"

"Spoilsport," he teased, and shifted to peer out the window. "No wave of soldiers crashing toward us so far. I wonder how long we'll be able to hole up in that motel before they—"

Snap cut him off, wisping out of the shadows into his seat with a quiver through the air. "Thorn's gone to the drop-off spot already," he said without preamble. "He thinks he saw the van heading this way."

I checked our car's clock and frowned. "It's way earlier than yesterday."

"Maybe they change up the times a little every morning to throw off anyone like us," Ruse suggested.

That was totally possible, but it didn't quash the prickling of my nerves. Sucking my lip under my teeth, I leaned toward my window, even though I couldn't see much of the street the van had taken from there. If Thorn was right, we'd find out what was up soon enough.

A rumble of an engine sounded, distant but getting louder by the second. Ruse rested his hand on the ignition. Snap hastily looped his seatbelt over his chest. We knew better than to count on a smooth drive.

As I waited for the pause in that rumble when the minivan would let Meriden out, my heart pounded as if it were chasing the passing seconds. The engine sound droned louder. Any moment now—

The gunmetal-gray minivan zoomed right by us, cruising on down the street without any sign of stopping. A startled noise hitched out of me just as a second car zipped after it—the baby blue compact we'd thought might be following us yesterday.

Fudge me sideways 'til Sunday. What the hell was going on?

"Ruse?" I said.

He was already starting the engine. "If we need to get going, we'll stage that getaway, but right now I think we'd better see where they're heading."

Thorn wouldn't be able to keep pace with the vehicles on foot, even through the shadows. As Ruse swerved into the road and around, I gripped the door handle, my pulse thudding faster. Snap grasped my hand again, this time holding on tight. Despite myself, I actually did find the gesture comforting.

We'd just pulled around the corner when the minivan jerked to a halt a few blocks ahead of us. A side door flew open; a slack figure tumbled out onto the sidewalk with a thump. Before the door had even slammed shut again, the minivan was tearing away.

They *had* made a drop-off—but I didn't like the look of that crumpled body. As we drove toward it, it didn't stir.

"Do we stop?" Ruse asked. The baby blue car had, just up the block from where the minivan had made its deposit. A slim figure in a white velour tracksuit hopped out, hood pulled up, but as the driver rounded the car, the wind tugged the fabric back just enough for a jolt of recognition to shoot through me.

"Stop. Stop!" I said.

The tires squealed as Ruse hit the brake. I scrambled out and found myself face to face with my best friend.

Vivi had wobbled to a halt on the other side of the fallen body, just ten feet away from me. Her gaze caught mine for a second, wide-eyed, and then dropped to the sprawled man. A tremor ran through her shoulders.

All I could see so far was the deathly stillness of the body and a reddish tinge along his hairline, but the sickly graying of her face told me to brace myself as I stepped closer.

I was pretty sure it was Meriden. The hair was the same color and cut as the guy I'd glimpsed exiting the minivan yesterday, his jeans and tweed suit jacket a similar style of clothing. Then his face came into view.

If you could even call it that. He barely had a face at all now. The front of his head—what I could see with it tipped toward the pavement—was a mash of splintered bone and bloody flesh. The only way you could tell it ever had been a face was its position relative to his hair and ears. His chin, nose, and forehead were caved in, his cheekbones crushed, all of it beaten in as if thwacked over and over by a baseball bat.

As my stomach lurched, a chilly realization crept through my nausea. His associates hadn't just smashed him up beyond visual recognition but shattered his jaw and teeth. Dental records wouldn't be any help. My gaze dropped to the hands that had twisted close to his skinny frame, and I flinched. Little red rivulets of blood streamed from his fingers where it looked as if they'd been shoved into a woodchipper all the way to the second knuckles. Forget fingerprinting too.

The people who'd dumped him here had ensured there'd be no definitive ID, not just for us but for any police force unless they happened to have the guy's DNA on file.

"Oh my God," Vivi was mumbling into the hand she'd clapped over her mouth. "Oh my God, oh my God, oh my God."

None of my shadowkind companions had joined us. Had they stuck to the shadows because of the additional witness? I wasn't sure whether to be grateful for that discretion or not. Their presence would raise more questions, but it wasn't as if there weren't a whole heap of those already. And I might have felt steadier with at least one of those powerful companions by my side.

I wrenched my gaze away from the mutilated man to focus on my best friend. "What are you *doing* here, Vivi? How did you— Whose car is that?" It didn't have rental plates, and she'd still been driving her long-time cherry-red Beamer when she'd picked me up for a trip out of town a couple months ago. Not that the car really mattered in the grand scheme of things, but it was the most concrete thing I had to latch onto in this crazy situation.

"My grandma's," Vivi said in a distant voice. "She let me borrow— I knew you'd recognize my regular one..." She yanked her eyes up to stare at me. "And you clearly didn't want me around. What the hell have you gotten yourself mixed up in, Sorsha? It's obviously incredibly fucking dangerous—why didn't you ask for help?"

I *had* help, but I wasn't going to mention that. "*Because* it's incredibly fucking dangerous. Obviously." I waved my hand at the body. "Do you think I want people who'd do that setting their sights on you?"

"But it's okay that they might come after *you*? You should have told me—told the Fund, if this is something to do with the shadowkind... Are these the hunters who came after Luna? Was this Meriden guy part of that somehow?"

Right, I'd told her I was looking into something to do with Luna when I was diverting her before. But— I knit my brow. "How do you know anything about Meriden?"

Her lips twisted. "I got it out of Jade after you talked to her—made it sound like we were looking into it together. Which, you know, even *she* thought had to be the case. Although I didn't realize it was *Meriden* like one word until I started asking around in his neighborhood—"

Her mouth snapped shut. She hugged herself, backing up a step from the body, but I was still staring at her. "His neighborhood?" She *had* been staked out there yesterday. "Just how much have you been spying on me, Vivi?"

"When I called you a couple days ago, I had one of the Fund's usual guys tracing it," she admitted. "And then I got him to poke around, and I did some asking—I went out there to scope it out and saw that car driving off to follow the van, and I figured it was you... Since you didn't show up today, I just followed the van."

"You realize how crazy that sounds, right? Like you're a psycho stalker."

"I just wanted to help you," she burst out. "You were shutting me out, and I could tell you were working on something big, something that made you nervous. I know you've got things you keep to yourself, and that's fine, but you don't usually lie to me, Sorsh. I was really freaking worried about you, okay?" A quaver crept into her voice. "And it looks like I was right to be. What's this all about? We'll figure it out together. You've got to tell me now."

"No, I don't." Another realization hit me, this one cold enough to freeze my gut. I'd never spoken Meriden's name to anyone outside my shadowkind trio except Jade, and then as "Merry Den" and a place. We'd kept a careful distance and a low profile when checking out his home. But Vivi— "How many people did you talk to about Meriden? Did you go right up to his house?"

Her expression twitched. "I called a few people in the Fund, and asked the guy who traced your call to look into it—he got me the address. After I lost you yesterday, I went back and talked to a few of the neighbors about him. Nothing too obvious, of course."

It didn't have to be obvious to tip off the people he worked for. My jaw clenched. "It's because of you poking around that they realized someone was onto him. That's why they killed him. That's the kind of people we're dealing with here, Vivi, and you crashed right in with this ridiculously obvious car and the questions and the following so close…"

"I didn't know—" she started to protest, but I didn't let her keep going.

"It doesn't matter. We're not working on this together. You've got to get out of town—maybe your grandma too, since they've probably looked up the car by now—lay low and hope I end up distracting them enough that they forget about you."

"No way. I'm not letting you go up against psychopaths like this on your own—"

"You're more likely to get yourself or both of us killed than to make things easier," I snapped.

Her hands balled at her sides. "I wouldn't have had to nose around if you'd just told me what you were doing in the first place!"

"I was trying to stop something like this from happening to you. For good reason, it looks like."

"Sorsha, whatever's going on, you can't handle it by yourself."

"Yes, I can." My voice came out taut. "And it'll be a hell of a lot easier if I'm not worried about what's going to happen to you while you're tagging along. Please, just leave, go somewhere no one will think to look for you. When this is over, I promise I'll tell you everything—but not until then."

Vivi wavered on her feet. Her expression tightened. But before she could keep arguing, a looming presence solidified in the air next to me.

Thorn placed a heavy hand on my shoulder. "Sorsha *isn't* alone," he said, his gravelly voice so low it was a threat in itself. "I, for one, would also prefer if you didn't make the job of ensuring she stays safe even more difficult than it already is. She told you to go. *Go.*"

My best friend gaped at the shadowkind and then at me. "You—He— You've got one of *them* working with you?"

I bristled at the way she said "them," as if all shadowkind really were the monsters that fables made them out to be, and felt Thorn's hand tense against me. "He knows what he's doing," I said. "Like you *don't*. So please, get out of here and find someplace safe to hole up until I get in touch."

"Or I can make sure that you do," Thorn added, glowering at her.

Vivi's mouth opened and then closed again. She swallowed audibly. Her gaze dropped to Meriden and his pulverized face, and she looked as if she barely held herself back from vomiting. She shot one last, desperate glance at me, and when I didn't soften my expression, she darted for her car.

The baby blue compact puttered away, leaving us in the docklands' eerie hush to contemplate the man who could no longer lead us to our goal and the savageness with which our foes had ensured that.

Snap and Ruse emerged from the shadows beside us. Ruse clucked his tongue at the body disapprovingly, but even he appeared to be momentarily lost for words.

"Now what?" Snap said quietly.

A huge lump had formed within the queasiness in my stomach. I swallowed thickly. "I don't know." All our work, all the clues we'd uncovered and the trail we'd followed—it ended here. Everything we'd done had gotten us nothing but a ruined corpse in a stretch of hollowed-out factories.

TWENTY-EIGHT

Thorn

Even without leaning nearer, I could tell there was a certain expertise to the savaging of this mortal's body. Blows chosen with care for maximum impact and to destroy specific zones. The zones they'd chosen, I couldn't account for. Mortals had strange inclinations.

None of the battering had ended this one's life. When I bent down by the body, my nose caught a faint but distinctive chemical tang that no human's senses would have discerned. He'd been poisoned in some way before the savaging.

Sorsha stood beside me, motionless other than a brief shiver that passed through her stance. Her jaw was tight.

"He's dead because of us," she said with an unexpected strain in her voice.

Ruse shook his head. "We took every possible precaution. From what your friend admitted to, you were right—her clumsiness must have tipped the sword-star folks off that someone was overly interested in Meriden."

"But Vivi wouldn't have been interested in him if she hadn't noticed that I was hiding something. If I'd faked it better—or maybe if

I'd told her the truth and managed to convince her to stay out of it—if that even would have worked..." She bit her lip.

I frowned at her as I straightened up. Why should this man be anything to her other than a fallen enemy? She appeared distraught by his death not just for the practical implications but for his own sake as well.

Mortals and their fickle emotions.

"What of it if *he's* dead?" I said. "The trail we were following is dead. All the answers we found centered around this man. Without him, we have no more than when we started at the bridge."

Snap stirred as if he might have argued that point, but then he grimaced. There *was* no arguing it. We'd been focused on his Merry Den from the start, narrowing in closer and closer on that target—and here we were. He'd already checked all over the bridge; that was the only distinctive detail we'd found to follow up on. We'd lost all direction.

It wouldn't have mattered if I'd been faster yesterday, if I'd managed to track Meriden's path from here to begin with. I'd lost *him* when it'd been our last chance to use him. Just as I'd lost Omen to begin with, lost our freedom when those hunters had descended on us afterward...

I had no justification for it. I'd failed again, pure and simple. While these ruthless mortals did darkness only knew what to Omen—while he might be barely clinging to life—if *he* wasn't already dead, that was. Every one of us standing around Meriden, even the lady, knew that the one we'd set out to save might have been dead before Sorsha had ever freed us from our cages.

He'd almost certainly end up dead regardless when I couldn't serve him better than this. I'd meant for this time to be different. I'd had a mere three colleagues to defend. It should have been the easiest task.

Sorsha's lips pursed, but the motion didn't change the hopelessness etched on her face. The incubus sucked in a breath and glanced down the street. He attempted to conjure a little optimism with his tone. "There is the minivan to consider."

"Do you really think they'll keep using the same vehicle after this?" Sorsha said. "Or that they'll have registered the plates in any way that would let us hunt them down? These are people who'll do this to a guy just to make sure their tracks are covered." She swept her arm toward the marred corpse.

The devourer shifted closer to her. "At least it wasn't you." His sharpened devotion showed in every inch of his posture, however that had developed.

He was right, though. I had achieved that one small victory: the mortal who'd rescued us from shameful captivity was still alive and reasonably well. For however much longer I could maintain that state of events.

"It's a long shot, but—" Ruse crouched down and checked the man's pockets, avoiding the bloody parts of the body as well as he could. Coming up empty, he sighed and straightened back up. "They thought of just about everything, like always."

As I was about to suggest we leave before our enemies also thought of sending a new pack of soldiers after us, Sorsha's chin came up. Her eyes gleamed with a ferocity that burned most of her despondency away.

"Just about, but not everything. They've never been able to predict *everything* we'd be able to do—the connections we've made, the skills we have."

She turned to Snap. "You can taste impressions off inanimate objects. I know there's something different about it with living beings, something you want to avoid—but he's not alive anymore. Can you test him and see what comes up, just like Thorn could take the drunk guy who attacked me into the shadows after he was dead?"

The devourer's eyes widened. He stared down at the corpse with a nervous flick of his tongue between his lips. "I don't know. I've never tried that before."

Ruse had brightened at the suggestion. "It certainly can't hurt to give it a shot, can it? It's not as if you could hurt him now. You certainly can't kill him any more than he's already been murdered."

I didn't know exactly what had soured Snap so thoroughly against his own greatest power, but his whole body had tensed despite the incubus's words. I squared my shoulders, preparing to order him to make the attempt with the full impact of my presence, but Sorsha spoke up first.

She touched his arm, her expression softening in a way that sent a twinge I couldn't explain through my chest. "The thought of doing it reminds you of whatever happened before, doesn't it?"

He nodded with a jerk, his gaze still fixed on the body. "I know it isn't the same. Ruse is right about everything he said. I should just—" And yet he couldn't seem to move.

"Don't think about that other time," Sorsha suggested. "Think about how it felt when you found Meriden's name or his house. Imagine how many useful impressions must be attached to him. You could get us so much closer to Omen, to stopping the people who worked in that lab."

"Yes. Yes." The devourer gathered himself, determination hardening the graceful lines of his face. He knelt by Meriden's back and leaned in.

Sorsha hovered over him, poised as if she thought she might need to leap in and steady him again, her lips curved in a gentle but elated smile. The fierceness I'd seen still shone in her eyes. Ruse watched the proceedings with eager anticipation.

The desolation that had come over our group had fallen away, just like that. *She* had defeated it, even though she'd been more affected by the death than the rest of us.

In that moment, while they all studied the body, I couldn't tear my gaze away from her—from the magnificent strength I hadn't completely perceived until just now. And not just strength. Snap might have gone through with this act under my orders out of fear, but she'd seen what he needed well enough to not just convince him but inspire him.

It shouldn't have been surprising. Our lady might be mortal, true, but she was the sort of mortal who broke into prisons and freed shadowkind from their jailors at risk of her own life and liberty. How could she be anything other than extraordinary? She'd managed to fill the gap left by our loss of Omen so surely and yet subtly it'd nearly escaped my notice.

Silly songs and flashy clothes and all, she brought something essential to our group. Something I suddenly had trouble imagining doing without, even after we had Omen leading the charge again.

But why would she want anything to do with us and the danger we'd thrust into her life once this quest was over?

The earlier twinge turned into a pang. Before I could examine it, determine just what it meant, Snap rocked back on his heels with a shaky gasp. His pupils had dilated, the brilliant green of his eyes in his true physical form glittering around them.

"I saw so much," he said breathlessly. "So many places. The house and the streets and halls that are bright but cold. Shadowkind in little rooms with locked doors. Shiny tables like in the office we searched, computers with streams of words and numbers and wriggling lines…"

"Where?" Ruse asked. "That's got to be the place they took Omen to."

"I don't… I don't know. It all came in fragments. It's hard to piece together." Snap went still, his forehead furrowing as he must have sorted through the barrage of impressions I had to assume an entire human body would have collected. "There was a place not yet built, all steel beams and walls half attached—maybe that was from farther back. There was another house like his but with a blue door. There was a grocery store, fruit with smooth skin in his hands. A book. A building coming up out of dirt ground, with concrete walls and doors shiny like those lab tables. Music rising from a wooden platform down below where people were sitting in rows with their instruments. And another building—I think it was important—he was nervous when he walked inside."

Sorsha latched on to that comment, sinking next to him. "When he walked inside where, Snap?"

His tongue flicked again, as if he could draw more certainty out of the air. "Big glass windows. Sale. Bright boxes in the windows with little figures like people and animals and cars. I think I can see the sign." He squeezed his eyes shut. "Fun Station Depot. He went there more than one time—I see it when it's light and dark and in-between. Worried. He had to tell them something, something about his work, he wasn't sure they'd be happy enough with it."

"Did you get much sense of what that work was?" Ruse asked.

"No. Only—shadowkind. Fear and awe of them. Needing to keep them contained." Another flick. "Walking into that building, the one that made him nervous, he'd be thinking about how the way to get in was iron. I don't know what that means."

The devourer's shoulders sagged with those last words, as if drawing out so many impressions had drawn most of the energy out of his body as well.

Sorsha tapped her lips. "Iron. A key, maybe, to wherever they do their illicit dealings."

"At this Fun Station Depot?" I said. "What is *that*?" It didn't sound like a military base or hunter's den.

Our mortal had already whipped out her phone. A laugh spilled out of her. "It's a toy store," she said. "A big outlet place—not too far from where I've gone bargain hunting for clothes with Vivi." She peered at Snap. "You think he went in there a lot for something to do with his work."

"Yes. It felt that way. I don't think the shadowkind were there… but wherever *they* were, he was less nervous about that."

"And at least for this spot we have a definite location. It must be a front for some part of the sword-star bunch's operations. They'd need money for all that equipment and the people they're hiring; they'd have to set up a legitimate business to launder it through, I guess."

She nibbled at her lip in thought and then glanced up at me with a twinkle in her eyes I wished I could capture. "What do you say we go toy shopping?"

TWENTY-NINE

Sorsha

"I don't like this," Thorn said for what was approximately the one millionth time.

I restrained myself from pointing out that he appeared to dislike pretty much everything as a general rule. "It doesn't matter whether you like it or not. From what you said, you *can't* get into the room that's got to hold the important stuff. So it's up to me. No need to worry. I've been training for this moment my entire life."

That was only a slight exaggeration. I tucked my ponytail under the knit cap that now hid all of my hair. Then I stretched my arms in the thin black top that was the centerpiece of my cat burglar attire, careful not to bonk my elbows in the relatively tight space of the car's back seat. I had my pouches with all my standard equipment—sans grappling hook and rope, since the place was only one story—attached to the thin belt around my waist. Piece of cake.

I'd just keep telling myself that until I was back here with the goods.

The warrior shifted restlessly in his seat. "I could dispatch the guards."

By "dispatch," I assumed he meant "punch their throats in" as per his usual M.O. But even if he didn't—" "No. Ideally, we don't want the sword-star bunch to know we ever found out about the store. If they realize we've gotten that far, they'll probably scrub every trail it could lead to before we have half a chance to follow them."

"There's got to be something major in there," Ruse said. "No business fills a few walls with silver and iron just for kicks."

"I still say I should at least go into the main building with you," Thorn grumbled. "Only the office was protected in a way I couldn't penetrate."

I leaned forward to poke his broad shoulder. "I need *you* patrolling outside the store in case reinforcements show up. It's a huge building —I can manage to avoid two security guards." The depot took up an entire block, the building sprawling across half and the rest a massive parking lot. From what Thorn had described, I'd have plenty of shelves and other displays to take shelter behind.

And I also needed to make sure he didn't get trigger-happy— knuckle-happy?—and bash up the guards even if I wasn't in serious danger.

Ruse patted the steering wheel. "I'll be ready to jet the second you get back, Miss Blaze." He gave Thorn a sly glance. "You, I'll leave behind if you're not back at the same time she is."

Thorn didn't look offended. "As you should. I can find my way to the motel through the shadows if need be."

"I can too," Snap said. "Isn't there anything I could do that would help you, Sorsha?" He gazed at me so beseechingly with those gorgeous green eyes that I wavered, though just a little and only for an instant.

I wanted my shadowkind trio out of my way so that they didn't cause unexpected problems during this heist, yeah, but that wasn't the only reason I intended on going in alone. The fact that the place even had a room protected against shadowkind showed they knew they might be dealing with beings of a monstrous sort. Who knew what kind of bullets the guards were packing in their guns—or what other weapons they might have on them? The building itself could contain other defenses that would weaken these guys.

I wasn't going to take that chance. I'd broken into plenty of buildings without getting caught. It was my specialty, really. If I went in there alone, it was only my hide on the line. If I screwed up, no one paid for it except me. I'd have been twice as nervous otherwise.

I squeezed Snap's hand. "You already found this place for us—and I know that took a lot out of you." It'd pained me, encouraging him to go against his fears, as necessary as it'd seemed. "I'm sure you'll be able to help with whatever I bring back."

Thorn was scowling, but apparently he was done arguing. "I'll go ahead and scout out the area one last time before you head in. Wait for my signal."

"Got it." I poked him again. "And don't you *dare* follow me in. If more guards come calling, do you really want to leave me unprepared until they're already in the building? If you see anyone coming after me out there, feel free to dispatch them however you'd like." If the alarm had already been sounded, leaving bodies behind wouldn't matter, only getting out alive.

His mouth tightened, but he nodded. I thought the reminder of his responsibilities would be enough to keep him patrolling where he shouldn't be in the line of fire. If I did my job right, there'd be no alarm and no reinforcements for him to do battle with.

He vanished, and I eased out of the car, shutting the door as softly as I could. We'd parked in a lot outside a kitchen supply outlet store where the nearest security lamp was burnt out. In the thickening dusk, I'd barely be visible in my black clothes against the black car.

I stared toward Fun Station Depot, watching for Thorn's go-ahead. The cooling breeze tickled across my cheeks. Just to pass the time, I touched each piece of my gear in turn to confirm I had it where I expected it to be.

A light flashed in the distance, there and gone. Thorn and the mini flashlight he'd helped himself to inside the store. All clear.

I gave the guys in the car a wave good-bye, unable to see through the tint if they returned it, and loped off. The soles of my sneakers made only the faintest rasp against the pavement. I veered around to the back of the kitchen supply building and crossed the street there, dashing through the lamplight.

My pulse thumped brisk but steady. I indulged in a brief spurt of song under my breath. "I can steal it, coming to your lair tonight, oh horde." The smile that came with the mangled lyric spurred me on.

As I reached the parking lot behind the toy store, I slowed. Thorn had given me a hand in one other way: he'd surreptitiously unlocked a door at the back of the store. I still had to make it through the stockroom, across the main retail floor, and into the office at the east end, but then I'd only have one lock to disable. *The way in is iron.* It didn't matter what kind of key that special room normally took—my picks would do the trick.

The parking lot was empty other than a charity donations bin the size of a small trailer in one corner. *Clothes for the Recently Deceased.* Now there was a cause if I'd ever heard one. Wouldn't want any corpses to have to wander around naked.

I slunk around the pools of security light, eased open the back door, and peeked into the dark stockroom with ears pricked. No sound reached my ears except the distant whir of traffic from somewhere behind me. Even two guards were overkill for nighttime security in a discount toy shop—reflecting the fact that the management had more they wanted to protect than just the merchandise—but neither of them hung out back here. That worked for me.

I crept between the high shelving units stacked with boxes of plushies, action figures, and Lego. Only the faintest streak of light showed beneath the door at the other end that led to the main retail area. I stopped by it, holding myself still and silent.

After a few minutes, footsteps tapped by. The guards weren't making any effort to conceal *their* movements—very helpful of them. How many months, even years, had they been on the job without ever actually needing to guard anything in here?

I smiled. Complacency was a thief's best friend.

When the footsteps had tapped away, I nudged the door open an inch to take a lay of the land. Packed shelves of playthings loomed on either side of an aisle right across from me. More stood at regular intervals to my left, but to my right, when I dared to fully emerge, I saw a cluster blocking my straight path to the spot where Thorn had said the office was.

I kept close to the end displays, peering down each aisle and then darting across the open space to make my way across the store. When footsteps tapped my way again, I ducked behind a cardboard stand of foil trading card packages. Catch 'em all—but no one would be catching me.

Slinking onward, I was feeling particularly confident for about five seconds. I slipped past the next display—and with a whir of mechanized parts, an electronic barking sound spewed out from the nearest shelf.

I flinched and barely restrained myself from smacking the thing. A little robotic puppy was stomping its feet and emitting that awful sound right by my shoulder. Because what could anyone want more than a yappy dog that couldn't even cuddle with you? Brilliant design.

Two sets of footsteps headed toward me, thudding rather than tapping now. I dashed for the nearest shelter: a life-size statue of a fashion doll poised next to rows of pink boxes containing her smaller counterpart. Thankfully, her ample chest and hips were more than wide enough to disguise my dark form behind them.

I held myself rigidly still, eyeing those curves. It'd better be true that these dolls were made in impossible proportions, because otherwise I definitely fell short.

The guards came to a stop by the yappy toy, which finally shut up. One of the men sighed. "Stupid dog. I swear all it takes is a tiny draft to set it off. I hope one of them haunts the asshole who designed those things."

"No kidding," the other said with a weary chuckle.

They poked around a bit, one ambling down my aisle, but Miss Giant Bosoms remained my savior. As I groped her butt while squashing myself farther out of view, I thought a silent *Sorry!* at her.

When the coast was clear, I edged out from behind her and headed for the cluster of shelves between me and my goal. They turned out to circle a play area with a ball pit, train table, and a few kiddie ride-on cars. Just beyond that spot, I caught sight of the door that must lead to the office. Bingo!

Approaching it, my heart sank. Snap had said Meriden had left a strong impression that the way into this place was iron. How could that be anything other than a key—one many shadowkind couldn't even touch, so very convenient? But maybe that had been for the outer door? The one in front of me had no keyhole at all, nothing for me to pick or even pop an explosive into, just a flat unbroken panel next to a keypad to enter a code.

Shit. I had a code breaker device that might have gotten me in if I'd had the time, but it could take hours depending on the model—if it would even connect with this one. I couldn't hang around with the not-so-deadly duo that long. Even if the guards didn't pose any more of a threat than they'd presented so far, they had plenty of friends who could pick up that slack.

Standing tensed, I glared at the door. Why the hell had Meriden been obsessing about iron coming in here? It being in the walls was a way to keep shadowkind *out*, not let anyone in. It was too late to go back and ask Snap if he'd happened to also pick up on a sequence of four numbers or—

Wait a second.

My pulse kicked up a notch as I bent over the lock. Sweet kit and caboodle, let this work. I-R-O-N: 4766.

The lock beeped faintly, making my pulse hiccup, and the deadbolt slid over. Yes!

I held back a fist pump of victory and pushed the door. It swung open to admit me without a squeak. Just like that, I walked inside, met with stillness crisp with an air conditioner's artificial chill.

Not knowing whether the overhead lights would show under the door, I opted for the smaller glow of my flashlight. It caught on a steel desk mounted with a computer and monitor, a leather office chair, a couple of filing cabinets, and a bulletin board pinned with a calendar and various sales announcements.

The computer would probably contain the motherlode. I took a quick skim through the filing cabinets just in case, but they were all filled with order forms and sales reports. Sinking into the leather chair, I tapped the mouse.

The monitor blinked on—to a password request screen.

Son of a basket weaver. Of course it'd be protected, and I wasn't any hacker. I'd never had to steal data during any burglar-ing mission before.

I typed in IRON, but that luck was only good for one point of access. The password window shuddered and informed me I needed to try again. I grimaced at it. How many tries would I get before it set off some kind of alarm or locked me out completely?

The odds of me guessing the password belonging to some people I knew zilch about was about five million to one. I could gamble with the best of them, but I knew when a bet wasn't worth taking.

So... I guessed I'd better take the whole damn computer until I could find someone better at this part than I was.

There was only so much I could carry. I could find another monitor someplace else. I unhooked the computer unit from the screen and heaved it up under my arm.

Ooof, yeah, time to start doing more push-ups. My bicep was aching before I'd even taken two steps. The corner of the heavy metal block dug into my hip.

As I moved around the desk, I spotted a clear plastic box with a stack of CDs labeled in sharpie. What if some of the necessary data was on those? I shoved the box under my arm on top of the computer. Now I had sharp corners digging into my armpit too—wonderful.

I snuck out the door again and closed it with the softest of clicks. All I had to do was schlep this haul outside, and I was home free. Still a piece of cake.

I'd only crossed a few feet of floor when the damned dog burst out yapping again.

That wasn't enough to throw me off. No, I had better nerves than that. But as I dashed for cover at the sound of approaching feet, the disc case that had already been wedged precariously against my side jostled out. It hit the floor with a clatter no one could possibly mistake for a tiny draft. As I swore to myself, one of the guards yelled.

Forget cake; forget stealth. It was time to run.

THIRTY

Sorsha

I SNATCHED UP THE BOX OF CDs, JAMMED IT BACK INTO MY ARMPIT, AND bolted for the back door. Unfortunately, one of the guards came charging around the play area's shelves at the same moment, blocking my way.

What could I do but make use of what was in front of me? Clutching my loot against my body, I dove for the ball pit.

As I shoved my free arm in, the plastic spheres rattled against each other and bounced over the walls. I snatched up one and then another to pelt the guard in the face as hard as I could. He stumbled backward in a mix of pain and—probably mostly, since they were kiddie balls—shock.

The other guard was pounding toward me from somewhere behind. In a matter of seconds, they'd have me cornered. I hurled one more ball, crashed straight through the pit, and braced a foot inside one of the ride-on cars: a rather stylish red convertible.

Pushing off with my other foot as if it were a scooter, I careened past the guard down the nearest aisle, smacking him aside with my elbow for good measure. He let out an *oof* and then hurtled after me.

The hiss of the car's wheels against the tiled floor must have tipped off the other guard, because those footsteps skidded and spun to follow in the neighboring aisle. I rammed my sneaker against the floor harder, pushing the toy car as fast as its wheels would go.

"Is it one of *them*?" the second guard hollered to his colleague, in a horrified tone that told me they knew what business their employers were really in—and they weren't any more fond of the shadowkind than the rest of the sword-star bunch.

"I don't know—doesn't matter. Just stop her!" the other shouted back.

Forget that. I whipped out into the wider space between the shelves and the checkout counters. The plastic wheels made an ear-splitting squeal as I swerved sharply with a jerk of my foot. I raced the car three aisles over, wrenched it around again to zoom down the one that would lead to the store-room door—and two of the wheels popped right off.

Clearly that ride wasn't built to stand up to a proper car chase. I flung myself off it, wobbling as I caught my balance with the weight of my cargo and wincing when the edge of the computer jabbed me harder. This machine had better contain what we needed, or I was going to shove it up its owner's ass. Assuming I got the chance to find out what it contained in the first place.

As I righted myself, my own ass bumped into a display of dark-cloaked action figures at the head of the aisle. "Intruder detected!" a host of them cried out in their tinny digital voices. "Fire when ready!"

For the love of gravy, the whole store was out to get me. But as I sprinted down the aisle, it occurred to me that their suggestion wasn't such a bad one. With my free hand, I snatched a dart blaster toy off the shelves. Already loaded with five foam darts—my lucky day.

A guard had reached the end of the aisle. I glanced back just long enough to take a couple of shots behind me. One of the foam bolts bounced off his shoulder, but the other hit the edge of his glasses, knocking them askew. Score!

I was almost in good spirits again when a second set of footsteps rounded the corner. I didn't look back, firing blind as I ran on, but the click of a safety releasing reached my ears clear as anything.

These guys were taking the whole "fire when ready" idea to a much more serious level.

With a lurch of my gut, I threw myself forward even faster. My feet slammed against the tiles, the impact radiating through the soles with an expanding ache. My arm holding the computer was outright throbbing now.

"Stop right there!" one of the guards yelled as they pelted after me—as if I were going to play nice now. I veered back and forth in an attempt to make myself a more difficult target, and I'd like to think that inspired maneuver was what saved me.

A *bang* split the air, and an instant later, a deeper agony than anything I'd experienced so far seared through my shoulder. On my right side, thank fluffy puppies, because if it'd been the left, I'd have dropped my sole reason for being here. As it was, my arm jerked with the impact, my fingers spasming with the rush of pain, and the toy gun tumbled to the floor.

Gritting my teeth, I tore onward. The door was in sight. I could make it—but I wasn't sure any more that simply leaving the building was going to guarantee my freedom.

I forced my fingers around the knob and yanked, a cry I couldn't contain breaking from my throat at the fiery sensation that stabbed through my shoulder at the effort. My head reeled, but I managed to stumble into the stockroom just as another shot rang out. The door vibrated with it.

Shit, shit, shit. My shoulder was on fire, tears prickling at my eyes. I dashed across the room for the outer door. The guards barged after me with a volley of shouts.

As I heaved the outer door open with a smack of my good shoulder that echoed into the wounded one with another flare of pain, a sharp little impulse shot up inside me.

Burn them. Burn the two of them down, right to the fucking ground. I didn't have my lighter in my hand, but the heat that pulsed through me with the frantic thrum of my heartbeat felt potent enough to leap straight from my fingers in a burst of flame.

The thought gripped me for a moment, and then I recoiled from it with a jolt of horror and the wash of the outside air over my face. Even if I *could* have done it—which obviously I couldn't have; how crazy would that have been?—burning people alive was a little beyond what I could stomach, even if they seemed intent on murdering me.

I choked down a sob at the pain now splintering right through my chest and raced into the parking lot with all the speed my legs could produce.

I could run pretty fast, even lugging heavy computer equipment under one arm, even in a haze of agony. But it was a big parking lot with no cover at all except for the *Clothes for the Recently Deceased* donation box way too far across that open stretch of asphalt. As the guards barreled out after me, it was only a matter of seconds before I became one of the intended recipients of the charity.

Pumping my legs even faster, I made for that one bit of shelter. Another gunshot crackled behind me, missing me but close enough that the tremble in the air crossed my cheek. Twenty feet left to go, my breath rasping in my throat... Fifteen... Ten...

Bang. A bullet I was instantly certain would mean my doom exploded from the gun—and a huge, speeding body crashed into me out of nowhere, slamming me off my feet and hurling us both the last short distance to the donations box.

The burly arms that had caught me managed to turn me as we whipped through the air and around the bin. I hit the ground on my back rather than face first, although the pain that lanced through my shoulder at the impact wasn't anything to celebrate. I choked on a groan and found myself staring up into Thorn's face.

I knew it was his face because of the scars that decorated it and the white-blond hair falling in disarray on either side, not to mention the hulking body looming over me. But the planes of his features had turned even harder than before, and amid them, the eyes that stared back at me smoldered as if they were made of dying embers—no pupils, no whites, just pure, dark red.

And then there was the fact that two immense, black-feathered wings had sprouted from his brawny back, arcing over us like a shield. Holy mother of mothballs. Of all the forms he could have revealed, I'd never have expected that.

The first inane words that fell out of my mouth were, "They could have shot you."

"They *were* going to shoot you," Thorn said. His voice had the same low gravelly rumble, but with a sort of reverb to it as if it were resonating through a majestic cavern. His eyes flashed an even starker red, and his lips curled back to bare his teeth. "They already did. They would have killed you."

Was there something wrong with me that I was abruptly all kinds of heated up myself with those bulging muscles just inches from my prone body and that kind of vehemence lighting his gaze? Maybe it was just the adrenaline messing with my head.

My next words weren't all that much more sensible than the first. "And here I thought you saw me as just a nuisance."

I felt the warrior's glower as much as saw it, washing over me in another hot wave, but a touch of gentleness came through the defiance in his tone. "You are irritatingly irreverent and infuriatingly obstinate, m'lady, but I'm finding that the thought of someone hurting you makes me want to rip out their entrails and choke them with their own intestines."

It wasn't heat but warmth that fluttered inside me then. He'd practically composed a poem for me. I beamed up at him, slightly delirious from the pain, and said, "Right back at you."

Something flickered in his expression, and I half expected him to lean in and kiss me. Then thudding footsteps reached my ears over the roar of blood rushing through my head. The guards hadn't given up the chase. Had they even seen what had dragged me to safety?

Somehow Thorn's hard features managed to stiffen even more. He sprang off me and charged to meet them with a bellowed battle cry that rattled my eardrums.

One of the men let out a yelp. They'd seen now. Then all I heard was the sickening squelch of smashed flesh and the crunch of shattering bone, followed by skin and muscle rending with a meaty tearing noise. Neither they nor Thorn spoke another sound.

I'd pushed myself up into a sitting position when Thorn strode back into view around the donations box. He'd returned to the mortal-ish form I was used to, nothing otherworldly about him other than the crystalline glint of his knuckles.

Two heads, ripped from their bodies, dangled by their hair from one of his broad hands, the stumps of their necks dribbling blood and smatterings of gore. He held them up. "I didn't know which one lodged that bullet in you, so I present you with both."

My stomach churned, but I couldn't say I didn't appreciate the sentiment. "Um, thank you. I think we can leave those here, though. I'm not really a trophy type of gal." At least not the bloody body part kind of trophy. "It's not as if we can avoid the people who own this place realizing something major went down here tonight anyway."

Thorn sneered at the detached heads and tossed them behind him. "You said I could 'come after' anyone who attacked you outside the building," he reminded me.

"Yeah, I did, didn't I? Good thinking, me." I rubbed my head. It was easier not to think about the wrecked bodies that were lying farther across the lot when I didn't have to see them. Easier not to care about their deaths with my shoulder still gripped in the jaws of agony.

At this point, he'd needed to kill them. If we'd left them alive, they'd have immediately sounded the alarm so the rest of the people could start damage control. As it was… we had until shift change to make the most of the booty I'd fled with.

The *computer* booty. Get your mind out of the gutter.

The computer in question had landed on the ground next to me. I examined the metal shell and determined it was only mildly dinged. In my not-at-all expert opinion, it should still work just fine.

Thorn scooped the device up as if it weighed no more than a kitten, putting my arm strength to shame. When I reached for the box of discs, he grabbed that too.

"We should return to the others," he said, holding out a hand to help me up. He'd reverted back to his usual cool demeanor, but I was too woozy to be offended this time.

He'd saved my life in the most literal sense. He'd slaughtered men on my behalf and offered me their heads as a gift of devotion. No matter how he liked to play it, he couldn't really pretend he wasn't a teeny bit fond of me.

"Ready when you are," I said, managing not to sway. "Let's bring these bastards down."

THIRTY-ONE

Sorsha

Patching me up turned into a group effort. Ruse picked up the necessary supplies while I lay grumbling and cursing on the motel bed, the one hand towel Pickle hadn't appropriated pressed to the entry wound and the dragon himself curled up against my head in an effort to offer comfort. When the incubus returned, Thorn and Snap sat next to me. After I'd swallowed a couple of painkillers and a swig of the vodka Ruse had also deemed necessary, the warrior slowly talked the other shadowkind through the process of removing the bullet and stitching my flesh back together.

Snap shuddered when he peered at the lump of metal that was apparently visible in the wound. "It's silver."

"Good thing I'm not a werewolf," I muttered. The guards had been at least a little prepared for supernatural intruders.

Thorn ignored my dry remark. "We wouldn't need it out otherwise. I don't want to leave anything in her that could make it harder for us to take care of her. It shouldn't cause any further trouble—no major blood vessels right there."

Snap sucked in a breath and brandished his tweezers.

His slender fingers did perform the job more gracefully than

Thorn's heavy hands could have managed, although I contributed quite a bit more cursing regardless. In between the throbs of pain, I couldn't help thinking about where the warrior must have picked up his knowledge in field wounds. A long time ago and probably in countries far, far away.

Thorn didn't look particularly fazed by the wound or the bleeding that had already slowed to a trickle by the time we'd made it to the car thanks to the pressure he'd applied. Snap, for all he kept his hands steady, was much more perturbed. At my every hiss and grimace, he winced in sympathy.

"You destroyed the ones who did this?" he asked Thorn with his new possessive fierceness.

The warrior offered a rare, if grim, smile that would have been answer enough. "Oh, yes."

The lump of metal Snap plucked out didn't look large enough to have caused half of the agony I'd been experiencing. The pain started to dull now that it was gone, other than the tiny jabs of the stitching needle. In a few minutes, I was sitting up with an ice pack over a gauze bandage, the muscle there turning nicely numb.

Piece of cake. Ha ha ha.

Ruse had been examining my loot. "So, our answers are in here?" he asked, nudging the computer.

"I hope so," I said. "They'd better fucking be after all this. The trick is going to be getting them out." I motioned to Snap. "Any chance you can get a sense of a password from that thing?"

Snap considered the metal structure with obvious skepticism. He leaned in, his tongue flitting past its surface here and there. When he straightened up, he shook his head. "It's mostly you, from when you were running with it. The other impressions are much duller. Nothing that tells how to open it."

Of course the owner wouldn't have been petting the computer while logging in or working out nefarious plans. If I'd thought to grab the keyboard too... But then, I'd barely made it out of the store with what I *had* carried.

I rubbed my mouth. "All right. We're going to need a monitor and a keyboard, and I guess I'll have to see if someone from the hacker cabal can talk me through breaking the password encryption... And fast." It was past eleven. At best, we had eight or nine hours before the sword-star bunch realized what we'd taken off with and started cleaning up shop.

Ruse cocked his head. "Wouldn't it be easier to bring the computer to the hackers and let them do the work?"

"I don't know where they are. I guess they probably know *someone* who could handle it in a city this big." I frowned. "If they'd agree to meet up with us anyway. If that would even be safe."

The incubus's eyes gleamed. "Get them on the phone, and I can handle the rest."

Every minute it took to wait for a response felt like years, but it'd actually only been half an hour before the Fund's contacts had hooked me up with a local associate who reluctantly agreed to a phone conversation. When the call came in, I handed the phone to Ruse.

"Hello there," he said in his smooth voice, and shot me an amused glance as he covered the mic area. "They're using a voice distorter—as if that'll help."

He sauntered around the room, rolling his cajoling words off his tongue, until he'd gotten an address and a promise that our new friend wouldn't mention the visit to anyone. "I'll return with all possible speed," he said, handing me back my phone and hefting the computer.

"Take the devourer with you," Thorn said abruptly.

Ruse looked at Snap, who blinked at the warrior. "What would I do there? I don't know how to get anything out of that box."

Thorn nodded toward Ruse. "He can pick up on whether this 'hacker' has had any contact with our enemies. If they have, we'll want you to test their home and possessions for any useful impressions you can glean that way."

The explanation sounded flimsy, and from the arch of Ruse's eyebrow, he thought so too. He wasn't inclined to fight with the larger shadowkind about it, though. "Come on then. My influence isn't quite as potent without visuals. We want to make sure we get there before it wears off."

Snap cast a concerned look my way, but the need for urgency cut off whatever arguments he might have made. "We'll be back soon," he assured me. "For now, get all the rest you can."

"Believe me, I have zero interest in running any marathons for the next decade or so."

They slipped out, leaving me with just Thorn, looming where he stood beside the bed. I raised my own eyebrows at him. "Couldn't wait to get me alone, huh?"

There was that familiar glower. He appeared to be waiting for something—the rumble of the car engine as the other guys drove away. Then he folded his arms over his expansive chest, but I couldn't feel all that intimidated just from his bulk when I'd seen what he *really* looked like.

"You won't say anything to the others about what I am," he said.

Interesting. "Why not?"

The glower deepened. "It's simply easier not to get caught up in the questions that arise. Even my fellow shadowkind are generally… taken aback."

So I wasn't wrong in being startled that his specific kind existed at all anymore. I scooted away from the pillow to Pickle's snort of dismay, gave the dragon a soothing pat, and gazed up at my avenging warrior. "All right, I'll keep quiet—on one condition. I want you to show yourself again."

Apparently it was Thorn's turn to be startled. "What?"

"You heard me. I'd like to get a look at you when I'm not half out of my mind in pain. Since this seems to be a once-in-a-lifetime-if-that sort of experience and all."

Thorn opened his mouth and shut it, appearing to think better of whatever protest he'd been going to make. He'd correctly labeled me as obstinate just an hour or so ago, after all. "Fine. But only if we're agreed."

"No blabbing your secrets—it's a deal."

I offered my hand to shake on it, and Thorn accepted the gesture with a twitch of his mouth that could have been amusement or irritation or maybe a little of both. His solid fingers engulfed mine in their firm grasp. Then he stepped back from the bed to give himself more room.

Unlike Ruse, he didn't need even the concentration of closing his eyes. The edges of his body flickered, and all at once he loomed half a foot taller, his frame filling out with even more of that sculpted brawn.

The smoldering red consumed his eyes. Where his hands had dropped to his sides, his knuckles glinted with their crystalline surface protruding farther and sharper, and the hardened lines of his scarred face caught the light with a diamond-like quality I hadn't seen in the darkness of the parking lot.

And those wings. He kept them partly folded, and still the arc of their dark sweep grazed the ceiling. The feathered tips might have stretched all the way from one end of the room to the other if he'd extended them.

I hadn't seen those wrong. My breath caught. I knew I was staring, but really, if there was ever an excuse to, this was it.

A wave of giddiness propelled my next words. "You're an angel."

Thorn's mouth tensed. "That word belongs to mortals. None of the trappings they add to it have any basis in reality. We prefer 'the wingéd.'"

He placed an archaic emphasis on the end of the word, saying it "wing-*ed*" rather than "wing'd." His voice resonated with the reverb quality I also hadn't imagined. It sent a tingle over my skin.

I hadn't had any reason to believe in a literal heaven even before he'd made his comment about trappings, but if anyone had ever sounded as if they came from on high, it was him.

"I didn't know there were any of you left," I said. "I heard... there was a war?"

The information the shadowkind passed on between each other and to the mortals they interacted with was limited, and where it did exist, the details were sketchy and probably skewed by myth and faulty perception. The little bit I'd gathered was that sometime several centuries ago, there'd been a brief but epic battle of some sort in which angels—okay, the wingéd—had fought in unison with the human factions... on both sides. The clash of uber-powerful beings had left most but clearly not quite all of them dead. No one who'd referenced it had any idea what they'd been fighting about.

If Thorn was a typical representation of his kind, I was going to guess the disagreement had been more serious than which way you hung a toilet paper roll.

He didn't add to my understanding. "Most slaughtered each other. I survived. It's not a time I care to talk about at any length, m'lady."

Fair enough. "And the others really don't know?"

He shook his head. "Not the incubus or the devourer. Omen knows. He was there."

My eyes widened. "Is *he* an ang—er, wingéd—too?"

Thorn chuckled—a sound I'd never heard from him before, thrumming from his throat with heavenly resonance. "No. He's— You'll see, if he wants to show you."

Someone had mentioned the man having claws at one point, hadn't they? I might have prodded the warrior further, but his good humor faded with the last few words. There was more he could have said but didn't need to.

If we ever do find him.

I didn't want Thorn dwelling on that right now. With a twinge from my shoulder, I pushed myself to my feet so I could step closer.

Thorn's stance tensed at my approach, but he didn't disguise his true form. As I reached with my good arm to trace my fingers over the slope of one wing where it left his back, he held himself perfectly still.

The surface of the black feathers was unexpectedly silky, only coarse along the edges, and the ridge of flesh beneath them emanated warmth. I couldn't resist the urge to stroke them more firmly. Was that a slight hitch in his chest, as if that spot might be particularly sensitive to the touch?

When was the last time he'd been close enough to anyone to let them offer this kind of caress, if ever?

"They're magnificent." I glanced up, my pulse stuttering at finding myself so close to that impenetrable face. "*You're* magnificent."

He peered down at me with those smoldering eyes. "Mortals usually flee in terror at this sight."

I grinned. My heart was still thumping double-time, but it definitely wasn't in fear. His musky, smoky smell had coiled around me, and every word that fell from his lips in that tone like low thunder was stirring heat in my core. The jolt of desire that'd rushed through me in the parking lot definitely couldn't be blamed on just adrenaline.

My hand drifted from his wing to rest on his bulging bicep. "Haven't you figured out yet that I'm not your average mortal?"

"It would be exceedingly difficult not to have noticed."

I walked my fingers down to his elbow teasingly. "And you like me, irreverence and obstinance and all, as hard as it might be for you to admit it."

He let out a sound that wasn't much more than a wordless grumble, and then he proved what I'd just said by clasping the hair at the back of my head and tugging me to him. His mouth collided with mine, hot and steady and unrelenting. I held onto his tunic for dear life and kissed him back, my senses overwhelmed.

Maybe it wasn't the sanest move I'd ever made. I'd already been canoodling with both of his companions, and just one monstrous lover was more than a handful. But—heaven help me even if it didn't exist— I wanted them all, and after tonight, I deserved a little indulgence. It wasn't as if any dalliance between a human and a shadowkind could turn into a real relationship in the long run. Once our battle with the sword-star bunch was over, who knew if I'd even see any of them again?

Thorn kissed me once more, with determined gentleness, before he drew back a few inches. His hand slid from my hair to stroke along my jaw.

"I almost didn't get to you quickly enough tonight," he said, with a rawness I could hear even through the reverb. "We still have farther to go to see this through. I won't insult you by asking you again to back down, but I hate the thought that next time I might fail to protect you."

"You've now saved my life at least a couple times over," I said. "I'm pretty sure any debt you owed me is fully paid."

He made a noise of consternation. "You're worth more than any debt. I didn't kiss you as repayment either."

A flutter passed through my chest with a softer sort of giddiness. "I'm glad we're on the same page, then. Maybe you take the whole protection gig to unnecessary extremes? All Omen could have asked was that you do your best, and I've never asked for anything at all."

"I..." His thumb that had been gliding along my chin halted. "I had friends in the war. Brothers and sisters at arms. I would have died for them—I *should* have—but I wasn't there when the need was greatest, and now they are gone and I am still here. I don't wish to repeat that mistake."

He'd spoken in his usual formal diction, but the weight of that loss rang through the words. A lump rose in my throat. How long had he spent roaming the shadow realm alone, tangled up in guilt and mourning? He'd been carrying that wound for centuries, and Omen's mission had brought the pain right back to the surface.

I touched his jaw like he had mine, finding the hardened planes of his face still had the warmth and suppleness of skin against my fingers. "I understand, but I swear to you that if something happens to me, *I* won't blame you for it. All right?"

Maybe it didn't matter what I thought if he'd blame himself anyway, but he inclined his head in acknowledgment. His wings vanished, his body contracting to his normal though still imposing height. The red faded from his dark eyes.

"The others might be back at any moment," he said, with more his usual brusqueness. "Snap was right—you should be resting while you can."

"Fine," I muttered, but my shoulder was starting to ache more insistently again. I could be satisfied with a couple of kisses for now. Getting more involved with the third member of my monstrous trio— I'd decide later how sane *that* idea was. If we got a later after wherever else our schemes led us tonight.

I sank down on the edge of the bed. As Pickle scrambled up onto my lap to curl up there, my thoughts veered toward my own friends. My best friend, who'd wanted so badly to fight for me too, even if those efforts had ended in disaster.

I grasped my phone. "I should call Vivi. Make sure she found someplace safe to hide out." Get in a few last words with her just in case they turned out to really be my last. It was late, but Vivi tended to be a night owl even when she didn't have a recently-witnessed murder to ruin her sleep.

"I'll give you the room," Thorn said, and wavered away into the shadows to his own room without bothering with the door.

I hesitated over my Frequent Contacts, where Vivi's welcoming face grinned up at me from the top spot. My stomach knotted.

Ten years ago, when I'd been barely more than a kid and she hadn't been much older, we'd been glued at the hip. I wasn't sure how I'd have survived this long without her friendship keeping me sane and human. The thought of someone putting a bullet in *her* still made my innards clench up with an icy panic.

But maybe she'd felt the same way about me potentially walking into danger. She'd screwed up and crossed boundaries, and I was still kind of pissed off about that, but at least she'd done it out of love rather than the intent to do harm.

I tapped the screen and lifted the phone. A few seconds later, my bestie's voice pealed into my ear.

"Sorsha! Are you still okay?"

I ignored the ache in my shoulder. "I've had better days, but yeah. Are *you*? Did you get out of town like I said?"

"Yeah, I grabbed Gran, and we took off for a cottage a couple of hours away that belongs to friends of the family. I—I keep looking out the windows just in case someone's coming." Her voice dipped lower. "I've been worried sick about you. I wanted to call, but I didn't want to interrupt you at a bad time. Obviously I'm not the greatest judge of when or how to interfere."

"You shouldn't have been interfering at all," I couldn't help saying, even though I hadn't meant to restart that argument.

Vivi sighed. "Okay, that might be true. And I'm really sorry I went all stalker on you. But *you* shouldn't have been lying to me. I thought you knew you could count on me... I wish you'd trusted me more."

The dejection in her voice made me wince. I swallowed hard. "It's not that I don't trust or count on you, Vivi. I do, for all kinds of things. But you saw how dangerous the situation is, what kind of people I'm up against... With the things Luna taught me"—and the trio of allies who'd turned up on my doorstep—"I'm better equipped to take them on. I was trying to keep you *safe*."

My best friend was silent for a moment. "I get that. I can even appreciate the thought. But Sorsh, what if I don't *want* to be safe if that means I can't help you when you're in trouble? How do you think I'd feel if you got hurt and I hadn't done anything to stop it? If we're working together, at least we can split the danger two ways instead of it all being on you."

"I don't think it works exactly like that," I said, but her words sent a twinge through me anyway. Had it really been right for me to take away her choice in the matter? I'd told myself she wouldn't fully understand the danger to know what she was getting into—but part of the reason she didn't was because of all the things I'd avoided telling her.

I hadn't liked Thorn trying to send me off to keep me safe, and he'd at least informed me of that decision rather than going behind my back.

"I'm sorry too," I added. "At this point, I think we're both safest if you lay low, but once the immediate crisis is over, we'll talk more. Okay?"

"That sounds like a compromise I can get behind. Are you… Are you looking after yourself?"

"As well as I can. And as you noticed, I've got some friends of another sort who've made that their business too." I smiled wryly. "You don't have to worry about them either. We've reached an understanding."

"If you say so." She gave a short laugh. "Ack, Gran's calling for me. I'd better see what's up. Call me again to touch base tomorrow so I don't go crazy wondering what's happened to you?"

"I'll do that." I'd be worrying about her too.

"Talk soon then. Ditto."

My smile turned painfully bittersweet. "Ditto," I replied.

I lay back against the pillow, Pickle snuggling into the crook of my neck, and closed my eyes. Despite the intermittent twinges of pain, I must have dozed at least a little. One second my mind was drifting through a highlights reel of the past week, and the next all three of my shadowkind companions had burst into my room, talking at the same time.

I sat up, blinking and swiping at my eyes. A glance at the bedside clock told me it was now nearly two in the morning.

We were running out of time.

I held up my hands. "Hold on, hold on. What's going on? What did you find out? Start from the beginning—just one of you."

Ruse came to a stop beside the bed and caught one of my hands in his. His smirk radiated victory.

"The hacker you found cracked all the codes, and we hit pay dirt. We know exactly where Omen is down to the cell number—we've even seen the blueprints to know how to get to it once we're there."

Snap was practically bouncing on his feet with eager energy. "At least, we think it's him. They're all called 'subjects' in the files. But 'Subject 26' was the only one brought in around the time he was captured, and some of the other details sounded like him."

"He's alive," Thorn said with undisguised relief.

"We found the building," Snap went on. "It was one of the other impressions I got from Meriden. Two of them together, actually. There's a big construction site"—he glanced at Ruse as if to confirm he'd gotten the term right—"and in the middle where you can't see unless you go right through, there's the building I saw with the concrete walls and shiny doors."

A secret facility hidden within a construction site? With all the building projects that went up around the city and then took forever to complete, I had to give the conspirators kudos. That was pretty brilliant.

"You *saw* the place?" I said as everything he'd said sunk in. A quiver of nerves raced through me even though the two of them had clearly returned unharmed. "You went in?"

"Not all the way in," Ruse said. "On the way back here, we swung by the address we got to scope things out so we could make more definite plans. We couldn't easily get into the actual building, though. They've got flood lamps all around the place so we can't get close enough to jump to any entry point through the shadows, and obviously we weren't going to stroll over and knock."

"Lots of guards too." Snap made a face. "Some of them standing around, some of them patrolling, with silver and iron protections and those weapons they used before."

"I can smash through their puny equipment," Thorn rumbled.

"Not with this many, even with these guns." Ruse punched him lightly in the arm. "We're going to need a better strategy than 'Charge straight in and hope for the best.'"

I thought of the construction of the toy shop office. "What about the building itself? Is there any silver or iron worked into it?"

Ruse hesitated. "We didn't pick up on anything from outside. The blueprints indicate there were special materials used in the cells, which makes sense. The rest of the building looked clear."

But of course we couldn't know for sure if they'd added more since then.

If the shadowkind couldn't simply slip inside unseen, then getting in would require my expertise. My first impulse was to tell them to lay out the route for me, and I'd get to Omen and release him myself. No need for any of them to risk the same assholes catching and caging *them*, especially when we didn't know how going into the building might affect them.

But as I looked around at the three men—and perhaps monsters—who'd crashed into my life uninvited days ago, the bizarre fondness that swelled in my chest was tainted with a pinch of shame.

I'd nearly gotten myself killed earlier tonight by insisting I go into the store alone. Shutting Vivi out had made more problems for us than it could solve. The idea of seeing anyone that I, yeah, cared about under threat still made every particle in my body balk. It made me think of my parents' cries and of Luna shattering into mere particles of the woman who'd raised me.

My lungs constricted with the memories. People around me, people who were trying to look after me—they died.

But these three knew the risk they were taking. How could I tell them it wasn't their choice to make—or try to take the choice away from them completely?

If we were going to outmaneuver the sword-star bunch and rescue their boss, it'd take all the wits and skills we had between us. Going in alone could be both a suicide mission and a guarantee of failure.

"We've gotten this far," I said. "No way are they stopping us now. Tell me exactly how the building is laid out and where we need to go, and let's work from there. We need to pull this jailbreak off before the sun comes up."

THIRTY-TWO

Sorsha

The steel struts of the construction site loomed above the lower rooftops of the neighboring buildings, reflected moonlight making them visible even from two blocks away. They gleamed faintly against the darkness of the night sky like the bones of some massive creature that had settled there to die and had its carcass picked clean. That image fit my mood perfectly as Ruse put the car into park.

"The end is nigh, but I'm holding on," I sang, but not even the inspiration of Blondie could stop my voice from sounding thin in the silence. At this hour, no other vehicles passed us on the road. Not the slightest breeze stirred the warm air. My shoulder still throbbed from the silver bullet Snap had pulled out of me.

The end of our mission was up ahead, sure, but for all we knew it could end *us*.

Out of all of us, I had to admit the one most likely to meet some dire fate was the owner of a mortal body—a.k.a., me. I was prepared for that, but a tightness wound through my ribs as my shadowkind trio moved to get out of the car.

I gave Pickle one last scratch between his wings where he'd perched on my lap and then shifted him to the middle seat so I could get up too, resisting the urge to cuddle him so close he'd squawk. We'd brought him and all my belongings with us because regardless of where this night led, returning to the motel after we faced off against the sword-star bunch directly seemed unwise. Leaving him there in the car, the constricting sensation crept up into my throat.

The three men had gathered around me on the sidewalk. I turned to them when I'd shut the car door.

"If something happens to me tonight," I said, "promise me you'll look after Pickle? He won't get very far on his own."

Snap's expression turned pained. "You don't need to worry about that," he insisted.

Thorn raised his chin, adding to the immense sense of his height. "I don't intend to return without you, but if it eases your mind, you have my word the little creature will be taken care of."

The hairs on the back of my neck rose with the implications of his initial statement. I knew he meant not just that he hoped to make sure I came out alive, but that if I didn't, it'd only be because he fell too.

We had a plan, and I didn't think we could have come up with a better one, at least not without days longer than the hour or so we'd actually had. But so much was still uncertain. Our enemies had caught us off-guard more than once. We intended to turn the tables on them tonight, but we hadn't pulled off anything quite like this before.

An impulse gripped me that I let myself follow, because who knew whether we'd have another moment of relative peace. I grasped Thorn's shirt and bobbed up to give him a light peck on the lips, swiftly enough that he didn't have the chance to return it or pull away, whichever he'd have decided on. I had no idea how he'd feel about the others seeing any softness from him.

The warrior glowered at me after, but the heat in his gaze felt at least as hungry as it did annoyed. Ruse was smirking, wider when I turned to him. He reached for me and tugged me to him by the waist, his eyelids lowering seductively.

"I'll take a little more than that, Miss Blaze," he said in the chocolatey tone that still made my skin tingle. But he let me be the one to lean in the last few inches between us and capture his mouth.

I'd almost forgotten how much skill the incubus could bring to a simple kiss. The press of his lips, languid as if taking his time and yet passionate as if reveling in every second, set a whole lot more tingling than just my skin. Wouldn't it have been nice to sink into that bittersweet cacao-and-caramel scent of him and leave death-defying capers for another night?

We didn't have any other nights before our enemies discovered how close to them we'd already gotten, though. Reluctantly, I eased back.

Snap's posture had tensed while I'd kissed the other guys. Glimmers of brighter green shimmered through his eyes with the intensity of the reaction he appeared to be reining in. "My peach," he said, shooting a look at the other two that dared them to deny him that claim. The defiance turned his heavenly face even more dazzling.

I touched his soft cheek. I'd saved him for last for exactly this reason. "My devourer?" I said. I wasn't entirely sure what that label meant yet, but the tension in his expression melted at the suggestion.

"Yes," he said with a brilliant smile, and tipped his head to nuzzle my cheek before he brought our mouths together.

I'd expected all sweet tenderness, but Snap was clearly determined to both make a statement and stake a claim. He parted my lips with eager determination, his tongue flicking in to twine around mine as he deepened the kiss. The stroke of the delicately forked tip sent a rush of giddiness through me. As he traced my jaw to tilt it at an even better angle, he all but plundered my mouth.

It was sweet, hell yes, and dizzyingly intense too.

When he released me, every inch of him was lit with satisfaction, deliciously fucking gorgeous. A laugh both delighted and terrified bubbled at the base of my throat until I swallowed it down.

I'd gotten myself an angel, a sort-of sun god, and a guy most mortals would consider a demon. What sort of being was waiting for us inside that prison if we succeeded in freeing him?

It was time to find out. I stepped back and motioned toward the construction site. "Let's do this thing."

As I strode toward the site, my companions wisped away into the shadows to draw less attention if anyone happened to look our way. The site itself was bordered by a solid fence some six feet high, but I made short work of the chain securing one of the entrances with my scorch-knife. Trusting that the trio was following close by, I squeezed inside.

I crept along a meandering path between metal beams and stacks of wood until I skirted a raw cinder-block wall and the glow of the flood lights came into view up ahead. With a few more steps, I made out the concrete walls of the squat two-story building Snap had first seen in the impressions clinging to Meriden's body.

It rose up out of a clear stretch of dirt in the middle of the larger half-finished building. The door on this side was indeed shiny—stainless steel, from the look of it—and the flat gray walls around it held only a couple of small windows, those on the first floor. The holding cells above must have offered no glimpse at all into the outside world.

Figures stalked along the edges of the harsh light that surrounded the place. I counted three patrolling in my view and two others stationed by the door. From what Ruse and Snap had reported, there'd be at least twice that many monitoring the entire area. They all wore helmets and vests that gleamed with plates of silver and iron.

I caught myself just shy of rubbing the bandage on my shoulder. Two guards had been trouble enough. But I wasn't alone here—and if we didn't get going, we'd lose all the advantage of the darkness and surprise.

I lifted my hand with an OK signal. That was Thorn's cue. Tucking myself as close to one of the nearby beams as I could, the metallic odor filling my nose, I braced myself for the chaos.

It started with a thumping like several boards toppling off a pile. All of the guards jerked their heads around to stare in that direction. As one man trotted over to investigate, a sharper clatter split the air. Drawing his gun, he motioned for two of his companions to follow.

They'd just loped out of view when something fell with a clang in the opposite direction. A shout carried from around the side of the building as more guards must have sprung into action. As long as they weren't heading anywhere near me, I was happy.

At an even more distant spot, there came a crash like shattering glass. One of the guards by the door spoke into her radio and then hustled off to help her colleagues. We were down to one between us and the entrance—but just distracting him momentarily wouldn't do the trick. If we wanted enough time to not just get into the building but get Omen and the other shadowkind prisoners out, we needed as many of our foes as possible caught up in a wild goose chase.

Thorn hadn't forgotten that part of the plan. A few seconds later, he charged over to join me, a dazed but thankfully not smashed figure dangling from his hands by the ankles so he didn't need to touch the helmet or vest that would have burned him.

Without a word, he dropped the man on the ground in front of me. Before the guy could regain his equilibrium, I yanked off the tight helmet and jerked at the snaps on his vest, gritting my teeth as the ache in my shoulder grew teeth. The protections hadn't been able to neutralize the warrior's physical strength, but none of my allies' supernatural powers would have any effect until we'd gotten rid of them.

The vest's clasps parted to reveal a faded Guns 'N Roses T-shirt. "Et tu, Brute?" I muttered.

As I tossed the vest aside, Ruse materialized out of the shadows. The guard took a swing at me, shoving himself more upright with a wobble, and Thorn clapped his hand over the guy's mouth the second it opened to yell. Before he needed to intervene any more than that, the incubus started speaking, staring deep into the man's widening eyes.

"Nice to meet you," he said in his cajoling tone. "Tell me, won't you, how many more guards are inside the building?"

The man's pupils had dilated. Thorn loosened his grip to allow him room to speak. "I— You—" he stammered.

Ruse knelt in front of him. The power rang through his voice so distinctly it tickled my ears even though it wasn't directed at me. "We're going to be very good friends. It couldn't hurt anything for you to tell me."

The guard's posture started to relax. "There are two people monitoring the security cams. Another patrolling the halls. Not that we've ever needed all this manpower on the site… before…"

Ruse made a swift gesture to recapture the man's attention and peered at him even more intently. "Before now. Indeed. Quite the catastrophe that's happening out here. Imagine how upset your employers will be if they find out you all let these intruders get away.

They're trying to break down the walls so anyone might wander in and see your secret base."

"No. We can't let that happen."

"Exactly. You know what you need to do? Put in a call on that radio of yours, get everyone you can out here. You can hear the invaders—they're all along the wall—you'll need to keep moving to catch up with them. Don't back down and keep everyone on their trail until you've nabbed them."

The guard nodded with a slow bob of his head. Then his gaze whipped away, his body stiffening all over again. He scrambled to his feet. "You're right—I hear them bashing at the wall right over there. Shit."

He raised his radio as he dashed off toward the outskirts of the site, hollering for every guard at the facility to join him immediately between pants for breath that only played up the urgency.

Ruse flashed me a grin. "And now…"

The last guard at the door hesitated and then hurried over. One, two, and then a third burst through the doorway to join the defense. Bingo!

Thorn hurtled across the stretch of packed dirt to slam the camera poised over the door into the concrete wall it was mounted on. I sprinted after him. Snap darted from the shadows to meet me by the entrance. With a flick of his tongue through the air over the electronic lock, he smiled and tapped in the code he'd gleaned. The bolt slid over, and I yanked the door open.

As the warrior sprinted back to the shadows to continue diverting the guards outside, Snap, Ruse, and I ducked into the building. We found ourselves in an entry room with lime-green walls and an antiseptic prickle in the air.

Ruse pointed to another doorway at the opposite end. "The stairs are down that hall."

We were hustling along it when a woman in a lab coat emerged, blinking, from one of the workrooms. She didn't have a chance to do more than gasp before I'd spotted the silver and iron badge pinned to her blouse, like a larger version of my own. I snatched at it and wrenched it off her with a rasp of tearing fabric.

"Everything's okay," Ruse said to her in a ridiculously soothing voice. "You have so much work to do. You should get back to it. Nothing's more important than that."

She drew in a shaky voice, her eyes glued to him. "But—"

"Trust me. Nothing going on out here interests you at all. Think of how much you want to accomplish before it's time to leave."

He nudged her toward her office, and she meandered inside looking intent if slightly puzzled. As the three of us jogged the rest of the way down the hall, I tapped Ruse's side with my elbow. "Very impressive. I haven't really seen you in action before."

He chuckled. "I don't normally have to skip so much of the foreplay. Turning the dial up this high is giving me an ulcer. Let's hope I don't have to charm too many more."

We didn't run into anyone else in the hall or the stairwell, but as we reached the second-floor landing, both Ruse and Snap slowed. Ruse's jaw tightened.

Snap gave a little shudder as I pushed open the door to the hall that held the shadowkind prisoners. "A lot of unkind metals in this place."

My gut twisted. "Can you keep going?" We'd known there'd be silver and iron in the cell walls to contain the prisoners, but we'd hoped the effect wouldn't seep into the space outside them. How could we get Omen and the other shadowkind prisoners out of their cells if Snap couldn't reach the locks? Hell, if I got the opportunity, I'd wanted to not just free every being in this place but grab whatever files we could get our hands on quickly to find out what the sword-star bunch had been doing here.

Snap squared his shoulders and marched forward, but I could see the effort it took in the clenching of his hands. Ruse followed, showing similar signs of strain.

The blank walls and solid metal doors offered no glimpse of the creatures inside the cells. I scanned the numbers on the doors as quickly as I could. "Cell 11 was Omen's, right?" He was our first priority. I didn't want to think through the implications of Subject 27 being in only the eleventh cell—or what might have happened to at least sixteen of the subjects before him.

The incubus gave a curt nod. "Let's find it fast. I'm definitely not digging the vibe of this place."

There. I rushed over, Snap close behind me. Fighting a cringe, he bent close to the keypad by the lock. On his first attempt, his tongue flinched back into his mouth before he appeared to catch anything. An even more determined expression came over his face, and he tested the air again.

"4-9-7-2," he spat out, hauling himself back from the noxious surface.

I tapped in the numbers, willing my hand not to shake. How long could Ruse's ploy and Thorn's shenanigans keep all the guards from noticing what we were up to in here?

How were we going to make it *out* of here if they came back too soon?

The lock whirred open. Hallelujah. As soon as we made sure this was Omen—and that he knew we were his people, coming to rescue him—I'd get Snap to move on to the next cell. If he could even tolerate testing the rest of the locks with all the toxic materials in this place, that was.

I tugged the door wide. The entire ceiling of the cell was one huge panel of light, which glared off the reflective walls and floor and nearly drowned out the twitching form like a streak of shadowy smoke in the middle of it.

"Omen?" I said. "Do you need help getting—"

Before I could finish the question, the blur of darkness flung itself at me with a guttural roar. Yellow-orange eyes blazed at me like twin flames; a clawed hand—or was that a *paw*?—smacked me aside with a scrape of pain through my arm that echoed into my injured shoulder. I stumbled into Snap, who caught me in a tight embrace.

"Omen!" he protested. "She's with—"

The blare of an alarm drowned out anything else he might have said. My stomach flipped over. Sweet stinking cheese. There must have been some other device we'd needed to disable to remove a prisoner safely.

The overhead lights flared twice as bright—and down the hall by the stairwell, a barrier of silver-and-iron-twined bars dropped into place with a clang, cutting off our escape.

"Shit," Ruse muttered. We bolted toward the stairwell anyway. The shadowy figure we'd released was still whipping around us, too swift and hazy to make him out clearly. One moment it looked like a hunched human form, the next some sort of muscular beast, its dark flesh streaked through with a fiery glow. A tail lashed in its wake, taut and sinuous with a triangular protrusion I glimpsed at its tip.

A devil's tail.

I couldn't think about that now. It didn't matter what Omen was if we all ended up dead or jailed tonight.

There was no time to try to free anyone else. Ignoring the guilt that jabbed through my panic, I yanked the scorch-knife from my belt, switched it on, and rammed it into the bars the second I reached them.

The people who'd designed this place had meant the barrier to hold off shadowkind with the power of its metals, not the width of its bars. I cut through one in a matter of seconds, drove the blade against it farther down, and kicked the large chunk out to clatter onto the floor. My heart seemed to be beating right in my throat, my pulse thudding behind my ears almost as loud as the alarm.

As I moved to the next bar, Ruse's voice carried from behind me. "Omen, pull yourself together. We've got you—we're taking you out of this hellhole—but it'll be a lot easier if you get a hold of yourself."

"They did horrible things here," Snap said, with a quiver of anger in his voice. "Horrible things to him. I don't even have to try to taste it."

I'd only cut out three bars when a door banged open below. Almost biting my tongue at the jolt of panic that hit me, I rammed the knife even harder into the fourth. One more and the space should be just big enough for the shadowkind to follow me through...

A guard barreled into the landing just as I severed the bottom of that bar. I punched it right into her face. As she stumbled backward with a grunt of pain, a form that now looked completely like a man sprang through the opening at her.

The shadowkind man who must have been Omen slammed the guard's head into the ground with a cracking of her skull. He launched his sinewy frame down the stairs, and the three of us bolted after him.

Another guard had just reached the lower landing. With a snarl, Omen crashed into him, slamming him into the door frame and snapping his neck a second later. He flung the body to the side and raced on.

Then, at the far end of the hall where we'd come in, half a dozen guards rushed into the space. Weapons of metals and light flashed in their hands. We all stalled in our tracks.

They stepped forward, wary but ready, a few more of their colleagues coming in behind them to join the blockade. My pulse lurched.

They were prepared for us now, and there were too many of them. I couldn't imagine tearing our way through the whole lot, no matter what Omen was.

My hands shot up instinctively, as if I could ward them off—and one of the guards at the front of the pack flinched as if I'd actually flung something at him. More chickenshit than I'd expected. Omen glanced back at me with eyes now icy blue, as if he'd only just noticed I was still with him and his companions.

But flinging my arms around wasn't going to help us more than that tiny distraction. The guards advanced on us with increasing speed.

"Sorsha!" Thorn's bellow carried through the walls, followed by the crackle of smashed glass. Omen jerked toward the sound. He sprang back to a door between us and him and shoved it open.

We dashed after him to find shards glinting around one of the small windows I'd observed from outside. Thorn stood beyond it, his harsh cheeks splattered with mortal blood.

"Omen," he said hoarsely at the sight of his boss. "Come on, all of you, into the shadows. Sorsha, I've got you."

It wasn't anywhere near the leap it'd been from the apartment building. He swept his arm across the window frame, clearing the splinters of glass. Omen hurled himself through, his form thinning as he soared out into the flood of light. The incubus boosted me after him. As Thorn caught me and swung me onto his back, Ruse and Snap dove after us. Their forms raced through the glow and vanished into the shadows of the construction site.

The alarm was still blaring, frantic shouts breaking through its rhythm. A shot like a sizzling bolt of light smacked the wall less than an inch from us.

Thorn didn't risk tangling with all these attackers. With me clinging to his shoulders for dear life, too grateful to have him to complain about the indignity, he charged off in the same direction our companions had gone. He dodged beams and boards, smashed through one of the gates at the edge of the site, and hurtled on down the street toward the car.

Ruse had already started the engine, the lights flashing on in the darkness. Thorn and I tumbled into the back seat, and he took off with a screech of the tires.

The bleat of the alarm pealed through my ears from deep within that giant steel skeleton. I couldn't catch my breath until the cacophony of our escape finally faded away in the depths of the night.

THIRTY-THREE

Sorsha

The fire crackled within the ring of stones in the derelict campsite we'd stumbled on, miles outside the city. Its heat, sharper than the warmth that lingered at the tail end of the summer night, grazed my face where I was leaning against the side of the car. Its light washed over all of us arranged around the firepit, including the man we'd risked life and limb to save.

Omen stood poised almost directly across from me, his arms folded over his chest as he watched Snap poke at the fire with a long stick. I couldn't have said he was quite as stunning as the team he'd gathered, though he wasn't exactly hard on the eyes. I suspected if I'd been a regular mortal passing him on the street, I wouldn't have given him a second glance other than maybe to check if his ass looked as fit as the rest of his body. But I wasn't, and something about his presence drew my attention like a moth fluttering to those flames.

Flames that brought to mind the flash of his eyes I'd seen when he first sprang from his cell. He was some kind of shifter, clearly, though not from what I'd glimpsed any standard werewolf or kitsune. And he had more to him than that. I remembered the eyes, yeah, and I also remembered that tail.

Those now icy blue eyes gleamed starkly beneath his sharp brow. His Cupid's bow lips would have looked dainty, his rounded chin soft, if it wasn't for the firm set of his jaw. A sense of power and authority emanated off him so intensely I could almost taste it, like a spike of adrenaline and a tang of blood. He'd been around several centuries ago during the war of the angels, and I'd be willing to bet ages before that as well.

He ran his hand over the short, tawny hair slicked close to his skull and raised his gaze to meet mine. My heart lurched under his penetrating inspection, but I held myself still as if it hadn't affected me. He hadn't bothered to apologize for or even acknowledge the way he'd lashed out at me when I'd first freed him, though at least the scrape of his claws had barely broken my skin through the sleeve of my shirt. Pickle, perched on my shoulder, squirmed closer to my face with a nervous chirping sound.

Omen's mouth curled into a smile as chilly as his eyes. "Would the three of you care to explain the mortal in our midst?" He gave the word "mortal" a disdainful taint.

"They needed a leg up navigating the city and figuring out where you'd ended up in it," I said before the others had to admit to how we'd met. A twinge of protectiveness filled my chest. He didn't need to know they'd gotten themselves captured too—and by ordinary hunters no less. "I was happy to help. I was raised by a shadowkind woman. I pitch in where I can."

I'm not afraid of you. Well, maybe a teensy weensy bit, but he didn't need to know that either.

"She's part of that group of humans that advocate for mortal-side shadowkind," Ruse put in with a wave of his hand. "The something-or-other Fund."

Omen grimaced. "The do-gooders who haven't the guts to do half enough good to make a real difference. I know of them."

I bristled at his bland dismissal, but Snap leapt to my defense before I had to. "I don't know anything about the people Sorsha works with, but *she* doesn't have any shortage of courage. Or any other useful quality. We wouldn't have managed to find you, let alone break you out, if it wasn't for her."

Thorn, looming by the hood of the car, inclined his head. "She's lost a great deal serving our cause and yet refused to back down. I wouldn't hesitate to fight at her side again."

Omen considered his three compatriots with the same piercing focus he'd aimed at me. I wasn't sure what they might have given away about the other directions our relationships had veered in. Maybe the fact that they respected me on any level irked him.

"I thank you, then," he said finally, turning his attention back to me for a brief moment—and not sounding particularly grateful. "Forgive me my skepticism. I've just spent the last innumerable weeks being tortured by your kind; I'm not feeling the friendliest toward anyone mortal at the moment."

His gaze lingered on me a little longer, as if searching for some reaction to that statement beyond my tight smile of acceptance. A creeping sensation ran over my skin.

"Is that all they wanted?" Ruse said. "To torture higher shadowkind? It seems like an awful lot of trouble just for that."

"Oh, no, I'm sure they had a much more complex agenda." Omen rubbed his jaw. "They were attempting to accomplish something with their torment, to *discover* something, but they were careful not to say very much about it in my presence, so I can't say what. I do know, given their techniques, it can't bode well for us. As I suspected, there are humans making some sort of bid to sway the balance of power between mortal and shadowkind."

My stomach knotted. And we'd left that place standing and full of other captive beings who'd be subjected to even more of that torment. The words tumbled out. "We have to stop them."

Omen raised his eyebrows at me. "You sound as though you're including yourself in that 'we.'"

I lifted my chin. "Of course I am. The same bastards *killed* the woman who raised me. Even if it wasn't for that, they deserve to go down. I'm already all in. The rest of the Shadowkind Defense Fund will help as much as they can too, whatever you think of them."

"So you plan to go running back to them. Or did you think you'd join our little company? Keep in mind that the way we're going won't be easy even for us."

The truth was, I hadn't had much of a chance to think my options over. I hesitated for a second, but the answer came with a swell of certainty.

Maybe it was the connection I'd started to feel with all three of my trio. Maybe it was the fact that I suspected sticking around would *really* piss off the man who'd asked the question, and the more he talked, the more the idea of annoying him appealed to me.

Or maybe it was simply because I had to believe that if I was dealing with a devil, I'd be better off having him at my side than anywhere else in this battle.

The other three shadowkind were watching me too: Thorn in solemn silence, Ruse with a slyly crooked grin, and Snap braced, his face aglow with an indomitable hope that suggested he'd tackle me if I made any move to go.

Not that he'd need to. I shrugged as if I wasn't concerned about how much danger I'd face and said, "I'm here now. We ended up making a pretty good team."

When Omen smiled, his teeth glinted, even and white. I hadn't yet located the shadowkind part of him that lingered even in this guise. "Welcome on board," he said, in a tone that seemed to say, *We'll see about that.*

In that moment, I wasn't sure whether I faced more peril from the jailors we'd just fought off or the shadowkind man we'd rescued from them.

SHADOW THIEF - BONUS SCENE

What was it like for the shadowkind men when Sorsha rescued them from the collector's cages, and how did they end up following her home? This bonus scene shows the events in Chapter 1 from Thorn's perspective.

Thorn

The manner in which I was being confined was nearly as great an indignity as the fact that I'd been taken captive at all. Trapped in a cage behind silver and iron bars like some creature in the establishments mortals called "zoos"—as if I were a particularly large *bird*… It made my being prickle with shame and frustration, even contracted as I was into the thinnest fragment of shadow I could compress myself into.

If any of my wingéd brethren had seen me like this… Well, they might have said I deserved it after my long-ago failures. Perhaps they'd even be right. I didn't like to dwell on that possibility, but there wasn't a great deal else to think about as I whiled away the days under my jailor's far-too-avid eyes.

I'd lost the comrade I was serving to our enemy and then succumbed myself not long after. I hadn't been able to defend my two companions either. Now we were all restrained and on display for the sake of mortal curiosity.

It might not have been as epic a failure as the catastrophe centuries past, but it stung all the more for its freshness.

I'd already tried flexing my strength against my prison, but the silver and iron twined through every aspect of the cage drained my might far too quickly. The burning beams from the lamps fixed overhead seared away every hint of darkness that might have provided an escape route. As much as I disliked giving up, it'd seemed wisest to conserve what power I had left in case the situation presented some new opportunity in the future.

Even holding myself out of view in my shadow form was wearing on my energy. I'd fallen into a sort of daze, paying little attention to my surroundings, and so I didn't notice the newcomer in the room until she was almost in front of me.

The curtain that separated the area with our cages from the rest of the room hissed faintly as an unfamiliar figure eased past it. I stirred out of my stupor enough to study her. She wasn't any of the colleagues our captor had brought to view us from time to time, showing off his prized collection. She wasn't moving as if she believed she had a right to be here at all. Every motion spoke of stealth.

As did her garments. Her athletically toned form was clothed in all black, a few wisps of bright red hair peeking from beneath her matching cap. An odd blade with a supernatural gleam to it glinted in her hand. She cocked her head, peering at our three cages with a furrow between her brows, as though she hadn't expected to see them.

What in the realms was she doing?

She stepped toward us cautiously—and trod on the rug that lay on the floor. A shriek blasted through the room that startled me as much as it appeared to her.

More of our captor's protections. No one had ever set the alarm off in my presence before. The vibration of the piercing sound warbled through my nerves in a most unpleasant way.

I expected the woman to turn heel and flee. It would probably have been the wisest course of action. She did dart backward off the rug—but then she jerked to a stop and switched directions, sprinting toward me instead.

She moved so quickly I barely understood what was happening. She reached my cage, wrenched her strange blade against the lock on the door, and suddenly she was flinging the door wide. The prickling pressure of the noxious metals lessened in that gap. I was about to hurl myself toward it when she eased my passage even more with a swath of dark material she whipped at the light overhead.

In the flash of darkness, I launched myself past the bars. I caught just the faintest sense of her essence as I brushed past her, all fiery adrenaline, and then I was free, out in the open room, nothing constraining me any longer.

A lesser shadowkind might have raced from that wretched place without a glance behind. But I was responsible for my companions—I needed to think of them as well.

I whirled around in the thin shadows and discovered that the woman had already leapt to the second cage, the one I believed Snap had been shoved into. She split that lock, performed her trick with the cloth over the light, and then dashed to the third that held Ruse.

The devourer flitted through the filmy patches of darkness to reach me, his bewilderment radiating off his presence, still vibrant even after the long stretch in captivity. "Where are we? What's happening?" he asked in a tone both anxious and thrilled.

"We're getting out of there, and that's what matters," I said as the woman threw Ruse's cage door open.

We leapt to join the incubus as he slipped out, somehow giving a languid impression even when his very existence was at stake. "Well, back together at last," he said in the breezy tone that normally got on my nerves. I was too pleased by this turn of events to be anything other than delighted to hear it in that moment. "This is quite interesting."

I could sense him watching the woman. We needed to get out of this building now that we were reunited, but I couldn't help glancing back to see what our liberator was engaged in now.

A tangy chemical smell reached my senses through the shadows. Then the rug with its treacherous alarm burst into flames.

"Come on," I said, yanking at the two presences on either side of me. They sprang with me out the nearest window into the thicker darkness of the night, which wrapped around me with a wash of relief.

I felt my shadow form expanding into it, taking up the natural space it'd been denied in our prison.

As we paused there to gather ourselves, the black-clad woman followed our route. She couldn't slip through the darkened slivers along the windowpane, of course. Instead, she smashed straight through the glass.

Shards burst into the air. The woman flung a hook attached to a rope and swung to a utility pole several feet away, leaving the house behind. The wisdom of her clothing choice was clear, seeing her in the night. She blended into the darkness perfectly.

In her wake, a furious roar echoed through the house. Our captor must have realized belatedly that his home had been breached. A small measure of satisfaction filled me at the thought of his humiliation, even though I'd had no hand in it myself.

As I watched the woman slide down the pole to the sidewalk, a jab of concern shunted away any pleasure I'd gotten from the moment. What would our jailor do to her if he found out who was responsible? She'd been quick on her feet and nimble with that knife, but her physique wasn't that of a warrior. Did she have the means to defend herself?

Even *I* hadn't, so it seemed unlikely that one lone mortal could be prepared for the full brunt of our enemies' wrath.

"We're well rid of that villain," Ruse said, with the impression that he was dusting himself off. "Shall we—"

"We need to follow her," I said, already propelling myself forward through the overlapping swaths of shadow so I didn't lose sight of our savior.

My companions hurried after me, the devourer with typical eagerness and the incubus with a hint of irritation. "Why would we do that? We're out now. We should recuperate in the ways that suit us best and then get on with tracking down Omen." I had the sense that Ruse had raised an eyebrow. "Unless you have certain carnal hungers you're looking to satisfy? I thought that was all my domain."

I grunted in dismissal. "I'm not looking to bed her. She released us from our prison. She risked her mortal life to free us, and now those who took us captive will want revenge. We owe her an immense debt. We will continue our search for Omen, naturally, but we must defend her as well as we can in the meantime. *We'd* be villains if we left her to her fate."

"Yes!" Snap said brightly as he kept pace with me. "She was amazing. I didn't know humans had weapons that could cut through metal like that."

"They typically don't," Ruse put in. "She's clearly not your average mortal." He paused in consideration as we rushed around a bend in our pursuit. "I suppose there could be something to be said for recuperating in the home of an unusual mortal who's also generous to the shadowkind."

I shot him a look I knew he'd feel even though we couldn't exactly see each other merged with the darkness. "*You* aren't to pursue your carnal desires with her either. She isn't there for you to use."

The incubus let out a bark of a laugh. "I assure you I never force myself on any of my lovers or leave them feeling bereft. I promise that any fun I get up to with our lovely heroine will be only on her invitation."

I supposed that was the best I could ask for from a being of his disposition.

We followed the woman for quite a while longer before she finally disappeared into a store-top apartment. We traveled through the shadows cloaking the building and arrived in what I determined was a kitchen. The warble of running water sounded from a different room down the hall.

"What do we do now?" Snap asked, shifting restlessly. "Should we go talk to her—thank her for what she did?"

"She may not appreciate strange men appearing out of nowhere in her apartment in the middle of the night," Ruse pointed out.

"Then we will make our introductions in the morning," I said definitively. "We should take the time to rest so that we can present a more impressive gesture of gratitude when she awakens."

Ruse muttered something to himself that he didn't bother to share, so I ignored it. I could already feel the energies of my being rejuvenating from the strain our captivity had put me through.

For the rest of the night, we lingered in the shadows of the kitchen, gathering our strength. By the time the sun was beaming through the window, Snap wasn't the only one who'd gotten restless while our liberator and host slept on.

I stalked through the lingering shadows around the building to confirm no threat had yet appeared. Then we all emerged into physical form so we'd be prepared for her return to consciousness.

I settled into one of the chairs at the small table and examined a knife that had been left there, which looked ill-equipped for cutting anything with more resistance than water. Snap exclaimed over the contents of the cupboards and drawers until Ruse quieted him by offering him a bunch of fruit with which to occupy his mouth. The incubus proceeded to fill the sink with water and soap, swishing it to create an abundance of filmy bubbles. The devourer watched with widened eyes, utterly occupied for the time being.

And that was how the lady found us when she finally arrived in the doorway.

TWILIGHT CROOK

FLIRTING WITH MONSTERS #2

ONE

Sorsha

I hadn't always wanted to end the world, even after it'd started to seem that a significant portion of the world wanted to end *me*.

The specific people who'd been after me most recently might still be lurking on the other side of the plywood wall I was now eyeballing from the sidewalk across the street. I couldn't see much other than the skeleton of steel girders rising up above it.

Construction workers perched in their neon vests at various points across that skeleton. That was new. Before, it'd looked like the construction site that hid my enemies' secret facility was just a front. Surprise, surprise: apparently all those beams and boards were actually going to construct a building.

"Okay," I murmured. "I'm going in."

If you were watching, it'd have looked as if I crossed the road alone. I was counting on my monstrous companions—four of them now, up from a trio to a quartet—slinking after me through the shadows. More properly called "shadowkind," beings like them had gotten the name both because of the darkness of their natural realm and their ability to sink into and travel through the darkness in ours.

Which also conveniently meant they could leap out of that darkness and tackle anyone who tried to tackle me.

We were pretty sure the crew of monster hunters and torture-happy scientists we'd faced off against wouldn't attack me in broad daylight with multiple witnesses, but I wasn't tossing all caution to the wind. Three cheers for supernatural bodyguards!

The buzz of a saw carried from deeper within the construction site. As I walked over to the half-open gate where the workers had driven a couple of trucks in, the tang of fresh-cut pine wood in the warm summer air tickled my nose.

I'd kind of hoped that simply strolling in would get me where I wanted to go. A lot of the time, looking like you knew you were allowed to be someplace would convince everyone around you of it too. No such luck today.

A guy with a gray helmet, an orange vest, and a moustache so bushy a squirrel could have borrowed it as a substitute tail stepped into my path and held up his hand. "Where do you think you're going, Miss?"

For those of you taking notes: you can get good mileage out of a well-placed giggle too. "Oh," I said with a little laugh. "I'm sorry. Something of mine blew over the fence—I just wanted to grab it."

A couple of the other workers sauntered over. Mr. Moustache glanced around. "Do you see it here? I didn't notice anything."

I tapped my lips, pretending to scan our surroundings. "No, maybe it drifted farther in. Couldn't I just take a quick look around? It doesn't look like you're doing anything at the moment that'd make me fear for my life." I raised my eyes to the girders above.

One of the younger guys chuckled, but the moustache dude shook his head. "Sorry, Miss, but we could get in a lot of trouble if we let pedestrians wander around. What is it you lost? You can give us your contact information, and we'll keep an eye out for it."

It needed to be something that could have easily slipped from my hand and been caught in the wind. The words tumbled out before I'd given them much thought. "It was a napkin. A paper napkin with a phone number on it."

Did they look skeptical? I folded my arms over my chest and put on my most convincing tone. "It was from a really hot guy, okay? I don't want him to think I couldn't be bothered to shoot him a text."

The guy who'd chuckled now waggled his eyebrows. "We could give you a few phone numbers to make up for the loss."

Very funny. In reality, I was getting more than enough action these days. Sure, it was from men these dudes wouldn't believe existed, but that was part of what I liked about my new lovers.

Before I could answer, Mr. Moustache handled the come-on for me. "We haven't got time for this messing around. After all the delays on continuing construction, they'll hand us our asses if we don't get on with it." He bobbed his head to me. "If you give me *your* phone number, I promise I'll only call if one of us turns up your napkin."

I sighed dramatically. "Oh, well, if it's drifted off that far maybe it's just not meant to be. Can't fight destiny! Thanks for your help, though." I sauntered out without waiting for their response.

Since it wouldn't exactly do for the regular mortals to witness my monstrous companions emerging from the shadows as if appearing out of thin air, I couldn't confer with them until I reached the dim alley a few blocks down the street. A trash bin farther down the narrow space was baking in the summer heat, giving off a lovely bouquet of broiled kitchen scraps. I wrinkled my nose and glanced around to make sure no one human had followed me between the looming concrete walls.

A moment later, four figures solidified around me like smoke condensing into physical form.

"A hot guy's phone number on a napkin—really?" Ruse teased, his hazel eyes twinkling beneath the fall of his rumpled chocolate-brown hair. "Or have you already gotten bored with the pickings here?" The incubus gave me his typical smirk, which cracked a dimple in his roguishly gorgeous face. I'd "picked" him a couple of times already, and I was happy to report that getting it on with a sex demon was everything you'd expect from the package and more.

Next to Ruse, Snap's forehead had furrowed, barely putting a dent in the divine beauty that made him look like a youthful sun god. "The napkin was made up," he protested in his bright voice, and turned his moss-green gaze on me. "It *was* made up, wasn't it?"

I patted his slim arm. "A total fabrication. I have no phone numbers whatsoever, nor do I want any."

The devourer made a pleased humming sound and stepped closer—not to touch me, but as if he simply wanted to soak up my presence. I'd *also* gotten it on with Snap not that long ago, in a tamer if no less satisfying fashion while he eased into the whole concept of physical desire. What could I say? I'd been busy lately... although with a whole lot more than *getting busy*, I promise.

Waking up Snap's carnal awareness had also stirred up a possessive instinct I hadn't counted on but couldn't help finding kind of sweet. He might stand a full head taller than me, but he was about as frightening as a gamboling fawn. Of course, at this point I knew more about the feel of his body than why the others called him a devourer, which was still a mystery to me. Whatever his greatest power was, just the idea of it made *him* shudder in terror, so he hadn't exactly been eager to chat about it.

As usual, the third member of my original trio was all business. "It didn't appear as though you got close enough to make out anything of the inner facility, m'lady," Thorn said somberly. The ruggedly handsome hulk of a man, a smidge taller even than Snap and filled out with muscles galore, had never met a subject he couldn't approach with grave severity.

He could be plenty intimidating without even trying, although right now his imposing air was impaired by the little dragon squirming from one broad shoulder to the other, displacing Thorn's long white-blond hair with little snuffles of discontentment. Pickle hadn't spent much time around anyone other than me since I'd rescued him from a collector ages ago. It'd taken a lot of coaxing—and quite a bit of bacon—to warm the lesser shadowkind creature up to Thorn enough for him to let the warrior carry him into the shadows, out of mortal sight.

"I couldn't see anything," I agreed. "But it seems like a bad sign that construction has started up again. I can't imagine the sword-star group would let the workers wander around the site if there was anything incriminating left to see." The covert group of hunters, scientists, and who the hell knew what else we'd spent the past week battling marked some of their equipment with a symbol like a star with sword blades for two of its points, which was the only way we'd found to identify them so far.

The fourth shadowkind in our group—the one I'd only met last night after we'd broken him out of the facility that'd been hidden in the construction site—shifted on his feet. His voice held a ring of authority as cool as his icy blue stare. "I think you should hold off on making sweeping assumptions until we've had an actual look inside the place."

I wasn't totally sure what to make of Omen, the guy my trio referred to as their "boss." He shouldn't have stood out in the bunch—not as tall or as muscle-bound as Thorn, not as languidly sensual as Ruse or as breathtakingly dazzling as Snap. Other than those piercing eyes, he was attractive enough with his tawny, short-cropped hair and sharp features, but hardly otherworldly. I hadn't determined what monstrous feature he'd been unable to shed in his mostly human form, either. No shadowkind could pass for fully human on close inspection, as Thorn's crystalline knuckles, Snap's forked tongue, and the curved horns that poked from Ruse's hair could attest to.

All the same, Omen radiated power and menace with every movement of his body, every word that fell from those Cupid's bow lips. When we'd opened his cell last night, he'd lunged out more beast than man—he'd slaughtered two of the guards in a blink. That capacity for violence lurked somewhere beneath the controlled façade he was presenting now. At least with Thorn, who could be monstrously brutal too, the warrior frame and the scars lining his face served as plenty of warning.

Thorn adjusted that frame now, giving Pickle a careful nudge to keep the tiny dragon from tumbling right off him. "We could slip through the shadows right now to survey it. Two of us go and two stay to watch over Sorsha." He'd already smashed through an apartment building and torn heads from men's bodies to keep me safe—he took his self-assigned job as my protector even more seriously than he took most other things.

Omen had held up his hand before the warrior had even finished speaking. "No. Whatever we find, we'll want our devourer testing it to see what he can glean, and he can't do that while there are human witnesses around." He glanced at the sky. "It'll be a little longer before their work day is finished. Since we'll want a vehicle of our own to rely on as we proceed, we may as well take the opportunity to pick up my car and then return."

He definitely lived up to the title of boss—as in, bossy. Since we *had* just met, and I wasn't confident he didn't have some supernatural power that would eviscerate me if I pissed him off too much, I meant to keep my mouth shut and go along with his plan. The trouble was, the next words out of his mouth were to me, with a slight sneering edge: "Since you can't travel through the shadows, I'll give you the address. You can meet us there."

I blinked at him. "You're telling me to head across town on my own?" The other three had refused to let me out of their sight for more than a few minutes since they'd shown up at my apartment, even when I'd *wanted* them to let me handle one thing or another alone.

Omen gave me a narrow look. "I would have thought a woman of your many supposed talents could manage a simple cab ride."

"Well, yeah." But the sword-star crew had a bad habit of showing up unannounced, weapons blazing. I was only alive thanks to the efforts of my trio—my shoulder throbbed dully where I'd taken a bullet yesterday before Thorn had yanked me out of the way of one that would have blasted straight through my heart. It was still daytime, though, and I sure as hell wasn't going to let Bossypants make me look like a weakling.

"Here's a thought," Ruse said, smooth as ever. "A cab can whisk any of us across town much faster than we can flit through the shadows. Why don't I charm a driver into zipping us to our destination as one happy family?" He slung a playful arm over my shoulders and grinned at Omen.

Omen frowned, but even he didn't have the authority to change the fact that motorized vehicles offered superior speed. "Get on with it then," he said with a flick of his hand toward the street as if it'd been his idea in the first place, and rattled off the address.

He must have made some other gesture of command, because as Ruse strolled past us, Snap and Thorn faded into the patches of darkness that lined the alley. Omen lingered a moment longer, eyeing me with an intentness that set my nerves twitching, and then vanished as well.

The boss had put Ruse on his team for good reason. It took all of a minute before the incubus had a taxi driver eagerly beckoning us into the back seat of his cab as if we were great friends and letting him give us a ride was a huge favor to *him*. Ruse swept his arm toward the open door. "Ladies first."

The other three stayed out of sight, but I assumed they hopped from the shadows along the street into the darker corners of the cab. We couldn't see them, but from what I understood, they'd be able to see us just fine. I doubted Omen would eviscerate me in full view of at least one unknowing mortal, so this seemed like the perfect time to pay him back for his obvious disdain for my presence.

"Nicely done," I said to Ruse as the cabbie hit the gas, and scooted over to grasp the silky fabric of his shirt. The incubus flashed a brilliant smile before meeting me halfway for the kiss I'd planned to claim.

The moment his mouth caught mine, it was definitely him doing the claiming. Holy mother of mistletoe, the guy could kiss. Sure, bodily pleasures were his stock and trade, but still, mark this one A with a thousand pluses.

For a few seconds, I forgot where we were. I forgot the onlooker I'd meant to piss off. I was lucky I remembered my name. My lips parted for Ruse's sly tongue, and my body melted into his, my skin sparking where he trailed his fingers down my side.

Why had we put a hold on our very enjoyable nighttime escapades again? Oh yeah, because he'd broken his promise and used his paranormal voodoo to take a peek inside my head. But he'd told me why with an explanation I could believe, and he'd been on excellent behavior since. I should definitely look into rewarding that behavior soon, shouldn't I, especially since the reward would be gratifying for both of us?

The driver gave a little cough, and that broke me out of the bliss enough to ease back. Heat crept over my cheeks. Ruse shot me another smile, but I'd swear even he looked a tad flushed. I gave myself a mental high five. If Omen was fuming right now, especially since he couldn't actually tell us to knock it off, so much the better.

The cab took us to a derelict storage facility on the outskirts of the city. Most of the garage-style doors were dented and rusted, many of them half-open with only dust and litter scattering the cement floors beyond. But the place must have been at least somewhat operational, because the unit Omen strode straight to had its lock in place and no sign of deterioration. He jerked up the door to reveal...

"You drive a station wagon?" I said, unable to keep the incredulous note out of my voice.

Omen shot me a frigid glance and patted the boxy brown hood. "Betsy here is as reliable as they come, and when evading one's enemies, that matters much more than glitz. She's also got a glamour on her windows that gives a false impression of who's inside, courtesy of a former fae associate of mine. I do *also* have a motorcycle, but that's kept elsewhere."

And it wouldn't really lend itself to carting all five of us around town, at least not when the others were in physical form. But seriously —he'd named his car *Betsy*? I held in a snicker, but the sharpening of his glare suggested he'd noticed the twitch of my lips. I did have to admit that the glamour spell would be awfully useful for keeping the pricks we were up against off our backs.

Thorn peered into the darkness of the storage unit, where wooden crates and metal chests were stacked along the walls around the car. "This space could also serve as a place for Sorsha to sleep—out of the way, and—"

Omen spun to face him, cutting him off with a curt voice. "Don't be ridiculous. Would you have her lead this group right to my stash? We shouldn't linger here any longer than we already have."

Thorn looked so stricken my throat constricted at the sight. It wasn't an expression that belonged on a man of so much strength. "My apologies," he said quickly. "I should have thought the matter through more carefully."

"It seems you haven't been very careful with your thinking in general these past few months, or I wouldn't have spent most of those months acting as a lab rat for a coterie of vicious mortals. Why don't you keep your mouth shut from now on and let me do the thinking?"

I hadn't realized it was possible for the warrior's face to fall even more. Bristling on his behalf, I lost control of my tongue.

"*You're* the one who got yourself trapped by those mortals," I said. "You have no idea how much Thorn has been busting his ass trying to get you back. He's the most dedicated person—being—whatever—I've ever met, often to the point of being incredibly irritating about it. So maybe you should shut up about things you apparently know nothing about."

I could tell Thorn had turned to look at me, but I didn't dare take my eyes off of Omen to check the warrior's reaction. I'd given Thorn a hard time about his single-mindedness in the past, but he'd proven he was holding in plenty of real emotion under that strict exterior—and plenty of passion I'd only gotten a taste of so far. He'd beaten himself up enough for failing to prevent Omen's capture without the very person he'd been obsessively trying to rescue adding to that agony. I wasn't going to stand around while this jackass laid into him for the one thing he couldn't possibly be criticized for.

If I'd thought Omen's gaze was frigid before, now it was cold enough to flay me down to the bones. His carefully slicked-down hair had risen in little tufts as if propelled by a swelling rage. My hands clenched at my sides as I braced myself for an onslaught of anger, but he kept his voice as tartly cool as before.

"If you hadn't insisted on crashing this party, none of us would need to worry about where you spend the night in the first place. Don't make yourself too much of a hassle."

The implied threat sent a shiver down my spine. Why had Omen agreed to keep me around anyway?

It could have been because of the emphatic references I'd gotten from his companions. Snap stepped closer to me, curling his long, slender fingers around my fist in solidarity. "It's because of Sorsha we managed to find and free you at all. She's just as important as any of us."

Pickle let out a chirping sound of what might have been agreement, fluttering his wings anxiously. He lost his hold on Thorn's tunic and ended up clinging to the warrior's hair in his panic to hurl himself back onto his perch. Thorn unfastened him with a long-suffering sigh, but a hint of a smile crossed his lips. I hustled over to take my sort-of pet off his hands.

Omen watched all of this with the same detached disdain and then shook his head. "We'll see," he said darkly. "For now—all of you, in the car. Let's discover what's left of my former prison."

To my relief, he drove with more care than Ruse did, making it back to the neighborhood of the construction site without prompting a single blared horn. By that time, I'd determined that the middle cushion in the back seat popped out to allow access to the trunk and had let Pickle scuttle through. The little dragon was now soothing himself by constructing a nest out of an old plaid blanket that'd been folded there. I decided I wouldn't mention to Omen that his beloved Betsy might end up with her felted trunk lining shredded.

The sun had sunk below the roofs of the nearby high-rises, but the summer evening was still warm and relatively bright. Thorn stole through the shadows around the site before giving us the go-ahead: no sign of the sword-star bunch. Around the back of the site, he hefted a section of the barrier wall aside to let me walk in while the others took the shadow route.

The half-finished framework of steel and cinderblocks wasn't exactly welcoming in the late afternoon light, but it provoked a lot fewer goosebumps than it had in the eerie glow of security lamps through the darkness last night. I suppressed a wince at the creak of the metal beams above in a gust of wind. Then my feet stalled in their tracks as I came into view of the facility we'd stormed last night.

Or rather, *didn't* come into view of it—because where the concrete building with its flood lamps had stood less than twenty-four hours ago, there was nothing but bare, packed earth and a shallow pit of rubble.

As I gaped, my shadowkind companions emerged around me. Ruse let out a low whistle.

A disbelieving laugh sputtered out of me. "These people don't do things by halves, do they?" Just yesterday morning, they'd battered one of their own men beyond identification to cover their tracks. I shouldn't be surprised.

We ventured closer, Thorn striding ahead to patrol the wreckage, but it didn't take long to determine that our enemies had left nothing incriminating or useful behind, only smashed concrete. Snap bent over various spots around the pit, flicking his forked tongue into the air just above the chunks to test for impressions that might still be clinging to them, but more hope seeped out of his face with each attempt.

Omen had lingered near me by the edge of the clearing, letting his companions do the work. No trace of emotion showed on *his* face—not discomfort at returning to the site of his torment, nor satisfaction at seeing the place in pieces, nor frustration at how utterly our enemies had obliterated the evidence of their activities.

There'd been several other shadowkind experimental subjects being held in the facility—beings we hadn't gotten the chance to free. We hadn't managed to figure out what exactly their painful experiments were meant to accomplish either.

"We have to find out where they've taken the other shadowkind," I said. "And then shut down the sword-star crew's operations completely. They can't keep getting away with this."

Omen didn't move. "Obviously."

That was all he had to say about it? I frowned at the barren stretch of ground. "It was hard enough getting just you out with the four of us working together. There are plenty of shadowkind who come mortal-side regularly or even live in this realm these days. Maybe we could ask around and see if any of them would join—"

Bossypants interrupted me with a dismissive snort. "Have you *met* many of our kind that linger in this realm? They're no less self-involved here than they are back in the shadows. All they care about is themselves and perhaps their immediate circle. The greater good of our people means nothing to them if it requires them to lift a finger. Why do you think I was tackling this menace with such a small group to begin with?"

I *had* seen those selfish attitudes in other shadowkind. The group of humans I worked with to protect the creatures that traveled into our realm had reached out to local shadowkind gangs and the like before, but they rarely opted to get involved unless it affected them directly. Still…

"This is a much bigger deal than solo hunters or small collectives snaring lesser shadowkind for profit. All the higher shadowkind are at risk. Don't you think that would matter to the others?"

Omen grimaced. "If it did, this 'sword-star crew' would never have managed to establish themselves as firmly as they have."

He vanished into the shadows, putting a definitive end to that discussion. Such a lively conversationalist.

With a grimace of my own, I picked my way along the fringes of the clearing. Maybe a bit of useful debris had blown this way in the midst of the destruction and been missed during the clean-up. I scanned the piles of boards and the interlocking beams to see if anything caught my eye, squinting into the lengthening shadows of the approaching evening.

I'd made it about halfway around the destroyed facility when a warbling sound from above caught my ears.

My head jerked up. I flinched and stumbled backward just in time to dodge a streak of fire that plummeted down at me.

The blazing thing whooshed past me close enough to singe a few flyaway strands of my hair before it hit the ground. My pulse lurched. The flames flared higher, and I scrambled farther back, my arms flying up defensively. A bolt of pain shot through my bandaged shoulder. The fire flickered in the opposite direction and then slowly dwindled as its fuel ran out.

As I lowered my arms and edged closer to the now only smoldering object, Thorn charged over with Snap and Ruse close at his heels. I clenched my jaw against the ache still burning in my shoulder, and we all stared at the thing that had nearly landed on me like a flaming toupee.

It was a charred... pair of work jeans? Yep, with a sharp chemical scent that indicated how the fire had caught on them so enthusiastically. The fabric must have been dosed in some kind of lighter fluid and then been tossed down from above.

Thorn sprang back into the shadows, presumably to search for my attacker. Snap checked me over carefully. His eyes stark with concern, he fingered the singed strands of my hair, which he'd admiringly compared to the color of a peach when we'd first met.

I took his hand in mine with a reassuring squeeze. "I'm all right. The jeans, not so much."

Ruse cocked his head, still considering them. "Well, that is something, all right."

I peered up at the gridwork and knit my brow. Who would have done that—*why* would anyone have done that? There were a hell of a lot more deadly things here than discarded construction pants.

A nervous quiver ran through my chest, but I wasn't going to be shaken by something this ridiculous, not if I could help it. Mangling the lyrics from my favorite '80s songs always bolstered my spirits. I waved my hand in front of my nose and sang a little tune: "This is what it smells like when gloves fry."

While Ruse snickered, Snap knelt down. His tongue flitted through the smoke. "A man was wearing them this morning—he spilled something sticky and black on them, had to change, left them in a waste bin. I can't sense anything after that." He frowned.

Omen had returned to join us sometime during the chaos. He contemplated the burnt jeans, the structure around us, and then me, his gaze so penetrating I could almost feel it digging through my skull. "Fire seems to like you."

"A lot of the time, I like it too, but only when I'm the one setting things up in flames." I resisted the urge to hug myself. "Someone's messing with us. Trying to keep us on our toes."

"You're lucky you didn't get the slightest bit burned."

What was he implying—that I'd been prepared for fiery legwear to fall on my head? "Three cheers for good reflexes," I said.

Thorn burst out of the shadows so abruptly the air rippled against my skin. "There's no one else on the site right now. Either it was another shadowkind who slipped away quickly or a trick set to go off automatically."

Ruse raised his hand. "Seeing as we weren't getting anything useful out of this ruin anyway, I'd like to vote that we take off before any other 'tricks' come at us."

I expected Omen to argue like he seemed to whenever anyone other than him suggested a course of action. Instead, he nodded. "We aren't getting any farther here."

He stared at me for a moment longer before shifting his attention to the incubus. "Why don't we make use of that computer adept you mentioned? Our enemies will have left a trail somewhere—we just need to pick it up, and quickly."

TWO

Sorsha

I WAS STARTING TO NOTICE THAT OMEN'S STATION WAGON HAD A particular smell to it. I inhaled deeply where I was sitting in the back seat, trying to place it. A hint of charcoal, a little salt, something a bit chalky, and a note that was maybe… meaty? Brick-oven pizza, I thought, except it was hard to picture Bossypants chowing down on a slice in his beloved Betsy. Anyway, the scent was too dry, no tomato-y juiciness.

While I contemplated the lingering odor, Ruse, who'd kept his physical form, gabbed away at his boss about the hacker he'd worked his charms on.

"Managed it over the phone," he said, leaning back in his seat with his arms crossed behind his head. "It only took a few minutes before we were such close friends she'd happily delve into an obviously stolen computer. A little internet tracing shouldn't be any problem at all. The original effect won't have worn off much yet, so it'll hardly be any work."

"Wonderful," Omen replied in a voice so devoid of emotion I couldn't tell whether he was truly pleased or being sarcastic, but Ruse's commentary had reminded me of another responsibility. I owed my one actual close friend a call.

I settled deeper into the worn leather cushioning of the back seat, which I had to admit was pretty comfy, and pulled out my phone. Vivi had inadvertently gotten herself tangled up in our conflict with the sword-star crew despite my efforts to keep her out of the line of fire. Okay, maybe even because of those efforts. My caginess had gotten her so worried about me that she'd tracked me down while we were following the bad guys and blown our cover. Since the baddies would have seen the car she was driving, which belonged to her grandmother, I'd ordered them both to go into hiding.

Vivi picked up on the first ring. "Sorsha?"

Hearing her vibrant voice sent a wash of relief through me. "The one and only. I take it you're still hanging in there out at that cottage?"

"Yeah, just bored." A matching relief sparkled through her laugh. "I'm so glad you're okay. I've been spinning out crazier than a cuckoo bird in a blender wondering what's going on."

Vivi had a way with metaphors. I cracked a grin. "Well, we solved one bit of the problem, but we've got a much bigger part to tackle next. The assholes who murdered Meriden are still on the loose, so you'd better hang tight."

"Actually…" I could practically see her twirling one of her tight ringlets around her index finger. "All this time cooped up gave me a chance to think about return strategies. I might have figured out a way I could come back—and give you a real hand—without doom raining down on me."

My chest tightened a little at the idea of my best friend back here in the line of fire, but I'd promised her I wouldn't keep shutting her out like I had before. And to be fair, staying clammed up hadn't protected either of us in the end. Vivi had grown up with parents who knew about and wanted to protect the shadowkind. Not the same as being outright raised by a fae woman like I'd been, but while she wasn't quite as comfortable with supernatural beings as I was, she did have a pretty clear idea of what she was signing up for.

"All right," I said. "Lay it on me."

"Well, I figure the main way these people have of identifying me or Gran is through her car. What if I go to the police and report that it was stolen a few days ago? I'll park it somewhere sketchy but obvious, maybe even call in an anonymous tip too so they'll find it fast, and then Gran has her car back but it sounds like we weren't involved in anything it was used for lately. Smooth as butter on a porcelain vase."

"Hmm." I kind of wanted to pick that plan apart so I had an excuse to keep Vivi where she was safe, but the truth was it sounded pretty solid. "Are you sure the baddies couldn't have seen it parked at your Gran's house in between your scouting missions? Besides the car, what about the questions you were asking Meriden's neighbors?"

"Nah, I parked it in a paid lot overnight just in case. And when I talked to the few people I spoke to in person, I had my hair covered by my hood and big sunglasses on—I don't think they could give a very accurate description of me. I can be a *little* stealthy."

I hesitated, wavering between the guilt over shutting my best friend out before and the guilt I knew I'd feel if I led her into more danger.

"Come on, Sorsh," Vivi wheedled. "Let me pitch in. You let me know what you need, and I'll be there, no other messing around."

She might be safer here in the city with a cover story for the car than she was staying in hiding with the sword-star bunch believing she was involved. "Okay. Handle the car thing like you said, and then don't do *anything* you wouldn't normally do until we have a chance to talk more in depth."

"You've got it." She made an air-kiss sound. "Ditto."

"Ditto," I replied, my smile coming back. Our shared love of corny movies included *Ghost*, which had inspired our trademark farewell.

As I hung up, Omen was just pulling up to the corner on a residential street. He glanced back at me, his gaze as intense as ever. "It never occurred to you that I'd expect you to keep quiet about our activities."

My shoulders tensed automatically. "That was my best friend—the one who already knows all about the shadowkind and that I'm onto something big?" He'd gotten most of the story in roundtable fashion from the four of us last night. "She's been advocating for beings like you her whole life through the Shadowkind Defense Fund. There may be ways she can help. After what she saw yesterday, she knows how serious the situation is."

"Having one mortal in the mix is bad enough."

"Well, she's involved now, so you're shit out of luck."

I kept my tone flippant, but Omen's eyes narrowed anyway. "If she compromises our mission, I'll ensure she can't interfere anymore."

My whole back stiffened. "You don't have to worry about that." *And if you lay one hand on my bestie, you'd better believe the next place you'll find that hand is rammed up your ass.*

Ruse cleared his throat and pointed to a house on the far corner of the block. "That's the place. Basement apartment, separate entrance. We want to encourage our hacker friend to dig up anything she can about the sword-star group's activities, right?"

"Particularly anything that could tell us where they're operating from," Omen said. "Any regular hunting groups or meet-up spots for their business dealings. But you don't need to remember all that. I'm coming with you. After everything that's happened, I think each of you could use plenty of supervision."

"Sure. Absolutely. The more the merrier." Ruse chuckled, but he'd tensed at the implied criticism.

"Thorn. Snap." Omen peered into the shadows next to me. Before he'd opened his mouth again, the other two shadowkind had emerged, so abruptly I found myself squeezed against the door to make room. Thorn could have used a whole back seat to himself.

Snap gave me an apologetic peck on the temple before turning to his boss with an eager gleam in his eyes. "How can I help?"

"I want the two of you patrolling the streets, making sure no one has followed us or takes too much interest in Betsy here. And since I'd like to keep this 'merry'—Sorsha, you're coming with Ruse and me. It may be useful to have a mortal around in this particular situation."

I rubbed my ears in disbelief, but his impatient gesture and Snap's proud beaming suggested I'd heard him correctly. "You'll see how much she can help," the devourer said. He pressed another kiss to my cheek before vanishing back into the shadows with Thorn.

"I'm sure I will," Omen said without much enthusiasm, and shoved open his door.

Somehow I suspected Omen's request was more about not trusting me alone in his car—as if *I* might shred the cushions like some kind of wild animal… or, well, like Pickle—than about him developing any respect for my talents. I wasn't going to look a gift horse in the mouth, though. The sooner I proved those talents to him, the sooner he'd put a lid on his condescending comments.

"This mortal is a little... quirky," Ruse said in a low voice as we walked over to the house he'd pointed out as the hacker's. "And I picked up on a certain amount of defensiveness about that. So, let me recommend that you keep any opinions about her clothing choices and décor to yourselves."

He'd called ahead so the woman would be expecting him. As he knocked on the back entrance that was down a flight of stairs from the backyard patio, I braced myself not to react to head-to-toe goth-gear, a raver's rainbow hair and glitter, or possibly a furry costume. It takes all sorts, after all.

I still wasn't prepared.

"Into the Cavern! Quickly!" hissed the figure who opened the door. A figure in full purple latex bodysuit complete with a yellow blaze of lightning on the chest, a glinting black utility belt, matching black vinyl platform boots, and a black cape she whirled with a dramatic *swish*.

Our hacker apparently saw herself as Superhero of the Cybernet, with all the trappings. I managed to keep my expression blasé as we stepped into her apartment, but it was a near thing.

She'd modeled the "Cavern" after the Bat Cave: a huge array of computer screens at one end, glass cases holding a couple of costume changes and assorted comic-book-esque weaponry next to it, slate-gray paint from concrete floor to ceiling, and light streaming in hazy beams from a circle of pot lights mounted overhead. A moped decked out with metallic black plating leaned against the wall by the entrance. Hoo, boy.

I brushed against the moped as we squeezed into the small space between all her equipment, and something flicked against my arm with a scaly swipe. I clamped my mouth shut before I could yelp in surprise, but Ms. Super Hacker here must have noticed.

"Don't mind Freddie," she said briskly, and plopped into a massive leather chair with an arched back that looked more suited to a super villain than a hero. I squinted at the moped and made out a hunched form with scales that blended into the black seat and the gray walls.

She had a pet chameleon. Named Freddie. Right. I should have brought Pickle along for a playdate.

The hacker chugged from an energy drink sitting on the workspace in front of her and waggled her fingers over one of her three keyboards. This one had a green glow around the elevated keys. She glanced up at Ruse with a grin. "What can I do for you tonight?"

The incubus obviously didn't need to do any more charming. He propped himself in front of the farthest screen and gave her a languidly warm smile in return. "It might be a little tricky, but I'm sure you're up to the task. We can't have anyone noticing what you were digging into, though. Our lives could be at stake."

The woman's expression turned more solemn. She nodded briskly. "You can count on me. I'd give my own life before I let those I fight for come to harm."

"Let's hope it doesn't come to that," Ruse said wryly. "We have reason to believe there are people in this city looking to purchase supernatural beings of particular power, as well as hiring mercenaries of some sort for security details. We'd also like to check for any mentions of activity around a construction site last night."

He gave her the address and a few other details that might help narrow down her search, and she dove into the world wide web as enthusiastically as if it were the Fortress of Solitude. The glow of the screens turned her pale face almost luminescent.

There didn't appear to be anything for me to do here. Of course, it wasn't as if Omen was contributing in some brilliant way either. He drifted over to the display shelves, running his finger over what looked like a ray-gun and then lifting a katana to study the arc of its blade.

"Hmm," Ms. Super Hacker said, more to herself than to us. "This could be—oops, no, I didn't need to see that many boobs all on one lady... What about—oh, that's a shipment of counterfeit plushies. Hmm... Yikes. 'Seeing you waiting at the bus stop, I couldn't help succumbing to the radiation of your smile'—nope, definitely not, lots of luck with that missed connection, weirdo. Hey, this is an interesting thread."

She leaned even closer to the screen, as if she might climb right into it in another minute or two. I ambled a little closer, but she was opening and swiping away windows too fast for me to make out much of what she'd unearthed.

Omen was still exploring her display cases with a rustle here and a clink there. I glanced around the rest of the room, searching for an opportunity to show I was more than dead weight. A stack of ramen packages sat on a little shelving unit in front of the moped. Maybe I could offer to cook her up a snack?

Wait, was I reading that right? She had… barbeque octopus balls flavor. And let's not forget the evergreen classic, mocha cheddar corn. Where the hell had she picked up those? More importantly—I averted my face so she wouldn't see me wrinkle my nose—*why*?

She tapped away at the keyboard some more with a rattle like machine-gun fire. I turned to examine the arsenal Omen had found so fascinating—just as he swiveled away from the cases with a metallic flash.

The curved dagger he'd picked up sliced across my bare forearm. A stinging pain sprung up along the line he'd carved. I did yelp then, yanking my arm back toward me so fast a fresh pang echoed through my other shoulder with its bandaged wound. Blood welled along the cut.

Omen swiveled the weapon in his hand with a practiced grace and set it back on the shelf. "I didn't see you there," he said, in the least apologetic-sounding apology ever, and grabbed my hand to yank my injured arm into one of the streams of light. "Let's see the damage."

Ruse had straightened up, eyeing Omen warily and me with a warmer concern. "We can't have you carving up our mortal. Are you all right, Miss Blaze?"

"It isn't much more than a scratch," I had to admit, but the pain was still nibbling across my skin with a similar sensation to the prick of Pickle's claws. Omen was studying the wound as if he thought he'd find the meaning of life in the slow seeping of my blood. An uneasy quiver raced down my spine.

Had that really been an accident, or had it been some kind of test to see my reaction? If it was a test, what in Waldo's name was he looking for?

And had I passed?

Our superhero had glanced up. Seeing my arm, she turned slightly green. She jerked her gaze away, her balance wobbling in her seat.

Fainting at the sight of a tiny bit of blood—not a great quality in a caped avenger.

"There's a first aid kit in the bathroom," she said in a tight voice, waving toward a door in the far corner. Ruse hustled over there while Omen raised my arm to catch the light better. He was frowning as if I'd managed to disappoint him somehow. Had he expected me to produce skin of steel?

Whatever he'd intended, he definitely didn't look remotely worried about my well-being. As Ruse returned, brandishing an adhesive bandage, my stomach knotted. Omen dropped my hand and stepped away, all trace of emotion vanishing.

I couldn't trust him, clearly—couldn't rely on him to care whether he chopped my arm in two. And as long as Bossypants held me in such contempt, I couldn't totally count on my trio either. As much as they'd supported me, they still followed his orders. They'd never leave me in danger on purpose, but all it would take was one risky situation where they couldn't get to me fast enough because he'd occupied them elsewhere, and my ass would be kaput.

As long as the shadowkind quartet were the only people at my back, at least. Vivi was coming home—and maybe I should start thinking about what other allies I could round up who'd follow my lead more than Omen's.

Ms. Super Hacker must have recovered from her blood-induced queasiness. She let out a cry of victory and drummed her hands on the console in front of her.

"I've got something. Someone's set up an exchange to happen in just a couple of days—potent creature of unusual inclinations. Isn't that exactly what you were looking for?"

A hint of a smile curled Omen's lips, but I couldn't say I found it reassuring. "I believe it is. Let's hear the full story."

THREE

Sorsha

I WAS STUMBLING THROUGH THE DARK HALLWAY OF A HOUSE. OUR HOUSE, the one Luna had rented the first floor of—and Luna was there by the door, so tense her skin had broken out in its supernatural sparkle. I could almost see the flutter of her fae wings behind her back.

"My shoes," I said, clutching the duffel bag I'd kept packed for emergencies, my head full of a sleepy haze. I had no idea what this emergency was, only that my guardian had shaken me awake with an urgent hiss of my name. "I can't find them—"

"Never mind that. Someone's coming, Sorsha. I can feel it. Wear these, and we'll go." She grabbed her sparkly sneakers off the shoe rack and shoved them at me. As I tugged them on, they pinched my toes. Her feet were at least a size smaller than mine.

"Are you sure we're actually in danger?" I whispered as she eased the door open. The only real concern my self-centered sixteen-year-old brain could process was: where the hell were we going to go *now*? "We've moved how many times already, and no one's ever—"

She tugged me with her outside, ignoring my protests. As Luna crossed the lawn, I stopped to try to wriggle my feet more solidly into the shoes. When I looked up, she'd reached the sidewalk—and several figures sprang at her from the night.

Whips that seemed formed of light slashed through the air; a blade flashed; someone hurled a glinting net. Luna whirled around with a shocked squeal. The bindings squeezed tight around her skinny form before I could so much as cry out. Her body shuddered—and then burst into a firework of sparks.

I jolted awake with my shriek still locked in my throat. The air around me was glittering, but it was the gleam of sunlight through crystal, not the sparkly shattering of my guardian's death. Sunlight through several crystals, actually—there were about a dozen of them dangling from silver chains in front of the window in the little cabin we'd found not too far outside of town.

The clang of horror faded from my nerves. I rubbed my forehead and sat up, but my stomach stayed clenched.

The fae woman I'd called Auntie Luna—the woman who'd saved me from the hunters who'd murdered my parents, who'd given me the best mortal childhood a shadowkind could, who'd never made me feel anything less than unreservedly loved—had died more than eleven years ago. I hadn't dreamed about that night in ages. It brought the same old questions back to nibble at me: if I'd just moved a little faster, left my own freaking shoes somewhere I could easily put my feet into like she'd reminded me a million times…

But all those what ifs didn't change the fact that she'd died at the hands of attackers with the same weapons the sword-star crew used, at least one of those weapons marked with that sword-star symbol. I might have screwed up, but *they* were the ones who'd killed her. While I couldn't change anything I'd done back then, there was plenty I could do to make them regret *their* life choices now.

They weren't going to get away with what they'd done to her or any of the other shadowkind. Including Omen, as big of an asshole as he could be. On the balance of things, I'd take him over the men with whips and nets any day.

Rolling my shoulders carefully to test the injured one, I got up. It appeared the property we'd ended up on had once been used for New Age-y retreats. Along with the crystals, three bunk beds were crammed into the single open-concept room between posters with nature photos and encouraging phrases like, "Believe in the sunshine of your spirit!" We'd found a heap of rolled yoga mats in the shed outside. But based on the dust that had coated nearly every surface and the weeds choking the driveway, no one had made use of the place in months, if not years.

I stepped out into the yard where Omen had parked the Oldsmobile under the shelter of an oak tree hung with fraying dreamcatchers. They swayed in the warm morning breeze. In that first second, it appeared I was alone on the property. Then my four shadowkind friends shimmered from the shadows into the daylight.

They didn't look all that friendly. Omen's mouth was set in a tight smile, his gaze holding its usual chill as it came to rest on me. The other three were watching him. Thorn stood with muscles tensed, his frown even deeper than usual, and Ruse's expression looked uncharacteristically serious. Snap's eyes had widened with worry.

"There's no need for all this fuss," Omen said, clearly picking up the thread of a conversation they'd been having out of my hearing. "If she's half as competent as you've spent so much time trying to convince me she is, she'll handle this without any trouble at all."

"But we shouldn't be trying to make things harder for Sorsha," Snap protested.

I walked over, raising my eyebrows. "What exactly am I supposed to be handling that's so very hard?"

Ruse's lips twitched as the incubus no doubt thought up a few suggestive remarks he could make in response, but he settled for a subdued smirk. Omen lifted his chin with the authoritarian air that was getting on my nerves more each day.

"We're attempting to turn the tables on our enemies at the hand-off tomorrow evening," he said. "Enemies who've already proven themselves very skilled at overwhelming us. If you're going to play any part in the ambush, I want to be sure your mortal clumsiness won't ruin our chances."

If I was so clumsy, he was lucky I didn't trip right now and accidentally ram my knee into his junk. But sure, he hadn't seen me in action—maybe it was understandable for him to be skeptical. I'd just bash that skepticism into the stratosphere, and if he was still being a jerk after that, then we'd see where my knee ended up.

I shrugged. "Fine. Hit me with your best shot."

Omen swept his arm toward the other men. "You see. She doesn't require your protection."

"She does occasionally take on more than even a shadowkind would think is wise," Thorn muttered. To be fair, it was true that he might not have needed to save me from any bullets if I hadn't insisted on handling that job alone.

"I'm sure Omen doesn't have anything *too* horrifying in mind," I said, and smiled sweetly at the other guy. "Do you?"

Omen gave me an expression even more openly disdainful than usual. "We'll start with this: my colleagues and I will take Betsy into the city. *You* will make your own way there, by whatever means you can come up with. I expect to see you at the Finger no later than noon."

It was a trip of nearly a hundred miles, and it was already past nine. Ruse tsked with teasing disapproval. "I did hear you like to play hardball with the mortals, Luce."

"Luce?" I repeated.

"Short for Lucifer." Ruse cocked his head toward Omen. "Not that the actual prince of Hell actually exists—or Hell itself the way humans conceive of it, for that matter—but from what I understand, our boss here used to make a game out of convincing mortals he held the title."

Omen cut his icy eyes toward the incubus. "That was a long time ago and is hardly relevant. I'd rather you did away with the nickname."

"But it suits you so well. You even have the tai—"

"Enough!" Omen barked. "You're wasting her time." His tawny hair rippled, a few tufts rising. So, there were a few topics that could get Bossypants emotional. Interesting.

And what had Ruse been going to say he had? The memory rose up of the tail with the devilish tip I'd caught a glimpse of when Omen had sprung from his prison cell in beastly form. Maybe *that* was the shadowkind feature he kept even in human form—the slacks he was wearing were loose enough to conceal it.

I yanked my gaze from Omen's behind to his face before it became too noticeable that I was checking out his ass, as fine an ass as it was. Such a pity it was attached to a massive jerk.

My time to complete his challenge was ticking away. How in holy heathens was I going to make it downtown in less than three hours without a vehicle? Even if taxis came out this far into the middle of nowhere, my phone had no reception here.

Back out now, and I'd never live it down. I waved toward the car. "Go on, then. I'll see you at the Finger by noon."

Omen strode toward the station wagon. The others followed more hesitantly, Snap lingering on the lawn until I shot him a smile more confident than I actually felt. He immediately smiled back, beaming back at me with so much certainty in my abilities that I had a spring in my step when I ducked into the cabin to grab my backpack full of my cat-burglar gear.

As I re-emerged, Betsy roared away down the dirt driveway. I slung the straps over my shoulders, careful of the bandaged wound, and set off at a jog. No time for dillydallying, as my Luna would have said.

It was hard to imagine what she'd make of the woman I'd grown into. Would she have been proud of everything I'd done to rescue the mistreated shadowkind in this world so far or horrified by how much I'd stuck my neck out? True to Omen's comments about shadowkind attitudes, during the time I'd been with her she'd never shown concern for anyone other than the two of us. I could easily imagine her racing past a hundred caged creatures to spare me from a splinter.

She definitely wouldn't have approved of the all-black outfit I wore for my thievery—I knew that much. Stealth and sparkles really didn't mix.

I headed down the New-Age retreat's overgrown driveway to a quiet road bordered by fallow fields, stretches of woodland, and the occasional farm house. As I loped alongside the ditch, I scanned all of those for anything worth putting those thieving skills to use on.

The sun crept up across the sky, and the heat intensified with it. Sweat trickled down my back.

I must have covered at least a couple of miles before I spotted my salvation: a mud-splattered bicycle leaning against a fence post, ratty tassels drooping from the ends of its handlebars. Not my typical plunder—I was more a gems and rare coins kind of gal—but right now I'd take that bike over the Hope Diamond.

No, let's be real: I'd take the Hope Diamond, but then I'd steal the bicycle too.

It was obviously a kid's bike, but a big kid's, at least. I couldn't have pedaled it while perched on the seat without hitting my chin with my knees. So, I gripped the gritty plastic handlebars and took off with my ass up in the air like I was about to race in the Tour de France.

As methods of transportation go, you'd be better off not following my lead. I bounced along the potholed country roads for the better part of an hour, until my thighs and back ached almost as badly as my wounded shoulder, and my eyes were stinging with sweat. Thankfully, my vision wasn't so blurry that I missed the delivery truck at the pumps of a gas station up ahead.

The delivery truck with its back door ajar.

There weren't many places around here that a truck that size would be taking its cargo to. I dropped the bike at the edge of the station and slunk over. The driver had his elbow leaned out the window as he chatted with the attendant who was running his credit card.

"Not my favorite type of load, but you've got to take whatever you can get these days. At least it's a short drive to the city."

Jackpot. I eased the rear door farther up and squeezed under it.

I found myself in a dim, hot space that smelled like straw and shit. Rustles filled the air all around me, punctuated by an occasional… cluck?

I was surrounded by chickens. A hen in the cage closest to me attempted to peck me through the bars.

"Mind your beak," I whispered at her, thinking various curses very intently in Omen's general direction, and hugged my legs to my chest as I prepared for a long ride.

By the time I made out city buildings through the gap under the door, I probably smelled like a chicken coop myself, but I'd made it to my destination with a half an hour to spare. I rolled out when the truck stopped at a red light, summoned an Uber while picking bits of straw off my clothes, and told the driver who showed up to take me to the Finger.

The Finger wasn't the official name of the gigantic statue that loomed in the middle of one of the largest downtown squares, but good luck finding anyone who could tell you what else it might be called. Erected a few decades ago by some avant-garde artiste, the tower of chunks of varnished wood held together by steel struts looked like nothing so much as a massive hand giving the buildings around it the middle finger. Naturally, it was the city's most popular landmark.

When I hopped out at the edge of the cobblestone courtyard at ten minutes to noon, several tourists were clustered around the Finger taking selfies. There was no sign of any shadowkind, but I wouldn't have expected to find them basking in the sunlight. As I strolled over to the structure, the four of them appeared as if they'd simply stepped from around its other side rather than straight out of the shadows.

"You see," Snap said happily if carefully, to make sure no one around us noticed his forked tongue. "Of course she made it."

With his baseball cap on to cover his horns in mortals' view, Ruse sauntered over to pluck something out of my hair. He tapped my cheek with a chicken feather. "I won't ask."

Funnily enough, Omen didn't look remotely pleased. "You cut it close," he said, as if even making it at the last second wouldn't have been an incredible feat, and immediately turned away. He jabbed a finger toward a police officer who'd paused to buy a hot dog from a stand at the other end of the square. "I hear you consider yourself some kind of master thief. Steal that cop's cap for me."

Oh, he wanted to up the ante now, did he?

Thorn tugged at the fingerless leather gloves that disguised his crystalline knuckles but always seemed to irritate him. "Omen," he started.

I shook my head to hold off the warrior's protest. "Not a problem. I'll just need a moment to prepare."

Omen crossed his arms, giving me a disbelieving scowl. I ignored him as I took the lay of the land. He was going to find out soon enough that I wouldn't give up—not until the bastards we were both after met a fate at least as horrible as they'd given to their shadowkind victims.

I could use a strategy I'd seen Auntie Luna turn to more than once when her fae glamours and other spells wouldn't do the trick. Collide and divert. I wasn't quite as petite and bubbly as she'd been, but I could pull it off nearly as well.

While the cop chowed down on his street meat, I jogged around the nearby streets until I found a performer with an open case strumming her guitar at an intersection. I held out a twenty and patted my wallet when she grabbed it.

"I'll give you four more of those if you scream as loud as you can, five minutes from now," I said, pointing at her watch, and added at her quizzical look, "Set it to music if you want. No scream, no cash."

There wasn't going to be any cash anyway, but hey, just the twenty was a lot of money when I'd lost nearly all my earthly possessions last week.

I hoofed it back to the square, watching the minutes tick by on my phone. When there was only one left, I took off across the cobblestones at a breakneck run.

The cop had just finished his hot dog. He dabbed at his mouth rather daintily with a paper napkin—and I slammed right into him, looking back over my shoulder as if I were paying more attention to something behind me than to where I was going. Still, I managed to swing my heel against his ankle to knock him right off his feet.

We both tumbled over, my arm flying up and smacking his cap to ensure it detached from his head. Since I wasn't a total fiend, I jerked my elbow to the side before it would have rammed him in the throat. We hit the ground with a shared grunt.

"Oh my God, I'm so sorry, so so sorry," I babbled, scrambling up. "It's just—There was—" I gestured wildly toward the direction I'd come from, widening my eyes as far as they would go.

The cop had barely righted himself when the street musician let out the scream I wouldn't be paying her for, high and shrill—and maybe with a riff on her guitar, but I didn't think the cop noticed that. He bolted up faster than anything, too alarmed to bother with his cap, and dashed off to see what devious crime was being committed two blocks away.

I swiped the cap off the cobblestones and ambled back to where Omen and the others were waiting. With a bow, I presented the prick with his prize. "Ta da. Please, don't hold your applause."

Ruse chuckled and clapped. Omen glared at me. "If you think this will—"

"I think," I said, already backing away, "that you've got nothing to complain about in my performance, and I deserve a little break as my reward. I'll meet you all back here at five—or I'll hitchhike my way back to the cabin, if you'd prefer."

I gave Bossypants a cheeky salute, and then I spun on my heel and hailed a passing cab.

Between his knife trick last night and this round of testing, Omen couldn't have made it clearer how he felt about my presence. I'd just have to show him what humans were capable of when they had allies of their own kind at their back. I needed a shower and a moment to breathe, and then I was going to steal myself a little mortal support.

Only after I'd already picked the lock to the apartment and snuck inside did it occur to me just how bad my approach to a surprise visit might come across to someone who wasn't in the habit of breaking and entering on a regular basis.

Ellen and Huyen, the married leaders of the Shadowkind Defense Fund, were film fanatics. They owned a second-run theater just down the street from the apartment, where they usually held the Fund's meetings to discuss how we could protect the shadowkind creatures in our realm from the humans who preyed on them. So it wasn't surprising to find their walls adorned with framed vintage movie posters and mounted memorabilia like a Godfather fedora and a license plate from North by Northwest. They even had a literal gun on their mantelpiece.

Based on the movies they'd chosen to display, it looked like suspense flicks and film noir were their favorite genres. Which meant they'd probably watched at least a dozen scenes where a character walked into their darkened home only to find an unexpected intruder waiting, sitting casually in an armchair, perhaps with a dramatic clicking on of a lamp.

I wanted to ask the Fund's leaders for their help, not give them a heart attack. At least it wasn't all that dark at three in the afternoon, when I knew they always popped back home for a late lunch break after the first round of matinees. Taking the sneaky route was the only way I could talk to them without any chance someone from the sword-star crew would see me with them and decide to make the two women their next targets.

I might have risked relocking the door and waiting for them in the hall, but before I'd quite decided, their key clicked in the lock. Oh well, I guessed I was stuck doing this the creepy way.

The couple walked in, Ellen in mid-sentence exclaiming about her ideas for new popcorn flavors to inflict on Fund members at upcoming meetings. Seeing me in the living room doorway, they both halted in their tracks. I raised my hand in an apologetic wave of greeting. "Hi?"

Ellen glanced between me and the door and back again, strands of her frizzy, graying hair flying around her face where they'd escaped from her loose bun. "Sorsha, what on earth—How did you—"

I held up both my hands before she could finish that question. "Let's not worry about that right now. I'm *really* sorry to surprise you like this. I just didn't think it'd be safe to talk anywhere else. There's something big going on—something that's hurting a whole lot of shadowkind."

I'd known that fact would override every other aspect of the situation. Ellen and Huyen were as dedicated to their cause as they were to their love of movies; they just couldn't show off the former anywhere near as openly. Ellen pursed her lips, but she didn't dial 911 or even tell me to take a hike, like most sane people would have.

"What's going on?" she asked in her throaty voice.

Might as well serve up the meat of it before they lost their patience. "I've found out that there's a large, well-organized group that's hunting not just lesser shadowkind but higher as well—capturing them and keeping them to run experiments. I've talked to a higher shadowkind who managed to escape"—no reason to mention that I'd orchestrated that escape; one case of breaking and entering would look bad enough—"and he's said it's basically torture. We don't know what they want to accomplish, but this is too huge and horrible to ignore."

Ellen's mouth had tightened too, but with obvious distress. "Hunting higher shadowkind—running experiments on them? Who *are* these people?"

"I'm not sure," I admitted. "They're very good at covering their tracks. That's why I'm hoping the Fund can use our resources to uncover more information and push back. But they—they already know I'm trying to stop them, and they've attacked me because of that. I didn't want to risk them tracing me to the theater. If we're going to meet to discuss this, it needs to be someplace else, and everyone who comes needs to be careful about it."

Huyen glanced at her wife, her tan skin graying. "I don't know. This sounds like it might be too big for us to tackle."

"Not if we're smart about it," I said quickly. "Not if we work fast."

"What did we even start the Fund for if we're not going to intervene when there's a major problem?" Ellen asked.

Huyen didn't look convinced. I sucked my lower lip under my teeth, my gaze skimming over the posters around us for inspiration.

"If *anyone's* prepared to take them on, it's you." I motioned to the Hitchcock pictures, to the spy capers and crime dramas. "You can put all the strategies you've watched to good use. We're the underdogs going up against the corrupt conspirators... Don't turn into one of the complicit wimps who tells the heroes they're on their own."

Resolve sparked in Huyen's dark eyes. "Okay, that's quite the pitch. I'm not promising anything yet, but why don't we all sit down, and you can tell us everything you already know."

FOUR

Thorn

"You went *where*?" Omen said. His voice had become even flatter and colder than it'd been for most of the past two days, but I'd known him long enough to recognize the crackling undercurrent of heat that ran through it. To say that he and our mortal lady were not getting along would be putting it very mildly.

Sorsha set her hands on her hips. She was always rather striking to behold, now that I'd allowed myself to acknowledge it, but I enjoyed watching her most when circumstances brought out the ferocity in her temperament. Unfortunately, recently those "circumstances" had mostly been our commander.

"They're the leaders of the local branch of the Shadowkind Defense Fund," she said. "If anyone can give us a hand with our investigations, it's them. We *are* dealing with mortal enemies, after all. Who better than mortals to figure out what they're up to?"

Omen rolled his eyes skyward. It wasn't the most awe-inspiring view, standing where we'd gathered in a laneway between a glossy office building and the slightly taller residential tower beside it. A rich but bitter scent wafted from the coffee shop on the office building's ground floor. The clientele exited through the front, though, and the tower had no balconies below the tenth floor, leaving the laneway quiet.

Which meant Omen didn't need to raise his voice even slightly for it to cut crisply through the silence. "It's bad enough having any mortals entangled in our affairs. I'm not interested in shepherding a whole flock of them."

"You don't have to see them or talk to them," Sorsha said. "I'm the go-between; I'll handle everything. You never asked me *not* to try to bring them on board."

His eyes narrowed. "I assumed you were sharp enough to realize that without my saying it. Apparently not."

"We got some useful tips from Sorsha's Fund friends before," Ruse put in. "They led us to the hacker. Why not see what they come up with?"

"Yes," Omen said with a sarcastic edge, "why not find out how quickly they can turn our efforts into a total clusterfuck?" He turned back to Sorsha. "You want to do things your way? I'm still not convinced even you can keep up with us. Do you think you're up to another challenge, or will you run away again?"

"I didn't *run away*." Sorsha sighed. "Lay it on me, Luce. What death-defying stunt have you got for me now?"

Omen's eyes narrowed at the nickname, and I restrained a wince. Of course the incubus with all his teasing would have brought that up—but our lady couldn't know just how charged that reference to our commander's long-ago exploits was for him. Omen had been quite a trickster himself when I'd first known him, but everything about his demeanor since he'd recruited me to his current cause showed how utterly he'd erased that past from his being. If he could have erased it from all memory as well, I expected he would have.

As he cast his gaze upward again, I braced myself. It seemed he had gotten something out of the view after all, because a moment later, he pointed toward the top of the residential tower. "There's a flower pot with an orange blossom on the highest balcony, by the far corner. Do you see it?"

Sorsha peered upward. "Yep. What about it?"

"I'd like to see you steal *that*... without taking advantage of the building's elevator or stairs. Without going into the building at all."

My defensive instincts sprang to the forefront with an inner clang of alarm. Sorsha might be able to scale the outside of the building—once she reached the lower balconies, it wouldn't require too much of a jump between them—but with each floor she climbed, she'd be tempting a fall. And by the time she made it to the twentieth or so floor, that fall would almost certainly be fatal.

Omen was smiling. It didn't matter to him whether she lived or died. I was starting to think he'd prefer her dead.

It'd become clear that arguing with him about Sorsha's worthiness wouldn't convince him. From the determined clenching of Sorsha's jaw, I knew she wouldn't refuse the trial. I was hardly going to stand here and watch her throw caution—and perhaps herself—to the wind without a care, though.

The thought of what I was about to offer sent a constricting sensation through my chest, but I could handle it discreetly. I stepped forward. "I'd like to confer with the mortal one for a minute."

Omen frowned at me, but I caught a flicker of curiosity in his eyes too. He knew I didn't bestow my loyalty liberally.

"Talk her out of the attempt for her own good," he said.

I ushered Sorsha farther down the laneway to where the others wouldn't hear what I had to say.

"You're not going to talk me out of it," she said before I could begin my appeal.

I let out a dismissive grunt. "Do you think after everything I've seen of you, I'd be witless enough to even try to? You'll retrieve that flower pot for Omen, m'lady. *I'll* see that you do. You only have to send Ruse and Snap off on some errand first."

Her brow furrowed. "Why? What are you talking about?"

"Omen wanted you to find a way to get to that balcony without entering the building. He didn't put any other limitations on the task. I can be your way. It would only require a matter of seconds—I'll fly quickly enough that no mortals catch more than a glimpse they'll believe they imagined."

Sorsha stared at me. "You're offering to show your true shadowkind form and fly me up to the top of the building, just to get a flower pot?"

I *had* impressed on her rather emphatically that I didn't want her revealing what she'd discovered about my nature to the others. The wingéd—what mortals tended to call "angels"—had a long-tarnished history, one I had no wish to open up to the incubus's teasing jokes or the devourer's unbridled curiosity. But I'd allowed my wings to come forth once before in the service of saving our lady's life. This was no different.

"It's more than retrieving a flower pot," I said. "It's proving to Omen that you belong with us. You've fought too hard by our sides for him to dismiss you now. If I can make the process easier—and less of a threat to your survival—then I won't hesitate."

The thought of the valor she'd shown throughout our time together outshone the irritation I'd once felt at her often flippant attitude. After everything we'd faced together, looking at her stirred a much deeper and more poignant emotion, one so unfamiliar I couldn't put a name to it. I only knew it would be a near thing not attempting to sever Omen's head from his body if she died because of his distrust.

That emotion gripped me even harder when Sorsha offered me her softest smile. A matching tenderness shone in her eyes. "I appreciate that, Thorn. I know you wouldn't make an offer like that to most people. But I really can handle this myself—and it'll prove much more to Omen if I do. Are you doubting my strength?"

She flexed her biceps and didn't quite conceal a wince. I couldn't hold back my protest. "You're *wounded.*"

"But feeling better with every passing hour." She patted her shoulder and then reached up to pat mine as well. Her touch brought back the quiver of sensation that had passed through me when she'd caressed my wings the other night, stirring a much more heated emotion I recognized perfectly well even if it hadn't come to me often. Ah, yes, that was desire.

I allowed myself just a fragment of remembering what her lithe body had felt like against mine when I'd captured her mouth so briefly, of imagining what it might feel like if I claimed her completely—and then I yanked myself back to the present.

"I was listening closely to Omen's requirements too," Sorsha continued. "I've got this. And on the off-chance I'm wrong, I trust that you'll catch me."

She bobbed up to give me a quick peck on the lips that sent an unreasonably hot flush through the rest of my body and sauntered back to rejoin the others.

"Just to be clear," she said to Omen, adjusting the straps of her backpack, "the only rule is that I *can't* go inside this building, right?"

He gave her a narrow look. "And you bring me the pot and flower unbroken. Those are the terms."

"Perfect. I accept. Now excuse me. I won't go in *this* building, but I am going into *that* one."

A delighted laugh escaped Snap as our lady sashayed over to the office building next door. Omen's expression turned murderous for an instant before he steadied himself with that nearly impenetrable cool calm he'd held in front of him like a shield since we'd first spoken to him after his escape.

"It still won't be easy for her," he said.

Ruse leaned back against the wall and tilted his head up to watch the balconies. "Oh, I wouldn't be so sure about that."

"This wasn't my idea," I told our commander. "I didn't know that's what she'd planned. She rejected my suggestion entirely." He didn't need to know exactly what that suggestion had been.

Omen eyed me, but he knew I wouldn't outright lie to him. He let out a huff. "Let's see what she thinks she can get away with like this, then."

Snap headed down the laneway where he could get a slightly closer look at the flower pot in question, and Ruse trailed after him. I glanced at Omen and judged it safe enough to say, keeping my voice low, "I can tell you that she's as honorable as she is determined. She—It came about that she witnessed my full form. I asked her not to speak of it with the other two, and she's kept her word."

Omen betrayed a hint of surprise at that. He gestured up and down toward my body. "She's seen you—wings and smoldering eyes and all?"

"Yes," I said. And she'd appeared to like what she saw, where most mortals might have screamed. A flicker of the heat she'd provoked raced through me again.

"Hmm." Omen went back to watching the upper reaches of the buildings, but I thought with a little less rancor.

It didn't take terribly long for Sorsha to emerge. She appeared at the edge of the opposite rooftop, a gleam of sunlight in the red hair she'd pulled into a tight ponytail. After giving us a jaunty wave, she swung a grappling hook she must have been carrying in that pack of hers across the distance.

It caught on the requested balcony with a clatter. She paused, but no one emerged from the residence. Grasping the rope, she leapt off the roof.

My breath started to hitch, but before I even had to recover it, she'd already planted her feet on the railing of the balcony below. She climbed the rope in a swift scramble, pausing just briefly with a suppressed wince only my battle-trained eyes might have picked up on, tucked the flower pot under her arm, and tossed the hook back toward the roof she'd descended from.

Less than five minutes later, Sorsha pranced out of the office building and held out the flower to Omen. "As you ordered. Now are we done with these stupid games or what?"

Omen glared at her. "For the time being," he said, as if he wasn't quite finished with her, and I knew it was too early to be truly relieved. When Omen put his mind to something, he was as unshakeable as— well, as a hound.

FIVE

Sorsha

"Wait," Vivi said, lowering her half-eaten butterscotch chocolate-chip cookie. "So, this badass shadowkind boss named his station wagon *Betsy*?" A snicker escaped her. Then she half-choked on the bite she'd just taken and sputtered several coughs, still managing to sound amused.

I grinned back at her. "That's right." Basking in the hot late-afternoon sun across the glass-topped café table from my bestie, I found it easier to let go of the uneasiness Omen had stirred up in me and simply laugh about him. Sweet cinnamon sparkles, had I missed having Vivi here to shoot the breeze with.

The only thing that might have elevated our reunion more was if we'd felt confident enough to drop in on our favorite dessert place near her parents' house, which we'd visited nearly every week when I'd stayed with her family in the first year after Luna's death. But this new spot, where we'd nabbed a table on the sunny back patio, had already more than met my best friend's approval. After one nibble, she'd declared her cookie was "the cream of the icing on the cake."

"And how does Omen feel about you hanging out with me, if he's so down on mortals in general?" she asked now.

My spirits sank a little, but I kept my smile. "I convinced him you'd cause way less carnage if I gave you the low-down than if you were running around the city without the full story. He still attempted to burn a hole through my head with his glare."

Vivi made a show of checking my face over. "Didn't work. Not so powerful after all, I guess." She paused, her own grin fading. "*Is that the full story now?*"

"All the important parts. If I went into every detail, we'd be here for a couple of weeks." And I wasn't sure I wanted to fill her in on every detail when those details included things like Thorn tearing the heads off of guards to avenge my shoulder wound. It was hard to see moments like that in a positive light if you hadn't been there.

I wanted Vivi to keep a positive outlook on my new companions specifically because I'd predicted her next question. She leaned her elbows on the table and gazed at me coyly through her eyelashes. "And when am I going to meet your incredibly hot new boyfriends?"

I'd skipped most of the details there too, but maybe I shouldn't have mentioned just how friendly I'd gotten with my trio at all. I popped one last bite of my blueberry pie into my mouth and waggled my fork at Vivi. "They're not exactly my boyfriends. It's not as if a mortal could really *date* a shadowkind guy, let alone three of them."

She waved my protest away. "Okay, your new cuddle-buddies. Whatever you want to call them, the question stands. I promise not to try to steal them away from you, but you've got to at least share the eye-candy."

"We'll see. I'm not sure I want Omen knowing any more about *you* than he already does." And I also wasn't sure she wouldn't think I was bonkers once she took in the full reality of the trio. I'd gotten to know them—in ways both literal and biblical—enough that their oddities didn't faze me, but Vivi had never been all that close with any shadowkind before. I didn't think she could even totally understand the bond I'd had with Luna.

For all the polite language they used and all the work they put into protecting shadowkind creatures, most of the Fund members never stopped thinking of those beings as monsters.

"Fine." Vivi wrinkled her nose at me and recovered her grin. "You are at least going to let me help out now, right? I need to get in at least one grand adventure before I hit thirty, or what the hell am I doing with my life? I can be very useful, I'll have you know. Look at me, all professional poise."

She gestured to her outfit, which as always was white from neck to toe: an ivory blouse and wide-leg dress pants over strappy sandals with a reserved twinkle of gold at the buckles. Even with the explosion of dark curls that burst at the back of her head from the tight braids along the rest of her scalp, she did exude a certain elegance that I doubted I'd ever pull off. Being raised by a shadowkind left a person a little feral in ways it was difficult to shake.

"I'll give you that," I said. "Let's see what comes out of the, um, meeting tonight, and I'll let you know where we need you."

She gave me a questioning look at that statement, but I held up my hands in a gesture for mercy. I wasn't shutting Vivi out this time around, but I sure as sugar wasn't dragging her off to a direct ambush of the murderous and potentially psychotic sword-star crew. Especially when she still saw this as an adventure, even if she realized it was a dangerous one now.

I had to get going to prepare for that ambush. As we left the café, I gave Vivi a tight hug, as if I could absorb her cheer into me to bolster me through the battle ahead. We said our "Ditto"s, and I headed for the spot where the quartet was meant to pick me up, singing a little song to inspire myself. "We'll touch and surround, I'm on the hunt this af-ter-noon."

Omen eyed me as I got into the back seat of the station wagon as if checking me over for mortal cootie contamination. I was mature enough at that particular moment not to stick my tongue out at him in return. The other three were sticking to the shadows as they often did in the car, but I took a little comfort in knowing I wasn't actually alone with the dude.

"Vivi's going to be chill," I told him. "She won't stick her nose in unless I ask her to—and I'll only ask her with something really specific that none of us can do."

Bossypants let out a grunt that seemed to say he couldn't imagine there being any task fitting that criteria and switched the car into drive. I drew in another sniff of that odd smell that clung to the vehicle's interior. Dry, smoky, a little savory, with that trace of minerals… Maybe he crisped chicken wings on a tray of scorching crystals in his spare time? It could be some weird shadowkind hobby no one had bothered to tell me about.

Ruse's charmed hacker had dug up the details of the hand-off we were heading to. It was supposedly taking place an hour after sunset in the parking lot of a mini-golf course. Not your typical spot for illicit exchanges of creatures the average mortal didn't even believe existed, but when we slunk over after leaving Betsy a short distance away, I could see why they'd picked it.

The course with its candy-bright painted fixtures—a windmill here, a castle there—surrounded the parking lot on two sides and was big enough that no one farther afield would have been able to see what was happening in the lot. A dingy warehouse offered a windowless brick wall on the third side, so no witnesses there. At the road, someone had conveniently left a dumpster full of construction rubble where it blocked most of the view of the span of asphalt, and the nearest streetlamps had burnt out. By a total coincidence, no doubt.

We'd arrived just as the sun was setting. The shadows of the miniature structures stretched twice as long as the actual fixtures across the patches of green. Ruse slipped through the shadows to unlock the gate so I could follow them in.

"Your only job is to hang back until we have our prize," Omen ordered me. He pointed to the roof of the hut that held the ticket sales booth and equipment. "Thorn will boost you up there. Stay out of view and watch the transaction. I only want to hear or see you if you spot something from up there that the rest of us need to know. Once we've trapped one of their number, then you can jump in to remove protective wards as necessary."

"And to open the cage to let their shadowkind prisoner out," Snap piped up.

"Yes, that too," Omen muttered as if annoyed at the reminder that I would be useful in more than one way. He fixed his stare on me. "Got it?"

"Aye, aye, captain," I said dryly. I suspected he'd have tried to lock me in the car instead of letting me tag along at all if he'd thought there was any chance that car could hold me for more than a minute. But even he couldn't deny the value of my immunity to the materials that deflected shadowkind powers.

Just in case I found a good use for it, I picked up one of the mini-golf clubs and swung it experimentally through the air. A little light, but it had decent heft to it. For good measure, I stuffed several of the small but incredibly dense golf balls into the pouches on my belt.

I'd decked myself out in full cat-burglar gear for this operation. If I didn't move or speak, I'd be nothing but a shadow on the rooftop, even my red hair hidden under the black knit cap. Thank flaming eels the evening was already starting to cool off, or I'd have been a puddle of sweat in a matter of seconds.

Thorn gave me a boost to the edge of the roof, and I scrambled across it to duck down behind one of the fake gables. Peeking over the protruding section, I could make out the edge of the golf course and all of the parking lot.

The shadowkind quartet had discussed their plans in more depth while I'd been chatting with Vivi. As I settled into my position, they vanished into the shadows. From what I'd gathered, they were going to station themselves in a rough circle around the parking lot. The idea was to watch the hand-off long enough to determine the sword-star crew's usual procedures, and then—unless the squad appeared too well-equipped—charge in, free the shadowkind the collector was selling to them, and snatch one of the sword-star employees for later questioning.

I shifted my position on the clay tiles a few times, my back getting stiff and my shoulder achy from my hunched posture. Every time a car rumbled by through the deepening evening dark, I froze. Finally, a black van that looked like the sort of vehicle used to transport large livestock pulled into the lot. It parked in the far corner where the golf course rubbed up against the warehouse.

Only one figure stepped out—the collector, I assumed. At first glance, he could have passed for an evil-genius supervillain from the type of comic books I was guessing our hacker had read too many of. The dome of his bald, bulbous head shone in the faint light from the far-off streetlamps, and he wore a gray suit with its square collar buttoned right up to his chin. I half expected him to produce a monocle from his chest pocket.

Then I noticed the sheen of perspiration that caught even more of the light than the pale skin of his scalp. The dude might have supervillain fashion aspirations, but super-confident he was not.

It took another ten minutes before a second vehicle growled into the lot: a white delivery truck with a bakery logo painted on the side. A fake business, or another front like the discount toy store the sword-star crew had run some of their operations out of? I made a mental note of the name in case it was the latter.

Five figures emerged from the truck. They wore the silver-and-iron helmets and plated vests that we'd seen before. All shadowkind found one if not both of those metals repellent, but they couldn't block Thorn's physical strength or whatever concrete tricks Omen had dreamed up.

One of the figures appeared to have a whip, probably one of those glowing laser-y ones, at his hip, but they weren't holding any weapons. It looked like they didn't anticipate dealing with any hostile parties in this transaction.

Exactly as we'd hoped.

The sweaty collector opened the back door to his van. Searing light spilled out—he'd have bright lamps set up all around the cage that must be holding the powerful creature to prevent it from slipping away into the shadows. The sword-star bunch wheeled a container like an oversized gym locker out of the back of their truck and set it facing the van. It looked like they meant to transfer the cage from the van into that box, which must have lights of its own.

Before they got that far, four shadowy forms hurtled into the lot. I couldn't make out much of their faces through the blur of darkness still clinging to them, but the massive shape bashing two of the sword-star crew off their feet was obviously Thorn.

The other three shadowkind didn't dare get quite as close to our enemies and their noxious armor. Ruse lashed some sort of rope at the collector's legs and yanked it so he tumbled onto the ground, his knees locked together. As the not-at-all-super villain started sniveling like a kindergartener, Omen and Snap tossed thick sheets over the two attackers Thorn had felled. Whatever those were made of, the material was heavy enough to hold the men in place.

Thorn was still dealing with the rest of the sword-star crew. He snatched the man with the whip by the wrists and hurled him over the fence to crash into the mini-golf castle. The dude slumped, one of the turrets wobbling and then plummeting to smack him in the head for good measure. Another asshole got a punch in the throat with the warrior's crystalline knuckles. A gurgle escaped the gaping wound as he collapsed in a bloody mess.

The last of our enemies had taken advantage of Thorn's distraction. The guy thrust a metal rod at the warrior's back, and sparks spurted against Thorn's tunic. The huge shadowkind shuddered, a spasm gripping his limbs for a second as he wrenched himself around. Meanwhile, the prick who'd broken the poor castle was managing to pick himself up, whip in hand.

Oh no, he didn't. "Thorn!" I called out in warning, springing to my feet. My hand had already shot to one of my pouches. My fingers curled around a golf ball, and I flung it at the guy with the rod.

It nailed him in the back of the helmet with a dull clang—I'd call that a hole in one. With a victory whoop, I pitched another few his way, pelting him for long enough that he wasn't prepared for Thorn's punch. The warrior's rigid knuckles smashed right into his face. I averted my gaze from the spurt of blood.

Good thing, because the castle dude was dashing back toward the chain-link fence, whip ready. I leapt from the hut's roof onto a plaster drawbridge and from there to the ground. As the guy moved to heave himself over the fence, I thwacked him across the ear with the golf club, just below the base of his helmet. His head swayed, and I aimed the putter at the top of the helmet this time. With one solid swing, I smacked the protection right off him.

Omen was there as if he'd been waiting for just that chance. The second the helmet careened off, our leader slammed the sword-star guy's forehead into the bar along the top of the fence hard enough to shatter his skull.

Okay, then. He might not have Thorn's bulk, but he wasn't lacking in bodily power. Note to self: don't get *too* far on this dude's bad side.

The two surviving members of the sword-star crew squirmed under the heavy sheets ineffectually. Omen stalked up to the collector, who was huddled by his van sobbing with shaky gulps for air.

"Tell all your collector friends that we see them, and we'll come for them, one by one," Omen said, his voice taut with threat. "Maybe if you scurry away and hide, we won't find you, but anyone who decides to do business with these people"—he pointed to the delivery truck —"from now on has sealed their doom."

I clambered over the fence and jogged across the lot to the van's open back door. The shadowy form of a large creature too distressed by its surroundings to show itself wavered amid the wash of light behind the silver-and-iron twined bars of its cage, which was nearly as tall as I was. It was either a smaller higher shadowkind being than my current companions or simply a very potent lesser shadowkind. Neither deserved the treatment it had gotten.

With a few hacks of my scorch-knife, the supernaturally enhanced titanium blade sizzling with heat, I carved out the lock. The second I threw open the cage's door, the shadowkind creature flung itself past me. It bolted off into the night without so much as a thank you. I guessed I couldn't blame it.

"Good," Snap murmured, coming up behind me. He set a gentle hand on my arm and nuzzled the back of my head in a way that sent a flutter through my abdomen that was totally inappropriate to the situation.

The others were standing around our two captives. Omen rubbed his hands together. "Get their gear off, and we'll see how much we can drag out of these miscreants tonight."

SIX

Sorsha

INTERROGATION WAS MUCH LESS PAINFUL WHEN YOU HAD AN INCUBUS IN play, both for those of us on the interrogator's side and, I had to assume, for the victims. No need for water torture or trolleys laid with knives and pliers when a little charmed conversation would get them spilling their secrets much more effectively.

Ruse had chatted up our two captives while they'd still been pinned against the ground. As soon as they'd been thoroughly under his thrall, we'd let them up and marched them into the back of their own truck. Now, we were parked in an isolated part of town, standing in a semi-circle facing the two star-sword dudes, who sat against the wall of the compartment.

The incubus might have softened up these two, but naturally Omen was determined to handle most of the actual questioning. His eyes gleamed, even narrower than usual under the stark glow of the one lamp we'd turned on—one that'd been meant to hold other shadowkind as prisoners under much harsher circumstances.

The specifics of those circumstances was clearly the largest question on his mind. He crossed his arms over his chest, appearing to just barely hold himself back from shooting the two guys a death glare. Ruse's illusion that we were all fantastic friends would only hold if Bossypants didn't push them too far in the opposite direction.

"What were you planning on doing with the shadowkind being you were buying from that collector?" he asked.

One of the men stirred, a hopeful expression coming over his face as if he wanted nothing more than to please his kidnappers with his answer. "We'd meet with the other truck and hand it off."

This was at least a two-stage manoeuvre, then. Not surprising, considering the lengths we'd seen these people go to for caution's sake before.

Omen frowned. "And where would the other truck have taken it?"

"We don't know," the other guy said. "The people who give us our instructions, they like to keep all the pieces separate. They say it's more secure that way. It's a good thing—what if someone who wasn't looking out for us had grabbed us instead of you?"

My lips twitched, but I managed to swallow a laugh. Had Ruse wiped the memory of what Thorn and Omen had done to their colleagues from their minds, or had he simply convinced them that those guys had been asking to have their skulls bashed in?

It would have been nice if we could have tracked down the second set of Company lackeys, but they'd have realized the hand-off had gone wrong by now. Wherever they'd been meant to meet these dudes, they and anything they could have told us would be long gone. So much for finding the new base of operations.

Omen didn't look remotely satisfied with the answer he'd gotten either. "Do your 'people' tell you anything about what they do with the shadowkind they're gathering once they have them?"

The first guy brightened. "Yes. A little. They're looking for ways to end the beasts' evil influence on our world. The Company of Light will eradicate all the monsters that prey on us. But they're slippery demons—just killing some here and there isn't good enough. They're looking for a better way."

I wasn't even one of those slippery demons myself, and I automatically bristled on behalf of my companions. Snap tucked his arm around my waist in a gesture of comfort, but his divinely sweet face was drawn. I squeezed his hand in return. He'd spent little time mortal-side before now—he might never have heard a human talk about how much they detested beings like him before. This supposed "monster" was more compassionate than most human beings I knew.

A hint of otherworldly smolder flickered in Thorn's eyes. The huge warrior took a deliberate step closer, looming almost to the roof of the compartment with an aura of menace, but Omen held up his hand. His mouth had formed a rigid smile.

He didn't like what the guy had said, but it was exactly the attitude he'd expected.

"The Company of Light," he repeated. "Is that what your organization calls itself?"

The man nodded. "We have to keep our cause secret, because backlash from the monsters could end us all, but with the work we're doing, our light will burn away all the shadows."

"But you don't know what exactly your Company's experiments are supposed to achieve."

"Experiments?" The man's brow furrowed. "That's not my area. I just know whatever they're doing, they're working toward destroying every fiend that dares set foot here—and maybe all the ones back where they come from too."

Lovely. A chill collected in my gut. He was discussing literal genocide as if it were the most glorious purpose he could imagine. Had any of these sword-star—excuse me, *Company of Light*—assholes ever even talked with a higher shadowkind?

I'd be the first to admit that beings like the four around me didn't subscribe to the exact same sense of morality humans did. And sure, some of their kind did prey on mortal beings. But plenty of mortals preyed on each other too. The answer was to fight back against the ones committing the actual crimes, not to mass murder everybody. I didn't think this Company would like it if the shadowkind turned their logic back on humankind.

"That does sound like an honorable goal," Omen said, his voice so edged with sarcasm I half expected it to slice right into our captives' flesh. He paced from one end of the compartment to the other as he considered his next line of inquiry. "Are these hand-offs with the collectors the only way you contribute?"

"They call on me once every few weeks for a job like this," the first man said. "Otherwise, I keep quiet and keep out of the rest of their business."

The shadowkind's gaze slid to the other guy. "And you?"

"I don't do anything else with the beasts, but I've done a little other driving—bringing equipment for the events and that sort of thing."

"Ah. What sort of events would those be?"

The guy shrugged. "I'm not sure. They have some parties with a bunch of rich folks now and then. With all the equipment they must need and the cash for buying off the collectors—I guess they've got to raise funds somehow or other."

Another laugh tickled my chest, this one sharper with irony. Of course the Company of Light would need to hold fundraisers just like Ellen and Huyen's group of defenders did. While we gathered money to protect the shadowkind, they gathered money to hunt and torture them. From the scale of our enemies' operations, they had to be a lot better at it than we were. Maybe we could pick up some pointers along the way.

Omen grilled the two more—about how they got their equipment, where they were trained in handling shadowkind, and anything else he could come up with relating to the structure of the Company of Light. Unfortunately, our enemies had been awfully sly all around. The training sessions happened at random locations that changed every time, the equipment showed up on the guys' doorsteps along with the orders for their next assignment, and they didn't know much else.

We stepped out of the truck to confer where they couldn't overhear us.

"It's not a total loss," I said. "We freed the shadowkind they were going to buy—we put the fear in that collector and hopefully a bunch more in his network. We know what their hand-offs look like now, and maybe we can get at them through these fundraising events somehow."

"It's still less than I'd like." Omen eyed the truck broodingly. "Maybe I can come up with another angle that'll be more productive."

A new chill tickled down my back. "What are you going to do with them when you've run out of questions?" I'd avoided prying into that subject until now, but that hesitance was starting to feel cowardly. The guys in there were prejudiced dicks, but they'd talked with us peacefully. I didn't like the idea of watching my companions slaughter them in their defenseless state.

Omen looked as though he'd like it just fine, but then his mouth twisted as if he'd bitten something sour. "It would be better if their 'Company' doesn't realize we held this interrogation. Ruse, you can charm them into keeping quiet about our chat, can't you? Convince them that they have to claim they drove from the scene of the attack unhindered?"

The incubus saluted him. "Give me a little more time, and I can manage it."

I glanced around at the darkened street. The shadowkind quartet didn't really need me here anymore—and there was something else I'd wanted to accomplish while Omen was distracted with this business. My stomach grumbled, giving me the perfect excuse. I hadn't eaten since that slice of pie with Vivi.

"Unlike the rest of you," I said, "I need dinner or I'll keel over. Meet you back where we left Betsy in a couple of hours?"

The thought of me fulfilling my mortal needs brought out Omen's disdain. He waved me off and yanked open the truck's back door again.

I trotted several blocks from the interrogation scene, weaving right and left at the intersections, and then called an Uber. I *was* planning on getting something to eat—but not anywhere Omen would have approved of.

As I settled into the car's back seat, something jabbed my leg in the bottom of my backpack. I felt inside, and my fingers closed around the cool, smooth surface of a little box. My throat tightened.

I drew out the box, the city lights outside the window catching on its pearly sides. My fingers moved automatically to pop open the lid.

This keepsake was the only thing I had of my parents'. There hadn't exactly been time to stop and pack when hunters had stormed into my parents' house while Auntie Luna and I had been playing in the backyard. At my mother's scream to her, Luna had grabbed three-year-old me and fled—but she'd had this box with the folded notepaper inside to offer me when I was old enough to read it.

The note didn't say much other than that my parents had loved me and wished things hadn't turned out this way but that Luna would protect me. They'd obviously realized there was a chance the assholes they'd stood up to would lash out at them.

I didn't know whether those assholes had been connected to the Company of Light just as Luna's attackers had been or whether they'd been just a random bunch of vengeful hunters, but either way, it only proved what psychotic monsters *humans* could be. And how much some of those humans needed to have their evil plans upended.

So I'd damn well use every tool I had, whether Omen approved or not.

I clicked the box shut again and tucked it into my purse this time, wanting to keep it even closer to me. The car slowed, just reaching the bar I'd given the driver the address to.

As I stepped through the doorway to Jade's Fountain, I scanned the room for anyone who didn't fit, but it looked like the usual crowd of quirky mortals and the occasional shadowkind partier who could blend in here. There was a mortal girl wearing a cat-ear headband, and two tables away a dude whose lizard-like eyes I suspected weren't contacts. Exactly as it should be. The burble of the water that cascaded down the far wall and the mineral scent in the air settled my nerves for the first time in days.

As usual, Jade was working solo behind the polished quartz bar counter, the dark green hair that would have marked her as a shadowkind to anyone who realized it wasn't dyed tumbling down her slim back. I headed to the seat at the far corner reserved for those of us already in the know.

The shadowkind woman ambled over a moment later. I thought her eyes were more wary than usual. Either she'd picked up word on the street about the hijinks I'd been caught up in, or those hijinks had made *me* more paranoid than usual.

"What'll it be tonight, Sorsha?" she asked.

"A Jack and Coke and one of those turkey paninis." I motioned to the little fridge where she kept prewrapped meals ready to pop into the toaster oven.

"Late dinner tonight?"

"It's been a busy one."

She hummed in response as she prepared the sandwich and poured my drink. When she set both in front of me with a clink of the glass, she lingered there, leaning one elbow onto the counter. "What's up?"

I paused to take a large bite of my panini and licked melted cheese grease off my fingers. Yum. "I know you don't like to get too involved in the Fund business and that sort of thing, so I'm not going to ask you to. I'm just going to say: if something major were going down—something that put *all* the shadowkind who've come mortal-side and maybe even the shadow-side ones in danger—do you know any higher kind who *would* want to stand up against the mortals involved?"

Her expression turned even more guarded than before. "Are you suggesting that something like that is happening *now*?"

I held her gaze steadily. "How much do you really want to know?"

She hesitated, and then her lips pressed flat. "Point taken. Maybe it's not worth the risk of even asking around, then."

"I guess you've got to weigh the odds. Would it be worse to do nothing at all and one day soon this bar gets stormed, or to just put out some very careful feelers that you can divert toward me?" I took another bite and chewed while she thought that over. Then I added, "I've never seen anything like this before, Jade. You know I wouldn't be making an ask like this if it wasn't important."

A couple of college-age kids with facial studs that might have been disguising an actual horn or two had come over to the counter farther down. Jade sighed. "I'll think about it—even if I check, I'm not sure I've got anyone for you. But if I do… I'll reach out to your private number?"

"You've got it. Thanks, Jade. I appreciate whatever you can do."

It was late enough that a few of the patrons were starting to sway with the music beside the tiled pond people used as both wishing well and, when drunk enough, wading pool. I hadn't planned to dance, hadn't planned to stick around longer than it took me to gulp down the rest of my meal, but as I tossed back the last sweet-and-sharp swallow of Jack and Coke, warm hands gripped me by the waist. The now-familiar bittersweet scent of cacao laced with caramel wrapped around me.

"I've finally got you alone," Ruse said in his equally chocolatey voice, tipping his head so his lips brushed the shell of my ear. Just that small contact, not even a kiss, sent an eager shiver through me.

I swiveled on the stool and looked up into his languid eyes. My heart might have skipped a beat at the heat in his gaze. Even with that silly baseball cap on his head to hide *his* very real horns, there wasn't anyone sexier I'd ever seen.

He couldn't have worked any of his seductive voodoo on me while I had my protective badge pinned to my undershirt in its usual place over my heart—just in case I happened on any shadowkind whose motives I *couldn't* trust—but he had plenty of totally non-supernatural charm to go around too. Taking the allure out of the incubus would have been as impossible as taking the purr out of a cat.

"We're hardly alone," I had to point out, motioning to the crowded room. "Did you follow me here? I thought you were taking care of your new best friends?"

Ruse grinned. "Oh, they're well taken care of. Sometimes I impress even myself. I just had a suspicion I'd find you here. I know who you turn to for information and reinforcements."

"I'm not sure I've gotten either." I gave his solidly muscled chest a nudge, more playful than designed to push him off me. "You've found me—what are you going to do with me now?"

His grin stretched wide. "Why don't we start with a dance? That seemed to work well for us last time."

The last time we'd danced together—in my old apartment after he'd put on an '80s dance mix to cheer me up—I'd pulled him into bed with me later that night. I still wasn't totally convinced that diving under the sheets with him again was a great idea. All the heights of bliss he could take me to were offset by that whole emotional manipulation side of his powers. He'd promised never to poke around inside my head again, but he'd promised that before the first time he'd done it too.

As he led me onto the dance floor, my uncertainty wavered. I'd forgotten just how good his hands felt against my body—trailing now from my waist over my hips and down my thighs. He stayed close as we shifted and swiveled with the music's haunting rhythm.

When I stopped for a moment as one song faded out, Ruse pressed a kiss to the bare skin at the side of my neck. I couldn't stop my breath from hitching at the jolt of pleasure.

"Hmm," he murmured against my hair. "The devourer has joined us in the shadows. I'm getting the impression he'd like to have you this close always. You know, my offer to show him the ropes between the sheets—perhaps literally, if you'd enjoy being tied to the bedposts—still stands. Imagine all the fun we—"

Before he could finish that torturously tempting offer, another of our companions pushed through the dancers toward us. Omen's eyes blazed so furiously in their icy way that even Ruse went still.

His boss came to a stop right in front of me and jabbed his finger at my chest. "What the hell do you think you're doing here?" he demanded, low but cutting.

"Dancing?" I said with an innocent smile.

"I know who runs this place. I know she talks with your *Fund*." He said the last word with a sneer. "I told you, we can't count on the other shadowkind for this. We're handling it ourselves."

"I never agreed to that. And anyway, I barely told her anything. I'm not an idiot."

"As far as I'm concerned, the jury's still out on that one." He jerked his hand toward the doorway. "Let's go. You've interfered enough for one night."

My body balked at the idea of following his orders, but his arrival had reminded me that it probably wasn't the safest for me to stick around here anyway. I was pretty sure the Company's people had looked for me here once before. From Ruse's reaction, he wasn't up for more dancing anyway.

"Interfering, huh?" I said, jabbing my finger right back at Omen. "That must be some brand-new way of saying, 'Provided an essential component to my masterplan.' You're welcome, by the way. Lucky for you, *Luce*, I'm ready to call it a night."

"You," Omen growled, but a second later he reined in the temper I'd known that nickname would provoke—even if I wasn't totally sure why—with a flick of his gaze toward the crowd.

He couldn't keep his cool forever. One of these days, I'd get under his skin enough to break the beast right open.

Maybe I'd better hope Jade had sent a few buddies my way before that explosion.

SEVEN

Sorsha

THE NEW-AGE CABIN DIDN'T HAVE ELECTRIC LIGHTS, BUT I'D SCROUNGED up a huge candle in a glass jar. The label said *Lawn Mower*, and the scent fit: like fresh-cut grass with a hint of diesel. I could tell why that one had been abandoned in the closet. It was better than the stale, dusty smell that had filled the cabin before, though.

As I blew out the flame for the night, Pickle let out a sleepy, squeaky murmur from the amethyst incense bowl now filled with shredded gauzy scarf. I'd set it in the shower stall in the tiny bathroom to give him the sense of a cavern. He'd have preferred a whole tub to trundle around in, but we were both making do with what we had.

I tucked myself in under the sheets on the cramped lower bunk, lay my head on the thin pillow—and all at once the warm weight of another body solidified against mine, making the space twice as cramped as before. I flinched with a lurch of my pulse. Then I registered Snap's breathtaking face gazing down at me in the dim moonlight that seeped through the cabin's window, his sweet but dark scent, like clover and moss, filling my nose.

He was already pulling back at my initial panicked response. Balancing precariously on the edge of the mattress rather than leaning against me like before, he stroked the side of my face in apology. "I'm sorry. I forgot that you can't tell I'm here until I come out of the shadows. It's started to feel so much like you're one of us that I find myself thinking you have the same awareness."

"That's all right." I didn't mind his company in my bed now that I knew it was him. I gave him a gentle tug toward me before his tall but slim frame tumbled right onto the floor. His body settled against mine again—chest to chest, one toned leg tucked over my thigh, those golden curls nearly brushing my cheek—and a hungrier heat formed low in my belly. I couldn't resist tracing my fingers along his smooth jaw in return. "Was there any particular reason you decided to drop in on me in bed?"

His smile looked a little sheepish, but his eyes gleamed with a hint of their monstrous neon green, unable to disguise his eagerness. "I was thinking—after seeing you and Ruse at the bar—I wanted to be that close to you again. We don't have to do anything other than this. I'd be happy to just lie next to you while you sleep."

Oh, my darling man—if I could even call him a man. I'd never have thought a being who was apparently capable of inflicting horrifying magic could be so enticingly adorable, but Snap somehow managed to be both in one.

I let my fingers trail down to where the collar of his Henley shirt splayed open over the lean muscles of his chest. "So you came here just to cuddle, huh? No interest in anything more?"

Another flash of neon flared in his eyes. "I didn't say *that*." His head dipped, his lips grazing my temple with his next words. "I would like very much to taste you again, Peach. Maybe in ways I didn't get a chance to last time?"

"Hmm. The truth comes out," I teased.

Snap drew back an inch to meet my eyes again. "Not just for me. That night, what we did together—it felt better than anything I've ever experienced in this realm or the one of shadow. But mainly because of how we connected so completely, sharing in the sensations. I want to do it again and again, but only if you're with me, wanting it too."

He spoke so earnestly it made my chest ache, both because of the adoration in his tone and because I knew how much of his affection was probably due to the novelty of the experience.

Sexual pleasure wasn't something shadowkind instinctively sought out in their own realm—it appeared to be the domain of mortals like me and mortal bodies like the ones he and his kind wore here. Many higher shadowkind sought out that bliss once they discovered it, and some like the cubi kind needed it to sustain themselves, but Snap hadn't spent enough time mortal-side to have stumbled on those desires until now.

"That attitude is a good one to have," I said. "But it won't only be me you can experience this with, you know. You'll find you can feel just as good with other women—maybe even men too—when you broaden your horizons."

He let out a soft huff. "No. There wouldn't be anyone else quite like you. I've never seen—the courage you show, so willing to fight for us even though we're not like you—your patience as we adapt to this world. You don't shy away even from the parts of us that make others call us monsters. You stand up with us against our enemies even without the same sorts of powers, no matter what you've lost… I only hope *I* can be strong enough to match you."

My throat constricted with a pang that shot straight through my heart. Okay, he might have made a pretty solid case there, even if I had trouble seeing myself as half as valiant as he did. Not being willing to stand by while living, feeling beings were caged and slaughtered was a pretty low bar to label someone a hero.

I caressed his jaw again, running my fingers up it and into his soft curls. "Well, I think you're pretty amazing too. This world can be a shitty place, but you manage to find every bit of beauty in the simplest things. You want to understand everything just for the sake of understanding it—most people only care about what's going to help them get ahead. I've never met anyone who wanted so badly to help and create joy in every way they can. I have no idea how I'm going to let you go."

I felt the ache of that uncertainty even more when he beamed down at me. He kissed my temple where his lips had teased me before, and then my cheek and the crook of my jaw. "Then don't."

For a moment, I tried to imagine what it would be like if the devourer didn't leave my life once this mission of ours was over. Could he really be a boyfriend, despite what I'd said to Vivi? Sharing an apartment with him, introducing him to all the other mortal pleasures like my favorite movies and music and—of course—food. Going out on the town with him, sharing in his wonder. Meeting up with friends...

How would I explain our relationship to anyone from the Fund? I wasn't sure even Vivi could manage not to be weird about it.

Would I get tired of his awe once I'd been around him for a while? Would he end up irritated by my many flaws as the initial glow of attraction faded? I'd had enough trouble making any kind of ongoing relationship work with actual human dudes. My track record suggested this would be the longest of longshots.

There was no point in saying that to Snap, though. It'd only ruin what we had right now. When we didn't know if we'd even survive to the end of the mission, it hardly mattered anyway. If we both got to have a future, one where maniacal organizations weren't attempting to eradicate his entire species, then we could worry about the practicalities—if we hadn't already determined that we were headed nowhere fast.

Right now, I wanted him as badly as he clearly wanted me. That was the only answer I needed.

Instead of talking, I drew his mouth to mine. He leaned into the kiss with all the eager passion I adored in him. As he deepened it, his tongue slipped between my lips, twining around mine with that skillful forked tip.

Mmm, yes, I definitely wasn't in any hurry to give this up.

The first time, days ago, we'd taken things slow while Snap explored his desire, and had gotten each other off with only our hands. The devourer had gathered confidence since then. As he kissed me again, ardently enough to coax a whimper from my throat, he was already tugging my undershirt up, placing his hands to avoid the silver-and-iron badge I left pinned to it out of habit.

The moment I eased back to pull it the rest of the way off, he palmed my breasts. In a matter of seconds, his long, lithe fingers had tweaked both my nipples into hardened nubs. Quivers of bliss flooded my chest, drowning out the twinge of my injured shoulder as I tossed the undershirt aside.

I yanked Snap into another kiss, but he didn't linger in it long before making good on his wish to taste me. He slicked his tongue over the peak of one breast and then the other, the forked end teasing my nipples even stiffer with the most incredible sensation.

I groped at his shirt, wanting to feel his naked chest against mine. Snap reached for the hem and then paused with a neon glitter passing through his eyes. He grinned with an unusual slyness, blinked—and the shirt simply disappeared.

Scratch that—*all* of his clothes had disappeared. I gazed down his sinewy frame to the erection jutting from between his thighs, and a fresh flush of desire washed through me. I'd known the shadowkind constructed the clothes they wore separately from their bodies when they emerged into the physical space, but I'd never seen that fact put to use to quite such enjoyable effect. Two thumbs up for instantaneous nudity.

"Very smooth," I said, and Snap looked even more pleased with himself for the second it took before he was kissing me again. He continued fondling one of my breasts to blissful effect while his other hand trailed heat down my side all the way to my hip. I arched to meet him automatically, and his knee slipped between my legs. His thigh pressed against my sex with the most delectable friction. I shivered in delight, unable to stop myself from rocking into that contact.

Snap smiled against my mouth and shifted his leg, his erection rubbing against my hip, moving with me until I moaned. Pleasure surged from my core. My fingers clenched where I was grasping his shoulder and his hair, my desire taking on an urgent edge.

The same urgency appeared to have gripped Snap. His breath stuttered over my lips. He kissed me again, hard, and then said in a voice so strained with need it rocketed my own hunger even higher, "Maybe more tasting can wait. I want to be inside you—that's how it's supposed to be, isn't it? That's what feels right."

My own breath was coming shaky. "Yes," I managed to say, never so grateful that shadowkind didn't reproduce the same way mortals did, because I sure as hell hadn't gotten a chance to stock up on condoms. "I mean, there are all kinds of ways that are totally right, but that's the one—that's what most people like best."

The devourer made a wordless sound of acknowledgement and yanked at my panties, which *I* couldn't conveniently will out of existence with a blink, more's the pity. I squirmed out of them and splayed my legs, reaching down to help guide him. As my fingers stroked the hot, silky length of his cock, Snap groaned, but his instincts led him well. Without any further direction, he teased the head of his erection over my slit and in, in, in with a deliberate care that had me burning for more.

When he'd pushed all the way to the hilt, pleasure radiated from where we were joined all through the rest of my body. He went perfectly still, his eyes locked on mine through the darkness, wide with a delighted sort of wonder. A short, breathless laugh escaped him. His rapturous expression choked me up all over again. I resisted the urge to buck against him and propel this union toward its climax faster than he seemed to intend.

"This," he murmured. "*This* is the best. With you."

"Snap..." I didn't know whether I was going to return that tender sentiment or beg him to drive me on to further satisfaction, but then it didn't matter, because, thank all that was taut and tingly, he started to move. Pulling back and pressing forward, gently and then with more forceful thrusts, watching my face with avid attention.

With each whimper that fell from my lips and each rush of bliss that sent my eyes rolling back, he adjusted his rhythm, his angle, his speed, until every plunge of his cock inside me set off rising waves of ecstasy. The bunk bed squeaked as our hips smacked together, and a giggle just as breathless as his laugh tumbled out of me. The realms really ought to thank me for waking up this potential in him, because he was fucking *brilliant* at fucking.

"If you get there before me, it's okay," I said around another gasp, but he shook his head. His features had tensed against his release even as he held the same rapt attention on my reactions.

He ran his fingers over my hair and across my thigh, fitting us even more tightly together. One thrust, and another, and another, each searing a headier pleasure through me.

With a little cry, I careened over the edge in a burst of bliss. Snap's groan and the clutch of my hair told me he'd followed.

His body slackened, but he held his muscles tensed enough to stop his full weight from squashing me into the mattress. He lowered his head to claim one more kiss. I reveled in it, my limbs gone boneless with release.

"There isn't much room," he said after, and I understood the question he was asking. He was a cuddler, as much as he enjoyed other activities too. Tonight, I could embrace that part of his nature. Maybe a small part of *me* could even believe I deserved this devotion.

"You can stay." I scooted over so my back leaned against the wall. Snap settled onto the mattress beside me, pulling the sheet back up to cover both of us. It was a tight squeeze, but our bodies interlocked as if they'd been meant to fit together. I nestled my head beneath the devourer's chin and brushed my lips to his chest. Snap's arm tucked around me, holding me there, secure.

Our breaths evened out in harmony. Shadowkind didn't need to sleep, but in physical form, they could. After a few minutes, Snap had relaxed completely against me. When I traced my fingertips over his bare torso, he didn't stir. My own eyelids drifted down. The ache swelling around my heart was nothing but contented now.

"It's quite the feat," I sang under my breath, snuggling closer. "In your eyes, I am so sweet." And maybe, come what may, that would be enough.

EIGHT

Snap

When I woke up, only a faint haze of dawn light showed through the window. Sorsha lay peaceful in my embrace, her red hair providing a bright frame to her pale face. Her fiery sweet scent lingered in my nose and on my lips.

I wanted to hold her like this forever. I wanted to slide back inside her and return to that wonderful, slick melding that had brought such pleasure to both of us. But the first option was impossible while we still had Omen's jailors to bring to justice, and the second would have meant breaking her much-needed sleep.

Instead, I settled for slipping away into the shadows and reforming outside, meaning to check the car for any food she might have bought and left there that I could offer her as a breakfast when she woke. That's what I would have done, except Omen was leaning against the car, his arms folded over his chest and his gaze piercing as it fixed on me. I might not have been an expert at reading emotions like Ruse was, but I could tell he wasn't happy.

"What exactly is this mortal's draw that all three of you are slavering over her?" he said in a cool, flat tone. "Even *you*. Are her nether regions laced with heroin?"

I blinked at him. I didn't like how hard and cold he'd been since we'd freed him. The Omen who'd asked me to help with his quest, the one who'd guided me through our first few ventures into the mortal world, hadn't exactly been cheerful, but he'd smiled with warmth. Made jokes now and then. Laughed at *Ruse's* jokes at least as often as he'd glared. He was angry because of what the other mortals had put him through, this Company of Light, and that made sense, but still, I didn't like it.

And also… "I don't know what that means."

He sighed and pushed himself off the car to straighten up. "Of course you don't. Never mind. The point is, you're awfully attached to this woman, aren't you?"

Did he simply know what we'd been doing last night, or had he managed to overhear some of the things I'd said to her as well? I wouldn't take any of them back.

"Why shouldn't I be?" I asked. "You haven't given her a chance—you weren't there to see how much she did for us, how incredible she's proven herself to be. Weren't your tests enough? Or how she helped us in the ambush last night?"

"That's not the point. She could deliver us the elixir of life and she'd still be a mortal. No good has ever come of a shadowkind getting hung up on one of them. We're not the same sort of being—we don't mix well. It's a losing game."

My hackles rose. "It isn't a game. I care about her."

He waved a finger at me. "That's exactly the problem. Caring tangles your fate up with hers. You haven't been on this side enough to know—mortals are fragile, Snap. Damned fragile. Why do you think they're always coming up with new ways to try to screw us over?"

"Because they think we're monsters?" I ventured.

"That's just the name they invented to justify how they feel. And how they feel is fucking terrified of us." He scoffed. "They're afraid of so much, and they want to destroy whatever scares them."

I paused, remembering a different sort of terror I'd sensed before we'd gotten Omen back. One he might have experienced as much as the creatures who'd left those impressions had. Was that what had changed him?

"I know what they did," I said quietly. "The Company, in their experiments—not every aspect of it or any hint of why, but we investigated one of their labs. I tasted... over and over again, so much agony to so many shadowkind. It was horrible."

"You don't need to tell me that," Omen growled.

"But I do need to tell you—Sorsha isn't like that, not at all. She hates the people who did that as much as we do."

"It doesn't matter. Even the ones who aren't outright hostile end up making more trouble than it's ever worth. The only thing it's worth doing with mortals is killing the ones out to harm us and giving all the others a wide berth. I guarantee you, she'll make you regret doing anything else."

"You don't know her. *She* isn't fragile." I couldn't imagine that word ever properly describing Sorsha. The power she wielded wasn't anything like Thorn's or Omen's—or any other shadowkind—but it was still power. I could recognize the determination and resilience in her as surely as I could glean impressions of the past from any objects in my grasp.

Omen had tried to hurt her or to put her into situations where she'd be hurt, but she'd overcome his challenges. Why couldn't he see?

"She is fragile," he insisted. "You just don't understand yet. It always comes out at the worst time. We've got too much at stake to risk it."

"We'd risk a lot more if we stopped her from helping us. And I might not be very familiar with the mortal realm yet, but I know enough to recognize that."

"Fine. She's helping us. I haven't sent her away, have I? Just have a little self-respect and stay out of her *bed* if you know what's good for you." He grimaced and stalked away.

A jittery sensation ran through my body in the wake of his words. The thought of Sorsha becoming fragile, of her breaking in some way, set all my nerves on edge.

I made myself investigate the car as I'd planned to. After a minute, I came up with a gas station store bag still holding some sort of chocolate cake-like confection that I expected would serve well enough, but I couldn't rouse much sense of victory. I flitted back into the cabin and set the food down on the little table under the window.

Sorsha had dozed on. There *was* a sort of delicateness to her features when they were relaxed with sleep, a vulnerability in the softness of her skin. When we shadowkind took physical bodies in this realm, we could be gouged and shattered too, but unlike her, we could escape into the shadows to avoid a blow.

I'd already had to dig one bullet out of her. That had been painful—for me as well as her. Perhaps that was what Omen meant about her supposed fragility causing trouble.

The answer was simple, though. It rang through me clear as anything as I gazed at her lovely form.

I wouldn't *let* the few who were vicious enough to wound this woman get close enough to do so. No mortal or shadowkind would uncover any frailty in her. She'd saved me from a cage that would have burned me and the searing of the lights in a collector's home—and I would save her when she needed me to. Over and over, if it came to that. When a battle turned bloody, it wasn't as if Omen needed my abilities in that moment to serve his purposes anyway.

Whatever other shadowkind he'd known who'd mingled with mortals, they must not have cared the same way I did. She was mine, and she'd called me hers, and nothing had felt more right in my entire existence. He didn't need to worry about how much she mattered to me precisely *because* of how much she mattered to me.

Satisfied with that conviction, I eased down on the bed next to her to soak up a little more of her warmth. If I was particularly lucky, she'd share a morsel of that chocolate delicacy with me when she woke up.

NINE

Sorsha

When I returned after placing the police cap I'd stolen a couple of days ago on the head of a ten-foot-tall horse-and-rider statue in the park, Omen barely gave it a glance, even though he'd given me the challenge. "All right," he said. "Now let's see you collect, oh, we'll say ten wallets. You never know when some mortal cash might come in handy."

I stopped myself just shy of glowering at him. It was a hazy afternoon, the sunlight filtering through a thin layer of grayish clouds overhead, but warm enough that plenty of people were roaming through the park around us. Nabbing ten wallets wouldn't be tough. But we really *didn't* need cash when Ruse could charm anything we needed out of just about anyone—and at this point I was pretty sure that Omen's tests weren't meant so much to confirm my abilities as to arrange my arrest or some disabling injury. Maybe he'd have liked both.

I'd thought he was done with the Sorsha Trials after yesterday's ambush, but apparently not. Ellen's phone call this morning appeared to have set him off. I'd only spoken to her for a few minutes to get the plans for a Fund meeting in an undercover location this evening, but Bossypants had been fuming behind his controlled exterior ever since.

My own patience was wearing so thin you could have severed it with the blunt end of a spork. I also didn't love the idea of screwing over ten random innocent bystanders who'd just wanted to enjoy the last few days of summer.

I set my hands on my hips and smiled thinly at Omen. "How about I do you one better? I'll steal the wallets, lift the cash, and return them without the marks ever knowing what they lost."

"A thief with a heart of gold," Omen said with a hint of snark. "I'll be watching to make sure you collect the full ten."

"I'm counting on it."

I slipped through the park, focusing on purses left by picnic blankets and on larger gatherings where I could blend in with the crowd long enough to score. I only took a bill or two out of each wallet rather than all the cash, because Omen wouldn't know how much I'd left behind. When I'd replaced the tenth and walked back to the edge of the park where he'd parked Betsy, I had a hundred and fifty bucks and no intention of playing this game any longer.

"Here you go," I said when he emerged from the shadows between the trees, and handed him the money. "Buy yourself a better attitude. Somehow I'm guessing you didn't put the shadowkind guys through half this much work to prove they belonged on the team."

"I *picked* them, knowing they already belonged." Omen grimaced at the bills as if he found them distasteful and stuffed them into his pocket. "You don't get to decide when we're done. I'm feeling like a snack. Get me a pie from that shop." He pointed to a bakery across the street.

Was he kidding me? I opened my mouth to tell him where he could shove his pie… and then realized there was an even better option. Instead, I gave him another smile. "Does it have to be stolen, or can I buy it? And any particular flavor you'd like, boss?"

Really, calling him "boss" should have tipped him off. I could almost hear Ruse's snicker from the patches of darkness nearby. But Omen either wasn't paying enough attention or assumed he'd actually persuaded me of his ultimate authority. He waved dismissively at me.

"An expert thief shouldn't need to spend any money, right? And I'll take apple or cherry."

So generous of him, giving me two options. I gave him a mock curtsey and strode across the street.

A beautiful cherry pie was sitting on the top shelf of the glass display cabinet beside the cash register. I asked for one of the tarts next to the pie, and once the clerk had opened the cabinet door, "accidentally" knocked her tip jar onto the floor. As she scrambled to grab a broom to sweep up the broken glass and scattered coins, I thought a silent apology at her and liberated the pie. If she'd understood what good use I was going to put it to, surely she wouldn't have minded.

When I returned, Omen was leaning against his car, looking way too smug. I had the perfect cure for that.

I gave him a broad grin as I crossed the street. "Here's your pie. Enjoy!" Then I lifted his just dessert and planted it smack-dab on his face.

I moved quickly enough that the unsuspecting shadowkind didn't have a chance to dodge. He jerked away an instant too late, sputtering as chunks of golden pastry and syrupy globs of cherry filling dribbled down his face and onto the front of his shirt. A couple of passersby snickered at the sight. He couldn't blink away into the shadows to remove the mess in front of witnesses.

His eyes flashed with the fiery glow I'd seen in the Company's facility. *"You."* With a wordless growl, he snatched my wrist and spun us around to slam me into the car.

The impact radiated all through my back, making my healing shoulder throb, but it was worth it—to see his sneering face covered in fruity gore, to watch his rigid control snap and let out the heated rage underneath. To prove *he* wasn't the perfect model of cool authority he liked to pretend he was. As he raised a fist, I stared right back at him, daring him to use it.

My trio ruined the fun. All three of them dashed from the shadows in the same moment. "Omen," Thorn said in protest, and Snap leapt to my side.

Ruse cocked his head, studying my masterpiece. "You did want her to show she can stand up for herself, didn't you? You've pushed her pretty far. Looks like sweet payback to me."

Omen's shoulders had already come down. His teeth flashed as he bared them, and then, with Thorn's massive form hiding him from view, he slipped into the shadows and back again so swiftly his body only seemed to stutter before my eyes. Just like that, the mashed pie was gone other than the bits that had fallen to the sidewalk. The lingering scent smelled pretty damn good. Almost a waste of a tasty dessert—almost.

Snap eyed the splatters on the ground as if he was thinking the same thing, but he stayed next to me, his arm coming around my waist. Omen glanced around at his supernatural companions, his expression back in its chilly mask but his stance tensed and the ice in his eyes searing.

"*I* decide when she's done," he said, and shifted his gaze to me. "Was that prank supposed to convince me of your self-discipline?"

"No," I said. "I was just getting the pie to your mouth in as speedy a fashion as possible. But it probably does show my self-discipline too, considering I'd been *wanting* to do something like that for ages. I've met all your challenges. Either I'm in or I'm out, Luce. Or are you not very disciplined at making up your mind?"

A renewed spark of anger danced in his eyes, but he held it in check. His chin rose to a haughty angle. "I was confirming how much shit you were willing to take. Always important to know the limits of those you're working with. That can be enough for now."

He didn't want to find out what he'd get in the face if he started up his tests again. I eased myself off the car and brushed my hands together. "Excellent. I'm glad we got that sorted out. You all can even enjoy a little bro time hitting up that hacker for more dirt while I'm meeting with the Fund tonight. Wins all around."

As hard as I'd been working to stay part of the shadowkind quartet's investigations, I had to admit I was looking forward to getting in some human socialization. Of course, I wouldn't have chosen to be climbing up walls while I did it.

I eyed the rock-climbing gym Ellen had told me to meet the group at skeptically before stepping inside. The vast room smelled like rubber and sweat. Carabiners clinked and voices echoed off the high walls. A pang ran through my still-healing shoulder. Well, I'd grinned and borne it through worse in the past few days.

Vivi was waiting by the check-in desk, decked out in a tee and velour sweatpants—both white, naturally. She bounded over at the sight of me.

"Interesting change in scenery, isn't it? Come on, sign the waiver and get your gear. Ellen and Huyen booked a private alcove, but we've still got to look as if we're using it to actually climb while we're talking."

I laughed. "A workout and a debate in one. This should be fun."

Vivi hefted a climbing harness over her slim shoulder. "Do you really think they're going to argue that much about getting involved? These Company of Light people are obviously into some seriously shady shit."

"Yeah, but I can't tell them about most of that without giving away how much I was hiding from them before. And you know how a lot of the members are—they don't want to extend any more effort than showing up to chat at the meetings and writing up a few outraged emails."

It didn't appear that all that many members had even made the effort to show up at this new location. In our reserved alcove, Huyen had already scaled nearly to the top of the wall. A few other regulars were poised at various points lower down, their feet braced against the handholds that looked like something out of an abstract art exhibit. Ellen and one of the younger guys were standing near the edge of the wall, the guy pitching an idea to her in a low, urgent voice.

"We'd raise so much more money that way. It's not *really* lying. Okay, so we wouldn't actually be trying to save the abused dogs in the photos, but we are rescuing some kind of creatures—and some of them are furry!"

Ellen didn't look convinced. Since most of the mortal population would never have believed the shadowkind existed—and the ones who lived mortal-side weren't in any hurry to draw attention to that fact—we couldn't be completely truthful about our goals when we campaigned for donations. Slapping photos of a cause that wasn't ours to gain sympathy points rubbed up against our leaders' conscience.

"Sounds like a great idea to me," I said as I passed them, clapping the guy on the shoulder and shooting Ellen an encouraging smile. Maybe that was how the Company of Light could afford a gazillion people on staff and fancy equipment out the wazoo: pictures of cute fuzzy animals in distress.

"Huyen and I will talk it over," Ellen said to the guy as Vivi and I picked our spots along the wall. "You know we try to avoid outright falsehoods—it could come back to bite us if anyone follows up."

Okay, so there were practical reasons to avoid blatant lies too. Knowing the Company as well as I did now, they just offed anyone who poked their nose too far into their business.

As I hooked up my equipment, another sort of hook-up slunk into the space with all the shine of a storm cloud. Leland dropped his harness at his feet and stared up at the wall gloomily.

After spending so much time around my supernaturally stunning quartet, it was hard to remember what I'd found particularly attractive in that boyish face and top-heavy physique. Especially since these days my ex-friend-with-benefits turned even more sour whenever he glanced my way.

He was all the evidence I needed that I had no idea how to make an even semi-romantic relationship work with a fellow human being, let alone a shadowkind. *All* we'd been doing was hooking up, and somehow I'd failed to handle that well enough to end things on good terms. I wasn't even sure what exactly Leland had wanted that I hadn't been delivering, since he'd never outright asked for us to become more —or acted interested in anything about me other than what I could offer between the sheets.

Men. Maybe I should stick to one-night-stands from here on out. How big a catastrophe could I create when I spent less than twenty-four hours with a guy?

Huyen had bounded down the wall with impressive springiness, and the other members who'd been partway up descended as well. Ellen beckoned us together into a circle.

"Why are we meeting *here*?" one of the other women asked. "Is something wrong with the theater?"

Both of the Fund's leaders glanced at me. "Sorsha came to us with a somewhat... unusual situation," Ellen said. She tapped her fingers against her lips, and I wondered what popcorn flavors she'd been experimenting with to stain the tips that shade of purple: lavender? Eggplant? "For the sake of caution, we decided it was best to discuss it in a setting we've never used before. Sorsha, why don't you explain the rest?"

I dragged in a breath and laid out the scenario to the other members the same way I'd explained it to Ellen and Huyen, as succinctly as I could. I was just finishing up when one of the gym employees ambled our way.

"Hey," she said. "Everything all right over here?"

It must be getting noticeable that we weren't using the equipment. "Just doing a little catching up before we climb some more," Huyen said cheerfully, and shot us all a look that said, *Get moving*.

Time for the fun part. I checked my rope and gripped it tightly before wedging my foot against one of the lower holds. Leveraging my weight with my good arm, I hefted myself up. Maybe I'd just hang out right here.

"We need to look into these people," I said over my shoulder to the others, who were gathering along the wall around me. "Find out where they're operating out of, how they're raising their money, and anything else we can about them. But we've got to be careful to make sure they don't catch on that we're interested. Whatever we find out, we can pass on to the higher shadowkind and they'll decide how to handle it."

Those higher shadowkind would just happen to be the ones I was currently shacking up with.

"I don't know about this," said a middle-aged guy named Everett as he edged his way from one handhold to another. "It sounds like this organization is very... intense. If they *do* find out we've been meddling with their business, how are they going to crack down on us?"

"Hey," Vivi said, bouncing a little against the wall. "We've managed not to clue any outsiders in to what we're actually working on for however long the Fund has existed, haven't we?"

I shot her a grateful look. "And we won't be *meddling*," I added. "I don't want us to stick our necks out that far—I agree that it's not safe.

Better to let the shadowkind"—*and me*—"handle any actual response. We'll just be information-gathering."

"If this is your pet project, I don't see why you can't gather information on your own," Leland muttered.

To my frustration, a couple of the others murmured noises of agreement. What the hell had they joined up for if they were going to turn chicken the second the shadowkind *really* needed us?

I bit my tongue against asking that out loud. Thankfully, I'd said as much in politer terms to our leaders the other day, and they hadn't forgotten. Ellen hefted herself a little higher and peered down at the rest of us. "This is the whole reason the Fund was created. We shouldn't claim we're out to support the shadowkind however we can if we won't get involved when they're in the most danger they've ever faced."

"We didn't realize we'd be up against some big, secret army or whatever when we joined," Everett protested.

"Yeah," said the woman who'd asked about the change in location. "Let the shadowkind deal with the info-gathering and everything else if it's so important to them. Half the time they don't even help *us* helping their own kind."

That was sadly true, as Omen well knew. "This is different," I started.

Leland cut me off with a scowl. "Only because you decided it is. These people have been operating for who knows how long already. If the shadowkind haven't figured it out yet, that's on them."

Did he really care about the beings from our sister realm that little, or was he taking his animosity toward me out on them? Ugh, why had I ever thought this dude was worth letting anywhere near me, let alone *into* me?

Vivi spoke up before I had to. "Look, you just explained why it's important that we pitch in. It's clearer than a crystal under a cloudless sky. The shadowkind *haven't* been able to figure the problem out on their own. They're not used to mortal-realm resources and strategies. We are, so obviously we could find out some things they haven't been able to."

"Exactly." I wished I wasn't dangling from a rope partway up a wall so I could have given my best friend a hug. Put a dunce cap on me for ever thinking Vivi wasn't up to facing off against this conspiracy. I'd gotten so caught up in trying to protect her, I'd forgotten how strong and smart she was.

Another round of murmurs carried along the wall, but this one sounded less decisive. Huyen, up at the top again, cleared her throat as she headed back down.

"As always, participation in our activities is optional. I think Sorsha and Vivian have made a reasonable case. We'll proceed with caution, of course, but we can at least put out a few feelers. Especially—how are these people raising their money? Coming at them from that angle could reveal all sorts of things the shadowkind aren't aware of, since it'll be all between the organization and other mortals."

Leland descended from his perch with a huff, but to my relief, at least a couple of the other members nodded, if hesitantly. Vivi's brilliant grin bolstered my spirits.

"I'm going to talk to my contacts tonight," I said. I wouldn't mention how much more intimate I'd gotten with most of them beyond talking. "I'll see if they know anything about the fundraising side that could point us in the right direction. You all could look through public records to check for any big events with a purpose that sounds suspiciously vague."

"And we should all know what that looks like from our own efforts." Huyen chuckled and soared through the air the rest of the way to the ground. "You heard her, people. That's this week's assignment. Let's not let ourselves down."

TEN

Ruse

"Well," I said, peering out of Omen's car at the farm we'd driven up to, "this place is gloom personified, isn't it? I have to say I preferred mini-golf."

By all appearances, the property was abandoned. The barn door hung open at an odd angle, and only weeds grew in the fields in uneven tufts, their yellowing leaves turned eerie by the moonlight. When I slipped out of the station wagon, the smells of dry dirt and old wood met my nose. A lopsided weathervane creaked as the night breeze briefly spun it.

Sorsha made a face where she'd gotten out beside me. "I see your gloomy and raise you ten creepies. But I guess the Company of Light needs the cover of darkness to do their dirty work."

We'd been directed here by the hacker girl who now saw me as the bestest friend she'd ever had. It'd been a particularly productive session on the computer, uncovering not just this hand-off with a collector who clearly hadn't gotten the message from the last one but also a fundraising gala happening in a few days. This Company had gotten away with an awful lot, but mostly because they hadn't faced off against an opponent who could really challenge them. The four of us with Sorsha in the mix were basically a dream team, if I did say so myself.

The location of our current ambush looked more like a nightmare. Thorn and Omen uprooted a couple of wilting shrubs to conceal the car more thoroughly where our boss had parked it behind a shed. The meetup was supposed to happen on the far side of the barn and not for another hour, but I wasn't going to argue against their caution. I had no desire to spend another second behind silver-and-iron bars.

Snap had ventured into one of the fields. He bent to sniff—and taste the impressions around—one of the taller weeds.

"Nothing has touched this except the wind and the rain," he said, and glanced toward the brick house in the distance. There might have been a FOR SALE sign outside it once, but it appeared to have fallen off the wooden post it'd hung from. "Isn't this a place for growing food?"

I came over, giving him a teasing tap with my elbow. "You're not going to find anything to eat here, my friend. I'd bet this place hasn't grown crops in years."

The devourer made a vaguely disappointed sound and headed toward the barn. We'd agreed that he would test the area for any sign of past transactions. There were only so many secluded spots in and around the city—the Company had to reuse some of them, especially if they'd been operating since the time when Sorsha's fairy guardian had been attacked.

We all stole across the field after Snap, Sorsha rubbing her arms even though there was only a slight chill to the summer night. Her gaze twitched at another creak of the weathervane.

"Doesn't it seem a little strange that they'd arrange another hand-off so soon after the last one?" she said. "If they were bringing in new shadowkind every week, they'd have needed a much bigger facility than the one where they were holding Omen."

"Many of them might be lesser shadowkind—smaller ones with some unusual or extreme powers," Thorn said.

Omen nodded. "Or they could have other facilities. They certainly moved their operations from that construction site quickly enough. It took the woman quite a while to dig up the details of this one, which I wouldn't expect if they'd wanted us to find it. But that is possible—

which is exactly why we're going to proceed with just as much care as always. Let's see where we can place our mortal so she won't create any catastrophes."

Sorsha shot him a withering look, but I thought he'd said it with a little less animosity than usual. As much as her trick with the pie had infuriated him in the moment, I suspected he'd gained a little more respect for her at the same time.

We'd just passed into the thicker darkness of the barn's shadow when Thorn, who'd taken the lead, barked a warning and lashed out with one of those rock-hard fists of his. I stiffened, expecting the meaty *whack* of that fist meeting flesh... but instead there was a soft *whoomph* and a woody cracking.

We hustled closer and found the lunk standing over his toppled foe: a tatty scarecrow with straw now burst from the split canvas of its head. I couldn't resist clapping Thorn on the back. The great hero of our time. "Excellent work. Now it won't hurt anyone else ever again."

The warrior glowered at me. Omen nudged at the straw with the toe of his boot. "Better overly fast reflexes than not fast enough. Let's see what our devourer has turned up."

Snap was still edging along the side of the barn. He moved from there to the sagging wooden fence, his normally cheerful face gone solemn with concentration. Finally, he straightened up and came to join us.

"I caught a trace of a person passing by in a few spots," he said. "Also, at one time there were younger humans who'd been drinking something with alcohol and were dizzy with it—they were gathering in the barn. I don't think they had any connection to the Company."

"Drunken teens? This would be the perfect place to party." Sorsha glanced around. "They cleaned up after themselves pretty well."

"We haven't looked *in* the barn yet," I pointed out.

"And it might have been years ago," Snap added. "I can't judge the timing all that narrowly. I didn't pick up anything to do with shadowkind, but if there've been other hand-offs here before, the people involved wouldn't necessarily have touched anything to leave impressions."

He drooped a little as if he felt he'd failed us by not discovering more. I'd have cracked a joke to perk him up, but Sorsha was already grasping his arm with the warm little smile she seemed to have invented just for him.

"You didn't pick up any sign of a threat," she said. "That's good to know."

He beamed back at her, his discomfort eased, and while I'd meant it when I'd told her that I was happy to see her take her pleasures wherever she could find them, the sight of them gazing at each other like that started an uncomfortable sensation nibbling at my gut. I wouldn't call it *jealousy*—what kind of incubus would I be then?—but it was something. Something I didn't want to look any more closely at. We had bigger fish to fry here.

Omen was in full admiral mode. He motioned to each of us in turn. "Thorn, watch the road and alert us if you see *any* vehicles heading this way. Snap, bring the rest of the equipment from the car. I don't smell any humans around the barn now, so it should be safe. Ruse, you figure out Sorsha's best vantage point with her. I'm going to check over the grounds farther afield."

My assignment suited me just fine. I offered Sorsha my elbow with a playful dip of my head. "Miss Blaze, if you would accompany me?"

Her lips twitched with amusement. Even as she rolled her eyes, she accepted my arm. "I think I can figure out my own vantage points, but I won't say no to having company. Maybe you can turn on that glow of yours so we can see in there."

She was joking, but Omen cut his gaze toward us anyway. "No special effects, please. We're trying to keep a *low* profile."

"Don't worry," I said. "I can manage to resist the urge to shine up the place." Besides, it would have felt strange shifting into my full shadowkind form anywhere other than in bed. We shadowkind revealed our true selves so seldom in the mortal realm that our more human guises were what came naturally after a while.

The inside of the barn *was* dark, though. Once we'd stepped much past the doorway, I could only make out the outlines of the shapes around us—some sort of large metal milk tank here, a row of stalls there. The odor of musty hay wafted around us. Not the most delightful perfume. Sorsha brought her hand to her nose as if stifling a sneeze.

I spotted a couple of squashed beer cans when I wandered close to one wall, but otherwise our mortal was right—the partying teens hadn't left much trace of their adventures here. Or else someone had come by since the partying and done a quick cleaning job.

A hay loft loomed high above our heads in the larger room, but if there'd been a ladder to access it, it was long gone. Sorsha frowned at it. "I think there's a window up there—that might be a good place for my stake-out. I just need a way up."

"We could have Thorn toss you," I suggested.

She swatted my arm and headed down the aisle beside the stalls. As I followed her, her pace sped up. "Oh, wait. Maybe that's—"

Whatever she was aiming for, she didn't make it there. One of the stall doors burst open as something large and heavy slammed into it with a metallic groan.

My supernatural skills might not be in the realm of combat, but I was still plenty quick on my feet. Sexual prowess required a certain nimbleness. The knobby monster of machinery careened toward Sorsha, and I dashed forward. I yanked her out of the way into a nearby stall on the opposite side—almost fast enough.

The mass of steel clipped her wrist, just shy of smashing her hand into the post beside her, and a bone snapped. We careened into the stall together, hitting the wall next to the door.

Sorsha gasped, the sound tight with pain. As she bit her lip, her eyes squeezed shut for a moment. Her left hand hung limp from her injured wrist, which was already swelling.

My pulse lurched. I held her motionless against the wall as another mechanical groan carried along the aisle with a heavy thump. If Omen had been wrong—if there were Company soldiers lurking in here—Thorn would be all the way down at the road by now, and the boss who knew where. I wasn't equipped for a fight.

Sorsha blinked, her lips parting with a shaky breath, and I caught her gaze. "We have to stay quiet," I murmured, and then, because it was the only way I could help her stay that way, I brought my mouth to hers.

I couldn't have imposed any of my supernatural intoxication on her to heighten the sensations while she wore that noxious brooch—and I wouldn't have regardless, having promised her as much—but I was plenty skilled as a lover without that enhancement. And I knew this woman now in ways I doubted even Snap did.

I swallowed any sounds she might have made and coaxed her tongue to twine with mine, leaning my body close enough to meld against hers, careful of her wrist and her still-bandaged shoulder. Her left arm stayed rigid at her side, but the rest of her melted into my embrace. I hadn't lost my golden touch yet.

As she kissed me back, her other hand came up to grip the back of my neck. She was throwing herself headlong into my attempt at distracting her from the pain—and damn if her response wasn't distracting me too. Why had I started this again?

No further noise reached my ears from the rest of the barn. Had the apparent assault really just been a precarious piece of farm machinery tipping over and not some kind of trap?

I didn't really want to stop this to find out. Sorsha's body adjusted against mine so pliantly, heat coursing between us. Shadows above and below, I'd never longed for anything more than to throw myself headlong into this burning, even though the tremors of energy that passed from her into me were barely more than a trickle thanks to her brooch.

No, I wanted to incite the passion in her just for the carnal satisfaction of it. To be inside her again—to feel her eager slickness around me—to know *she* wanted to be that close to *me* despite everything else...

A chill cut through the flames of my desire. That last longing, to be embraced fully by her not just in body but mind and heart as well—I had no business thinking that way. That kind of desire had nearly wrecked me before.

I'd learned my lesson. I damn well better have.

I pulled back, leaving Sorsha flushed and breathless against the wall. A faint glint caught in her eyes in the darkness—a shimmer of tears that had formed before I'd taken her mind off her injury.

"No one's coming," I said. "I think it was just an accident, not an attack. We should do something for that wrist. I mean, something more permanent than my immediate efforts."

I winked, and she managed to grin at me, her mouth twisting as the pain must have caught up with her again.

"I can still do my part in the ambush," she insisted in a strained voice as we crept out of the stall. "I'm not letting any of you tell me otherwise."

How was my heart supposed to be still when she talked like that, all ardent defiance? But I hadn't spent centuries dealing in desire to fail at curtailing my own, even if it wasn't quite the desire I was used to. I made a flourish with my hand for her to leave the barn ahead of me, as if this had all been a bit of fun.

When Omen returned, he didn't even try to argue with Sorsha. He knew battle wounds well enough to fashion a rough splint for her wrist, glaring at the limb the whole time even though I'd made it clear she hadn't been remotely careless. But it turned out none of us had any parts to play. The hour of the supposed hand-off arrived and passed, and another hour after that, until each passing minute left my stomach balled tighter.

"They're not coming, are they?" Snap said finally.

Omen scanned the farmyard, his expression grim. "No, it appears they aren't. Let's hope that means they got scared off by our last ambush and not that they have something worse planned. Time to move out—and make sure that as far as they can tell, no shadowkind were ever here."

ELEVEN

Sorsha

My nerves stayed jittery the whole way back to the cabin. I didn't like that the Company had apparently changed their plans, not at all. They'd never been the fickle type before.

Omen took the windingest of winding routes, and every honk or laugh that carried from the street around us had me jerking around with a hitch of my pulse. Which wasn't great, because every sudden movement took my probably-broken wrist from the deep but dull ache it'd settled into back to sharp, stabbing throbs for the next few minutes. I couldn't even bring myself to ponder the mystery of the car's smoky-savory-minerally car smell.

But even though the eerie stillness of the farm had been supremely suspicious, we made it back to the New-Age retreat unobstructed. I wouldn't have minded popping into a hospital on the way, but Omen seemed determined not to make any more stops tonight, and I wasn't going to tell him I couldn't take the pain.

"First thing in the morning, we'll find a quiet little clinic where I can 'encourage' a doctor into giving you a proper cast," Ruse assured me when we got out by the cabin.

"I might have a better solution than that," Omen said curtly, and didn't follow up that proclamation with any further detail. Just Bossypants being super helpful as always.

I yawned and considered both the makeshift splint and my exhaustion. "Well, I think I'm tired enough to sleep as long as I don't put any pressure on it." I paused, eyeing both the incubus and Snap. "So, I'll need the whole bed to myself, no company. Just FYI."

Ruse let out a chuckle that sounded oddly emphatic. "Have no worries on that score, Miss Blaze."

"Do you need anything else?" Snap asked, as if he could have produced whatever I asked for out of the woodlands around us.

"No, rest and a doctor in the morning sounds perfect. But thank you." I gave him a quick peck for good measure. When I glanced at Ruse, meaning to offer him the same gesture, he averted his gaze and turned as if to inspect the trees. All righty then. I could recognize a brush-off when I saw one, even if I had no idea what bee had gotten into the incubus's bonnet.

Picturing Ruse swapping his baseball cap disguise for an actual bonnet and taking way too much amusement from the image, I headed into the cabin. By the bunk bed I'd been using, I stopped to fumble with my cat burglar outfit's belt. Maybe I should have asked one of my lovers to join me for just a little platonic action. Undressing one-handed was pretty tricky.

I settled for only removing the belt with its dangling tools and stuffed all that into my backpack with a sharp tug of the zipper. At the sound, Pickle came scampering out of the bathroom. I'd barely had time to give him a scratch under his chin when the world went to hell around me.

A crash split the air, then a thump and a volley of shouts, most of them voices I didn't recognize. My heart stopped. No time for that rest right now after all, unless I wanted to be doing it six feet under.

I snatched up my backpack and my purse—and, shit, Pickle. Scooping up the little dragon one-handed, I tossed him into the purse with so little grace he squealed in protest. As I wheeled around, pawing at the backpack for the tools I'd just put away, a figure in silver-and-iron armor crashed through the cabin window.

Shards of glass pelted the arm I raised to protect my face. Thankfully, my fighting instincts kicked in, honed by the self defense classes Luna had made me take—I sent up a silent apology to her spirit for ever complaining about those. The guy lunged at me, and I knocked his feet out from under him with a swipe of my leg. As he caught himself on the post of one of the bunk beds, I groped with my good hand for any hard object I could turn into a weapon.

My fingers collided with a big, jagged hunk of rose quartz on the tiny dresser. Time for it to do something other than look pretty and emanate loving vibes.

The guy swung at me again, but *his* weapon—one of those blazing whips—wasn't much use in the tight space. Before he could fling it at me, I walloped him in the head with the pointy end of the crystal. He swayed but managed to throw a punch that clocked me in the jaw.

I reeled backward, my head spinning, and he smacked the crystal out of my hand. I grasped hold of the next nearest object, which turned out to be my lovely lawnmower candle. Thank goodness for thick glass jars. I mashed that right into his nose, hard enough that blood spurted from his nostrils.

As he swore at me, I fled out the cabin door. Pickle squeaked in distress at the bumping of my purse against my ribs, but I didn't have a chance to steady him, especially when my one functional hand held my only means of defense.

Outside was even more of a shit-show. The moonlight glinted off protective helmets and vests all across the clearing. Thorn let out a bellow as he thwacked a few of our attackers off him, but their weapons had slashed across his bulging arms deeply enough that even in the darkness I could make out hazy mist trickling out of the wounds.

Shadowkind didn't bleed like we did, not that red liquid mess. Sever what should have been a vein or an artery, and their essence wisped out as black smoke.

Another form careened through the night, chomping and gouging unshielded calves and bellies left and right. I'd barely seen more of Omen than a blur when he'd first barged out of his jail cell, and then he'd been flickering somewhere between his shifted form and his more human appearance, but I knew this had to be him—and now he was all beast.

The enormous, hound-like demon-dog could have stood

shoulder-to-shoulder with me, and I was no shorty. In place of the icy blue eyes I was used to, its gaze blazed a fiery orange. The same searing glow coursed amid its dark gray fur like rivulets of molten magma across a volcanic plane. Fangs as long as my index finger gleamed with each snap of its jaws. The devilishly pointed tail I remembered lashed through the air, wrenching a knife from one attacker's hand.

I'd never seen a shadowkind like that before, but Luna had told me stories of some of the more frightening creatures you could encounter, mostly to dissuade me from begging her to find a way to take me into the shadow realm so I could experience it for myself. I was looking at what most mortals would have called a hellhound.

In the midst of the chaos, I was struck by a fleeting eureka moment. So *that* was the source of Betsy's smell. Instead of your typical doggy odor, Omen's presence had marked it with sulfur and hellfire.

The Company's people clearly hadn't caught him by as much surprise as during their first ambush, but despite his ferocity and strength alongside Thorn's, our attackers were closing in on us. They hadn't skimped on manpower.

One guy sprang at me, and I beat him off with the candle jar, just as another came charging toward me from the other direction with one of the Company's nets. Did he figure *I* was a shadowkind, or did they just want to take all of us alive for questioning? My breath hitching in my throat, I lobbed the jar at his face.

He must have been holding a lighter or something that I hadn't seen. The candle's entire wick flared to life as the jar's mouth smacked into him, and hot wax splashed into his eyes. He dropped the net with a howl.

Thorn barreled toward me just as another attacker swerved my way. The warrior pummeled him three feet in the air with one of his mighty fists and spun to shield me. "Take cover—the car!"

Abandoning him to keep fighting on my behalf sent a jab of guilt through my gut, but *he* wouldn't leave until I had a safe route out of here. And the station wagon was my only hope of a quick escape.

A figure already sat in the driver's seat—a blond surfer-looking dude. Confusion washed over me for a second before I realized it was the disguising spell on the windows. The guy inside had to be Ruse, having slipped inside through the shadows now ready to make a getaway.

I was just a few steps from the door when the Company people must have noticed my mad dash. A louder shout rang out, and something shrieked through the air over my head. I had just enough sense left in my spinning head to duck, my good arm coming up over my head.

Whatever explosive our attackers had hurled, it hit the hood of the station wagon—and blasted a burst of flame all across poor Betsy. I hit the ground, my skin stinging from the heat. A lance of pain shot through my injured wrist, a duller throbbing waking up in my bandaged shoulder. I hissed, nicking my lip with my teeth.

Someone grabbed my good arm—Ruse, his cacao smell turned smoky from the wafts of heat streaming off the station wagon. "This way!" He hauled me onto my feet and toward the drive.

I glanced back toward Thorn and Omen. "But—"

"We're not leaving them behind. I'm a firm believer in back-up plans."

Snap wavered out of the night up ahead and beckoned us onward. "I found it! There's only one man there—I think he has the keys—" He gazed past us to the crackling mess that had been our previous method of transportation. "And we need them, don't we?"

"Lead the way," Ruse said. "And make it snappy, Snap."

The devourer had enough sense of humor left to give a flicker of a smile as he whipped back toward the road. "Down the road this way," he said, pointing.

The gray shape of a large van came into view beyond the trees. Ruse smiled. "Perfect. We'll go through the shadows and only emerge when we're as close as we can get. Between the two of us, we should be able to knock him over. Sorsha, you can get his gear off?"

I gripped the strap of my purse, crisscrossed with the backpack I'd never gotten the chance to take off, thank Merlin's magic. My jaw was aching from clenching against the pain in my wrist. "I'll do my best."

Ruse nodded and turned to Snap again. "Then I can convince him we're all just having a friendly party. As soon as he's subdued, you bring Omen and Thorn."

Without another word, they both vanished into the darkness again.

I pelted onward, sweat beading on my brow. "Just another manic run-day," I sang to myself under my breath, but even The Bangles' bouncy tune couldn't lift my spirits right now.

The guy guarding the van looked up at my footsteps when I was still a short sprint away, but my shadowy companions had gotten there first. His hand jerked up, a pistol clasped in his grip, and Ruse and Snap appeared right behind him, slamming his legs so he toppled over.

I dropped to my knees to wrench off his helmet. Ruse grasped the man's head and Snap sat on his legs while I fumbled with the snaps on the vest.

"A lot easier with two hands," I muttered, but after what felt like a million years, I was yanking that off too.

The incubus immediately started speaking in his smooth, cajoling tone. A magical thrum resonated through his voice. "We're all just having a little fun: a night-time game of tag. You and your partners had the wrong idea coming in here. No one wants to hurt anyone else. Happy times all around."

I raised my eyebrows at him, but the guard was already falling into a subdued daze. "Yes," he said. "I'm sorry. No one passed on the message."

Snap flitted off into the darkness. As Ruse kept charming the guard, I checked the guy's pockets for the keys to the van. "Don't mind me. Just a little friendly groping."

He didn't look offended. I fished the keys out and opened up the driver's side door. *I* obviously wasn't driving in my current state, but I'd shit silver dollars before I let myself be crammed in the windowless cargo area.

I settled my purse and the deeply disturbed Pickle on the floor by the front passenger seat, tucked my backpack beside them—and ducked as a gunshot rang out from someplace much closer than I'd ever have preferred.

Ruse's voice rose. "If you could do me a quick favor, pal? Run on over there and tell your colleagues that there are more shadowkind coming from the north. If they hurry, they can tag 'em all."

"Yes, right, of course," the guard said, and trundled off toward the figures I could see just emerging from the driveway.

"Buckle your seatbelt," Ruse said breathlessly, diving in behind the steering wheel. He obviously didn't trust that his gambit would delay our pursuers long enough for us to laze around.

I shoved the keys into his hand, he gunned the engine, and to my vast relief, three figures popped into the space behind us with a whiff of Snap's mossy scent, the sulphuric odor I now knew belonged to our hellhound shifter, and far too much of Thorn's smoky blood.

Ruse hit the gas and hauled at the steering wheel. The van screeched around in as tight a U-turn as he could manage, engine sputtering, and roared off down the country road with bits of gravel rattling like machine-gun fire against the undercarriage.

Two more shots rang out behind us. One clipped the side mirror beside my door, and I flinched. But then we skidded around a bend and left our enemies far behind.

"Well," I said, with as much optimism as I could summon, "we all got out alive. And in one piece… I hope?"

Omen's cold voice carried darkly from behind me. "All of us except Betsy. Any thoughts on how you're going to repay that debt, mortal?"

TWELVE

Sorsha

"Just keep quiet and let me handle everything," Omen said as we walked down the street, the others trailing through the shadows around us.

I grimaced at him. "I know, I know. You've been telling me how much I should shut up ever since you brought up these friends of yours."

"They're not my *friends*. They owe me a favor. A few favors, really. Which is a good thing for you, considering I'm down one heavily enchanted car."

"Hey, I'm not the one who must have led them to our hide-out."

He stopped in his tracks to glare at me. The late morning sun searing off his blue eyes turned them almost as fiery as when they'd been the color of flames last night. My skin itched with the suspicion that if I pushed that line of thought harder, he might transform into his hellhound self so he could literally bite off my head.

"It was your human hacker contact who pointed us in the wrong direction," he said. "And we wouldn't have needed a hideout in the first place if your mortal body didn't require sleep. I don't think it's in your best interests if we start tallying up the full score."

I didn't see how it was *my* fault his car had gotten blown up. How the hell had I been supposed to get to it without running toward it? But to be honest, while the shadowkind boss had grumbled plenty about the loss since we'd ditched the Company's van in the wee hours of the morning, he hadn't been quite as caustic with me as I'd have expected.

Another suspicion itched at me: something was up. Maybe he was being slightly less awful to me for the time being because he was about to offer me up to his past associates as dinner?

He set off again, walking fast enough that I had to hustle to keep pace. Then I saw the building he was leading us toward, and all other questions fell to the wayside.

"*That's* where they run their business?"

The parking lot he'd moved to cut across sprawled outside of a sleek, dusky block of a building with a sign that would have been lit up in neon if it'd been opening hours yet. A sign with a buxom lady in a bikini holding a martini glass, next to the words, *Paradise Bar & Dancers*. If you looked up "strip club" in an encyclopedia, it'd probably have a picture of this place.

"*Quiet*," Omen said in a harsh undertone, and added, equally low. "It's not for the male members of the gang. They've got a succubus in the mix—this allows her easy feeding."

Right, and I was sure the shadowkind men who ran their criminal syndicate operations out of the place didn't get so much as a smidgeon of enjoyment out of the boobs and butts on display.

Maybe Ruse would perk up in the presence of another cubi type. He'd seemed a little down this morning, his smirks pale around the edges. Unnerved by the fact that the Company had tracked us down yet again despite all our precautions? Or was whatever had turned him standoffish last night still eating at him?

I did manage to keep my mouth shut as Omen rapped on the glass door. A woman in a dress designed to draw your eyes to exactly the few body parts it covered opened it and waved us in with a bored expression. Omen had called ahead so his friends—excuse me, owers of favors—would be expecting us.

The woman who'd let us in didn't appear to be the succubus he'd mentioned. She went over to one of the little tables by a platform ringed with soft purple lights. A few other ladies with big hair and bigger cleavage were sitting there, nibbling at a plate of nachos. The tangy scent of the salsa hung in the air alongside sour notes of alcohol. They didn't go for the bah-dah-boom music during off-hours, though—in weird contrast to the setting, a classical flute piece was lilting from the speakers.

Pickle squirmed in my purse, and I set my hand on it to hide his movement. I didn't see anything supernatural about the gathered dancers. Omen strode straight past them and the stage to a door at the back of the main room.

Just before he reached it, a man opened it. Or maybe I should say a goliath. The dude filled the entire doorframe, taller even than Thorn's six-foot-and-quite-a-few-inches and equally muscle-bound.

Not one of the wingéd, though. His skin had a faintly blue-ish cast that I knew from experience meant *troll*. How he explained that to the mortals he dealt with in his gang's activities, I didn't know—but maybe when you were that big and scary, people tended not to hassle you about the exact hue of your skin.

"Omen," he said in a thick baritone, his narrow gaze jerking from the hellhound shifter to me. "And friends." He must be referring to the others he could sense in the shadows.

"Good to see you, Laz," Omen said in his usual cool, even voice. "I appreciate you all making the time at such short notice."

A sharper male voice with a hint of humor carried from the room behind Laz. "Aw, come off it, Omen. We know as well as you do that there'd be hell to pay if we forgot what we owe you, possibly literally. Get yourselves in here, already. Let's have a look at this troop you've assembled."

The troll stepped back, and we walked into a back room that disproved Omen's spiel about the strip club front being all for the woman in the bunch. Pin-up posters hung on the plaster walls, a few of them of hunky dudes showing off the full kit and caboodle, but mostly sprawled women with come-hither eyes.

To avoid having my own eyeballs assaulted by too many pairs of perky nipples, I trained my gaze on the group lounging on the leather sofas that created an L along the far walls.

My nose told me before anything else did that there was a

werewolf in the bunch. I'd had dealings with a couple of them before through the Fund's work, and anyplace they spent much time always took on a distinctive smell, like musk and pine and a hint of wet dog. Soon appearing as a new candle scent, no doubt.

From the look of the three figures on the sofas, Mr. Wolf was the guy with the scruffy brown hair and scruffier beard whose eyes glinted an eerie yellow. At his left sat a slim man with skin so pale it was nearly translucent. I wouldn't be surprised if he was fae or some related being.

Reclining on the other sofa was the succubus Omen had mentioned, a voluptuous woman in a lacy baby-doll dress who hadn't bothered to pause in painting her toenails at our entrance. The fall of her wavy honey-blond hair didn't quite disguise gem-like protrusions twinkling like rubies just behind the corners of her jaw. She must pass those off as some kind of piercing.

The trio shimmered into their physical forms around Omen and me. Snap stuck close to my side, his arm tucked next to mine, and when the succubus finally looked up, Ruse tipped his head to her with a knowing glance. Thorn, who was no longer smoking from various body parts thanks to the shadowkind's quick recovery time, flexed his shoulders and appeared to size up the troll. The other dude might have a few inches on him, but I'd bet all my worldly goods—limited as those were at the moment—that the wingéd's fighting skills could overcome that difference no problem.

The werewolf stood up slowly as if he didn't want to look too eager to welcome us. His voice was the one that had called us in—he must be the leader of this pack.

"Quite a collection," he said, and gave Omen a slanted grin. "Even a mortal. Although I see you've managed to break her already."

My jaw clenched at the mention of my bandaged wrist.

Omen shrugged with a casual air. "That's one of the reasons we're here. Birch, you can handle a wrist fracture, can't you?"

The pale man sprang up like a tugged branch swinging into place, and I caught the rustle of the few silvery leaves mixed with his ash-gray hair. Not fae—dryad. The shadowkind with affinities to plants often had healing abilities—something to do with the whole sprouting to life thing.

"I'll need to remove the splint to take a proper look," he said.

Omen nudged me, and I held out my arm. Bossypants was using one of his previous favors to fix up my wrist? Awfully weird when he'd just spent the last few days doing everything he could to set me up for a fall. But while he was offering—

I motioned to my shoulder. "I've got a bullet wound that's still sore while you're at it, if you have the chance."

"That wouldn't take long. Melding flesh is easier than bone." Birch led me to the sofa and sat me in the spot the werewolf had vacated. As he began unwrapping my wrist, I gritted my teeth.

"Broken and shot at," the werewolf said with obvious amusement. "You're usually more careful than that, Omen."

"She's something of a disaster, but useful in other ways," Omen said, lucky I was too busy holding in a pained gasp to chuck something at his head. "And 'careful' wasn't enough to completely protect us last night. There's a particular group of mortals who've taken their vendetta against our kind to another level entirely."

As the dryad gripped my wrist and threads of a warm tingling sensation wound through the pain, Omen gave the gang's inner circle the low-down on the Company of Light. He managed to avoid mentioning the fact that its members had captured and imprisoned him for weeks on end, I noticed.

"We're all under threat," he finished off. "It's clear these mortals won't be happy until they've eradicated every shadowkind in existence."

The werewolf had listened intently to the story, but now he scoffed. "They don't stand a chance."

"You haven't seen the resources they've gathered and the techniques they've worked out for overcoming us, Rex." Omen motioned toward me. "We have to rely on *her* to make it a fair fight. And from what I've heard about the experiments they're running—it's not a simple matter of them looking to kill us all. They've got something more complex they're working toward. Maybe something we can't be prepared for."

"It's horrible," Snap said, a waver running through his bright voice. "The things I've sensed from the places where they worked—they enjoy hurting us and want to hurt us more."

The werewolf—Rex? Well, I guessed that was better than "Fido"—gave the devourer a skeptical look. "I doubt you need to worry your pretty head about it too much, Sunshine." He raised his eyebrows at Omen. "Where'd you dig *that* one up?"

Okay, now they were both lucky the dryad still had a firm grasp on my arm. "I don't think you'll be making jokes about it if they come for the bunch of you and stick you in their silver-and-iron cells," I said.

"I've fought many battles across many centuries," Thorn added in his grim tone. "I can confirm that the strategies this Company of Light is using are particularly—shamefully—effective against our kind, even those of us with strength beyond that of any human."

"Only if they hassle us," Rex said. "It sounds like they've come after you because you've been stirring up shit with them. Why are you sticking your neck out if it's going to get chopped? Any shadowkind stupid enough to get snared can face the consequences for themselves."

"When they run out of the easy pickings," Omen started, but his argument was cut off by a grunt from the troll.

My head jerked around at the squeak that followed. Shit on a soda cracker—while I'd been distracted by Birch's healing efforts, Pickle had squirmed his way out of my purse where I'd set it on the floor. Now he was bounding around by the troll's feet, flapping the wings that couldn't carry him more than a few feet thanks to the collector who'd had them clipped.

"What is *this*?" Laz asked, his lips curling in apparent disgust.

"He's mine," I said quickly, and then, remembering Thorn's initial offense at the idea that I was keeping a shadowkind as a pet, "I mean, because he decided that. I couldn't get rid of him even if I wanted to."

Ruse chuckled. "He appears to like you, Laz."

The troll attempted to ease Pickle away with a push of his foot, but the little dragon just scuttled around it and squeaked at him some more. A smile tugged at my lips. Now that we'd gotten Pickle friendly with Thorn, he probably figured all hulkingly intimidating shadowkind had bacon somewhere on them.

"Pickle," I called with a cluck of my tongue. Proving my point about who called the shots in our relationship, the creature completely ignored me, now nipping at Laz's pant leg.

"Oh, pick it up and give it a few pats," Rex said dryly. "It's clearly not taking no for an answer."

The troll bent rather stiffly and scooped Pickle onto his bulging arm. The dragon immediately scurried up to perch on his shoulder, where he chirped happily. Laz straightened up, his jaw working as if he was holding back a cringe, and watched the creature warily from the corner of his eye.

I stifled a laugh. *Not such a tough guy after all, huh?*

As the dryad shifted his attention from my now-numbed wrist to my shoulder wound, Omen launched back into his appeal. "I've heard the way these mortals talk. They aren't going to stop until they've wiped us all out—and one of their goals with their experiments is probably to find easier ways to identify us. They won't leave you alone to mind your own business. We have to strike back against them hard and soon, before they become even better at incapacitating us."

Rex clapped the hellhound shifter on the arm. "I know you've been through a lot and seen a lot in your time, Omen, but we've been living on this side for decades. I know mortals inside and out. If they come for us, they'll regret it. This city is ours now—let them try to take it from us or us from it, and we'll paint downtown with their blood." His teeth bared in a fierce grin.

"They already are taking shadowkind captive right within this city," Thorn said.

"The beings who haven't bothered to offer our crew their loyalties can buck up or leave. Most of *them* are a nuisance anyway." Rex turned back to Omen. "I owe you, sure, but not enough to dive into a war of your own making."

"*They're* the ones making it," Omen muttered, but I could see the resignation in his expression. He'd told me from the start that there wasn't any point in turning to other shadowkind for help. But he'd tried to convince this bunch anyway—because seeing them stay alive mattered more to him than it did to them, apparently.

As the faint throbbing in my shoulder fell away with the dryad's magic, a prickling sensation rose up from my gut. The frustration spilled onto my tongue before I could hold back the impulse.

"You know what happens when all you think about is looking after yourself and your friends? You look around one day when everyone who could have used your help has been killed or caged, and guess what, there's no one left to help *you*. But sure, go ahead and ignore the people who've actually dealt with the threat you're dismissing. I'm sure you know *so* much more about what we're up against than we do while you're sitting here in your titty bar playing gangster."

"I'll have you know we've got a lot more than just titties," the succubus said in a wry tone, but Rex whirled on me.

"*You* are just a hanger-on playing at being part of something special and supernatural," he snarled. "I don't need lectures on politics from a mortal."

I stared right back at him. "This mortal hanger-on survived being shot with a silver bullet. Think you could do the same, wolfie?"

Ruse raised his hand to his mouth to cover a snicker.

Omen sighed and shook his head. "Don't mind her. She doesn't know when to shut her mouth. I've still got more favors to call in. We need something to drive and someplace to stay that won't call attention to who or what we are. I assume you can offer that much?"

Rex turned to him without bothering to answer my last question. "Yes, that much I can do for you. In fact, I've got something that'll count for both." He snapped his fingers at Laz. "Quit playing with that little beasty and get me the key to the Ford."

The troll poked tentatively at Pickle, who merely nuzzled his fingers, probably wondering when the bacon was coming. Thorn stepped in to lift the dragon off the troll's shoulder. With visible relief, the big guy hustled away and returned with a key on a leather fob.

Rex motioned for him to hand the key over to Omen. "It's yours, and we're square. You can pick it up in the back left corner of the lot at King and Washington."

Omen palmed the keys and glanced around at the others. "You all relax here while I collect our new ride. You might as well get a breather in after the night we just had. Except you." His gaze settled on me. "You're coming with me before you burn any bridges all the way down."

I didn't have any interest in hanging out with these jackasses anyway. "Thank you," I said only to Birch, because I could be polite *and* an ungrateful bitch. As I tramped after Omen out of the strip club, I reveled at the easy roll of my shoulders. The dryad had some magic, all right. The numbness was already wearing off around my wrist, but that joint moved with only a slight ache now too.

I waited until we'd traveled another block before I said anything in response to Omen's cold silence. "I *mostly* kept quiet. Don't pretend I didn't say exactly what you were thinking anyway."

The corner of his mouth curled upward. Was that a hint of a real smile?

"You did," he said. "If I minded, I'd be reaming you out right now. You saved me having to say it myself. Not that it made any difference—which is why I wouldn't have said it."

All right then. I would have left it there, the silence feeling less tense if not quite companionable, but Omen shot a penetrating look my way. "If you're willing to say all that to a bunch of supernatural gangsters, when are you going to tell me about your fire powers?"

I blinked at him, struck by both confusion and something deeper, something more chilling than his eyes—because I wasn't totally confused. "What are you talking about?"

That slight smile came back, but I didn't like it this time. "You know. I wasn't so caught up in the fight last night that I would miss you lighting that candle with nothing but strength of will. You hide it well—I started to think I'd imagined the wave of heat you sent at the pricks in the Company's facility—but the cat's out of the bag. You're obviously not a shadowkind, or you couldn't handle the metals in their armor. Is it sorcery?"

Wave of heat… I remembered the way the one guard had flinched that night as if burned, but I'd put that out of my mind as just a weird random happening. Like the weird way the fires I set when taking my leave of the collector houses I'd raided sometimes behaved too. Because assuming those incidents were anything other than random, that they had anything to do with *me*, would mean something was very, very wrong.

"For it to be sorcery, I'd have to be a sorcerer, wouldn't I?" I said. "I don't have the faintest idea how to summon shadowkind to do my bidding. I've never even known a sorcerer. So, sorry, I think you're just imagining things. But while we're talking about interesting powers, what's the deal with the whole hellhound thing? Are you going to rain down hellfire on me the next time I piss you off?"

I didn't really believe he would, but changing the subject made for excellent deflection. Usually. Omen *was* rather dogged...

Forgive me the horrible pun. Could you have resisted?

"No," he said. "Although if you try to touch me in that state, I will sear your skin off. But you know one power I do have? I can smell fear. You don't actually think your connection to fire is nothing. You're terrified of the fact that it's *something*."

I folded my arms over my chest. "For your information, the only things I'm *terrified* of are sharks and being forced to go into witness protection someplace with no decent Thai restaurants."

"Say whatever you like. But if you deny it, you're being nearly as bad as Rex and the rest. You could use that power to help our cause."

"I don't *have* any power," I said, tamping down on the icy jolt his words had provoked in my gut. I couldn't have any sort of supernatural skills. It was impossible by any measure I knew of, and I knew more about the shadowkind and magical goings-on than just about any mortal alive, so it simply... couldn't be true. "And look, here's the parking lot Rex mentioned. Let's get on with more important, *real* concerns like what we're going to be driving."

"You're not going to dodge the subject that— Oh, boils and brimstone."

Omen stopped dead halfway across the lot, which was the point when it'd become obvious what "Ford" Rex had meant and how it was going to serve as both vehicle and home. Parked in the far corner was a vehicle even dorkier than his station wagon had been: the patchy blue shell of a squat camper van.

THIRTEEN

Omen

I could always feel a rift between the mortal realm and our own, even before it came into sight. There was a quiver in the air and a subtle flavor that tasted like salty steam. Here in the docklands, it mingled with the warble of the evening breeze over the river and the marshy scent of algae.

Rex had done me one better than handing over his clunky camper van. He might not want to stick his neck out for the rest of shadowkind, but he always had his people keeping their ears to the ground for potential threats, and he'd gotten a few reports of odd activity near this particular rift that sounded very much like the ambush I'd been caught in. The Company of Light had a few clear patterns, including that they liked to hunt near the rifts, presumably hoping to catch shadowkind who were still disoriented from the transition and so easier to disarm.

We didn't know how often the Company's hunters made the rounds here, but the past reports had all been from Thursdays—and all well before we'd staged our own ambush, so I didn't think the Company had planted that information like they must have for the hand-off at the farm the other night. We'd just have to hope we got lucky. I wanted to hear from someone who could tell us about more of their operations instead of just spouting anti-"monster" bullshit.

My shadowkind associates were surveying the area through the shadows, ready to dart back to me if they spotted suspicious movement. I'd opted to stay in my physical—human-ish—form, staked out on a low rooftop over one of the derelict factory garages, so that I could put the screws to my mortal ally a little more.

Said ally was crouched next to me by the low brick wall that ran along the edge of the rooftop. Sorsha flexed her slender wrist as if she still couldn't quite believe that Birch had mended it.

She knew magic, had been raised by a woman with shadowkind powers, and yet seeing them in practice was still somewhat otherworldly to her. So otherworldly that she seemed determined to deny that she could wield any powers herself.

I knew what I'd seen—not just during the attack by the cabin, but when we'd been escaping the Company's experimental facility and the day afterward, when I'd tested her with that falling fire. The effect *had* been small enough that I could see how she might have explained it away. I'd nearly explained it away after my slicing of her arm had revealed human blood rather than the smoke of a well-disguised shadowkind. None of my other tests had provoked her to using deliberate magic—or relieved me of the problem of deciding what to do with her.

But then the candle. And I'd seen in her reaction when I'd confronted her that she knew there was something more than human about her, as much as she wanted to deny it. I'd just have to prove it to her beyond her ability to deny it.

First I had to figure out what brought out those powers in the first place, since she didn't appear to activate them consciously.

"Shut up," she said before I'd so much as opened my mouth. "I know why you decided to stick with me, so you should know I'd rather tongue-bathe a tiger than talk about *that* anymore."

"Funny that you seem to think you have any choice in what I decide to talk about," I replied. If the universe had seen fit to send me a secret weapon with unpredictable powers, couldn't it have offered up one slightly less mouthy? "We could be facing off against Company people again tonight—people prepared to capture shadowkind. Are you really going to hold up your hands and play the powerless mortal if they get one of their nets or whips around us?"

She shot me with a look as fiery as that red hair of hers. "I've never acted *powerless*. I just don't have any super-special hocus pocus, no matter how much you want to believe it."

"Have you ever really tried to work some 'hocus pocus'? Why don't you see if you can set that stick up in flames?" I nodded to a bit of the debris that was scattered across the asphalt surface around us.

"Why don't I throw it and you go fetch it, dog-breath?"

The worst part about the insult was it did bring out my inner hellhound. My hackles rose, and my lips started to curl with a growl before I caught the searing surge of my temper.

She sparked all sorts of fires. I'd spent ages reining in the wildness that ran through my nature. I was *not* going to let one upstart human blast all that effort to smithereens in the course of a week. It was bad enough that both she and my shadowkind associates had seen me in a bout of unhinged fury when they'd first broken me out of my prison cell. I wasn't going to live that down until I'd shown just how in control of myself and *them* I could be.

I hadn't enjoyed browbeating them back into line, but sometimes harshness was a necessary component of leadership. If they didn't see me as fully in command, they might hesitate to follow an order when far too much depended on it. I hadn't devoted my current existence to this cause to see my efforts fall apart because I placed kindness over authority.

Besides, if I let my temper loose and incinerated the mortal, she wouldn't be any kind of secret weapon at all.

Before I could compose a perfectly calm and controlled yet scathing response, Snap flickered out of the darkness. "Men," he said breathlessly. "With the protections the Company has used before. They're moving toward the dock just east of the rift."

I peered in the direction he'd indicated. Beyond the glow of the nearest streetlamps, a few figures slunk through the darkness and vanished onto the abandoned boats still roped to the docks. Planning to hide out in that shelter while they watched for any beings that emerged, presumably. I frowned.

They'd come in enough numbers to overwhelm me during that first ambush. We had the advantage of surprise this time, but that wasn't a guarantee of victory. They'd shown how formidable a threat they could present at the cabin the other night too. As much as I'd hated it, especially after what they'd done to Betsy, turning tail and running had been our only hope of surviving with our freedom.

We did have the river to work with here, though. Those vests and helmets were pretty heavy—the men wouldn't be eager to swim in them. I cocked my head, considering the possibilities.

"Get Thorn and Ruse, and go through the shadows around the dock to the boats. Cut them loose—push the two far ones toward the middle of the river so they can't reach the dock and the one nearer this way, toward the shore. We'll give them a fine welcome." I jerked my hand toward Sorsha. "Come on."

As Snap vanished, we hurried to the stairs. "Getting a few flames going on that boat would keep our enemies even more distracted from shooting or slashing us," I pointed out. "Is it really so important to convince yourself you don't have the power that you won't even try to pitch in?"

Sorsha's eyes flashed at me in the darkness, but I thought I heard a hint of hesitation in her voice with her next protest. "I think it's better I focus on the ways I can actually help rather than imaginary super powers."

"Funny, of all the things I could criticize you for, I hadn't taken you for a coward."

Her shoulders tensed. That blow had landed. Now if only it'd push her enough.

Falling into silence out of caution, we slipped out the factory doorway and edged along the side of the crumbling brick building toward the water. As we reached the sprawl of the shipyard that lay between us and the river, shouts rang out from the dock. My boys were getting down to work.

I set off across the yard at a lope, assuming Sorsha would follow, determined as she was to help in one way or another. In the dim light, I made out the motorboat careening across the water toward us. Three figures were scrambling across it, one of them yanking at the chain on the motor, which coughed its last wheeze of gas and died again.

Another brandished a gun. I'd take care of him first.

"You know the plan," I said to Sorsha. "See if you can add to it."

She stared at the boat, but if she was attempting to stir up a fire, I didn't see so much as a glimmer. Fine. We could do this without any magical help from her. That was *our* area of expertise, after all.

I reached the edge of the concrete yard just as the boat came within leaping distance. One of the men gave a yell at the sight of me, but I was already springing across the gap.

I tackled the prick with the gun, knocking the weapon out of his hand and into the water. Thorn appeared next to me an instant later. He heaved another of the men by his bare arms onto solid ground, a few feet from where Sorsha had come to a halt.

The man landed on his side with a grunt, but he was sprier than we'd given him credit for. Ruse appeared with one of our lead blankets on one side, Sorsha dove to snatch off his helmet from the other—and he swung his leg around so fast he managed to kick the back of her knee. She stumbled, yanking herself out of the way of his next blow, and skidded right over the slick metal lip that jutted over the water.

She fell with a yelp and a splash, the water swallowing her up. Thorn rammed his fist into one of the other men's faces, crushing his skull, and spun to dive for her, but Sorsha had already heaved herself back to the surface. With an angry hiss, she grasped a post to haul her dripping body out of the water.

Ruse had managed to trap the first man under the blanket. The one I'd disarmed threw himself at the shore. He snatched at Sorsha as she swung her legs out of the water, she smacked out at him with her hand —and just then, a tiny flare glinted along the collar of his shirt.

It was there and then gone. I wasn't sure Sorsha had even noticed it, but I grinned—both at the momentary flame and at the crunch of Thorn's fists pummeling the prick into the pavement a second later.

Sorsha picked herself up. Her drenched shirt clung to her chest and hips, emphasizing every curve of her athletic but undeniably feminine body, and a different sort of heat stirred in me.

Oh, she was something to look at. I wouldn't try to deny *that*. She could light all sorts of sparks, indeed. But those ones, I had no interest in pursuing. She already had enough shadowkind under the spell of desire.

I motioned to the man we'd trapped. "Their friends will be on us any minute now. Get the iron and silver off him and let's go!"

FOURTEEN

Sorsha

We held our second interrogation in the back room of a funhouse. The summer fairgrounds had shut down for the season a few days ago, but they left enough supply trailers and other structures on site year round for the camper van to blend right in.

Omen stalked back and forth in front of the chair where we'd plunked our now perfectly willing captive down. "The docklands, the bridge in the park, and the strawberry-picking place south of the city. Are those really the only rifts your people check regularly? You never go farther afield?"

The Company of Light guy let his head list to one side as he considered with a frown of concentration. Once Ruse had chatted with him long enough, he hadn't even minded having his arms and legs tied to that chair. Bossypants was insisting on extra caution.

"I went out to a town just north of Pittsburgh with the guys once," our captive said, "but I wouldn't call that regularly. Covering those three every week takes up plenty of time as it is. We don't catch many of the monsters, but the Company is happy with what we bring in."

An edge of frustration was creeping into the hellhound shifter's voice. "All right. Let's run through all the Company higher-ups you've dealt with. Names, descriptions."

"It'll make helping them so much easier," Ruse put in with a twinkling of charm, shooting Omen a look of warning not to get too brusque in his questioning.

Pickle, who'd been watching the proceedings with me where I was standing beyond the glow of the single overhead bulb, scrambled from one shoulder to the other with a prickle of his claws and a nervous twitch of his tail. Tension hummed through the small, barren space, most of it wafting off of our leader. After everything we'd risked, this captive wasn't proving much more useful than the first one.

My phone vibrated in my pocket. I stepped out into the evening air with a little relief at the excuse to leave. It wasn't much fun listening to the Company jerks spout off about eradicating "monsters"—and even though they appeared to all be prejudiced and potentially murderous assholes, seeing them in that charmed daze for hours on end unnerved me.

I had my protective badge pinned to my undershirt to ward off supernatural powers, and I trusted Ruse not to use his on me anyway, but still… under certain circumstances, he *could*. He had on at least a few innocent people who had no opinions about the shadowkind whatsoever in the past couple of weeks in the service of our cause.

The phone's screen glowed in the deepening darkness outside. It was Vivi calling. My heart leapt. Kicking at crinkly concession-stand bags, I wandered farther across the desolate concrete yard that had held a Ferris wheel a few days earlier and brought the phone to my ear.

"Hey, Vivi. Did everything go okay?"

"Oh, yeah. They ate up my posh persona like I was caviar with a cherry on top. I told you I could work a crowd."

"You did," I agreed, and I'd known it was true. Vivi's brand of poise seemed to endear her to people almost as well as Ruse's charm. She'd been out this afternoon at a fundraising event. Between the connections the Fund had started tracing and the information we'd gotten from our local hacker, we'd been pretty sure it was a front for the Company of Light. "No one asked any awkward questions?"

"Nah. I've been around this kind of crowd before—just like the folks my uncle would schmooze with when he was running for state office. As long as you look the part, they assume you're some rich professional like them. And they do like to talk. I think I might have picked up a couple of tidbits your little team will find useful."

I perked up, ignoring Pickle nibbling at my ear. "Oh, yeah? What did you get?"

"Well, I made friendly with some of the catering staff and was able to sneak a look at some of their paperwork to check the billing name and address. Not sure how far that'll get you, but it should be worth tracing. And there were some pictures in this slide-show they did—they were claiming they're raising money for a special treatment center for kids with cancer. Maybe Ellen and Huyen should reconsider the whole 'no outright lying' policy for *our* appeals, because man did it work—"

"The pictures?"

"Right, yeah." Vivi laughed at herself. "I wondered if they might have used any from their actual buildings, since they wouldn't want anyone to recognize a place they know isn't really a cancer treatment facility. So I snapped as many pics as I could of *their* pics with my phone. I'll email all that and the billing info stuff to you. I know it's not a ton, but I didn't want to get too pushy my first time out."

"You shouldn't get pushy, period," I reminded her, but a smile had touched my lips despite the desolate atmosphere around me. We were building a real team here. With enough people—mortal and shadowkind—on our side, eventually the Company wouldn't stand a chance.

"I know, I know. Safety first. I did find out they're holding another event like this next month, so I can try to dig up more leads—in non-pushy fashion!—then."

"Perfect." Next month—that felt like forever away. Of course, it felt like it'd been at least one forever since my shadowkind trio had barged into my life in the first place. I was already down an apartment, most of my belongings, and my sense of certainty about who I was.

That thought led me right back to the insinuations Omen had been making—the last thing I wanted to dwell on. As I shook my uneasiness off, Vivi kept talking.

"I stopped by our favorite bar too—a certain someone there wanted me to pass on a message. I guess whatever she wants to tell you, she didn't feel comfortable talking about it except in person? She wants you to meet her in the FoodMart five blocks east of her place at eleven thirty tonight."

Jade wanted to meet at a grocery store? Well, I'd had dealings in weirder places recently... like right now, looking up at the giant clown face on the front of the funhouse. The shadowkind woman might have come through with something for us. I checked the time on my phone—I wouldn't have to rush to make it there. "I can do that. Thanks for letting me know."

"If there's anything else I can help out with in the meantime..."

"I know, I know. You're eager to get in on the action." But I still wasn't in any hurry to pull my best friend that far into the fray, as hungry as she might be to get a taste of adventure. "I'll keep you in the loop."

I ambled back around the funhouse and slipped through the back door just in time to see Thorn plunging his fist into our captive's smiling face.

Plunge was absolutely the right word. His crystalline knuckles caved in the guy's forehead and nose with a sickeningly wet crunch and squelched at least a few inches farther into his skull. The man's body slumped—a body that was still tied tightly to the chair. It wasn't as if he could have been any threat.

My stomach lurched. "What the hell!? Since when were we going to kill him?"

Thorn stepped back, blood and gore dripping from his hand to patter on the floor, his mouth tightening as he looked at me. Beside him, Omen—who must have given the order—offered only a casual shrug.

"Since he was a genocidal bastard out to destroy all shadowkind?" he said. "He coughed up everything useful he knew, and some of his colleagues saw us take him—they'd never believe he escaped before we'd raked him over the coals. From the sounds of your past exploits, they'd have killed him for being a loose end. This way he ends up in the same place without spilling anything about us."

He was still spilling—spilling brains all over the concrete floor. I averted my eyes, swallowing down the bile that was rising in my throat.

Omen had a point. The Company had murdered their own people before for compromising the organization through no fault of their own. I'd seen Thorn himself murder several Company employees in the past couple of weeks. They'd just always been actively trying to murder us at the same time, so it'd been easier to keep down my dinner at the thought.

"Well, I'm going to need a ride downtown in about an hour," I said. "I think I'm going to tour the sights outside until then." I turned on my heel and marched back out before any more of the fleshy stink could reach my nose.

Meandering around the vacant fairgrounds didn't do much to lift my mood, even with the good news I'd gotten from Vivi. I lobbed discarded pop cans at a target game that had been left in place while Pickle rummaged for treats by a snack stall with empty racks. Exerting my muscles distracted me a little, but that gnawing uneasiness lingered in the back of my mind.

I let my voice carry across the concrete yard. "In a messed-end town in a dread-sent world, the beast-blend boys can stress their girls..." Nope, even warping lyrics was taking me in a gloomy direction.

This was my life now: murder and mayhem and never setting my head down anyplace any other human wanted to be. Maybe I wouldn't have anything like a normal life back in a month—maybe I wouldn't next year.

It'd been easier not to think about long-term plans during the hunt for Omen's captors when we'd had no idea who we were up against, and then when it hadn't seemed all that sure I'd even be alive in a few days' time. Easier not to wonder if I was meant for a normal human life at all when I hadn't had an obnoxiously domineering shadowkind insisting I had some kind of supernatural power.

That *was* impossible, wasn't it? The uneasy quiver rose through my chest again, but the memory of Omen calling me a coward hardened my resolve. I glared at a tattered popcorn bag drifting across the concrete and pictured it going up in a burst of flames.

Burn. Burn!

Not so much as a flicker of heat wavered off the paper shell. With a surge of relief that maybe was a tad cowardly, I shook my head.

Of course I couldn't set a piece of trash on fire with will alone. The rest... it had to be a string of coincidences. Heck, when you played with fire as much as I did, was it really surprising that now and then something strange would just happen to happen?

My restless rambling led me back toward the funhouse. As I skirted an ancient-looking transport truck someone had left parked between the building and the now-deserted go-kart track, voices reached my ears. I paused out of view to listen. Hey, long-time thief here—why would you expect me to be above a little eavesdropping?

The first voice was Thorn's, even more somber than usual. "—pick them off a few at a time, and it hardly seems to make any difference."

"We're getting there," Omen replied. "Even I didn't know how complex this mortal conspiracy was going to be. But all that picking away at them will get us closer to shutting them down completely."

"It's not the kind of war I'm used to fighting. *They're* not the kind of opponents I'm used to going up against. To kill one who's been talking to us cheerfully as if we're his comrades..."

"Just because they don't fight the same way as the armies of times past doesn't make them any less formidable. If anything, they're more so, don't you think? If they came at us in a horde with swords swinging, you'd make mincemeat of them in an instant, and we'd be done with it."

"That's true."

My hackles were starting to rise at the thought of Omen badgering Thorn into acting against his conscience when the shifter's voice softened.

"I do appreciate all you've offered to me and this cause already, old friend. I wouldn't have called you out of your seclusion if I didn't think you could save so many more now than were ever at risk back then. Not that *I* believe you owed anyone more than you gave all those eons ago. You definitely don't owe me anything. While you stick with us, we do things my way—but if *you* need something from me to make the sticking easier, just say the word."

Thorn sighed. "It feels as if time has passed so quickly and yet so little of it has gone by. Someone needs to stand up for our kind, and

I'm more equipped than most. I'd just wish for a clearer way if one were available."

"Wouldn't we all?" Omen said with a chuckle, and then paused. "How do you think the others are holding up? You've spent more time in their company than I have by now." To my surprise, he sounded honestly concerned, as if he cared about Ruse's and Snap's well-being beyond how well they could carry out his orders.

Thorn took a moment before answering. "The incubus is difficult to read, but he's seemed happy enough. Maybe a little *too* merry at times, if anything. The devourer remains steady as long as he's not prodded about his greater power. He has more resilience to him than I might have expected."

"All right. If you get the sense either of them is faltering, let me know. I didn't start this crusade to ruin the only shadowkind willing to stand with me."

Holy hiccupping hellfire, the boss had a heart and a conscience after all. What would he say about *me* when he thought I couldn't hear?

As much as I'd have liked to indulge that curiosity, I had a covert meet-up to get to. I strolled around the truck as if I'd only just arrived back at the funhouse.

Omen's expression immediately sharpened at the sight of me. Thorn drew himself up even straighter as if he felt the need to look extra imposing after the doubts he'd expressed to his boss, but I'd stopped being intimidated by his size days ago. Mostly.

"I've got to get back to the city now," I said. "Important news from a friend—something too delicate to be passed on over the phone. Who's driving?"

I hadn't really figured Omen would volunteer, no matter how much heart he'd hidden behind that authoritarian attitude. "Ruse," he barked. "The mortal needs someone inhuman to drive that human vehicle."

"Hey," I said. "We can't all learn everything. Unlike some of you, I've only been in existence for twenty-seven years, and for all but eleven of those, driving would have gotten me thrown into juvie."

Omen ignored my attempt at defending my honor. As Ruse materialized by the camper van, the hellhound shifter motioned to

Thorn. "You go too. Make sure our walking disaster doesn't cause any new catastrophes."

Snap poked his head out from the funhouse doorway. "I can—"

"You," Omen said, "are going to sample that corpse like you did the man that led you to my prison. Maybe he'll be slightly more informative now that he's dead. Let's get to it."

Snap shot me a pained apologetic glance, but he couldn't exactly claim he'd provide more protection than the warrior. I hopped into the passenger side of the van, and Thorn vanished into the shadows in the back. It held two padded benches—one of which was going to serve as my bed tonight—and various cupboards Pickle darted off to continue exploring.

Ruse arched an eyebrow at me. "What are we up to tonight?"

"The thrilling art of grocery shopping," I said.

"Hmm. Maybe this is more Snap's area after all."

Despite his initial joke, he flipped on the radio and drove from the fringes of the city toward the downtown core without attempting any additional conversation. When I made a wry comment here or there about the passing buildings, he offered a smile and a quick response, but nothing to encourage his usual flirty repartee.

The most he spoke was when he had me call up our hacker ally and put her on speakerphone so he could bolster his supernatural influence before I sent her the address and photos Vivi had passed on. "Everything you can find out, as soon as you can find it," he said, his voice dripping with charm. "Your help has been absolutely invaluable."

As I hung up the phone after our next steps were all set, I studied him from the corner of my eye. Maybe this newfound reserve of the past few days meant he was starting to take our current circumstances more seriously than Thorn had given him credit for.

Or maybe, despite all that initial flirting and the heat I'd thought I'd felt between us just a few nights ago in the barn, he was bored of my mortal companionship already. He'd been with who knew how many other women before me, after all, and he didn't usually stick around for much chitchat after the deed was done. I should have felt honored he'd invested as much attention in me as he had.

But to tell you the truth, it only added to the uncomfortable hollow in the pit of my stomach. Call me greedy, but it seemed *I* liked each member of my trio more than was probably wise.

Any worries about Ruse's interest in me or lack thereof vanished when the glowing windows of the FoodMart came into view up ahead. The downtown grocery store took up half a city block, open from the wee hours in the morning until midnight. I guessed even Jade might use it for purposes other than covert meet-ups—shadowkind might not *need* to eat, at least in the traditional mortal way, but many of them enjoyed doing so simply for the pleasure of chowing down. It was just hard to picture the bar owner's sleek, green-haired form amid the aisles of canned veggies and jars of pasta sauce.

There she was, though. I spotted her within seconds of heading inside, Ruse and Thorn following invisibly through the shadows. Her dark hair swallowed up the artificial light, turning the green almost black.

She caught my eye for just a second and then drifted farther down the aisle to contemplate the cereal boxes. Lucky Charms were on sale—now that *was* lucky. I picked up a box and pretended to be fascinated by the nutritional information. What vitamins did they stuff into those marshmallows?

"What's up?" I asked quietly.

Jade turned and inspected a container of peanut butter. "I know this is ridiculous, but we've had a few mortals come into the bar asking rather pointed questions. I think it's best you steer clear of the Fountain until this situation you've gotten yourself into is... cleared up."

My throat tightened. I'd already suspected the Company might have asked around about me at Jade's, but I hadn't meant to bring more trouble to her doorstep. "Understood. I'll be a stranger until it's safe again."

"I do have some—well, possibly—good news too. A couple of occasional patrons stopped by yesterday talking about a conflict with mortals, and I told them you were working on something like that. They seemed interested in joining forces. I'll let you figure out how to reach out to them. Here's Glisten's number."

A shadowkind named Glisten? What sort of shiny being would that turn out to be?

"Thank you," I said with intense gratitude as she surreptitiously passed me a slip of paper.

The corner of Jade's mouth quirked up. "Wait to thank me until after you've met them. They might be of some use. Take care of yourself."

With that, she set the peanut butter back on the shelf and walked away. I gazed longingly at my box of Lucky Charms for several seconds longer, but that was made for people who had things like bowls and spoons and, y'know, fridges in which to keep milk. A.K.A., people other than me at the present moment. Sighing, I put it back and headed for the door.

I came around the corner by the cashiers and stopped in my tracks with a stutter of my pulse.

A lanky man with shaggy black hair was just handing his credit card over to the woman at the counter. A man I'd recognized from his posture in an instant, but he turned his head enough for me to see the profile of his face and remove any doubt.

I'd lived with that man for almost a year, until I... hadn't. It'd been years since I'd last seen Malachi. Our paths hadn't crossed since he'd left—mostly by his design, I suspected.

I'd been as over our relationship as I could have been without any kind of closure, but seeing him out of the blue sent a flush that was half shame and half anger surging through my body. No way in hell did I want to deal with him *now* of all the possible times I could have run into him. A significant part of me would have liked to run him *over*. I spun around and darted for the entrance before he finished paying.

As I clambered into the van, Ruse reformed on the driver's side.

Thorn loomed over my seat with a worried frown. "Are you all right? It looked like—"

"I'm fine," I said quickly. "It has nothing to do with... with anything important. Please, let's just get out of here."

Ruse took one look at me and shifted the van into drive, and I left yet another piece of my old life behind.

Good riddance.

FIFTEEN

Sorsha

Red and purple lights flashed in the old fortune teller booth. The mechanical figure with her cracked plastic cheeks and glittering turban jerked a little to the left, still running on some reserve power source in the fairgrounds.

I popped in a quarter. "Who'll they cast in my role when they make a movie out of this craziness?"

The crone's creaky voice was starting to outright sputter as she ran out of juice. "The answer lies in your hea-a-art."

I nodded sagely. "Okay, so an Eastwick-era Michelle Pfeiffer then." Dye her hair red—it could work. We'd just need to invent time travel first.

I readied another quarter. "Am I even going to survive to see that movie?"

"All things are possible if you find the w-w-will inside yourself-f-f."

The fortune-teller was basically a Magic 8-ball with a face. Since my restless wandering had led me through the night to this part of the fairgrounds, she'd answered my previous questions with cryptic remarks like, "Your chances will rise with your spirits," and "Sadly, my ancient eyes cannot see that far." It was a good thing she only cost a quarter. And also that her owner had left the money collection panel open so I could retrieve my few quarters for repeated rounds.

But maybe I didn't want real answers. Maybe that was why I was interrogating her rather than getting some much-needed sleep. If I lay down with nothing to occupy myself, it'd give my worries a chance to really dig into my brain.

Not that they weren't jabbing plenty of spades into me as it was. As I pushed in one more quarter, my throat tightened just a bit. My next question came out in a rough murmur. "What am I?"

"Seek with an op-p-pen mind, and the truth will become c-c-clear," the fortune teller informed me.

Another voice followed on the tail end of her response, low and sly. "But clearly you're a tall drink of water up way past her bedtime."

My pulse skittered, but only for a second. I knew that voice. I folded my arms over my chest. "Very funny, Ruse."

The incubus sauntered from behind the booth wearing his typical smirk. "I didn't mean to startle you. You've seemed disconcerted ever since we left the grocery store. I figured I'd make sure you hadn't wandered off too far." He cocked his head, taking me in, and of course at that exact moment a yawn I couldn't hold back stretched my jaw. "And you *should* be in bed, shouldn't you?"

"With you there too, you're suggesting?" I said, not totally against the idea.

The brief tensing of Ruse's features tied a knot in my stomach. *He* was against it, apparently. "I suspect you do need some actual rest at this point," he said.

"*I* suspect I'm not going to be able to get to sleep until I'm at least twice as exhausted as I currently am."

"Let's see if we can't tire you out some more then." He eyed the crone in her plastic box. "This old gal doesn't seem to be doing the trick. Come on."

I was already tired enough that I couldn't be bothered to protest. We wandered across the vacant lots where various carnival rides had once stood until we reached a sort of plaster hill about ten feet high that must have supported some part of a track.

"Mountain-climbing is good, solid work," Ruse said, clambering halfway up the lumpy side and then offering his hand to me to help me. I waved it away and scrambled up to the top on my own.

The peak had enough room for at least three people to sit side-by-side. One of the ride operators must have used it as a lounging spot before we'd discovered it—an open beer can was wedged into a notch at one side. I drew my knees up to my chest and peered out over the desolate fairgrounds in the thin glow of the moonlight.

Ruse settled in next to me, leaving what felt like a careful space between us. Was he shunning all physical contact now? What was up with *him* these days?

Or maybe the problem was me thinking the incubus had to still be into me after our intense but admittedly short entanglement.

I resisted the urge to scoot closer to him, as good as it might have felt to have one of those well-toned arms around me. Which was the right choice, because a moment later, he said, "It has something to do with the man you saw in the store, doesn't it? You knew him, and it wasn't with happy memories."

Since he wasn't touching me, he couldn't feel how much my body tensed up at the question. I gazed determinedly at the city lights in the distance. "There were some happy ones," I said finally. "A lot of them. At least, I thought they were happy at the time."

"Do you want to talk some more about that? Get it off your chest?"

I didn't really want to talk about Malachi any more than I'd wanted to see him, but it could be I didn't have any more choice about the former than I'd had about the latter. As long as I held the thoughts in, they'd keep gnawing at me. It wasn't as if Ruse was going to judge me for my failures in committed relationshipping.

I shrugged, picking at the tab on the beer can. The sour smell of the stale alcohol fit my mood perfectly. "He's the only serious boyfriend I've had. We were together for two and a half years, lived together for almost a year of that... Everything seemed to be going great. I was in love with him, thought I was going to spend the rest of my life with him. I hadn't told him about the Fund stuff or Luna yet, but I figured we'd get there."

Ruse sprawled back on his elbows, watching me with a mild expression. "I sense a rather large 'but' coming this way, and not the sort I enjoy checking out."

I rolled my eyes at him, but my lips twitched at the joke. "Yeah. But." The memory came back to me, so sharply it stole my voice and my breath. I braced myself, summoning all the detachment the years afterward had allowed me to cultivate.

"One day I got home from the job I had back then, manning the cash register in an ice cream shop, and it was like... like he'd erased every trace of his presence from the apartment. All his clothes and books, his shower stuff, the armchair his dad gave us—gone. Oh, except that he'd bought all the dishes and silverware, but he was kind enough to leave me one plate with a knife and fork." I grimaced.

Ruse blinked, looking genuinely taken aback. "Totally out of the blue—no arguments beforehand? Not that up and leaving that way would be normal even under those circumstances, as far as I understand it."

"Nope. As far as I knew, nothing had changed. He left a note..." I swallowed hard. "He said he felt like he was lying when he told me he loved me, that he couldn't seem to fall in love with me because I wasn't quite what he needed. That's the last I ever heard from him. He ghosted me completely. I hadn't even seen him again until tonight."

"This may not be much comfort, but if that's how he deals with his problems, I'd say you're better off without him, Miss Blaze."

"Obviously. I just..." I just had never quite been able to shake the question of what I'd been lacking that had made me unlovable. But maybe I knew now. Maybe there was something not quite right about me that he'd been able to sense even if he couldn't have put it into words.

I didn't want to linger in the chill of that possibility.

"It would have been hard to take when you were so fond of him," Ruse filled in for me.

"Well, yeah." I gave myself a little shake and forced my tone to turn wry. "It doesn't matter. What's so great about a normal life anyway? I'm having way more fun fleeing murderous psychos on a daily basis."

Ruse chuckled. "Your involvement with the shadowkind has brought a certain sort of excitement into your life, hasn't it?"

That was one way of putting it. But I did want him to know— "I don't regret breaking you three out of those cages one bit. I let some of the things that *should* have mattered slide while I was with Malachi, not wanting to risk him getting caught up in any trouble I got into. It was only after he left that I really started going after the collectors, emancipating their zoos and all that. So I suppose you could say I've decided to be married to my work."

"We'd certainly be in a much worse position if it wasn't for that," Ruse said with amusement, but the intentness of his gaze suggested he hadn't totally bought my nonchalance about the break-up.

For a minute or two, we sat in silence. A plane flew by far overhead, its tiny light flashing. Then the incubus said, "It *might* make you feel better to know that from what I've seen, love doesn't come all that easily to anyone."

I raised an eyebrow at him. "You haven't exactly been pursuing that kind of relationship to speak from experience."

He smiled crookedly. "Not generally, no. But—and I'll thank you not to mention this to any of our companions—there was one woman, a little more than a century ago. She enjoyed our initial interlude so much that I found myself returning to her, and now and then we would talk before or after… or during… and I found I enjoyed much more about *her* than the physical satisfaction."

It was my turn to blink at him. An incubus falling in love? I wouldn't have thought the cubi kind were even capable of that—but maybe that was my own prejudice, as enlightened about the shadowkind as I liked to believe I was.

Ruse didn't meet my gaze, still staring up at the sky. "It was ridiculous, of course. When I attempted to spark something beyond our encounters of the carnal kind, she made it very clear she only wanted me around for getting her off. Put me right in my place. An embarrassing blip in an otherwise illustrious career, but I guess we all have our lessons to learn."

I studied his roguishly handsome face, trying to picture what kind of woman would turn any of Ruse's attentions away. He'd gotten *me* off impressively well between the sheets, sure—I had no complaints there—but my fondest associations with him had nothing to do with the bedroom. There'd been the night he'd gotten us all dancing to one of Luna's old CDs to lift my spirits. All the ways he goofed around to counter Thorn's sternness. The delight he seemed to take in filling Snap in on all the weird and wonderful parts of the mortal realm.

The fact that he'd come after me tonight and made sure I was all right—and that he'd done it without turning it into a big to-do.

"She didn't know what she was missing," I said in all seriousness.

Ruse flashed another smile at me. "How kind of you to say."

"I mean it." And driven by an instinct I couldn't deny, I leaned in to kiss him.

I half expected him to pull back from the kiss, to confirm the disinterest I thought I'd picked up on earlier. I couldn't have been more wrong.

The second my lips brushed his, Ruse pushed himself up to better meet me. His mouth seared hot against mine, and his fingers teased into my hair to urge me closer. I found myself gripping his shirt, lost in the wave of sensation he could provoke so easily.

"You're perfect," he muttered against my lips. "Don't let any mortal prick convince you otherwise."

There were other pricks I was much more interested in paying attention to right now—one in particular, behind those fitted slacks. As he claimed my mouth even more scorchingly than before, I let my hand trail down his chest to his fly, just to be completely clear that I was up for more than a quick make-out.

My fingers grazed the erection already hardening behind the smooth fabric, and Ruse groaned low in his throat. The sound of his desire—his desire for *me*—sent a tingling rush through my chest. His grip on my hair tightened, the pressure drawing sparks through my scalp.

He rolled us so he was nearly on top of me, and right then I'd have happily welcomed him on top of that plaster mountain or up against it, or any other way he wanted this to go down. My worries about him using his abilities on me, messing with my mind, seemed absurd now.

No wonder he'd been nervous enough to break his promise and take that one peek inside my head that he had, if the only other time he'd believed a woman might want more than his sexual talents, he'd had *his* heart broken.

Ruse delved his tongue between my lips and eased his thigh between my legs to pay back some of the friction I'd offered him. I gasped, arching into him automatically.

My hand came up to find one of the curved points of his horns where it protruded from his hair just above his ears. He'd seemed to enjoy it when I touched those. I curled my fingers around it, his tongue twined with mine, and for a few seconds, nothing else in the world existed.

Only a few seconds, though. Without warning, Ruse's shoulders tensed. He drew back, his breath momentarily ragged while he gathered himself.

"Not the best place for this," he said, a twinkle dancing in his eyes. "And I *really* shouldn't be keeping you from your sleep anymore. Darkness knows Omen will be whipping us off on some new quest first thing in the morning."

I sat up, my giddiness fading. As we climbed down from the fake mountain and headed back toward the camper van, I couldn't shake the impression that those excuses hadn't been the whole truth, or maybe even most of it.

Ruse had told me more than he'd admitted to any of the shadowkind tonight, but there was something else going on with our incubus—something he didn't want to say to anyone at all.

SIXTEEN

Sorsha

Occasionally, my dreams were pretty damn delicious. A three-foot-high stack of waffles layered with custard and blueberries and drizzled with enough syrup to give Snap a spontaneous orgasm? Who cared if it was obviously unreal?

I searched the table for a fork, and suddenly in that way dreams had, it wasn't waffles but all three of my trio stretched out before me. Mouth-wateringly naked. Eyes come-hither. Still being drizzled with syrup.

Um, yes please, I'd take a bite out of *all* that. I leaned in to lick a trickle of sweetness off Thorn's massively muscled chest—and fuck all that was just and juicy if some asshole didn't yank me awake before I got even a taste.

A harsh voice was rasping by my ear. "Sorsha!" My pulse stuttered, and I thrashed aside the blanket I'd curled up under on one of the camper van's padded benches.

Omen loomed over me in the thin dawn light, his brimstone scent sharp around us. He hauled at my arm again. "Get up, they're on us—get out of here unless you want to be barbeque."

A crash and a metallic crunching reverberated through the air from somewhere beyond the van walls. My blearily sleep—and syrup—deprived mind couldn't quite process what was going on other than it was something very bad and apparently staying here would make it even worse. I lurched off the bench and dashed out the back of the van with the shadowkind boss.

He leapt up the funhouse's steps, tugging me with him, and propelled me through the entrance into the darkness. "Go, go, go!"

Go where? I sprinted through the shadowy halls, his urgency spurring me on even though I had no idea why it made any sense to be running away in here. Was this another dream? If so, I really needed to have a chat with my subconscious about appropriate transition points.

A figure sprang out of the darkness, hurtling right toward me. I flung myself to the side—and slammed into the cool glass of a mirror. The figure in front of me heaved sideways and winced too.

Oh, that was my reflection. Not looking so hot on three hours of sleep.

I whirled around in the hall of mirrors, barely able to make out more than blurred impressions of movement in the darkness. Were those shapes all me?

No—that one darted at me with a slash of some glinting blade. I threw myself past it, smacked my hand against a nearby mirror to push myself around a corner, and nearly pinged off another reflective panel.

An explosive sounding *boom* echoed through the walls, rattling the glass. My heart thudded faster.

As my breath stung in my raw throat, I dashed on. Something thwacked my shoulder. A searing hiss wound through the air from somewhere overhead.

I veered around another corner and pelted at full speed into a room full of hanging punching bags painted with smirking clowns. Welcome to heart-attack land! I pummeled my way through the dangling obstacles, the bags battering me this way and that as they swung back into me.

A metallic screech from behind me made my nerves jump. I bashed my way past the last of the freakish clowns and bolted into the next room, only to find myself swaying back and forth as if I'd careened onto a raft on stormy water.

The floor—the floor itself was warped into weird undulations, bending this way and that under my feet. I teetered to my left and almost fell to my knees.

Omen's voice rang out from somewhere in the distance. "Sorsha, hurry! Get to the roof!"

Then a distinctive squeal sounded almost directly above me. Panic raced through me with an icy jolt.

Pickle! What were these fuckers doing to my little dragon?

I scrambled onward across the topsy-turvy floor. By the time I reached the far end, I wasn't just exhausted but woozy too, as if I'd had a couple of shots too many.

There was a stairwell. I pounded up the spiral steps to the second floor, ignored the rest of the wacky gauntlet for the door that must guard the route to the roof, and rammed my heel into the knob. To my momentary relief, the door burst right open.

Another squeal reached my ears, even more terrified than before. I hurtled up the steps to an open doorway where the faint dawn sunlight shone across the staircase. Before I'd even reached the top, the prickly scent of a fire flooded my nose.

I burst from the doorway into the wavering heat on the concrete plane of the roof. Pickle was perched on an overturned plastic bucket several feet away, flames crackling in a ring around him. His clipped wings fluttered in terror.

If I'd been thinking clearly, I'd probably have noticed that it made no sense at all for my shadowkind creature to be here or for a fire to have somehow flared up around him like that. But at that point I was running on pure adrenaline, and all I knew was I had to rescue him.

I raced toward the fire with a swipe of my hand, willing it away from him with all my might.

And just like that, the flames parted. They bowed to either side of a blackened patch they'd marked on the concrete in front of me, and Pickle sprang through the opening into my arms.

As I skidded to a halt, four forms shimmered out of the shadows along the edges of the roof. The nearest one, Omen with his cold blue eyes gleaming bright, slashed a pocket knife across my forearm where I'd wrapped it around the dragon.

I yelped as much from surprise as the shallow sting of pain. As I moved to leap backward, Omen caught my wrist, wrenching me into place and turning the cut to the light in the same motion. My eyes caught on the narrow, red line—and all I could do then was stare.

The line *was* red with the blood welling up across the wound, but that liquid wasn't all that was seeping from my skin. A thin but unmistakable trickle of black smoke snaked up from my arm into the air.

Smoke, like shadowkind bled.

My heart had outright stopped for a few beats. It revved up again with a tremor through my veins, but the adrenaline rush was already fading. With fatigue closing in on me again, the smoke dwindled and disappeared, leaving only a streak of proper human blood across my pale skin.

"Well, fuck," Ruse said from where he was standing by my other side with Snap and Thorn. Even the incubus didn't seem to know what to say after that.

"We all saw it," Omen said, his voice taut. "Both the fire and the smoke."

"But I can't— It isn't *possible*," I said. My voice sounded hollow. As Pickle clambered onto my shoulder, I brought my arm close to my chest to inspect the cut. My entire abdomen felt hollowed out. "None of *you* would bleed actual blood like this if you were cut. Shadowkind never do."

"No human would bleed like smoke, though," Thorn said, his stern face frozen in an unusually stunned expression.

I guessed he should know from all the epic battles he'd fought long, long ago. I swallowed thickly. "I don't understand."

Omen flicked the pocket knife shut and tucked it into his pocket. "Neither do I, but you can't deny the evidence any longer. There's *something* about you that goes beyond normal mortal bounds. I don't think it's just a spell laid on you either, with it twined that deeply with your essence. It seems to only come out when you're particularly worked up. At least, for now. We'll see if we can work on that."

My idea of who—and what—I was had just been unavoidably flipped upside down, and he was already making plans for how he'd put me to use? "I don't—I've got to think about this."

"What's there to think about?" he demanded. "You have power. We need all the power we can get if we're going to take down the people intent on ravaging the entire existence of shadowkind. You've already wasted enough time with your refusals to admit it."

"Well, maybe I'd be a little more interested in exploring the possibilities if you had any idea what this means. But you don't, do you?" I glanced from him to my trio. "None of you knows how the hell this could happen."

The three pairs of uncertain eyes that gazed back at me held no more answers than Omen had offered.

I let out a ragged breath. "Right. I assume we're not actually under attack, and this was all just a ploy to freak me out enough to run your little test?"

"For now," Omen said. "The Company of Light *could* attack at any—"

"I *know*. But they're going to have to wait too. I need at least a few minutes to process this identity crisis. Just—just leave me alone."

I spun on my heel and stalked to the stairwell. Hurrying back through the funhouse, I barely registered the punching bags brushing against my shoulders or the warped reflections showing me only my own wan face. As I stepped out of the building by the camper van, my legs wobbled. Once I'd climbed inside the back of the vehicle, I tugged the door shut and burrowed under my blanket, cuddling Pickle against me.

The tiny dragon squirmed around and nuzzled his scaly head against my chin. I gave his neck a comforting rub. "The boss man was awfully mean to you, sticking you in that fire, wasn't he?" I paused, and a lump lodged in my throat. "Is that why you like me so much, Pickle? Because somewhere inside me I've got smoke for blood?"

Had Luna known and simply never told me—was that why she'd been willing to raise me? What did it mean about my parents? *Were* they even my parents? Did I have parents at all? I'd never heard of a shadowkind of any sort being born rather than simply coming into existence out of the ether of their native realm—never heard of a single mortal-shadowkind pregnancy despite the many liaisons between the cubi kind of both sexes and their lovers-slash-meals.

But of course, I obviously wasn't a shadowkind, at least not much of one. It was only a fragment of my being that emerged in tense situations.

I'd never heard of anything like that before either.

Even under the blanket, I felt it the moment another presence wavered from the shadows into the van.

"Sorsha?" Snap said, his voice tentative.

I forced myself to uncover my head. The devourer sat on the bench opposite me, his golden curls glowing with the rising sun but his moss-green eyes dark with concern.

He probably didn't even understand why any of this bothered me. Working supernatural voodoo and bleeding smoke was business as usual for every being he'd spent much time around before me.

"Can I do anything?" he asked, softly and simply, and somehow that was exactly what I'd needed to hear. He couldn't *really* do anything, but—maybe I didn't actually want to be left alone right now, not completely.

"Come here?" I said, scooting as close to the wall as I could to make room on my bench.

Snap smiled and moved to join me. Pickle scuttled away with a little snort, presumably deciding he wasn't interested in being the filling of our cuddle sandwich.

There was even less room on the bench than we'd had on the bunk back in the cabin, but Snap managed to lie himself down beside me without toppling over the edge. He slipped one arm around my waist and tucked his chin against my forehead, cocooning me in his bright warmth.

"Omen wanted us all to make it seem like there was some kind of attack, to scare you," he said. "I told him I wasn't going to help, but he went ahead anyway. He gets very... determined sometimes."

I leaned into his embrace. "I guess he wouldn't have gone to those lengths if I hadn't been so stubborn about insisting I couldn't do anything magical."

The devourer was silent for a moment. "*That* scares you. That you could influence fire in some magical way?"

Okay, so he could understand more than I'd given him credit for. It was fair to say I was scared. Possibly even terrified, not that I wanted to admit that out loud.

"And that there might be other powers I don't know about. Just... not knowing what I might be capable of, what I even *am*, and what else from my past must be either a lie or a total mystery."

"I think it's amazing that you have a force like that in you. You're even more special than I already realized." He pressed a light but possessive kiss to the top of my head. "But not knowing if you can control a power, one that could also hurt people... It feels pretty horrible, doesn't it? I believe Omen only wants to help you learn how to find that control. Or I could help, if you'd rather that. I'm not sure how to, but I'd try."

The lump in my throat returned with a pang of affection. I hugged him even tighter. "I appreciate that. I've never been scared of *you*, you know. No matter what power you have that you've decided you shouldn't use, it's obvious *you* can control it. I've never worried that you'll hurt me."

"I'm glad," Snap said, "but I hurt people before, and I can't forget that. That's how I make sure it doesn't happen again. I don't think you would in the first place, though."

His faith in me made my heart ache even if I couldn't say he was right. There'd been plenty of people I'd *wanted* to hurt over the years. In the heat of the moment, if I knew I could with barely any effort at all... but then, that was all the more reason to learn what the hell I was doing from beings who were experienced in the supernatural arts, wasn't it?

Maybe dealing with this puzzle wouldn't be so bad with Snap by my side. And Ruse... and Thorn...

My thoughts slipped back to the delicious dream Omen had woken me from, and then to last night when I'd been ready to give myself over to Ruse yet again. Was my greediness fair to the guy holding me right now and all his passionate devotion?

"Snap," I said. "Does it bother you that I might hook up with Ruse again, or even Thorn? It's not that I don't want you—I do, a hell of a lot. I just..."

I wasn't sure how to explain it. But Snap seemed to already understand that too. He shifted against me, fitting me even more perfectly against his body.

"I've seen you with them," he said. "And I can tell—the energy you have with them is a little different than with me. There's something you *get* that's different." He paused, his embrace tightening. "I wish very much that I could give you every conceivable thing, but I'm not sure that's possible. And if it's not, I don't want to take anything away from you. That would be incredibly selfish, wouldn't it?"

"For a lot of people, wanting to keep a lover to yourself would be a pretty normal feeling."

His hum reverberated from his lean chest into me. "I'm not a person, and I don't want to be like those sorts of humans. What I like the most when I'm around you is seeing you happy, and if they bring extra happiness that I can't, then that's a good thing." He ducked his head, his lips grazing my forehead. "As long as you're still mine."

I wouldn't have thought I'd ever agree to that kind of claiming, but who was I kidding? The possessiveness in his tone only set off a warm glow around my heart. The devourer had made an indelible mark there, one I suspected no supernatural voodoo could ever erase now.

"You've got me, all right," I said.

I felt his smile against my skin. "At least I know the two of them—I know they're worthy of having you too."

A better question would be whether I was worthy of any of them. Snuggled up against Snap, I wanted to be. I wanted to be a woman who could not just stage jailbreaks and sway fire to my will but also handle the hearts of those who cared about me with the care they deserved in return.

That kind of cherishing might be hard, like Ruse had suggested last night. It might even be impossible. But an hour ago I'd thought it was impossible that a human being like me could manipulate fire with my mind, so maybe I shouldn't draw any conclusions just yet.

If I was going to be that woman, I knew where I'd need to start. Hiding under a blanket wasn't going to cut it. I couldn't stand by my lovers properly if I was denying who I even was.

"Let's hope you're right about that," I said, tugging Snap upright with me. "I'd better see what Omen thinks he can teach me."

SEVENTEEN

Sorsha

Saying my first official training session didn't go well would be like saying the Pacific Ocean was a teensy bit damp.

Omen marched me out into the deserted yard next to the funhouse, where a stray Ferris wheel car had been pummeled almost out of recognition. I guessed that was how Thorn had produced the crashing noises I'd taken as part of a Company attack earlier this morning. A rusty old delivery truck parked nearby seemed to hold a look of relief that it'd been spared in the slant of the dust smears on its windshield.

Omen clapped his hands together. "All right. We know you *can* work this power. Let's see if we can get you working it on purpose."

I thought of last night's failed experiment with the popcorn bag. "I'm not sure I can, at least not out of the blue with no real reason to. Didn't you say it's activated when I get 'worked up'? I can't make myself panic over nothing."

The hellhound shifter's expression suggested he thought I'd been pointlessly overwrought plenty of times already, but he managed to keep at least a little of his disdain to himself. "You'll need to get familiar with the specific feeling of manipulating—or producing—fire until you can summon it up without a bunch of panic around it. But for now, we'll start by triggering it first."

He gave me a thin smile, and then he started pelting me with beanbags he must have found at an abandoned game stall.

Having the bags smack into my chest and legs—oh, and that was the side of my head—definitely pissed me off. I snatched one out of the air and flung it right back at Omen. It clocked him in the nose.

"That's not what we're looking for," Bossypants snapped. "Focus on the projectiles, not on me. They're what's hitting you. If you light one up, I'll stop."

"Promises, promises," I muttered, not really believing him, but it didn't matter anyway. I squinted at the beanbags as they whipped toward me until I thought I was going to go cross-eyed, but my irritation didn't come with the rush of energy that'd coursed through me a few times in the past. If that even was the feeling I was looking to stir up. I hadn't exactly been meditating on my inner state while I was dashing to save Pickle's life.

After a while, Omen gave up on that tactic and ushered me back to the funhouse rooftop. He shoved a slip of paper into my hand and motioned for me to get up on the low railing that circled the roof's edge. "Walk along there and see if you can get the paper burning."

I took a brief glance at the ground a couple dozen feet below. No biggie. With nimble steps, I crossed from one end of the building to the other in less than a minute. I looked back at Omen, my heartbeat barely elevated. "This is supposed to work how?"

He was glaring at me, a few tufts of his tawny hair poking up from the smooth surface he'd slicked it into. He swiped his hand back over them, failing to tame them, and stalked over. "Most people would be a little unnerved walking along up there."

I rolled my eyes at him. "You watched me pilfer that flower pot for you, and you still thought I might be afraid of heights?"

"Come on then, Disaster," he said in a growl. Apparently that was my new nickname—oh, joy.

After several more exercises that all seemed to involve battering or tripping me in some way, Omen resorted to getting into the camper van and roaring toward me at full speed. I watched him come with a slight hiccup of my pulse, but even as my body tensed, nothing supernatural woke up inside me.

He hit the brake just in time to screech to a halt a foot from where I stood. I waved my hand with the slip of paper that was now grayed and creased, and it proceeded to remain as unburnt as it'd been when he'd handed it to me.

The shifter threw open the van's door and loomed on me. "What the *hell* is wrong with you?"

I stared right back at him, my jaw clenching. It wasn't as if I'd been having a ball with what he'd put me through over the past several hours. "I thought we'd already determined that none of us has any idea."

"That's not what I— For fuck's sake, can't you get a little nervous even with that thing barreling toward you?" He waved toward the van.

I shrugged. "I knew you weren't going to actually run me over. That would kind of go against the whole 'use Sorsha to turn the tables on the baddies' plan, wouldn't it?"

An inarticulate noise of frustration spilled from his mouth. "How are you so fucking aggravating?"

The retort shot from my tongue automatically. "Because you're fucking infuriating and it's contagious?"

But this wasn't just some annoying jerk at the office. This was the highest order of shadowkind with multiple centuries of honing his might. He really did growl then—the sort of dark, grating sound I'd have expected his houndish form to emit, with a flare of his eyes from blue to scorching orange and a baring of his teeth to reveal fangs that hadn't been there a moment before.

I'd almost forgotten just how much coiled power that compact human frame contained before it hit me. A slap of otherworldly heat lashed my skin, and my pulse really lurched for the first time since I'd leapt to save Pickle.

So naturally, I did the thing any sensible person would have done: I set Omen's shirt on fire.

It was only a little fire—a flicker of flame that shot up from the hem and disappeared the second he'd whacked it with his open hand, leaving only a tiny scorch mark on the maroon fabric. It happened so quickly, like always, that I couldn't have said what exactly I'd been feeling when I'd done it, other than both incredibly frustrated and abruptly sure the guy was about to rip my head off, grand plans thrown to the wind.

When Omen raised his head from examining his shirt, his shoulders had come down, though they were still rigid, and his eyes had returned to their usual piercing blue. His voice came out tightly controlled. "I don't suppose you have any idea how to do that again, preferably to something other than me."

I splayed my hands in a helpless gesture. "It just… happened."

Running his fingers over his hair, which was now utterly ruffled, he let out a brusque huff of air and turned away. "Take a breather. I suppose you need to eat something by this point anyway."

I had wolfed down a few snacks here and there in between his various torture sessions, but I wasn't going to argue with the chance to indulge in a proper meal, even if I didn't totally understand his decision to retreat. Maybe he'd decided I was hopeless after all.

I clambered into the back of the van in its new location, murmuring a few soothing words to Pickle, who scuttled back and forth with his wings trembling. What did I have left in the stash I'd grabbed during our last gas station stop?

As I dug into the bags, Ruse appeared by the open door, a box balanced on one upturned hand. A pizza box. The second the combined smells of melted cheese, rich tomato sauce, and spicy pepperoni hit my nose, I was salivating. I could have jumped him in gratitude, except I was hungry enough that I'd rather jump the pizza.

I hopped back out, Pickle at my heels. To no one's surprise, Snap materialized out of the shadows a second later, his eyes eagerly intent on the pizza box. "What is *that*?" he asked.

Ruse chuckled. "And this is why I got a large. The mortal realm has plenty of fantastic food beyond fruits and sweets." He caught my gaze. "I'd have gotten you a spread of Thai, but that would have been much more unwieldy."

"No complaints here! Pizza is my second favorite." And definitely much more suited to digging into when you didn't have much in the way of furniture… or utensils.. or, well, anything.

Ruse stacked a couple of crates into a makeshift table and opened the pizza box there. Soaking up the fading rays of the late-afternoon sun while chowing down on a crisp slice gooey with mozzarella was the perfect combination. From the speed with which Snap downed his first slice and his euphoric expression as he reached for his second, he agreed.

"While you and the boss were busy playing, we heard back from our hacker," Ruse said. "She traced that address your friend got to a shell company—and some of those photos are buildings that company or some connected shell owns. We'll have to scope those out."

"Great, I'll pass the info on to the Fund too so they can make their own inquiries." I swallowed another tasty mouthful and glanced around, not wanting to exclude the third member of my trio from the meal. "Where's Thorn?"

The incubus waved his hand dismissively. "He got one of his 'feelings' and went off patrolling, as if he doesn't feel the need to patrol every second hour regardless. They've never attacked us by daylight before, but try telling the lunk that."

I glanced toward the funhouse, where the final member of our larger quartet was looking at something on the cellphone he'd picked up during our recent travels. I didn't feel particularly inclined to invite Omen over to our impromptu dinner, and anyway, if he'd wanted a piece of it, he'd have marched over and demanded it. Still, as I took in his frown at whatever he was looking at, some of my lingering irritation faded.

He was a hard-ass and a beast—literally—but it was mostly in the service of saving all shadowkind, something most of the rest of his kind weren't willing to put in any effort to accomplish at all. And... as much as my trio had glommed onto me and become fond of me, none of them had picked up on the hints of powers even I hadn't been ready to acknowledge. Probably because they couldn't conceive of a mortal *having* that kind of power.

Omen had noticed when he'd barely even known who I was. For all his disdain of humankind, he'd been open-minded enough to keep me around and push me—however obnoxiously—toward uncovering those powers further. He'd spent all day doing whatever he could think of to help me control them. It might not have been fun, but I doubted he'd considered it a laugh riot either.

With a little less generosity, he could have written me off as a hopeless mostly-human being. It wasn't as if the four shadowkind didn't have plenty of supernatural voodoo between them without me contributing.

Omen raised his head as if sensing me watching him, and I jerked my gaze away—just in time to see Thorn leaping out of the stretching shadow of the camper van.

The warrior strode toward us, his voice ringing out with a force that thrummed through my nerves. "We've got to go! There's a squad coming this way—it looked like they were—"

Before he could finish that thought, something shrieked through the air behind him to crash into a side window of the camper van.

Ka-boom!

An explosion shattered the van's other windows with a burst of fire that rocked the tires. Another one biting the dust. Sweet scorching salamanders, these people *really* meant business now.

For a second, I stood frozen, stuck in the uncertainty of where to run when our expected means of escape had just gone up in flames. One frantic thought hit me—*Pickle!*—but at the same moment, the little dragon brushed against my ankle with a quavering squeak, having followed the pizza brigade over here. Then a volley of shouts and the rattle of gunfire from the direction the missile had flown from spurred me into action.

I scooped Pickle into my purse—which I'd picked up out of habit, thank God—and whirled toward the only other vehicle I'd noticed anywhere nearby: the rusty old truck by the funhouse. My backpack with my cat-burglar equipment was still in the van, but it'd be ashes in another few heartbeats if it wasn't already. Losing the scorch-blade I'd spent three robberies' worth of ill-gotten income on hurt, but not as much agony as if one of those missiles hit *me* going back for it.

My feet pounded across the pavement. Snap vanished into the shadows, as Omen appeared to have too, but Ruse dashed alongside me in physical form so he could speak. "I already checked it—there are no keys. So unless you're as good at hotwiring as you are at breaking and entering…"

"Nope." But I did have some idea. My thoughts had slipped back to the winter years ago when Malachi's car battery had kept dying and we'd gone to a guy down the hall to jump-start it four or five times. I'd watched them hook things up; I had a basic idea of where the power needed to flow. A little jolt was all it needed.

A little jolt like a flash of fire.

I had no idea whether it would work, but jumping on a carousel horse wasn't going to get me anywhere. I sprinted faster, hoping Snap and Omen would head to the same destination too in their shadowy way.

Just as I reached the truck, Omen appeared in the driver's seat. He groped along the dash in search of a key, clearly not prepared to rewire the thing either. I turned as I yanked the passenger side door open—and my stomach flipped over with a surge of horror.

Thorn was charging after us across the lot. He'd stayed in his physical form too, no doubt expecting he could fend off any attacks that came his way and shield the rest of us from them at the same time. But the mercenaries who'd just come into view back by the burning van weren't looking to capture any shadowkind they got their hands on this time. No, from the size of the machine guns they raised, we'd made enough trouble that they were perfectly happy to wipe us all off the face of the earth now, even if it was a waste of experimental subjects.

Thorn hadn't looked behind them—Thorn didn't know. If the machine gun bullets were the same silver the guards in the toy store had fired, they'd tear him to pieces.

My heart pounding, I threw myself forward to catch his attention. "Thorn, into the shadows!" The words tore from my throat, and my hand slashed through the air at the same moment in a gesture of pure desperation.

The gunmen had just pressed their triggers. The rat-a-tat of machine gun fire pealed out—and cut off just as abruptly as the van's flames roared out at them. Fire lashed across the yard in a vast billow. The gunmen scrambled away with cries of pain, a hell of a lot more than their shirt hems on fire.

Thorn had vanished. I had to assume he was on his way to us and not fatally wounded by those first few shots. I leapt into the truck, slammed my palms against the dash without letting myself second-guess or really even think, and pictured another flare of heat setting off a spark deep beneath the hood.

The engine sputtered to life. My chest hitched with it. "We're all in," Ruse said from the cramped back bench, and I found just enough wherewithal to tug my door closed as Omen hit the gas.

The truck tore around with a groan and rattled toward the fairgrounds entrance. Snap formed on the seat behind me. "Thorn's hurt," he said in a stricken voice, and my pulse lurched all over again.

"I'm *fine*," the warrior said gruffly a second later, emerging into being on the back bench so abruptly his massive form shoved Snap and Ruse toward the windows. Which was all well and good for him to claim, but smoke was trailing off his back as if someone had set *him* on fire. At a jostle of the truck's rickety undercarriage, he winced.

Oh, hell, no. I grabbed my purse, which did have a few useful bits and bobs in it, set Pickle on the floor, and motioned Thorn back through the door that led to the truck's cargo area. "You're not bleeding out—or up, or whatever—on my watch. Get back there where we've got more space to work before you keel over."

"I need directions, stat!" Omen added. As I got up from my seat, Ruse leapt through the shadows to take my place. He snatched up Omen's phone, and I followed Thorn into the dim cargo area.

The boxy space was swaying so violently that I nearly tripped over my feet. Thorn sank down against one bare wall, and I dropped down next to him with as much grace as I could manage, which wasn't a whole lot. More shots stuttered behind us, but they sounded farther away now. At least, I hoped I was judging that right.

"Let me have a look," I said—briskly, to cover up the panicked thumping of my heart. A little light seeped through the small window on the cargo door at the back. The space around us was empty except for a few crumpled cardboard boxes and a couple of canvas sheets that I could cut up into bandages if need be.

"I *will* be fine," Thorn insisted as he twisted at the waist to show me his back. "You warned me in time—they only clipped me. And I heal quickly."

He wasn't lying. I'd known about shadowkind resilience already, but it was still a little startling to see it in action. I knelt beside him, taking in the tatters of his tunic—and the already closing wounds that dappled the edges of his shoulders and back amid numerous scars of all sorts of shapes and sizes.

The streams of smoke had slowed to a trickle. By the time I made a single bandage, the gouges where the bullets had caught his flesh would probably be closed completely.

He was okay. Not dying, not even that badly injured. My breath whooshed from my lungs in a rush. Thorn shifted so his back rested against the wall again, and I tipped my head against the warrior's broad shoulder.

The muscles there had tensed, even harder to the touch than usual. Thorn's voice came out in a low, terse rumble. "You shouldn't have needed to warn me. I should have been more aware of our enemies' movements."

"You can't be looking everywhere at once. Anyway, none of us had any idea they'd up the ante that far."

"I should have considered it—it was to be expected after we'd proven ourselves such daunting opponents."

I tucked my hand around his massive bicep. "It doesn't matter. We got through it. I'm just glad I *could* warn you."

The frustration in Thorn's tone didn't fade. "It matters because you had to put your energy toward protecting *me* when my job is meant to be protecting you—and the others. Yet again, I have—"

He cut himself off, glowering at the opposite wall, but I thought I could fill in the blanks. He'd told me a little about the long-ago war he'd fought in and how ashamed he felt that he hadn't been there to battle to the death alongside so many of his fellow wingéd when he might have made more of a difference.

Did he really think he'd *failed* just now, even with all of us alive and no longer bleeding smoke all through the atmosphere? I wasn't sure whether to be more sad or offended about that.

"Hey," I said, and waited until he shifted his gaze to me. "You need to loosen up on yourself. You did enough. If you hadn't gone patrolling, they'd have caught us completely by surprise. And it shouldn't be only your responsibility to keep me—or anyone else—safe. Aside from the fact that I can look after myself just fine lots of the time, we're a team. That means we all look out for each other. We've got a much better chance of making it through *this* war that way. You watch my back, and I'll watch yours too—as well as I can, anyway."

Thorn blinked at me. His eyes slid away, his expression still so solemn I braced myself for further argument. But after a stretch of silence, he said, "I don't believe you need to worry about your capabilities. That was quite the blast you sent at the mortals who were shooting at me. I'm honored to have such a valiant warrior on my side."

I sputtered a laugh at both the idea of being valiant and being a warrior myself. "Don't count on me ever pulling off something on that large a scale again, at least not when we actually need it." The only way I seemed to be able to use my power was by not thinking about using it at all, just doing it… which was hardly a reliable strategy.

The truck jostled, and Thorn tucked his arm around my waist to hold me steady. It stayed there, his thumb tracing a gentle line up and down my side. "You did save my life, m'lady. Quite literally this time."

"Please don't tell me you now have another huge debt to repay."

An unexpectedly light note entered his voice. "Oh, I do. But I swear I won't mention it except under exceedingly urgent circumstances." He paused, and his usual serious demeanor returned. "Thank you. I wouldn't have expected—but I should know by now not to underestimate you."

"You really should," I agreed, and eased back to look at his face. "Just so we're clear, I *will* be looking out for you, but I don't think I'm ever going to live up to your standards as a warrior. Stealthily making sure I'm never even seen is much more my thing than direct combat."

The corner of his mouth twitched upward. "Maybe so. It doesn't change the fact that I'm still here because of your quick eyes and action. I suppose I can admit there's something to your point about teamwork, but there's no need for you to be a warrior when that's not your nature. It's not the incubus's or the devourer's either, but they have their own strengths I can't match."

"Because you're so strong at being strong." I poked him in the pec. "I do wish that me being mortal—however much I am, which seems to be a fair bit—wasn't such a liability in a battle. I guess there's not really any getting away from that, though." My fingers lingered on the muscles of his arm just below the sleeve of his tunic, trailing over the pale scars that marked his tan skin there too. "How far do these go back?"

"To my very first battle. Any time I'm wounded badly enough to draw out the smoke, the reminder is etched in my physical form. I haven't added many to it in centuries, though."

"Not since the wars way back when. Until now." I grimaced and, to distract myself from morbid thoughts, teased my fingers up to his neck and along his jaw where even more pale nicks and notches told the story of his valor. As hard as his features looked, his skin was warm and smooth, only lightly textured by the scars. I let my hand venture farther, into the thick fall of his hair.

Thorn made a rumbling sound from deep in his chest. His voice came out even lower than usual. "When you touch me like that, I'm glad for your body's softness."

My pulse kicked up a notch, but there was nothing fearful about its pounding now. My skin warmed where his arm still held me close. Gazing into his near-black eyes, I found I couldn't come up with anything cleverer to say than, "You'd better be." Then he was drawing me to him, his mouth claiming my lips before anything more inane could fall from them.

In that moment, the shudder of the truck's walls and the battle we were fleeing fell away. I gave myself over to the firm heat of his mouth and the stroke of his hand along my abdomen. It rose until his thumb skimmed the curve of my breast. Need condensed, sharp and hungry, between my legs, even though this wasn't the ideal place to indulge that desire.

"For the record," I said, my lips grazing his, "I think you're good at a few things other than fighting. And I'm *very* glad about that."

"Is that so?" Thorn said, and tugged me back to him with a kiss so demanding that glad wasn't the half of it.

At the screech of the tires and the jolt of the truck stopping, we pulled apart from each other. Thorn glanced toward the door that led to the front of the truck with a regretful air. "I suppose we'd best see where we've found ourselves—and where we're going from here."

"Yep." I heaved myself to my feet, but as he stood up beside me, I couldn't resist giving his cheek one last caress and saying, "To be continued. So please do your best not to get shot any more before I can make good on that promise."

EIGHTEEN

Ruse

I might not have shared Omen's contempt for most things mortal, but the community center where Sorsha's Fund had gathered for their current meeting definitely wasn't the highlight of this realm. The stale sweat smell reached my senses even in the shadows, and the pounding of the basketballs in the gym next door filtered through the conversation so loudly I couldn't make out some of the words.

It did beat the smell of burning camper-van upholstery and the blare of machine-gun fire we'd left behind at the fairgrounds yesterday—I'd give it that.

One thing was clear without hearing any of the words: most of the members weren't happy. The leader with the black hair and sharp eyes had her hands on her hips as she spoke to Sorsha. "That was your apartment, wasn't it—that building that caught fire, where they found those dead bodies? And the victims found by that mini golf—they were smashed up the same way..."

Her wife and co-leader with the frizzy hair grimaced. "I saw the photos. Those injuries look like they were caused by shadowkind strength. What are these beings you've gotten yourself involved with?"

Sorsha was standing on the other side of the room's long table, only her friend Vivi next to her while they faced off against not just the group's leaders but the several other members who'd shown up and appeared equally disturbed. Clearly those people had no appreciation for Thorn's skill with his fists. What was he supposed to have done—tied up our attackers with a silk ribbon and asked the police to pretty please toss them in the clinker?

Our mortal—or whatever exactly she was, unexpected powers taken into consideration—looked as stubbornly stunning as ever, even though she'd had to rush off here with barely any notice. Her hands had clenched where she'd rested them against the table.

"We've been attacked," she said, dodging the question. "Repeatedly and violently. The people the Company of Light has sent after us have practically killed *me* at least half a dozen times at this point. Anything you've seen in those reports was self defense."

The ones that hadn't been strictly necessary, like the dope Omen had asked Thorn to off after we'd questioned him, we'd been able to dispose of more carefully since we hadn't been fleeing for our lives at the same moment. I could tell from the tension in Sorsha's jaw that she hadn't forgotten those deaths, even if she wasn't going to mention them to her fellow Fund members.

The Company assholes would have seen all shadowkind tarred, feathered, boiled in oil, and hung for good measure if they'd gotten the chance. Why should any of us be wracked with guilt over their loss of life? Mortals and their tender hearts.

Not that I minded Sorsha's. She had plenty of steel in there too... and if that heart hadn't been at least a little tender, she'd never have forgiven me for my broken promise.

"We've only got your word on that," one of the other members said. "None of us has seen any evidence that this 'Company' is doing anything at all to shadowkind."

"*I* saw what they did to one of their own guys," Vivi piped up. She might have screwed us over a little with her initial nosiness, but the flash in her dark eyes as she defended Sorsha earned her plenty of points. "They killed him and mutilated the body—these aren't anyone you'd want to make friends with."

"Do you even know for sure it was mortals who killed that guy?"

asked the stout young man with the soft, gloomy face. "Or did you need Sorsha to tell you that too?"

He was the one Sorsha had once had some brief dalliance with. Not the massive asshole who'd vanished on her with a brief note about her vague inadequacies, whom I'd have liked to tar and feather myself, but the almost-as-massive asshole whose emotions churned with resentment and indignation—but not a hint of regret about his *own* behavior, funnily enough—whenever he'd looked at her. Leland something-or-other.

It'd been a pleasure to trip him in the movie theater where the group had met a couple of weeks ago. I slunk closer in case I got another chance to poke a foot from the shadows and knock him face-first onto the floor.

Vivi gave him a look as if she were contemplating doing the same thing. "Are you suggesting that Sorsha—the Sorsha who's worked with the Fund for more than a decade without getting into trouble—is suddenly orchestrating some kind of huge conspiracy that includes murdering random men, all to take down a bunch of people who've actually done nothing wrong?"

Leland shrugged, his expression turning even more sour. "She might not know either. The shadowkind *can* be manipulative."

Oh, I'd show him manipulative. I'd like to see him licking his own ass after I'd had a little charmed chat with him. From the emotions clouding his mind now, I didn't think he was even considering that Sorsha's story about the Company *might* be true. As far as he was concerned, she'd snubbed him and that meant she must be misguided in all things—just a dupe of vicious shadowkind.

He'd gotten to share all those bodily intimacies with her, but he didn't know her at all.

"Yes, some can look to mess with ours heads. That's why I wear this." Sorsha tugged down the neckline of her blouse to show the silver-and-iron trinket pinned to her undershirt. Probably for the best that she didn't mention the few times she'd taken it off—and what she'd gotten up to with me and sometimes Snap during those times. "Believe me, I'd like this fight to have a lot less blood in it, but that's not on us. The shadowkind just want to survive."

The first of the leaders had raised her pointed chin. "I'm afraid that given the evidence we've encountered, none of us feel comfortable pursuing this issue any further. And I think it'd be best if you got yourself out of whatever you've become mixed up in too."

Sorsha's mouth tightened. *You don't need these putzes*, I thought at her, but some part of her seemed to believe she did.

"*I'm* not willing to walk away from the shadowkind when they're facing this kind of threat. Did you find out anything else with all the digging you obviously did?"

"Yeah," Vivi said. "What about the addresses Sorsha passed on— did you get anywhere with those?"

The addresses our hacker had uncovered from us thanks to Vivi's efforts. The twitch of the older woman's eyes told me she knew something, all right, but she locked it away with a purse of her lips. "The matter is closed. We'll resume our regular meets at the usual time and place this weekend. You're both welcome to join us for our regular business there—it's up to you."

"Huyen," Sorsha protested. "Ellen. Please. I swear—"

The frizzy-haired woman was shaking her head. Sorsha took in their expressions and must have come to the same conclusion I had about ten minutes earlier: this bunch was useless. With a curt sigh, she stalked out of the room.

"Really?" Vivi said, glowering at her colleagues, but the other Fund members held steady. She flounced out after her best friend.

Which was why it was a good thing Sorsha had agreed to let us stake out this place—me inside the rec center and my three companions patrolling the neighborhood around it. You couldn't get a more perfect spy than a shadowkind lurking in dark corners.

Ellen rubbed her mouth, the only one who looked at all conflicted about what had just gone down. She turned to Leland. "We should keep an eye on the activity around that building in the docklands, as much as we can, just in case. I wouldn't have thought Sorsha would get involved with anything disturbing. If there *is* an organization hunting the shadowkind on this scale…"

Leland snorted. "All I found was a record of some trucks arriving at the place ten days ago. No way of knowing what was in them—and it's not like trucks are a strange sight on Wharf Street."

Ten days ago—that'd be right after we'd stormed the facility to break Omen out. Exactly when the Company would have needed to move its other captives. And one of the addresses our charmed hacker had matched to the Company's shell organization was on Wharf Street. Thank you so much for the tip, my glum friend.

A little more muttering followed between the various Fund members, but nothing of much interest. I slipped along through the shadows after them as they left. They wandered off in different directions, Leland heading across the street in the same general direction as the spot where I was supposed to meet up with Sorsha and the others. I followed right beside him, watching for a good moment to send him stumbling.

He rounded the corner—and stopped in his tracks. I peered through the slightly blurred view of the world beyond the shadows to make out what had startled him.

Oh. Sorsha's red hair was just visible down the alley where we were meant to meet, as were Snap's golden curls. The devourer had just leaned in to steal a kiss.

Leland's hands balled into fists at his sides. He couldn't have known from that glimpse that Snap was shadowkind—but maybe he could guess it, knowing what sort of beings Sorsha had been canoodling with lately.

Before he could move again, the two figures headed deeper into the alley where I'd need to join them. A scowl twisted Leland's lips. He strode on by with an aura like a storm cloud, fury and betrayal radiating off him so thickly I barely had to reach out my powers to taste it.

As if she owed him anything at all at this point. *I* had far more reason to wince at the sight than he did, and I barely had any at all. I'd told her to take all possible pleasure wherever she could receive it, after all.

But I did wince a little as I flitted toward the alley. Not because of the kiss with Snap. Not because I'd sensed the closeness between her and Thorn continuing to develop as well. Hell, at this point I didn't think even Omen was unaffected by her presence.

That would have been fine. She could have been kissing thousands of shadowkind, and I'd have said, "The more the merrier"... If I'd been letting myself kiss her too.

Okay, so I might not have exerted the greatest self-control in that area. My lips had stumbled into hers once or twice despite my best intentions. But every time they did, the deeper longing inside me welled up more potently.

If I couldn't have the fun without the pain tagging along, I had to go cold turkey on the whole endeavor. Let the longing be just a pang at moments like this rather than a full-out heartache. Who the fuck ever heard of an incubus with an aching heart anyway? Much more of this and I'd be a disgrace to my kind.

If there'd just been a way to enjoy her without those other desires creeping in as well…

I told the little voice in the back of my head to shut up and sped through the alley's shadows to our meet-up spot. The other four had already reached it. As I materialized next to Thorn, setting my mouth in a triumphant smile at the thought of the news I had to share—and shoving all other feelings down as far as they would go—Sorsha looked up from her phone.

"I just heard back from the shadowkind Jade said might be up for joining the cause. They're ready to meet us. Why don't we go see if they'll be more help than our mortal allies?"

NINETEEN

Sorsha

The first words Omen muttered when our potential new allies came into sight by the looming wood-and-metal mass of the Finger were, "Fucking tourists. Of course."

We paused on the opposite side of the street from the courtyard, waiting for Thorn to give us one final signal that the coast was definitely clear. After the Company had managed to find us on the fairgrounds, we weren't taking any chances even when it came to other shadowkind.

I glanced over at the hellhound shifter. "Tourists?"

The two shadowkind hanging out by the fountain didn't look like my stereotypical image of tourists: no Hawaiian-print shirts or cameras dangling from neck-straps. They would have fit in pretty well at Jade's bar, actually. The guy was a burly teddy-bear type with a glossy chestnut mane of hair that spilled over his scalp from a loose mohawk. The girl, slim and doe-eyed, had dyed her spiky bob with streaks of so many hues I couldn't tell which was the base color. Their casual but well-tailored clothes gleamed with even more color and, in the girl's case, a heavy dose of glitter.

I suspected she and Luna would have gotten along well. If Thorn hadn't already identified the two as "equines" when he'd reported back to Omen, I'd have pegged her for a fae like my former guardian.

"Easy to tell from the look of them," Omen said with a hint of a sneer. "The type of shadowkind who come mortal-side like it's a recreational endeavor: take a little trip, indulge in the mortal lifestyle for a week or two when it suits their fancy, then back to the shadow realm before any of the logistics get too difficult. They don't care about anything other than enjoying themselves."

I could think of worse reasons to come to the mortal realm, but given Omen's general attitudes, I wasn't surprised that sort of cavalier traveling irked him. "Well, these two care enough about something else that they told Jade they wanted to take action. That's more than your gang buddies offered."

"I told you before, they're not my bud—" Omen started.

He cut himself off at a flash of a signal from Thorn by the other end of the courtyard. The warrior and our other two companions were going to stick to the shadows, ready to spring out as need be, while Omen and I talked with the newbies. We'd picked this central location for our meet-up hoping that it'd be way too public for the Company to stage any sort of attack here with all the human tourists around.

Omen started forward. "Come on. Let's see what these doofuses you dredged up think they're getting into."

The two shadowkind had been leaning against the wooden base of the statue, seemingly oblivious to the passersby who'd stopped to try to read the plaque they were blocking. As we approached, they straightened up, probably recognizing Omen's otherworldliness with just a glance and a sniff.

"Hi," I said with an awkward little wave. "I'm Sorsha. This is Omen—he's sort of—"

"I'm the one who calls the shots," Omen broke in, staring down both members of the couple in turn. "I don't know what you heard, but this isn't fun and games. There won't be any prancing around or sight-seeing or whatever else you usually get up to on this side of the rifts."

"Obviously," the girl said in a voice that practically twinkled, her doe-eyes growing even rounder. "You're after the jerks who took Cori, aren't you? We're not going to mess around when it comes to getting him back."

"Cori?" I asked.

"Coriander," the guy said with a droop of his head and his voluptuous mohawk. "Our best bud. We've partied all across the mortal realm with him, but just a few weeks ago, these dudes in silver-and-iron clothes grabbed him out of nowhere." His expression turned sheepish. "That night, we were all high on the LSD a little more than was really good for the reflexes."

Ah, so we were talking partying hardcore. Omen's mouth flattened at the mention of drugs, but his tone stayed even. "Who—and what—are *you*?"

"Bow," the guy said, pronouncing it so the W at the end of the name was obvious. His gaze flicked to judge the distance of the nearby mortals, and his voice lowered. "I'm a centaur, sir."

"Glisten, unicorn shifter," said the girl with less concern. "I prefer to go by Gisele if you don't mind."

She held out her hand in an offer to shake. As I accepted the gesture, I noticed the shimmering braid of what appeared to be hair wrapped around her wrist—hair that was growing from the underside of that wrist? Found her shadowkind trait. And I was guessing Bow's mohawk was literally a mane.

Fantastic. I knew of centaurs and unicorns, obviously, but the way all kids do from storybooks. I'd never met the real deal in the flesh before. What were the chances I'd get to see either of them in their shadowkind forms?

Possibly pretty low if Bossypants here had anything to say about it. Omen adjusted his stance, looking as though he wasn't sure whether to be more mollified by the "sir" or offended by the fact that Gisele had taken on a mortal name. "And what exactly do you think you can do for us?"

"Whatever you want, sir," Bow said eagerly. "I'm pretty strong, and Gisele is awfully fast and fierce when she's shifted, and, well, we'll try just about anything if it helps us get Cori back from those hunters or whoever they are."

Gisele nodded. "And if we need a getaway vehicle, there's plenty of room in the Everymobile."

Omen raised his eyebrows. "The 'Everymobile'?"

"You'll see! Come with us."

As Gisele bounded off across the cobblestones, Omen shot me a pointed look. I held up my hands. "Let's see what they've got. There's strength in numbers, right?"

"Depends on what those numbers are made up of," he grumbled.

The vehicle Gisele stopped at, parked half a block from the courtyard, looked for all the world like a typical city bus, though empty with a *Not in Service* message blinking on the display over the windshield. Gisele swiped her palm across a spot next to the door, and it hissed open for her. "All aboard!" she called out, and glanced at the shadows around us. "And I do mean all of you, unless you'd rather creep around in the dark spots out here instead."

The trio took the hint. As we tramped onto the bus, they reformed just inside—in a space that was several steps up from any public transportation vehicle I'd ever ridden on.

Behind the front seat with its violet velvet covering, the bus opened up into an immense RV. We were standing at the edge of a living room-slash-kitchen with a full sink surrounded by slick counters that sparkled like Gisele's blouse, hardwood cabinets, and a semi-circle of padded pearl-gray sofa-bench large enough to seat eight, which curved around a sleek table. A narrow hall led from there to a few other doorways, the open one offering a glimpse of a four-poster bed.

"Holy mother of manticores," I said, taking it in. "You've got yourself a mansion on wheels. It has a glamour on the outside?"

Gisele swept her hand toward the dashboard. "Programmed with multiple variations!"

The multi-colored buttons were carefully labeled. There was *City Bus*, naturally, as well as *Tour Bus*, *Cargo Van*, *School Bus*, and some particularly unexpected options like *Train Locomotive* and— "Military Submarine?" I couldn't help reading out loud in disbelief.

"We've never had the opportunity to use that one so far," Bow said from where he'd shut the door behind us. "It's too bad. It looks pretty amazing."

"Very slick," Ruse said with approval, and promptly sprawled out on the leather sofa cushions. "I approve. We did need new digs."

"Assuming our walking disaster here can manage not to get this latest vehicle blown to smithereens too," Omen muttered, but even he couldn't hide a glimmer of awe as he took in the space. "How did you two manage to get yourselves a ride like this?"

Gisele shrugged. "We already had the RV. Mortals have a tendency of wanting to make me happy. Cori crafted it bigger than it was before with his magic. But we were getting into trouble finding places to park it around the cities where we usually wanted to hang out. Then we helped a fae lady through a bad trip, and she repaid us with the glamouring."

I guessed knowing your way around psychoactive substances could have its benefits too.

Bow peered into one of the cupboards. "Do you all want anything to eat?" Beside me, Snap immediately perked up. The centaur licked his lips. "We've got grass and hay and a little clover with the flowers still on it..."

The devourer's expression fell again. Bow glanced back and caught our lack of interest in what I guessed were delicacies to equine types. A slyer smile crossed his lips. "We do also have the *other* kind of grass, that's not actually grass. Good stuff."

"None of us except the lady need physical sustenance," Thorn put in.

"Oh, the point of smoking this stuff isn't to fill your belly. Although I've made some pretty good brownies with it before."

I guessed Omen had decided the vehicle was too useful to pass up even if its owners weren't his cup of tea. He cleared his throat. "We're glad to have your assistance, but I think we'd better hold off on addling our minds until we've decided on our next course of action. Ruse, you mentioned a solid lead on our way over here."

"Yes!" Ruse straightened up with a clap of his hands. I dropped onto the sofa next to him, and Snap squeezed in beside me. Our hosts settled in across from us.

"That dark cloud you call an ex spilled the beans after you left," the incubus said with a tip of his head toward me. "There's a factory on Wharf Street that had a bunch of trucks arrive the day after we broke into the facility where they were holding Omen."

Thorn's attention jerked to us from where he'd been studying the street outside through the window. "One of the addresses the computer adept gave us lay on Wharf Street, didn't it?"

"Right you are, my friend."

For the first time since we'd fled the fairgrounds, Omen's mouth curved into a smile. "We'll have to scope the place out surreptitiously to confirm, of course," he said. "That's work for tonight, when we can hope at least some of the employees will have gone home for the day. But now we've got the perfect cover for cruising through the neighborhood."

He patted the Everymobile's sparkly counter and, shockingly, deigned to turn his smile on the tourists he'd snarked about less than an hour ago. "I'd bet the Company of Light has your friend there too. I think it's time to crash *their* party."

TWENTY

Sorsha

"And then while we're getting the prisoners out of there, the virus your hacker programmed can be spreading all through their computer systems, erasing their data!" Gisele bounced on the RV sofa, her eyes sparkling with enthusiasm. "It's the perfect plan."

I thought her confidence might have been a little overboard, and Thorn appeared to agree. "We still have many details to determine," the warrior said from where he was standing propped against the back of the driver's seat.

"We'll get there," Omen assured him with the restrained smile he'd been showing more often over the last day. "It's all coming together."

It'd better be. After scoping out the docklands building as well as we could around the Company's protections and surveillance, we'd spent most of the last couple of days piecing together how we could best break in and unleash the many shadowkind they held captive. The contribution from Ruse's hacker friend meant we could also destroy any hazardous information their experiments had uncovered so far—if we got the chance to use it. But having nearly twice as many people on our side this time around and significantly more experience tangling with Company guards made the mission feel less daunting.

"I just wish I still had my scorch-knife," I said, making a face at the thought of the blasted camper van.

Omen was close enough to jovial to give me a playful pat on the shoulder. "Maybe we'll find you a new one, Disaster."

"It's time to celebrate, then!" Bow sprang up from where he'd been chowing down on a salad of clover and strawberries and beckoned to Gisele. "If we're not storming the gates until tomorrow night when the next delivery comes by, it should be safe. Where's the good stuff we just picked up?"

As they pawed—or hoofed?—through the contents of their cupboards, I glanced up at Omen, who despite his good cheer hadn't relaxed enough yet to actually sit down. It was hard to resist needling him, so I didn't. "Still pissed off that I talked to Jade about getting help?"

He glowered at me, but only for a moment. His expression lightened again as his gaze traveled around the RV. "It didn't exactly bring us a heap of seasoned warriors... but I'll concede that I'd rather have these two joining us than be going it alone. Especially since I doubt Rex has any more camper vans for you to get blown up."

I elbowed him in the hip, which was as high as I could comfortably reach from the sofa. "I had even *less* to do with that act of destruction than I did with Betsy."

He hummed to himself as if to say we'd see about that, but the glint in his eyes might have been actual amusement. Even if I hadn't tamed the beast, I'd at least gotten him wagging his tail.

Before that thought could lead to me ogling his ass again—just to check whether he had a real tail at the moment, nothing more, shut up —I yanked my gaze back to our hosts. Gisele had produced a caramels tin she popped open to reveal a hefty stack of joints.

Ah. The other kind of grass indeed. No surprise that was how these two celebrated.

"Who wants in?" Bow asked, grabbing one. "We're happy to share."

As he lit the joint, sending a whiff of that pungent musky smoke into the air, I shook my head. "I'll pass. Not really my thing." And even though we were parked in a lot of city buses looking very city bus-y ourselves, I didn't totally trust the disaster Omen had been teasing me about not to descend on our heads.

Apparently our hedonistic incubus wasn't one for the MJ either. Ruse waved off the offer with a crooked grin. "Even the good stuff makes me queasy. Believe me, no one's sadder about that than I am."

Snap considered the rolled papers with tempered curiosity. "I've never tried this before."

"Go ahead," I said, tapping his calf with my foot under the table. "Just take it easy."

As he accepted the joint Bow passed him, Thorn loomed closer. "What possible purpose does this serve?"

Gisele smiled at him. "It's just for fun. Helps you relax and gets your mind thinking in creative ways. Maybe we'll figure out those details that are missing while we're flying high."

Or maybe they'd only be inspired to make a run for Cheetos and French fries, but I was willing to wait and see.

Thorn paused, his gaze shifting to me for a second. Thinking about my suggestion that he needed to loosen up? At his evident wavering, Bow added, "It's easy to shake off the effects if you need to. Popping into the shadows and back eliminates the chemicals from your system." He giggled, the weed's effects appearing to have kicked in. "As long as you can remember that you *can* pop into the shadows. Oh, that *is* good stuff."

"I certainly wouldn't become so muddled as to forget that," Thorn said with sudden resolve, and held out his hand. Son of a jacked-up jaguar, I wouldn't have predicted that, but I was plenty interested in discovering how it'd pan out. What could possibly go wrong?

Snap took one drag from the joint and shoved it back to Bow with a hacking cough. "That is—that is enough," he said weakly as Ruse clapped him on the back. "I don't suppose you have any more strawberries?"

Thankfully, the equines did. While Snap made short work of those, Thorn sucked away on the spliff with a slight flush creeping across his tan skin.

"I can't see that it makes any difference at all," he announced after a few minutes, but a few minutes after *that*, he was chuckling to himself while he peered at the sparkly countertop. "I never realized it before. It's as if you could connect each glint to find the source," he informed us, whatever that was supposed to mean.

Pickle scampered across the table, his head weaving as if he'd gotten a bit high off the atmosphere too. Omen rolled his eyes and went up front to study the maps on the Everymobile's GPS some more.

By the time Thorn was lying on the floor beside the cabinets discussing horse feed, favorite forest terrain, and the slant of the evening light across the ceiling with our hosts—all with equal enthusiasm—the stink of the smoke was getting a bit much for me. Snap stirred restlessly, eyeing Thorn with obvious bewilderment, and Ruse… The incubus was smirking at his companion's newfound state of levity, but there was something muted about his glee at the situation. It could be the smoke was getting to him too or more of that odd reticence I'd noticed coming over him.

A burst of confidence rushed through me that might have been a tiny bit bolstered by a slight second-hand high. We knew where our enemies were. We had a plan to smash them tomorrow night. Even with new allies on our side, it was going to be absurdly dangerous. We all deserved to enjoy ourselves thoroughly before then.

I stood up. "Ruse, Snap, come on. I think we should have our own non-smoking celebration."

Snap leapt up, an eager glow brightening his face. Ruse's smirk took on a sly slant, but he got up more slowly, maybe with a little hesitance?

Well, we'd see what we could do about that. He'd only ever hesitated before because he'd thought *I* wasn't fully committed. How could I have forgotten that?

I motioned for them to follow me and sauntered down the hall to the RV's second bedroom, where I'd slept the past two nights.

You could tell the current owners had been responsible for decorating the space. The comforter had a dreamy purple cloud print; the built-in wardrobe had received a coating of silver glitter. The gauzy curtain over the small window sparkled with matching spangles in the afternoon light. The only other illumination came from a circle of fairy lights fixed to the ceiling.

Not really my taste in décor, but when our hosts had managed to provide me with a double bed in a freaking *RV*, I had no complaints.

Especially now that I might get to share that bed with not just one but two of my new lovers. As they came in after me, I sat down on the edge of the bed, my heart beating faster.

I'd never done anything like this before—but wasn't that all the more reason to try? If Thorn could get high, I could handle a threesome.

If the men involved could handle it, that was. Snap beamed at me but then glanced uncertainly at Ruse. "How did you want to celebrate, Sorsha?"

I reached up to grasp his hand and turned my own gaze on Ruse, who looked oddly uncertain too for a creature whose natural habitat was bedrooms. "I think your soundproofing ability would come in handy right about now." One of his supernatural skills allowed him to ensure the sounds of lovemaking didn't escape a given room, thank all the glitter around us.

"And then I'll play voyeur?" he asked.

I kicked him—lightly—in the shin. "That wasn't what I was thinking. Haven't you offered on half a dozen occasions to teach Snap a few advanced techniques? No time like the present."

The incubus and the devourer considered each other. I couldn't tell which of them was more torn—or why Ruse was torn at all when this had been his idea to start with. Oh, well. If he left, that was up to him. Snap and I could still enjoy ourselves perfectly well.

"If it helps your decision any..." I said, and tugged off my blouse and undershirt together to remove my protective badge as well. Might as well put the assets on display. I leaned back so my boobs perked up even more in my demi-cup bra.

Snap made a hungry noise low in his throat and moved to join me without another second's hesitation. He trailed his fingers down my back, kissed my shoulder, and peered up at Ruse again. "I *would* like to know what you can show me. For Sorsha."

"Looking to put me out of a job, huh?" the incubus joked, but his roguish face had softened. When he met my eyes again, the gleam in his brought an unexpected flutter into my chest. "I did offer, didn't I? I suppose a tutoring session can't hurt anything."

Did he think some other kind of hook-up *would* hurt? I wasn't sure how to ask that question, especially in front of Snap. And then Ruse leaned in to capture my mouth, and questioning his exact phrasing was the last thing on my mind.

He kissed me with such intensity it left me breathless, all my nerves quivering in anticipation of what would follow. He nudged me over on the bed so all three of us could sprawl there side by side and glanced across at Snap.

"The first and most important lesson: explore. There are no perfect spots or motions that get every woman off. You caress here and kiss there to see how she responds. The sounds she makes. The speed of her pulse. The heat of her skin." His smirk came back. "For your first round of homework, put that advice to test while I enjoy these lovely lips a little more."

He claimed another kiss, easing us both right down on top of the comforter. The intoxicating pressure of his lips turned even more potent with the stroke of Snap's hand up my side to my chest.

The devourer had already proven he was an intrepid explorer during our previous encounters. He unhooked my bra and, attentive to Ruse's advice, teased his fingers not just over the sensitive peaks of my breasts but all along the curves, across my ribs, down my spine, as if he were charting every plane of my naked skin.

His lithe fingers woke up tingles of sensation everywhere he touched, but when a particular spot made me hum, he lingered there a little longer. Soon it felt as if my whole body was thrumming with awakening pleasure. When Snap finally returned to my chest with a flick of his thumb over one nipple, I gasped into Ruse's mouth.

"The student learns quickly," the incubus murmured, and dipped his head to attend to my other breast.

Snap scooted higher, and I turned my head to meet his softer but no less passionate kiss. His forked tongue slipped between my lips, drawing lines of bliss inside my mouth.

I dug my fingers into his silky curls, into Ruse's shoulder as the incubus swiveled *his* tongue to urge the peak of my breast even stiffer, wondering what miracles I'd worked in some past incarnation to be worthy of this moment.

Snap kissed me harder and tweaked my nipple again. As he left my mouth to nibble along my jaw, Ruse slid his hand lower. When he reached the waist of my jeans, a sharper heat jolted between my legs. My hips canted upward of their own accord.

"Patience, Miss Blaze," Ruse teased, jerking my zipper downward. "We'll set you alight in all sorts of places."

Snap paused in his attentions to watch Ruse help me squirm out of my pants. The neon glint came into his eyes.

"You tasted her here before," he said, his fingers gliding down my abdomen to the hem of my panties. "I want to try that—I want to learn how to make her feel as good as when you did it."

"Hmm." Ruse branded my breast with another scorching kiss. "I'm sure that could be arranged, if our mortal has no objections."

I let out a laugh that turned into a gasp when Snap grazed his fingertips over my clit through the thin fabric. With just that light touch, my entire sex woke up with a pulse of pleasure. "No objections whatsoever," I managed to say. "Instruct away."

As he pulled my panties down, Ruse trailed his lips across my belly and over my hip. Each point of contact lit a giddy glow beneath my skin, just as he'd promised.

Snap bent by my thighs and pressed a tentative kiss just below my belly button. He inhaled deeply, and my nerves tingled at the way he appeared to revel in my scent.

"The word of the day is still 'explore'," Ruse said in that chocolatey voice of his. "Sample every bit of the terrain to see where she reacts most enthusiastically. Soft or forceful; lips, tongue, teeth, and fingers—make use of every tool at your disposal in every way. But carefully until you're sure you're onto something. Even the strongest of women have some rather delicate pieces down there." He waggled his eyebrows at me.

Snap's head dipped lower. He slicked his tongue over my clit, the forked tip encircling it for an instant, and an even giddier heat rushed through my core. A whimper shuddered out of me.

As he suckled me harder, I returned my hand to his head, tangling my fingers in his hair and expressing my pleasure with both the pant of my breath and the tug of his curls. The latter became more important when Ruse eased up beside me and reclaimed my mouth.

Within moments, I really was blazing everywhere. Between my legs, Snap coaxed more and more pleasure with each increasingly confident swipe of his tongue and nibble of his teeth. He delved one finger right inside me, his other hand stroking my hip down to the sensitive back of my knee. As bliss spiraled up from my sex, Ruse's mouth on mine and his skillful fondling of my breasts drew out even more to join it. My body practically vibrated with the heady waves.

I jerked at Ruse's shirt to get at the sculpted muscle underneath. He nipped my earlobe before stripping it off. As he leaned over me again, Snap's long finger hit just the right spot inside me, in perfect concert with his lips on my clit.

"That's it," I said, unable to stop my hips from arching up. "Right there. Oh…"

And then I couldn't speak at all with the flood of bliss that rose up over me, surging higher so swiftly it stole my breath. With one more swipe of his tongue, it crashed in a burst of ecstasy that knocked all thought from my head. My hand clenched in Snap's hair.

As I lay there, momentarily jellified, he peered up at me. A hopeful smile curled his glistening lips. "That was a good one?"

A laugh tumbled out of me. "They're all good ones, but that one definitely makes at least the top five." A different sort of hunger gripped me, gratitude and desire mingling. "Get up here. You should find out how good being 'tasted' can make *you* feel."

Snap scooted up the bed, and I sat up, yanking at his Henley shirt. He let me tug it off him, but when I reached for his pants, he blinked, and the rest of his clothes vanished in the same trick he'd used in the cabin. Even if there was no syrup to be had here, my mouth watered at the sight of his long, lean frame on display, cock jutting eagerly from his slimly muscled hips.

Ruse chuckled. "I guess this is where I take my leave."

I grasped his wrist before he could get off the bed and caught his eyes. "I want you too. If you're up for it, I mean."

His hazel eyes glimmered with a hint of their unearthly shadowkind glow. "Always," he said softly. "How do you want me?"

An eager shiver shot through me at the thought of the possibilities. "Inside me. I'll leave the rest up to you. I know I'm in good hands." I grinned at him and turned back to Snap.

I kissed the devourer on the mouth first, taking my time to revel in the passionate intentness with which he returned the gesture. As I made my way down his trimly toned chest, pecking more kisses against his smooth skin, Ruse knelt behind me. The incubus ran his hands down my back, over my sides, and up my torso to cup my breasts. His squeeze of my nipples left me growling for more.

When I circled the head of Snap's erection with my tongue, the devourer's chest hitched. "Oh, that is—That is *very* good."

"It gets even better," I assured him, and took his cock right into my mouth.

The tender skin there held the same fresh, sweet taste as the rest of him with its darker mossy undertone. Delicious. I pressed my tongue to the veins on the underside and swiveled it around. Snap groaned. Then I was groaning too, as Ruse tested my slit with his fingers and slid his own cock inside me in one practiced thrust.

We moved together in an erratic rhythm that slowly came together: Snap's hips jerking up and his hand squeezing my shoulder, my head bobbing over his cock while I sucked him farther down, my body rocking as Ruse plunged deeper into me. Every eagerly desperate sound that escaped the devourer's mouth, every ecstatic stutter of the incubus's breath as he drove us both toward release, sparked my own bliss even hotter than the delectable friction inside me could generate on its own. The whole room seemed to have lit up with our pleasure. Well, maybe the profusion of sparkles had something to do with that too.

When Ruse sped up his thrusts, his fingers slipping around my hip to stroke my clit, it wasn't just sparkles but twinkling stars that formed behind my eyes. I moaned around Snap's cock, sucking harder.

We all careened into release together. Snap's head tipped back into the pillow as his salty cum flooded my mouth. I swallowed and gasped with my second orgasm pealing through me. Ruse bent over me with a satisfied sigh and a few last lazy pumps of his hips to extend the bliss a little longer.

I slumped next to Snap, and Ruse sank down at my other side. The devourer looped an arm across my waist, the incubus rested his hand on my thigh, and for a few minutes as we lay there in the afterglow, we felt perfectly connected. Like a single being, no push or pull of competition. I didn't figure it would last, but I'd enjoy it while I had it.

Snap was just shifting closer to kiss my temple when my ringtone carried from my purse. I grimaced but waved at Ruse for him to retrieve it from the floor. No one much called me, so if someone was bothering, it might be important.

The number on the display was Huyen's. Maybe the Fund's leaders had come to a change of heart? But when I squirmed onto my back and raised the phone to my ear, it was the voice of one of the other members that spilled out.

"Sorsha? I don't know what the hell you've gotten into now, but I thought you should know—Ellen was attacked this evening."

TWENTY-ONE

Thorn

As soon as we arrived in view of the tall, white hospital building, my combat instincts shot a twinge through me. I materialized on the vehicle's sofa by the driver's seat and thumped the back of that seat. "Keep driving past. Someone's watching. We don't want them realizing there's anything odd about this vehicle."

Bow nodded, the centaur's hands tight on the steering wheel. Had it only been minutes ago that we'd been chuckling and exclaiming over… I couldn't remember what now, only the exhilaration that had come with the supposed brilliance we'd stumbled on. Diving into the shadows and back out again had felt like leaping through the frigid flow of a mountain waterfall, wiping my senses clean.

That "grass" the equines had given me had been potent in its effects. It had certainly loosened up *something* in my mind while I'd inhaled the smoke, but the uncertainty of what I'd actually been thinking in that loosened state left my nerves on edge. Perhaps not a substance I'd partake of again.

Sorsha sat rigid at the other end of the sofa, her fingers curled around the edge of the leather seat. "Did you see Company people out there?" she asked.

"I'm not sure of the exact threat, but someone hostile toward us is monitoring the place. Several someones. And I can't imagine what other party would match that description."

She shifted her weight. "I have to get in there. I have to see her and make sure she's okay."

"What good will that do?" Omen demanded, his posture tensed where he was leaning against the kitchen counter across from us. "You aren't a doctor, and your powers have nothing to do with healing. You can't help her with her injuries. Company people have seen you before—they'll notice if you go in. And given how thorough they are, I think we can assume they're watching every entrance."

"It's my fault they attacked her," Sorsha said. I didn't fully understand why this meant she needed to visit the woman—wouldn't it be more sensible to steer clear and avoid drawing further danger?—but her voice was so raw it squeezed my heart.

Omen did not appear to be similarly affected. He motioned sharply at her. "So, get whatever details we might need to inform our plans over the phone, and leave it there. She abandoned our cause. You don't owe her anything."

Sorsha glared at him. "Maybe not in shadowkind terms, but humans don't work like that. I've known Ellen for more than a decade—she and Huyen helped me get back on my feet after Luna died. I owe her a hell of a lot more than the last few weeks can decide. I'd be an actual monster if I didn't make an effort to show I care."

"Well, it looks like you'll have to do *that* over the phone. Because you're not walking through any door on that building."

I glanced back toward the hospital, taking in the rows of glossy windows all the way up its dozen or so floors… and the neighboring office building, darkened at the end of the day, standing right next to it. The memory of Sorsha snatching the flower pot from the apartment balcony flashed through my mind.

"Maybe she doesn't need to use a door," I said before they could keep arguing. "I could slip into the place through the shadows, find a room that faces the building next door where I can open a window, and she could jump across." I looked at Omen. "I'd make sure our mission remains uncompromised." I wasn't sure how well I could hold to that statement, so I didn't make it an outright promise.

Omen's jaw worked, but Sorsha had perked up a little from her despondence. "That's perfect," she said. "I'll just pop in, see if there's anything I can do or anything they can tell us that'll help us crush these bastards, and pop back out. You know Thorn would never let me get up to anything ill-advised." The smile she gave me was both sweet and a little sly.

"I could drive around the other side of the block and park there," Bow offered. "The tour bus guise is pretty multipurpose—we can stop just about anywhere without looking strange."

Omen threw his hands in the air. "Fine. A quick 'pop'-in. But if you're not done in half an hour, we're leaving without you and you can find your own way back."

Bow brought the bus to a surprisingly smooth stop less than a minute later. Sorsha sprang up immediately. "Be careful," Snap said with a worried frown.

Ruse moved to stand. "It might be easier with more than one of us—"

"Everyone else stays put," Omen said in a cutting tone. He jerked his head toward the doorway as he fixed his gaze on Sorsha. "Your half hour has started. Get a move on."

Sorsha mouthed a quick "Thank you" to me on her way out, already opening up the pack of lock-picking tools Ruse had gotten her this morning to replace her old ones. Our lady was so sure of herself and so stubborn. By the realms, I hoped I hadn't made a mistake in offering to orchestrate this surreptitious entrance.

Whether I had or not, the thing needed to be done swiftly. I stepped back into the shadows and trailed behind her out through the general haze of the dusk across the street. She ducked down an alley to weave toward the office building out of view, and I raced straight to the bright walls of the hospital.

It wasn't, I realized once I'd squeezed through the shadow around a doorway, the most ideal environment for a shadowkind. Stark lights glowed all across the hall ceilings and reflected off the pale walls. I leapt from one thin patch of darkness to another until a trolley of operating equipment carried me the rest of the way to a stairwell. It was fortunate that the size of my physical form had no bearing on how I filled out the shadows.

The caller who'd notified Sorsha of the attack had told her that her injured friend was on the fifth floor. I rushed up that far and then dashed through the patient rooms on the side of the building that faced the offices. Finally, I entered a darkened room where the bed lay empty. I emerged from the shadows by the window, yanked out the screen, and shoved the lower pane high.

Sorsha spotted me from a fifth floor office room farther down. She gave a quick wave there, vanished, and reappeared directly across from me in a matter of seconds.

The buildings had only a five-foot gap between them. I stepped to the side, and she threw herself across that space with only a slight *oomph* as she caught the window ledge with both arms. She scrambled inside, bobbed up to peck me on the cheek, and hurried out to the hall.

I had the distinct impression that I'd hardly go unnoticed with my broad human body in the clothes I'd chosen for comfort several centuries ago, but I wasn't going to let her charge off completely undefended. With another leap into the shadows, I followed her to her friend's room.

A few figures from those meetings of hers stood outside the doorway. They all stiffened at the sight of Sorsha.

"What are *you* doing here?" asked a young man whose soft face didn't show any of the strength he'd built up in his musclebound body. During my time on the battlefield, that would have marked him as easy pickings, barely worth the time it'd take to knock him off his feet. I might have judged it worth the effort anyway after his sneer at the lady.

"I had to come," Sorsha said, her back stiffening. She glanced past him to the other figures. "How's she doing? Is she awake?"

"Huyen's in with her now," one of the women said flatly. "From what she said, Ellen is still pretty out of it. They hit her hard—concussion, broken ribs, all that."

At that moment, another woman strode out of the hospital room, her face tight with worry. Her mouth pulled even tighter when she saw Sorsha. Without a second's hesitation, she grabbed our mortal's arm and yanked her farther down the hall. The soft-faced man slunk closer, presumably to listen in, which only increased my desire to punch his face in.

"You have to get out of here," the woman snapped in a harsh undertone. "This is all because of you and your crazy crusade."

Guilt flashed through Sorsha's expression. "I didn't mean—I tried to make sure we were careful."

"Obviously not careful enough."

"I'm so sorry, Huyen." Sorsha set her jaw. "I know it doesn't make up for the attack, but—you can tell her we're going to bring down the assholes who did this tomorrow night."

The woman sucked in a sharp breath. "Are you kidding me? Do you want to screw us over even more? The people who attacked her asked her to pass on a message: to tell you and your friends to stay out of their business. They nearly *killed* her, you know. I didn't even want you coming here—Lila shouldn't have called you."

Sorsha swallowed audibly, her shoulders drooping. "I'll go. I just wanted to see—when I heard—" She shook her head. Then her gaze jerked back up with a flicker of concern. She raised her voice so it would carry to the cluster by the door. "Did anyone call Vivi?"

The woman who'd spoken to her earlier nodded. "I tried. Went straight to voicemail. Either her battery's dead or she was on the subway or something."

"Okay. Okay." Sorsha looked as if she wanted to make a run for the injured woman's room after all—I collected myself in the shadows in case I needed to clear the way for her—but then she spun around and hurried to the other room where she'd entered.

As soon as she'd shut the door, she pulled out her phone. I emerged into the physical realm next to her.

She answered my question before I had to ask it. "They went for Ellen—why wouldn't they go for my best friend too? If they've identified the Fund members, they're not going to buy Vivi's phony story about her grandma's car getting stolen anymore. Shit, shit, shit." She grimaced at the phone, which I supposed hadn't connected with Vivi, and shoved it back into her pocket. "I've got to go to her place. They jumped Ellen right outside her apartment. Vivi would usually be working late today—if I can get there first—"

"Where are we going?" I asked as she clambered into the window.

Sorsha glanced back at me. "I don't expect you to come. Omen was pretty clear that he didn't approve of getting even this involved. You can let the others know I'll meet you all at the bus lot on Lincoln Road."

If she made it back to the lot at all. Did she really think she could tackle a band of attackers on her own—or that I'd let her attempt it?

"No," I said firmly, striding over to join her. "We have each other's backs—isn't that how you put it? We'll do this together. Omen can wait."

"Are you—oh, fuck it, there isn't time. Thank you." She shot me a smile and leapt back to the office building.

I flung myself after her, stretching myself to cross the entire space as little more than a blur of thicker darkness in the hazy evening dimness. On the other side, Sorsha dashed straight for the door she must have jimmied open.

"Thank heavenly heathens Vivi just had to live right in the middle of downtown," she said, racing toward the stairs. "Her apartment is only six blocks from here." A wild laugh hitched from her chest. "We might even make it back before Omen's thirty-minute deadline is up."

We sprinted through the alleyways and along a busy street lined with restaurants and shops, Sorsha's sneakers smacking the sidewalk and me soaring through the shadows where I could move faster and without obstruction. She only slowed on the fifth block, with another jab at her phone's screen. I hurtled ahead of her but stopped where I could still hear her voice as it pealed out with relief.

"Vivi! Please tell me you're not home yet. Oh, geez, if you squint you'll probably see me down the street." She started walking again at a brisk clip. "Don't come any closer. We've got to—"

I'd already peered ahead to where a familiar figure with a puff of black curls and a sleek white outfit stood outside a shop at the other end of the next block. Or rather, she was standing outside it when my gaze first located her. An instant later, two figures in plated vests charged from around the side of the nearest building.

Sorsha's voice cut off at her friend's shriek. She propelled herself forward as fast as her mortal feet would carry her.

I reached the attackers even more swiftly. Leaping from the shadows at the last second, I plowed my fist straight into the nearest miscreant's throat.

The man fell with a sputter of blood, but the other attacker hauled

Sorsha's friend through the doorway next to him. Sorsha and I charged after them—and two more Company combatants rushed in after us, the first raising a gun and the other flicking one of those whips of light that made my entire being twitch with discomfort.

A thick, meaty scent filled my nose. We'd barreled into a butcher shop. I managed to kick the gun from the one man's hand with a snap of the bones in his wrist. Then I raced after the man who'd grabbed Vivi, who was now hauling her through another doorway at the back.

Sorsha and I burst into a room of hanging carcasses, vibrant red and pink etched with paler lines of fat. The smell rolled over us in a thick wave, but Sorsha didn't hesitate even as she coughed. She launched herself straight at her friend's captor.

My first instinct was to hurl myself after her and take the fellow down for her, but I forced myself to stop and quite literally have her back instead. I ripped a thigh off one of the cow carcasses and slammed it into the man who'd come in behind us before he could slash either of us with that unnerving whip.

The strategy worked out well enough, as Sorsha clearly had her side of the battle under control. She dodged to the side at the last second and heaved an entire carcass into Vivi's attacker, pummeling him in the head with the raw meat.

The man grunted and teetered; Vivi tore free with a yelp. When the man lunged after her, his hand jerking upward with a pistol in its grasp, Sorsha tackled him.

Sparks shot up. The waft of heat she'd conjured browned the carcasses above them, turning the raw meat stink into barbeque.

Our attacker with the whip hadn't been dissuaded yet. He flung the arc of light toward me, and I dove under it, ramming into his legs. As he toppled, I threw myself around both the weapon and the venomous plates of his armor. I rammed the beef thigh into his mouth hard enough to puncture the back of his throat.

"Eat that, villain," I said, and swiveled around to discover that Sorsha had managed to bury her foe under three of the heavy carcasses. The cords they'd been hanging from dangled with blackened ends where they'd been burnt through.

She caught my eye, and I found myself smiling at her, a rare sense of elation filling my chest. I hadn't *enjoyed* combat in eons. But this...

this had been good. What a battle was meant to be: comrades conquering evil side by side. Protecting each other wasn't all it came down to. I had to give my companions room to be the warriors they were capable of becoming too.

Perhaps I could make sure *this* war was won the right way after all.

Vivi was braced against the far wall, breathing hard, her sleek white outfit now streaked with blood. "Sorsha?" she said tentatively, her eyes wide.

The lady held out her hand. "Come on, Vivi. We're getting you out of here."

TWENTY-TWO

Sorsha

"Well, this is… something, all right," Vivi said, taking in the walls in the low-ceilinged living space, which looked—and smelled—like they were pasted with dried algae. From her face, I suspected she was resisting the urge to wrinkle her nose.

Gisele pranced around the room, which otherwise held an odd collection of rattan furniture with cotton cushions that at least appeared to be cozy. The unicorn shifter's perky voice gave no sign that she'd noticed Vivi's hesitance. "Kaiso said we could drop in and use the place any time. He's got houseboats all over the world, so he's not here that much."

"A big fan of water living, huh?" I adjusted my balance as the floor rocked under us with the shifting currents of the river.

"It makes sense. He's a kappa, after all."

Vivi's eyebrows shot up. "Um, are you totally sure he won't be back while I'm staying here?" Temperaments really varied even across shadowkind of the same sort, but kappa did have a reputation as tricksters at best and murderers-by-drowning-mortals at worst.

"Oh, I'm sure it won't be a problem even if he does," Gisele said. "Just tell him you're a friend of ours."

Vivi didn't look any more certain about that strategy than I felt—who was to say the water spirit would ask for introductions before getting down to drowning—but Omen stepped into the boat's interior then. *He* didn't hesitate to wrinkle his nose as he glanced around.

"You should be safe from any shadowkind who come wandering this way," he said. "I've marked the place with my power as a warning. There aren't many who'd purposefully risk the wrath of a hellhound."

Marked the place? What, had he peed on the deck in hound form to leave his scent? The image made the corners of my mouth twitch, but I decided it was better not to risk his wrath right *now* by sharing it. Too much gratitude was tickling up through my chest.

I hadn't expected Omen to even participate in finding Vivi a safe place to hide out, let alone use his influence to protect her.

"Thank you," I said, meaning it.

He shrugged and stalked back out without another word. "I guess the other guy got all the friendliness on offer when they came into being, huh?" Vivi said with a quirk of her lips. Ruse had been by a few minutes earlier to drop off food and a couple of changes of clothing he'd gathered for her, which he'd presented in his usual charming fashion.

"Something like that." I glanced at Gisele. "This is great. Thank *you* so much too. Can you give us a little while to talk?"

"Of course!" The unicorn shifter bobbed her head with its rainbow of hair to my best friend. "A pleasure to meet you." She trotted out after Omen.

Vivi flopped down into one of the rattan chairs. "My God, what a night. Out of the frying pan and into a five-alarm blaze."

The comment pinched at my gut. I knew she only meant it as an expression, but I also wasn't sure if she'd noticed the spurts of heat and flame I'd been able to produce while I was taking down her attacker in the butcher shop. She hadn't brought it up, and I'd figured it was better not to heap any more craziness on her than she was already dealing with… and also I wasn't super keen on seeing how our friendship might change if I revealed I might not be completely human after all.

"Ruse will bring more supplies around if you need them," I said.

"And I'll always have my phone on me. But hopefully what we're going to do tonight will get us a huge step closer to taking down the Company of Light completely, and then we won't need to worry about them coming after you again."

"You think so? They're a hell of a lot more organized and vicious than any hunters we've tangled with before."

"Well, if we can free a bunch of higher shadowkind they've been torturing, that's tons of new allies right there. And we're going to get all the info we can out of the people working there, whatever files they have on site, and then hopefully erase everything on their end so all their experimental data is kaput… We're a lot better prepared than we were before."

"You had things figured out well enough to get to me before the jerks strung me up or whatever the heck they were planning, so I have all possible faith in your plans." Vivi reached to pat my arm as I sat down beside her, but her usual energy was still dampened.

A sharper jab lanced through my stomach. If I hadn't pursued the Company and kept helping Omen and the others work out how to take them down—if I hadn't gone to the Fund asking for help—right now, Ellen would be at the theater getting everything ready for the day. Vivi would be able to go back to the apartment she'd decorated with so much flair. Neither of them, or any of the other Fund members, would be living with the fear of murderous psychopaths in silver-and-iron armor rampaging into their lives.

"I'm sorry," I said. "I didn't realize—I thought taking this to the Fund would be safe with all the precautions we took. The last thing I wanted—"

Vivi held up her hand. "I'm going to stop you right there. I *begged* you to let me be a part of this, Sorsha. Ellen and Huyen made their own choices too. The whole point of the Shadowkind Defense Fund is supposed to be to stop assholes who treat the shadowkind as worse than vermin, and these Company people are clearly the worst of the lot. Do you really think it'd be better if we stepped back and let them run their experiments and murder anyone else who stumbled onto their scheming? Because I don't. I'm still 100% on team Crush Those Assholes To Smithereens."

I had to smile at that, but my fingers tightened against my pocket where my phone formed a flat, silent lump. "You're the only one out of the Fund who feels that way, as far as I can tell. The only people who answered when I tried to reach out this morning didn't have much to say other than to fuck off."

"Aw, they'll get their heads on straight when you expose everything the Company has been up to. And those who don't are just chickens."

Her vehemence eased my guilt a little. I sank back into my chair with the rocking of the boat. Thankfully it was docked far down the river from the place we'd be crashing into tonight.

"So..." Vivi prodded me with her index finger. "How many shadowkind groupies do you have now?"

I rolled my eyes at her, ignoring the faint flush that crept into my cheeks. "Still just the three. You don't think that's enough?"

"Why stop there? That Omen guy is pretty hot in an I'll-rip-your-face-off sort of way."

I was pretty sure Omen had literally ripped plenty of people's faces off, but maybe Vivi realized that. "We can barely have a conversation without wanting to punch one another. I think I'll stick to three." I rubbed my face. "It's weird enough that I'm having any kind of relationship with a bunch of monsters in the first place, isn't it?"

Vivi shrugged. "Nothing wrong with having unusual taste in men. Leaves more of the typical hotties for the rest of us. Now that I've met them, I can definitely see the appeal." She shot me a wide smile.

"Believe me, they're more trouble than they look," I muttered, but the complaint was half-hearted. I couldn't say I regretted that the trio had barged into my apartment and my life those weeks ago—not even a little bit, the loss of that apartment and just about everything else I'd counted on notwithstanding.

And we had much bigger trouble to tackle tonight. I'd have loved to linger there on the plump cushions, ignoring the algae smell and chatting with Vivi as if this were some unexpected aquatic holiday and not an attempt to save her life, but I really should get back to our final preparations.

I pushed myself off the chair. Vivi got up too so I could squeeze her in a hug. She hugged me back just as hard.

"You lay low completely this time, all right," I ordered, wagging a finger at her. "Don't set one foot off this boat—unless the bad guys set foot *on* it, of course."

"Aye, aye, captain," she said with a cheeky salute. Then a cloud crossed her expression, a hint of the fears she was suppressing. "Ditto."

"Ditto."

As I crossed the houseboat's deck, my own fears swelled inside my chest. I'd only just barely protected Vivi this time. If the Company tracked her down here...

We'd just have to make sure they didn't get the chance to so much as try.

As I headed for solid ground, I spun a lyric around and sang the newly mangled version under my breath to bolster my spirits. "Stand up and burn 'em down, never let them see us frown. Ne-eh-ver. Ne—"

I stopped in my tracks when I saw Omen waiting for me on the road. The Everymobile had vanished, leaving just him—and the motorcycle he'd apparently retrieved when I wasn't looking. He straddled the old but well-polished Harley, one foot on the ground and one propped on the footrest. All he'd need was a beat-up leather jacket, and he could have driven straight out of a '70s biker flick.

Not my decade, but I could appreciate the vibe all the same.

I ambled over, crossing my arms. "Decided it was time to lean into the bad-boy persona, did you? This does look more your style than good ol' Betsy."

He grimaced at me. "You will not besmirch Betsy's good name. She gave us her all. This is Charlotte."

I swallowed a guffaw. "Do you name all your vehicles?"

"All two of them that I used to have, yes. Do you think you can manage not to get this vehicle blown up, Disaster?"

"The other ones weren't even my fault," I felt the need to point out. "Why are you letting me near dear Charlotte if you're concerned about that?"

His gaze sharpened. "Thorn mentioned that you used your powers again to fend off your friend's attackers. You seem to be getting better at bringing them out—it's just the control bit that needs work. It occurred to me that the bike might be a good way to get some concentrated practice."

"How so?"

"You can't drive, so I'm going to guess you're not quite as confident *on* a speeding vehicle as standing in front of one. And I've got plenty of tricks to get your heart thumping. Get on." He tapped the seat behind him and then a strip of paper he'd taped to the end of the right handlebar. "When you're agitated enough that you can feel your power, see if you can light *this* on fire—not me. I've got more where it came from once that one's good and crispy."

It actually sounded like a reasonable plan... except I wasn't only hesitant about the whole riding on a speeding motorcycle thing but also having to cling to the man in front of me while I was doing it. I couldn't exactly hope to perch daintily on the back—no, this was going to require full body contact.

I wasn't going to let Bossypants see that hesitation, though. "Fine," I said, and hopped on.

As I settled my knees against his hips and wrapped my arms around his waist, Omen turned to face ahead. His entire abdomen was packed with solid muscle. This wasn't a man I'd ever expected—or wanted—to be embracing, but I couldn't say it was an entirely unpleasant experience. Here was hoping I didn't, like, drench him in sweat in the summer heat or something.

"No helmets?" I asked.

He chuckled. "And here I thought you had a hard-on for danger. We're going to do a little death-defying today."

Without another word or any warning, he sent the bike roaring forward.

My arms jerked even tighter around Omen's frame in an instinctive bid to, y'know, *not die*. My legs pressed in too, my body shifting forward to meld against him for security's sake. Well, now I could say I'd had the fourth member of my shadowkind quartet between my thighs, even if it wasn't in the way Vivi had been teasing me about.

As we tore down the street and around a corner, the shifter's hellish scent filled my nose, plenty dangerous in itself. His muscles flexed beneath my fingers. My heart was thumping all right, but it might have partly been because my jerk of a brain couldn't help wondering how Omen would react if I dipped my hands a little lower and found out what *he* would get a hard-on for.

Then the hellhound took another turn with a rev of the engine and a lurch of the bike to one side, and all thoughts of anything other than surviving fled my mind. Seconds later, he whipped around a curve dipping so low I'd swear my hair grazed the pavement.

My pulse stuttered. With his shadowkind strength, he'd probably recover from a high-speed tumble. Did he comprehend how easily *my* head would crack open?

Yes, yes, he did. That was the whole point of veering so close to this guardrail that I could see the traffic passing below the bridge as vividly as my life flashing before my eyes. For one specific purpose.

Focus, Sorsha. I *wanted* to master this force in me.

With my next jolt of panic at a risky maneuver, I trained my attention on the strip of paper now flapping wildly in the wind. Heat flared in my chest alongside the clanging of adrenaline. I narrowed my eyes—and the paper went up in a burst of flame.

Omen slowed at a traffic light and fished another slip out of his pocket. "Good. Let's do it again. After a few times, we'll see if you can manage it when you're slightly less terrified."

"I'm not *terrified*," I objected, and lost the rest of my protest and probably all of my credibility when the bike took off again with a squeal of burnt rubber that shocked a yelp from my throat.

As much as I was tempted to whack Omen across the head for the wild ride, it did work. By the time I'd fried my fourth slip of paper, the surge of power from my gut to my chest was becoming familiar. True to his word, the hellhound shifter eased up on the stunts, and even with the—okay—terror dwindling to a tamer uneasiness, I managed to summon enough sparks to burn up a few more strips by dredging up that sensation.

I hadn't realized he'd swung around to arrive at the bus lot until he parked just outside it. I pulled myself away from him and clambered off the bike, figuring a little space was in order now, but the smile he shot me—the brightest and most genuine one I'd seen from him so far—brought back that pulse-thump of attraction.

That was okay, wasn't it? I didn't have any plans to actually jump his bones or anything. Why couldn't a gal simply have unusual taste in men, as Vivi had put it?

"You're getting a handle on it," he said.

"Maybe not such a disaster after all?"

"We'll see how it goes tonight." He said that part dryly, but his gaze didn't feel quite as icy as usual as it lingered on my face. "You have kept up all right so far."

Coming from him, that was the highest of praise. Had I brought the hound to heel?

I found myself grinning back at him. "And you only took a *little* convincing."

He snorted, but then his good humor seemed to fade. He motioned me toward the lot. "I've got to stash Charlotte. See if the others have made any progress with the final details. We've wasted enough time getting your issues sorted out already."

Then he drove off without another word, leaving me caught in a different sort of whiplash.

TWENTY-THREE

Sorsha

Our hosts only looked a little put out when Ruse opted to make a run for Thai take-out instead of the rest of us digging into their stash of actual grass and other fine greens. "They make a great salad too," Bow said, holding up his plate of foliage. He studied the containers of rice noodles and creamy curries with a puzzled expression as if he couldn't work out why anyone would choose to put those things into their bellies.

"I need protein for brain food," I said. "It's... a mortal thing." It seemed politest not to mention that eating grass and clover wasn't a human thing in any scenario I was aware of.

Omen was flipping through the photos and blueprints we'd gotten for the Wharf Street building on a tablet Ruse had charmed out of our hacker-on-call. "Don't feel bad for her," the incubus had told me. "She has a stack of them twice as tall as your dragon." Snap tucked his arm around me on the RV's sofa.

I gave in to the urge to feed the devourer a tidbit of green curry chicken off my fork. His tongue flicked over his lips to absorb the lingering traces of spice, and his pupils dilated.

"It has a sweetness, and also so much heat." His smile took on a sly slant. "I can see why you like it, Peach."

"Shut up," I said, and kissed him on the cheek so he'd know my light tone meant I was joking.

Ruse had tucked himself in at the table by my other side, not quite as cuddly as Snap but with more of his usual laidback air. Whatever he'd been tense about before, our recent interlude of three must have cured it. His eyes twinkling, he swiped his thumb over a speck of sauce at the corner of my lips and sucked it into his own mouth.

Oh, yeah, I was made of heat. A wash of it had pooled between my thighs before he even rested a teasing hand on my leg under the table.

"The best place to get some fiery action going would be here," Omen said, zooming in on an image. "How close do you think you'd need to get, Sorsha?"

If I *could* get the building burning in the first place? I sucked my lower lip under my teeth as I considered. "I don't know. I moved the flames on the camper van from something like fifty feet away, but that was just propelling what was already there—plus I was trying to stop those guys from murdering Thorn. I don't think I'd like to go at this with the same inspiration. But maybe, if we come down this alley, I could get a lot closer than that without getting caught anyway."

"While the rest of us stay in the shadows. That could work. And where would you dodge to—oh, let me guess, that window wouldn't be too much of a scramble for you?" The corner of his mouth curved upward.

"You've gotten to know me so well," I said with amusement, but something *had* transformed in the dynamic between us since this morning, his brusqueness after the bike ride aside. We'd been bouncing ideas back and forth all afternoon with a familiarity that was starting to feel almost comfortable. Not an adjective I'd ever thought I'd associate with Bossypants here.

Snap, as always, was looking out for my well-being more than I tended to do. "We don't know what guards might be stationed on the second floor there. Sorsha could end up jumping right into their midst."

"I'll take the same route she does," Thorn said, shifting his shoulders as Pickle galivanted from one to the other. He shot the little creature a glower, but that didn't stop him from reaching up to scratch Pickle's chin. "They won't be expecting us, and it'd be poorer tactics than the Company has ever shown to have many guards grouped at the same point without reason to anticipate entry. Between the two of us, we'll tear right through any there."

"As soon as we've got our brethren free, we'll have even more strength in numbers," Omen said.

I drummed my fingers on the table. "But remember, we don't want to stick around long enough for the Company to bring in reinforcements, and we need all the data we can get about their operations. As soon as Ruse has the virus uploaded onto the first computer we find, we'll want to grab any other computer equipment we see before he activates it. We can figure out what we'll get out of their records when we've hauled the equipment back to the Everymobile."

Omen nodded. "Snap, you determine which equipment is the most vital if we have to prioritize. Bow and Gisele, we'll want you two wrangling the escapees and making sure they stay on track. But I think this should pull together well." He paused and then lifted his gaze to catch my eyes. "You do understand that we won't be leaving any humans alive in that place if we can help it, don't you?"

A chill ran down my spine at the coolness with which he made that statement, but I'd been prepared for it. Slaughtering the building's mortal occupants was the easiest way to ensure our own safety both during the attack and afterward. The more we reduced the number of people working for the Company of Light, the harder it'd be for the Company to keep running and the easier for us to disrupt any other parts of the organization we needed to destroy.

A quiver of queasiness passed through my stomach—and faded with the memory of the asshole who'd rammed his gun at Vivi, of the descriptions I'd gotten of Ellen's injuries.

Anyone working in that facility knew they were torturing conscious beings that had all the self-awareness humans did, and had been party to who knew how many horrors inflicted on actual humans as well. I didn't enjoy the idea of spilling their blood, but I wasn't going to shed tears over their deaths either.

"If that's what we've got to do, then we do it," I said firmly. "I'll fry a few of them if I have to." If I could.

The hellhound shifter tipped his head approvingly and started going over a few more points with Thorn, who leaned over to peer at the screen. I forced down another mouthful of pad thai, but it dropped heavy into my stomach.

The last time we'd stormed one of the Company's buildings, we'd had fewer people and less idea what to expect—but I'd also had less time for the enormity of what we were taking on to sink in.

I squeezed between Snap and the table to squirm off of the sofa, snatching a kiss from him as I passed. "Bathroom break. Don't leave without me."

As Gisele tittered at that unnecessary request, I ducked into the little RV bathroom and yanked the door shut behind me. The compact space was the only part of the vehicle its shadowkind owners hadn't expanded or spruced up, probably because they had little use for it. I sat down on the closed toilet seat, one knee bumping the sliding door to the shower stall, and dragged in a deep breath.

I could do this. I could generate fire out of nothing—I'd done it plenty of times before, and tonight I'd do it again, as many times as I needed to. That was all there was to it.

I tugged a square of toilet paper off the roll and held it up in front of me. All I needed was to remember the sensations from that motorcycle ride. Stir up the emotions that brought the flare of heat into my chest. Think of Vivi being grabbed by those assholes—of that hall of cages in the experimental facility—of Snap's expression when he'd gleaned impressions of the pain the Company's experiments had caused. Of the hail of machine gun fire aimed at Thorn.

My lungs constricted with a hitch of my pulse. All those fuckers *deserved* to be burned to a crisp.

I glared at the square of floppy paper, and a flame spurted up along its edge.

Beautiful. I'd need a lot more fire than that to raze the Wharf Street building to the ground when we were through, but I'd have a lot more motivation when I was in the middle of the fray. And if my newfound powers faltered once I was in the building, I had a new lighter and bottle of kerosene to speed things along.

I doused the flaming toilet paper with a spray of water in the sink and stepped out to find Snap waiting for me in the hall just outside. His eyes took me in with unusual intentness.

"Are you all right?" he asked.

My most devoted lover was nothing if not attentive. I rested my hand on his chest, smiling up at him. "Absolutely. We've got this."

He brushed his fingers over my hair, gazing at me with such affection that my heart skipped a beat for much more pleasant reasons. "I'll look after you out there too. Not just Thorn. I won't let anyone hurt you again."

"Hey, if I take any more bullets or break any more bones, that dryad can always patch me up again, right?"

When his intensity didn't soften at my teasing, I leaned even closer, trailing my hand up to his shoulder. "Don't worry. I'll be fine."

He hummed to himself. "You can't always be fine. But when you're not, I'll be there for you."

That simple but determined statement sent an echoing rush of affection through me. I tugged him to me for a proper kiss, but it didn't feel like enough.

I had to make sure I had my devourer's back too, like the sort-of agreement I'd made with Thorn. Hell, any one of my quartet and our new companions might need protection at some point, supernatural powers or not. I'd be ready if that happened.

With all final loose ends tied as tightly as we could manage ahead of time, we drove the RV out of the lot. I did my best not to fidget in my seat on the sofa. Pickle curled up on my lap, bumping his head against my stomach as if sensing the tension and attempting to reassure me. Omen paced from one end of the living space to the other with only a slight sway when the RV turned.

I'd sat myself down so I could see part of the view from the front windshield. The Finger came into view up ahead, a looming F-you against the dwindling dusk. The ring of lights around the outside of the courtyard barely touched the enormous statue. Halfway there.

My phone chimed. Vivi? I tugged it out as quickly as I could.

It wasn't my bestie's number but one I didn't recognize. I hit the answer button, a new thread of uneasiness already winding through my gut. "Hello?"

"Sorsha? Oh, good, I got you."

It took me a second to place the voice with its odd wavering distance. She must still be woozy from the medications the hospital would have doped her up on. "Ellen! How are you? You have to know I'm so—"

"Don't worry about that. That isn't—" She coughed. "You're right. These people—we can't let it continue. But I overheard—Leland was talking near the doorway—he said something about making sure you don't get anyone else hurt. It sounded as if… he meant to do something… something he probably shouldn't."

Something that had troubled the Fund's leader enough that she'd reached out to me despite her injuries. My throat constricted. "Thank you. I—I'll keep that in mind. You get some more rest, okay? We need you better."

As I lowered the phone, the Finger slid by outside the RV's windows. I'd just opened my mouth to say we needed to stop and take stock with this new warning when the roar of another engine penetrated the wall across from me.

The RV jolted and lurched to the side with a crunch of steel ramming steel.

TWENTY-FOUR

Sorsha

The crash threw me back into the sofa cushions, my phone spinning from my fingers. I threw my arms over my head just in time to shield it as the entire RV careened over.

I tumbled toward the roof, and the window next to me shattered. Metal screeched as the vehicle skidded on its side across the asphalt.

"It's them!" I gasped out over the throbbing where my recently healed shoulder had slammed into a ridge in the wall. "The Company. They knew we were coming."

My shadowkind companions whirled around me, flashing in and out of the patches of darkness. Footsteps were thumping outside. "Can you get up, Sorsha?" Thorn hollered, and I shoved myself onto my feet, snatching up a trembling Pickle as I did. Given the way the Company had blasted our last two vehicles, I had no reason to believe I was safer in here than out there on the street.

Omen had already bashed the door open in what was now the ceiling of the toppled RV. I ran to it, and Thorn heaved me up onto the steel side that still, miraculously, looked like a city bus.

The others had darted outside through the shadows. Maybe it'd be better if they stayed there. Figures in typical Company of Light armor were rushing all around the RV, spilling from the armored truck that must have rammed us. "Get back, get back!" more distant voices were yelling at pedestrians who'd been nearby.

Taking in the chaos in those initial few seconds, my first chilling thought was that the shadowkind should leave me. Get the hell out of here as fast as they could, and let the Company take out their frustrations on the one being who couldn't slip away through the shadows. There were too many of the mercenaries—they'd caught us too off-guard—

But Thorn leapt out of the RV in his solid form without any hint of considering abandoning me. The swing of his fist gouged out the face of one soldier who'd been springing at me. As another clambered onto the overturned vehicle, he slammed his heel into the back of the man's head.

On the ground, someone… rode by on horseback? Holy mother of a mongoose, no, that was *Bow*, charging at our attackers with a battle cry and an actual bow notched with an arrow that seemed to have appeared alongside his full shadowkind form. His human-like torso emerged from the shoulders of a chestnut stallion's body.

With a scream that was somehow silvery sweet, another horse charged into the soldiers' midst—a graceful ivory animal with tassels of hair sprouting above her slender hooves and a brilliant horn sparkling where it jutted from her forehead. At least, it sparkled for the instant I saw it before Gisele stabbed her horn into a man's gut. The equines apparently had no intention of giving up their Everymobile without a fight.

The unicorn jerked back with a squeal of pain as the man's armor banged her. The twined metals left a black mark just below the slick of blood dripping from the rest of her horn.

"Come." Thorn hefted me onto his back, presumably to make our escape, but he'd only just jumped to the ground when a barrage of attackers came at him. As he whipped around to fend them off, the jolt of the abrupt motion loosened my grip. I tumbled onto the cobblestones of the courtyard.

I scrambled up, spinning this way and that in search of shelter or, better yet, a clear direction to flee in. As long as I was vulnerable, my companions would make themselves vulnerable protecting me. My gaze caught Snap blinking out of the darkness for just long enough to slap the gun from one soldier's hands—a gun that had been pointed my way.

Another attacker came at me swinging one of those horrible laser-like whips. I managed to duck under it and hurled myself at the guy's legs. We toppled together, his helmet falling off with a clang as it hit the ground. Omen hurtled past us in hellhound form with a slash of his claws to open the guy's throat.

But there were still more—still way too many fucking more of the pricks. I grabbed the dagger my latest attacker had strapped to his hip and pushed away from him just in time to see a clot of the Company soldiers tossing one of those glinting nets around Bow.

The centaur staggered to a halt with a clomping of his massive hooves. His captors closed in around him, and a jolt of horror rang through me. Without hesitating, I sprinted toward them.

The centaur shuddered in the toxic metals' grasp, and a furious heat surged through my body. I threw myself between two of the men holding the net, grasped one silver-and-iron strand, and propelled the searing sensation out through my hands with all the force I had in me.

The soldiers around the net yelped or barked with pain. Their hands jerked from the bindings, whiffs of burnt flesh reaching my nose. I wrenched at the net and managed to yank it off Bow before they recovered.

The centaur staggered away, shaking himself, and then wheeled with renewed resolve. As a couple of the men whose hands I'd barbequed launched themselves at me, Bow charged between them. One kick of his powerful hind legs shattered a man's hips. His fists sent the other reeling backward to meet Thorn's crystalline knuckles.

Was that the wail of a siren somewhere in the distance? The Company of Light couldn't have stopped every spectator from calling in the crash and the following fight. Once emergency services got here, our attackers would have to skedaddle or start offering explanations I didn't think they wanted to. If they wouldn't give us room to make a dash for it, we just had to hold on that long.

I dodged one way and another, yanking off a helmet here, tripping an asshole there. My focus narrowed down to the flurry of combat around me and the thump of my pulse, hard but steady. Skewered lyrics to match its beat trickled through my mind and off my tongue. "Once I ran you through, now to stun some crew…"

The words buoyed my spirits. I tossed out a few more lines with the weaving of my body. An elbow to a nose here, with a satisfying crack. A knee to the balls there with an even more satisfying groan. "…And that's not nearly a-a-all!"

A mass of movement on the other side of the courtyard's immense wood-and-metal sculpture caught my eyes. A new wave of attackers was racing toward us from beyond the Finger. The streetlamp light glanced off their armor—and more nets, more knives, more guns. Shit.

My pulse hiccupped. Strength flared inside me. I shoved my arms forward, intending to hurl a tsunami of flames to stop them in their tracks.

What came out wasn't quite a tidal wave—more like a wavering. And that wavering firelight smacked mostly into the wooden struts of the looming statue rather than the attackers charging around it. Flames leapt up over the boards with a plume of smoke. I'd lit up one of the city's most beloved landmarks.

Oops.

Before I could attempt to summon any more of my fiery power, the second squad of Company soldiers was on us. Thorn, Omen, and Gisele ripped through the front lines, but more converged on us from all around.

Why the hell weren't those sirens getting louder faster? Couldn't they see the entire damn Finger was now blazing away, the flames licking higher than the buildings around the square?

Which, yes, was my fault, but do we really need to keep score here?

The shadowkind couldn't hold the front on all sides. An armored woman barreled around the toppled RV straight at me. Her pistol shot went wide, but the next instant she was bashing the gun across the side of my head.

I stumbled but managed to punch her hard enough to compel a spurt of blood from her nose. Ruse flashed out of the shadows for long enough to kick her legs out from under her.

Another two attackers were already running at me. I knocked one back with an uppercut, but I wasn't fast enough to handle both. The second grasped my wrist and heaved me toward the blade he was holding—more silver and iron, it looked like, but those would sever my mortal soul from my body just fine if he filleted me with it.

I yanked away from him. The blade slashed across my chest, slicing through my shirt and drawing a line of blood across my sternum and down my ribs. Pain spiked all across the cut.

I gasped and flailed again, but the man held on tight. My first punch dislodged his helmet, but he evaded my second and flipped the knife in his hand to plunge it straight into my heart.

Snap flickered out of the shadows in a flash of golden curls, his eyes wide and face pale with panic. "No!" He snatched at the blade and hissed through his teeth as it seared his fingers. My attacker landed a kick to the devourer's belly that sent him slamming into the underside of the Everymobile.

The mercenary spun back toward me. I lashed out with my free hand again, my fingers curled to claw out his eyes if I could, but he jerked me into the swing of his knee. It pummeled my gut so hard the world swam before my eyes. His blade rammed down—

And a sinewy figure loomed over the man with an unearthly shriek.

It was Snap. Even in my momentary daze, the golden curls and heavenly face were unmistakable. But his body had stretched, serpentine, to even greater heights. As I watched, his face stretched too, his chin lengthening to a sharp point. His eyes blazed neon green around the slits of his shadowkind pupils. Long, twig-like fingers clutched my attacker's shoulders.

Then his mouth yawned wide open, his jaw unhinging and dropping even farther to reveal rows of spindly gleaming fangs. With an audible creak that shivered through my nerves, he snapped them around the man's skull.

My attacker's eyes bulged. His own jaw dropped with what looked as if it should have been a scream, but the sound came out so thin and strained it barely split the air. It carried on and on as his face purpled. The scream got even thinner and higher but never ceased, as if the pain of whatever was happening was so great it'd seared through his voice. The hairs all over my body stood on end.

I'd gotten a front-row seat to the showing of why the shadowkind called my sweetly innocent lover a devourer.

TWENTY-FIVE

Snap

The kick to my gut and the slam of my back into the RV sent more shock than pain through my body. I'd kept to the shadows for most of our altercations before—I'd never felt what it was like to be tossed around in the fray.

An instinct shot through me to dodge back into the darkness where our enemies couldn't reach us. Then my gaze caught on Sorsha buckling at another blow from her attacker, his knife gleaming as he moved to stab it down into her—

No. The protest rang through my entire being. I'd promised to protect her; I'd promised I'd keep her safe. I couldn't let her loyalty to us bring her death.

She was *mine*—my peach, my Sorsha—and I refused to lose her.

I flung myself forward on a surge of alarm and defiance. My hands clamped on the man's shoulders—and a very different instinct kicked in.

The shift into my full shadowkind form raced through me like a rough wind. Rising, lengthening, *sharpening*... I yanked the man backward into my hold and clamped my gaping jaws around his head.

The second my teeth pricked his scalp, a wallop of sensation drowned out the rest of the battle. I gulped flickers of memories full of color and sound and here and there a smell or taste: grass baking in the sun in a park, a scramble up the stinging surface of a slide, a party full of other children with flames dancing over a cake, a flush of shame as a presence—*Mommy*—snapped angry words.

Each shred flowed into me with an underlying quiver of resistance and agony as my jaws sheared the mortal's soul away bit by bit. That silent wail of pain was the seasoning on the feast, turning every moment I devoured more poignant. I drank it in with an answering clang of satisfaction all through my limbs.

It'd been too long. Years and years since I'd indulged like this that one time. How had I ever given it up?

More and more impressions flitted through me, now with little spasms of anguish through the man's body. I wrenched more and more from him, tearing away at his being particle by particle, swallowing it all down. A spilling of notes from a long, thin instrument under a spotlight on a stage. A kiss and a hot fumbling in a darkened parking lot. A lacing of heavy boots while a curt voice barked commands. All mine now—*mine, mine, mine.*

Slivers reached me of how he must have come to stand with the Company in their silver-and-iron armor. He'd brushed up against some sort of shadowkind creature—a man had spoken to him of a grave threat in tones that both soothed and terrified him. The promise of destroying the things he thought of as monsters pealed through him like joy until I tore it away.

I ripped more and more from him as if peeling off his skin in curls. The pain that mixed with the cocktail flooded faster in turn. That was mine too. None of it belonged to him any longer, not now that I had him in my grip. I would ravage him until nothing remained but a black hole of emptiness and the vast well inside me overflowed.

His soul was dwindling. The impressions had a tang of recency to them now, a little clearer and more vivid. Standing in a room with several humans who awed him—a sense of elation as someone said, *We'll hollow them out. Hollow the danger out of those beasts and make them ours*— the perfect sweetness of a summer plum, its juice dribbling down his throat—*It'll spread and claim them all. There'll be no stopping it once we have it right*—a looming mansion of gray brick with a turret rising from the righthand side, a place he was honored to protect—wind whipping past him as his legs pumped a bicycle—fading, fading, into a spiral of searing torment.

The torment *I* was causing. As the flow of sensations ebbed, more of my broader awareness crept back in. The physical stomach I'd nearly forgotten I had turned with a fit of nausea.

All the agony and horror reverberating through the final moments of this being's existence—I'd brought that on him. I'd wrung it through his *entire* existence, from his very first memories onward, as I'd savaged my way through them.

Even then, I couldn't will my jaws to open. I couldn't let go of that delectable thread until it petered out completely, leaving my prey nothing but a husk.

My jaws unlocked. The man collapsed as if boneless. I contracted back into the human form that fit this world better and found myself staring at Sorsha… who was staring back at me.

She'd fallen to the ground when I'd pulled her attacker off her. Her hands had tensed where she'd braced them against the pavement, the knuckles white. There was so much white in her eyes too, gleaming starkly. Her throat worked with a thick swallow.

Any pleasure I'd gotten from the devouring shattered into a thousand icy shards. Oh, no. That wasn't—I'd *sworn* I'd never again—

And yet underneath the chill, a tiny part of me wondered what it would be like to consume her existence too, every morsel that made her the fascinating woman I'd only barely scraped the surface of. The keening hunger pealed through me. I felt my tongue flick against my sharpened teeth before I could catch it. *Yes.*

My gut lurched, and the impulse vanished under a fresh wave of horror. A shout reached my ears alongside a blare of sirens—flashing lights at the other end of the courtyard.

The men in their poisonous armor were racing back to their truck and wherever else they'd come from. Thorn charged past me with a bellow to Omen. "Help me push!" He glanced at us. "Snap, Sorsha, get out of the way!"

I didn't know what he meant, but I scrambled in the other direction. Sorsha heaved herself to her feet and followed, her gaze sliding away from me. But I could still see her expression in my mind's eye: the shimmer of the whites of her eyes, the stiffness of her features.

She'd been looking at me as if I were a monster.

With a creaking and a thud, the RV righted itself. Or rather, Thorn must have pushed it upright with Omen's help. Ruse appeared at the window by the driver's seat. The engine growled, and he flashed a grin, but it faltered when he glanced outside.

Thorn and Omen had dashed back around the RV. As they rushed across the cobblestones, ignoring the hollers of the uniformed workers streaming out of the flashing vehicles beyond the blazing statue, Sorsha sprinted over to join them.

Bow was swaying toward us, smoke streaming from his injuries—but even more billowing from the crumpled form he held in his broad arms. Gisele lay limp, her shadowkind essence draining away into the night air in great gusts that showed no sign of slowing.

I leapt forward and then hesitated, torn about which direction it'd help more for me to go in. Omen solved that problem an instant later by waving me toward the RV. "Get on. We've got to take off, *now*."

I darted through the shadows to the living area, which had become a jumble of shattered window glass, leaves from the cupboards, and takeout cartons. Pickle huddled in one corner, shivering. When Sorsha dashed on board, she spotted him immediately and scooped him up. As she cuddled him against her, the others materialized on board.

"Go, now—go!" Omen yelled at Ruse.

More sirens were screeching nearby. The roar of the RV's engine couldn't drown them out, but it could carry us away from them. The vehicle heaved forward and tore down the street.

Sorsha's gaze followed Thorn and Bow as they rushed Gisele's battered form into the main bedroom. "Is there anything—"

"We'll do what we can, which might not be much," Omen snapped, barging past. "Too many hands will only make more confusion."

I guessed that applied to me too. I watched the door slam behind them and glanced down at Sorsha. Her face drawn, she slumped onto the sofa with the dragon. She was bleeding too in her human way from a cut partly visible through her slashed shirt. Her nerves had apparently calmed enough that her wound wasn't smoking, if it even had been before, like that time on the roof. It'd been hard to make out details in the dusk—and I'd been so caught up...

I wavered, wanting to reach out to her, afraid she'd cringe away from me.

Before I'd decided what to do, Sorsha extended her hand to grasp mine. She tugged me down onto the sofa next to her and rested her head against my shoulder. "Thank you," she said. "For— That guy would have killed me."

Even with her saying that and with a pang of longing radiating through me to absorb even more of her warmth, I couldn't bring myself to put my arm around her. I'd saved her, yes, like I'd meant to do, but the way I'd done it— And there'd been a piece of me that had wanted to inflict the same torment on her for my own satisfaction.

She'd looked at me like I was a monster because I was one.

That thought filled my head, blotting out everything else. I'd tried so very hard to exorcise the ferociously hungry side of myself. The one time it had happened before, I hadn't known where the instinct would lead. I could have believed it was a mistake. Now I knew that wasn't true.

I was a devourer. I couldn't stop being one, no matter how long or thoroughly I denied the hunger. Sorsha was in danger while she stayed with us, yes, but not because of our enemies. Because of us.

Because of *me*.

I could hurt anyone around me if I was pushed the wrong way at the wrong time. Not just her but her friends, her colleagues... Maybe even my own companions. I had no idea how my power would work on a shadowkind, but that didn't mean it wouldn't.

The windows darkened as we left the brighter streets of downtown behind. Omen and Thorn emerged from the bedroom, and Sorsha straightened up.

"She's not well, but she seems to have stabilized there," Omen said before she had to ask about Gisele. "We stemmed the bleeding. She hasn't regained consciousness yet. I'm not sure if she will."

As Sorsha muttered several colorful swear words under her breath, our leader's gaze shifted to me. Before he'd even spoken, the cool glint in them told me he'd seen my performance of my full powers.

"This might not have been a *total* catastrophe, thanks to Snap. Did you get anything useful from the one you devoured?"

I'd taken in so much. My mouth opened and closed again with the rush of memory and the sickening mix of relish and guilt it stirred up. I wanted to lick my lips and also to vomit.

"I think he was someone fairly close to the important people in the Company," I ventured. "It seemed as if he was there for meetings, hearing about some of their plans… something they're going to do to take away our powers, maybe?"

Sorsha's head jerked around. "That could be what the experiments are for—to figure out if they can destroy your abilities somehow."

"There was something else they said…" It was all a jumble now, and it hadn't totally made sense to me even as it was careening through my head. "Something they wanted to spread and 'claim'—but maybe that wasn't about us. I don't know." I paused. "I saw one building a few times that he was honored to have the chance to guard. Big with gray bricks and a turret on the right side, a lot of grass around it. I think a tall fence?"

"We didn't see anything like that when we looked at the places connected to the shell company," Ruse said, clearly following our conversation from where he sat behind the wheel.

"I don't know how it fits in," I said. "There might be more I'll piece together. It all comes so fast."

Omen squeezed my shoulder. "Let me know if anything else comes to you that stands out. More of it might make sense as we make additional discoveries via other avenues." He folded his arms over his chest. "They knew we were coming. They knew what bus to look for."

Sorsha tipped her head back against the sofa with a groan. "It was Leland—my ex, from the Fund. Ellen tried to warn me, but it was too late."

Thorn's expression managed to darken even more. "He told the Company our plans? I should have—He was listening at the hospital. He must have heard you tell the other woman we were making a move tonight. And then we were talking in the other room after. If he came over to the door, he might have heard some of that too."

"I think I mentioned the lot where we'd been staying with the bus. Shit." Sorsha's mouth pulled tight. "From the things Leland was saying at the last meeting, he figured *we* were the real villains, beating up on innocent humans. He must have decided he had to protect the Company from us."

"Mostly because he resented you caring what anyone other than him wanted with you, not out of the goodness of his heart, I'd imagine," Ruse said in a disdainful tone.

A fiery sheen had lit in Omen's eyes. "Mortals," he spat out, and then raised his chin, his posture rigid. "We won't return to the same lot, then. What else did—"

"Sorsha's wounded too," I broke in. "Before you ask her any more questions, someone should see to that."

Not me. Someone who posed less of a threat.

While Thorn sprang to inspect her and grab bandaging supplies, Omen paced, and Ruse shouted suggestions from the front, I slipped away into the shadows. The mishmash of voices from the devouring still jostled in my head, but one fragment pealed clearer than the rest.

Hollow the danger out of those beasts.

My focus curled around the words as if they formed a lifeline. Could the Company do that? Could they carve out the pieces of me that made me truly a monster?

If they could, wouldn't it be worth the torture that came with it? It wasn't as if I didn't deserve to face the same agony I'd inflicted on my victims.

I pulled deeper into the darkness, stitching together a path through the impressions I'd devoured that might take me someplace where I wouldn't be a threat to anyone.

TWENTY-SIX

Sorsha

I woke up to a spray of grit pattering against my cheek. As I swiped it away, the morning sun seared my eyes through the broken window above me.

I'd fallen asleep on the RV's sofa, one arm cradling my head and the other tucked against my bandaged belly. I couldn't remember deciding to forego the actual bed—everything after the ramming of the armored truck into the Everymobile had turned into a blur.

Birds were chirping outside, and the next gust of wind brought a wash of pleasant warmth along with more grit. I sat up and squinted at the scene outside.

Right. Somewhere during our hasty flight last night, Ruse had switched the RV to its school bus setting. We'd parked in the lot outside a sprawling rural elementary school well outside the city limits. A stretch of trees beyond the lot blocked any view of the nearest buildings. On a Sunday, no one would be bothering us here.

At least, that should be the case. Leland might have overheard us talking about the city bus lot, but I didn't see how he could have figured out what glamours the RV held unless he'd developed some unexpected supernatural power too. The best we could figure, he'd directed the Company to keep an eye on the Lincoln Road lot last night, and they'd tracked what would have looked to them like a city bus until they'd been able to get into a suitable position to ambush us.

Lord only knew what the people around the square had thought of the chaos afterward.

Pickle leapt up from the floor and tucked himself close to me, resting his chin on my thigh. As I scratched between his ears, three of my higher shadowkind companions materialized in the living space around me. Ruse took a glance into the kitchen cupboards and appeared disappointed with his findings. Thorn surveyed the inside of the RV as thoroughly as I suspected he'd just been investigating the grounds outside, his expression typically grim.

Omen brushed his hands together. "We appear to have evaded any additional assaults for the time being, but I don't think we should count on that luck holding."

If you could even call what we'd experienced so far "luck." My gaze darted to the door to the master bedroom. "How's Gisele?"

Thorn grimaced. "Still unconscious. I've seen shadowkind in a similar coma a few times before when they're badly wounded… Sometimes they manage to regain enough energy to restore themselves, and sometimes they fade utterly into smoke in a couple of days."

"At least we had the RV to drive off in before the mortals ended her completely." Omen patted the wall. "You managed not to get one of our vehicles destroyed, Disaster. So far, anyway."

I wasn't in the mood to return his snark with more of the same. Bow must still be in the bedroom watching over his—friend? Wife? They'd never really clarified their relationship.

Shadowkind didn't tend to pair up in a romantic sense in their own realm, but for mortal-side enthusiasts, who knew what human customs they might have gone in for beyond the horse feed and the other kind of grass. Whatever the case, the centaur and the unicorn shifter clearly cared about each other a lot.

My stomach clenched at the thought that next time it might be one of my trio who drew the short straw in facing off against the Company. And speaking of that trio…

I glanced around. "Where's Snap?"

"Dozing in the shadows to sleep off that big meal, apparently," Ruse said with amusement. "Hey, devourer, time to rejoin the physical realm!"

No slim figure emerged to answer his call. Ruse cocked his head and vanished into the dark patches himself. When he returned several seconds later, still alone, the clenching sensation crept up to the base of my throat.

"He wouldn't have gone far," the incubus said. "He's always stuck close to the rest of us before. And we've all seen he's particularly stuck on you." He shot me a smile, but it was tense along the edges.

Thorn was frowning. "I didn't encounter him during my sweeps of the area around the school. Where would he go?"

"Perhaps he heard there was a country fruit stand nearby," Omen muttered, but his cool eyes betrayed more concern.

I got up to check the view from the windshield as if the others might have somehow missed him shooting hoops in the school yard. "When was the last time anyone saw him? I know he was in the RV with us when we took off from the square."

I'd held onto him briefly then, confirming to myself that he was still the same passionately gentle man I'd found myself welcoming into my bed and my heart—and doing my best to reassure *him* that I knew it. I might have been startled by seeing his full shadowkind powers in action, and what he'd done to that guy hadn't been pleasant to watch, but he hadn't used them lightly. His regret over taking that step had been written all over his beautiful face afterward.

Ruse's brow furrowed as he thought back to the previous night. "We talked about what he saw during his devouring. Then you two started patching up Sorsha's wound, and I don't think I heard anything from him after that. When we parked here for the night, I assumed he'd taken to the shadows to get some rest."

"We were focused on helping Sorsha and finding somewhere safe to pass the night." Thorn rubbed his chiseled jaw. His frown deepened. "I don't recall taking note of him after that initial conversation either. It never occurred to me that he might leave."

Fucking hell. A lump rose in my throat, almost choking me. "He was so ashamed of his power. You all saw the way he would react when it came up. He was so adamant that he'd never use it again, and then for him to feel like he had to…" Because of me.

It was all because of me, wasn't it? Leland had tipped off the Company because of his grudge against me. The shadowkind had stayed by the RV instead of escaping into the shadows to protect me. I should have been paying more attention to Snap after—I should have noticed he was slipping away from us.

I dropped my head into my hands. Pickle nuzzled my arm as if sensing my distress, but the gesture didn't give me much comfort. "Where would he have gone?" I asked the RV at large.

"I don't know," Ruse said. "I don't think he's been mortal-side long enough to have regular haunts."

Omen's voice had turned even flatter than usual. "If he isn't in his right mind enough to stay with us, he'll be easy pickings for any Company hunters prowling around. Let's hope we find him—or he finds his way back to us—before they do." His shoes scraped the floor as he swiveled. "You two take my bike back into the city. Try to follow the same route we took and watch for him. We also need to check the Wharf Street building so we know whether it's still a valid target."

I glanced up at him. "You're letting *Ruse* drive 'Charlotte'? What are *you* going to do?"

As Ruse and Thorn tramped out to detach the motorcycle from where Omen had clamped it to the back of the RV yesterday, hidden under the glamour, the hellhound shifter fixed his narrow gaze on me. "I've got to see how much more power we can drag out of you, mortal. If we've lost the element of surprise *and* Snap, we're going to need you outright blazing to take the Company down and get him back."

The last thing I felt like doing at this particular moment was tap dancing to Bossypants's tune, but the look he gave me warned off any arguments. And he might have a point. It wasn't as if I'd be doing Snap any good by sitting around and moping.

I marched after him out into the parking lot. He ushered me toward the school yard. Chalk marks from the previous week's recesses colored the pavement in pastels: creamy hopscotch boxes, jagged pink and purple flowers, a mint-green abomination of a kitten. That kid better not have any dreams of art school.

The yard gave us plenty of space to work with. The sprawl of pavement stretched all around the brick school building and out to a larger stretch of grass, where football goal posts jutted toward the clear blue sky. I rolled my shoulders and shook out my arms, trying to shed the guilt twisting through my innards.

"Okay, here we are. What crap are you going to put me through this time?"

Omen had turned to face me. His eyes flashed. "I hardly think you can call it 'crap' when it's gotten you this far. You could barely summon a spark to save yourself before, and last night you started a bonfire. It'd just be ideal if next time you could light up our enemies instead of random civic sculptures."

He motioned to a piece of blue construction paper the breeze was nudging across the ground, doodled with gawky stick figures. "Let's see if you can get a blaze started now without an immediate crisis hanging over you."

He didn't think Snap's disappearance was a crisis? Maybe I should try setting his shirt on fire again. But as much as my emotions were churning inside me, it wasn't the sort of distress that got my heart thumping. I glared at the shifter and then the paper, but no heat stirred beneath the gloomy funk that had come over me.

"What does this even matter?" I demanded. "We should be out there looking for Snap too—covering as much ground as we can."

"It appears he's been gone all night. He's got too great a head start if we head out on foot, and we only have one vehicle I feel comfortable sending back into the city to simply meander around, thanks to this friend of yours and his loose lips."

That provoked a flare, but of my temper rather than any voodoo. "He's not my friend. He's fucking *nothing* to me." Which was exactly what had pissed Leland off. How had I ever been attracted to anything about him?

He'd seemed normal. Safe, as long as there were no strings attached. Look how wrong I'd proven to be about that.

"Nonetheless, my point stands." Omen jerked his head toward the field. "Let's at least get your pulse going, then, and see if that's enough to jump-start your inner fire. Sprint between the goal posts a few times."

To my irritation, my feet started to move automatically. I caught myself and planted them on the pavement. "No."

The ice in Omen's gaze hardened. "No?"

"You heard me, Luce. N. O. You ran me ragged at the fairgrounds, and that got us diddly squat. The only thing you've actually tried that worked was dragging me around on your motorcycle, which you've already sent off with someone else—oh, and getting all houndish up in my face, if you want to see if I'll light *you* up again."

He sneered. "I'd like to see you try. Is that what you need—for me to get in your face? Rain a little hellfire down on you and see what catches?"

He stalked toward me, all controlled aggression, everything from his stance to his predatory expression setting off a clang of warning bells in my head. Maybe I should have taken the sprint while I had the chance.

Fuck that regret to Fiji and back. I wasn't letting him terrorize me, no matter what kind of deadly beast he was.

I backed up, but slowly, my hands rising as they clenched. "What do you think you're going to do to me, huh? Take a few swipes with those puppy-dog claws? Gnash your great big fangs? Somehow I'm not shaking in my boots yet."

"You should be," he snapped with a hint of a snarl that chilled my blood. Then he socked me right in the shoulder.

His fist wasn't chilly—it slammed into my body with a blast of otherworldly heat. Apparently *he* could blaze just fine even in human form.

I stumbled, clamping my teeth against a gasp as the impact radiated through the still-healing cut across my abdomen. Then I lunged right at him.

I wasn't totally sure what I was hoping to accomplish. I just wanted to pummel something or someone, and Omen was there acting like such a dick it was hard not to see him as an ideal target. I lashed out with my own fist, skimming his jaw as he dodged to the side. He gave me a shove—not too hard, just enough to send me staggering backward.

"Come on then, little mortal," he taunted. "Where's your fire now? Am I going to have to thrash it out of you?"

I didn't think so. As I circled him, my heart was thudding like the rhythmic pumping of bellows raising flames from a furnace's embers. My inner fire burned through my gut and trickled through my veins, turning me molten.

"Such a fantastic teacher," I shot back at him. "Five minutes in, and you're beating up on your only student."

"If it's the only lesson that'll work..." He feinted and snatched at me. His fingers bruised my arm as he yanked me toward him and spun me around. I barely wrenched myself out of the way of the kick he aimed at my ass. "Seems like you need a little more toughening up, anyway."

I swung at him, and he caught my knuckles. With a chuckle and a heave, he sent me stumbling sideways. "Nice try. Is that the best you can do?"

"You haven't seen anything yet. Let me remind you that I've done more for *your* people in the last few years than you've managed so far."

That blow landed even if the physical ones hadn't. An orange light flashed in his eyes, but his voice stayed tight. "If you think that, then why are you so afraid of giving this battle your all? Let that fire out, Disaster. Show me what you've got."

He came at me then like a hound unleashed, no sign that he intended to stop until I forced him to. His first smack across my cheek whipped my head to the side. The next sent a lance of prickling pain through my collarbone.

I did my best to block him, to dodge him, but I'd never fought anyone like this. My self defense classes had focused on a few quick moves to disable your attacker so you could run for the hills, and I couldn't land a single one of those against the onslaught of this shadowkind.

He must have been able to tell he was overwhelming me, but he didn't let up. A fist to my jaw. A heel to my toes. Fresh jolts of pain marked my body with every huff of breath he released.

The flames inside me flared hotter on the combined fuel of frustration and panic. I slashed my hand at him, and his sleeve caught fire. He slapped it out and pushed me toward the school building. "Not enough. Let's see more of that. I want to see *everything*."

The welling sense of power was starting to sear right through me from the inside out. Why couldn't he lay off me for one fucking second?

Why did Leland have to be such a vengeful asshole? Why hadn't I steered clear of him to begin with?

How could I not have realized Snap needed more from me last night?

Such a fucking mess. Burn it down. Burn it all down.

The urge rolled over me in a wave so visceral it brought a jab of terror with it. The certainty gripped me that if I gave Omen what I was asking for, if I let loose everything that was raging inside me, I could burn even this man with all his powers to a crisp.

A flare of heat slipped out—a flame shot up from a tuft of his hair that had risen from the slicked-back strands. He shook it away and punched my other shoulder. "Still not seeing what makes you so great."

"I don't think you want to. I don't think you'd survive it."

"Oh, ho, big talk from the mortal." He swiped at my temple, hitting me hard enough to send my thoughts reeling. "Try me, then."

The heat scorched my throat. I couldn't swallow it down. My rising terror flickered higher alongside those flames. "No, Omen, I really don't think—"

"Come *on*, Disaster! Why can't you do this one thing? Or were all those grand rescues before, letting out the collectors' prizes, only about the glory of pulling the capers off? Don't you care whether you can help any more shadowkind? Or whether we ever see Snap again?"

"Don't *you*?" I burst out. "All I see is a fucking bully who doesn't have a clue what he's doing if he can't badger everyone around him into falling into line. As far as I can tell, you're the problem here, not the solution."

A growl escaped him, and suddenly he was *really* on me, hurling me into the wall with a slam that spiked pain all through my back. He pinned me there, the thrust of his hands nearly shattering my wrists, his eyes burning and his teeth bared. His hot breath spilled over my face.

There—there was the beast I knew was in him. Somehow seeing his cold front fall away dampened the fury in me.

Not so much for Omen. He wrenched himself back a step a moment later, cursing under his breath. His hair had bristled; his chest was heaving. He blinked, but the orange haze wouldn't quite clear from his eyes.

I let my arms drop to my sides. He leaned in again, his palm against the bricks just inches from my head, his conflicted gaze holding mine.

"What is it about you that you always have to bring out the worst in me?" he asked in a ragged voice.

"I don't think this is the worst," I said honestly. "Right now? You feel like you're being real. I *like* you angry—way better than I like the ice-cold prick who orders people around from his high goddamned horse, anyway."

He guffawed, the sound equally raw. "You like me better when I'm on the verge of literally biting your head off."

I shrugged, my shoulders scraping the wall. I might have liked him better, but I still valued my life too much to try to push past him right now. My anger had dwindled, but fear was alive and well, thrumming through my pulse. "It's become increasingly clear to me that I have unusual tastes. But yeah, I do. Although I'd also prefer that you didn't actually bite my head off, if it's all the same to you."

Omen's own head bowed, dipping closer so his forehead almost grazed mine. The heat of his body radiated over me. It wasn't entirely unpleasant, to tell you the truth.

Yep, the poster girl for unusual tastes, right here.

"If you had any idea how hard I've worked to get here..." he muttered.

"Get where?" I asked. "The state of being an asshole?"

"See, that— You—" He let out another growl, but it was a subdued one this time. Then he eased back just a little. A flicker of something I hadn't seen in him before crossed his expression. Was that... concern?

He fingered the side of my shirt, his fingertips brushing my side for the briefest of seconds. "I opened your wound again."

I glanced down, more surprised than I should have been by the streak of bright red spreading across the center of the bandage. The sight of it brought the sting of the wound into sharper awareness. My mouth twisted. "Well, hey, what's it matter if another mortal is spouting blood, right?"

Omen's tone was gruff but firm. "You know you're more than that."

I supposed I did. And that was clearly the only reason he cared—because of my superpowers and how they might help his cause. "I'm sure I'll survive, because or in spite of that."

"No doubt." He hesitated, still looming over me by the wall, as if he couldn't quite tear himself away but also didn't know what he was doing there. "I was taking out frustrations I shouldn't have directed at you, at least not entirely. I wish… that I'd been less of an 'ice-cold prick' toward Snap lately. Maybe he thought he'd crossed some line I wouldn't abide by, and I'd made him feel he couldn't even check with me to see where he stood."

I would have laughed if I hadn't been so shocked that Omen was lowering himself to admitting any regrets at all. "You think I haven't been beating myself up as much as I tried to beat up you? If I'd been more careful what I said around my ex—if I'd paid more attention to the state Snap was in last night—"

Omen interrupted me with a hoarse chuckle. "Suffice to say there's plenty of blame to go around. Maybe you didn't send me up in flames, but you put up a pretty good fight."

I guessed that was a high compliment coming from him. I wasn't completely comfortable with the flames that *had* been surging through me just minutes ago, though. If I'd let myself hurl the full force of them at him, just how bad would it have been?

Then he raised his hand to my hair, and those thoughts fell away. My awareness condensed to the warmth of his knuckles grazing my cheek as he fingered a few stray strands—not so different from how Snap had the first morning we'd met.

Omen's gaze slid from his hand against my face to my eyes. The fiery light had faded from his, but the pale blue didn't look quite so icy now. I found my hand drifting forward to rest against his chest, taking in the slowing rhythm of his breaths beneath the taut muscles.

What the hell was I doing? I couldn't tell you. Whatever it was, it seemed to draw Omen nearer. He leaned in, his fingers sliding down to stroke across my chin, and a new pulse of heat flared in my lips. I wet them, my pulse kicking up a notch, not entirely sure what I wanted but wanting it *very* much at the same time.

His breath tickled over my face. Then he shoved the hand he'd leaned against the wall to push completely away from me, his gaze jerking toward the RV.

"We should get you patched up again before you make any more of a mess of yourself, Disaster," he said, back to business as usual.

I peeled myself off the wall with only a smidgeon of disappointment. Whatever line *we'd* come close to crossing just now, I couldn't help suspecting it might be better if we stayed on this side of it.

"And then back to training?" I suggested.

Omen shook his head. "No. I think we've both had enough of pushing you around. I know you'll fight as well as you can when the need is there."

I wasn't sure whether to be relieved or insulted by him throwing in the towel. I was trudging after him toward the Everymobile, debating just how suicidal I'd be to put up an argument, when the door flew open and Bow stared out at us.

"Please—Gisele—I think she's getting worse."

TWENTY-SEVEN

Sorsha

Other than a glimpse as the other shadowkind had hustled her onto the RV, I hadn't seen Gisele since the start of the battle. At the sight of her lying crumpled in the master bedroom, horror overwhelmed any sense I'd had of my own discomforts.

Her slim, graceful body had deflated, limbs limp and cheeks sunken. What skin I could make out had lost its pearly sheen to a creeping gray undertone, as if her entire being had clouded over. Most of her, though, was covered with rough fabric wrapped tight and dappled with yellow-green smears.

From what the shadowkind had said, those bindings had stabilized her before. Now, thin trails of smoke were seeping through the cloth. Omen took one look at her and made a noise of consternation.

As he grabbed a jar off the bedside table, Bow hovered uneasily nearby. "I wasn't sure if it was a good idea to put on even more…"

"We do this and give her a chance to recover, or she leaks away into nothingness," Omen said. "It's not much of a choice."

I didn't understand why there was any debate at all until he started slathering the pale green paste from the jar onto the bandages. Gisele's face remained flaccid, but her arms twitched, her shallow breaths stuttering. Bow winced and turned away as if he couldn't bear to watch.

"It's hurting her?" I asked quietly.

"The herbs in the salve are toxic to shadowkind," the hellhound shifter said without looking up from his task. "Normally we'd avoid them—they'd weaken us. But in a case where someone is already severely weakened and in danger of wasting away, in small amounts they can repel our essence back into the body. The hope is that before too long, that body can heal itself enough to stem the bleeding on its own."

The treatment was poisoning her as much as it was curing her. My stomach turned. But Omen's efforts had clearly accomplished their goal—the wisps of smoke faded away. A tremor ran through Gisele's body, and then it sagged even more lifelessly into the mattress.

Bow was swiping at his eyes. He sat down onto the bed next to her, the haggard expression on his usually jovial face almost as painful to look at as his companion was. Omen set down the jar with a sharp rap. He stalked out of the room to wash his hands with a hiss of the faucet and returned a moment later, brushing his reddened fingertips against his pants. The stuff had burned his skin too.

"Next time, you start applying the salve the moment you notice any seepage. She can barely afford to lose the little essence she still has."

The centaur's head drooped more, but he nodded. "I'm sorry. I—I panicked. We've never gotten more than a scratch here before. I didn't know what it would be like."

"This is war," Omen said. "Don't imagine it can't get worse." His tone softened just slightly. "We'll continue doing what we can for her. I've put a call in to a dryad with healing skills—if he's willing to stick his neck out this far after we've become such a target. I'm not sure how much even he'd be able to help her at this point as it is. She seemed strong. She may manage to pull through."

He spun around, and I followed him back to the living area.

"If she starts bleeding again, I could put the salve on," I said. "It wouldn't hurt me at all."

Omen glanced at his fingers, where the flush of irritation was already fading. "It's a minor discomfort. Better that I handle it, or

Thorn—we can judge what's a reasonable amount from how it affects us."

"I guess you have experience with this sort of thing from the wars before."

He gave me a sharp look. "Not something Thorn would want you discussing with anyone else."

I grimaced at him. "I figured *you're* safe enough, since he told me you were there. You already know what he is."

"That's hardly—"

An engine sounded outside, and he cut off whatever other criticism he might have added with a rough breath. "Enough of that. Charlotte's back—and let's hope our wingéd, our incubus, *and* our devourer are with her."

Had the others found Snap? As I hustled to the door, my heart leapt with more hope than I knew was sensible.

When I stepped out onto the pavement, Ruse was just driving the motorcycle into the lot. He parked it, and Thorn emerged from the shadows around the undercarriage where he must have been riding —alone.

"No sign of Snap," the warrior reported to Omen without preamble. "And no sign of activity at the Wharf Street factory either. I ventured inside, and it appeared to have been very recently gutted."

Omen swore. "They guessed that was our target."

"This Leland twerp could have told them everything the Fund was looking into on Sorsha's behalf," Ruse said. "Everything her friend discovered at the fundraising gala."

"Then we can assume that anything important they were keeping at the other locations under that shell company has been cleared out or will be shortly too." The shifter started to pace. "In some ways that could be good. We've got them on the run; they'll be getting short on property where they can carry out their operations and stash their prisoners. They may be having to cut corners on certain security measures to avoid places we might know about."

"Except they'll be cutting it at places we *don't* know about," I couldn't help saying.

"Yes, that is the primary problem."

Was that my fault too? We wouldn't have known to make that

factory a target if I hadn't gotten Vivi and the Fund involved in the first place, so... maybe it all evened out on the scale of horribleness and personal responsibility?

That thought didn't exactly lift my spirits.

Thorn stepped forward, worry turning his expression even more somber. "Sorsha, you're bleeding again."

Oh, right. Gisele's much more urgent injuries had diverted Omen and me from the whole patching-Sorsha-up plan. I set my hand on the top of the bandage. "It just needs a change of dressing. I'll be fine. It only stings a little." And maybe there was a bit of throbbing in there too after all this bustling around, but he didn't need to know that.

Despite my reassurances, the warrior ushered me back into the RV like some kind of hulking matron. As he unwrapped the wound, he tutted under his breath. He added a few careful stitches where a couple Omen had sewn in last night had broken and dabbed antiseptic cream over the whole slash. When he'd wrapped a layer of gauze around the new sterile pad, Ruse set a paper bag on the table by the sofa. I straightened up, a buttery, cheddar-y scent reaching my nose.

"I liberated some breakfast for you," the incubus said, his tone jaunty but his hazel eyes darker than usual as they lingered on my face. "I know it's no substitute for our beloved devourer, but you do need to look after the inside of your belly as well as the outside."

I couldn't deny that—and on a better day, my mouth would have been watering at the savory smell. "Thank you," I said, unwrapping a breakfast sandwich of biscuit, egg, and melted cheese. It sure beat hay-and-clover salad.

As I took a bite, the two remaining members of my original trio stood on the other side of the table like stalwart guardians—or wardens, ensuring I didn't leave until they were satisfied I'd taken care of myself. The crumbly pastry dissolved on my tongue, and the cheese added the perfect amount of bite to the creamy scrambled egg. For a guy who used human sexual satisfaction for sustenance, Ruse was an excellent judge of actual food.

But each gulp stuck in my throat before dropping into the hollow in my gut. I'd only made it halfway through the sandwich when the lump expanding inside me felt almost too heavy to bear.

I set the sandwich down, figuring I could at least take a breather, and Thorn's brow knit. "You don't look well. Your sleep can't have been satisfactory lying on that bench all night. You should take some rest in your bed."

"I'm really not—"

"No arguments, this once," he said, and swept me off the sofa into his bulging arms as if I weighed no more than Pickle did.

"Thorn," I protested, ineffectually trying to squirm out of his hold. Exerting just enough strength to stop me from bending at the torso and straining my wound again, the warrior marched me to the second bedroom without a word.

"Sleep tight!" Ruse called after us with audible amusement.

Thorn set me down gingerly on the bed. When he moved to leave, a more piercing resistance shot through me. My throat closed up, and my arm darted to grasp the side of his shirt before he could get very far.

"If you want me to rest, you'd better stick around and make sure I do."

Thorn peered down at me. "Sorsha…"

I tugged on his shirt. "I'm not tired, just worried and upset and…" I had to pause to steady my voice. "I don't really want to be alone right now."

The firmness in the warrior's expression vanished under a wash of tenderness. He sank down onto the edge of the bed next to me and managed to make only a small disgruntled sound when I pushed myself into a sitting position.

I tucked myself against Thorn's broad, solid chest. His musky smell with its trace of smoke filled my nose, and when his arm came around my shoulders, his warmth enveloped me too.

Having him with me like this didn't make up for Snap's disappearance any more than the breakfast sandwich had, but in the power coiled through his brawny body, I could feel the certainty that he wouldn't give up until the devourer was back with us where he belonged.

Thorn held cautiously still for a moment and then allowed his hand to stroke up and down my arm from shoulder to elbow. He tipped his head so his chin rested against my temple. "Snap was incredibly dedicated to our cause—and, from what I saw recently, to you. If he can make it back to us, I doubt he'll stay away very long. And if those bastards have imprisoned him, we'll get him back. They didn't manage to break Omen in all those weeks."

"I know," I said. But Snap wasn't Omen. He meant so well, and he felt things so deeply. "I was startled… and maybe a little scared when I saw his full form. With how horrible he feels about devouring already, he might have convinced himself *I* think he's horrible."

Thorn grunted. "He couldn't believe that for very long if he's been paying any attention at all. I'm no expert in affection, but *I* could see how much you cared for him. He means a lot to you."

"You all do." As the words spilled up, the truth of them swelled inside me. When the trio had shown up out of nowhere in my kitchen, I'd seen them as nothing but a hassle. Now, it was hard to imagine going on with regular human life once this was over and never seeing them again.

Thorn's hesitance to accept the affection I was offering *him* even after I'd asked him to stay twisted me up inside even more. I raised my head to gaze up into his ruggedly handsome face. "You realize that, don't you? That if something happened to you—if you left or the Company hurt you—I'd be just as upset as I am over Snap."

He opened his mouth and closed it again as he appeared to gather his thoughts. His dark eyes held mine. "I don't have the gentleness and joy the devourer exudes—I can't offer the incubus's skill with words or caresses. How could I expect to provoke the same fondness they do?"

I made a dismissive sound. My hand came up so I could trace my fingers over the faint lines of the scars that framed his face. "You know, *they're* the outliers. I never really went for cheerful sweethearts or suave smooth-talkers before. Give me a strong silent type any day."

He grunted doubtfully.

I tapped his cheek. "I've seen how much emotion you carry under that stoic front. I've never known anyone, human or shadowkind, half as resolute or loyal as you."

"Only to make up for where I failed in the past."

"I'm not convinced you actually screwed up so very badly back then in the first place, but believe me, an awful lot of human beings go through their much shorter lives totally disregarding the people they let down along the way." Or even lashing out at those people as if they were to blame. Thorn—and Ruse and Snap, and maybe even Omen—was worth a thousand Lelands. When you compared him and his vengeful sabotage to them, how could you say the shadowkind were more monstrous?

My tastes might be unusual, but why the hell should I want a generic jerk when I could have a magnificent monster—or, you know, three?

Thorn brushed a lock of my hair behind my ear, the skim of his fingers tingling over my skin. His voice dropped to a husky note that sent those tingles deeper. "You contain plenty of tenacity yourself, m'lady. A steely will and yet so much compassion as well. You were a worthy ally before we knew you had any unearthly power."

"Only an ally?"

His hand teased along my jaw in answer, tipping up my chin so he could claim my lips. I hadn't known how much I needed this until I was kissing him back, melting into the planes of his muscular frame.

His mouth branded mine, as determined as if he were pouring all the affection he had for me into that one kiss. His fingers trailed down my back, tucking me closer to him, and my knee slid up over his thigh. A rush of heat flooded me.

Yes. Yes. Just for this moment, I wanted to revel in what I still had instead of brooding over what I'd lost. I wanted to see that steely, compassionate woman Thorn took me for reflected in his eyes.

I shifted even closer, running my hand over his chest, and drew my lips from his just far enough to say in a voice so thick with need I barely recognized it, "Thorn, can we—"

The desire ringing through the words must have said enough before I even finished the question. Thorn grasped me and swung me right onto his lap, capturing anything else I might have said with another kiss. As I straddled him, he stroked my thigh while his other hand tangled in my hair.

I slid forward, and my sex settled against the substantial bulge of his groin. Even through the layers of fabric, the feel of that hardness was enough to make me groan.

I arched into him, extending the friction, and Thorn groaned too. His mouth plundered mine, but there was still a carefulness to the way he held me, even as the squeeze of his fingers around my thigh urged on my rocking against him.

He eased my face back an inch, still close enough that the heat of his breath flooded down my neck. His voice came out strained. "I don't want to hurt you, Sorsha. This body is made for fighting, not love-making."

I'd seen how large my warrior was in *every* area a few weeks ago when he'd sprung out of the shadows nude. The memory only spurred on the ache of need between my thighs. "I think it's made for whatever you decide to do with it," I murmured, splaying my hands against his abdomen. "Let me worry about how much I can handle. If anything's too hard or too fast or too… large"—my palm slid over his erection—"I'll let you know. But so far I have no complaints."

"As m'lady wishes," he breathed in return. It came out like a prayer, so different from the reluctant tones with which he'd once offered that term of respect that delight trembled through me.

I stripped off his tunic, eager to see all that sculpted flesh on display again, and he managed to tug my blouse open above the bandage on my stomach with surprising deftness, though his thick fingers fumbled with my bra. I unhooked it for him and gasped as his hands engulfed my breasts. The swivel of his calloused palms against my nipples raised them to points with a surge of bliss. The sensation shot to my sex, and the lingering pain of my wound hazed away in the wake of that pleasure.

I kissed Thorn again, still rocking against him, the heat between us turning searing. I'd waited too long to get this intimate with the last of my lovers—I had no patience left. My mouth skidded against his lips, a whimper tumbled from my throat at the powerful sweep of his thumbs over my breasts, and then I was groping at the ties of his trousers.

Sweet simmering symphonies, medieval clothing was a devil to unravel. At my muttered curse, Thorn let out a chuckle and flicked the knot loose as if it were nothing—through some supernatural voodoo, I was sure. I didn't spend much time worrying about it, because the next second I'd delved inside his underclothes to free that massive cock.

It was magnificent, thick and corded with veins and so fucking hard I thought he might explode as I gripped it. His erection twitched at my touch, and a ragged breath shuddered out of the warrior.

"M'lady," he whispered, and that time it sounded like a plea. One I was all too happy to answer. We could play around with more possibilities some other time.

There would be other times. I swore it by whatever was still true in my soul.

I scrambled out of my jeans and panties, and Thorn pulled me to him, the strength even in that controlled gesture taking my breath away. I ran my fingers up and down his cock. He kissed me so hard his teeth nicked my tongue, and then I lowered myself onto him with as much haste as my body allowed.

Just the head of his cock penetrating my slit stretched me more than I'd ever experienced. I stopped there, adjusting. Pleasure pulsed through me as my channel relaxed to accommodate him.

The warrior was a perfect gentleman, as torturous as the wait must have been for him. He kissed the side of my neck and massaged my breasts, adding to the blissful sensations coursing through me.

I sank a little lower and a little lower still, each inch stretching me farther with a burn that was increasingly ecstatic. My head tipped against Thorn's shoulder, sweat dampening my brow. "You feel so good," I said, my lips brushing his skin. My fingers teased over his belly, his pecs, his pert nipples, any way I could pay him back for the intense pleasure he was offering me with his patience.

Another groan slipped out of him. "As do you."

The impulse flitted through me to feel all of him pressing down on me, to lose myself in the surge of that massive body over and inside me, but I wasn't sure I was quite ready for that yet. I settled for dropping even lower, a pleased sound reverberating from my chest.

I felt full to bursting in the most giddying sense. The only question left was how well we could move together.

I eased up and down, up and down, a little more each time. The bond between us turned slick with my expanding arousal. As I hit a rhythm, Thorn found the confidence to raise his hips to meet me, gently at first and then, when he saw how I whimpered at the additional motion, with more force.

I bit my lip, struggling to hold in the louder cries of pleasure that wanted to peal from my lungs. The walls in the RV weren't thick enough to disguise those without Ruse's soundproofing magic.

I didn't have to hold them in very long. The ecstasy building inside me was spiking higher, racing me toward my peak with a momentum I couldn't rein in. I bucked against Thorn, clutching his shoulder, his side, and he was right there to meet me. His lips crashed into mine, the thrust of his hips sent me spiraling even higher, and I came so hard my vision whited out with the flare of bliss.

As my sex clenched around him, the warrior's fingers dug into my thigh. He jerked me to him, impaling me so deeply his cock set off a second orgasmic wave just as he spilled himself inside me.

I sagged into him, alight with the afterglow. Thorn cupped my cheek and kissed me with a softer determination. As I nestled against his broad chest, the doubts and self-recriminations that had gripped me earlier scattered into the distance.

I was strong—hell, yes, I was. Strong enough to take a legendary warrior as my lover. No shitty ex was going to beat me down.

Leland had used the conflict with the Company of Light to act out his resentment against me. Maybe it was time to turn the tables right around and see how we could use *him*.

TWENTY-EIGHT

Sorsha

Omen watched me climb onto the motorcycle behind Ruse with obvious reluctance. I gave him an optimistic thumbs-up. "Don't worry! We'll take care of Charlotte."

"I don't think you'd enjoy finding out what'll happen if you don't," he retorted, but he turned away rather than continuing to stew about the situation. This plan required only Ruse and me, and as much as the hellhound shifter might have wanted to tag along to supervise from the shadows, it didn't really make sense to put anyone else at risk. The Company people were a hell of a lot more likely to notice us in the city than way out here in the middle of nowhere.

In my attempt to avoid drawing their notice, I fit the helmet the incubus had been kind enough to obtain for me over my head, where a black knit hat already hid my red hair. Ruse sported a helmet himself, a situationally appropriate way to disguise his horns. He gave Omen's retreating back a salute, patted my knee to confirm my position against him, and gunned the engine.

It was way easier to relax against the incubus's lean back than when I'd been clinging to Omen yesterday. For one, Ruse didn't drive the bike like a, well, demon. He might not have been the smoothest at lane changes, but he was concerned enough about keeping a low profile to stick to the same speed as the cars and avoid any flashy moves.

And considering how intimate we'd gotten on multiple occasions, I didn't have a whole lot of modesty left when it came to having my arms wrapped around his chest or my thighs pressed against his hips.

He followed the directions I'd given him to Leland's townhouse without a hitch. The sight of the narrow, gray building on the end of the row made my chest constrict.

How many times had I rung that doorbell ready for a quick jump in the sack—a dozen? Twenty? It had never felt like anything other than scratching an itch, and then even that enjoyment had turned sour with Leland's caustic disappointment in me.

My current feelings toward him went well past sour and into "raze it to the ground" territory, but I wasn't here to mess with his living space. At least, not yet. We'd see how this visit went first.

I knew my ex-friends-with-benefits's schedule well enough to have anticipated that he'd be at the gym on a Sunday afternoon. We left the bike a couple of blocks over and slunk into Leland's backyard, Ruse sticking to the shadows now. As I waited for him to slip inside and unlock the door for me, I set my shoulders, gathering my chutzpah.

We had a plan—one that should get us to Snap if the Company had grabbed him. No uncomfortable memories were going to shake me out of accomplishing that. Leland had no idea what he'd set himself up for.

Ruse opened the door with a little bow, and I marched inside.

Had the place always held this stale grease smell? Maybe I'd never been close enough to the kitchen before to notice it. Wrinkling my nose, I passed through the space with its tarnished steel appliances and into the living room off the front hall where I intended to wait.

I clearly hadn't spent enough time on the first floor in general, or the framed photographs along the mantel would have been a tip-off that this guy wasn't worth my time even as an easy lay. Each of those photographs was of Leland, on his own: posing at an amateur weight-lifting competition, leaning over beneath the open hood of a car I doubted he had the slightest idea how to fix, giving a victory sign on the deck of a speed boat. He might as well have built a little shrine to his ego—a testament to how much he thought the world should revolve around him alone.

Ruse ambled over to contemplate them closer up. "Such a catch," he teased. "What a mistake you made in letting this fine specimen go. At least, *he* clearly thinks he's the finest specimen around."

"No kidding." I socked him lightly in the shoulder. "No need to rub it in. I did find the good sense to move on to greener pastures."

The incubus wiggled his eyebrows. "And I've been delighted to plow you." As I choked on a laugh, one of those eyebrows arched higher. "Speaking of which... I take it you got something other than grumbles and glowers out of our Incredible Hulk."

My interlude with Thorn. A faint flush crept up my neck. "We tried to be quiet."

"Don't worry your lovely head about that. I have especially keen senses when it comes to my area of expertise. I lent a little magic to give you the privacy I figured you'd want to have."

"Oh. Thank you." I paused. "That didn't require you to be in the room, did it?"

Ruse held up his hands. "I enjoy participating in the act, not so much watching it from afar. Consider the favor my contribution to the public good. Thorn's needed a good lay for at least a few centuries, I'd estimate."

I socked him again, but his banter had helped distract me from my uneasiness in this place. When Snap and I had gotten close, the incubus had told me that he was happy for me to seek pleasure wherever I could find it. It sounded like that applied to the warrior as well, as much as their attitudes tended to clash.

The gaudy brass clock standing between the photos showed it was quarter past three. "Leland will be here soon," I said. "You'd better stay out of sight until I give the signal that his badge is off." I didn't know whether he'd be wearing it just to walk around the city, but after screwing us over as badly as he had yesterday, I wouldn't be surprised to find him extra cautious.

Ruse nodded and vanished. I prowled around the living room until I found an ideal spot where I could crouch beside a side table. The position gave me a clear view of the hall so I'd know what I was dealing with before I sprang into action, but should hide me from a casual glance. Then all I had to do was wait.

As the minutes ticked by, I twisted a lyric and sang softly into the silence. "Waiting for that final woe sent, you'll say the words that lie and prey." Leland would probably claim siccing our enemies on us had been a heroic act. Well, he'd lost any hope of screwing me months ago, and now he was going to lose any chance of screwing *us* over again.

Ruse blinked into the physical space just long enough to say, "He's coming down the street," and then vanished again. I tensed in my hunched pose. My fingers curled toward my palms.

A key clicked in the lock. Leland strode in, all puffed up on an endorphin high from the weights he'd have been hefting. As he tossed his gym bag to the side of the hall, his shirt shifted, and I caught a glint of silver at its V neckline. He was wearing his protective badge pinned to an undershirt like I often did. No other metallic gear gleamed on his person.

That was all I needed to know. I sprang up and leapt across the few feet between us.

Leland stiffened in surprise—wrong reflex, dude. "Sorsha," he sputtered, and I was already on him, smacking his defensive hand away with a quick swipe while I yanked on his shirt. With one swift jerk, the badge snapped off the layer of cotton underneath. I flashed it through the air to signal Ruse.

"What the fuck are you doing?" Leland snapped, lunging at me. Too bad he spent all his gym time bulking up and not developing his inner Jack Be Nimble. I darted out of the way just as Ruse materialized in the space between us.

"Hello, my friend," the incubus said in his most cajoling tone, so strung through with supernatural power I could feel the vibration of it in the air. "As you can see, we're all going to get along here. We came out of concern for your well-being—you need to listen to us or you could be in grave danger."

Leland swayed on his feet, his boyish face tensing. The voodoo hadn't totally enraptured him in one go. "You're one of the shadowkind she's working with. I don't think you should be here. Either of you. You—"

Ruse held up his hands in a placating gesture. "We'll certainly leave as soon as we've settled things with you. You've been in contact with very malicious people, and we couldn't bear to see you get hurt because of that. I know you and Sorsha have had your differences, but can't you see how much she still cares for you?"

I fought back the urge to glare at him for that remark and gave Leland the sweetest smile I could summon. Which probably wasn't very sweet, since I was also inclined to puke on the jerk's shiny trainers at the idea of caring about him, but it appeared to be enough to smooth Ruse's spell along.

"I always knew she must, somewhere in there," Leland said, peering back at me with his own smile, which was so self-satisfied I nearly did puke.

Thankfully, Ruse stepped in before any expelling of bodily fluids became necessary. As he nodded, a sly thread crept into his voice. "And you must care about *yourself* enough to prioritize your safety, no? Look at this magnificent display of your past achievements." He motioned to the photos on the mantel.

Leland's gaze followed the gesture. "We have to celebrate our victories," he said. "Pep ourselves up to take on even more. Or to step in when other people are going too far." He glanced back at me, drawing himself up with a pompous air. "You were ruining people's lives. I couldn't stand back and let that happen."

I bit my tongue to avoid pointing out that *he'd* potentially ruined dozens of lives by enabling the Company's attack and preventing us from freeing their captives. As much as he'd pretended to care about defending the shadowkind, their lives clearly didn't mean all that much to him. Maybe he only saw them as worth protecting when they were small and inept. Maybe it'd always been about gaining a sense of magnanimity and never about kindness at all.

Ruse grinned. Confident he now had the other guy completely under his sway, he pointed Leland to the photos again. "I need to see just how dedicated you are to yourself before I know how we can help you. Take your favorite image and give yourself a kiss."

"*Ruse*," I whispered in protest. We had more important things to do here than goof around with my ex on puppet strings.

The incubus ignored me, and it *was* kind of satisfying watching

Leland rush to grab the photo of himself on the boat deck and give it a hearty smooch. My lips twitched despite myself.

Ruse applauded. "Perfect. Now, do you think you could show us a headstand? It's very important for ensuring we give you the most helpful strategies for protecting yourself…"

Leland was already bending over to set his head on the rug. He braced himself and heaved his bulky legs into the air. They flailed this way and that for a few seconds before he toppled over onto the rug with an audible *whoomph*. Then he was leaping up again as if ready for another go.

I elbowed Ruse. As much as I'd like to watch my ex make a fool of himself for hours, we were here on business, not pleasure.

"All right, all right," the incubus said, and motioned Leland over. "Just one more thing I'd like to check. If you wanted so much for Sorsha to offer you the full girlfriend experience, why didn't you romance her like a boyfriend would? An honest answer, please."

Leland's expression turned vaguely puzzled, but he was charmed enough to answer without balking. "Why should I have to put in that work first if she didn't appreciate what she already had? I didn't hear any complaints about our hook-ups. I've got a good job, I work out—I'm a goddamned catch. I'm not going to chase someone who can't be bothered to give me a foot massage or cook up a meal to pay back what they're getting out of me. She obviously has delusions about deserving all kinds of fawning. I bet that's how these creepy shadowkind sucked her in."

That time I bit my tongue so hard I winced at the jab of pain. What I'd been getting out of him? Last I'd checked, he'd gotten off at least as much as I had from our hops into bed. Was I supposed to have been so honored that he'd stuck his dick in me that I'd decide to play merry homemaker—and without a single indication he even wanted that until he started sulking that it wasn't happening?

Ruse had my back in his own way. "I see," he said. "You really are a prickish piece of work, aren't you?"

Leland faltered. "What? I—"

The thrum came back into Ruse's voice. "Say it—that you're a prickish piece of work. Like you mean it."

"I'm a prickish piece of work," Leland said emphatically.

"Wonderful! Now let's get down to work. These people on Wharf Street I assume you contacted—how did you reach out to them? It'll help us so much to know."

Any uncertainty that had crossed Leland's face with the past instruction faded. "I wasn't sure I'd get someone in charge if I just called. It seemed like the message should go to someone higher up. So I went right down there."

He'd gotten a look at the building? "What did they do when you got there?" I asked.

"They were pretty tense about the whole thing." Leland frowned. "I guess it makes sense they would be when I showed up out of nowhere. When I told them I had vital information, a different guy came out to talk to me in the yard."

Ruse's eyes gleamed intently. "You didn't go inside?"

"Nope. I told him that I had reason to believe a woman working with some hostile shadowkind was going to attack his operations tonight, and that they definitely knew about the Wharf Street location and a few others—the ones the Fund checked out. Do you think that's why they'd be out to get me now—because I was involved in doing that research, even though I realized what the right side was?"

"Could be," Ruse said sagely. "Although if you went back there now that they've foiled the attack and seen you gave them good intel, maybe they'd be more friendly and let you in on their plans."

Leland dashed any hopes we'd had of sending him out into the field as an unwitting double-agent with a chuckle. "Oh, they're not at that place anymore. They were pretty upset about what I told them, and I heard one guy say to another as I was leaving something about having nowhere to move now except Gorge Avenue. But I have no idea where on Gorge Avenue they were going. That wasn't an address the Fund had."

No, it wasn't. I hadn't seen or heard anything about Gorge Avenue before—but it sounded like that was where the Company would have taken their prisoners.

"Did you overhear anything else? Anything at all?" I pressed.

Leland shook his head. "They shooed me off pretty quickly. Even the guy who made that comment shut up really quickly afterward. And now they're after me? I was only trying to help them. I thought

—" His forehead furrowed as he tried to connect what he'd believed before to what Ruse's charm was forcing him to feel. "Have they actually been hurting people? It wasn't just Sorsha getting caught up with the wrong sort of shadowkind who wanted her to think that?"

"Unfortunately for you, these people are the worst of the worst, and it turns out they didn't appreciate that help," Ruse said in his most apologetic tone. "But I've determined that there's a simple way you can ensure they don't interfere with your life one bit."

Leland breathed a sigh of relief. "Thank you so much. I was trying to take the hassle *out* of my life by cutting off Sorsha's false crusade, not add to it. She'd already gotten the Fund too tangled up in all that. I never should have started investigating... Well, I guess if this Company of Light really *is* part of some kind of conspiracy... But that's more than I'm prepared to deal with anyway."

Right, because God forbid *he* experience the slightest discomfort while shadowkind were caged and tortured. He didn't sound even slightly regretful that he'd turned us in to people I'd warned him repeatedly were up to no good. I glanced at Ruse curiously.

The incubus rubbed his hands together in a way that would have tipped off anyone not under the spell of his charm that he was up to no good. "It's very simple. You must fix a pair of your underwear on your head and keep it there like a hat for at least three days. Oh, and only drink coffee that's as dark as you can brew it with no cream or sugar, left to cool for two hours first. Finally, call in sick from work while you're undergoing these steps and be sure to tell your boss exactly what you truly think of him."

I had to clap a hand over my mouth to hold in a laugh. The puzzled crease returned to Leland's forehead, but Ruse's voodoo gripped him tightly enough that he didn't argue. "Thank you. These people work in strange ways, I guess. I'll do all of that."

"Excellent. Don't mention we were here or your visit to Wharf Street to anyone. And may you find a romantic partner who's everything you deserve!"

The stairs creaked as Leland headed up to his bedroom to obtain the boxers that would serve as a hat. Ruse held in his snicker until we'd reached the back door.

"I'd have come up with a more public humiliation," he murmured to me, "but I think it's best if we don't call attention to our magical meddling."

"You didn't have to do any of that," I said. "All we needed was the information."

He made a skeptical humming sound. "Just be glad the defending of your honor was done my way and not Thorn's. I had plenty of my own bones to pick with the jackass at this point, you know."

"Fair." A twinge of affection shot through my chest. "And thank you."

"Think nothing of it, Miss Blaze. You're worth a hundred thousand of that putz." Ruse looked in the direction we'd left Charlotte. "What do you say we take a detour along Gorge Avenue?"

"Sounds like the perfect next step."

Once we'd reached the outer reaches of the suburbs where Gorge Avenue was located—nowhere near any actual gorges we could toss our enemies into, sadly—it wasn't long before we realized that Snap had left us with one last gift. The motorcycle crested a low hill, and at the sight of an estate that sprawled across the entirety of the next block, I squeezed Ruse's arm.

It was a mansion of gray brick with a turret on the right-hand side, the one Snap's victim must have guarded in times past. And from what Leland had overheard, the Company had nowhere left to run if we came for them here.

TWENTY-NINE

Omen

"WE'VE GOT THEM," I SAID, TAPPING THE RV'S TABLETOP AND LOOKING around at my three associates. A sense of triumph rippled through me. "This puts us in an even better position than if we'd taken them on in that factory building by the river. We've backed them into a corner, and they'll have consolidated all their equipment and resources in that one building, ripe for destruction."

"They'll have consolidated all their security there too," Thorn pointed out, ever the man of practicalities and glasses half empty. "Especially if—you said you think the man who owns the property may be the head of the entire Company of Light?"

After Ruse had returned from his venture with Sorsha, he and I had driven out to see what further information his hacker dupe could unearth. With her charmed dedication, she'd found enough records to clarify the situation.

I nodded. "He's covered his tracks well, but we came across money trails that convince me that this Victor Bane is behind the biggest operations the Company has conducted in this city. Either that, or someone with immense influence over him was pulling his strings, which amounts to the same thing."

Restlessness gripped me, and I had to tense my legs to stop myself from pacing. This was only the first glimpse of our real victory. We wouldn't achieve the rest until we got down to action.

But Thorn was right. We couldn't charge in, eyes and fists blazing, like the wild fool I'd once been. I dragged in a breath. "And he'll have plenty of security, yes. But most of the guards won't be used to working there. We can still make use of parts of our original plan, like the various diversions to divide and conquer. It may be difficult, with fewer of us…"

My gaze lifted to the bedroom doorway down the hall. The unicorn had proven herself a fierce fighter—I'd give her credit for that—but even if her body healed, she'd be in no condition to leap back into a battle for several days at a minimum. I wasn't sure the centaur would join us in venturing that far from her bedside either, even to avenge her injuries.

And Snap… The day had crept into evening and then dusk with full night looming over us, and our devourer hadn't reappeared.

When I'd asked him to enlist in my team, I'd known that he had lingering reservations about the most potent part of his nature, but I'd thought his eagerness to help save our kind would override that if he ended up needing to use his greater power. Evidently he'd been more fragile—or the Company's hunters swifter—than I'd anticipated.

"We'll make the best of what we have," I went on, and then, as I drew in my next breath, a knock sounded on the RV's door.

Both Thorn and Sorsha sprang up, but their demeanors couldn't have been more different. Thorn's muscles flexed, his body braced to meet an attack—as if our enemies would have *knocked* before attempting to blow us to smithereens.

As Sorsha obviously realized. Her face had lit up with hesitant but obvious hope. In that moment, I didn't see any of the mouthy mortal who pushed me to the limits of my temper or the cocky thief who laughed at deadly threats, only a woman whose heart was leaping at the possibility that our missing companion had come back to us unharmed.

The sight wrenched at me more than I'd have liked. When had I ever seen a mortal that earnestly dedicated to any of the shadowkind? But I didn't think it was Snap out there—I doubted it would have occurred to the devourer to knock with his return either. And perhaps there was also an incredibly small yet niggling sensation with the knowledge that she'd have looked nowhere near that enthusiastic if I'd been the one who'd vanished.

You didn't win wars by courting affection. My job was to kick her ass into getting those powers up to speed—a job I might already have backed off on more than I should have today.

I strode to the door and yanked it open, my other hand balled at my side ready to launch my claws. With my first glance outside, my stance relaxed, but only slightly. "What are *you* doing here?"

Rex was standing just outside the RV's door, his arms folded over his chest and a particularly wolfish gleam in his keen eyes. "You put out a plea for help, didn't you, Omen? Are you going to let us answer it or not?"

As he said "us," he stepped close enough for his companions to converge around him. By brimstone and hellfire, it looked as if he'd brought his entire outfit along for the ride. The inner circle stood at his flanks—Birch the dryad, Lazuli the troll, and Tassel the succubus—and at least half a dozen of the gang's lower underlings encircled them.

"I remember reaching out to see if Birch would lend his healing abilities," I said. "Are the rest of you along to provide him with moral support?"

The werewolf rolled his eyes. "Why don't we discuss all this inside before some country-dwelling mortal drives by and wonders what's going on with the party at the school bus?"

He had a point, but my hackles rose instinctively at the thought of letting so many powerful and self-interested shadowkind onto the vehicle I was starting to consider mine. Of course, technically it belonged to the tourists in the back, and power was relative. In the grand scheme of shadowkind existences, Rex with his century or so of experience was still a gangling teen, and he was the most established of the bunch. Thorn and I would have stood a decent chance at decimating this pack between the two of us.

That was an evaluation the werewolf could likely make for himself with the experience he did have and his knowledge of me. And I *had* asked for at least one of them to make an appearance. I restrained my inner hound and stepped back to let them in.

The inner circle kept their physical forms, coming to join the four of us by the sofa. At Rex's gesture, the underlings flitted into the shadows as they followed. I could still sense their presence lurking around us, but at least we weren't being squashed into the space like sardines in a tin.

Both Thorn and Sorsha stayed on their feet. Maybe I shouldn't have been surprised that even faced with several shadowkind she barely knew, our mortal was the one to push them into action.

"You should take a look at Gisele right away," she said, motioning to Birch. "They hurt her really badly. Omen and Thorn patched her up as well as they could, but…"

Her voice faded as she led him to the master bedroom. Rex glanced at me with a slight arch of his eyebrows as if amused that I'd let the human call any of the shots, but he didn't remark on it.

"That was quite a ruckus you stirred up downtown last night," he said instead.

I grimaced. "Not by our choosing. We meant to ravage the pricks on their own turf, but they caught wind of our plans and ambushed us on our way there. We still managed to do plenty of ravaging, though, just not the rescue effort we'd hoped to include."

"They've moved their prisoners again," Thorn added with a grumble of frustration. "And they may have captured one of our own."

Rex's gaze skimmed over us. "Oh, yes, your ray of sunshine is missing, isn't he? What a pity."

A squeak sounded as if in agreement. Sorsha's shadowkind pet had been huddled in a corner of the sofa at the arrival of the newcomers. Apparently having recognized them now, the little dragon scampered across the floor to twine around Laz's ankle like a cat. The troll stared down at the creature with an expression of such anguish that I had to suppress a laugh. So much for the tough-guy front.

Sorsha slipped out of the bedroom alone, her face drawn, and moved to rejoin us. I tipped my head to Rex with all the authority I could emanate. "Why exactly are you all here, Rex? Does your dryad require this much protection or were you simply wanting to gawk at us? Because we have more plans to make and battles to carry out on behalf of all shadowkind that I'd like to get back to."

The werewolf chuckled, but the arrogance in his pose deflated a little in recognition of who was the greater alpha here. I didn't push the matter far enough to force him to outright cower in front of his associates. There might be times when it'd be useful to call in a favor from this man in the future. Aggression got you farthest in the long run when tempered by diplomacy.

"We're not here as bodyguards or to gawk," he said. "I got the impression last time we spoke that you wouldn't mind a little assistance with all this battling. Well, here we are. We can battle on our own behalf. Just point us at the bastards who need gutting."

I had to stiffen my expression to hide my shock. He was willing to step into a conflict that didn't directly involve him yet—and not just offering his own allegiance, but that of his followers as well?

"I got the impression you didn't give a shit what happened to the rest of the shadowkind as long as you and your comrades weren't affected," I said, keeping my tone dry. "What changed your tune?"

"Oh, we're affected now." A growl crept into the werewolf's voice. "This is our city, and those assholes think they can burn down the fucking *Finger*? Maybe I'm not going to join you on any epic quests to win justice for all, but they clearly need to be taught a lesson."

I managed to stop my gaze from twitching in Sorsha's direction. From the corner of my eye, I could see her lips had pressed tight. It seemed wisest not to mention that it was one of *my* associates and not the Company who'd reduced the better part of that monstrosity of a statue to ashes.

"So they do," I said without missing a beat. "And who better to deliver that lesson than you and your followers." A smile curved my own mouth. "I'm looking forward to seeing how much damage we can inflict on them together. If I have it my way, they'll never light so much as a cigarette around here again. Let's get down to work."

We'd just finished filling the gang in on what we knew and our plans so far—"Infecting their computer system," Tassel purred. "I like it."—when Birch emerged from the master bedroom. Somehow his nearly translucent skin looked even paler than it had when he'd gone in. His voice seemed to have faded too.

"The unicorn shifter will live," he murmured roughly. "She woke up enough to exchange words with her partner. It may take another day or two before she can even move around on her feet, though. I've suggested they retire to the shadow realm until she's fully recovered, as soon as she's strong enough to make the leap through a rift."

"You've got yourself a *unicorn* shifter?" Rex gave a disbelieving guffaw and then snapped his fingers at the troll. "That reminds me of something. Laz, fill Birch in on what he missed. Omen, a word?"

We stepped into the second bedroom—and damn if I couldn't still scent a trace of the passion Sorsha must have shared with at least one of my shadowkind companions in the past couple of days. I willed it out of my awareness before my thoughts could linger on the moment in the yard when her body, her lips, had drawn me in with a nearly magnetic pull before I'd broken out of the spell. "What?"

The werewolf rubbed his hands together. "On the subject of unusual and powerful allies... I don't remember many details—this was at least a couple of decades ago, though not so long it couldn't be relevant. The Highest were searching for a particularly virile and apparently unpredictable shadowkind in this realm back then. I got the impression this one had caused some kind of chaos they needed to settle. Can't remember the name they asked us about... A red stone of some sort. Jasper? Garnet?"

"Is this story going anywhere?" I asked, as though my interest wasn't already piqued.

"I'm getting there. From what I heard from my contacts, they were looking for this red-stone-name all over the country. Maybe farther out too. And they specifically told us not to engage with the shadowkind if we got any word. It was too great a risk, and we should let them handle it." He grinned. "I never heard that they caught that one. If *you* could track this Jasper or Garnet or whatever down... That'd be someone to have on your side in this war with the mortals, don't you think? Could be almost as much a rebel as you are."

I had a vague recollection of hearing murmurs about this subject, but I'd mostly been shadow-side during that time. As it probably had back then too, the first thought that flitted through my mind was of a being long-gone. I didn't think the Highest had ever taken issue with anyone more than they had with Tempest, my once some-time partner-in-crime, and she'd gone through guises like mortals shed clothes... but I'd watched the minions of the ancient ones batter her to a pulp centuries ago. The sphynx was long gone, and we were likely all better for it. I doubted she'd ever have reformed.

Whoever this newer rebel was, it certainly sounded as though they had energy and guts to spare. Stumbling on them would be a longshot, but a possibility to file away all the same.

"I'll keep that in mind," I said. "If we need the extra assistance in the first place. I say we crush the bastards tonight and end things there."

"That works for me." Rex bumped shoulders with me hesitantly, as if half expecting me to take a bite out of him for his forwardness. I settled on a simple glare. He hadn't needed to offer anywhere near this much help. I could allow a little chumminess.

And maybe not just with him. When we returned to the living room, my eyes settled on Sorsha—sitting cozied up to Ruse now, poking Thorn in his massive bicep without any fear of the wingéd's power, shooting a snappy response back at something Tassel had said. Like she belonged here.

Could I really say she didn't? Correct blame for the fire aside, I doubted *Rex* would be here at all if she hadn't laid into him about his self-centeredness.

Our mortal and her hope springing eternal.

I just had to keep a careful eye on all the other emotions her presence tended to stir in me. There was no room for distractions. We had a conspiracy of humans to destroy—and I intended to see them fall before the night was done.

THIRTY

Sorsha

In taking on the Company of Light, we'd faced old office buildings, modern lab facilities, and now what might as well have been a castle, set well back on its sprawling lawn. I wouldn't be surprised if the man who owned the old mansion figured he really was some kind of king. Victor Bane—that was a super-villain name if I'd ever heard one. If that even was his real name and not yet another layer of subterfuge.

Thanks to Birch's healing efforts just before we'd headed out, my no-longer-wounded stomach could rest against my thighs in my crouched position without pain prickling through it. I scanned the yard from my perch on the branch of an oak tree in Bane's neighbor's backyard. Thorn's initial scouting through the shadows had shown him about twenty armed guards on the premises outside the building, and I could make out several of them stalking along in their patrols.

No big deal. We were more than ready for them. Bane or whoever couldn't know that we'd more than doubled our numbers since the Company's last assault on us, or I suspected he'd have called in every man he could.

Of course, maybe he already had. Thorn, Omen, and the others had torn through quite a few last night.

We had to crash their party before they got the chance to find out about our latest plans. The Company had eyes and ears in too many places—nothing we did seemed to stay secret for long. The only times we'd really turned the tables on them was when we'd acted on our information right away.

I just wished this plan didn't depend so much on my powers kicking in when they should. Or on keeping those powers secret even from our new allies.

Omen had pulled me aside after we'd finished settling our strategy, in which he'd claimed responsibility for setting a few things alight once we were at the Bane property.

"You know which parts you were meant to handle," he'd said in a dark undertone. "Stick to the original plan on that count—I'll be with Thorn focusing on cutting down as many of the guards as we can. But don't let Rex or his lackeys see you at it if you can help it. Easier for us to keep you as our ace up our sleeve if word doesn't get out too widely."

I already didn't love the way Rex tended to eye me as if speculating how he'd carve me up into steaks given the opportunity. Keeping any additional attention off me sounded just dandy.

I would hold my own tonight—I'd be more an asset than a liability, even if some of the help I offered went under most of our allies' radar. If we lost anyone else tonight because of my actions or my mortal limitations...

My jaw tightened. No, I wasn't even going to think that far. It wouldn't happen. I wouldn't let it.

To begin with, our main trick would be creating small enough diversions that the shadowkind could pick off one or two guards at a time without them realizing they were under attack. We'd rather no one clued in that an assault was underway until we'd reduced their numbers already. If we could make it all the way to wherever the Company was keeping its imprisoned shadowkind, even better—but I didn't expect our luck would stretch that far.

The shadowkind could pull off a hell of a lot of their own, but they were going to need me to open those silver-and-iron cages, and I couldn't waltz in through the shadows unseen. Without Snap to taste the locks, I wasn't even sure how long it'd take me to break into whatever cages the captives were currently being held in. We might have to rely on Ruse charming an employee who happened to know the entry codes or Rex's techie guy to find the details in the computer system.

So, yeah, the more of our opposition we picked off ahead of time, the better for all of us. Particularly, for me making it out of this alive and without taking anyone else down with me.

A light flickered on and off around the back of the Bane property. I tensed on my perch. That was my cue. I was supposed to wait ten seconds.

As I counted, I sang under my breath to bolster my nerve. "We'll laugh and flare, woo-oah, giving them a scare."

Holy mother of margaritas, did I wish I had Snap's upbeat presence by my side now. If these assholes had caught him in their nets and hurt him in any way... I'd happily join the shadowkind in the bloodier part of this rampage.

That thought sent a little spurt of adrenaline through me, just enough to kick my pulse up a notch—and to fuel my inner flames. With the narrowing of my eyes, I flung the energy out toward the electrical wire that cut across the sky from a nearby post.

Sparks leapt from the cable. Then a lick of fire spurted up, sizzling over the rubbery coating.

Shouts volleyed across the lawn. Some of the security force had noticed. My heart thumped even faster as I aimed my attention at the post itself. Another flame flickered into being where the cables hooked onto it.

Just a little electrical issue threatening to cut off the entire property's power. Wouldn't want to have to explain to the big man how they'd let that happen.

Someone was talking into a phone in urgent tones, and a few of the guards approached the front gate. That was right—just walk on out past the wall like it's an ordinary night, just a little hassle with the utilities...

The gate's metal bars clanged shut behind them, and my perked ears caught the faintest grunt as a couple of the shadowkind must have toppled that bunch. I didn't have time to waste on wondering how the skirmish was playing out or how horribly my allies might be eviscerating the Company dudes right now. My gaze darted across the grounds to the trees closest to the utility post.

A little smoldering here, a little flare of heat there. At least, that's what I wanted to happen. The branches stayed dark and unburnt as ever.

Come on, come *on*. I gritted my teeth and thought again of Snap—of Snap on one of those metal tables where the Company did their experiments, pinned with silver and iron bindings so he was in too much distress to be able to shed his physical form, his body pierced with scalpels and needles and whatever other horrors these people inflected on their prisoners—

Flames darted across a few twigs at the top of the trees, as if they'd leapt from somewhere along the burning cable. I willed them higher until another round of shouts rang out.

A few more guards headed out through the gate to their doom, and a handful more hustled into the stand of trees near the northern wall by me, where monsters lurked in the darkness.

The distraction part of the plan wasn't *all* on me. A motor growled, and footsteps thumped around the back of the yard too, where Ruse would have activated the ride-on lawnmower. On the far side of the mansion, a few of the gang members would be standing on the other side of the wall hooting with laughter and smashing bottles against the stones like drunken hooligans.

How many of the guards had we drawn away between all our efforts? I edged farther along my oak branch, readying myself to spring onto the top of the wall and then down when I got a signal that the coast was clear.

Hardly any guards were in sight now. The two I could see striding across the lawn to check on their colleagues toppled abruptly under the impact of two burly shadowkind who burst from the shadows. Silver and iron might protect these people from shadowkind voodoo, but it couldn't do anything to stop those fists from smashing their skulls in.

A molten orange glow streaked across the grass toward the building's side door—Omen, making himself visible in hellhound form just long enough for me to see him. We were heading inside. Time for the hard part.

I threw myself onto the wall and then landed with a thump on the grass just inside the property. A voice started to bellow in alarm, but the sound was cut off with a bloody gurgle. Fickle fates willing, no one up at the house had taken note of that first sound the guard had barely managed to get out.

The grass whispered under my sneakers as I darted across the lawn. The side door swung open, its lock released, just as I reached it. Quieting my rasping breath, I ducked into the hall on the other side.

Thorn solidified completely just long enough to give me a nod and an encouraging squeeze of my arm. *We'll be right there with you*, he'd said when we'd discussed this phase of the mission, and the same sentiment was etched all over his face.

Here I was, the most essential piece in the plan and also the most breakable.

The shadowkind intruders had already gotten to work on clearing my way. I darted past a body slumped against the wall, her gut gouged open beneath her metal vest, and pushed through the doorway ahead of me.

In the first second as the wavering blueish light washed over me, I thought I'd stumbled on a mad scientist's lab already. Then my eyes adjusted to the dim light—and the stink of chlorine. The bastard had his own indoor pool, for fuck's sake.

I skirted the still water and the glow of the lights beneath it. I'd made it halfway around the pool when a guard pushed past the far door. From his stern but not frantic expression and the energy to his stride, he was concerned about whatever he'd come down here to investigate but not yet aware it was an all-out invasion.

At least, until he spotted me. "Halt right there!" he shouted, his gun hand jerking up.

He had better instincts than Leland, but not good enough. I'd already grabbed a life preserver that'd been mounted on the wall beside me. I hurled it at him like a massive discus in time to smack his arm to the side.

The good news: I remained bullet-free. The bad news: His finger still squeezed the trigger, sending one of those bullets into the far wall with an unmistakable boom that echoed through the building around us.

There went our advantage of stealth. Our chances of victory were really ticking away now.

I dove at the guard's legs, aiming to stay out of the line of fire while I knocked him on his ass. Unfortunately, there are rules about running on pool decks for a reason. My feet skidded on a slick patch, and I tumbled over on my ass.

Ruse materialized beside me looking ready to come to my defense however he could, but at the same moment, Bow leapt from the shadows in full centaur form. "I can't touch your head in that helmet, but the diving board doesn't have the same problem," he declared, and spun so he could slam his hind horse legs into the guard's gut.

The man hurtled across the water. The back of his skull smacked into the edge of the diving board so hard the helmet dented halfway through his head. He dropped like a sack of potatoes into the pool. Bow wiped his hands together with an unusually vicious expression.

Possibly too vicious. "Maybe a little lighter on the hoof power next time?" Ruse said as we dashed to the door the guard had emerged from. "We need at least one of these fools alive—and conscious enough—for me to charm them into leading the way to their prison."

"Sorry," Bow said, not looking as if he meant the apology all that much. "I just—I think that's one of the guys who attacked Gisele."

"And payback was a bitch. Just remember the best payback will be getting the rest of our kind free *before* we cave in the rest of their skulls."

They both slipped back into the darkness. I hustled through a small change room, down a short hall on the other side, and burst through the next doorway into—a personal *bowling alley*?

Victor Bane must take plenty of time for his recreational pursuits in between attempts to destroy all shadowkind.

Three guards were just charging in from an entrance across the room. I ducked behind one of the bowling ball dispensers by the two lanes, the tang of wood polish saturating my lungs.

Another shot rang out—and then a gasp and a fleshy ripping sound reached my ears. Maybe I should question my life choices when that sound was actually familiar at this point.

I bobbed back up to see Laz twisting the neck of the third of the guards, gripping the man by the jaw so he could wrench his head off without touching the toxic metals of the man's helmet. Two other headless figures already sprawled on the floor, leaking blood all over the gleaming boards.

The troll, whose skin had deepened to a darker blue and who'd grown at least a foot in both height and width in his full shadowkind form, grinned to reveal two rows of uneven teeth and tossed the heads one by one down the lane. The first clanged into the pins helmet-first and scored him a strike.

Ruse had reappeared. "Again," he chided, "could we please be at least a tad more careful with the mortals? Spare one for me to do my work?"

Laz grunted. "Either I go straight for the throat or the gut, or they bash me with their stupid weapons before I can do much. Fucking armor makes it pretty hard to be subtle. I don't see *you* felling any of the pricks."

"Fair. Come on, let's keep moving."

We came out into a wider hall at the base of a stairwell. Thorn appeared next to us a second later. "We've searched the entire basement. Wherever the cages are, they're not down here."

I raised my chin, ignoring the increasingly frenetic beat of my heart. "Upward and onward it is, then."

Footsteps thundered toward us before we'd made it to the first landing where the staircase split in two. Thorn took one side and Laz the other, and a moment later two more gouged bodies tumbled down next to Ruse and me.

"It's raining corpses," I said with a shudder.

"As long as they're not ours." The incubus grasped my arm. "Better catch up before they tear through the entire population of this building."

We rounded the corner after Thorn, and Omen blinked into being at the top of the stairs. He'd kept his human-ish form, but traces of his hellish nature showed all over his body, from the orange blaze in his eyes to the mottled lava-gray and magma-glow twining across his skin.

"This way," he said with a jab of his hand, fangs glinting in his mouth. He sprang back into the shadows in the direction he'd pointed to.

Racing after him, we found ourselves in a music room: a grand piano at one end, a circle of wing chairs at the other, books of music and a few other instruments propped along the wall. But we didn't arrive alone. More guards dashed after us inside.

As Thorn introduced his crystalline fists to two of their throats, I snatched up a violin by the neck. When I whirled around, the nearest guard was almost on me, brandishing one of those brilliant whips. My pulse hiccupped, I slashed out with my free hand, and he jolted backward with a flinch at the wave of heat I'd sent at him without thinking.

I couldn't care at this point whether Laz or any of the other gang members who might be watching from the shadows had noticed. Without missing a beat, I swung the violin at his helmet, knocking it to the floor and giving him a good wallop to the temple at the same time. The groaning of the violin as it cracked matched that of Thorn's current opponent, who was crumpling at the warrior's blow.

The guard I was facing off with swayed but righted himself, just in time for me to land a kick that smacked the whip from his hand. I threw myself at him with all my weight to knock him to the floor. While I yanked at the clasps on the silver-and-iron vest, Ruse danced around me, wavering in and out of view as he alternately dodged other guards and attempted to prevent our allies from obliterating this one.

The jerk managed to clock me hard enough in the head that my thoughts scrambled, but I wrenched off his last piece of armor at the same time. Ruse dropped with his knees, pinning the man's chest, and gazed intently into his startled eyes.

"Hello, friend," he said with the full force of his cubi charm. "You're going to help us free the poor wounded creatures locked up somewhere in this place."

"Hopefully quickly," Omen snapped. He'd shoved back a bookcase at the far end of the room to reveal a hidden door. His gaze snagged on me. "Let's go, Disaster. It's time for you to take the starring role."

I wished my gut hadn't lurched so much at that statement. Wished this was one of my usual capers where it was just me vs. one minor asshole collector and not a mission where the fate of all shadowkind—of Snap, of Bow and Gisele's friend, of the many other beings the Company might have captured and those they wished to destroy—hung in the balance. But here I was. I couldn't even say I hadn't signed up for it.

Resolve swelled inside me as I met Omen's eyes. "Ready when you are."

I skirted pools of blood and gore on my way across the room, the stench of ruined human flesh making my stomach churn even more than it already was from my nerves.

Just focus on the doorway. Focus on the beings in need on the other side.

In just a few more minutes, I might have Snap with me again.

Ruse's voice rose and fell in lilting tones as he and his increasingly charmed companion followed me. The doorway Omen had revealed led to a narrow flight of stairs down into a second, hidden basement.

As I descended, cool air licked over my skin, raising goosebumps on my arms. A chemical scent tickled my nose.

The room we emerged into had clearly been prepared in a rush. Crates and cardboard boxes had been shoved into stacks on one side somewhat haphazardly. The rest of the room was full of what looked like huge freestanding lockers, similar to the one the Company had brought to their hand-off with the collector. Their outsides gleamed stainless steel, but I'd be willing to stake my life and my love of curry on there being plenty of silver and pure iron embedded inside.

They were locked with keycode panels on the right side of the doors. Those gleamed less severe shades of gray, the base of the pad silver and the keys iron. No one on this mission would be able to touch them except me—or our charmed guard.

I jerked the guard over to one, my eyes watering in the glare of the overhead lights. Ruse came along too but with a grimace at the toxic vibes the metals must have been giving off around us.

"Do you know the codes?" I demanded.

"No," the guard said. "None of us—they were so strict about that—but I believe—it should all be on the computers. I don't know the password for that either—"

He'd motioned to a flashy, high-tech set-up on a desk in a corner beyond the cells. "Rex!" Omen barked.

The werewolf appeared a moment later with one of his lackeys at his side. "On it," he said, and gave the guy a shove toward the computer.

Thanks to his tech guy's expertise, we shouldn't need to run off with any equipment, only grab the data before destroying it—and hopefully the data on every computer in Bane's network as well. The lackey dropped into the chair and launched his digital assault with a clatter of the keyboard.

I turned back to Ruse and the guard. "They'll figure out that we're down here sooner rather than later, even with the doorway closed again. We should get this guy to divert the others—to say he's seen us moving to a different part of the house." Might as well make as much use of the dude as we could.

As Ruse cajoled the guard into giving frantic commands over his radio, the guy at the computer raised his hands with a brief whoop. "And we're in! Codes for the cages, where are you...?" His fingers resumed their clattering.

Omen frowned at the blank steel sides of the cells. "How will we know which code is for which cage? They don't appear to be conveniently numbered." He snapped his fingers toward Ruse. "Get that man back over here."

Ruse nudged the guard toward us. The man drew in a shaky breath. "How can I help?"

Omen's fiery eyes had simmered down now that we'd reached our goal, but they lit with a new glint that might have been partly amused at the guard's cooperative attitude. "These metal boxes have got to be labeled somehow. How do you tell which is which?"

The guard's head bobbed in eager agreement. "There are dots on the sides of the keypads. Blue first and then red."

I squinted at the edge of the panel and made out the little flecks of paint now that I knew to look for them. "This one is 3-5 then." There had to be close to twenty of the things in this space. I glanced toward the computer guy. "Do you have those codes for us yet?"

"Working on it, working on it." He tapped vigorously, sucking his lower lip under his teeth. The spines that poked from his hair at the nape of his neck quivered.

Thorn and Rex both vanished into the shadows, I assumed to fend off any guards who headed this way despite our efforts. I paced, my chest constricting.

Omen cast me a baleful look. "Too much excitement for you, mortal?"

"No," I said. "I just want us—all of us—out of here." He should know as well as I did that every passing second might mean fewer shadowkind freed—might mean our plan failed altogether. Last time we'd only managed to get him out before we'd had to run for our lives.

"There!" the computer guy said with obvious relief. "Okay, I'm going to start the virus uploading while I read out the numbers. The code for cage 3-5 is 6-9-0-2."

I braced myself as I typed in the code. Omen had already moved to the next cell, dragging the guard with him. He bent close, flinching just at being close to the toxic metals, and read off the number on the keypad there. The metals in the keys would have burned him—or any of our other shadowkind companions—too badly for him to use them, but at least we could free the captives twice as fast if the guard was punching in codes too.

As the lock thudded and the cell door in front of me swung open, Ruse stepped up to peer inside with one of his warmest smiles but wary eyes. Shadowkind didn't tend to be in a friendly state when they'd been locked away for who knew how long.

Even starker light filled the inner space from a panel up above. A streak of darkness quivered in the center of that light where the captive being had drawn its least substantial form in on itself. I couldn't make out any of its features, but somehow just looking at it, I knew we hadn't found Snap—not yet, anyway.

"Please, my friend, make your escape," Ruse said, extending his hand. "We're getting all of you out of here. And feel free to enact a little revenge on your captors as you flee."

The patch of shadow hesitated and then sprang from its confines with a shudder of knobby haunches and a clicking of scales. I didn't wait to see how it would react to its newfound freedom—I was already rushing to the next cell.

Omen and I volleyed numbers back and forth with the tech guy, and one by one the cell doors gaped open. After the first, I leapt to the next the moment the lock clicked over, not waiting to see who might be inside, as much as I might have wanted to.

A couple of the freed beings lingered in the room, watching our progress: an emaciated fae man hunched by the stack of boxes, shivering, and a shifter woman with cat-like irises prowled back and forth with darted looks toward the staircase as if she wasn't convinced it was actually any safer up there than down here. The others vanished straight into the shadows.

"Don't hang around here too long," Ruse called to them. "Take a few jabs on your way out if you like, but don't give these bastards a chance to snare you again."

We were down to the last few cells when voices crackled from the charmed guard's radio loud enough for me to hear. "The east basement! All units head there now!"

Shit. They'd realized we'd made it this far. "The rest of the numbers, fast!" I shouted, darting to another cell.

As the computer guy rattled the digits off, my fingers flew over the keypad. There were only two cells left. The guard hesitated as Omen urged him to open the cell they were at, and the hellhound shifter snarled.

"Type in the fucking code!"

Panic flashed across the guard's face. Ruse dashed over, seeing his magical influence fracturing.

I waved the computer guy on. "I can do the rest. Hurry!"

Despite the cool air, sweat trickled down my back as I jabbed in the last two codes, not even waiting to make sure they worked first. "That's it!" the computer guy shouted to me after the final one, and mashed at the keyboard a little more. "I've downloaded all the other data I can, and the virus is in the network. Should I activate it?"

"Yes, yes, get on with it!" Omen said. "We're going to burn this whole place down... in every possible way."

He shot a meaningful glance at me. At least this part I could do by regular means, no worries about uncertain powers or witnesses.

"Everyone out, now!" I hollered, just as the first figures in the new wave of guards barreled down the stairs.

Thorn, Laz, and other shadowkind I couldn't recognize from a glimpse shot in and out of the shadows between them, mashing a skull into the wall here, cracking a spine in half there. The less combat-inclined beings hurtled past them. I caught sight of smoke streaming from open wounds on Thorn's back and stiffened against the urge to run to him. I had other work to do.

I splashed the kerosene from the pouch at my hip across the crates and boxes and lit them up with a flick of my lighter.

I'd gotten too used to the struggle of using my power for the same purpose. The flames roared up faster than I was prepared for. I yanked myself backwards, slapping at a few sparks that singed my hair, and bolted for the stairs my shadowkind allies were just clearing.

My foot slipped on a smear of blood, and then Thorn was whipping me up into his arms. He barged up the stairs with me over his shoulder, smashing past another guard who'd just appeared at the top. But as he tore through the music room, a man he hadn't seen sprang from behind the piano and hurled a huge net at my warrior.

It didn't quite cover Thorn's hulking form, but it fell over enough of him that his muscles locked up with a spasm of pain. I wrenched at the silver-and-iron cords, shoving them off him as quickly as I could. More smoke poured from the fresh wounds on his back and face that would add to his collection of scars. He fell to his knees, and my feet hit the ground too.

As I hauled the net the rest of the way off the warrior, Omen leapt from the shadows to slash a claw across our attacker's throat. "Out the front!" he shouted at us, and flashed out of sight again.

Thorn staggered upright. We ran out into the hall together, his hand clutching mine as tightly as I was clutching him. With the amount of essence billowing out of him, I wasn't sure he could have carried me now if he'd wanted to.

"Did you see—" he said roughly. "Was Snap—?"

"I don't know," I said, but the hollow in my stomach didn't hold much hope. If Snap had been in one of those cells, surely he'd have stayed long enough to show himself and reunite with us properly?

If we didn't get the hell out of here, there'd be none of us left to reunite with *him*, wherever he was. Silver and iron glinted everywhere

I looked—armor, nets, knives. The remaining guards were converging on us.

I wasn't finished with this place, though. We'd meant to see the whole building burn. The thick cement walls in the secret basement wouldn't let the fire seep from below into the rest of the mansion.

I grasped at my bottle of kerosene—and it slid from my hasty fingers to rattle across the rug and under a hall table behind us. Behind us, where a dozen or so guards were currently storming our way. Sayonara to that one.

We burst into a grand entrance room with woven tapestries hanging from the walls and an actual red carpet slashing down the middle of the marble floor. Ahead of us, the double doors hung open to the night, but another dozen guards stood between us and that escape.

In seconds, we'd be surrounded. I spun around, a searing heat mingling with the burst of panic in my chest.

These assholes had destroyed who knew how many beings, had tormented Omen, had nearly killed Gisele, and if they'd gotten their hands on Snap…

My jaw clenched as the heat flared into a surge of fury. They had no idea who they were dealing with. *I* could clear our way this time, and I didn't need so much as a match to do it.

I flung out my arms and hurled all the searing rage inside me at our attackers.

The carpet and the tapestries went up in a blaze. So did most of the bodies between us and the door. The guards stumbled, toppled, or flailed with shrieks of agony as the flames ate across every part of them not made of metal.

A horrified lump clogged my throat, but this was what I'd wanted. It wasn't anywhere near as horrifying as the genocide they'd planned to enact.

If I'd been thinking clearer, I might have been a little more careful. Flames raged across the entire room around us, cutting off our escape as well. I tightened my grip on Thorn's hand. He squeezed mine back with a curt nod.

"And so we dance into the fire," I muttered, and threw myself toward the doors.

The flames snagged on my sleeves and the pouch at my hip. As I soared through the doorway, I let go of Thorn so I could flip into a roll. The cool blades of the lawn's grass snuffed out the hungry tufts of fire.

I sprawled on my back, staring up at the mansion. I'd incited my blaze even higher than I'd realized. Yellow-orange light roared through broken glass on the second-floor windows. More flames leapt out to crawl across the roof.

We'd done it. We'd taken back what the Company of Light had stolen and then razed their data and their last hide-out to the ground.

And now I'd better get the hell out of here before anyone gave me the same treatment.

A few figures had charged out of the building in my wake. The guards stared at me, one of them pointing. He dashed away while the other two came at us.

Thorn swung around so swiftly you'd never have guessed he was producing nearly as much smoke as the entire mansion. His punch slammed into one guard's face, but in the warrior's weakening state, his knuckles only scraped her cheek instead of crushing it. I grabbed his elbow.

"We've got to get out of here, now!"

Laz and Rex flickered from the shadows to topple our attackers. With the mortals' shrieks and the warbling of the fire following at our heels, we ran across the lawn, leaving the remains of the Company to sink into its own ashes.

THIRTY-ONE

Sorsha

At a glance, the gathering of figures around the Everymobile looked more like a summer barbeque than a conspiracy of monsters.

Ruse had driven the RV well out of the city and parked it in a fallow field in the countryside where no buildings stood in sight. Other than him, me, and Rex's tech guy, who'd sat bent over a laptop on the sofa for the whole drive, the other shadowkind had ridden with us in the shadows. Now, coming out after a brief doze in the second bedroom, I found the entire company spread out around the vehicle.

At least, I thought it had to be the entire bunch. Omen and Thorn stood talking with Rex and a couple of his underlings near a drooping tree. A few feet from them, Ruse was shooting the breeze with Laz, Birch, and assorted other gang members, as well as the few liberated prisoners who'd decided to stick with us in our escape. To my right, Bow was sitting on the ground with Gisele lounging on his lap, her face still drawn but brighter than I'd have thought possible after the way she'd looked the last time I'd seen her. Her beaming was probably thanks to the petite, twiggy young man they were chatting with—their long-lost friend, Cori.

Everyone was smiling and laughing, their stances relaxed—except

Tech Dude, who hadn't left his hunched pose on the sofa behind me. The dawn light turned the edges of the landscape golden, matching the triumphant vibe perfectly. I dragged in a deep breath of the cool early morning air, a smile of my own crossing my lips, but a twinge shot through my gut at the same time.

Snap was still missing. My instincts had been correct—he hadn't been in any of those cells in Victor Bane's mansion.

If the Company hadn't captured him, where had he gone? All the way back to the shadow realm? Was I ever going to see him again?

I'd been prepared for us to part ways when Omen's mission here was done, but the loss still gnawed at me. I hadn't gotten to say good-bye. Maybe if we'd talked, if I'd been able to talk the devourer through his doubts, I wouldn't have *needed* to say good-bye, at least not right away.

The Company of Light wasn't the only force malevolent toward the shadowkind in this world, only the largest one I'd encountered. We might have decimated them, but I wouldn't be surprised if Omen and his crew found other ways to stay busy rather than heading straight home.

And maybe I was kind of hoping they'd count me as part of that crew for as long as they stuck around. What did I have left to go back to anyway? A burned-down apartment, a handful of sort-of friends and colleagues who'd turned their backs on me...

Well, one very dedicated best friend as well. I should call Vivi and let her know it was safe to leave her watery safehouse now.

As I fished out my phone and stepped out onto the untamed grass, Pickle scuttled after me. I bent to give him a scratch between his wings before he scampered off in Laz's direction. My smile grew with the amused anticipation of the troll's nervous reaction. I brought up my contacts on the screen—

—and the tech guy burst out of the RV behind me, his laptop held up like a signal flag, gasping for breath as if he'd just run miles rather than five feet.

"Everyone! It isn't over. This isn't— That place was just *one*—"

My hand dropped to my side. As I stared at him, the others drew in closer, Omen and Rex at the front of the crowd.

The hellhound shifter's good humor had faded. "What are you saying? Spit it out—a little more coherently, if you can manage that?"

Computer Dude swiped a nervous hand across his mouth. The spines on the back of his neck jittered. "It's just—It took me a while to really dig into the files. There were a lot of layers of protection. And at first I didn't totally understand what I was seeing, with all the code names and the rest. But—there are definite references to other facilities in other cities—New York, Chicago, San Francisco, New Orleans…"

"All the best locales," Ruse murmured. Any place that attracted a decent number of artsy or otherwise quirky humans tended to appeal to the shadowkind as well—easier for *their* quirks to blend in.

My stomach had balled into a massive knot. "You're saying the Company of Light isn't alone? There are other organizations like them?"

"No, that's all the same organization." The guy swept his hand through the air. "The Company of Light has… let's call them branches in at least seven other cities in the US. It doesn't look as if all of them are currently holding higher shadowkind captive—the operation here seems to have been one of the biggest—but they're all experimenting on lesser beings and hunting around the local rifts."

The buoyant mood that had filled the gathering deflated. I exchanged a grim look with Thorn and Ruse. This hadn't been our final stand after all. The operations we'd burned down here had only been one piece in a massive puzzle of awfulness. Shit.

Omen cleared his throat, taking charge with a typical authoritarian vibe. "Have you at least determined what all this experimenting is for—specifically? How do they think they're going to conquer the shadowkind?"

Computer Dude's fingers tightened around the laptop. "They… they've been testing all sorts of things to see what drains our essence the most, in an attempt to create a sickness that could be passed between the shadowkind and deadly enough to kill any that encountered it in the mortal world."

A deeper hush fell over the crowd. "It'll never work," one of the gang underlings said after a moment. "We don't get sick."

The guy shrugged. "They have made progress. Nothing we'd need to fend off immediately, and the virus I sent into their computer systems may have passed on to the rest of the organization over the internet and damaged their research overall, but—I won't feel comfortable while they're still working on it. They've already created bacteria potent enough to make lesser shadowkind weaken."

There was a moment of total horrified silence. It'd obviously never occurred to the assembled crowd that even that much could be possible. A shiver ran down my spine.

"Fine," Omen said. "The assholes are dangerous—we already knew that. If we didn't topple the kingpin last night, we'll just have to do that next. Did you find some indication of who *is* running the whole show?"

"It does appear that Victor Bane was in charge of operations here. The records stay pretty vague about who holds the ultimate authority, but… based on the scale of operations, my best guess is they're located in San Francisco."

"Road trip!" Ruse said, raising his fist in the air, but even he couldn't summon much enthusiasm into his joking tone.

Murmurs spread through the crowd. As Rex took them in, he nodded. "We fought the battle we came here to fight—we kicked the bastards out of our city. The rest I'm going to have to leave to you. We've put enough on the line as it is."

The werewolf's gaze settled on me. So had that of a few of his companions, I realized. Their expressions had tensed in a way that only amplified my uneasiness.

"Especially when you've got a sorcerer working with you," Rex added, and it clicked. Of course the shadowkind who'd seen me summon fire in the entrance hall would assume I'd used sorcery, bending a shadowkind to my will. They'd seen plenty of evidence that I was mortal, and that was the only way mortals were supposed to be able to use magic.

I pulled my posture up straighter. "I'm no sorcerer. I—I'm not totally sure what I am, but I wouldn't manipulate shadowkind for power."

Rex's eyebrows shot up. "You're trying to tell me that you're a human who can conjure fire on her own steam?"

"Well, more like smoke, but…"

"It's true," Omen said brusquely. "Do you really think I'd work with a sorcerer, Rex? I'd rather eat them for dinner. If you're not sticking around, I can't see how it matters anyway."

The murmurs had heightened, more gazes turning my way. Thorn took a step closer as if he thought I might need a bodyguard, but Rex waved his people silent.

"You're right. It's your business, not ours. Come on, folks—let's leave these do-gooders to their crusade."

He wavered into the shadows. Most of the gathering followed him. I guessed they'd find a vehicle of their own to steal to shorten the trip back into town.

Let the selfish pricks have it their way. A deeper chill was sinking into my bones that had nothing to do with any shadowkind.

"Omen," I said. "At least one of the guards who saw me use my magic got away last night. I didn't worry about it because Thorn was too injured to go after him—with everything else destroyed, I didn't think it would matter. But if he tells everyone else in the Company… At the very least, they'll be ready for it next time."

"One more in a whole heap of worries. We'll deal with that along with the rest."

Someone cleared their throat. Omen turned and scowled as he noticed the Tech Dude standing nervously at the base of the RV's steps, not having left with the others. "What?"

The guy bobbed his head. "I thought you'd want to know… I think the being you were hoping to find on the Bane estate, the devourer? It looks as though they did capture him—or one of very similar description. Whichever it is, they shipped that shadowkind to Chicago yesterday afternoon. Maybe they were worried you'd be able to trace his presence if they kept him too close."

My throat closed up. "Snap." He was in one of those cells after all, pinned by the silver and iron and the searing lights—and whatever else they were already using to torment him.

"Thank you," Omen said, and the computer guy darted off after his boss. The hellhound shifter pressed his hand to his forehead. "When I get my claws into the rest of these people…"

Thorn's shoulders flexed. "It'll be a pleasure to tear them limb from limb."

"We have to get to them all first. Seven cities." Omen's mouth tightened. "Well, maybe if we shatter what they have in San Francisco, that'll be enough…"

His gaze slid past us, over the few rescued shadowkind who were standing uncertainly at the fringes of where the crowd had been, and stopped on Bow, who was just walking up to us with Gisele still cradled in his arms.

The unicorn shifter, not the centaur, was the one who spoke, her voice reedy but still silver-bright. "I think we might be able to help you out a little bit more—as a thank you for bringing Cori back to us." She shot a smile over Bow's shoulder at their friend.

"You can't try to fight when you're still recovering," I protested, but she waved me off.

"Not like that. We only… We only need the Everymobile while we're here in the mortal realm. The dryad was right—I'll heal faster shadow-side. If you can drop us off at the nearest safe rift, we're happy to lend her to you as long as you need her." She rested her hand against the vehicle's side. "Maybe I'll even bounce back fast enough to jump back into this war of yours."

Omen considered her for a long moment. Then he dipped his head, just slightly but with obvious respect. "Thank you. You've already contributed more than most would have." He swiveled back to face Thorn, Ruse, and me.

The words tumbled out before I'd thought them through, but I wouldn't have changed them anyway. "We have to get Snap back. We can't leave him in the hands of those assholes when we've got no idea how long it might take to shatter the whole Company."

I braced myself to have to argue practicalities on my lover's behalf —to point out how much *he'd* already contributed to Omen's cause and how much more he might if he got the chance, as if that mattered more than the fact that he was now facing who knew what kind of torture because of the hellhound shifter's crusade. But I didn't need to.

A tense smile curved Omen's lips. "I agree. It looks like we do have a road trip in our immediate future—and head of the Company be damned, our first stop will be Chicago. We're not leaving our devourer behind."

TWILIGHT CROOK - BONUS SCENE

While Sorsha was off visiting with Vivi in Chapter 5, Omen questioned Ruse about her involvement with his three underlings. Read on to find out how that conversation went down...

Ruse

If I'd accused Omen of sulking, he'd probably have bared those hellhound fangs and attempted to tear my head off—and possibly succeeded. But there really wasn't any verb that more accurately described his current mood.

He was putting on a show of keeping busy, puttering around his car making sure everything was properly oiled and greased and whatever else the thing needed. Vehicular maintenance wasn't my forte. His attempt didn't disguise how his mood had dampened after Sorsha had gone off to chat with her friend. Or rather, how it'd dampened when he'd failed to argue her out of doing so.

Sooner or later, he was going to have to learn that Miss Blaze didn't bend to anyone's will but her own, and that we were all better for her imperviousness. Preferably sooner. I didn't mind speaking up on her behalf, but it did put me at greater risk of those snapping jaws than I totally enjoyed.

Our indomitable leader had sent Thorn and Snap off to conduct a preliminary survey of the site of our upcoming ambush so that he could make most of his plans ahead of time. I wasn't totally sure why he'd kept me around to witness his vehement not-sulking until he finally opened his mouth.

"You're the expert on all things desire. If your head's not too turned by your own obsession with this mortal, maybe you can explain to me why not just you but the rest of my squad are chomping at the bit for her?"

I managed to hold in a laugh, but I couldn't quite contain my smirk as I leaned against the wall of the vacant store he'd parked next to. "I wouldn't have thought it was that much of a mystery."

Omen glowered at me over the top of the car. And when the hellhound glowered, his eyes literally lit up with little flames. "I've rarely seen *any* shadowkind this enamored with a human. Three at once—the three I specifically picked for their dedication for seeing our mission through..." He cut himself off with a growl. "It's absurd."

I refrained from suggesting that he might be protesting a little too much. I'd seen how his gaze had burned into Sorsha when she'd told him off and risen to his challenges, and as an expert in desire, I felt confident in saying that it hadn't been only anger simmering behind his eyes. Of course, he'd say that was even more absurd.

Instead, I focused on the other point he'd made. "We're still just as dedicated to the mission. Sorsha is going to *help* us complete that mission, so vouching for her is working toward that goal, not against it."

"And are you going to tell me that fucking her is also an act of devotion to the cause?"

Devotion to the cause of having a spectacular time, certainly. My tongue flicked over my lips at the thought of getting to enjoy my new lover as thoroughly as I had in the past all over again now that we seemed to have mended the damage I'd caused to our partnership.

"We can't be hunting our enemies every hour of every day," I said. "Even shadowkind need a chance to unwind to be at their best. So a few indulgences with her may also be in the service of your mission, sure."

Omen growled again and went back to polishing the side mirror, which I was pretty sure was already clean enough that you could have licked whipped cream off it. If that was your thing.

"You, I understand," he said after a minute. "You needed to refuel, so you'd have been seeking out *some* kind of connection. But the devourer's barely ever been around humans at all. I don't think he even knew what all they do in the privacy of their bedrooms or why. And Thorn..." He stopped himself, maybe recognizing he'd almost said more than he wanted to about who and what exactly our lumbering giant was. "He's been all duty, all the time for as long as I've known him."

"Then maybe it's a good thing he's loosened up," I said, and received a glare even more blistering than the glower. I held up my hands in surrender. "All I can tell you is that she's not like any other mortal I've ever encountered—and you know I've dallied with a lot of them. She brings out something in the two of them that even they didn't expect, I'd imagine. But it isn't a bad thing. You've seen how patient she is with Snap. She thinks he's fucking adorable even when he's being so naïve I want to smack some sense into him."

"Which happens about once an hour," Omen muttered, and sighed. "So that's it? She's *nice* to all of you, and that's all it takes to turn you into shadow-putty in her hands?"

Possibly he didn't realize how appealing the thought of being molded by those skillful hands actually was. If he'd meant that as a shaming remark, he'd failed.

I grinned at him. "It isn't about being *nice*. She understands us. She's more comfortable with shadowkind than plenty of *shadowkind* I've met. When you mix that with other qualities well worth admiring... She's got passion to spare, which I'm naturally a sucker for. She seeks out excitement and new experiences like Snap. And underneath the attitude, she's as dedicated to protecting shadowkind as the bunch of us, which is probably what softened Thorn to her. It's hard to tell with that lunk."

"She puts on a good show," Omen said, as if he was one to talk in his current state. "When the going gets really tough, then you'll see what she's actually made of—or not made of."

He had no idea how tough the going had already gotten. Sorsha had made it clear that she didn't mind us… revising our account of our adventures before we'd freed our boss, so that the three of us appeared somewhat less incompetent than we might have otherwise. But I wasn't sure even the full details would have convinced the hellhound.

I didn't think *anything* was going to convince him right now, but he'd keep dragging this increasingly boring conversation out until he'd gotten all his grumbling in… unless I made him feel it was better shutting up about his frustration with our lovely woman.

I folded my arms over my chest and tipped my head to the side, taking on a provocative tone. "It could be that it's impossible to fully understand her appeal until you've indulged in it yourself. Perhaps you should try turning on the charm rather than the flames and see whether—"

"I have no interest in getting caught up in a charade of intimacy with some mortal," Omen snapped, but for the first time, he looked more than just irritated. His eyes flared brighter, and his tawny hair ruffled as if a gust of smoke had coursed over it.

He swiped his hand over the tufts and turned away, tossing the rag into a nearby dumpster. "Just make sure you don't forget why we're here. It won't be good for you or her."

I couldn't tell whether that was a threat or what he saw as a simple statement of fact, but one thing was perfectly clear: our fiery-furred boss wasn't anywhere near as unaffected by the mortal in our midst as he wanted to be.

DUSK AVENGER

FLIRTING WITH MONSTERS #3

ONE

Sorsha

I wouldn't have thought my journey toward ending the world would involve a glamoured RV plastered with copious amounts of glitter, but hey, we couldn't always choose our fates.

At least the glitter was all on the inside—as far as I knew, anyway. At this point, I'd only seen the outside in its various glamoured states. With a push of the button on the dashboard, the luxurious ride could appear to be anything from a school bus to a military submarine.

We hadn't tried out the latter of those just yet, more's the pity.

Right now, the RV was in its tour bus guise—an excellent multipurpose façade that could fit in just about anywhere. Like, for example, the parking lot outside a state park's nature center. The building with all its displays about local flora and fauna was closed for the night, but we weren't here to brush up on our environmental acumen anyway. About half a mile off one of the forest trails lay a rift that connected this mortal world to the shadow realm.

The seven beings who stood around me—or in the case of my little dragon, Pickle, *on* me, in his favorite perch on my shoulder—all belonged to that other realm. Only three of them were returning to it this evening, though.

Gisele adjusted her stance next to her partner, Bow, who had his arm around her torso to help her keep her balance. A few days ago, the unicorn shifter had been nearly mortally wounded in a battle with the Company of Light, a secret organization we'd discovered that was dedicated to ridding all worlds of the shadowkind by whatever means necessary. Gisele, Bow, and their friend Cori were heading back to their natural home so she could hurry along her recovery.

She gave the RV one last mournful glance. "You take good care of the Everymobile, all right?" The three of them were kindly lending us their vehicle, glitter and all, to continue our quest to take down the Company. As a thank you slash apology, we'd fixed up the broken windows and other bits that'd been battered in that recent skirmish.

Ruse shot the unicorn shifter one of his typical smirks, making his gorgeous face even more roguish, and patted the RV's side. "We'll treat her like a member of the family—the best of everything."

I jumped in before Omen, the leader of our little group, could bring up the fact that I'd supposedly gotten two of our previous vehicles destroyed—as if it were somehow my fault the Company's mercenaries had decided to target our means of transportation.

"You've been healing so fast," I said. "I bet you'll be back to collect her in no time."

"Back to rejoin you in crushing those assholes," Gisele muttered, her voice managing to keep its sparkle even when she was grumbling. "There are consequences to messing with a unicorn."

Omen tipped his head with its tawny, slicked-back hair to her—just slightly, but a major show of respect from the hellhound shifter, who was the most powerful shadowkind I'd ever met. An air of menacing authority radiated off him, as consistent as his breath. "We'll continue paying out those consequences until you return. We've got plenty of bones to pick with the Company."

"I'm looking forward to clobbering many more of them," Bow announced. He'd done a good deal of clobbering already with the massive haunches and hooves of his full shadowkind form. After seeing him as a centaur, I couldn't quite accept the standard human appearance he took on to blend in with mortals. Like all the shadowkind who traveled here, he did keep one of his monstrous features no matter how human he tried to pass as: in his case, a glorious mohawk mane of chestnut hair.

Thorn, the third of my current companions, straightened his considerable height even taller with a flex of his bulging biceps. The moonlight glinted off the one shadowkind feature *he* couldn't hide: his crystalline knuckles, also highly useful for bashing our enemies. His deep, gravelly voice came out as somber as always. "The villains have much to answer for."

They did. Just remembering Gisele's crumpled form after the ambush, smoke billowing off her like blood would have poured from a mortal, sent a prickle of angry heat through my chest. The sensation flared hotter at the thought of what the murderous Company pricks might be doing to the fourth member of my monstrous quartet now.

Snap had been the sweetest, gentlest being I'd ever met, humans included—even if, yes, he was also capable of inflicting inexpressible pain by devouring mortal souls. He'd been so ashamed of using that power to save me that he'd taken off on his own and been captured by the Company. Their scientists ran torturous experiments on the shadowkind they imprisoned. Imagining the devourer on one of their steel lab tables brought the searing heat to the base of my throat.

In the last week, I'd discovered a supernatural power inside myself, one no mortal should contain. So maybe I wasn't all mortal, even if neither I nor the shadowkind with me had been aware that was possible. I didn't know *what* I was, but I did know I'd happily send anyone who laid a hand on Snap up in flames. I didn't think it'd even be difficult to summon the fire inside me now. The Company had messed with the wrong gal.

As if sensing my mood, Pickle squirmed from one shoulder to the other and pressed his scaly neck against my cheek. As we waved our good-byes to the equines and their friend, I reached up to scratch the dragon's belly. He let out a pleased snort.

Maybe I should have been sending him back home along with the others. He wasn't equipped to fight in what had become a full-out war. But there was a reason I'd kept him after rescuing him from one of the collectors of the supernatural whose menageries of beasties I'd enjoyed freeing. His jailor had gotten Pickle's wings clipped so he could barely fly. I suspected that on the other side of the divide, he'd quickly become prey to other sorts of predators.

Could I even call the shadow realm his "home" now that he'd spent the past two years living here with me?

Gisele glanced back at us one final time and blew us a kiss I'd swear twinkled in the deepening dusk. Then she and her companions vanished into the shadows between the trees. The late-summer breeze twined around us, cool enough now to raise goosebumps on my arms. We turned back toward our ride.

Omen folded his arms over his chest and gave the RV a rare approving look. "We've got a long road ahead of us, Darlene."

I bit my lip and exchanged a glance with Ruse, barely holding in a snicker. Omen liked to name his vehicles, from his now-demolished station wagon—R.I.P., Betsy—to the motorcycle he called Charlotte that was currently mounted on the Everymobile's back end. Of course, this time there was one small issue that I couldn't help raising.

"You know, I don't think you should really be naming things that don't belong to you."

Omen let out a huff. "She does for the time being. All right, folks. Let's get on this thing and point her toward Chicago."

A shadowkind who knew his way around computers had been able to determine from the Company's files that Snap had been sent to the Windy City. Before we tackled the head of the murderous organization, who as far as he'd been able to determine operated out of San Francisco, we were getting our devourer back.

Of course, that was easier said than done.

As Ruse took the driver's seat with a twirl of the silver spangle dangling from the rear-view mirror, I sank onto the white leather sofa that curved around a sleek dining table. Omen propped himself against the kitchen's marble counter. The hellhound shifter seemed to be most comfortable on his feet.

"How hard do you think it'll be for us to find the facility where they're holding Snap once we get to the city?" I asked. In my hometown, I'd relied on the connections I'd spent over a decade developing, and Omen had been able to call in a favor from a local shadowkind gang that had owed him. I didn't know anyone in Chicago.

There was probably a branch of the Shadowkind Defense Fund there, but I couldn't expect the people back home to provide introductions. I'd burned through a lot of bridges—metaphorically speaking, but we wouldn't get into what I'd *literally* burned—in the last few days.

"It's easy enough to sniff out the beings with the most influence if you know what to look for," Omen said with his usual aloof confidence. "If they haven't picked up on any hint of the malevolent organization rounding up their own, then they barely deserve to be called shadowkind."

Thorn had come to stand beside the sofa. He squeezed my shoulder with one of his large hands. "We'll rescue the devourer, m'lady—and make the miscreants regret ever ensnaring him. No matter what it takes."

Yes, we would. We'd managed to take on a local head of the Company operations and raze his home to the ground—and that after freeing all my city's imprisoned shadowkind and uploading a virus that would decimate their computer systems as well. But my stomach stayed knotted.

It was possible that Snap's capture was a teensy bit my fault. We'd gotten… close over the weeks since he and his companions had shown up in my apartment unannounced. In every meaning of that word. He'd become as devoted to me as he was to sampling every edible item he could get his hands on. I didn't know exactly why he'd left, but I wouldn't be surprised if it had at least a little to do with the fact that when I'd first seen him in full devourer form, I'd been horrified. And I probably hadn't hidden my reaction all that well.

My momentary horror hadn't changed how much I trusted and cared about Snap. I'd tried to show him that, but in the chaos afterward, he'd slipped away before I'd gotten much chance. If he'd had any idea how much I missed his divinely golden beauty, the possessive tenderness with which he'd doted on me, his awe at every new discovery he made in the mortal realm…

My throat constricted. *I* hadn't realized just how much I'd miss him either. I wasn't in the habit of getting all that emotionally attached to my lovers since years ago, when a long-time boyfriend had ghosted me out of the blue, leaving nothing but a note and our apartment half-empty. Snap's earnest affection had been like a balm on the wounds that had never quite healed in my heart.

But we'd be on the road all night before we made it to Chicago and could even start our search for him. There were other people I cared about that I might be able to help right now. As I sank deeper into the cozy leather cushions, Pickle cuddling against my thigh, I dug my phone out of my purse.

"I'd better touch base with Vivi—let her know what's happened."

Omen made a derisive sound at the mention of my mortal best friend and turned away to consult his own phone.

"I'll keep watch over the road behind us," Thorn said, and stepped into the shadows to give me a little privacy.

Vivi answered on the first ring. I guessed she didn't have a whole lot to keep her energetic mind occupied on the houseboat we'd turned into a sort of safe house for her after some Company goons had attacked her.

"Sorsha!" she said. "I've been going crazy here wondering what's going on. What's happened? Did you crush the bad guys?"

The corner of my mouth twitched upward, but the knots in my stomach tightened at the same time. Vivi was an enthusiastic supporter of our cause, but we'd had a bit of a falling out over her treating the conflict like an adventure rather than a potentially lethal clash.

"We got all the shadowkind out," I said. "And we destroyed as much of the Company property as we could. But... it turns out their organization stretches way beyond the city. They've got other bases of operations all across the country."

"Shit." I could practically see my bestie's grimace over the phone. "They're like some kind of cockroach hydra, more creepy hairy legs springing up every time you think you've cut one off."

Vivi had a way with metaphors. I couldn't say that one wasn't accurate.

"Yeah." I made an answering grimace at the cupboards across from me—which probably still contained the equines' treasured stash of grass, hay, clover, and... the other kind of "grass." "So, that means it *might* be safe for you to go back to life as usual, but I don't know for sure. Maybe they'll focus on ramping up their security everywhere else, or maybe the other 'legs' will send more people your way looking to strike back any way they can."

As usual, Vivi didn't sound particularly fazed. "I'm keeping in touch with the Fund people. If no one comes sniffing around—or worse—in the next couple days, I'll risk showing my face again. I've got enough food here to last that long, but I can't hide away forever." She paused. "Ellen got out of the hospital, by the way. They say she's recovering quickly."

A rush of relief swept through me. "That's really good to hear." The co-leader of our branch of the Fund had nearly been another casualty of my involvement in this war. The Company had beat her up to send a warning my way—and turned the rest of the Fund members against me in the process.

"What are our next steps?" Vivi said, breaking into my uncomfortable reverie. "How are we taking down these assholes?"

The "we" made me wince. What had happened to Ellen—and nearly happened to Vivi—was exactly why I had to give her an answer I knew she wouldn't like.

"I'm already on the road with my shadowkind friends to see about that. You just focus on staying safe. If there's anything you can do to pitch in from there, I'll let you know."

"What, you took off on me? Sorsha…" Vivi couldn't disguise the disappointment in her voice.

"I couldn't ask you to uproot your whole life when this feud has already sent you into hiding twice," I said quickly. "You've got a job; you've got family—and we don't know what else these psychos are going to throw at us."

"Hey, if *you* can stand up to them, there's no reason why my mortal self can't too."

Other than that I wasn't sure exactly how mortal—or not—I was. But I hadn't told Vivi about my newly unearthed powers. Either she'd get all excited like they were a cool new app I'd downloaded into my personal operating system, or… or something would shift in her tone the way it did when she talked about the shadowkind. Because she'd see me as something not-quite-human too.

I kept my tone breezy. "No reason except for the ones I just gave you. Trust me, the best thing you can do for the cause right now is keep out of trouble and be ready for when a good opportunity for you to step in *does* come up."

"All right, all right. But I expect regular updates. No holding out on me, Sorsh."

"Of course," I said with a pinch of guilt.

When we'd said our good-byes, I tucked my knees against my chest and gazed gloomily out the window at the darkening sky. I didn't like this weight of worry pressing down on me. I was the Robin Hood of monster emancipation—I laughed in the face of danger.

It was just a heck of a lot easier to do that when the danger was only coming at you and not everyone else you cared about too.

I pushed my posture straighter and gathered my resolve. Auntie Luna, the fae woman who'd raised me—and who'd died evading the Company's hunters—had given me a lot of things, not least of which was a thorough indoctrination in the joy of all things '80s. There was nothing for honoring her contributions to my life and pumping up my spirits like mangling an excellent song lyric or two.

"Never gonna give it up, never gonna fret and frown," I sang into the quiet of the RV, ignoring the face Omen pulled in my direction. "Now we're gonna run you down and see hurt through!"

I pictured Snap standing beside me while another building burned down in front of us. One more Company facility destroyed; one more set of baddies slaughtered. The villains had it coming to them.

Without even trying, a surge of heat seared through me. My fingers curled around the edge of the seat. I closed my eyes, the swell of sensation inside me so intense that I lost my breath.

Burn it. Burn it all down like they deserve.

In that moment, I felt as if I could have leveled the entire city of Chicago with one blast of the rage inside me. My pulse hiccupped. The flames were rising higher, slipping between my ribs and out through my skin, faster and more furious than I could control—

A sharp sting shot across my fingers. I jerked my arms toward me, biting back a yelp. My gaze dropped to my hands, and a chill settled over me that doused that inner fire.

Holy mother of magma. My fingertips shone red, still stinging with the brush of the air. As if I'd set *myself* on fire.

TWO

Sorsha

Walking up to the clubhouse of Chicago's premier shadowkind criminal syndicate, I had trouble telling whether the gang had been going for unsettling or brutal with their décor. Either way, it was safe to say they'd shot well past the mark on both.

With the narrow two-story building tucked in between a tattoo parlor and a motorcycle dealership, they definitely had their clichés in order. But the front of the place was painted entirely black—including the first-floor window, because apparently curtains weren't enough for these dudes—other than stark white skull symbols on either side of the door and threads of pale gray that crept across the darkness like a massive spider web. They hadn't bothered with a sign or any other pretense of this being a regular place of business.

I stepped inside half-expecting a collection of Halloween store paraphernalia, but what I got wasn't much better. The walls of the small front room were painted the same black as the outside. No spider webbing here, but the single lightbulb overhead cast a red glow over the room's limited furniture, which included a metal desk that had rust creeping along the corners, a matching bench sporting spikes on its supposed arm rests, and a display rack of ornate swords and daggers that looked much more authentic than anything our superhero hacker associate back home had owned.

A sour, slightly metallic scent lingered in the air, as if the room had recently hosted a blood bath. Not exactly a place of friendly welcomes.

Omen didn't look concerned, though. He stalked into the middle of the room and stood there, his eyes narrowing. He'd told us the shadowkind who operated this syndicate would be expecting us, and I could tell he wouldn't be happy if they kept us waiting long.

Before it got to the point of his hellhound fangs coming out, three figures wavered out of the shadows to meet us.

The one in the middle was obviously the leader, nearly as tall and broad-shouldered as Thorn, though packed with leaner muscles. The speckling of pale stubble on his scalp gleamed in the crimson light, and a patch of scales glinted on the backs of his hands just below the cuffs of his suit jacket. Reptilian in nature, presumably.

He was flanked by two other men. The slender, sallow one on the left I immediately pegged as a vampire—which wasn't hard when his lips had curled back to bare his fangs in implicit threat. That explained the painted-over window and the weird lighting. The guy on the right was trickier to pin down—literally. His eyes darted this way and that, his wiry body never quite settling from its twitching and fidgeting even while he stood in place next to his boss.

When his gaze did come to rest in one spot for a couple of seconds here and there, it was on me. The vampire was ogling me too. Possibly Boss Man was as well, but it was impossible to tell thanks to the thick sunglasses that hid all hint of his eyes. I was pretty sure Omen would have given this bunch a heads up about the mortal he was working with, but I was used to the extra scrutiny my presence provoked. You didn't see shadowkind and humans getting chummy all that often—if you could call my relationship with Omen anything as warm as "chummy."

Omen was sizing up the syndicate guys in turn. "You'd be Talon?" he said with a nod to the boss and a razor-edged tone that suggested the dude had better be or there'd be hell to pay.

"As you requested," Boss Man replied in a liquid voice so dark it seemed to blot out the dim glow of the bulb overhead. "What brings us to the attention of a hellhound and his cohorts? We don't have much time for entertaining unexpected visitors."

Despite myself, a shiver shot down my spine. Unlike the other gang leader we'd dealt with, this one didn't speak with any noticeable deference to Omen. For him to have agreed to his impromptu meeting in the first place, Talon must have recognized the hellhound shifter as a larger power, but he wasn't offering much in the way of respect besides that.

As happened sometimes, being intimidated annoyed me, and when pissed off, I didn't always make the choices most likely to keep my innards intact. I'm sure you have your flaws too.

I waved to the closed door behind the syndicate dudes. "What, have you got a full schedule of polishing torture devices and laying down a few more coats of black paint? You know, putting so much effort into showing how badass you are only makes it look like you're trying to distract anyone from actually measuring your dicks. Maybe if you cared a little more about what's happening out *there* and not how cool you look wearing sunglasses in a room that's barely lit, we wouldn't have needed to interrupt your busy day in the first place."

The boss's head turned in a smooth, serpentine motion. He was *definitely* looking at me now, whether I could see his eyeballs or not.

"The sunglasses," he said, equally smoothly, "are to ensure I don't extinguish your life with a glance—unless I absolutely want to. But I can remove them if you'd prefer to play that game of Russian Roulette. With an attitude like that, I don't think your odds are great."

Son of a shih tzu. As Thorn stepped closer to me with a threatening flex of his muscles, the details added up in my head, and I almost bit right through my tongue. Luna had told me plenty of stories about her shadowkind brethren over the years. I hadn't forgotten the tales she'd spun of basilisks, giant lizards that could kill you with a look, although I'd never met one in the flesh before.

Probably best to avoid getting into a pissing contest with one. I gave him a little smile. "My apologies. I wouldn't want to let any games distract from our very important mission."

Omen cleared his throat, shooting me a glare *he* might have wished could kill me. "Maybe you can manage to keep your mouth shut for the next five minutes?" He turned back to Talon. "If you have as much sway over both shadowkind and mortals in this neck of the woods as I hear, I assume you'll have caught on if there were humans gathering our kind in a far more organized way than the typical hunters."

The twitchy guy finally gave in to his restlessness and drifted over to the display of weapons. He plucked up a dagger and spun its blade on the tip of his finger. "There's the type with the nets and the whips. Obsessive bastards."

Thorn frowned, his muscles appearing to bulge even more. "Those would be the ones we're after."

"I don't suppose you've done anything to rid the city of them," Omen remarked.

Talon shrugged. "They catch little pests that are no concern of mine. The occasional higher being they might sweep up should have been watching its step better. I protect those who seek our protection—what happens between mortals and the rest is their business."

That was the standard line of mortal-side shadowkind. Why should they think of the greater good—or the good of anyone at all who wasn't licking their boots?

To be fair, there were an awful lot of humans who approached life that way too.

The tightening of Omen's jaw was the only sign of his disgust with that kind of self-interest. "Understandable. We need to tangle with them, though. They've come into possession of one of our associates, and we intend to get him back."

"Well, I certainly won't stop you from tearing a few heads off if that's what gets you off," the basilisk said.

No offers to pitch in, not that I'd really expected one. Ruse gave my ponytail a teasing tug and leaned over my shoulder. "I don't suppose you gents with all your connections could direct us to this group's center of operations? That would speed along the tearing of heads quite a bit."

"I suppose that wouldn't be too much trouble." Talon turned to his frenetic companion, who was now flipping the dagger from hand to hand. "Jinx, a moment?"

The wiry guy tossed the weapon back at the display—in a perfect arc that sent it dropping right back onto the metal pegs that had cradled it. "What're you after, boss?"

"See if you can fetch Grit—he's the one we had keeping an eye on the museum. Maybe he can cough up a few more details for these 'gents'."

As Jinx darted into the shadows to follow that order, my ability to keep my mouth shut ran out. "Museum?" I asked. "We're looking for living shadowkind, not stuffed ones."

The vampire let out a chuckle almost as dark as his boss's voice, but he didn't bother to enlighten me. I got the distinct impression that Talon had rolled his eyes behind those shades.

"Humans work in bizarre ways, as you should know, mortal," he said. "The museum gives them a front—a large building to work from and presumably a reason for money to change hands. I doubt many of the beasts that go in come out alive, though."

And I'd bet I'd freed more of the lower beings of his kind than he'd ever lifted a finger for. But with another warning glare from Omen, I managed to keep that thought to myself.

A jitter through the air that made the blades rattle in their holders, and Jinx reappeared. "Grit is stationed down by the lake today. I can take you to him if you make it snappy."

Through the shadows, he meant. I opened my mouth to protest, but Omen held up his hand. "You don't need to be involved in every piece of this operation. Wait for us back on Darlene."

Oh, he was doubling down on the name, was he? I might have had a few choice words about that, but before I could voice any of them, Talon approached me. He peered down at me through his sunglasses, cocking his head. My shoulders stiffened, but you'd better believe I held my ground.

"Can I help you with something?" I asked, raising my chin.

I might not have been able to see his eyes, but I thought I could feel his attention pass over me like a cool draft grazing my skin. His mouth tightened into the kind of smile that ate children's laughter for breakfast.

"There's a burning inside you," he said. "But it might not stay in for long. If you're not careful, you're going to sear away with it when you decide to let it loose."

THREE

Sorsha

The Company of Light's main Chicago facility resembled nothing so much as a shoe box—albeit one the size of a city block. That resemblance might have been intentional, because their front wasn't just any museum. It was a Museum of Footwear.

As we cruised by, I squinted at the pale gray walls from the window over the RV's sofa. "Why would anyone think you need a building that big just to show off a bunch of shoes?"

Ruse chuckled from the driver's seat. "You fail to recognize the multitude of items mortals have worn on their feet over the centuries, Miss Blaze."

I rolled my eyes in his general direction. "I'm sure there are plenty of interesting slippers and sandals and galoshes or whatever, but who wants to spend a day looking at them all?"

"Enough people to keep the Company's front in business," Omen said from where he was standing near the door, watching the street through the windshield. "The dwarf said quite a few ordinary-looking humans go in and out on an average day."

"Well, there's no accounting for taste, I guess. I don't see much in the way of security on the outside, at least not right now." There wasn't much room for guards to take up posts along the narrow strip of lawn between the building and the sidewalk. I'd spotted a figure just inside the glass front doors, though. "If they mostly stick to lesser shadowkind here, maybe they haven't felt the need to really lock the place down."

Thorn appeared across from me so suddenly that Pickle startled where he was curled up on my lap. The warrior must have leapt straight from the shadows along the road into the RV and then into physical form so fast even his fellow shadowkind hadn't been prepared.

"The building appears to have an inner sanctum," he reported without preamble. "The galleries form a square around an area that only a single locked door leads into. The door and the walls around that area contained enough noxious metals that I couldn't slip past while the entrance was shut. No telling how many mortals might be stationed within, but I counted six guards patrolling the outer rooms."

A thin smile curled Omen's lips. "They're definitely not expecting us, then. The Company must not have realized how far we got into their computer system before we burned that last place down. It'll be simple enough to blaze through this spot to wherever they're holding Snap."

His words were enough to set off a flash of heat in my chest. My hands tightened around Pickle.

A couple of days ago, I'd have welcomed the searing power that stirred with my anger. After scalding my fingers and hearing the basilisk's warning, my body recoiled at the sensation.

I'd only just discovered this power—or acknowledged it, anyway—a week ago. I'd barely scraped the surface of learning how to work it. Which was to say, I didn't have much of a clue what all I might be capable of, for good or ill.

Besides, did I really want to go charging at every enemy we faced from now until the end of this quest, burning them alive as my opening move? The shrieks of the people I'd sent up in flames in the last facility echoed through my memory, leaving me faintly queasy. Omen and Thorn wouldn't have batted an eye at that tactic—Ruse and

Snap might not have either—but murder was a tad more taboo among humans than it was among the shadowkind.

Just how much of a monster was *I* going to become while we saw this mission through?

An unnerving prickling crept over my skin with that question, as if some of my inner fire was already rising to the surface. I wet my lips. "Before we do any blazing, could we find someplace for me to get in a little fire-throwing practice? I'd like to make sure I still have a good grip on my powers after the downtime."

No need to mention that I already suspected I was losing my grip.

Omen frowned as if he resented the delay, but then he sighed. "It isn't as if we'd go barging in there five minutes from now anyway. You can toss your flames around while we discuss our plan of action. The dwarf did mention a place where we should be able to park Darlene without being observed or disturbed."

He pulled up the map on his phone and barked a few directions at Ruse, who gamely drove us through a sprawling residential neighborhood and out to a strip mall where all the store windows were boarded up. They formed a perfect C around the parking lot Ruse drove into. Plenty of room and no witnesses—just the way we liked it.

I stepped out into the cool night air and rolled my shoulders, willing my nerves to settle. That little accident the other day was no big deal. So my powers were a little capricious still. What else would you expect when I was some weird type of mortal who occasionally bled smoke as well as blood?

There was no guidebook on being... whatever the hell I was. I just had to get used to my unexpected abilities. And as for Talon and his sunglasses, he'd probably been pulling crap out of his ass, hoping he'd freak me out as payback for mocking his interior design sense.

There'd been a time only days ago when I hadn't been able to summon a flame except under terror of death. Now, I fixed my gaze on a paper bag drifting along the asphalt, and the surge of power swelled inside me so swiftly my heart started thudding *because* of that magic instead of the other way around.

"Burn," I murmured with a flick of my fingers.

Heat shot through my arm, and the paper bag exploded into flame. In seconds, it was nothing but a little heap of charred black flakes.

Ruse clapped his hands for me where he was conferring with Omen and Thorn beside the Everymobile. "Bravo!"

I grinned at him in return, but my face felt stiff. The prickling sensation that had welled up inside me before was spreading all through my chest and down to my gut.

As long as it stayed there, I was just fine. No self-roasting today; no problem.

I swiveled around in search of more targets. A tattered flyer for a small-time theater production—with one sharp look, it was ashes. A paper plate with grease stains in the shape of a slice of pizza—cinders. An empty pop can that rattled as it rolled in a gust of wind—why the hell not?

I stared at it, my gaze narrowing to a glare. Heat blazed from my chest through my throat to the back of my eyes, and—

A rush of fire burst up not just on the can itself but several inches around it too. The heat of those flames flared so intensely that it lashed across my body from five feet away.

Or was that the heat *inside* my body flaring at the same time? The sensation whipped up in a whirl that sizzled up my spine and across my shoulder blades, and pain stabbed through my back.

A cry caught in my throat. I winced, drawing my arms toward my chest, and both the pain and the fire around the pop can shimmered down.

Or rather, around the smear of melted metal that marked the ground where the pop can used to be. Holy liquified lizards, I'd reduced the aluminum to a puddle in just moments. A little more practice and I wouldn't even need to miss my titanium scorch-knife with its magically heated blade anymore.

A slightly hysterical giggle tickled up from my chest. Watch out, Company of Light.

As I adjusted my stance, the fabric of my shirt shifted against my back, and a fresh sting jabbed across my right shoulder blade. I tensed instinctively. With careful fingers, I prodded the flesh just below the collar of my shirt.

Even that tentative touch provoked more stinging. Small ripples met my fingers, as if the skin there was blistered.

I wasn't just melting down metals—I was barbequing myself.

That had never happened when I'd used my powers in the first several days. Why was the fire lashing back at me now? A scorching churn remained inside my gut even though I wasn't trying to summon it now, fierce enough that my stomach lurched with the thought that it might not be just my skin getting scalded.

Maybe this was just how this impossible power of mine worked— the more I wielded it, the more it leached from me in turn. Why not, when mortals were never supposed to work magic in the first place? At least the burns on my fingers had healed with shadowkind-esque swiftness. I hadn't done any permanent damage to myself.

Of course, that didn't mean I *couldn't*.

When I looked up at the strip mall, the heat inside me bubbled up eagerly. The sense came over me that I could have burned that whole stretch of buildings down with just a little push of my will...

I closed my eyes. Fuck this. I was all for kicking butt and pummeling the assholes who treated shadowkind as lab rats and worse, but a gal needed to have some kind of limits. I didn't understand what was going on inside me, and the more my powers grew, the more dangerous that ignorance became. Playing with fire was only fun if you were truly in charge of the matches.

We had other options beyond bringing a full maelstrom down on the shoe museum, right? There had to be room for a little subtlety in between "stand back and do nothing" and "burn everything and everyone to ashes."

As I walked over to the shadowkind men, I braced myself. I could predict how at least one of the three would react to the suggestion I was going to make.

Thorn had been saying something, but he fell silent as I reached them, looking to me as if he realized I had something to say.

Omen considered me with his icy blue eyes. "Finished your flambé practice?"

"For now." The jolt that rushed through me at those words, both giddy and rattled by the impression of all the things it could be in my capacity to incinerate at this moment, only bolstered my resolve. "I think it might be best if we come up with a plan that doesn't count on me using my powers."

The hellhound shifter grimaced before I could get any further.

"Don't tell me you're doubting your abilities all over again. You burned down a whole mansion a few days ago. I saw you lighting up trash over there just now. The fire's in you—you know how to use it. What's the problem?"

The heat inside me flared with a prickle of frustration. I resisted the urge to hug myself as if the press of my arms would force the inner flames to simmer down. "The problem is it feels... different from before. Bigger. Fiercer. I know how to bring it out, yeah, but I'm not sure how well I can keep it in check once it's out there."

Omen shrugged. "So you might char a few other establishments around the museum. The mortals never seem to care how many shadowkind they mow down in their crusades."

"You might care if I charred *you*," I retorted.

"I think I'm safe from your incredible talents. I know you think very highly of yourself, but you *really* don't need to protect me from you."

Would he be so sure about that if he could feel the building inferno of my power the way I could?

"I think I do," I said stubbornly. "Especially since you can't be bothered to listen to me. I don't think it's safe for any of us—including *me*—if I keep throwing my powers around when none of us has any clue how I even have supernatural skills in the first place."

Omen squared his shoulders. "Look, Disaster," he said, his voice flat but cutting. "I know the fact that there's something not entirely human in you unnerves you. The fact that the rest of you is human unnerves *me*. I've gotten over it, so you're going to find a way to come to terms with it too. Preferably soon. Stay focused and committed, as little practice as I'm sure you've had with that kind of discipline, and you'll control yourself just fine."

"Maybe if you were focused on something other than giving me a hard time, you'd be able to think of a plan that's better than 'fry all the villains to a crisp.' Brute force isn't the only skill we've got. Look at... Look at how far Ruse has gotten us with his incubus charm. Why don't we have him beguile all the guards into being on our side, and then we'll be able to waltz right through the place and get the cells open without running for our lives at the same time?"

Ruse blinked at me, apparently startled that I'd singled him out. He ran a hand through his rumpled chocolate-brown waves, past one of the small, curved horns that poked through them. "As much as I appreciate your faith in me, Miss Blaze, I can't easily charm more than a couple of mortals at the same time—not to the lengths we'd need to override their devotion to their cause."

"You wouldn't have to win them all over at once," I said. "They're not expecting us to be here. We have time. We watch the museum, follow the guards when they go off duty so we know where they live, and you can bring them around to our side one at a time. If we can get a few of the syndicate's followers to help us track them down, we could probably have them all dancing to your tune by tomorrow evening."

The incubus tapped his lips, but a soft smile was starting to tug at them. "You know, that might work. And I *would* love to see a whole company of Company goons following my every command."

Omen still looked skeptical. "We have no idea of their shift structure or how many staff might be working in the inner chambers of that place. Miss one, and we'll still have a mess the second we get in there."

We might have been able to sort that out if we'd had weeks to survey the museum's comings and goings, but I wasn't going to leave Snap at the Company's lack-of-mercy for that long. I spread my hands. "So what? You and Thorn can take care of one or two stragglers if they get in our way, can't you? Or we let the guards deal with their own." I liked that way better than being responsible for several deaths-by-charbroiling—and who knew what other havoc on top of that.

Thorn cleared his throat and rested his hand on the small of my back, a solid, comforting pressure that offset the faint stinging still radiating through my shoulder blade. "You know I'm most at ease with physical combat, Omen, but I believe Sorsha's plan has its merits. The incubus has proven just how much influence he can wield. We'll have more time to uncover information on our enemies' weaknesses and policies if we enter through non-violent means. Any records we can obtain could make the difference between succeeding against the larger organization."

For the warrior to support a strategy that involved him standing back while someone else took the lead role was as huge as, well, the warrior himself. I would have kissed him if I hadn't suspected that would only undermine his larger point with his boss. I settled for giving his brawny forearm an affectionate squeeze instead.

Omen's mouth went as flat as his voice had been. I hated it when he ramped up the cold-and-hard-as-ice façade he turned to more often than not. Hated it so much that I'd never been able to resist poking at him until I found the right angle to provoke some of his own inner heat to the surface.

To be clear, dealing with a hellhound shifter in a rage was no laughing matter. But I'd take being terrified over condescended to any day.

We could get along; we'd proven that while making our final plans to take out the facilities back home. But Omen had been particularly stick-up-ass-ish when it came to my unexpected voodoo skills from the start.

"Are you sure this isn't all about giving you more excuses to hide away your powers?" he demanded. "Because it sounds an awful lot like that."

I gazed right back at him. "I've gotten so far from hiding them that a whole bunch of shadowkind and at least a couple of human beings who are still alive witnessed my flame-throwing last time. And I've spent my whole life toeing the line between risky and outright suicidal, so you'll just have to trust that I know when I'm on the verge of crossing it."

"Maybe you simply need a little more practice at exercising that discipline you struggle with." He loomed on me abruptly, a flash of orange light darting through his eyes, and somehow my body reacted with both a panicked hiccup of my pulse… and a tingle of a different sort of heat low in my belly.

We should probably get this out of the way up front—I have a unique taste in men. Deal with it.

I hadn't given in to any of those flares of attraction the hellhound shifter occasionally set off, though, and I wasn't about to start simpering now.

"Let's go," he said, jerking his hand toward the open lot behind us. "We'll see what you've got."

I jabbed him in the—very well-built, I had to admit—chest with my forefinger. "No. I've had enough for today. I need some simmering down time, not more stoking of the flames."

"So you say. There's one very simple way to get over the fear that you'll somehow reduce me to cinders. Give it a shot—your best one."

My power shifted inside me with an uncomfortable crackling. I swallowed hard and played one card I knew for sure would rankle him. "Leave it, Luce. Haven't you ever heard that no means no?"

A while back, Ruse had mentioned that long ago, Omen had pretended to be Lucifer—the devil himself, who apparently didn't actually exist—to frighten old-timey mortals. Usually pulling out that nickname was a sure-fire way to break him out of his own taut self-discipline. Tonight, a few tufts of his hair rose from its slicked-back surface, but his gaze kept its cool blue. A slightly dry note crept into his voice.

"I say when you're done. Come on and get this over with, Disaster. There's nothing you can—"

"I said *no*," I interrupted, with a burst of heat I hadn't meant to unleash. Flames sprang to the surface, but not on Omen. My clenched hands lit up like glowing embers—and with agonizing throbbing as if embers were burning against my palms.

"Shit." I pressed them to my body as if I could extinguish a fire that hadn't even leapt all the way to the surface of my skin and choked on a gasp of pain at the contact. The agony faded with the glow, leaving my hands faintly pink and my heart pounding all over again.

Omen considered my hands with an unreadable expression. His gaze rose to meet mine. For just an instant, he hesitated.

"All right," he said brusquely. "You're frayed enough for one night, then. We'll deal with your fears and whatever else tomorrow. It can't hurt to have Ruse pave our way into the facility whether you bring your blaze or not. Go get some rest."

Both Thorn and Ruse were eyeing me with obvious concern. "M'lady?" Thorn started, but I waved him off.

"I'm fine. But I *could* use that sleep. Go track down some guards while I get my mortal beauty-rest, all right?"

I kept my tone breezy, but as I climbed into the RV, my lungs had clenched. *I'd* thought the new direction my powers were taking was freaky, sure, but this was all new to me. Omen had hundreds of years of supernatural exploits under his belt… and what he'd seen in me had freaked *him* out enough that he'd backed off without one more word of argument.

Just how fucked was I?

FOUR

Ruse

"Two down, three more to go," I said, taking in the squat brick home our next target had vanished into after leaving guard duty at the museum. "This is the one we think will be working the inner rooms, isn't it?"

Sorsha nodded where she was lounging on the RV's sofa next to me. "That's where he was this morning, anyway."

"You'll want to prime him to not just let us pass but also so that he'll bring any colleagues he's working with out where you can work your charms on them too," Omen reminded me, leaning to eye the building over my head. "I can't believe it'll just be him in the inner sanctum. And since our Disaster here wants to spare the poor little mortals…"

Sorsha shot him a half-hearted glare over her shoulder but didn't bother to comment. The movement sent a whiff of her fiery sweet scent into the air. Fucking delicious. What I wouldn't have given to be spending the next hour in the bedroom down the hall, drinking that scent right off her skin from every part of her body, rather than chatting up another of the Company's dupes.

We did have our devourer to break out of imprisonment, though.

And besides, even if I had let myself indulge in Sorsha's allure alongside Snap not long ago, I suspected making a solo venture of it wasn't the wisest idea. Not if I wanted to stamp out the longing tug in my heart that no incubus had any business feeling—something I should have been doubly sure of after the last time a mortal had turned my head around.

Still, I allowed myself the luxury of a fond smile and pretended it didn't send a ridiculous giddiness through me when she returned the gesture. It was because of her suggestion that I'd ended up spearheading our current plan of action.

I hadn't really seen myself as the leader type. It'd certainly been less pressure hanging back in the shadows during our previous operations and only popping in for the rare occasions when my talents were needed. There was a bit of a thrill in knowing that when we stormed the museum facility tomorrow, it'd be my persuasive skills rather than Thorn's brute strength and Omen's houndish savageness that paved the way.

And maybe there was also a thrill in knowing Sorsha had believed in those skills enough to point to me rather than them in her moment of uncertainty.

"I remember the whole strategy we discussed," I told Omen, and gave him a teasing salute. "Off I go to meet my fate."

I leapt through the shadows, peered through the slightly hazy view of the world they gave me until I was sure no one was nearby to see, and emerged into physical being on the house's doorstep. Since we already knew this fellow's feelings about shadowkind, I'd brought my favorite cap into being with me. As Sorsha caught up with me, ready to take on her mortal part in this role-play, I adjusted the hat's angle over my horns and knocked on the door.

The sinewy young man who opened the door frowned as he looked the two of us over, clearly not expecting any stunningly handsome gentlemen callers, at least not in the middle of the afternoon. His gaze lingered on me. I couldn't read his emotions at the moment, but his expression suggested he didn't find me entirely unappealing, if I'd happened to swing that way—and if I hadn't had other more urgent concerns.

I couldn't read his emotions or work any of my other skills on him just yet because he was still wearing a protective badge made of silver and iron over the general area of his heart. Not the same design as the one Sorsha tended to keep pinned to her undershirt, but for the same purpose. How kind of him to have left it uncovered so we could carry out this part of our plan with minimal struggle.

"You've got something on your shirt," Sorsha said as if spotting an embarrassing stain, and jerked the badge off with one deft yank.

The guy had barely let out a yelp before I let the full force of my seductive power trickle up my throat and into my voice. "I'm sorry to interrupt you, sir, but there's a matter of grave importance I need to bring to your attention. Lives could be at stake."

From the conversation with a colleague I'd overheard while watching him from the shadows, I'd already known he saw himself as some sort of champion of the people. The appeal to his heroic aspirations gave my magic an extra hook into his mind. He still looked discomforted, but he appeared to have forgotten Sorsha's manhandling already. An avid gleam had come into his eyes. "What are you talking about? How do you even know me?"

"There are many of us who study the Company of Light and reach out to its most promising members," I said, letting my smile turn conspiratorial. "Are you ready to step up to the next level in the war against evil?"

Dashing darkness, was he ever. The peek I took inside his head only confirmed the eagerness that lit up his blotchy face. "Absolutely," he said. "Come in—whatever you need, I'll do what I can to help."

Sorsha's part here done, she gave my arm an affectionate squeeze and hustled back to the RV. I ambled after our target into a living room with a leopard-print sofa, a zebra skin rug, and a very large cat—no, by the realms, that was a living, breathing tiger cub bounding across the floor to pounce on a ragged chew toy.

"Oh, don't mind Elsa," my host said with a careless wave. "She never bites that hard."

Our aspiring hero was also an owner of illegal wildlife and possibly a new Tiger King in the making. Wonderful. If Omen didn't end up tearing his throat out when this was through, I'd bet Elsa would once her fangs had grown. I only regretted that I wouldn't be around to see it.

I settled onto the sofa and put on my "serious business" expression, mainly inspired by Thorn and his vast range of sternness. Another thread of magic wove through my voice. "It's particularly important that you don't mention our meeting to anyone. Not everyone in the Company of Light is worthy of our trust. Which is precisely why we need your assistance with a vital matter…"

It took more than half an hour of tempting and cajoling before I was sure the hopeful hero was 100% committed, but by then I could have told him the security of the planet depended on him jumping off the roof of the museum, and he'd have happily run off to do it. Luckily for him, the use I needed to put him to was much less hazardous to his health, at least in the immediate moment. What the rest of his Company would do to him if they realized he'd been compromised— well, I expected he'd receive his just desserts for his horrible life decisions.

As I sauntered out of the house, the sun had just touched the rooftops of the buildings opposite. I kept walking until I was out of view and then dashed through the shadows back to the RV where Omen had brought it around the other side of the block.

As soon as I appeared with an okay signal to Omen, he revved the engine as if the vehicle were his motorcycle and not the sort of thing in which retirees took off to Florida. It rumbled on down the road, and Sorsha poked her head out of her bedroom.

"Did it go all right?" she asked.

I gave her a thumbs up. "Got him eating out of my hand in no time. He had an important bit of info to pass on to us, too. They're expecting an inspection from a couple of higher-ups tonight. They run most of their experiments overnight when there wouldn't be any patrons around if a creature escaped. Smaller staff during the day. In light of that news, I primed him to make our introductions tomorrow while the place is open."

I glanced in Omen's direction with a flicker of anxiety that the boss might not appreciate my taking that initiative, but his grunt of acknowledgment was approving enough. He might be the man of plans, but I had enough wits to contribute in that area too, didn't I? More than just a pretty face and a sweet voice, thank you very much.

As Sorsha had clearly trusted. There was no surprise tempering the relief that crossed her face. "Less than twenty-four hours until we get Snap out," she said. Then her exhilaration dimmed. "Assuming he's still there. Assuming they haven't been even more horrible to him than the other shadowkind."

There was definitely something wrong with my incubus inclinations that her fretting wrenched at me as much as it did. Well, our companions didn't need me until we made it to our next target. I went over to her.

She leaned back against the closed door with a dip of her head. "I know, there's no point in worrying about it when we won't find out until tomorrow anyway."

I brushed a few locks of her red hair back from her cheek and let my hand linger against her warm skin. "Of course you're worried about him. We know what these fiends are like." And as much as our mortal had woken up passions I never would have expected in the devourer, he'd woken up a tenderness in her that I wasn't sure she'd ever expected either. Something softer than the playful affection she'd offered me as she'd started to open up to my attentions, but why shouldn't it be?

She sucked in a breath and appeared to gather herself, resolve steadying her posture. Never did she look so gorgeous as when she was preparing for battle, and damn if I hadn't had plenty of opportunities to witness that in the past few weeks.

"They have no idea what hell they brought down on themselves when they took him." Her gaze darted to Omen in the driver's seat. "Maybe literally if it comes to that. And they'll deserve every bit of it." She shifted her attention back to me. "*You* know I didn't suggest a change in tactics just to avoid having to fight, right?"

Rarely had I wished quite so much that I could take a glimpse of the contents of her head without breaking her trust. Something about her powers had unnerved her since we'd come to Chicago, but I wasn't sure why now or what exactly was going through her mind.

It didn't matter, though. I could still answer truthfully, "Of course. I'd be less surprised by you giving up your '80s tunes than by you running from a brawl where you're needed, Miss Blaze. Woe betide anyone who messes with our mortal." I stroked my fingers down her jaw, resisting the urge to lean in to claim more than just a caress. "We'll get Snap back. These pricks don't stand a chance. And just imagine how overjoyed he's going to be to see you again."

"The feeling will be mutual," she said. From the momentary dreaminess that came into her eyes, she was picturing that reunion right now. If Snap could have seen her like this, he'd never have doubted her devotion enough to run off in the first place.

If she could accept all the monstrous parts of him—the jaws, the whole eviscerating of mortal souls bit—was it possible she might accept all that I was as well, without the lingering fear of how I might pry inside her mind or sway her to my whim? The one thing I knew above all else was I wouldn't want this woman coming to me on any terms other than her own. It wouldn't have been worth it to win her by magic, not when I'd had a taste of utterly unclouded yearning.

I shook that desire off like I had so many times in recent days. It was nothing but noise and clutter. But perhaps it wouldn't be such a bad thing if I presented a distraction in this moment that we'd both enjoy quite a lot?

The ring of her phone served as a cockblocker. I managed not to glower at it as she pulled it out of her pocket to check the number. Her jaw tightened.

"Vivi," she said, and to my surprise, hit the button to dismiss it.

"Did you two have another argument?" I asked.

"No, nothing like that. I just—with everything that's going on—" She made a face as if she couldn't find the words to express her reasoning. Then her phone pinged again, this time with a text alert.

As Sorsha read the message, she let out a disbelieving laugh. "Oh my God. I can't believe I forgot." Shaking her head, she looked up at me with a twist of her mouth. "She's wishing me a happy birthday."

My eyebrows jumped up. Then a smirk crossed my lips. I could give her something even better to take her mind off everything that troubled her. "It's your birthday today? Oh, Miss Blaze, you'd better believe I'm not letting that pass uncelebrated."

FIVE

Sorsha

"This really isn't necessary," I said as Ruse guided me down the street with his hand shielding my eyes.

"Oh, no, I think it is," the incubus said by my ear in his chocolatey voice. "Since you met us, we've lost you your apartment, your friends, and practically your life on multiple occasions. The least we can do is give you a proper birthday celebration to make up for it."

He said "we," but as far as I'd been able to tell, he'd been doing all the actual planning. While Omen had stayed at the wheel of the Everymobile, Ruse had confiscated the hellhound shifter's phone to do some research on the city, with Thorn looming over him offering not much more than uneasy humming sounds. Once the incubus had worked his charm on the last two guards we'd been able to track down, he'd given Omen directions that the hellhound shifter had accepted with a long-suffering sigh.

I wasn't sure how much of a birthday celebration I wanted in the first place. Normally I'd have gone out with Vivi and maybe a couple of the other younger Fund members to chow down and let loose, but the thought of the friends I'd left behind made my gut twist now. It was hard to say no to the incubus when he was charging full speed ahead with all his charming enthusiasm, though.

Now we were at our first destination, although I couldn't tell where the heck that was since Ruse had insisted on escorting me over to it blind.

"You could at least let me see where I'm going," I groused.

The incubus chuckled. "But making it a surprise is more fun."

"Maybe to some humans. I prefer a full view of my surroundings."

"Don't worry, Miss Blaze. I'm sure the lunk here is doing enough scanning for danger to protect us all."

The "lunk" let out a wordless grumble. "You look ridiculous," Thorn said. "I really don't see why—"

"Oh, the mortals around will understand how we're playing. We're fine. And... ta da!"

Ruse whipped his hand away from my eyes. For a few seconds, I could only blink at the mass of lights gleaming against the deepening evening across the face of a... tiny palace?

No, not an actual palace, but a restaurant in the shape of one. *Regal Thai* said the sign that was almost lost in the glow over the arched doorway.

A hint of curry drifted to my nose, and my mouth immediately started watering. Maybe a little celebrating wouldn't be such a bad thing if we were going to do it in there.

Ruse ushered me inside while he sang the restaurant's praises. "It's just opened—with a top chef who spent ten years running a four-star establishment in Bangkok—and as you can see, they've pulled out all the stops with the décor too."

The smells grew even more enticing when we stepped inside. I managed to keep my drool in my mouth, but it was a near thing. Columns painted in what I assumed were traditional Thai designs of gold, red, blue, and green stood in rows down the eating area, marking off sections filled with booths painted the same hues.

The hostess ushered us to an alcove where we settled onto seats padded with scarlet silk cushions. Sweet silver sand dollars, the fabric was so soft it felt like a crime to sink into it.

Our server gave Ruse's cap a bit of a side-eye, but he'd exchanged his typical baseball one for a subdued black number that gave the impression of religious significance. I couldn't have told you what religion or whether that religion even existed outside of the incubus's imagination, but it was convincing enough that the woman didn't comment.

Thorn rubbed his hands together in the fingerless leather gloves that hid his knuckles as he contemplated the menu. Ruse snatched it from under his gaze. "I believe Sorsha should do the ordering. She's the one who'll get the most satisfaction out of this meal, after all."

Just a glance over the offerings had me drooling all over again. "I can order us a perfect feast," I promised, and started making a mental list of all my favorites.

When the dishes arrived, they were delicious, but the best parts of my birthday dinner had nothing to do with the food. There was watching a warrior angel—excuse me, *wingéd*—attempt to manipulate the traditional spoon and fork between his massive fingers, and the look of awe Omen quickly tried to disguise when he lowered himself to tasting the pineapple fried rice. And what could be better than letting an incubus offer a morsel of fried banana while his hazelnut-brown eyes lingered on my face, as sweet as the dessert tasted?

By the time the last dishes had been cleared, my stomach felt as if it'd expanded to about ten times its previous size, but the ache was more satisfying than painful. I leaned against the silky cushions and patted my belly. "Okay, you did well, Ruse. Just as long as Omen's not going to roast me now that you've stuffed me."

"Don't tempt me," the hellhound shifter said, but the slant of his lips was *almost* a smile. We'd come a long way from the early days when he nearly had gotten my ass roasted taking on his tests.

Ruse grinned and pulled out a handful of cash that I was probably best off not asking the source of. "Better to support good food than the putz who contributed this," he said to me with a wink as he set the money on the tray with the bill. "And we're not done. You're going to peel yourself off that seat so I can stuff even more fun into this evening."

I groaned. "I'm not sure I can walk at this point."

Thorn glanced up with a hopeful expression, looking pleased to have found some way he could contribute to the party. He moved as if to scoop me up in his bulging arms. "I could convey you back to the vehicle, m'lady, if that would—"

I miraculously found the motivation to shove myself onto my feet after all. "No, no, that's totally okay, thank you all the same." As much as I enjoyed the feel of those muscles against me, I'd like to keep a little of my dignity.

I wouldn't have thought the night could get much better, no matter what the incubus had planned next, but my heart leapt when the RV pulled up at our next stop: a karaoke bar decked out with neon lights. Not that singing was my most favorite activity—it was the thought of watching my companions take a shot that had me grinning.

"We've got to take equal turns," I announced as I bounded to the Everymobile's door. "No one sits out, or you'll have a very sad birthday gal."

"We wouldn't want that, now would we?" Ruse said with amusement.

My demand worked on two thirds of my shadowkind crew. Omen plonked down in a corner of the private room Ruse had booked and refused to do anything with his mouth other than scowl. But it was pretty easy to ignore his lack of participation when I got to belt out "I Love Rock 'n' Roll" to Ruse's enthusiastic whooping and Thorn's applause, followed by the incubus strutting around with the microphone as he instructed us all, "Don't you forget about me."

The highlight, though, had to be Thorn gruffly but gamely giving "Sexual Healing" his best shot while he held the mic as if he expected to need to club someone with it at any moment. Believe me, you've never seen any performance to top that.

I nearly exploded holding in my laughter, but the flush that darkened the warrior's tan face made me want to offer him a little sexual healing to his ego after he'd finished. I wasn't quite so wanton as to get down and dirty in a karaoke booth, so I settled for planting a kiss on him long enough to bring a rumble into his chest before I went to pick my next song.

When our hour there was up, it turned out Ruse wasn't done with us yet. "One more stop," he said, with an affectionate tap of my chin. "But you can stay there as long as your feet will hold you up."

I understood what he meant when Omen parked the RV across the street from a dance club. A dance club with a sign in the window gleefully announcing that tonight was '80s night. The smile that sprang to my lips brought a bittersweet pang with it.

It was impossible to indulge in my love of all things '80s without thinking of the woman who'd passed on that love to me. Before I'd really had friends, when we'd moved from city to city so often I didn't have the chance to get close to anyone, my birthdays had been spent eating ice cream cake that Auntie Luna glamoured glittering sparkles onto and having private dance parties in the living room of whatever house or apartment she'd managed to arrange for us in that town.

She should have been here to celebrate more of those birthdays—to see the woman *I'd* become. The Company had stolen her in a way I could never get back.

Ruse obviously hadn't realized the connection I'd draw. His own smile faltered when he took in my expression, which must have shown a little of my sense of loss.

"It's great," I told him before he could think I was at all disappointed with his choice of activity. "It's perfect. Just brings back some memories."

I'd dance for Luna and amp myself up to strike tomorrow's blow against the organization who'd caused her death.

Thorn studied the building's front with obvious hesitation. "I don't know if it would be wisest for me to—"

"Nope, no backing out now—I want to see *all* of you on the dance floor." I grabbed his hand and tugged him toward the door. "If you're not sure what to do, just shuffle from side to side a little. No one's going to dare to even think anything judgemental when they take a look at you, I promise."

Omen stretched where he was still sitting in the driver's seat. "I'll come, but only to keep an eye on the rest of you fools."

"The fool is often the one who sees things most clearly," Ruse informed him with a smirk that practically twinkled, and led the way across the street.

It wasn't that late in the evening yet, but the place was already packed. I squeezed into the center of the dance floor and let the familiar music wind around me. Ruse kept pace, his hands grazing my waist, my hips, and my arms as he moved with my rhythm.

Thorn, well… Thorn did a very good job with his side-to-side shuffle. He even bobbed his head a little with the bass line. I gave him a thumbs up when I caught his eye, which I figured he deserved for the effort.

Putting in absolutely no effort at all was our defiant hellhound leader. After a few songs, I shimmied on over to where he'd staked out a spot by the wall between the pink-lit bar and the coat check.

"All right," I declared. "Onto the floor with you. You've been around umpteen centuries—you've got to have at least a few moves."

Omen didn't budge. "It might surprise you to hear this, but the fact that it's your birthday doesn't put you any more in charge than you were before."

"Maybe it does. How would you know? Shadowkind don't have birthdays, do they? Maybe it's a rule you just never heard about." I prodded his arm and then, with a rush of boldness fueled by the synth-pop beat, grabbed the front of his shirt, willing myself not to notice the sculpted muscles of his chest my fingers brushed or just how far I'd stepped into his aura of dominance.

The song playing over the speakers gave me the perfect lyrics to spin to my purpose. "Get up on your feet," I sang with a teasing edge, giving him a tug. "Yeah, step up, don't cheat. Boy, what, will you flee?"

Omen's eyes flashed, whether at being called a "boy," accused of turning tail, or simply because of the way I was manhandling him, I wasn't sure. He gave me a little shove backward—but he followed, to the fringes of the crowd.

Content with that victory, I did a spin and sidestep, daring him with a glance to keep up with me. His eyes stayed narrowed, but his body started to sway with the rhythm. When I swung closer to him again, he caught my elbow and added a little heft to my whirl. His touch left a tingling heat coursing over my skin.

This was playing with an entirely different sort of fire, but taunting flames had been one of my favorite pastimes. I sashayed around the hellhound shifter, trailing my fingers across his back, wanting to wake up more of the passion in him. Where he ended up aiming that passion, well, we'd just have to wait and find out, wouldn't we?

"Like what you see?" I asked with a waggle of my eyebrows, turning so he could check out the whole package. My gaze slid over the crowded floor—and caught on a glint of golden hair with a stutter of my pulse.

The jolt of emotion only gripped me for a second. It wasn't Snap—how could it have been?—but a young woman with gleaming curls twice as long as those the devourer had sported. But the momentary association had already sent me tumbling back through my memories to the night a few weeks ago when Ruse had set up an impromptu '80s dance party in my apartment living room.

Snap had joined us then, with a sinuous, unself-conscious style that had fit his godly beauty perfectly but would have looked awkward on anyone else I could think of. No one around me now could match it, that was for sure.

All these people dancing away with no clue or care what torment was being inflicted on all sorts of beings from beyond this realm...

A ripple of a much sharper emotion raced through me, propelled by my inner blaze. It surged up so suddenly I lost my breath, my skin seemed to crackle—and a couple dancing next to me leapt apart with a gasp and a scream as flames leapt across both their shirts.

My heart lurched, and my arms seared from wrists to elbows. Other dancers spotted the fire with more cries of alarm. As the girl sobbed in pain, Omen grabbed me with a solid arm around my waist.

"Let's get you cooled off," he muttered, his breath tickling over my cheek, and hauled me toward the exit.

"But—" I started to protest. It was my fault. I should do something. What, I didn't have the faintest idea—and one of the bouncers was running over with a fire extinguisher, already taking care of the catastrophe I'd almost sparked. As the hiss of escaping foam melded with the music, Omen dragged me out of the club.

The hellhound shifter didn't let go of me until he'd yanked me into the alley beside the building. He let me go so abruptly I stumbled into the wall. As I whipped around to face him, he rounded on me.

"What kind of crazy stunt were you trying to pull in there?"

I gaped at him. "I didn't do that on purpose. Do you think I'm a total idiot? I just—it just came out, out of the blue. I don't even know why." I'd barely even been aware of feeling anything like the kind of anger or panic that had riled up my powers before. "This is why I've been balking about using my powers. They keep doing crap like that."

Omen leaned in, his proximity and his dry sulphuric scent sending my pulse into overdrive all over again. As his gaze pinned me in place, an orange light flickered in his eyes. "If this is some stupid move to convince me not to push you to get your act sorted out…"

"Of course it's not," I snapped. "I didn't want to set random people on fire, for fuck's sake."

"Well, maybe if we hadn't been spending the whole night wasting time on inane mortal pursuits, you wouldn't have had to worry about that."

Was he kidding me? "None of this was my idea. If you have a problem with tonight, take it up with Ruse."

Omen let out a growl that left my skin quivering in ways somehow both eager and unnerving at the same time. "He was busting his ass to please *you*. You seem to think you can have us all wrapped around your finger and doing whatever you want, but what I say still goes here, and you're not shirking your part."

The quivering had brought back the sting in my arms. I wrenched them up to thrust my forearms between our faces. "I'm not shirking anything. I'm trying not to be the fucking *disaster* you keep calling me."

Even in the dim light, the reddened, blistered skin made my stomach lurch. I hadn't realized I'd burned myself quite that badly this time.

The sight seemed to stop Omen in his tracks too. He paused, taking in the burns. With surprising gentleness, he slipped his fingers around mine to lower and turn one arm and then the other, studying both sides.

"Why would you do this to yourself?" he demanded, but the accusatory note had left his voice. He sounded almost… concerned. About me? Let demons sing "Hallelujah."

"I don't know," I said. "It just keeps happening now. Maybe… Maybe I wasn't meant to wake up those powers after all."

"No. You don't get a gift like that unless you're meant to use it." He raised his head to peer into my eyes again. I wasn't sure what he was searching for. He might not have been quite as stunning as my original trio, but there was no denying he was a looker too—and doubly so when his icy mask fell away.

"Would have been nice if it came with an instruction manual, then," I heard myself saying, and miracle upon miracles, something that might have been a smile tugged at the hellhound shifter's lips.

He was still holding my hand. His thumb stroked across my knuckles in a firm caress. "We'll figure it out," he said. "Lucky you—you've got the expertise of three incredibly skilled shadowkind to help guide those shadowy powers. Four, when we get back our devourer tomorrow."

"Assuming I don't incinerate us all while we're trying to accomplish that."

"I don't think you need to worry about that."

I restrained a grimace. "Because you don't believe it could get that bad?"

"No, because I'm saying you don't have to try to use them. In fact, consider that a direct order. We're taking your 'charming' approach tomorrow, and if anyone ends up needing to be destroyed, you can leave that to Thorn and me."

"Oh." I hadn't expected him to give in that far, even after this incident. "Well, er, thank you."

His mouth twitched. That was definitely a smile now. "So polite when you get your way."

I did grimace at him then, but it didn't diminish the weird fondness that was rising up in me. "I mean it. I…"

I didn't know how to express my appreciation of this non-dickish side of him other than to push off the wall and brush my lips against his.

I couldn't tell you what kind of response I was anticipating. Omen's hand shot to my hair, and I started to brace myself for him to yank me away—but instead he jerked me closer, taking the kiss from a peck to a branding in an instant.

A fire I didn't mind at all flared all through my body at the hot crush of his mouth. I would have reached for him in turn if he hadn't ripped himself away a second later.

The orange glow faded from his eyes, but his tawny hair had become thoroughly mussed without my even touching it. His jaw clenched at a harsh angle. There was Mr. Ice again.

He swiveled on his heel as if we hadn't been twined like lovers just a moment ago. "We're gathering up the others and getting out of here. That's been enough commotion for one night. We've got a shoe museum to scuff up come tomorrow."

SIX

Sorsha

As we strolled up to the museum entrance all casual-like, Ruse offered me his elbow as if he were a Victorian gentleman. The effect might have worked better without that goofy baseball hat perched over his horns.

"M'lady?" he said in a near-perfect imitation of Thorn's somber voice.

I poked him with my own elbow instead. Thankfully, with some aloe and the healing powers that seemed to come with my ability to barbeque myself, the burns on my arms from last night were already pretty much gone. "Let's save the joking for *after* we've gotten Snap and all the little beasties out of here."

"Ah, you wound my heart," he teased, but his warm eyes took in the foyer with total alertness. For all his playful nature, he was taking this operation seriously.

There were actually a shocking number of patrons browsing the glass cases holding various styles of shoes. A tourist couple snapped photos while their two kids tugged on their shirts, looking like they'd rather be anywhere else. A young guy in sneakers so puffed up he could have pulled off an excellent Donald Duck imitation exclaimed about the history of sporting footwear to a girl with glazed eyes. Good luck hitting a home run on this date, dude.

We passed boots worn by soldiers—not anyone who'd seen much action, from their pristine condition—and slippers supposedly possessed by emperors, with an obscene amount of gold thread. The celebrity hall of fame boasted diamond-encrusted stilettos worn by some pop star on a recent tour. Did she still have working ankles after stomping around a stage with those things strapped to her feet? Or vision, for that matter? Their sparkle was blinding. Luna would have approved, anyway.

We came up on the inner sanctum, its doorway discreetly tucked down a little hall between *Put Those Soles To Work* and *A Watery Good Time*—boat shoes and diving fins for the win!

Ruse didn't give any noticeable signal, but he must have primed the guards he'd charmed well. A muscular woman in a tan uniform approached us with a respectful tip of her head.

"Everything's in order, sir," she said. "Let me know when you're ready to begin your final inspection."

Ruse put on an expression of total professionalism, but a hint of his roguish smirk showed through. I bit back a smile.

"I'd like to meet the other guards on duty out here first," he said. "Everyone except Mack, I already spoke with him. If you could escort them over to the vestibule one at a time, so we can keep this discreet…?"

"Absolutely, sir, absolutely."

"The vestibule?" I repeated with another twitch of my lips as she hustled off.

Ruse let his grin slip out. "One of my favorite words. Can't go wrong with a good vestibule. Now let's get over there so I can have the rest of this contingent singing our praises."

There were only two other guards patrolling the collection during the day—the Company must have thought it was unlikely anyone would risk an invasion while there were so many witnesses around. Of course, that fact worked in our favor now. And once we had what we needed, we could clear the innocent bystanders out of the place with a pull of the fire alarm before any real fires got started.

As long as we kept the situation totally under our control.

Ruse made great friends with the other two guards in a matter of minutes—easier when he only needed the influence to last for an hour or so now. As much as I hated these people who'd dedicated their lives to eradicating the shadowkind, watching the incubus work his charm was still a little unnerving. I couldn't completely suppress the faint but chilly quiver as I remembered the other shadowkind who'd toyed with me as a child using his own brand of persuasive voodoo.

But Luna had chased the jackass off, and I emerged unscathed, and Ruse wasn't anything like that prick. I couldn't imagine him harassing a child, even if he did let his sense of humor come out when it came to the real villains.

He watched the second guard amble off with a mischievous glint in his eyes. "I could have them marching through the halls singing Christmas carols if I wanted to."

I elbowed him again. "As much as I'd like to see that, it won't get Snap out. You can start your carol group once the cages are open."

"Oh, fine, you spoilsport."

He gave me a fond peck on the temple with a tenderness I hadn't been expecting. The incubus and I had gotten about as intimate as any two beings could be, but lately he'd had more standoffish days than not. Even after last night's celebrations, he hadn't made a single come-on to prompt an invitation into my bed.

I wasn't totally sure what was going on with that or with this brief PDA, but puzzling over it could wait for later too.

It was just five minutes to noon now. We sauntered back toward the door to the inner sanctum, and at twelve on the dot, Ruse knocked with a one, one-two, one beat. A signal he'd arranged with his new friend he'd been calling the Tiger King, the ropey-limbed guy who opened the door with a rasp of its lock a moment later. He wasn't wearing his own armor—Ruse had instructed him to shed it before he let us in.

"I haven't said a word to anyone," he murmured as he ushered us into a brightly lit, white-washed room packed with glass desks and computer equipment. Ruse gave a restrained shudder, now surrounded by the silver and iron embedded in the walls. "A couple of the guys might give you some trouble—I don't think they're in on the bigger picture. I'll bring them over like you asked, and you can decide—"

What he thought we were going to decide was lost with the click of the door at the other end of the room. I caught a faint whiff of chemicals with the breeze that emerged, my body tensing with the understanding that the lab—the experiments, the captives, *Snap*—lay that way, and then the two figures who'd appeared in the doorway gave a shout of startled concern.

"What are you doing—who are these people?" one demanded, striding forward. Both of them were drawing their guns. Okay, then. Plan: Peaceful Intrusion had just gone down the drain.

"A hand with your colleagues?" Ruse said to his charmed guard, his voice thrumming with renewed energy.

The guy leapt at the guard who'd barreled toward us with some kind of karate chop that sent the other man's gun flying from his hand. The third guard's gun hand jerked up—and Thorn leapt from the shadows in full brawny glory, smashing his fist down on the man's arm so forcefully I heard the crunch as the bone shattered.

The charmed guard had wrestled his other colleague to the ground and was now shoving off the guy's protective helmet. "It's for your own good!" he was declaring. "There's so much they haven't told us—so much we haven't seen…"

Thankfully, he seemed to be too busy wrenching at the ties on the guy's vest to see the next swing of Thorn's fist, which drove the warrior's crystalline knuckles deep into the underside of the third guard's jaw. The man slumped with a bloody gurgle, no de-armoring necessary.

I leapt in to help remove the last of the second guard's protective gear. The second he was free of silver and iron, Ruse's cajoling voice rolled out again.

"There's so much at stake—we have to hurry. These monsters are toxic, but they'll burn away if we drive them out into the sunlight. Quickly, quickly, before the people who wish to keep them here and protect them can stop us from doing what is right."

The appeal to the man's hatred of the shadowkind worked so well it made my stomach turn. He sprang to his feet and dashed for the door to the lab area without another word from Ruse. The sight of the mangled flesh on the body Thorn had dragged out of the way didn't exactly inspire my appetite either, but in that moment it wasn't hard to remember why my qualms about taking the bashing-their-skulls approach had worn thin.

We pushed into a larger room full of steel tables, shelves of lab equipment—and a full wall of silver-and-iron cages. There had to be at least thirty smaller ones and then several larger enclosures at the end. They all blazed with artificial light, thin shapes of shadow jittering in its glare.

Snap had to be in one of those big ones. "Open them up!" I said to the guards. "Come on, let's go!"

"You heard her," Ruse added with more voodoo in his tone. "All of the beasties out, and then we'll drive them into the daylight to vanquish them for good."

"We don't have the keys or the codes," the guard said with an anxious stammer, waving to the cages. The large ones had keycode panels—the small ones only little locks with holes.

Ruse spun on his original ally. "You said you had access."

"To the rooms! You didn't ask about the cages before."

He hadn't wanted too much detail in case one of the guards let our plans slip ahead of time. Shit.

Omen rippled out of the shadow. "Who has them, then?" he demanded, but a surge of fury and frustration seared up through me, burning all need for that question away.

"It doesn't matter," I said tightly, ignoring the prickle of pain that came with my power. "I can open them."

I grasped one of the little cages, fire flaring from my palm. The metal warped like the pop can melting the other night. With a yank, I opened a gaping hole in the interlocking bars.

With enough space now to pass by the toxic metals, the shadow within flitted past me without so much as a thank you. That was fine. I didn't need one. Gritting my teeth, I grabbed the next cage and poured more of my searing power into my grasp.

"I don't know if this is going to work on the big ones," I gritted out. Those had solid walls, no bars. I had no idea how thick the metal was there.

"The computers," Ruse said with a brisk gesture toward the other room. "Both of you, get on those devices and see what you can find. And if there's nothing useful there, then—"

The door to the largest cage in the row swung open with a mechanical whir. None of us had been standing anywhere near it. I wrenched the cage I'd been holding open and jerked around, my hands rising to face some new threat, but the figure that emerged was completely the opposite.

A tall, slim blur of shadow solidified into Snap's golden-haired, green-eyed form. He stared around him in a daze. My heart leapt, the impulse to engulf him in a hug ringing through me—but he was out now and there were still dozens more creatures to save. I settled for shooting him a smile of pure gratitude and reached for another cage.

Omen swiveled around, his body tensed, his lips curled as being surrounded by so much of the aversive metals was wearing on even his vast stores of strength. "Someone did that on purpose—someone knows we're here. They're watching us." His head snapped around toward the guards. "Is there another room?"

"I... don't think so," the first guy said uncertainly.

Thorn frowned. "This space doesn't seem large enough to account for the dimensions I charted from the outside. There should be more... there." He pointed to the wall beyond the lab tables where a fridge and a couple of large cabinets stood. Clenching his jaw, he flexed his muscles—and charged straight at the wall.

I'd seen the warrior smash through concrete and brick before, but never anything quite like this. As his massive form crashed through not just plaster and beams but plates of silver and iron too, his flesh hissed. Smoke puffed up from the wounds. A groan escaped him, but he'd managed to bash a big enough hole for us to stare through into one more white room with desks, computers, charts and maps on the walls, and two figures in lab coats staring at us wide-eyed.

"You should leave here now," one of them spat out, her hands clenched at her sides. "We've notified the rest of the Company. There'll be dozens of people here ready to fight you off in a minute."

She only cared about saving herself, then, not capturing us? Was that why they'd freed Snap—in the hopes we'd take just him and leave before we found them? I could respect that sense of self-preservation, but that didn't mean I was going to cater to it.

"They'll have the keys," I said, with a wild motion to the guards. "Grab them, help me get these open."

The two charmed men charged through the smashed opening to comply. As the scientists yelped in protest, I heaved another cage open by my own power. A few moments later, I had two helpers scrambling to shove keys into as many locks as they could. Which was a good thing, because the heat blazing from my hands was starting to rush through the rest of me with unsettling intensity.

"What's this about?" I heard Omen ask. I glanced over my shoulder just long enough to see that he'd stepped into the hidden room and was peering at a map that showed the whole world. "What do these markings indicate?"

One of the scientists sucked in a shaky breath. "We can't—we're not supposed to—"

"To hell with that. Ruse, make them *want* to tell me."

The incubus clapped his hands. "My good friend Justin, I need your services for a moment."

The Tiger King guard shoved his key ring toward me—I reined in my power as quickly as I could so I wouldn't melt the thing—and hurried to help his new favorite person. The ripping of fabric told me someone's protective badge had been removed from their clothing in a violent fashion. I checked the numbers on the keys, jammed another into a lock, and hurled the cage open as quickly as I could.

Snap had lingered in the room, watching us, his expression still hazy. I glanced at him and offered as much reassurance as I could manage. "We'll get out of here with you as soon as we have all the other shadowkind free. Just hang tight."

"Hang tight," he echoed in a faint but curious voice.

Figurative language wasn't the devourer's strong point. "Stay there," I said. "You'll be safer leaving the building with the rest of us."

Ruse had been speaking in cajoling tones to the scientist his guard had disarmed. Omen spoke up again, his voice on the verge of a snarl. "Explain the map to me. What do these blue marks mean?"

"Oh, those are the locations of Company facilities," the woman replied in a much chirpier voice than before. "And the red dots indicate areas where we've detected recent shadowkind activity. It helps us quickly identify patterns and decide who should investigate."

"They're not just here in the US. You've got polka dots all over Europe as well."

"Yes. That's where the Company started, as I understand it. The president of operations runs everything from over there."

Wait, the Company of Light was run from someplace overseas? We'd thought we'd have to go all the way to San Francisco to deal with the ultimate head honcho… I hadn't bargained for a trip across the ocean.

Neither had Omen, clearly. His voice came out with a sharp edge of sarcasm. "Wonderful. *Where* 'over there'?"

"I don't know. I've never talked to him directly. I got the impression he travels around a lot. With a mission this crucial, how could he stick to just one place?"

Omen swore under his breath. I wrenched open the last of the smaller cages. "Are you done with her yet?" I called. "We need these bigger ones opened."

The scientist sprang into action before Ruse even needed to prod her. He must have done quite a job on her with his hocus pocus.

"I can control the locks from the computers," she said, bending over a keyboard. Her colleague made an incoherent sound where he was sprawled on the floor—under the charmed guard, who'd taken a seat on the guy's back.

One cage door whined open, and then another. Thorn cleared his throat. He swung his hand toward a row of monitors mounted higher on the wall. "These TVs, they show what's real—what's happening now?"

This time Omen swore louder. Whatever he'd seen there, he didn't like it. "Unfortunately, yes. You, open those last two. Everyone else, let's go. We've got a lot more jackasses incoming from the Company than I'd like."

It was hard to tell whether all of the creatures had left or only retreated into the nearest shadows. "Out, out, all of you!" I called to them. More fire stirred in my chest at the thought of our enemies closing in on us.

Ruse hollered at his charmed allies. "Head out there in front of us— divert the attackers as well as you can!" He grabbed Snap's wrist, and they vanished into the shadows a moment later. They'd herd any creatures who'd lingered out, I had to assume.

The guards and the charmed scientist dashed for the entrance to the outer museum. I ran after them, Thorn and Omen alongside me. A fresh jab of guilt that I was the only one who couldn't slip away into the patches of darkness hit me.

"You can go," I said. "I might be able to dodge them."

"You didn't see the security footage," Omen muttered. "We're not leaving you behind, Disaster."

We burst out into the hall between the galleries. Shouts echoed off the walls as the onslaught of enemies shooed the visitors out of the museum. Footsteps pounded on the floors. Two squads of guards hurtled toward us from either side.

My pulse stuttered with a flare of adrenaline. I wasn't dying here, not after all this—not when I hadn't even gotten to welcome Snap back. Fuck these assholes and the shit-show they rode in on.

Without my even consciously willing it, flames whooshed up over three of the figures racing our way. I tuned out their shrieks with a wince. Thorn threw himself toward the other attackers at our right, and my gaze stopped on a broad window that looked out onto the street just behind them.

"Thorn!" I said. "We can crash right through."

There'd been a time not that long ago when Thorn would have been too caught up in his own combat focus to pay attention to any suggestions I made. We'd established more of a mutual having-of-each-other's-backs since then. He followed my motion, made a quick nod of agreement, and swung both fists to gash open two of the guards' throats. Then he snatched up a couple of steel-toed shoes and hurled them at more distant opponents with a kick hard enough to break their noses.

Omen was slashing through the wave of guards coming from the other direction, but there were a lot of them. They all wore their protective armor, and a few carried the laser-like whips that raked through the shadowkind's bodies in ways most other weapons couldn't.

I gritted my teeth, and another two of our attackers vanished into an explosion of flame, along with a couple of displays that let off a whiff of charred leather. My skin tingled, but I didn't seem to have caught fire myself this time. Having clearer, more deserving targets seemed to help keep that scalding energy focused away from my own body, thank tasseled toe shoes.

The smell of burning flesh wafted through the smoke. Bile rose in my throat, but I ignored my queasiness. I just had to get to the window, and we could be done with this.

Let them all burn. Why the hell shouldn't they, when that was what they wanted to do to every shadowkind in existence?

Thorn battered a couple more guards and hurled himself past them to the window I'd pointed out. The slam of his fist brought down a hail of broken glass. I sprinted toward it.

A movement by one of the display cabinets next to the window brought my fury back to the surface. I whipped my hand out, and a pair of ancient miner's boots turned into a fireball that careened toward—

A little boy. It was one of the tourists' kids: a scrap of a thing all round eyes and flyaway hair, who couldn't have been more than seven years old. My boot-iful fireball flashed toward him where he'd crouched trembling beside the case. A look of pure terror took him over, and a cry broke from my lips. *No, no.* I hadn't meant to—

Something in me heaved with that shock of panic, and the flaming boots veered just enough that they skimmed the boy's legs rather than roaring right into his face. He squealed, slapping at his jeans.

I'd still hurt him. What if he—

I didn't get to find out whether I had enough conscience left to make sure I hadn't flambéed a child. Thorn caught me around the waist and hauled me through the broken window. The fresh outside air slapped me in the face, waking me out of my conflicted anguish.

Get to the RV. Get to Snap. Then it would all be over.

I dashed alongside the warrior around the corner. Omen flickered in and out of view, loping along in his hellhound form, just long enough to show he was with us. As we came into view of the Everymobile, Ruse flung the door open for me and then dove back into the driver's seat. Thorn vaulted into the shadows around the steps, I threw myself up them and jerked the door shut behind me, and the RV lurched forward with a screech of its tires.

My heart was still thudding. I swayed over to the sofa and collapsed onto it. "Where's—where's Snap?" I managed to ask.

The devourer blinked into sight at the other end of the sofa in response to my question. Relief choked me. I found enough energy to shove myself over to him and dragged him into an embrace. His delicately dark scent, like a sunny meadow hiding mossy depths, filled my nose, fantastically familiar. It sent a pang through my heart.

"I'm so glad we got you out," I said, pulling back so I could look him in the face.

Snap regarded me, cocking his gorgeous head. "So am I," he said brightly. "It was very kind of you." His gaze slid from me to Ruse and then Thorn and Omen, who'd stepped out of the shadows on the other side of the table. "You all went to so much trouble to help me... Who *are* you?"

SEVEN

Sorsha

THORN BRANDISHED THE FRUIT LIKE IT WAS A SWORD. "*THIS* IS A BANANA."

Snap took the yellow crescent from him and brought it to his nose. He breathed in, and a dreamy smile crossed his lips. "It smells delicious. Is it for eating?"

Ruse chuckled where he was standing next to Thorn by the RV's kitchen, but the sound came out a bit strained. "Absolutely! You ate one of those when we made our first appearance in Sorsha's apartment. Jog any memories?"

Snap raised the banana to his lips, taking a bite right through the peel like he had that first time what felt like ages ago. Watching him, my breath caught in my throat. At this point, I didn't really expect a light of recognition to spark in his eyes—the way it *hadn't* after all the previous memory-jogging we'd attempted—but it was hard not to hope for it anyway.

He chewed thoughtfully, every motion like the shadowkind man I'd come to know and to care about a lot more than was typically my policy. Then he shook his head, regretful as always that he was letting us down in some way he didn't even understand. "I don't believe I've had one of these before. It's fantastic, though!"

My stomach clenched tighter into the ball it'd been forming since Snap had first shown that he had no recollection of who any of us were. He *was* the same person—monster—whatever. It was just as if months, possibly years, had been wiped from his mind.

As the devourer downed the rest of the banana with equal enthusiasm to the one he'd pilfered from my kitchen, Ruse and I exchanged a glance. His was as fraught as my inner state. Omen had been held prisoner by the Company for weeks longer than Snap had, and *his* memories hadn't been addled as far as any of us had noticed. But who knew what additional tortures the scientists might have devised? It could have been some new tactic in their scheme to infect all shadowkind with a deadly plague or an unintended side effect from one of their experiments.

I stroked Pickle's back where he'd hopped onto my lap and tried to ignore the growing gnawing of the question I least wanted to face: What if Snap had lost those memories for good? All the work he'd done toward taking down the Company... All the intimacies and affection we'd shared...

When I'd first met him, he hadn't even realized what physical pleasures his body was capable of. I wasn't sure he'd felt anything for me other than gratitude that I'd helped free him—and he didn't remember *that* now either. I was a total stranger who meant nothing to him, and there was no way to replicate the scenarios that had brought us to our unexpectedly passionate union.

"If our equine friends had left us behind some dish soap, I'd make you a bubble stew," Ruse joked. "You liked those last time too."

Snap's forked tongue flicked over his lips. "Is this 'bubble stew' as tasty as the banana?"

"Ah, no, it's not for eating—that one's just fun to look at. Little shiny globes floating through the air."

The devourer laughed. "For a place without magic, the mortal realm has a lot of marvelous things! So many different flavors and colors... So much vivid sound. This contraption that carries us great distances without us having to move our bodies at all." He patted the RV's table with an awed expression.

The Everymobile wasn't carrying us anywhere right now. We'd

parked it in the lot by the derelict strip mall while we sorted out what to do next. Omen stepped up to the table, his arms folded over his chest.

"It's unfortunate that you don't remember anything about our cause or the rest, but we do have to get on with that mission. Our enemies know we're in Chicago now. When I first sought you out in the shadow realm, you agreed to help me investigate the disappearances of our people. Now we know who's behind it—the same people who locked you up. Are you going to stick with us and make them pay?"

A flicker of uneasiness passed through Snap's expression and vanished just as quickly. I hadn't been able to tell whether he remembered all the way back to his first devouring, the one that had made him so horrified with himself that he'd sworn never to use that power again. Hints like that suggested he might, but he hadn't mentioned it.

"Of course," he said now in his brightly eager voice. "The way those mortals treated the shadowkind in that place—it was awful. So much pain…" A shudder rippled through his slim frame.

I had to resist the urge to take his hand. Would the gesture comfort him from a woman he probably associated more with the mortal villains who'd captured him than his shadowkind comrades? A quiver of anger shot through the ball of my stomach.

Snap recovered himself with a set of his shoulders. "They should be stopped. I'll do my best to help with that. I don't know what I can tell you right now. With all the energy of the metals in that place, I couldn't bring out any of my powers to test their equipment."

"That's all right," Omen said, so brusquely I'd have liked to punch him. Too bad I was on the other side of the table with a tiny dragon on my lap. "I'll let you know when you can pitch in." He turned to take in the rest of us. "So. We have an even larger challenge than we anticipated ahead of us. It appears the Company of Light has been doing their wretched work not only all across this country but on the other side of the ocean as well."

"So bloody many of them," Thorn muttered.

"Exactly." Omen paused. "I think our mortal disaster here might have had the right idea in our past operations, recruiting whatever help we could get. I never expected us to be confronting an organization this widespread, and I don't think the five of us will be enough to shut them down once and for all. More skills, more insight, and simply more beings in play will allow us to put together a more complex strategy. We need to seek out more allies. We managed it before—I'll be optimistic and assume we can find others willing to lend a hand at least briefly."

I should have been gratified that he was admitting out loud that I'd been right about something. He'd groused enough about my ideas while I was putting them forward before. But any pleasure I might have gotten from his acknowledgement was swallowed up by the overwhelming sense of all those pockets of shadowkind-torturing psychos spread out across the planet. So many fucking mortals so determined to ruin everything in their path—maiming and killing and whatever they'd done to Snap—

There was so much they needed to pay for. And sweet shredded seashores, did I want to be there delivering that payback.

The fire inside me roared from a quiver to a blaze in an instant. A burning sensation flared through my limbs—and Pickle squeaked, flinching so violently he tumbled off my lap onto the sofa cushions.

My heart lurched. My palms were prickling with the heat that must have burst from them. Pickle nuzzled his side—oh, God, were his shiny green scales faintly singed?

"Hey," I said softly, reaching out to the little creature in the hopes of offering some sort of apology. He leapt back with a widening of his beady eyes. My throat constricted. "Pickle?"

He stared at me, his head weaving from side to side on his slender neck, and then he sprang off the sofa-bench completely and scurried down the hall toward the bedrooms.

Tightly as my stomach was balled, the bottom still managed to drop out of it. He'd been *scared* of me.

My hands clenched at my sides. Ruse and Thorn had been talking, sharing their ideas about who we might turn to for assistance first, but when I glanced up, Omen's gaze was trained on me, his ice-blue eyes as piercing as ever.

"They might at least contribute a few of their underlings," Ruse finished. "That Talon gent didn't seem like the type to want to leave his home base unsupervised for long."

Omen nodded. "Yes, we'll speak to him again and see if he's willing to offer anything." He made a beckoning gesture toward me. "Disaster, a word outside? You two, have another go at stirring loose a memory or two in our devourer's head."

Oh, this was obviously going to be a laugh riot of a conversation. Did the RV have an escape chute?

Even if it did, I wasn't going to give our leader the satisfaction of thinking he'd intimidated me into pulling a runner. I'd managed to coax the big bad hellhound onto the dance floor last night. I'd kissed him and survived to tell the tale.

And there wasn't anything he could say to me that would feel any worse than what was already going through my head.

Thorn shot me a look of mild concern, but I gave his arm a light squeeze in reassurance as I passed him. "Is this a super-secret meeting for discussing mortal strategies?" I said to Omen, following him out in the cooling evening air.

The hellhound shifter made a point of not only shutting the door but also stalking across the lot to give us distance as well. With more than a little trepidation, I walked after him to where he came to a stop outside a hair salon. Its broad front window was plastered with posters of individuals who, based on their 'dos, needed to re-evaluate their personal style. A long-squashed shampoo bottle lying on the concrete walk outside gave off a soured honeysuckle scent. Way to set the mood.

I crossed my arms in imitation of Omen's typical authoritarian stance. "What's up? Was I not joyful enough that you finally recognized my genius?"

Omen rolled his eyes. "I'm just glad not to have you crowing about how you told me so."

"Oh, don't worry, that might come later. I'm waiting for my moment."

"Sorsha."

Something about the way he said my name, crisp and solemn, put a cap on my snark. When did he *ever* address me by my name and not "mortal" or "Disaster" or when he was having a particularly uncreative day, "you"? A chill tickled over my skin, but honestly, that was better than the flames I couldn't seem to stop from leaking out.

"What?" I said, serious now. "I'm listening."

He studied me for a little longer with a cool gaze incisive enough to cut into my skull. "You really are losing your handle on your powers, aren't you? More than you've let on. It's not just when you're trying to use them. Something happened that startled your dragon just now, didn't it?"

I couldn't stop the cross of my arms from turning into hugging myself as I dredged up the answer. "I didn't just startle him. I burned him—I hurt him. And no, I didn't mean to do anything at all. I've tried to tell you a bajillion times already. There's more fire in me than I know what to do with or how to contain, and sometimes it just bursts out. Even when I *am* fighting, it's getting ahead of me."

I hesitated, and Omen's gaze sharpened. "What?"

"I almost fried a little kid in the museum," I said, the words scraping my throat raw on the way up.

"That was a reaction in the middle of a battle. You can't expect to be able to take the same care there."

Oh, now he thought it was time to go easy on me? I raised my eyebrows at him. "Would you let yourself off the hook for messing up your control like that?"

But the shifter stayed impervious. "I wouldn't be worrying about which mortals I took down, whatever their age, to begin with."

"You know that's not what I meant." I let out a rough sigh. "I realize you find it hard to believe that I could have enough power to be a danger to anyone when I don't mean to be. You probably still find it hard to believe that any mortal has powers at all. But I do have them, and—I don't like the way it feels now. It isn't a wonderous talent I can bend to my will. Sometimes the flames come out of nowhere, and I can't shake the impression that they could totally explode. That I could flatten the whole city if I didn't catch the fire in time."

Omen didn't retract his previous skepticism, but at least he didn't argue with me. "It's been hurting you when you're using it—how often?"

"Most of the time, lately. And when I'm not, when it has those surges, too. But at least I heal from the burns quickly." I rubbed my forearms where the skin had been blistered last night but was now only faintly pink. "That kid wouldn't have recovered. Pickle wouldn't if I burned him badly enough."

The hellhound shifter sucked in a breath. He started to pace the width of the walkway, his expression intent. "I don't like it," he said finally. "We have too much at stake to bring a destructive wild card into the mix."

My back stiffened. "If you're going to try to tell me to take a hike after all this—"

He held up his hand. "Cool your jets, Disaster. I pushed you into bringing this power out; I can take responsibility for that. And you still contribute more to the cause than I can dismiss. But before these unusual reactions take hold any further, I think we should see if you can get a handle on them so that you can use them to destroy our enemies and not yourself. For that, we need to understand them. Understand you and what you are. Do you know where you were supposedly born?"

That wasn't the direction I'd expected this conversation to go. "I'm not sure. I was three when Luna escaped with me, and she refused to tell me very much—she didn't want me going back there. I think she figured the hunters who murdered my parents might still be looking for me. But I remember a few things. We might be able to figure it out."

"Good. Then we can add that to our list of goals alongside building our base of allies. There must be someone in that place who'd know more about this fae woman and your supposed parents, and therefore how you came to be. If we're going to get answers, I have to imagine they start there."

"Okay." A tingle shot through me, both exhilarated and uneasy at the thought of digging into my history. Even if I got answers, that didn't mean I was going to like them.

"I'm glad we're agreed," Omen said in a slightly wry tone. He'd actually been pretty... considerate about the whole thing. And that wasn't a word I'd ever thought I'd associate with the hellhound shifter, at least not when it came to his attitude toward me. But we had been through a lot, hadn't we? We'd found a pretty good rhythm for working together until my powers had started turning me into even more of a pyromaniac.

My gaze had drifted to his mouth: those perfect Cupid's bow lips. The lips that had branded mine with a heat that still made my knees weak remembering it.

He was turning away to head back to the Everymobile. "Omen," I said quickly. "About last night outside the club—"

His gaze shot back to me with a flash of orange fire that didn't look at all welcoming. Maybe that'd been designed to cut me off, but he should know by now that keeping my mouth shut wasn't a particular skill of mine.

"I take it you want to pretend it never happened," I went on.

He spun the rest of the way to face me again. His eyes had settled back into their usual cool hue, but a heat wafted over me that I was pretty sure had come from his well-built body. If he wanted me to believe he had no emotions at all about our split-second encounter, he was being about as convincing as a dog drooling over a forbidden bone.

Except I wasn't forbidden, definitely not where boning was concerned. So what exactly was the issue?

"Do you have any alternate suggestions?" he asked. "Because if you think you're going to reel me in like you somehow did my associates, you can incinerate that idea. Even if anything *did* happen between us—which it won't—it isn't going to buy you any special favors."

I blinked. "Hold on. Why would you figure I was looking for favors, special or otherwise?"

He shrugged. "You do seem to be making a habit of seducing some rather powerful shadowkind. Do you really need one more just for the hell of it?"

He was lucky I didn't incinerate *him* for what he was implying. I glowered at him. "I didn't kiss you—or do all the *many* things I've done with the others—for some kind of personal gain, unless you count the gaining of fine times between the sheets. It isn't part of any plan. It just… happened. And I liked that it happened, so I didn't see any reason to stop more happening when the occasion arose. This situation is already crazy enough. Is there really something wrong with taking part of that craziness in an enjoyable direction now and then?"

"I suppose not. What was last night about, then?"

"I don't know. Sometimes you're appealing in a very annoying way. Sorry if that bothers you. I kissed you because I wanted to, plain and simple. If you're looking for a huge conspiracy, you're not going to find it there. But if it was so distasteful to you, I'm sure I can restrain myself in the future. As you've pointed out, I have plenty of other supernatural beings to kiss if the urge strikes."

Omen's mouth twitched. There I went, staring at those damn lips again. When I met his eyes instead, a hint of their orange glow had come back.

"I didn't say it was distasteful," he said, in a carefully restrained voice that spoke of so many emotions he might be tamping down. "But if you're concerned about how many blazes you set off, perhaps you should pick your dance partners more carefully. Let's have it end where we left it last night."

"Fine," I said. I definitely wasn't disappointed about that. All right, all right, maybe a teensy weensy bit. "I just thought we should clear the air. Look! Clear as crystal. Now back to our regularly scheduled programming."

That twitch of his mouth was in the direction of a smile. And maybe it would have gotten all the way there if Ruse hadn't hurried over to us from the RV right then. The fire in Omen's eyes went out as swiftly as a doused campfire.

"No luck with Snap?" he said, taking in the incubus's expression.

"Not exactly." Ruse ran a hand through his already rumpled hair. "I didn't want to say this in front of him in case it made things worse."

My pulse hiccupped. Was there more wrong with Snap beyond just his memory?

Ruse looked at me and then back at Omen. "I took as good a read as I could on his inner state. It's not easy picking up emotions and the rest from shadowkind—most of us keep our minds too guarded. But you know our devourer is pretty much an open book. I think… I think he's in there. All of him. The Company jackasses didn't burn those memories out of them. He's just buried them so deep even he can't dredge them up again, for whatever reason."

"Why would he do that?" I asked.

"I don't know. Maybe he was trying to pull his consciousness away from the torment and he overshot by a couple of miles?" Ruse let out a short laugh that had no real humor in it. "In essence, you could say he devoured himself."

EIGHT

Thorn

If Talon's fidgety comrade didn't stop sneering at Sorsha, I was going to have to apply my fist to his skull and enjoy the billow of his essence escaping. Our lady wouldn't like it, but I was starting to feel it'd be worth weathering her disappointment.

The syndicate boss himself wasn't cultivating my good favor either. He'd grimaced and sighed through Omen's explanation of our need, and now he was working his jaw in thought with his basilisk eyes still hidden behind those dark-paned glasses.

You couldn't trust a being who wouldn't look you in the eyes—even if it was a look that could kill. He'd have been thinking rather highly of himself if he believed he could fell any of us shadowkind in attendance.

But of course one of our number was not shadowkind and thus not of the same bodily durability. And Jinx—who, based on his frenetic movements and the quivers of energy that rippled off him with a faint lemony tang, I'd become increasingly sure was a poltergeist—absolutely delighted in reminding us of that.

"Not sure what you need allies like us for when you've got this one already," he mocked, waving his hand toward Sorsha. "Interesting strategy, bringing a human along to fight enemies who can topple even higher shadowkind. Makes me wonder what other screws you've got loose up there."

Now he'd managed to insult both my commander and my lady in one go. We could discover how amusing he'd find the situation when he was leaking smoke all over his clubhouse.

I took a step forward, my hand clenching, and Sorsha caught my arm. She gave me a little smile with a sharpness I suspected was intended for the other shadowkind. "Leave him be. He doesn't know how much he doesn't know."

Jinx squirmed at the affront to his intelligence and shut his mouth, which satisfied me enough for the moment, even if it was mostly because of the stern glance Talon sent his way. Omen might not be terribly pleased if I thrashed one of our potential allies in the middle of negotiations either.

Or perhaps we were already at the end of those negotiations. The basilisk turned back to us, his mouth still twisted at a not-at-all-promising angle.

"I hear your concerns," he said. "But I've already offered plenty of assistance within the city bounds. My base of power is here—I can't say I have any resources on the other side of the ocean. I'm not about to leave my operations here untended, and I'm hardly going to ask even the employees I can spare to traipse off across the world on some potentially suicidal quest."

"*Not* tackling the Company of Light as soon as we're able to could be even more suicidal," Omen said, but I could tell from the weary edge to his tone that he was even less optimistic now than he'd been going into this place.

When he'd first brought us together, my old associate had said the four of us would be enough to see through his mission, that the shadowkind who refused to recognize the impending catastrophe would only slow us down. The urge gripped me to say we didn't need any of these buffoons, that we should continue as we had been after all. Suggesting otherwise had made me uneasy to begin with, as much as Sorsha had proven her case before. I'd chosen to follow Omen on this path because I trusted he would lead us well.

And I knew far too well the consequences of questioning one's superiors. It was because I'd gone to seek out another possible solution to the conflict—against the orders of the wingéd generals—that I hadn't been there for the final slaughter in the wars that had demolished my wingéd brethren. I'd chased a hope of a better way rather than standing by my comrades, and they had died without me standing by them while I'd lived with fewer scars than I'd deserved. If I'd been dedicated enough to stay the course, would it have gone differently?

I'd thought that if this time I devoted myself completely to a figure smart and strong enough to be worthy of that faith, it would be my redemption. But this course had turned out to be much more complicated than I'd expected.

"You could at least tell your underlings about the problem and see if any of them would be willing to pitch in without being ordered to," Sorsha said. "Or is your grip on your operations so shaky you couldn't spare even a few shadowkind to make sure you don't all end up in cages?"

"*No one* is going to cage me," Talon retorted, a threatening hint of a hiss creeping into his voice. "You can make your own invitations. I have better things to do than cater to your crusade."

"Fine," Omen said flatly. "Can you at least answer one question before we leave you to your oh-so-important business? I hear the Highest were making inquiries with the mortal-side shadowkind some twenty or thirty years ago, looking for a powerful and potentially dangerous being. Possibly by the name of Jasper or Garnet or similar? Did you catch wind of any of that?"

Talon frowned as he appeared to consider. "That does ring a bell of some sort. I remember the word going out... I seem to have gotten the impression the search was mostly to the south."

"Do you remember if you heard that the being was apprehended?"

"No, nothing more after the initial questioning. What do you want with that one anyway?"

Omen's lips curled with the subtlest of sneers. "I'm wondering if he'd have the balls to go up against a conglomerate of mortals, unlike some others I won't mention."

He turned on his heel and stalked out without another word. Sorsha and I followed, my lady shooting a derisive glare Talon's way for good measure. As we headed back to the vehicle where Ruse had stayed with our befuddled Snap, she gave herself a little shake as if to release the tension of the encounter, the sunlight flashing in her lovely hair.

The stresses of our mission had appeared to weigh on our lady more than usual these last few days, even before we'd discovered the devourer's unexpected predicament. I hadn't wanted to impinge on her honor by revealing that I'd noticed when she clearly was attempting to master those concerns on her own. Still, I was glad that she'd seemed more settled since her talk with Omen earlier today.

"Who—or what—is the Highest?" she asked him now.

"The oldest of the shadowkind," he replied. "Some say they were the first ones, the only ones that have existed from the beginning. There aren't many of them, and they don't have much to do with the rest of us, generally speaking. They only intervene from time to time when they get the idea someone's making quite a bit more trouble than they'd prefer."

"I've never even encountered one of the Highest," I said. We all knew, perhaps by some instinct, that it was best not to venture too far into the deepest depths of our natural realm. The ancient beings there preferred not to be disturbed.

"And you should be glad for it," the hellhound shifter said darkly.

Sorsha hummed to herself. "So why are you really interested in this shadowkind they were looking for?"

"Essentially the same reason I gave that trumped up lizard. If the Highest take issue with this being's behavior, he's got to be something of a rebel. Maybe that means he won't care about our cause either, but at the very least, I doubt he'd beg off out of fear of disrupting the status quo." Omen let out a huff of breath. "As we've witnessed yet again, most of our kind are useless when it comes to paying attention to anything other than their own self-interest."

"We found allies before," Sorsha insisted. "There'll have to be others who'll care enough."

She always challenged him so easily, without the slightest fear. And she *had* been right. I didn't know if we'd have managed to destroy the main facility in that last city without the assistance she'd worked to obtain, often against Omen's direct command.

I hadn't tended to question my own capacity for bravery, but this mortal lady sometimes put me to shame. Watching her was making me start to wonder if the problem all those centuries ago hadn't been that I'd ventured to question what we were doing but that more of my comrades *hadn't* questioned it. Which I supposed was why when I opened my mouth, the remark that fell most easily from my lips was, "I believe there are potential allies out there, as difficult as it may be to find them."

Omen gave me a sideways glance as if in askance, but he'd clearly come around to agreeing with our lady's perspective on this matter, even if he still muttered about it now and then. He didn't bother to argue. "Then it's a good thing we'll have plenty of time to ask around while we're dealing with our diversion. We need to work out exactly where we're going next to unravel your mysterious history, Disaster. Let's hope it won't be too catastrophic."

Sorsha made a face at him as she climbed onto the RV. "You obviously wouldn't have any frame of reference for this, but a three-year-old human's memories are pretty vague. We can go over the bits and pieces I do remember, and—"

She stopped in her tracks in the space between the driver's seat and the living area. Ruse had just emerged from the shadows farther down the hall, Snap popping into view behind him, but Sorsha wasn't looking at them.

I peered over her shoulder to observe three pairs of shoes lined up on the floor beside the cupboards. From their size and their neon hues, I guessed they were possessions the unicorn shifter had left behind.

I was about to ask Sorsha what had disturbed her about them when two of those shoes leapt up in the air and switched places. Then three of them started hopping around in a little dance. They flipped over each other, smacked the floor in a rhythmic beat, and suddenly all six of them flew up two at a time to stack into a wobbly tower. It held, swaying, for a few seconds before the shoes tumbled back to the ground.

A figure about the size of a partly-grown human child blinked into view beside them, spiky orange hair sticking up from her rounded head and skinny arms flung out to grab at the shoes. Her voice came out thin and squeaky. "Darn it, darn it. Never get the balance right."

She glanced up at us—at Sorsha, mostly—and gave a grin that stretched far into her cheeks. "I hope you were a little entertained by the trick anyway."

"Um," Sorsha said, apparently at a loss for words.

I wasn't going to brandish my fists at a figure this pathetic, but security was my job. Stepping up beside my lady, I cleared my throat. "Who are you, and what are you doing on our vehicle?"

"Oh, I—" The figure fumbled with the shoes and then shoved them all into one of the cupboards with an exaggerated sigh of resignation. She sprang up to her full height, which only brought her about level with Sorsha's waist. Still grinning, she gave us both a brisk salute. "Antic, at your service. Here to help in whatever ways I can."

"An imp," Omen said from behind me with a note of distaste.

Ugh. Imps were mischief-makers, always seeking human attention in the most obnoxious ways. Since they liked to scamper around mortal-side and I'd rarely crossed the divide in centuries, I'd thankfully had few dealings with them.

"You didn't entirely answer the second question," I said. "Why are you here? Our human doesn't need your version of 'entertaining'."

The imp raised her pointed chin. "I did answer. I'm here to help. You're looking for help, aren't you? I heard you talking about it. And you obviously know what you're doing, the way you marched into that awful room where they had me shut up behind bars. If you're going to stick it to more of *those* kinds of humans, count me totally on board."

"I don't think your sort of helping is exactly—" Omen started.

Sorsha held up her hand. "Wait a second. Weren't you just complaining about how few shadowkind want to get their hands dirty? She just proved she can move things around invisibly, even if her shoe towers need a little work in the steadiness department. There's got to be *some* way she could contribute."

Ruse had ambled closer. He peered down at the little being with a smirk. "I don't get any sense that she has motives beyond what she's offering."

"The question is whether she'll contribute more than she'll make us long for a quick sword to the chest," Omen said, echoing my own reservations.

"Hush, you," the imp said, as if she wasn't speaking to a hellhound shifter more than twice her size and approximately a thousand times more powerful than she was. She bounded up onto the sofa and sat there with her scrawny legs dangling. "The human wants me to stay, and that's good enough for me."

"No one asked your opinion," Omen muttered. "Really, Disaster?"

Sorsha gave him a firm look. "Really. You can't moan about not getting enough help and then moan that the help we get isn't in the perfect package." She turned back to the imp. "Thank you. *I* really appreciate it."

The imp beamed at her. "How are we sticking it to 'em first?"

Sorsha sank down on the sofa across from her. "Well, we need to figure out where we're going next—for a sort of side mission. Maybe you can even help with that. I'll mention all the things I can remember about the place, and if it sounds like anywhere any of you have been mortal-side, speak up."

As I propped myself against the counter by the sink, keeping one eye on the imp in case she turned out to have more malicious intentions—you could never be too sure—Sorsha rubbed her mouth.

"All right. There was someplace we got ice cream at least a couple of times—there was always a line-up and I'd get impatient, and it had a bright red sign. I remember things about the inside of our house, but that won't help anything. Um… there was a park near the house, with a slide my mom said was too tall for me to go on yet. Some kind of festival we went to with lots of music, in the summer I think—my hair got all sweaty. And there was a big bridge I loved… something about it at night, like smoke rising across the sky?" She knit her brow. "I know that's all incredibly vague. I do have the box with the note my parents left me, too."

She reached for her purse, but Omen brushed past me to touch her shoulder. "Hold on. Say what you did about the bridge again. As much as you can remember."

Sorsha frowned in concentration. "It was definitely big—although hard to say how much of that impression is relative to when I was a preschooler. I only remember it when it was dark. Maybe not full night but evening. And that smokiness moving toward the sky—"

"That." His fingers tightened where he was gripping her. "There's a glamour on your memory. I can feel it coming through when you try to verbalize the scene. Your fae must have put it there."

"Why would Luna have messed with *that* memory?"

"That's the question, isn't it? Maybe to make sure you didn't go back. All the more reason I should break it. A nearly twenty-five-year-old bit of fae flim-flam shouldn't be too difficult to dispel. Keep focusing on that image."

Sorsha tensed. "What are you going to do? Is this some kind of mind-reading trick you never mentioned?"

Omen shook his head. "Don't worry, Disaster. I've got no interest in unraveling the entire contents of your head. I can simply sense the magic there when you're concentrating on the information it's clouding. And I can break it, if you'll let me."

She exhaled slowly. "All right then."

Her eyes closed as she must have brought the memory back up, and Omen's did too. The rest of us watched silently—even the damned imp, though she was squirming in excited anticipation.

Our commander's hand gave a little tug on Sorsha's shoulder, and her eyes widened. Then she laughed. "It wasn't smoke. It was *bats*. A whole cloud of them, soaring up past the bridge."

Ruse snapped his fingers. "I know where that is. It figures you'd have come from a city with plenty of shadowkind." He nudged the devourer. "Sounds like we're heading down to Austin."

"Austin," Sorsha repeated as if trying out the word. She smiled, but hesitantly. Maybe wondering the same thing I was.

If her fae guardian had taken steps to meddle with that memory, what else might she have hidden in our lady's mind?

NINE

Sorsha

It was going to be a long drive from Chicago to Austin, so I figured I might as well find something useful to do with the time. Only because I was such a hard worker, and not at all to distract myself from the fact that the woman who'd raised me had distorted my memories without telling me, of course.

Why had Luna been so adamant that I never return to the city of my birth? She'd never given me reasons, just obscured that key image so I had no choice, no way of knowing where to go. Would she *ever* have talked about it with me if she'd lived to see me all the way to adulthood, or had she planned to take that secret to her grave regardless?

I couldn't ask her now, and I didn't think Omen would appreciate it if I asked him to listen to my entire life story up until age sixteen to find out if she'd glamoured other blanks into my memories. So I just wouldn't think about it. Piece of cake. Ha.

I wasn't really looking forward to the call I was about to make either. Vivi had told me that Ellen was home from the hospital, so I should be able to contact her at her regular number, but that didn't mean the co-leader of my local branch of the Shadowkind Defense

Fund would be happy to hear from me. Being attacked by Company goons as a warning would tend to sour a person to the gal who'd drawn that attention in the first place.

But Ellen had gone to the trouble of reaching out to me when she'd realized I was in danger, even while she was still in the hospital. I couldn't be totally out of my mind to think she might help us again.

I pulled my legs up where I'd tucked myself into one corner of the sofa-bench and brought my phone to my ear. At the other side of the sofa, Snap was examining a coffee mug Ruse had handed him in the game of Let's See If You Remember This that had been going on without any wins all day. Rather than remind myself of the innocent bemusement so often in the devourer's expression now, I gazed out the window. The lights along the freeway flashed by through the thickening dusk.

To my relief, Ellen picked up on the second ring. "Hello?" she said with an unusual tentativeness that made me wince inwardly.

"Hey, Ellen," I said, suddenly tentative myself. "It's Sorsha. I'm sorry I haven't checked in on you sooner—hell, I'm sorry about all of it. Things have gotten pretty... crazy."

Understatement of the century.

Ellen made a dismissive noise. "I know you hadn't expected any of us to get hurt. This group you've clashed with—they're obviously much more of a menace than we've dealt with before. *None* of us expected that." She paused. "Did you get my warning about Leland in time? He didn't turn up at the last meeting. I'm not sure if he's sided with this Company of Light completely now."

I *hadn't* gotten her warning soon enough—not in time to save us from getting T-boned by an armored truck, anyway. And my ex-FWB hadn't shown up because he must still be staked out in his townhouse wearing boxers on his head and drinking cold, stale coffee as Ruse had instructed him to do for his "protection." It seemed better not to mention either of those facts, the former for Ellen's benefit and the latter for mine.

"Who knows, with him?" I said with a stilted chuckle. "I really appreciate you looking out for me, especially considering the state you were in. Are you doing okay?"

"Oh, yes, no permanent damage here. I'm made of stronger stuff than those criminals realized."

A sporadic crackling sound carried from the background. Was that... popcorn popping? A smile tugged at my lips despite my guilt. If Ellen was experimenting with popcorn flavors again, she couldn't be feeling too bad.

Lord only knew when I'd get to sample any of her new combos again. When would I be welcome at another Fund meeting? Assuming I made it back home in the first place...

I shook off the gloom of that thought and focused on my main objective. "About those criminals—we've found out that their operations are spread out much farther than we'd guessed: across the country and even overseas. I know a lot of the Fund members aren't feeling all that friendly toward me or that cause right now, but if *any* of you would be willing to lend a hand even in some teeny tiny way... We'd make sure you stayed out of the line of fire, of course."

The moment the words came out of my mouth, I felt like a shit heel. She'd just been beaten to bits, and here I was suggesting she might do me another favor. What had I been thinking when I'd come up with this ridiculous plan?

Well, I'd been thinking that Ellen was just about the only ally with much in the way of resources that I still had that I could call on, but that didn't make it an act of compassionate genius.

Ellen was silent for a moment. I was debating asking Ruse if he could take a break from shoving assorted paraphernalia in front of Snap to charm the Fund leader into forgetting I'd ever brought up the subject when she finally cleared her throat. "Something needs to be done about them. I don't know what we'd be able to offer on our end, but—I'll give it some thought and make some discreet inquiries."

"*Very* discreet," I emphasized. "I don't want anything else happening to you. Don't—don't mention the Company or take any action against them, not right now. Just let me know when you know if you've got anyone who still *wants* to take action, and I'll work out the details from there."

Even with that cautioning and Ellen's willingness, I ended the call with a lump of nausea in my stomach.

Ruse was now dipping his fingers into a cup of water and

sprinkling droplets over Snap's head. "There was this time it started raining while we were scouting out one of the disappearances, and you were so surprised you stayed right in it instead of vanishing into the shadows like a sensible being."

Snap laughed, shaking his head as the drops hit his curls. "I wish I could remember that. The water falls right from the sky?"

"Unfortunately," Thorn muttered. I couldn't tell whether his grimness was due to the devourer's continued forgetfulness or his distaste for mortal realm weather. Maybe a little of both.

Past him, near the driver's seat where Omen was at the wheel, Antic the imp was hopping from one foot to the other like a kid trying to avoid the urge to pee. She turned a map in her hands. "The next exit," she said determinedly in her squeaky voice. "You want to get on the 24. Oh, it's a pretty one."

"I don't care what it looks like as long as it's going to get us to Austin," Omen said.

I didn't know where Pickle had gotten to. He hadn't come scampering to me for pets since the accidental burning this afternoon. So much for two years of back rubs and bacon.

My phone, still in my hand, pinged with an incoming text. Another one from Vivi. *I know you're probably very busy saving the world, but could you shoot me a quick message letting me know you're okay? Ditto!* Kissy-face emoji.

As I looked at the words, my throat tightened. My best friend's effortless cheer felt leagues removed from anything my life resembled at this moment. What might I inadvertently do to *her* if we ever hung out again? The image of one of her trademark all-white outfits singed to brown and black flashed through my mind, and the constricting sensation ran down to my chest.

This was what my life had become: monsters and mayhem... and maybe this was what it should have been all along. I didn't know what to say to her anymore.

Still alive, I forced myself to write back, because a reassured Vivi would be much safer than a panicked one. *Reasonably okay. Not much to report yet. You hang in there. Ditto.* The sign-off was our homage to one of our favorite cheesy romance flicks, and I couldn't *not* say it when she did. You could consider that a sacred pact, no matter how far I veered into monsterdom.

"And then we make a right at those shiny lights," Antic said to Omen's wordless grumble.

Ruse slid onto the sofa beside Snap and gave the devourer's hair an affectionate ruffle. "You know you're all right now, don't you? We'll make sure those assholes never get their hands on you again. There's no need to be hiding away."

Snap blinked at him with one of those puzzled looks that wrenched at my heart. "Is someone hiding? I'm right here." He spread his arms as if in demonstration.

My dear, sweet shadowkind. If Ruse was right that Snap had essentially devoured everything about himself from the past however many months, was it even possible for him to spit himself back up, so to speak? What would it take? If I needed to put on a full-blown musical production or sacrifice a crow or some other hocus pocus, someone had better fill me in quick.

The incubus glanced across the table and caught my look. Whatever my expression showed, it turned him as grim as our warrior companion. He opened his mouth as if to speak, but at the same moment, Omen's voice barked from up front.

"That sign says we're heading toward Atlanta. I might not be a geography expert, but I'm pretty sure that's a hell of a lot more east than we want to be going to get to Texas."

Antic let out a squeal of apology and fumbled with the map. "I think—I think—*Texas*. Yes. Right. I had it turned the wrong way. We don't want to be on *this* road at all."

Omen's next growl suggested that if the imp gave him one more direction, he'd be picking her bones out of his teeth in a minute. Ruse arched his eyebrows at me, his expression still more solemn than usual, and sauntered over to lend a hand.

"We're not too far off track," he said, and grabbed Omen's phone from the dashboard. "But you know, even if we don't need sleep, we could use a break from the highway. Let that road rage simmer down and all. It's been a stressful day. I'll charm us a space in a hotel so luxurious it'll mellow even *you* out, Luce."

He flashed a grin at his boss, who bared his teeth in a much more menacing fashion in response. The incubus retorted with some gesture I couldn't quite make out but knowing him was probably obscene.

The hellhound shifter sighed. "Fine. But mainly because *Darlene* could probably use a break. I expect us to be up and on the road again at sunrise." He glanced over his shoulder at me. "If *you* had ever bothered to learn how to drive, the rest of us could have slipped in and out of a rift and been there already."

I stuck my tongue out at him, although sadly he didn't get to see my show of immense maturity because he'd already returned his gaze to the road. "As if you'd leave 'Darlene' in my disastrous hands anyway."

"Good point," he said, in a tone I chose to believe was more amused than annoyed. "Work your magic, incubus. If you can shock our mortal speechless for a minute or two, I'll consider that a victory."

TEN

Sorsha

I wouldn't say I was struck speechless, but Ruse hadn't been lying when he'd said he would aim for luxury. The place he led us into a half hour later boasted sweeping velvet-carpeted staircases around marble pillars so wide the ancient redwoods would have been envious. I resisted asking the concierge if they'd stolen their lobby furniture from the Palace of Versailles.

The penthouse suite the incubus had charmed our way into wasn't any model of restraint either. The main lounge area stretched wider than my entire apartment back home—before, y'know, I'd burned it down and all—with leather furniture so buttery soft a person could melt right into the cushions. The bathroom sported a small, marble-tiled swimming pool I couldn't imagine anyone in their right mind calling a "bathtub." And the bedroom…

"Where the magic happens," Ruse said with his typical smirk, sweeping his arm toward the king-sized canopy bed draped with gauzy silk on the other side of a Persian rug so thick I was in danger of drowning in it. Holy mother of majesty, we were living like the crustiest of upper crusters tonight.

Pickle, who'd accepted being carted in via my purse, charged across that red-and-gold expanse and promptly tumbled head over heels as his tiny feet sank deeper than he'd anticipated. With an indignant snort, he changed course and trotted off to the bathroom, where he had designer towels to shred into a very high-class nest.

"Good night!" I called after him, but the little dragon didn't glance back. Apparently we still weren't on speaking terms.

Snap took the whole place in, beaming with wonder. "What a fantastic building. Mortals do make things so much more bright and colorful than anything in our realm. I think I'll explore the rest of this… 'hotel' from the shadows." He paused and looked at the rest of us with evident concern. "Unless there's something you need from me."

Always thinking of how he could help everyone else first. A renewed ache woke up in my heart.

"No, no, you've done plenty, whether you remember it or not," Omen said, more gently than I was used to. Sometimes I forgot that underneath his preferred cold exterior, he really did care about the members of the team he'd assembled. He gave the devourer an awkward pat on the shoulder and walked with him toward the door. "But since we don't want to lose you again, maybe I should make the rounds with you. It wouldn't hurt to keep an eye out for any suspicious activity."

"Yes, we can do both! Explore and investigate." Snap beamed even brighter.

My heart might as well have been broken into pieces and fed to a pond of koi. "You be careful," I said, unable to stop myself.

"Of course," Snap replied cheerfully, and vanished into the shadows.

Maybe forgetting everything that had happened since he'd first ventured among mortals—not just forgetting me and his original companions but the way he'd used his power too—made things easier for him. With the pang in my chest, a lyric swam up and twisted in my mind. It came out mournful when I sang it. "You were always in a bind. You were always far too kind."

Antic had leapt onto the bed and was now bouncing on the mattress, the satin sheets rustling beneath her feet. She grabbed the silk drapes of the canopy. "What shall I make for you? A clown on a surfboard? A fish falling from a skyscraper?" She vanished behind the fabric while swinging it into a shape that did somehow resemble that second offering.

"Er, I think I'd like to just relax, like we planned," I said. "I don't need a show."

The imp harrumphed and popped back into view. "I'll go see if someone else in this place would enjoy some antics from Antic, then." She jabbed her finger in Thorn's direction as she skipped past us. "I *will* be back at dawn when we ride again!"

Thorn managed not to grimace until she'd slipped out of sight. He gave me a baleful look. "And you think she'll be a valuable addition to our plans?"

I threw my hands in the air. "I haven't got a clue. If worse comes to worst, we can tell her building shoe towers is an essential component and let her occupy herself in the mall while we do the real work, right?"

"With allies like these, who needs enemies," Ruse teased. His gaze had lingered on the bed. A thread of heat ran through my body at the thought of all the ways he could help me, ahem, "relax" between those sheets, but he turned as if to leave the room.

"Ruse," I said. When he met my eyes, his were warm and maybe even intrigued, but something in his face struck me as uncertain. I found I didn't know how to follow that up, and not only because his gorgeous face could steal my breath.

A deeper, sweeter emotion than desire welled up inside me. Even without peeking inside my head, I doubted it'd escaped his notice that my mood had gotten pretty dour during the drive. None of the shadowkind really needed pit stops. He'd come up with this scheme as much for my benefit as the fun he'd planned for my birthday last night. Why?

I wasn't really sure, but I did know how badly I wanted to show him I'd noticed and what it meant to me. How much *he* was coming to mean to me. I could have invited him into my bed, but that was just a night's work for an incubus, wasn't it? He'd indicated before that no other mortal woman had ever wanted anything from him *other* than his talent for pleasure.

So maybe it was time he got to experience what it was like to be at the receiving end of that kind of attention. I could invite him into bed after all.

I held out my hand to him. "Come here. You arranged all this—I think you should get to enjoy it as much as anyone."

He cocked his head. "What exactly did you have in mind, Miss Blaze?"

The suggestive lilt he gave the nickname sent a tingle all the way down to my toes. Even if I was focusing on him, I was still going to enjoy this a hell of a lot myself. "Get over here already, and you'll find out."

Thorn coughed. "In that case, perhaps I should—"

Ruse gave the warrior's arm a tug as he ambled over. "I don't see any reason for you to go anywhere, my friend. Our mortal here has been known to require, shall we say, additional servicing." He winked at me.

He seemed more at ease saying that—like he'd relaxed more when I'd asked him to join me and Snap last week. If he preferred the company, I sure as sugar wasn't going to say no. I peeked at Thorn through my eyelashes as coyly as I was capable of. "The more, the merrier?"

The warrior's tan complexion flushed slightly pinkish. He glanced between us as if waiting for one of us to laugh and say it was all a joke. When we didn't, he took a step closer. His voice came out with a roughness that got any part of my body that hadn't already been tingling on board. "If m'lady wishes it…"

Ruse did laugh at that. "Just get your medieval ass over here, my friend."

I poked the incubus in his deliciously sculpted chest, prodding him toward the bed. "I'm starting with you. Now strip."

"Oh, getting bossy, are we?" He raised his hands to the buttons of his shirt, the glint in his eyes turning more heated.

He didn't move fast enough for my liking. Before he'd finished unbuttoning his shirt, I was reaching for the fly of his slacks. Ruse let me undo it and stepped out of his slacks gamely, finally shedding that shirt so nearly all the well-muscled planes of his body were on display.

"This doesn't seem quite fair," he remarked as I pushed him the last few steps to the bed, but when he reached for my blouse, I shook my head. He glanced past me to his comrade for assistance. "Thorn, are you going to get to work on her or what?"

Thorn let out a low rumble of a chuckle from where he was standing behind me. I rarely heard a laugh out of him—it turned my earlier tingling into an eager flare of desire.

"I don't believe you're in command of this encounter, incubus," the warrior said.

I smiled. Indeed he was not. "Down you go," I instructed Ruse.

The incubus sprawled back on the bed, everything on display other than the bulge hidden behind those briefs, so languidly sensual in his pose I practically orgasmed just looking at him. He shot another remark at Thorn. "But don't you *want* to see that lovely form on full display? I doubt you're in this to ogle *me*."

That much was true too. Thorn rested his broad hands on my waist, grasping the hem of my shirt. "May I?" he murmured, his gravelly voice full of promise. Who was I to argue?

I raised my arms so he could pluck the blouse off me and then squirmed out of my undershirt with its silver-and-iron badge before he had to deal with that. I stayed put just long enough for Thorn to cup my breasts through my bra and press a kiss to my shoulder, soaking in the strength that emanated from his brawny form with an encouraging hum, but I had another lover I'd meant to attend to.

I crawled onto the bed next to Ruse, and Thorn sank down at my other side. The incubus teased his fingers into my hair as if to draw me to him, but I knew how easy it was to get lost in his skillful kisses. I diverted my mouth to the edge of his jaw, then the side of his neck. The bittersweet cacao scent of his skin flooded my senses.

As I charted a path across Ruse's drool-worthy chest, Thorn unhooked my bra and palmed my breasts skin to skin, the roughness of his calloused hands adding a spark of friction to the caress. I sighed happily against the incubus's toned stomach and raised my head to tug at his briefs. "These need to go too."

Ruse lifted his hips to help me peel the undergarment off. He pushed himself up on his elbows and reached for my jeans, but I brushed his hand away, doing some ogling of my own. His cock had come to attention, jutting at its eager angle like a glorious leaning tower of pleasure. I couldn't wait to be the one generating that pleasure tonight.

The incubus peered at me with what looked like genuine puzzlement. "Where are you taking this, Miss Blaze?"

I lowered my mouth to his hip, then his thigh, and ran my fingers up the straining length of his erection. "I'm taking care of *you* like you've always been taking care of me. About time we did a little role reversal, don't you think?"

Before he could respond, I skimmed my fingertips back down his cock and wrapped my lips around its head. The cacao flavor of him was even more intense on that sensitive flesh, with a tang of salt when I teased my tongue over the tip.

He sucked in a ragged breath. "You don't owe me this."

I looked up at him, slicking my saliva and a bead of his precum down his cock with my hand. "I know. I want to do it. And even if I'm not the most talented gal you've ever been with, I'd imagine I can make it reasonably satisfying."

"That's not—" His mouth twisted into a crooked grin. "You don't have to worry about being compared. Not many of the women I've been with would have thought to offer this. But why should you forego your own pleasure?" He beckoned to me, his eyes glinting slyly. "Turn around, and we can at least make this a mutual love-fest."

The fact that so many of his past lovers wouldn't have thought beyond getting their own rocks off only made me more sure of my intentions. I didn't budge, giving his cock a firm pump that made it twitch against my hand. "I'm getting off plenty just knowing how good I'm making you feel. And I'm sure Thorn can add to that as he'd like. For once, *you* are going to do nothing except lie back and enjoy yourself."

I bent over him again, taking him into my mouth as deeply as I could. Thorn had eased back to give me room, caressing my naked back with rhythmic strokes, but at my invocation, he leaned closer. He followed my spine with scorching kisses, one hand fondling my breasts again and the other sliding over my belly. The pleasure he stirred fueled my desire into headier flames.

I swiveled my tongue around Ruse's cock, cupping his balls, and he groaned. When I glanced at his face, his eyes were flashing between their hazel guise and their natural glowing gold. Faint shimmers of that same sheen flickered over his skin as if he was struggling to hold himself back.

"Go ahead," I said. "Let your shine out. You know I like it."

His body flared in response, his incubus glow lighting up every part of him, even the cock I sucked down again. It curved at its sharper shadowkind angle in my mouth, the bump of his pubic bone protruding, all designed to give his partners the most possible satisfaction. But he'd fed plenty from me in that way in the last few weeks. He'd had his sustenance—now he deserved a treat.

His supernatural glow brought a giddying warmth with it. The sensation spread through my mouth and all through my limbs as I bobbed over Ruse's thighs. Thorn fanned the flames higher with the pressure of his hands and mouth. His fingers trailed lower to tease right between my legs. I gasped against the incubus's cock and reached back to caress the warrior's arm in return.

As I sped up my rhythm, Ruse bucked into my mouth. I tightened my lips around him and sucked harder, and he came with a flood of bittersweet heat that I swallowed down. Before I could do more than give his cock one last swipe of my tongue, he'd sat up to tug me to him, his mouth claiming mine at long last.

Thorn was undoing my jeans. Melting into the kiss, I kicked them and my panties off, but my warrior seemed to think his work was done there. I snatched at his arm before he could withdraw and pulled him back. My lips left Ruse's so I could twist around and capture the wingéd's mouth for myself, my fingers tangling in his white-blond hair.

"I want you," I said with a stutter of breath as Ruse pinched one of my nipples. "I *need* you." My core was throbbing now, aching to be filled—and no one could fill me like Thorn.

"I think you'd better attend to our lady," Ruse said, his amusement coming through the smokiness of his shadowkind voice.

Thorn dipped his fingers right between my legs from behind and groaned approvingly at the slickness of my arousal. He jerked at his trousers. "As m'lady desires."

I did desire—oh, I desired every bit of his massive form. He bent over my back, easing his thick cock into me with that incredible searing stretch, and the bliss of it radiated through me. I moaned.

One of these days I was going to have to take him in *his* full form, even more massive as that was, but I knew he didn't want Ruse seeing what he was.

As Thorn began to thrust into me, Ruse's mouth crashed into mine. I arched to meet the warrior, my fingers slipping up to grip one of the incubus's horns. I was locked between them, all that immense power looming over me and the giddy glow beneath, and yet I couldn't imagine feeling more free. The pulsing rush of pleasure swept me higher and higher—

I tipped over the peak with an even sharper surge of ecstasy and a cry I couldn't contain. My sex clenched around Thorn, and his arm tightened where he'd looped it around my waist. He drove into me again. Ruse's tongue tangled with mine, and I came apart all over again as the warrior found his own heated release.

As Thorn sagged down beside me, I rolled over to kiss him properly. He stroked his fingers down the side of my face, the gentleness of that touch a perfect contrast to the force of his mouth on mine.

Ruse slung his arm around me and kissed my shoulder. I snuggled in between my two lovers and clung to this moment of contentment before the thought of the lover I'd lost could creep back in.

ELEVEN

Snap

From the short while I'd gotten to enjoy the mortal realm, I had to say it was a spectacular place. Why did anyone return shadow-side when they could have all this? The bright colors and soft textures of the expansive room the incubus had gotten for us... The intoxicating mix of scents from the platters of items something called "room service" had delivered just moments ago... It was nothing short of its own sort of magic.

I'd admit the first experiences here I remembered, being shut away under brilliant lights with a prickle of poisonous metals all around, had been rather disturbing. But if I hadn't endured that, I'd never have gotten to taste this miraculous object Thorn informed me was a breakfast sausage.

I chewed on the meaty bite, salt and savory juices mingling on my tongue, and my smile stretched wider. Yes, this world was a paradise for a devourer.

A cool quiver shot down my back at that thought, there and then gone so quickly I couldn't have examined it even if I'd wanted to. Why should I bother with that discomfort, though? It didn't feel as if the impression wanted to be prodded. And I had a great deal more breakfast to eat.

"And this?" I asked, tapping a heap of lumpy yellow stuff that smelled much more appealing than it looked.

Ruse glanced over and chuckled. "Scrambled eggs. I think you'll like those too."

The little imp we'd picked up before we'd left that last city bounded around the table. "Is there anything he *doesn't* like? He'll be having the table next!"

"And he may have it, if that's what he'd like," the incubus declared.

The mortal woman came over, still tugging at her red hair, which always drew my eye. It was more vibrant than even the furnishings in this extravagant room. She was tugging at it, I'd gathered, because she'd woken up to find the imp had woven it all into a mass of little braids while she'd slept.

Antic watched her work at untangling the strands with a huff. "*I* thought it looked nice that way."

"It's just—not my style," Sorsha said. I got the impression she was trying to spare the imp's feelings, which she seemed to do rather often, although I wasn't sure why. The two of them hadn't appeared to know each other already. The mortal obviously had a certain kindness to her. I liked that—and I liked her hair down in its loose waves best too.

She let go of the strands long enough to paw through the offerings on the table. "Didn't we get a fruit salad? There it is. You can't skip this, Snap."

She pushed the shiny bowl with its glistening rainbow of chunks toward me, an emotion coming into her eyes that I saw quite a bit when she fixed them on me. Something hesitant but also hopeful, as if she were waiting for something she didn't actually expect to happen. I hadn't figured out what, but it made her sad, and that didn't seem right.

All of them wanted more from me than I'd been able to give. They knew me from a long while before this, and I hadn't known them until they'd pulled me from that prison.

I furrowed my brow as if that might push the memories to the surface, but I had nothing. Nothing except the journey on the large, sparkly vehicle and before that, the harsh lights in the uncomfortable cage—and before *that*, the stretch of hazy gloom in the shadow realm that I'd wandered through not knowing all the delights I was missing.

There must have been more experiences that I simply couldn't remember. Ruse and Thorn had shown and told me so many fascinating things I couldn't have imagined but had apparently encountered before. I supposed I'd have to seek out those they couldn't immediately supply all over again. That didn't sound like a horrible burden.

I popped a piece of banana into my mouth and reveled at the soft sweetness of it, even better with the peel removed. Oh, yes, I was looking forward to rediscovering everything that had slipped my mind. Even if this physical body had its quirks. A tiny itch had woken up in my forearm again. I scratched at it absently and reached for a perfect grape.

A small green shape launched itself onto the table with a warble of ineffective wings and a scrabbling of little claws against the polished wood. "Pickle!" Sorsha cried, leaping at the little dragon. He snapped up a piece of bacon before she managed to grab him. "You've had plenty already. Leave some for the rest of us."

The shadowkind creature gave a snort of disagreement and scuttled away under the table as soon as she'd set him down. That made her appear sad too. No, I didn't like that look on her at all.

"Are you going to have some eggs?" I asked. I was never sure how much I should say to her, since it seemed to both cheer and dishearten her when I spoke. I thought she might have grabbed a morsel or two in the midst of her work on her hair, but I'd been too absorbed in my own meal most of that time to pay attention.

"Nah, I'm more of a sausage gal myself," she said, spearing one of those with a fork, and shot a grin at Ruse. The incubus guffawed as if she'd said something funny, which didn't make much sense to me.

"I prefer the sausages too," I offered, and suddenly Ruse was laughing so hard his breath sputtered, and Sorsha swiped her hand across her mouth as if she were holding back a snicker as well.

I turned my gaze to Thorn, who shrugged with a resigned shake of his head. I couldn't tell whether that meant he didn't understand the joke either or he simply didn't approve of it. There appeared to be a fairly large number of things the large shadowkind didn't approve of, from what I'd seen so far.

"Sausages, sausages!" the imp started to sing in her chirpy voice, and the dragon let out a sort of bugling noise from under the table, and I could laugh at that.

Omen stalked into the room in the midst of the mirth and surveyed us with his mouth flat. His aura of power and authority filled every space he entered. I quieted out of respect. I hadn't determined yet what sort of a shifter he was, although I could tell he was one—it felt rude to outright ask—but whatever it was, there was clearly a reason the others looked to him as the leader.

And he had wanted *me* to join this team of his. I couldn't say how I'd be of much use, but I hoped I'd figure that out. It must have been an honor to be chosen by a being so formidable.

"The sun's rising," he barked. "Let's get a move on. You've lounged about long enough."

"I don't imagine Austin is going anywhere while we eat breakfast," Ruse replied in a teasing tone, but I noticed he got up quickly all the same.

Sorsha sighed and grabbed her purse. She knelt down by the table, clucking her tongue to coax Pickle into it. Not wanting any of the precious refreshments to go to waste, I snatched up the bowl of fruit salad and tipped its contents into my mouth.

I was just gulping down the last of that riot of flavor when the door crashed open with an explosive *bang*.

A horde of figures in shiny helmets and vests charged into the room, tools glittering in their hands. The metals sent a wash of vibrations through the air that dug through my skin down to my bones. Pain prickled through the sensation.

I sprang to my feet with a jerk, some instinct in me rearing its head with a vicious shudder—and another impulse yanked me backward. A chill gripped me even more potent than the poisonous energies of those metals.

I flung myself into the nearest shadows and away—away from the clang and crackle of the battle, away from the beings who'd acted like my friends, *away*… Because deep down in some cold, dark place in the center of me lay the certainty that my presence would only mean a far greater pain for those around me.

They all were safer with me off in the distant darkness than they were if I stayed among them.

TWELVE

Sorsha

The second the Company mercenaries burst into the hotel room, my fighting instincts took over. Heart thudding, I snatched up two of the brass platters our breakfast had been delivered on, briefly lamented the waste of delicious food, and slammed them into the faces of the men who'd lunged my way.

Metal clanged and eggs squelched. An invisible force I assumed was Antic followed my example and started hurling more dishes off the table at our attackers. Delicate china cups smashed left and right. Tea and butter splattered the ornate rug.

Well, what do you expect when you open up a penthouse to a bunch of monsters?

An instant later, the tea and butter was joined by a gush of blood. Thorn gouged one crystalline fist through one soldier's neck and bashed the other into a second man's face. Omen tore through the room in a maelstrom of hellhound brutality, raking his claws across thighs and calves, sinking his jaws into one woman's belly. The magma-like streaks that seared through his dark gray fur blazed with fury.

Our efforts might not be enough, though. As I ducked down and knocked the feet out from a gunman with a sweep of my leg, the sight of more figures charging through the doorway made my gut lurch. One of them was already hefting a silver-and-iron net to toss over the fighting shadowkind.

A crackle of fire rushed through me in response. I hadn't meant to risk burning the place—and all the other, perfectly innocent guests—down, but flames spurted across the guy's shirt before I had any chance to rein them in. His colleagues shoved him to the floor to drop and roll, one snatching the net from him as they did.

Shit. If I let out more than that, a lot more than just the Company assholes might end up incinerated on this fine morning.

As I swung the brass plates again, willing down the vicious heat inside as well as I could, my gaze darted across the room. At the other end, the gauzy curtains drifted in the cool breeze where we'd left the balcony door ajar. Inspiration shot through me like a bolt of lightning.

Just this once, I didn't need my supernatural allies to ensure my mortal self made it out of this alive.

"Get out of here!" I shouted. "You don't need to wait for me. I've got my own escape route; I'll meet you at Darlene."

Not that I approved of the Everymobile's new name, just to be clear—it was only a way to avoid tipping our enemies off to where we were heading.

"M'lady," Thorn called out in protest, apparently unwilling to take my word for it. Time to get a move on anyway.

"Just *go*!" I said, snatching up my purse with a sputtering Pickle in it, and dashed toward the balcony.

It helped that our attackers had entered from the main door and were opting for a "mow them down" approach rather than "surround them." I only had to dodge a couple of fists and one gleaming whip before I was springing past the curtains into the crisp dawn air. My devoted shadowkind defenders had better take the hint and escape into the shadows now that I'd exited the room.

Leaving the balcony looked to be slightly more difficult than reaching it. Our lovely penthouse stood twelve stories above the sidewalk I'd like to end up on, and I hadn't brought my grappling hook and rope. Note to self: All occasions are good occasions to have the cat burglar gear on hand.

The thunder of impending footsteps told me I'd better get going one way or another. I glanced down, ignored the flip of my stomach—I was no chicken when it came to heights, but I generally wasn't prancing around on buildings *quite* this tall—and vaulted over the balcony's railing.

With a grasp of the bars and a swing of my legs, I launched myself onto the smaller balcony below. One floor down, eleven more to go. Too bad the rest of the windows below me only featured Juliets—who in their right mind called that little stub a balcony anyway?

The inhabitants of the sub-penthouse had left their balcony door locked, but even in a hotel this fancy, those things weren't really built for keeping people out. Who expected robbers to descend from the sky? I gave the handle a well-practice kick, grinned at the snap of the lock, and shoved the door wide just as shouts hailed down from above.

I sprinted through the room of some hotel goer who was lucky enough to still be sleeping at this hour—at least, until my pursuers crashed in—and down the hall to the stairs, not wanting to risk the elevator. My feet had never flown faster. On the ground floor, I peeked out through the window, spotted the metal-helmed figures by the front doors getting stares from the desk clerks, and eased the door open just far enough to make a run for the kitchen.

The staff who'd provided our delightful breakfast were clattering around fulfilling other room service requests. "Thanks for the lovely meal!" I hollered to them as I sprinted past. As I'd hoped, a door at the far end of the room offered an exit into an alley that held a dumpster and exactly zero Company assholes. For now.

Thankfully, we'd taken the precaution of parking the Everymobile —in cargo van guise—a few blocks away from the hotel. I loped over there before our attackers could get their act together and figure out where I'd snuck off to.

As our vehicle came into view, tension prickled through my muscles. The shadowkind *had* all hoofed it out of the penthouse when I'd left, hadn't they? I couldn't remember even seeing Snap in the fray. If we'd lost him again, or any of the others…

The door flung open to admit me, Thorn standing on the other side with an urgent beckoning. I spotted Ruse in the driver's seat behind him, foot poised over the gas.

Neither of them looked at all concerned about getting anyone on board other than me. Thank holy hamburgers. I accepted Thorn's hand, he yanked me on board, and the RV peeled away from the curb the second the door had thumped shut behind me.

"We all made it?" I asked, just in case.

"All present and accounted for," Omen said tersely from where he was standing by the kitchen. Snap was sitting on the sofa-bench with a vaguely bewildered expression, and Antic… was bouncing on her heels right on the table.

She shot me an eager smirk when she saw me look her way. "I gave them a good lesson with those teacups, didn't I?"

"You were great," I said. No need to pick apart exactly how much each of us had contributed to the skirmish. I dropped onto the sofa across from Snap and released Pickle from my purse.

Omen was frowning. "Hey," I said, aiming a teasing kick at his calf. "We just escaped a vicious ambush with all lives and even body parts intact. What more could you ask for?"

He swiped his hand across his narrow jaw. "I'm more concerned about how those pricks found us in the first place. There's no way they should have been able to determine that we'd head to Austin from Chicago, and even if they had, we weren't on the right course." He aimed a particularly icy glance at the imp.

I hadn't had enough time to recover from the whole fleeing for my life bit to consider the implications of the attack. "That's true. I didn't mention where we were headed to Ellen or Vivi, so it couldn't have come from them."

Ruse glanced back toward us. "The hotel was the first place we've been in one spot for any significant length of time since we stormed the museum and then hit the road. Could the Company have tracked your phone, Sorsha?"

I shook my head. "I've had it off except when I was using it while we were on the road, just in case."

"It's possible they were tracking something else." Omen's gaze settled on Snap. "Didn't any of you find it odd that our devourer's cage opened on its own to release him when we came for him? The Company's scientists had already called in back-up. Why would they *want* us to leave with him rather than be caught?"

"I figured they got scared that we'd find them before back-up arrived," I said. "But yeah... They didn't have any reason to worry at that point. It was *because* his cage opened that we got suspicious."

Snap had stiffened against the leather seat. "I wouldn't have helped the people who locked up me and Antic and the others in those metal boxes."

"Of course you wouldn't have, not on purpose," Omen said in the same unexpectedly gentle tone he'd used with Snap before. He stepped closer to the devourer, studying Snap's lean frame from head to toe. "But you might have without even realizing it. There's a trick I've seen hunters use when they want to collect a lot of little shadowkind at once. Some of the lesser creatures tend to congregate together. They catch one and fix a tracking mark of some sort on it, then release it and let it lead them to the others."

I'd heard of that too. They marked the creatures' bodies with a little silver ink that wouldn't vanish even if the creatures slipped in and out of the shadows and that created a resonance they could detect with a specialized device. A shiver tickled through me. "You think the Company scientists put a tracker mark on Snap? Wouldn't he have noticed?" The lesser shadowkind might ignore a little discomfort in their relief at being freed, but Snap was more aware than that.

"Possibly not, if it was small enough. He hasn't used a physical body long enough to be all that aware of what's normal in the first place." The hellhound shifter motioned for Snap to stand up. "Let me check you over. We don't want them tracking us any farther than they already have."

Snap got to his feet, his eyes wide. "They attacked us because of me? I never thought—if I'd realized—"

"We know." I scooted close enough to take his hand, although I didn't know how much real comfort that would give him. Still, I ran my thumb over his knuckles in as soothing a gesture as I could offer while Omen leaned in, practically sniffing the devourer with his houndish senses.

"Here," he said abruptly, grasping Snap's other arm and turning it to tap a spot just below his elbow. "There's just the faintest hint of it..." He grimaced. "Not on the flesh, but there's a bit of a regular scar here. They must have cut you open and etched it right on the bone."

A shudder ran through Snap's body. "There is something there—a bit of an itch. I thought that must be normal." His head jerked up. "I can't stay. You'll have to go on without me. I could return to the shadow realm—they won't be able to follow me there. Then you'll all be safe."

Like when he'd run from us when he'd been afraid of how we—how *I*—would see him after he'd devoured that man in front of us? Panic jabbed through my chest, and my grip on his hand tightened. "No. There has to be a way to get it off." I just didn't like thinking about how bloody those ways might be.

Omen glanced at Thorn. "You know your way around a blade."

The warrior bowed his head. As he opened the drawers beneath the kitchen counter, I tugged Snap down beside me. He turned to me. "I had a feeling, in the hotel room—I *knew* it was dangerous for me to be with you. You all could have been captured or killed, and it would have been my fault."

"Not your fault," I said firmly. When his gaze started to slip away from me, I touched the side of his face to bring his attention back. "Hey. It'd be the fault of the assholes who put that mark on you. I know you don't remember it, but you've helped us so much. We need you. Don't you want the chance to see them totally shut down?"

"I don't know how much more I can do."

"I do." I kept all my focus on his moss-green eyes. "And even if you weren't going to stay with us, would you really want them to be able to track you down any time you came mortal-side again? *You'd* never be safe here again." I couldn't imagine Snap having to give up everything he'd taken wonder from in this world. He'd make that sacrifice if he thought it would protect us, because that was how he was, but he'd never stop missing the color and flavor his home realm lacked.

Just like I wasn't sure I'd ever stop missing the passionate devotion he'd brought into *my* life.

That thought brought a lump into my throat, but I kept holding his gaze. "If we can get the mark off you, do you think you can handle the pain?"

He hesitated, his forked tongue flicking across his lips. "Yes," he said softly. "Yes—to be able to stay here. To keep up with the mission. To have all the fantastic things I haven't gotten to experience yet."

"Good. Then think about all the fantastic things you *have* had already, and I'll keep holding your hand, and we'll pretend Thorn isn't even there."

Snap drew in a breath and squeezed my hand in return. His eyes became distant as he must have thought back to some favorite of the new memories he'd accumulated in the past day—the grandeur of the hotel? The rush of the RV's speed? Or maybe the simple pleasure of his fruit salad, knowing him.

As I watched his face, I could see Thorn applying a carving knife to the devourer's forearm at the edge of my vision. I restrained a wince at the smoke that unfurled from the cut. Snap blinked, and his jaw tensed —the only sign that he'd felt it. He could be as stoic as the warrior when he needed to be.

"Tell me your favorite things here," he said abruptly.

Recently? *Lying on a cramped bunk bed with your arms around me. Seeing your face light up at a taste of honey.* I swallowed hard. There were plenty of other things too.

"Listening to music," I said. "Letting the beat move through me. Singing along, finding ways to play with the words. You haven't gotten to do any of that yet. Opening those cages and watching the beasties big and small leap free. Burning the places that belong to the assholes who built those cages down to the ground."

Thorn had opened up a gash wide enough that the smoke was billowing now. His expression was as pained as I felt seeing it.

"There's the mark," he said. "Barely larger than the head of a pin. I think I can scrape the silver off with the edge of the blade."

He braced himself, and a flinch ran all through Snap's body. The devourer closed his eyes with a hiss. His fingers clutched mine so hard my hand ached, but not half as much as my heart did.

Then the warrior was tossing the knife into the sink. Omen stood ready with the roll of gauze they'd procured for *my* injuries days ago. He'd smeared a little of the green paste that helped contain shadowkind essence on the pale fabric.

As he bandaged Snap's arm, the devourer's shoulders sank down. His head dipped toward me. "Thank you," he murmured.

I wished I could kiss him. I wished that was still something he'd take joy from. "Any time," I said with forced cheer.

"You should rest," Thorn said gruffly. "After losing some of your essence…"

"Yes." Snap stood, took a step, and wavered. I followed him, ushering him down the hall to the RV's main bedroom.

He sat down on the edge of the bed and then didn't seem to know quite what to do with himself. An impulse gripped me, so insistent I couldn't ignore it.

I sat down next to him and wrapped my arms around him, tucking my legs over his lap. Almost like that time in the back of our long-ago borrowed SUV when the friction of me jostling against him during a getaway had woken up his sense of carnal desire. His fresh yet mossy scent filled my nose.

Fruit and flattery hadn't unearthed his memories. Would something about this embrace do the trick?

Snap gazed down at me, stroking my hair, but the gesture felt more absent than affectionate. "Are *you* all right?" he asked me.

So much for that idea. I'd stop throwing myself at him now.

I pulled back and gave his hand one last squeeze. "Just making sure you are. Lie down—it's easier to rest that way. And don't you dare go anywhere."

"I wouldn't," he said, with a determined assurance that killed me. "Whatever I can do here, it's so much more than I could ever offer where I came from."

I didn't really want to go back to the others just yet. Thorn would probably look at me pityingly, and the devil only knew what Omen was thinking about my soppiness. I retreated into the second bedroom that had almost become my own and flopped down on top of the purple cloud-print comforter. It didn't *feel* all that cloud-like. After the heavenly linens in the hotel, this fabric was scratchy against my skin.

Damn. Penthouse life had ruined me for the plebeian existence in a matter of hours.

Someone rapped on the door. "Still alive in there, Disaster?"

I rolled my eyes at the ceiling. "Yes, *Luce*, as much as you might hope otherwise."

Omen didn't bother with opening the door—he slipped in through the shadows, his well-built form solidifying at the edge of the bed. I supposed I should be glad he'd bothered to knock at all. I looked at him without raising my head from the pillows, which to be honest strained my eyeballs, but I didn't feel like giving him the satisfaction of sitting up at attention.

"I thought we'd established that I don't particularly want to see you dead," he remarked with a coolly casual air.

"More like that you think I'm too useful to get rid of, regardless of what you'd personally prefer."

He let out a soft huff at that but, I noticed, didn't put up an argument. Then he just stood there, as if waiting for *me* to figure out why the hell he'd come in.

"Was there something you wanted?" I asked.

He folded his arms over his chest. I braced myself for whatever criticism he had for me now, but what he actually said was, "You handled yourself well in the ambush. And—with Snap. You know how to… settle him down. Keep his head on straight."

At that admission, I couldn't help propping myself up on my elbows so I could look at the hellhound shifter without giving myself a headache. "It's easier when your first priority isn't being the most ice-cold bastard in the room."

Was that a wince he'd suppressed with the tightening of his lips? "That may be true," he said evenly.

It might not have been totally fair, though. I'd seen him making an effort to be kinder with the devourer in his uncertain mental state. "You haven't been quite as much of a bastard to Snap as you generally are to everyone else," I conceded. "And I appreciate the recognition of my many talents."

That time I could tell it was a smile he'd caught. "Ice-cold bastards get things done, you know. Better to have one than none." He turned to leave.

"Omen," I said before I was sure what I was going to ask. He paused, and I pushed myself all the way up, tucking my feet under me to sit cross-legged.

He'd come in here for a reason. Just to pay me a compliment? I didn't completely understand, but the moment felt vital yet tenuous, like a chance I shouldn't let slip through my fingers.

What did I most *want* to ask? I turned the possibilities over in my head before settling on a topic.

"Why did you decide you needed to become all ice-cold anyway? You obviously don't take to the chill naturally—the other day, you talked about how hard you worked at it. And I know from some of the things the others have said that you were a lot more laissez faire with your abilities however many eons ago."

"The incubus and his loose tongue."

I couldn't hold back a smirk that would have made Ruse proud. "Oh, don't complain about his tongue. He puts it to all sorts of wonderful uses."

Omen glowered at me, but he stepped away from the door to prop himself against the bed's footboard. "I didn't come to the decision lightly," he said. "I *did* use to be much more careless with my powers, playing with mortals for entertainment." He paused, looking toward the wall with a distant gaze. "I had a lot of power to work with and an associate who enjoyed the revelry of horrors even more than I did, always encouraging fresh intrigues."

"Not Thorn." The warrior was the only shadowkind I knew Omen had associated with ages ago, but I couldn't imagine the stalwart wingéd instigating mayhem.

Omen snorted. "No. And you don't have to worry about meeting her. In the end, Tempest was too caught up in her cleverness for her own good. She was a sphinx, but taunting mortals with riddles wasn't thrilling enough—she shifted her form I don't know how many times, riding humans to their deaths as a night mare, riding doom through their towns when she led what they called the Wild Hunt, and the Highest only know what else. Which was the problem. The Highest caught on to how much hell she was raising and sent a pack of wingéd to take her down, back when there still were enough wingéd around for them to form packs."

"And you decided you'd rather not end up bashed open by a hail of crystal knuckles, so you committed to changing your ways?"

"Not exactly. I wasn't quite as flamboyant as her. I thought I could stay beneath their notice. But there was a night—"

He halted as if grappling with the memory. I gave him a good long stretch before impatience got the better of me and I prompted, "A night?"

"I'd messed with a lot of the mortals in one settlement, and they came to get retribution. Instead of finding me, they stumbled on a cluster of lesser shadowkind who'd been drawn by my energies. The humans slaughtered every creature there without a moment's hesitation. And I realized the Highest were right in the little bit of enforcement they do enact across the divide."

His gaze was still fixed on the wall, his tone as even as ever, but his hand had come to rest on the bed frame, the knuckles paling where he'd clenched his fingers. I waited another moment before asking, "How so?"

"It was my doing," Omen said. "The mortals were brazen fools like so many of them are, and they deserved all the havoc I brought into their lives, but in wreaking that havoc I stirred up their distrust and hatred of all shadowkind. How many hunters took up hunting because I hurt them or theirs? How many humans simply blundered into causing massacres like the one I witnessed that night in fits of rage? So many lesser creatures and no doubt some higher ones as well paid for my crimes more than I ever have."

Ah. I tried to imagine what it would have been like, arriving at a personal revelation on that scale, and couldn't. His voice had only gotten flatter as he spoke, but I'd been around Omen well enough to know that meant he was clamping down even more control over emotions threatening to leak out.

"So this is your penance?" I said. "Making yourself a model of self-restraint and ordering everyone around while you save the shadowkind you can?"

"Something like that." Omen's gaze finally slid to me. "I was selfish and undisciplined and foolhardy—all the worst qualities mortals have in abundance. By provoking them, I was sinking to their level. Yes, I have plenty to make up for, but mainly I want to be as little like those pricks as I possibly can be."

I guessed that could explain why so many parts of my mortal self—impossible supernatural powers aside—irritated the hell out of him. Or the hell *into* him?

Whatever. I glanced down at my hands and then back at him. He hadn't needed to tell me any of his history. Maybe he was already regretting that he had. I could avoid driving that regret home.

"I see your point," I said. "For what it's worth, the being I've seen when you let the ice crack isn't *anything* like the worst human beings I've met. Do you ever think you could ease up on yourself a little after all this time?"

A gleam lit in his eyes. "And ease up on the rest of you as a natural consequence?"

I spread my hands. "You said it, not me."

He did smile then, a gesture that only curled one side of his mouth but that I'd take as a victory anyway. In that moment, the vibe between us felt almost companionable. Then he straightened up.

"Get some rest. I got the impression you didn't spend all that much time in that big hotel bed *sleeping* last night."

The thought that he'd been paying any attention at all to my interlude with Ruse and Thorn sent a flicker of heat through me that wasn't exactly comfortable but not totally unpleasant either. "Spying on us, were you?"

He scoffed. "It isn't exactly difficult to put the pieces together with certain scenarios."

I leaned back on my elbows again with a tingling awareness of my body laid out on the bed. "Next time, maybe you should join in."

I was mostly joking—but a little part of me wasn't. And there was no joke in the flash of orange that lit in Omen's eyes before he jerked his gaze away.

"Less snarking and more napping," he said in a definitive tone. "We'll want you sharp when we get to Austin."

THIRTEEN

Ruse

If the chaotic events of the past twenty-four hours had made anything clear, it was that no matter how much of himself Snap had swallowed into the deepest depths of his being, the devourer still had a puzzling but valiant habit of caring about everyone else's welfare more than his own. This despite the fact that as far as he could remember, he'd only known the bunch of us for those twenty-four hours.

That observation led me to a spark of inspiration. None of the items I'd offered him so far had jogged any familiarity loose. My reassurances that he was among friends hadn't cajoled his old self free. But maybe if he believed our lives depended on him dredging up times past, whatever force was holding them down in his gullet would shatter.

It was worth a try, anyway. Every time Sorsha looked at him with the loss shining in her eyes, I wanted to shake him until he snapped out of it. I would have if I'd thought there was any chance of that tactic working. I'd always liked the devourer well enough, but starting over from scratch with his naively precocious self was getting rather irritating.

I got my chance to try out my new strategy when we stopped at a gas station-slash-burger joint just past the Texas border to fill up both the RV and our mortal. My job, of course, was to persuade the establishment that they didn't need any money for their trouble. Snap stepped out of the Everymobile with Sorsha and me and tipped back his head to bask in the midday sun.

"Wait right there," I told him. "I'll find a tasty snack for you too."

He beamed at me so brightly you'd have thought I'd offered him a ten-course banquet on a week-long tropical cruise. He had always been easy to please.

It wasn't pleasing him I was after, though. I had a little chat with the man at the counter, watched him call out our order eagerly to the cook staff, and left Sorsha to collect the goods. As I reached the restaurant door, I threw myself forward, bursting out into the parking lot as if I'd run all the way to the entrance.

At the sight of me dashing over, Snap straightened up with a jerk, his body tensing. "What's wrong?" he asked, buying into my gambit before I'd even had to really sell it.

"Sorsha," I said in a breathless voice. "The Company goons were waiting for us—they've grabbed her, and they'll be coming for the rest of us any minute now."

The devourer turned even more rigid. "What should we do?"

I waved at him frantically. "Quick! There was something you picked up about a guy named Meriden before—I think if we could show we knew him we could get them to back down—"

It had to be a real fact, or it wouldn't connect with his smothered memories. A fraught expression crossed the devourer's pretty face. He opened his mouth and closed it again, his hands moving at his sides as if groping for an answer in the air.

I almost thought I had him, that something was jostling loose, when he let out a choked sound of dismay. "I don't know. Meriden, Meriden—there's nothing."

"Just give yourself more of a chance. It's got to be in there somewhere."

"I don't know." The furrows in his brow dug deeper as the seconds slipped by. He shook his head and spun toward the RV. "We have to tell Thorn and Omen. They'll know how to push those people back and get Sorsha away from them."

Throwing the whole group into a panic wouldn't solve anything. I grabbed Snap's arm before he could reach the door. "There isn't time. Even if you have the slightest sense—tell me anything that comes to you. It could make all the difference in saving her."

"Saving who from what?"

The restaurant had worked faster than I'd anticipated. Sorsha was walking over, a paper bag dangling from her hand and a crease forming in her own brow as she looked from me to Snap. Her grip on the bag tightened. "What's happened? Do we have to get out of here?"

Snap brightened with such intensity the brilliance of his smile stung my eyes. "You're all right! Did the Company people let you go? You have the food…" He trailed off and then looked at me uncertainly.

I made a living out of lying, but I had to admit the hint of betrayal in his expression provoked a prick of guilt. I gave him a tentative pat on the arm. "Just a little… prank. I was hoping it would jumpstart your memory. She's been perfectly fine the whole time."

"Of course I'm fine." Sorsha grimaced at me. "All you did was freak him out. The last thing he needs is more stress after this morning."

The prick of guilt expanded into a sword-like stabbing. Although the wound where Thorn had scraped out the silver mark on Snap's arm hadn't leaked any smoke since being bandaged, it was true that this morning's events had been far from a pleasant stroll in the park for the devourer. And the look our fiery mortal was giving me was the exact opposite of the sort I'd have wanted to elicit.

She didn't need more stress in her life either.

I dipped into an apologetic little bow. "I'm sorry. I only wanted to give every possibility a shot, and we seem to be running low on them." I glanced at Snap. "We'd all like to have you back with full history intact."

"I'm sure we'll have plenty of other chances that don't involve giving him a panic attack," Sorsha said, and shot Snap the soft smile that seemed reserved just for him.

Snap's head drooped. "I'm not sure whatever you've been looking for is still there to be found. I've tried… I truly have."

"I know." She swallowed audibly and then made an attempt at cheerfulness. "Good thing I'm not the kind of girl who gives up just like that." Her gaze came back to me. "No more staging supposed attacks. We've had enough of the real thing."

"What's the hold up?" Omen barked from inside the RV. "Let's get a move on!"

"All right, all right," Sorsha hollered back—and a little flame licked from her palm to her elbow.

She suppressed her flinch so quickly I might not have noticed it if I hadn't been watching her already. She pulled her arm to her torso, snuffing out the flame, and all that remained was a thin pink line over the sensitive skin. I might have offered to kiss it better if the clenching of her jaw hadn't warded me off from any teasing remarks.

"Just—just behave yourself for a little while," she grumbled at me, and handed Snap his bacon cheeseburger before clambering on board.

The devourer and I followed, Snap gulping down his lunch in a few swift bites and then looking mournful that somehow the meal was already gone. He licked his lips. "The different types of meat do make an excellent combination, especially with the cheese and the fluffiness of that bread."

I clapped him on the shoulder. "A little more practice and we'll get you writing a food blog."

"Blog? Is that some kind of fallen tree? Why would someone write on one?"

Good old Snap. "Don't worry yourself about that."

We stopped in the kitchen area. Sorsha had kept going, disappearing now into her bedroom with a flash of her scarlet hair. I suppressed a fresh jab of guilt. If my gambit *had* worked, she'd have been overjoyed. It'd been worth the chance. Snap clearly wasn't traumatized in any lingering way.

Snap was watching *me*. "You like her," he said in his direct, well-meaning way. "Quite a bit."

I yanked my gaze back to him. "You did too," I felt the need to point out. "You and her…" I didn't know how to describe the bond that had appeared to be forming between the two of them, partly because those sorts of tender feelings weren't my domain… and partly because remembering that fact sent an uneasy twinge through me.

"Come on," I said to distract him. "Let me show you the best view we can get from this thing." I motioned to him and leapt into the shadows. The least I could do after my trick was give him a more enjoyable experience to make up for it.

Snap trailed after me into the shadow around the small sunroof positioned over the hall. From the top of the RV, the suburban landscape we were passing through sprawled out on all sides, every bit of it visible without us needing to move an inch. The clear blue sky and the warble of the wind faded as they reached our senses through the patch of darkness, but I'd take that dulled view over risking a tumble in my physical body at the speeds Omen drove at.

A serpentinely slim presence beside me, Snap made a sound of approval. For a few minutes, we simply crouched there, taking in the sights of the mortal world with the colors of early fall whipping past us and the faint tang of gasoline rising from the freeway.

"It's too bad the mortal can't join us up here," Snap said. I felt his attention shift to me. "Why is she particularly important to you?"

I suspected he was really asking why she'd mattered so much to *him*. Was that the way to get through to him—to remind him of the devotion she'd enflamed?

"She's proven herself to be a—how would you put it?—a particularly fantastic being of any sort," I said. "She's been standing up to and sticking it to the people who collect shadowkind for years. Even when we turned up in her home out of nowhere, she held her own and refused to be intimidated. You saw just now that she doesn't put up with any crap from me."

Snap nodded. "She protects all of us in every way she can."

"That's one way of putting it. But she's hardly all severity like Thorn. She has a playful spirit to her, a bountiful capacity for amusement and enjoyment..." I had to smile, thinking of her absurdly switched-up songs, all the banter we'd exchanged. Of the passion that radiated from her in the bedroom, so eager both to give and receive pleasure...

Maybe I'd answered the question he'd actually spoken as well.

"It's hard not to care about her, even when it's not the wisest idea," I finished.

Snap was silent for a moment. "What's unwise about it? Everything you've said makes her sound like a worthy mate, if you wanted one. Is it not accepted for shadowkind to have relations with mortals? I thought I'd heard of others forming bonds, from talk in the shadow realm—maybe I misunderstood."

"It's not that," I said automatically. "*I'm* just not made for that sort of connection. My nature is to focus on bodily gratification."

"Well, I don't know anything about that, but you seem to be affected by her words and feelings as well."

"That doesn't matter. What matters is *she* wouldn't want a being like me."

I had the sense of Snap blinking at me in confusion. "Why would you say that? I haven't noticed her treating you differently. Did she say that to you?"

"Well, no, I just—"

I cut myself off, feeling vaguely ridiculous that I wasn't managing to hold my own in a debate with *Snap* of all beings. I could even play out his counterarguments in my head. *There was another woman*, I'd say, and he'd reply, *What does that have to do with Sorsha? Do they share the same mind?* And I would point out—

I didn't even know what else I'd point out. The truth was that Sorsha *hadn't* ever treated me as anything less or different because of my inclinations. Last night… She'd offered up an experience that was all about pleasuring me without a second's hesitation. She'd seemed to revel in the bliss she'd provoked.

Remembering sent a flare of heat through me that wasn't entirely lust.

How could I say she was yet another mortal woman who'd see me as little more than an extremely extravagant vibrator when she'd already proven she cared about me so much more than that? It wasn't ridiculous that I couldn't convince Snap to believe me. It was ridiculous that I'd convinced myself to suppress all the tenderness that had been growing in me with every passing hour I spent in her presence.

Was I really such a coward that I'd push away the one woman who'd enjoyed my company at least as much outside the bedroom as in it—all because of some harlot more than a century ago who couldn't have held a candle to Sorsha anyway? Why was I so intent on throwing away the exact thing I'd wanted so badly all those years ago now that I had it for real?

What a relief it would be to stop reining those unexpected feelings in and… and simply love her.

A sense of release was already spreading through me, loosening more tension than I'd realized had tangled up inside me. Yes. Screw anyone who thought they could decide what an incubus was capable of or deserved. If she wasn't going to be governed by the rules of what made mortals mortal and shadowkind of the shadows, then I could sure as hell take a slight deviation from the typical cubi path. It'd simply be in the name of a different sort of satisfaction.

"You know," I said, with a broader smile, "you might actually have a point."

Now if only we could get the devourer to remember how deeply he'd fallen for this woman too.

FOURTEEN

Sorsha

"Remind me again what *possible* use these pathetic attempts at heroes could be?" Omen said as I checked myself over in the RV's narrow hallway mirror.

As far as I could tell, I looked reasonably civilized in the clean blouse and jeans Ruse had obtained for me, but I couldn't say I totally trusted my ability to judge these days. Not that I could ask Omen—I'd have even less faith in his assessment.

I swiped at my hair one last time, smoothing an unruly wave, and turned to face our leader. "I get that you don't like mortals, and we had some issues with my usual branch of the Fund—but my friends there *did* help us. Heck, even my asshole ex turned up information that helped us decimate the Company's operations. All I'm going to be asking these people is whether they know anything about my parents."

"And you're so sure they'll have something to tell rather than just screwing us over?"

"They've got no reason to screw us over," I said. "Since thankfully I haven't *screwed* anyone in this bunch. Even if they're not superheroes, I think we can assume they generally want to avoid outright hurting shadowkind, or they wouldn't be in the Fund. And yeah, this is the best shot we have at finding out anything about my parents. They wouldn't have been murdered by hunters if they hadn't been working against the douches, and that sounds like Fund work. They probably met there."

Assuming the two people who'd raised me for the first few years of my life really had been my parents. But even if they hadn't been, I still needed to know who the Mom and Dad from my vague memories and the note in my trinket box were. That should lead us on the path to discovering where I'd actually come from—and how I'd ended up with magic powers and blood that turned to smoke when my adrenaline blared.

Ruse came up behind me. He gave my ponytail a flirtatious tug. "Woe betide anyone who fails to give you answers. I've seen how quickly you can dig up the truth, Miss Blaze. And I'll be right there in the shadows to hear if any secrets come out behind your back."

"Just restrain yourself from tripping anyone," I said, not that I'd really minded seeing him knock my treacherous ex on his ass at the first Fund meeting my shadowkind companions had followed me to.

"I'll do my best to behave… while we're there, at least." Smirking, he set his hands on my waist and leaned in to press a kiss to the crook of my jaw. Sweet silky champagne, the incubus did know how to light up every inch of my body with one small touch.

The tenderness of the gesture sent a flutter of warmth through my chest that wasn't just lust. Our interlude with Thorn at the hotel hadn't seemed to change anything at the time, but today Ruse had been back to his affectionate and demonstrative self—the man I remembered from the early days of our… association.

Maybe even more affectionate, or simply in a way that felt more like an expression of his own happiness rather than an attempt to work his charms. I wasn't sure what had made the difference, but I wasn't going to complain.

"I'll keep an eye on the incubus," Thorn said in a rumble, a note of amusement emerging in his usual somber tone. "And make sure none of the mortals cause any trouble for Sorsha."

"There you go," I said to Omen, folding my arms over my chest—

and maybe leaning just a *little* into Ruse's embrace to stretch out the enjoyment. "I'm well-protected."

"One might even say… in good hands," Ruse murmured, trailing his fingers up my sides to set off a wave of heat to join the earlier warmth. He kissed me once more, on the side of my neck, before easing back. "But of course I shouldn't let those hands distract you from your mission."

I shot him a look through my eyelashes. "Save that for later."

Antic skipped down the hall between us, flickering in and out of her invisible state. "I want to meet this bunch of mortals too! So many new humans to play with. If I entertain them, maybe they'll feel more friendly?"

"Er…"

I was saved from needing to answer by Omen, although he took a harsher approach than I would have. He fixed the imp with his cool stare. "Has your 'playing' *ever* put its recipients in a better mood? Think hard now."

She pouted at him. "I do my best. Sometimes they simply don't appreciate a good joke."

"I think we should save the jokes for when I've gotten to know them a little," I said, jumping on that excuse. "So we can make sure you cater to their specific sense of humor."

Omen raised an eyebrow at me as if to ask why I was even bothering to humor the shadowkind he saw as a pest, but he didn't argue with my framing.

Antic sighed and plopped down in the middle of the floor. "I suppose you're right. I just feel my talents aren't being put to full use."

A glimmer of inspiration lit in my head. "Why don't you spend some time exploring town, chat up the local shadowkind you meet—see if you can find anyone who was around twenty-five years ago and might have heard about the murders?"

"I could do that!" She jumped up again and gave me a sharp salute. "I won't let you down."

The hellhound shifter's gaze followed her as she flitted away. "Are you sure you want *her* making our first impressions for us?"

"At least the shadowkind won't flee in terror at the sight of her like they should with you, right?" I knuckled his bicep teasingly as I headed past him to the door. "I'll try to keep this short."

Nothing about the city beyond the Everymobile was exactly familiar. I only had those few wavery fragments of memory from my childhood to go by, and no doubt the place had changed plenty in the twenty-five years since I'd last set foot here. But still, walking down the bustling street past café patios and various vibrant stores gave me a sense of homecoming, as if my body knew I belonged here. Maybe it was all a delusion because I knew I'd started my mortal life here, but there was something enjoyable about it all the same.

After our business with the Company of Light was done, maybe I'd have to spend some time getting to know the city of my supposed birth all over again.

I'd gotten the contact information for someone in the Austin branch of the Shadowkind Defense Fund from a list all Fund members received once they'd participated in the organization for long enough to show their dedication. When I'd reached out last night as we'd approached the city, the woman had told me their next meeting would be in the gaming shop I was walking up to now. The plastic figures of orcs and trolls poised in the windows looked like caricatures of the actual "monsters" living among us.

I walked up to the counter as if I belonged in the place and smiled at the guy behind the counter, who was buff enough to have wielded a sword in real life as well as with a roll of a die. "I'm here for the 4pm gaming session. The password is Dragonlance."

The dude gave me a thumbs up and motioned to a door behind a rack of LARPing instruction manuals behind him. "Head on in. Most of the usuals are already here."

I braced myself and pushed open the door. I hadn't told my contact —just "Monica," since the contact sheet didn't include last names— anything about myself other than that I thought my parents might have been involved in the Austin Fund a while back. My branch back home didn't have any reason to believe I'd left the city, let alone that I'd come here. I didn't *think* anyone would have sent out a general warning when as far as anyone there knew, the worst I'd done was get mixed up with some brutal local shadowkind. But if our experiences with the Company had taught me anything, it was that I was better off being careful than not.

From the size of the room and the—small—number of "usuals" who looked up at my entrance, this branch wasn't as active as the one I'd left behind. The space held two tables, one like a dining table with eight chairs around it and a small card table off to the side that right now held assorted pop cans and a couple of bowls of chips that laced the air with a salty potato scent. Only four of the chairs at the larger table were occupied.

The woman at the head of the table had to be Monica… because she was the only woman in the bunch. She squinted at me through owlish glasses and then leapt up with a grin. Relieved at the thought that she might get a respite from testosterone dominating the room?

"You must be Sorsha!" she said eagerly. "Come in, come in, no need to be shy."

You could tell she hadn't met me before.

The three guys who got up more slowly might as well have been the personifications of a few of the more current mortal legends. The first had on a black suit and shades with a grim expression like he was auditioning to join the Men in Black. Across from him, a short, stout dude with wild, curly hair could have passed for one of Santa's elves in that ruffled green shirt… which was especially noticeable because the burly man next to him was doing an excellent impression of Father Christmas himself with that bushy white moustache and beard.

My hopes sank before I'd said one word. Everyone here except Saint Nick looked to be under forty—too young to have been active in the Fund when my parents would have been.

I gave them a little wave. "Hey. Nice to meet you. Is this the whole group?"

Monica's hands twisted where she'd clasped them in front of her. "I know our branch isn't super impressive. There are a couple other people who come around maybe once a month, but they're not quite as dedicated. Things have been pretty quiet around here lately, I guess. Not many humans stumbling on the shadowkind and ending up connecting with us these days."

The man with the beard let out a low chuckle. "Back in the day, we'd have ten people show up and that was a small turnout. No accounting for how things change." He dipped his balding head to me. "Welcome to our humble abode. My name's Klaus."

Of course it was. I could picture Ruse snickering in the shadows. I managed to keep my own smile friendly rather than incredulous.

"If anyone here can help me, it's probably you," I said. "I don't know how much Monica told all of you—I think my parents were part of the Fund before I was born. Maybe for a little while after too. That'd have been almost thirty years ago. Were you working with the branch that far back?"

"I've been a member since I was twenty-two—which, I'll thank you not to tell anyone else, was a whole forty-five years ago now." He stroked his beard thoughtfully, only amplifying the Santa Claus look. "What were their names?"

I bit my lip. "I'm actually not sure... They died when I was three. From what I understand, they were murdered by hunters, presumably as revenge. I don't know much about them other than that, but that's why I thought they must have been working with the Fund. Why would hunters come after them unless they'd been getting in their way to help the shadowkind?"

For a few seconds, the four humans just stared at me. I guessed colleagues being murdered wasn't a subject that came up a whole lot. To be fair, no one in the Fund back home had died for the cause in the eleven years I'd worked with them—I'd never even heard of anyone there getting hurt in the line of duty until the Company of Light had come for Ellen.

Then Klaus's eyes widened. "*That* must be what happened to Philip. My God. It never occurred to me—maybe I'm naïve."

My pulse stuttered. "You knew them?"

"I knew *him*." He leaned his weight against the table as if he couldn't hold himself all the way up while he thought back. "He was with the Fund for about five years, if I remember right. Near the end he stopped coming all that much—mentioned something about a woman he'd met, getting serious with her. I saw her once, at a distance, when she came to pick him up after a fundraising event. She had red hair like yours. You don't see many with that color. She must have been your mother."

"So, she wasn't part of the Fund?"

He shook his head. "And from what you've said, it must have been around the time you were born that he stopped coming to meetings altogether. We kept in touch a little over the phone, but the last time I called him, his number was out of service. That was back when we still used landlines for most things... I assumed he'd just moved out of town. If I'd had any idea—*murdered*—"

There mustn't have been any major coverage of the slaughter on the news, then. Maybe no one had realized what had happened. The hunters could have covered their tracks. The Company's employees did so very effectively on a regular basis.

And for all I knew, it hadn't been random hunters but the Company themselves who'd come for my parents. Luna had been afraid that whoever had killed them would target us next, and it'd appeared to be Company mercenaries who'd attacked her.

"Do you have any idea what they might have gotten into outside of the Fund that would have pissed off hunters or other people out to harm shadowkind?" I asked.

"Can't think of it. Philip definitely wasn't the type to go for violence... I remember how much he'd grouse when he had to deal with even a little blood from a papercut. He was more about the research, so papercuts were a fairly common thing. But I don't know what your mother might have gotten up to. And maybe he developed a stronger stomach for direct confrontations after he left us."

Well, that answered another question I might have asked—whether the guy had definitely been human. If Kris Kringle here had seen my dad bleed, he couldn't have been any typical shadowkind, anyway.

"Papercuts are about the most painful injury known to mankind," I said.

"He'd have said that, I'm sure." Klaus squinted at me. "I can see him in you now. You might have your mother's coloring, but that nose and jaw... I'll have to see if I have any photos I can give you. We don't record our activities in all that much detail, as I'm sure you understand."

"Right, of course not." A sensation squeezed my lungs, thrilled and yet uncertain. I'd found a lead already—I knew my father's name now. But where did that actually get me? Klaus clearly didn't know anything about the circumstances of my birth. He hadn't even known I existed.

And if I took after my mother *and* this Philip guy... then I really was human. Or I'd started that way, at least. Well, I had already realized I couldn't be a shadowkind, what with being able to handle silver and iron and generally bleeding human blood myself.

Had one of my parents or someone else done something to create the power in me?

Jolly old Saint Nick here wouldn't have a clue. I sure as hell wasn't going to go spilling the beans about my fiery voodoo to this bunch. Some first impression that would make.

Monica glanced at Klaus. "Is there anyone from that generation you're still in touch with? Maybe someone else stayed in closer contact with Philip and could tell Sorsha more about what happened after he left the Fund."

"I can't think of anyone. He always kept his life outside of our business to himself. Like I said, I didn't even know he was still working on behalf of the shadowkind after he left, but if hunters came after him, he must have been. We never carried out any operations that would have provoked them that much. No one still with the Fund was hassled."

Maybe that was why Dad had left. He'd had a bold side under his bookishness and had gone vigilante, knowing the Fund wouldn't approve of pushing back harder against the people who threatened the shadowkind. Just like I'd always kept my breaking-and-entering to free collectors' menageries secret from the rest of my branch. Like father, like daughter?

I swallowed hard. "What if I told you that I think the people who murdered him and my mother might still be around? That they've hurt a whole lot more people—and shadowkind—since then?"

The Man in Black straightened up. "Well, then we'd have to do something about them, obviously. We haven't seen anything major happening here, though. You think they've managed to keep it hidden?"

"I'm not sure how much they're doing in Austin right now," I said, measuring out how much I told them with an eye to caution. "The people I think are responsible have built up quite a network across a bunch of different cities. I think I know where they're the most active here in the US—there are a few of us who're going to travel there and see if we can stop them from continuing."

The green-shirted elf-guy frowned. "Stop them how? If they're that entrenched..."

"Clearly we'd have to try!" Klaus drew himself up straighter. "We haven't had more than minor incidents to deal with in years, and not many of those. We could make a trip for a greater cause, couldn't we, Monica?"

The woman blinked, her eagerness fading, but then she lifted her chin. "I suppose I don't see any reason we couldn't... in one way or another. There have to be steps we can take without making a commotion out of it."

Right. Because here just like back home, avoiding a commotion took precedence over actually protecting the shadowkind from murderous psychos.

The tension in my chest condensed into a lump that settled into my gut. I was human—and right now all I could see was how right Omen was to disparage my kind. They hadn't even noticed when one of their own members was *murdered* right under their noses. And now that they did know, they'd gone straight to figuring out how they could address the issue with as little disturbance to their own lives or the villains' as possible.

I'd accomplished more in defense of the shadowkind in the past month than these people would in a lifetime.

But they were willing to pitch in somehow or other, and if that was good enough to bring Antic on board, it was good enough with our human allies too. I had to look at this glass as half full.

"Great," I said. "I'm going to do some more poking around in the city to see what else I can find out about my parents, but when we have a plan for tackling their killers, you'll hear from me."

And maybe once the idea had sunk in, they'd care a little less about commotions and a little more about justice.

FIFTEEN

Sorsha

All the questions still hanging over me cast an unsettling gloom. Still, I put on my best upbeat front when Omen demanded a report of the meeting and through the other conversations that followed, both with my shadowkind companions and the various mortals I encountered as I made what I could of Klaus's information.

Unfortunately, none of that talk got me anywhere. Klaus sent me snapshots of a couple of old photos he'd found that included a skinny guy around the age I was now with shaggy blond hair and copious freckles, but seeing my dad didn't tell me all that much about him, let alone myself. My Saint Nick couldn't even recall Philip's last name.

I checked the public records I could find through the city's administration, but there'd been no Sorsha born or any kid at all born to a Philip on or around the day I'd always believed was my birthday. Was that a lie, or had my parents simply refused to document my birth?

Given what I was, the latter didn't seem totally unbelievable. But it did mean I had nowhere to go from here—no way of tracking down other relatives or even having good questions to ask.

By the time we'd had dinner, the weight of the uncertainty was wearing on me. I retreated to my bedroom to gather myself.

Pickle might have forgiven me a little since I'd accidentally toasted his scales, but we weren't back to best buds just yet. When I scooped him up for a cuddle, he squirmed out of my arms, scampered across the bed and around the room a few times, and finally darted under the bed where he'd been building a nest out of a heap of gauzy curtain fabric the equines had left stashed down there.

I lay back and tried to clear my head, but the dragon's restlessness had infected me. After several minutes of shifting around and not finding any position that felt relaxing, I got up and went back out into the RV's common area.

Ruse and Snap were sitting at the table, both with a handful of playing cards. The incubus had decided that since his attempts at unearthing Snap's memories hadn't panned out, his next project should be teaching the devourer poker. They were placing their bets with blueberries from little bowls by their elbow. Snap probably preferred winning those over money anyway.

"I see your three and raise you five," Ruse said, waggling his cards, and glanced up at me.

"Where'd everyone go?" I asked. "Or are they just lurking?" Even after all the time I'd spent in shadowkind company, knowing they could be around and watching without my having any way of telling was a bit unnerving.

The incubus shook his head. "Thorn went to conduct a wide patrol, because of course he would. The imp set off to search for shadowkind in the suburb we passed on the way out here, and Omen got it into his head that he needed to make some kind of inquiries of his own. I'm not sure where he headed—he wasn't very loquacious about the decision."

"That is generally his style."

"Indeed." Ruse motioned to the table. "Want to join a friendly game?"

I wavered, but I wasn't sure I was in the mood to exchange banter right now. "I think I'll just take a walk. I won't go far."

"Don't be gone too long, or Thorn'll have a conniption."

The corner of my lips quirked up. "I'll do my best to avoid that."

We'd parked on the outskirts of the city in a secluded treed area not far from the river. I ambled past a picnic bench, which from its splintering edges and dirt-crusted boards hadn't been used in years, and followed an overgrown trail down to the water's edge.

The breeze murmured through the leafy branches and licked cool air across my face. The crisp, earthy scent of autumn was starting to emerge through the last whiffs of summer. It was all very peaceful until a chorus of frogs that somehow sounded both wheezy and hoarse started up. Excellent mood music.

The sun had nearly descended behind the distant buildings to the west. I walked in the other direction, dodging fallen branches and clumps of bushes, which gave me plenty to focus on other than how exactly I'd come to be the impossible being I was. When the breeze turned chilly enough that I wished I'd worn a jacket over my thin tee, I turned and headed back the way I'd come.

I'd nearly made it to the path when the last rays of sunlight caught on a head of golden curls moving toward me. Snap's face brightened when he saw me, but there was something tentative in his expression too. Not a typical look on the being who liked to throw himself headlong into anything that caught his interest.

Keeping up the breezy, nonchalant front was harder with him than with the others. Every time I pretended we were just casual associates, my stomach knotted all over again. But that wasn't his fault.

"Felt like stretching your legs?" I said with my best offhandedly friendly smile.

The devourer smiled back, but the tentativeness lingered. He came to a stop just a few feet away from me. "I wanted to see how you're doing. You'd been gone for some time."

"Oh." I wouldn't have thought this Snap paid enough attention to me to be concerned, but maybe I'd been unfair. I held out my arms in demonstration. "I'm fine. Just needed some air."

"Are you going back to the Everymobile, then?"

I'd thought I was, but my legs balked. The gloom didn't weigh as heavy out here. I wasn't in a hurry to return to it. "I might just sit by the river for a little while longer."

Snap paused. "I could sit with you if you'd like company."

His presence brought a different sort of weight, but I found I couldn't send him off when he'd offered so sweetly. "All right. Thank you."

We settled in on a grassy patch by the remains of a concrete wall, just a few saplings between us and the rippling water. I leaned against the crumbling surface. Snap fingered a spiky flower that had sprouted nearby, careful not to detach it from its stem.

"I guess you must need a break from the rest of us sometimes, huh?" I said when the silence started to itch at me. "Always badgering you about things you can't remember."

"I would like to remember," Snap said. "I don't resent you for trying to help me. It bothers all of you too." He glanced up at me. "Especially you, I think."

It wasn't a question, but I felt the need to address it anyway. "We'd… gotten to know each other pretty well before all this. You're still *you*, but the way it happened—I don't know if that can be replicated. Maybe we'll never end up in the same place. But that's okay. It isn't your fault. If anything, it's mine."

He blinked. "What do you mean?"

"Well, I…" I drew my gaze away and tugged at a few tufts of grass near my knee. "The worst part we can obviously blame on the Company assholes. I know that. But they only captured you because you'd gone off on your own, and I think if I'd handled certain things better, you might not have."

"I'm sure if I left it was for reasons completely my own. You couldn't have forced me."

"Of course not, but— It's hard to explain." How could he understand how emotionally entangled we'd gotten when the being he was now had reverted back to having no concept of intimate relations? "But, you know, we've got bigger problems to worry about. It'll be however it'll be."

Snap considered me for a long moment. "I don't know what I would have done or said before, but I do know that I don't like seeing you upset." He scooted a little nearer to me. With a deliberateness that made me suspect he was bringing to mind a memory of seeing Ruse or Thorn taking the same action and was afraid of getting it wrong, he took my hand in his.

The simple gesture that would have meant so much more a week ago brought a lump into my throat. I swallowed thickly. Maybe it was okay if I just tipped my head slightly to the side so it could rest against his shoulder.

Snap didn't pull away, but he didn't tug me closer the way he would have done before. I closed my eyes, breathing in the smell of him, clover sweet with its mossy dark undertone. An ache filled my chest. Was this making things better or worse?

"I miss you," I couldn't help saying. The words were too true to hold down.

I supposed Snap with his literal mind couldn't help his answer either. "I'm here."

Yes, the most essential parts of him were here: the gentleness, the wonder, and the compassion. Just not the man who'd wanted to claim me as his own, who'd seen me as a shining hero, who'd been both so fierce and so tender in his devotion. The man I'd started to imagine building some kind of life with when all this was over, regardless of what realm he came from.

I'd woken up lust and passion in him, sure, but hadn't he woken up plenty in me at the same time? I'd started seeing things, enjoying things, wanting things I'd never have thought of before… or maybe that I just wouldn't have *let* myself think of.

The ache expanded down to my gut and up to the base of my throat with a more wrenching truth that could have followed my first admission. But what was the point in saying that? This was my chance, from here onward, to pretend it wasn't true. To step back from the path I'd been hurtling down where my life would have been entwined with my shadowkind lovers far beyond the mission we were on.

Wouldn't it be better to sever that connection here and go back to some kind of normal human existence as soon as I could?

The question passed through my head, and all of me tensed in rejection of it. I *wasn't* a normal human—and whatever I was, it was okay. I'd rather be that than one of the people so afraid of risks and consequences.

I could admit this much: Even if I couldn't have Snap the way we'd once been together, I wished I could.

I opened my mouth, but the words stuck in my throat. I hadn't said them to anyone since Malachi, years ago—since the man who'd decided I wasn't even worthy of a conversation had erased himself from our shared life. A sliver of a lyric came easier, twisted to almost the thing I meant to say.

"Somehow I've stayed like glue-ue-ue," I sang softly, gazing through the trees toward the river. "Full of snow and frost I was until I found you."

"Sorsha?" Snap said without moving to dislodge me. Moonlight glimmered across the ripples in the water, and my chest constricted.

Mangled lyrics didn't cut it. Just say it. Once, out loud. He deserved to know, even if he couldn't really understand it.

My fingers tightened around his. My lips parted, and the words fell out. "I love you. Just as you are, with everything that makes you a devourer too. I should have told you back then, when it mattered a whole lot more, but—this is the best I can do. I love you."

Snap had gone rigidly still beside me. Shit, I'd probably terrified him with the seemingly random declaration. His hand released mine, and I lifted my head to give him space—should I apologize? How did I apologize for *that*?—but before I'd had a chance to say anything, his arms were wrapping right around me, tugging me into a full embrace.

My heart skipped a beat. I wanted to look up at him and take in his expression, but I was afraid of shifting in his hold and breaking the moment.

His chin had settled in a familiar position on the top of my head. A faint shudder ran through his body, and his arms squeezed tighter. His next breath came with a hitch. Then he spoke, his bright voice so faint it sounded as if it were coming from a deep, dark hollow inside him.

"My peach?"

My pulse hiccupped. Had I heard that right? He couldn't have—unless someone had told him about the nickname he'd given me?

There was only one possible answer. "My devourer?"

Another shudder passed through him, and then all at once he was pulling me right onto his lap, turning me at the same time to face him. "Sorsha," he said, still strained but with a ferocity of emotion I hadn't heard from him since we'd rescued him. Like a demand. Like a claim.

A burn crept into my eyes. "Snap? Do you—?"

I forced myself to raise my head despite my fears of shattering the moment. Snap stared back at me with a look so fraught yet full of longing that the hope I hadn't quite dared to let loose before flooded me.

I touched his cheek, and he leaned into my caress, the edge of his jaw coming to rest against my temple. His breath stuttered in a warm wash down the side of my face. His embrace tightened.

"The look on your face," he murmured. "I—" He jerked back with a flinch. His arms fell to his sides, his expression tensing with a neon glow flaring in his moss-green eyes. "I'm a monster."

The admission cut through me. I swiveled around in his lap, gripping his face when he made to move even farther away. That was why, after all—not the Company's torments, although no doubt they'd contributed.

He hadn't devoured himself just to escape their experiments. He'd devoured the moment he'd become the thing he'd hated about himself and accidentally taken everything else about the last few months with it.

"Yes," I said, looking straight into his eyes. "You're a monster. So are Ruse and Thorn and Omen. Some days, so am I. I love you with all the monstrousness included. I didn't—I was just startled. I hadn't known what to expect. It didn't change how much you matter to me, not one bit."

"I didn't just kill that man," Snap said. "I shredded apart his soul bit by bit, and every moment of it was agony for him."

I gave him a grim smile. "And I've burned alive more people than I can currently count. I don't imagine they enjoyed that experience very much before it killed them."

"I *liked* doing it. I reveled in it, in all the pieces of his life I got to consume. I—" His voice dropped. "For a moment, I wanted to devour *you*."

That would be the ultimate act of making me his, wouldn't it? I wasn't going to volunteer, but the admission didn't stir any of the horror he'd obviously expected it to.

I stroked my fingertips over his cheek again and into his golden hair. "But you didn't. Do you have any idea how many awful things *I've* wanted to do in my entire lifetime? No one has control over what ideas or feelings pop into their head. We are the things we say and do, not the things we don't. The fact that you wanted to and didn't shows what really matters to you, more than if you'd never wanted to in the first place."

"It could happen again. I thought I could make sure I never gave in to that hunger again, but I was wrong. That's why… The things I gleaned from that man's memories—I thought maybe the Company knew how to destroy the dangerous parts of me. I went to ask them, to show— But they didn't give me a chance to say anything."

I bristled on his behalf even as my heart wrenched for him. "Of course they wouldn't. They don't *want* to believe any of you could be anything other than a total beast."

"I know that now. They wrapped me in one of those jabbing nets and shut me in that glaring box, and when they took me out there was only more pain, and more, and…" He flinched just at the memory. "I wanted so much to get away from that, from what I'd done before, all of it. I didn't mean to forget that completely. I'm not sure what I even did. It just… happened."

"I don't blame you for doing whatever you could to get through their torture. And I don't blame you for what you did to that asshole either. If some prick is on the verge of gutting me again, I hope you *do* shred his fucking soul into as many little bits as you can manage."

The neon flare returned to Snap's eyes. His forked tongue flicked between his lips. He still didn't look completely convinced, though.

I pushed myself off his lap and tugged him with me. With his slender frame and heavenly beauty, it was easy to forget just how impressively tall he was until he was standing right over me, his chin hovering above my forehead. But he was here. My devourer. He was with me completely like I'd started to believe I'd never have him again, and that felt like nothing short of a miracle.

I took a step back so I could catch his gaze again. "You saw how I looked at you when the change surprised me. Why don't you see how I'll react to you now? Bring out your devourer form. I know you won't hurt me."

"Sorsha…"

I walked my fingers up his lean chest. "Please, my devourer?"

I didn't know whether it was the plea or the claiming that decided him, but he inhaled sharply and eased backward to give himself room. His shoulders stiffened. For a second, he looked so uneasy that I almost took back the request. Then the eerie green light that had glinted in his eyes shimmered over the rest of him.

His body stretched upward the way I remembered until he towered a good two feet over me. His face lengthened to accommodate that monstrous jaw that could unhinge to encompass an entire human head. His pupils had narrowed into slits around the neon glow in his eyes, and his fingers stirred restlessly at his sides, long and spidery.

Maybe I should have been horrified. But he hadn't lost his golden curls, and the planes of his face still reminded me of a stunning sun god, if a more vicious version. I could see Snap all through the form that was his more natural state, even though he'd rather have shunned this side of himself. He looked brutal and unsettling and unnervingly but undeniably gorgeous.

Not your type? Not a problem. He was all mine. Just let anyone try to take this monster away from me.

Reaching up, I could just trace my fingers along his treacherous jaw. "*My* devourer," I said again. And then, softer, because somehow it was still hard to say it, "My love."

The light in Snap's eyes blazed. He contracted in on himself with a rush of air, his body barely returned to its more human-like state before he'd caught me up in his lithe arms.

He kissed me like he'd been suffocating and I was his only air. In all the passion he'd shown me before, he'd never been quite this intense. As I kissed him back, I tangled my fingers in his soft hair and held on for the ride.

"My peach," he said against my lips. "My Sorsha." Then he dove back in to capture my mouth just as utterly a second time.

I let one of my hands trail down his chest, and a savage sound reverberated up his throat. Still kissing me, he swept me around. I found myself pressed up against a tree trunk, the bark rough through my shirt and my legs splayed around the devourer's waist.

Snap adjusted me against him, his hands on my thighs, as he dropped his mouth to the side of my neck. The flick of his forked tongue seared across my sensitive skin. His groin pressed against my sex with an unmistakable bulge that sent a wave of heat tingling up from my core.

"Too long," he muttered. "Too many days I lost with you in that awful prison and then forgetting. I want to taste you everywhere again and make you gasp in so many ways, but for now I simply need to be inside you."

"Please," I said, with a perfectly good gasp just from the friction of his erection pressing between my legs through the layers of fabric.

His nimble hands made short work of my pants. He had to ease away to let me kick off those and my panties, but the second the clothes dropped to the ground, he hefted me up against the tree again. As he gripped my ass on one side, he delved the slender fingers of his other hand inside my slit. They curved into my slick channel to find the point of deepest pleasure within. When they stroked against that spot, I moaned at the flood of bliss.

Snap rocked his hand inside me and swallowed whatever other sounds I'd have made with another scorching kiss. It felt so fucking good, but it wasn't what he'd promised me.

"Snap," I said when he released my lips, a whine of need creeping into my voice.

He understood. With a blink, his clothes vanished—he formed them with his shadowkind magic and could dismiss them just as easily. He grasped my hips and plowed his rigid cock into me, not slow and lingering like the first time we'd fucked but all the way to the hilt in one go, thank all that was firm and fanged. The thrust set off a fresh surge of pleasure that knocked my head back against the tree trunk.

Once we were joined, though, the devourer's urgency seemed momentarily quelled. He hummed happily, the sound carrying from his chest into mine, and traced a giddy path along my jaw with his tongue.

"My Sorsha. I love you too. More than any peach."

A laugh tumbled out of me, even though my body was aching for him to ravage me to my release. "That's pretty impressive, but only peaches? What about bananas? Strawberries? Mang—"

He let out a rough noise that was almost a growl and plunged deeper into me, exactly the way I'd wanted. "More than any fruit. More than anything. You are mine, and I am yours."

"Mmm." As he thrust again, more pleasure seared through me, and I couldn't find the concentration to tease him any more. But one other point that I needed to make swam up through the ecstatic haze clouding my mind. "You don't leave again. No matter how worried you are. You'll stay and talk. Promise me."

"I won't leave," he agreed. "I swear it." Then his mouth descended on mine, our breaths and tongues mingling, and we were both completely done with conversation.

My hips bucked to match Snap's thrusts, and if my backside was getting rubbed raw by the tree bark, I didn't give a damn. I couldn't feel anything but the bliss spiraling through my body with each pulse of his cock inside me. As I clutched his shoulders, I sped toward my peak faster than a hurricane.

My whole body quivered as I came, an electric shock of the most exhilarating kind jolting through me. The cry that broke from my throat probably carried all the way back to the RV. What the hell. Let them know our devourer was himself again.

Himself and mine.

Snap followed me over the edge to release with a groan of satisfaction. His fingers clenched around my thighs as he poured himself into me. He held me there against the tree for a minute longer, nuzzling the side of my face, as gentle now as he'd been ravenous moments ago.

"I suppose we should return," he said regretfully as he lowered me so my feet could touch the ground. "The others will worry."

"About you as much as me." I bobbed up to give him one last quick kiss and groped for my pants. "We wouldn't want to cause them any panic attacks. Anyway, I do have a room in the RV, and we haven't got any plans for the rest of the night, so…"

Snap beamed at me with a slyer slant to his mouth than usual. "We have a lot of time to make up for."

"We do." Struck by a wave of gratitude and affection too powerful to ignore, I wrapped my arms around him in another embrace. Tears that were mostly joyful this time formed behind my eyes. "In case I haven't made it clear enough, I'm so glad to have you back."

And who knew how much time we'd get to make up what we'd lost before the Company or some new catastrophe came hailing down on us.

SIXTEEN

Omen

AFTER SPENDING MUCH TIME MORTAL-SIDE, IT BECAME OBVIOUS JUST HOW dreary and amorphous most areas of the shadow realm were. How could any setting have the same impact as even the mortal world's more mundane sites in a world where our interactions were reduced to vague impressions and ephemeral sensations?

So, it said something that the deep, sprawling hollow of the place where the Highest dwelled still managed to strike me as imposing. The shades of darkness lay somehow thicker and blacker there than in any other part of the realm. The shadowy planes seemed to loom over you and simultaneously threaten to suck you down. If I'd been mortal side, the scent that drifted through the filmy air here would have made me think I'd stumbled onto a rotting old ocean-liner: a combination of salt and rust and wet loam that spoke of the immensity of the sea.

Had this area arisen this way naturally, or had the shadows collected more densely and pungently because of the ancient nature of the beings that dwelled here? Or maybe the Highest had constructed the atmosphere in some purposeful way. They did enjoy wallowing in their self-importance.

I waited at the edge of the depths, the innate scorching heat of my shadowkind form holding off what might have otherwise been a chill in the darkness. The scrap of a demon lackey who'd run off to inform the Highest of my arrival was taking so long I was considering eating him for dinner if he ever returned. The Highest drew in enough fawners that they weren't likely to notice one minor being missing.

I was equally tempted to turn around and head back to the rift I'd leapt through—to return to the crisper air and the vivid colors and sounds that I had to admit I often preferred to this place even if I wasn't terribly fond of most of the mortal beings that inhabited that world. But if Sorsha could swallow her pride and turn back to her Fund for as many answers as she could get, and even the damned *imp* was willing to spend hours scouring the streets for a shadowkind who might have information, how could I shy away from making at least this one attempt to support my greatest cause?

It was a matter of dignity.

The unimpressive demon didn't return after all. Perhaps one of the Highest had decided he'd make a nice snack. Instead of a lackey coming to usher me in, the call arrived in an echoing swell of a voice that I felt wash through me more than heard.

"Hellhound, you may come."

So kind of them to allow this meeting. As I traveled forward, I suppressed the snarky remarks my old self would have liked to make. I wasn't sure I *would* have made them, even back when I'd had a hard-on for making trouble. Not after my first meeting with the Highest, anyway. I'd been smart enough even back then to prefer toying with beings who couldn't turn around and bite me in two.

The attitude that came over me when I sensed the massive, ponderous presence of the Highest ahead of me was more than shrewd caution, though. There wasn't much dignity in it at all.

I'd heard one of the humans I'd conned long ago speak about how he reverted into the postures of his childhood when he visited his parents, as if their expired authority over him could reduce him from his current status as an adult. While I'd never been a child in the same way as mortals, and the Highest had nothing to do with my existence, confronting their enormity made me contract inside myself instinctively, as if I wasn't one of the oldest beings in the realms besides them. My hellish heat shrank back beneath my skin; my fingers curled their claws against my palms. I didn't quite tuck my tail between my legs, but an embarrassingly large part of me wanted to.

I couldn't help imagining the choice remarks Sorsha would have made about that. Which annoyed me even though she wasn't around to actually make them, doubly so because of the other emotions that stirred at the memory of the glint that lit in her bright eyes with her teasing.

Our mortal ally had tangled herself up far too much in my thoughts.

"You return, hellhound," one of the other Highest rumbled. They towered so close together I'd never been entirely sure how many of them there were. "Have you tired of your quest?"

I drew myself up with as much confidence as I could exude without crossing the line into insubordination. "Not at all. Actually, that's what I came to talk to you about."

There was a general rumbling between more than one of the beings —a chorus of disgruntledness. I thought it was a different one who spoke up next.

"When we permitted you to take your leave on this endeavour you requested to pursue, it was with the understanding that we had no interest in it ourselves."

The "permitted" remark rankled, even if it was technically accurate. "I know," I said. "But I thought you might be interested now that I've discovered more. The harm I thought was being done to our kind—it's much more serious and widespread than I ever suspected."

Another of the Highest let out a sound that could only be described as a grunt, which even the echoing quality of their voices couldn't make portentous. "Are there rabble-rousers like yourself fanning the flames of ire again? We can send a host to bring them in line—"

"No," I cut in, instinctively bracing myself. For good reason, because an instant after my failure of manners, a jab of pain coursed across my throat like the jerk of a choke chain—if that choke chain had been buried within my flesh.

I barrelled onward. "I haven't seen any of our kind inciting the conflict at all. The offense is all on the mortals' side. There's a large collective of humans spread out across the mortal realm, determined to destroy not just every being of our sort on their side but the entire shadow realm as well."

"Hrmph. Not surprising after all the work you and your ilk did to stir up those hostilities in the past."

My jaw clenched. I didn't need them to remind me of my complicity in the problem. That was exactly why I couldn't back down now and let the Company do their vicious work unimpeded. I'd helped set the stage for them, and I'd damn well yank it out from under them if I possibly could.

"What these mortals are attempting goes far beyond any damage the shadowkind ever caused them. They're attempting an outright extermination. And from what we've uncovered, they're close to achieving it. They're even working on ways to extend their influence through the rifts. They want *all* of us dead."

And that includes you, I thought but kept in. The Highest could read between the lines. The last thing they'd appreciate was a being beneath them suggesting they were in any way vulnerable.

One let out a bellowing sort of chuckle. "They could never penetrate our home. You may disdain the creatures, hellhound, but you give them too much respect at the same time. They are frail, waning beings who barely breathe before they're gasping their last."

It would seem like that to the Highest when they'd been around who knew how many millennia. As if a human lifetime wasn't plenty long enough to wreak all kinds of havoc.

Some part of me abruptly wished that Sorsha *were* here, just to see what she'd say to these lumbering ancients. Better that she wasn't, though, if it'd even been possible. I'd get to admire her brashness and the flare of that flaming hair for about two seconds before she was down one of these leviathans' gullets.

I hadn't really expected any other answer. But for the sake of being at least as intrepid as that one mortal, I gave it a final go. "I think they might come up with a way. But even if they don't, they're tormenting and killing all sorts of mortal-side shadowkind."

The sublime presences of the Highest loomed even larger over me. "That is not our concern. We regulate the rest of *you* when we must, but we don't trouble ourselves with mortals. If one of our kind has been intensifying the problem, then perhaps we would step in, as we did with you... and your associates. Otherwise those who choose to pass through the rifts must own that risk themselves."

Naturally. They would police and even slaughter their own kind if other creatures complained about the turmoil we were stirring up, protecting the mortals from *us* as much as those creatures from the mortals, but ask them to shield us from a direct, organized onslaught of maliciousness from those same mortals...

What did these ancient goliaths know about any of this anyway? None of them had ever ventured mortal-side, as far as I knew. They laid down laws and punishments about a world they'd never even experienced.

I would simply be thankful that they'd provided a convenient opening for the other topic I'd wanted to raise with them, one I thought I might get a smidge farther with.

I picked my words carefully. "On the subject of our kind causing problems... I've heard a few beings mention one you were searching for not that long ago. A shadowkind you wanted reports of but warned others to stay away from because of the danger—the name might have been Jasper or Garnet... some sort of red stone?"

That question elicited a much more energetic rumbling. My throat prickled as several sets of senses focused intently on me. Their voices blurred together.

"What have you heard? Has someone located that being? What destruction has it already wrought?"

They were definitely worked up about this rebel shadowkind—and obviously their minions hadn't located it yet.

"Nothing that I'm aware of," I said quickly. "And no one I spoke to had any idea of that one's current whereabouts. I simply wanted more information so that if I saw evidence that might point you in the right direction, I'd recognize it to pass it on."

There was a moment of silence I couldn't help feeling had a skeptical edge to it. Then one of the Highest responded. "It was in the region the mortals call 'America' when last we heard, but that was some span ago by mortal time. The name you must watch for is Ruby. And even you should not challenge this one. If you catch any sign, bring the matter to us at once."

"As you request. I want nothing to do with anyone who's raised so much of your ire. What has this one done, if I might ask, so I can be particularly wary?"

"That is none of your concern." The attention on me shifted, with another pinch of pain around my neck. "*You* haven't been disturbing the mortals again during your quest, have you, hellhound?"

Darkness save my soul if they ever found out just how much mortal blood had already spilled at my hands—and claws and fangs—in the past few weeks. Not enough that it would have mattered to them if it wasn't for my history, but with that hanging over me...

I forced a smile I wasn't sure they'd notice and lied through my teeth. "Of course not, oh Highest ones. I'm keeping within my bounds. I'll return to my quest, then—and do my best to ensure none of the shadowkind affected by these treacherous operations ever need to call on your help."

"Very well. That is satisfactory."

I had the impression of them turning their backs on me, and the tension that had coiled through my chest released. Breathing more steadily again, I loped out of their hollow as quickly as I could move without looking as if I were fleeing.

Despite all their power, that was the only thing the Highest really cared about in their old age: being left alone. Even telling their lackeys how to carry out their orders was an imposition to them. All the better for me that they'd let much of their surveillance of the mortal realm dwindle over the past century.

But it was clear we wouldn't find more allies against the Company of Light among them. We'd just have to hope we could track down this "Ruby"—and that the enemy of my enemies would turn out to be a friend to us.

SEVENTEEN

Sorsha

I DIDN'T THINK I'D EVER SEEN ANTIC QUITE SO INVIGORATED, WHICH WAS saying a lot considering she was the most excitable being I'd ever met. She bounced up and down on her little feet as she led us through the thinly forested area that bordered a post golf course. The teenage son of one of the players blasted a jaunty ska tune from his phone for a minute or so before the employees hustled over to scold him, and the rollicking tune matched the imp's exuberance perfectly.

"The gnome said he's been living in this city for almost fifty years," she exclaimed breathlessly. "He must have been here when you were born, Sorsha. Maybe he knows about the hunters who killed your parents!"

I'd also never heard anyone speak quite that cheerfully about a double homicide. "Maybe," I said, tugging at the hem of the starchy button-up blouse I'd had to wear for this adventure. My shadowkind companions had been able to slip across the grounds to the shelter of the trees invisibly, of course, but I'd needed to disguise myself as one of the staff to avoid questioning. As long as no one asked me to distinguish between a putter and a driver, we were good.

Under the canopy of leaves, this section of the grounds was cooler and dimmer than the grassy stretch under the morning sun I'd left behind. I eased aside a low branch blocking my way and continued that thought. "Or at least he might have known my guardian. Luna could have told him something about them or me, or..."

Or how I'd come to be the only human being I'd ever heard of with magical powers.

"If he has any answers, we'll get them out of him," Omen said. The words could have been menacing—they usually would have been, coming from him—but his tone was mild, almost as if he was trying to reassure me. Hold the presses! The ice-cold hellhound might be softening up after all.

It didn't seem totally fair to think about him in those joking terms anymore, though. He *had* accepted this substantial detour in his quest to let me investigate my heritage. Now, that might be in large part because he didn't want his secret weapon incinerating herself before we were done destroying the baddies, but I'd take the generosity anyway.

"Are gnomes dangerous?" Snap asked by my other side. "I don't think I've ever met one." His grip on my hand adjusted to twine our fingers more tightly together. As pleased as all our companions had been to find out he'd come back to himself, he'd stuck like glue to me since last night—and I couldn't say I minded. I was still wrapping my mind around the fact that I had my devourer back and that the intimacy we'd shared might not be so fleeting after all.

"The worst he's likely to do is bite her knees," Omen said with a crooked smile.

Snap squeezed my hand. "I won't let him do that!"

The hellhound shifter shook his head in exasperation. "I don't think we really need to worry about that unless our mortal here decides to start using *him* as a soccer ball. But if he's a particularly rabid one, I think we can manage to save her."

"I'll restrain myself from playing any contact sports with our informant," I said.

We'd decided not to bring the full group on this excursion-slash-interrogation so as not to intimidate the gnome too much, but naturally Bossypants couldn't allow anything to happen without being there to oversee, and Snap had refused to let me out of his sight. Thorn and

Ruse were patrolling the edges of the golf course at a greater distance. I definitely didn't feel in any danger from the being we intended to meet.

Antic halted by an aged stump about the height of my waist and knocked on it. From the thump, the thing was hollow. "Hello there!" she chirped. "I'm back with my friends that I told you about."

Omen couldn't manage to stop his lips from curling in disdain at being referred to as one of the imp's "friends," but he schooled his expression into something if not friendly than at least emotionless rather than openly hostile.

A little man wavered out of the shadows around the stump. And by "little," we're talking *little*. Like, the dude barely came up to my knees. Although I guessed that did put him in the perfect position to bite them if he decided that was a fun way to pass the time after all.

Other than the absence of a pointed cap, he looked disturbingly like the garden gnomes—you know, the ceramic kind—I was more familiar with than the real deal. His chubby cheeks were rosy above a tuft of silvery beard, his eyes twinkled, and his diminutive body was stout and plump beneath his bright blue jacket and emerald trousers.

Despite the twinkle in his eyes, which I guessed was a permanent feature and not an expression of joy, he was frowning. "What's this all about?" he muttered in a reedy voice. "I don't like showing myself when there are mortals around."

Unlikely he'd been fast friends with my parents, then. I crouched down so I wasn't towering over him quite so much and flashed him a smile. "I'm really sorry. We just wanted to ask a few questions about things that happened quite a long time ago. There aren't very many shadowkind who've stuck with this city with as much dedication as you have."

The flattery got me somewhere. The little man puffed up his chest, and his frown faded even though it didn't disappear completely. "I know when I've got a good thing. What is it you wanted to know?"

"There was a fae woman who lived around here about thirty years ago. Her name was Luna. In her shadowkind form, she had filmy wings and she was pretty sparkly… well, like faeries are. I don't suppose you ever ran into her?"

The gnome rubbed his chin. "Luna. Luna. I can't say that name sounds at all familiar."

As my heart sank, he waved a finger in the air. "I know who you might ask, though. She's rather fickle, as faeries are too, but they do often gravitate to their own kind. There's a fae by the name of Daisy that hangs around out back of the lighting store over that-a-ways. It's been a time since I went that way, but she's been in this city almost as long as I have, I think, so I don't see why she'd have left. You could try her."

He motioned to the east toward this lighting store. Well, that was the start of a trail, at least.

As I straightened up, Omen cleared his throat. *He* didn't bother lowering himself to the gnome's level. "One more thing. At least a couple of decades ago, powerful shadowkind might have come through the city asking about a being they'd have said was dangerous—one named Ruby."

The gnome paused, and then his eyes widened. The recollection made him quiver on his feet. "Oh, yes, I didn't like those ones that asked about it. Three times they badgered me—a lot less politely than you lot."

"Three times?" Omen repeated. "Did you know something about Ruby?"

"Not at all. But they seemed to be making the rounds over and over thinking they'd turn something new up. I can't say why. It must have been over the course of at least a month they kept coming around."

"How long ago was that?"

"Like you said, years and years ago." The little man grimaced. "I'd put it out of my mind."

"All right. That's helpful to know." Omen gave the gnome a slight but definite tip of his head in thanks.

"I guess we'll have to hope this fae who might or might not be at the lighting store will have more dirt to dish," I said as we headed in the direction he'd pointed us.

Snap cocked his head to one side. "How do humans sell *light*?"

I wasn't going to get into the extent that we actually did, or I'd end up needing to explain the entire science of electricity. "They just sell fancy ways of generating that light for inside our houses. Lamps and ceiling fixtures and all that."

"Ah, yes! They had many glowing things like that in the hotel that were lovely to look at." The devourer beamed so brightly at the memory that we probably could have put him up for sale in the store.

Omen, on the other hand, was frowning now as if the gnome's expression had been contagious. "We do know more than we did before. There must have been a reason the Highest's minions would have focused on this city more than others. If there was a definite sighting of 'Ruby' here, or more than just a sighting—we might be able to pick up that trail while we're here too."

I didn't know why he'd frown about getting closer to this shadowkind he figured might help us, but with Omen, sometimes it was better not to ask.

The lighting store was easy to spot: a big building with massive amounts of crystal fixtures glittering in its broad windows. Snap re-emerged from the shadows in time to take in the view in all its splendor with an awed inhalation, careful to hold his forked tongue out of sight.

Antic had vanished from view with the others while we'd headed out of the golf course. As we came around the back of the store, she sprang into sight again, pointing at a little house that was really more of a hut, wedged between the rear end of two neighboring shops. The paint on its clapboard front and slanted roof had dulled and faded, but I could tell it'd once been a vibrant pink and blue. That looked like a fae's design sense, all right.

"Is she around?" I asked without thinking the question through.

"I can pop in and check!" the imp offered, and sprang toward the closed door.

"Hold on!" I said quickly. I should have remembered she didn't have much sense of boundaries. "I'd imagine it'll give a better impression if we're polite enough to knock rather than barging right in."

Antic shrugged as if it was all the same to her and rapped her small fist against the door. "Daisy?"

Omen stepped closer. No visible hint of his shadowkind form showed, but his aura of power intensified enough that the energy tickled over my skin. "We know you're here, and you know we're shadowkind," he said to the patches of darkness around the house. "We only want to ask a few questions. I'd rather not have to get more insistent about that."

I smacked his arm. "What did I just say about politeness?"

He gave me a baleful look. "I phrased that threat very politely." He turned his gaze back to the house. "To be clear, I'd much rather keep things peaceful."

What was he going to do if the fae woman didn't emerge—dive into the shadows and wrench her out by force? She'd be just overjoyed to answer our questions then.

I made a face at him and attempted my own plea. "We wouldn't be asking—or being assholes about it, in the case of someone I won't name—if it wasn't important. It's about a fae named Luna who used to live in Austin a long time back. A gnome suggested you might have known her."

For a moment, nothing happened. Then a form shimmered into being in front of us.

The fae woman wasn't Luna's twin or anything, but she had enough of the same fae features that I could have believed they were cousins. Her pale hair sparkled in the pigtails she'd wrapped with shiny pink ribbons; actual glitter gleamed all over her frilly dress. She'd draped several strands of crystalline glass that looked as though she might have stolen them from the store's chandeliers over her shoulders as an opulent sort-of necklace. Her features were delicate except for her eyes, which were just a little too large to look comfortably human. Those eyes fixed on me.

"You know Luna?" she said in a tinkling voice that reminded me of my guardian too, so much that my lungs constricted. "It's been so long —I kept hoping she might come back."

The constricting sensation deepened. She didn't know that Luna couldn't ever come back. "Luna… looked after me when I was a kid. But she was taken down by hunters several years ago. I'm sorry. Were you close when we lived here?"

"Oh, no. She's gone?" The woman's face fell for a moment before she seemed to recover. Her makeshift finery tinkled as she shifted on her feet. "I couldn't say we were *really* close, but, you know…"

She tipped her head to the side and gave me a dreamy smile that sent another wave of recognition through me. I hadn't really talked to any fae women other than Luna—I hadn't realized how much she simply represented her kind rather than her own unique approach to life. Apparently coyness was another common trait.

"I always wished we could be better friends," the fae went on. "She had so much energy; it was lovely to be around her. But she was so busy too…"

I fought past the eerie resemblance to focus on my search for answers. "Do you know who else she spent time with? Was there anyone in particular?"

"Let me see, let me see… It was so long ago!" She tapped her lips with another cutesy tip of her head to send her pigtails bobbing. "She mostly stuck to the downtown area. I can't think of anyone still around who'd—oh. There was the elf. I always wondered why she bothered with *him*. But I saw them together a bunch of times."

I'd take whatever leads I could get. "And this elf is still in the city? Where we could find him?"

"Oh, he came from the worst place. I don't go out that way anymore, but he never moved that I knew of. He might still be there."

"*Where*?" Omen demanded, the threatening edge coming back into his voice.

The fae woman let out a faint huff, and I was afraid she'd vanish rather than tolerate his tone. But she wanted to dish her gossip more. "He lived in the *sewer* of all places. Near the spot where the busy road crosses the river." She shuddered. "The one time I talked to him, he said no mortals would ever oust him there, but *I* could never tolerate it."

"Thank you," I said, and then, since the hellhound shifter had at least tried to support me in his overbearing way, added, "I don't suppose you know about anyone named Ruby? Shadowkind might have come around asking about that name a while back too."

"Ruby… Ruby… That does sound familiar. I thought if it'd been an actual ruby, I'd have cared more." She tittered. "They were so insistent about it, but I don't keep track of every being in this place."

Nothing more than the gnome had told us about that one, then. Even less, really. "Thank you," I said again anyway.

She bobbed her head and blinked away, shooting a hint of a glare at Omen just before she vanished. He simply rolled his eyes.

"I wonder why anyone was so interested in this Ruby shadowkind," Snap said as we headed to the Everymobile. "It doesn't sound as if the local beings even knew about them before the Highest sent their underlings around to ask."

I knit my brow. "That's a good point. If—she?—did something so offensive that the Highest shadowkind wanted to bring her in, wouldn't someone have heard about what she actually *did*?"

"I think you're missing the obvious," Omen said in a dark tone.

"What do you mean?"

He looked over at me, his expression grim but not cold. "The search for this Ruby happened somewhere around the same time as your birth. We haven't determined yet how you got your powers, which no mortal should have. Maybe Ruby was in the habit of imbuing shadowkind skills on beings that weren't meant to have them."

A chill pooled in my gut. "You're saying—"

"I'm saying our two mysteries might almost be the same one. It's starting to seem like an awfully big coincidence otherwise. Whoever this Ruby is, maybe it's because of *her* that you are as you are."

EIGHTEEN

Sorsha

We figured the "busy road" the fae woman had mentioned was probably the highway that cut through the city—at least, it'd better be, because otherwise we'd be down in the channels of excrement for days. As Ruse drove along it toward the river, I peered out the window for promising-looking manholes. A mix of nervousness and excitement gripped me as tight as a toddler clutching her blankie.

We were going to talk to a shadowkind who might have been Luna's closest friend, as shadowkind went. If anyone would know more about her history here and what had gone on with my parents, it'd be him.

Which also meant that if he *didn't* know, the trail might run totally cold.

I drummed my fingers against the top of the sofa-bench and sang to settle my nerves. "Drive it by, we'll watch for you, don't plead or even move."

Ruse let out a chuckle from the driver's seat. "Are we going to ask this elf some questions or hold him up?"

"If we let Omen do the talking, it might end up being a combination of both."

Antic smothered a giggle where she was perched on the edge of the table.

Omen bared his teeth at me, but only a little. Progress! "You're assuming I'm coming with you into that dank place."

I raised my eyebrows. "You'd actually let me off the leash to handle things on my own?" I teased. "Not afraid of all the catastrophes I might cause down there?"

"You have occasionally managed to handle yourself acceptably."

"I think you mispronounced 'amazingly.' Anyway, you'll miss an excellent opportunity to show off your authority and all."

"Perhaps I'd rather use that authority to avoid treading through sewage." A glint lit in his eyes that was uncharacteristically playful. "I'd almost think you're afraid to go down there by yourself, with all these attempts to badger me into coming along."

Oh, he thought he could turn the tables on me that way, did he? I resisted the urge to stick out my tongue at him. I could be slightly more mature than that, this once.

"I won't be alone. I'll be accompanied by the shadowkind who think getting answers that could help us take down the Company is more important than steering clear of shit." I patted Snap's thigh where he was sitting next to me and Thorn's elbow where he was standing beside the sofa at my other side. "Maybe 'boss' doesn't mean the same thing it used to."

"I'm pretty sure delegation has always been part of the job description." He glanced toward the front of the RV as Ruse slowed to a stop. "But don't worry, Disaster. Since you're so keen on having my protection, I'll sacrifice a few minutes to the stench."

"That's not what I was saying," I groused—and holy heretic hounds, was that a hint of a *grin* from the hellhound shifter, despite our argument?

"I *could* hang back then," he said as he pushed himself away from the counter across from the table. "Darlene needs protection more than you do while you're around."

"Oh, no." I gave him a light shove toward the door. "You said you'd come, and you've got to be a man of your word. Come on. You'll get to do so much glowering and growling. Probably mostly at me. It'll be fun."

He caught my hand before it'd even finished grazing his back and pushed it back toward me—not roughly, but firmly. The heat of his fingers blazed over my skin, making the banter suddenly feel electrically charged. "You won't want to misplace this where we're going."

"A gentleman would offer his elbow," I informed him.

"Good thing I've never pretended to be one of those, then."

"M'lady," Thorn said, offering me *his* elbow and looking as if he took the whole gentleman thing as seriously as he did most other subjects.

I smiled up at him and rose on my toes to kiss his cheek. "I already know you're perfectly chivalrous. But you'd better stick to the shadows unless we need defending—it's going to be hard enough getting down there without anyone asking why we're messing around with city property."

Ruse appeared on the steps by the door, apparently having already scoped out the area. "There's an opening to the sewer down one of the quieter streets," he said. "We can go through the shadows and push it up for you, and if you're quick about it, there aren't too many people around to notice."

"Sounds like a plan."

The other shadowkind vanished, except for Snap, who rested his hand on my hip with his arm around me. I tipped my head back to put my face at the perfect angle to receive a kiss, and he didn't disappoint me.

"I'll be fine," I told him. "You'll all be right there—and I'm just walking down the street." And disappearing into a manhole of some sort, but I'd rather not dwell on that too much ahead of the stink. Slipping stealthily through the gap shouldn't be any trouble after all my thieving practice.

"Of course you will," Snap said with automatic confidence. "I only wondered…"

When his pause stretched on, I poked his arm. "What? You've wondered a lot of things, and I'm always happy to answer."

He wet his lips with that tempting tongue. "Have you and Omen become closer? The way we are, and how you are with Ruse and Thorn?"

The memory of the hellhound shifter's hot fingers just now—and of the moment days ago when he'd responded to my kiss—tingled through me. "Not like that," I said. "Why?"

"It's only—there are times when the two of you have that energy between you, for what Ruse calls mating." The devourer looked abruptly, adorably awkward. "I wouldn't be upset. He is... very different from me, and very powerful, and he's doing so much for all shadowkind. I couldn't say I'm worthy of your affection and he isn't."

I gave him a wry smile. "I think it's more whether he thinks *I'm* worthy of his. That's all right. The three of you are plenty to keep me occupied. And he's a jerk at least as often as he's tempting."

Snap hummed. "He carries a lot of weight on his shoulders. It's made him hard. But he's been good to me." He pressed a peck to the top of my head. "I'd better catch up. Hurry to meet us."

I shut the door of the RV—currently in tour bus form—carefully behind me and made for the ridged metal surface that stood out against the asphalt just down the street. As I reached the manhole, the heavy cover lifted to show an inch of darkness and the faint gleam of Thorn's white-blond hair.

A couple of teens were ambling down the street toward me. I gestured for the warrior to wait a moment, became fascinated by the closed storefront next to me until the teens had passed by, and then made an upward motion with my hand.

The second he'd raised the cover higher, I squeezed through the gap and found myself wrapped in Thorn's free arm, pressed to his brawny torso. He lowered the metal disc, his body braced between the tunnel's walls with his back and feet at opposite sides, and adjusted me against him.

"I'll convey you down, m'lady."

"Thank you ever so much," I said with a grin.

It was hard to keep that good mood intact as the sewer smells closed in around me in the dimness. Only a few thin streaks of light fell from the little holes in the manhole cover. Thorn set me down on a stretch of dingy concrete, his mouth set as if he were restraining a grimace at the stench. "It is very dark from here on. The others have gone ahead to search for our elf."

"Let's hope they find him soon." I had no qualms about

wrinkling my nose. Breathing through my mouth to dilute the stench, I pulled out my phone and switched it to flashlight mode. I wasn't afraid to go tramping around in these tunnels, but if I could avoid taking a wrong turn into a trench full of literal crap, I'd prefer that.

Up ahead, one of those trenches held a turgid flow of murky water. Well, water and lots of other things much less appealing than H2O. Was that the swish of a crocodile's tail?

Better not to look too closely.

I crept along the walkway beside it, my stomach starting to churn for reasons that had nothing to do with my nerves. After what felt like a hundred and one years, a figure emerged into view up ahead: Omen, a hint of his hellhound magma glow making him stand out against the darkness. "Here he is," he said in a dry tone that didn't give me much idea of what to expect.

The skinny man who stepped out beside him could best be described as "sullen." Everything about him seemed to droop, from the fall of his black hair, the bags under his eyes, and the slope of his jaw, all the way down to the floppy tongues of his miraculously spotless sneakers. True to elvish form, his ears had sharp tips aimed toward the ceiling. If we had to take this meeting out in public, maybe Ruse could give him some hat pointers.

"He says his name's Gloam," Ruse said, materializing just behind me. He rested his hand on my waist with the sweep of his thumb in a fond caress. "I asked to make sure, and surprisingly enough, it's definitely not 'Gloom'."

I held back a snicker with a twitch of my lips. "A fae woman by the lighting store told us you were good friends with Luna."

The elf sighed, the sound heavy with disillusionment. You'd have thought we'd just told him his house had burned down and his car exploded. Although given where he was living, maybe that had already happened.

"Luna," he said in a dour voice. "I thought I mattered more to her than to be *abandoned* without a second thought. But off she went to who knows where and left me all alone."

Antic popped out of the darkness with a tsk of her tongue. "She's dead now, elf. So maybe it's better you didn't go with her, huh?" She tweaked his sagging shirt sleeve and shot me a smile as if seeking my approval of the point she'd made.

Gloam appeared so depressed already it was hard to tell whether that news affected him. "Some mortals say to die is to go to a better place. It could be that's true."

"Let's hope it is," I said, aiming to speed things along. "And she left in a rush because she thought she was about to get murdered *right then* by hunters who were in the process of murdering other friends of hers. I take it that you did know her pretty well?"

"We explored the human nightlife together. She said I was the only one she could talk to who wouldn't think she was strange." He sighed again. "Everyone thinks *I'm* strange. Who am I to judge anyone else? Not that it stops them."

I wasn't sure "strange" was the right word for the impression he gave off, but getting into a debate about it didn't strike me as a good use of my time. "I'm sorry to hear that. You don't happen to know about other people she was friendly with in the city, do you? Maybe a man named Philip... a human man?"

"Oh, yes," Gloam said, as if this were common knowledge, so why was I bothering to ask him? "The human man. She talked about him. One of her daytime companions, since my company isn't good enough then."

His head drooped farther. How had perky Luna ever ended up friends with *this* dude?

Omen looked as though he were restraining himself from grabbing the elf's shoulder and shaking the answers out of him. "What did she say about him? Did she mention anything to do with his wife?"

"That's the only reason she knew him—his wife. Not that she was his wife to begin with. Who would have thought? But these things—sometimes it's strange..." The elf shook his head dejectedly. "Luna made it sound like the most wonderful experience, not that I'll ever have it."

Antic gave him a jab in the belly with her finger. "What experience?" She made a face at me. "I think he's trying to make us all just as miserable as he is."

"No. No, no one should ever have to feel as I do right now." He rubbed his mouth. "Ember was Luna's *best* friend, really. How could I compete with an ifrit? And then she goes and has this romance with some human man—Luna found that so fascinating—but she stopped talking to me all that much, she got so wrapped up in helping *them*..."

My heart stopped. "Wait, you're saying the guy named Philip that Luna knew—he married an ifrit? A shadowkind woman?"

"It does happen from time to time," Gloam said, as if he couldn't imagine any fate more tragic. Or maybe he thought the tragedy was his own lack of romance? It was difficult to tell through the general haze of melancholy. "All hush hush, of course. Luna barely let it slip even to me. Augh, maybe I shouldn't even have told you." He dropped his head into his hands.

My pulse started up again, but its beat kept stuttering. Naturally it was Snap, ever curious, who asked the question we must all have been thinking in that moment. He might not even have realized how ridiculous it would sound to anyone more familiar with shadowkind-human relations. He set his hand on my shoulder and leaned past me toward the elf. "Could the human man and the ifrit have had a child?"

Gloam laughed, but somehow he turned even that noise despondent. "Everyone knows shadowkind don't produce children. But it's funny that you ask. Luna said something once—looking up legends of when fae and the like had supposedly mingled with mortals to that extent—I suppose they might have been looking for a way. I doubt they found one, though."

I swallowed hard, staring at him, not yet ready to look at my companions and see what they made of that revelation. No doubt rose up in me. What he'd said wasn't definitive proof, but the pieces fit together in a way I couldn't deny.

I bled both blood and smoke. I could hold iron and silver, and I could generate fire by will alone. I was human, and I was also shadowkind.

My parents and Luna had found a way.

There was my answer—and it was just as much a puzzle as it'd been before I'd started this quest. How could anyone tell me what being a hybrid of human and shadowkind would mean or how to handle my powers? Even this elf, who was apparently the only being still alive who'd known that secret, had dismissed it as utterly impossible.

NINETEEN

Snap

How could I ever have forgotten the tempting spicy sweetness of Sorsha's skin? Thinking back to those days when everyone and everything I'd known in the mortal world had felt so unfamiliar sent a jarring sensation through my mind.

So I put the thoughts out of my mind and focused on the much more enjoyable sensation of slicking my tongue across the nub of my beloved's breast.

Sorsha's breath caught with the hitch I loved to provoke, her fingers tightening where they'd twined with my hair. I gave the risen nipple a little nip I'd discovered could bring out even more delightful sounds and eased up to claim her mouth again.

My hand delved through the tangle of sheets on her bed to tease between her thighs. The slit where we both found so much pleasure met my touch slick and ready. Mmm, I would have to start our mornings off this way more often.

Sorsha's knee rose against my hip, but she pulled her face slightly back from mine with a rough inhalation. "Snap—I think we're going to need to be more careful from now on."

I couldn't resist dipping one of my fingers into that hot slickness within her. The way she bit her lip made me want to kiss her all over again, but I wasn't sure what she'd meant. "Careful how?"

"Well—what we found out about me. That from the sounds of things, my parents discovered some way that my mother could have a kid even though she was a shadowkind. It sounds like it must have been pretty difficult to manage, but—we don't know whether I could get pregnant. So probably better not to risk it."

Right. This act of merging bodies was how humans created life. Could what we did here, what we'd already done mingling so closely and passionately, bring about a being that was somehow both her and me?

The idea sent a quivering thrill through me. She *was* my beloved, in every sense of the word I understood. She'd told me she loved me even when faced with my most monstrous form, even after I'd admitted how harsh and selfish the hunger inside me could be. And I didn't know what else this other hunger—tender and selfless instead, wanting to possess her but only as much as the act would please her too—could be.

Love barely seemed a big enough word to encompass the feeling that lit me up with a warm glow whenever I looked at her.

I kissed her temple and eased my lips down until I could nibble her tender earlobe. "Would having a child be so awful, Peach?"

Sorsha laughed and tugged my mouth to hers so she could kiss me back. "Maybe not, someday *way* down the line," she said. "You have no concept of what babies are like, do you? They take a lot of work, and they need a lot of attention and security. Not really a good fit for our current lifestyle."

"Hmm. But perhaps later. When there's no more Company of Light to worry about?"

"We'll see. I never really saw myself starting a family, at least not… not recently. But it's starting to feel a little more possible. I mean, assuming we all survive this war we've ended up in."

"We will," I said, wishing I felt as certain about that as I did about my adoration of the woman beside me. I worked another finger inside her, testing the sensitive inner flesh for the spot that sent the greatest flush of bliss over her skin. "How do we be 'careful' in the meantime?"

Sorsha arched into my touch. When she managed to speak, her

voice was thick with desire. "For now, we'd better stick to hands or mouths. Which you're doing a *very* good job of, by the way. And I'll have to pick up some condoms—we put those over you"—she stroked her hand across my erection, drawing it even stiffer with a surge of delight—"and then no worries about babies."

I could follow those rules—and perhaps adapt them to my purposes to even more enjoyable effect. I pulled myself down her body, still stroking her between her legs. "How about hands *and* mouths, then?"

"I'm sure as hell not going to argue—"

I flicked my tongue over that other responsive nub just above her slit, and her agreement cut off with a gasp. I transformed the gasp into a moan by adding the pressure of my lips.

Her taste filled my mouth, even more fiery down here. The most delicious thing I'd ever tasted.

Something clanged from the kitchen area down the hall. Ruse's voice filtered through the wall. "I come bearing breakfast! Who's ready to eat?"

I was too busy savoring this delicacy to be tempted by whatever he was offering. But Sorsha would need to fill her stomach simply to keep her strength up. I wouldn't keep her from her sustenance very long, then.

I suckled harder, pumping my fingers in and out of her while adding a third. Sorsha let out a guttural sound. Her body clenched around me and then sagged with a shudder of release. More wetness seeped over my fingers as I withdrew them. I licked it off and smiled. "All the breakfast I need."

Sorsha laughed again and tugged me down next to her. Her hand trailed over my chest to my still-rigid cock. When she wrapped her fingers around it, a groan tumbled from my lips. I would so much have liked to delve that wondrous part of my physical body right inside her. Perhaps Ruse had some of these 'condoms' around, given that sexual intimacies were his specialty?

But that thought led me back to the reasons we needed that protection and the possibilities of how Sorsha herself had been conceived. Even through the expanding swell of pleasure, my mind latched onto a memory from before we'd ever become so intimate.

I stilled her hand before I could lose the thought in my distraction. Sorsha looked up into my face with a question in her expression.

"It makes sense now," I said.

"I'm glad my hand job came with bonus enlightenment. What does?"

"The impressions I gleaned from that pretty box that your parents left for you." I might not have known just how much I'd come to value Sorsha's existence at the time, but I'd still been honored that she'd trusted me with the treasures of her past. "The strongest sense was that they'd taken a lot of risks to bring you into their lives—that it almost hadn't been possible at all. Because of how difficult it must have been for the two of them to conceive you at all."

"That's true. I'd forgotten you took your reading of the box." She paused. "You didn't get any sense of someone else being involved in that process—someone they owed a debt to or wished I could have met or anything like that?"

"You mean if the Ruby shadowkind was connected to them and helped them somehow?" I shook my head. "It was all focused on you and their bond with you. But that doesn't mean Ruby wasn't involved. It was so long ago, the impressions were quite vague."

"I get it." She grimaced. "I remember that you also told me there was someone from Luna's past that she missed. I wonder if that was the lighting store fae or our gloomy elf. I never thought to ask her about the things she left behind—somehow I always took it for granted that her whole life should be dedicated to me."

I stroked my hand over Sorsha's hair. "From what I know of shadowkind, I don't think she'd have made the sacrifice if you weren't *much* more important to her than anything she gave up."

Thinking about her losses had dampened my desire. I could fulfill it to greater effect once she'd gathered her protections anyway. I sat up, tugging her with me. "You should have your breakfast before it gets cold."

Sorsha arched an eyebrow at me. "Are you sure?"

I stole one last kiss. "I have everything I need. For now."

We emerged from the bedroom to find that Ruse had laid out his bounty on the RV's table—and Omen had returned to join us. The hellhound shifter had gone off on his own again not long after we'd finished questioning Gloam, who'd had no contact with the shadowkind named Ruby either, at least as far as he'd admitted. From our leader's stern expression, I suspected his independent search hadn't turned up any new information either.

Sorsha must have made the same assessment. "No sign of our mysterious Ruby?" she said as she slid onto the sofa-bench. I sat beside her and picked up a particularly delectable-smelling pastry with syrupy cherries in the middle.

Omen sighed. "As far as I can tell, none of the shadowkind in the city even *saw* her, let alone noticed any catastrophe she caused. It could be that the Highest's lackeys cleared out any other being who'd been drawn into her schemes... but I'd have expected there to at least be rumors of that kind of round-up."

"Perhaps it was a false rumor that brought them here to begin with," Thorn suggested. "Or a piece of information they thought was related to her but wasn't after all. We don't know how many cities they conducted a more intensive search in. The fact that they did here, where Sorsha was born, might not be that great a coincidence."

"True enough. For all we know, they harassed shadowkind across every metropolitan area in this half of the country." The hellhound shifter's next breath came out in a huff. "I suppose there's no point in continuing to go out of our way looking for Ruby. Whatever trail there was is long cold. We'll have to make do with what we have. Rex's hacker thought the command center of the Company was located in San Francisco. We'll scope them out and decide how to proceed from there."

Sorsha had picked up a wrap stuffed with cheesy scrambled eggs. She stopped in mid-bite, her stance tensing, and lowered her meal with an audible gulp. "You want us to leave now?"

Omen eyed her across the table. "It seems we've achieved all we can here. We have a basic sense of how you came to be what you are and no way of quickly determining any of the details. Did you really think we'd forget about our primary mission while we searched out the key to an incident that no shadowkind I've ever heard of has stumbled on before or since?"

"It might not be *that* hard to figure out. How many shadowkind have wanted to have kids anyway? I thought I'd at least talk to the local Fund branch again. Klaus might remember more if I ask him some leading questions. And we could use their help *with* that primary mission too."

Omen made a scoffing sound at that idea. "It was hard enough getting the humans who knew you to contribute when we were in their own city, Disaster. What are these mortals going to do for us when we take on San Francisco?"

"I don't know. It just seems worth a try. Trying did get us somewhere more than once before, as you've admitted yourself." She waggled the wrap at him.

"And let's hope I never have to again," he said dryly. "They have your contact information if they feel spurred to action, don't they?"

"Well, yes, but—" Sorsha hesitated, the fierceness in her eyes dimming. I was about to put down my pastry and reach out to her when she found her voice again. "We still don't know why my powers have been acting up. I don't know how much help *I'm* going to be if I can't be sure I'll burn up the right people when people need burning."

Omen propped himself against the kitchen counter, looking unconcerned. "I think we've got enough of an answer for that. Obviously your human parts are having trouble accepting the shadowkind parts. It's the conflict of our species all over again."

"Wonderful explanation, but it doesn't help me avoid setting myself on fire."

"Sorsha." Omen's gaze turned momentarily intent, his tone serious enough that my ears pricked to even closer attention. "The fools in the Fund won't be able to help you with this. You can handle it. *We* can handle it. I'll just keep training your impossible self until your control improves. I'm not letting you go down in flames. All right? I'd just like us to take the training sessions in the direction of our ultimate goal so we can tackle more than one bird with the same stone."

Sorsha blinked at him. "Oh. Okay." Then her smile came back. "As long as these training sessions don't involve pummeling me into a pulp like you've attempted in the past."

Omen rolled his eyes skyward. "I think I can manage to keep you safe from that threat as well."

I inhaled slowly, tasting the energy that shivered through the air between them. It was such an odd mix of antagonism, comradery, and amusement that I had trouble knowing what to make of the stew. It wasn't at all like the steady vibe of fondness and support that flowed between Sorsha and Thorn or the sensual heat she and Ruse could spark with just a glance, but it held echoes of both of those flavors along with so many others.

Maybe they didn't know where to go with that chaos of emotions either.

"I'd still like to touch base with the Fund people here, even if it's just briefly," Sorsha was saying when her phone beeped with some sort of alert. She picked it up and read something off the screen. As her face fell, my heart sank too.

"What's happened?" I asked.

"It's—" She swiped her hand over her mouth as if trying to push away her frown, but it didn't quite work. "It shouldn't really matter. I didn't expect anything. Ellen from back home just texted me. She's decided that as far as our conflict with the Company goes, she and the rest of the Fund members from my old branch are staying out of it completely."

TWENTY

Sorsha

A SPURT OF FLAME LEAPT UP FROM THE BALL HURTLING TOWARD ME—AND at the same time, a crackling heat washed over my hand. As I dodged out of the way of the now fiery projectile, I clapped my fingers against my shirt and restrained a wince at the stinging.

"You're not keeping your focus," Omen said from where he'd leaned against the wall of the batting cage a few feet away. "You can't expect to maintain control if you're not even paying attention."

"Sorry for having a few other things on my mind the day after I discovered I'm some kind of never-before-heard-of human-shadowkind fusion," I shot back, and waved my hand in the air to dispel any lingering heat.

"If you're not up to continuing, we can leave things here."

"I didn't say *that*." Imagine the party he'd throw if I ever admitted I couldn't meet one of his challenges. Oh, no, this gal was in it to win it. Even if I wasn't totally sure what "winning it" would look like. Not frying myself at random, presumably.

The batting cage training session had actually gone pretty well at first. As Omen had set up the ball launcher to, well, launch balls in the approximate direction of my face, the other shadowkind had come out to watch. With Antic's eager cheers, Ruse's sly praise, and Thorn's and Snap's quieter but powerful support, I'd been able to put what I'd learned about my history and Ellen's refusal from my mind.

But now the daylight was dwindling. The time was creeping closer to the Fund meeting Omen was grudgingly agreeing to let me attend, and it was getting harder to tune out the niggling uncertainties.

And look what that got me. Scalded fingers—nice work, Sorsha.

I squared my shoulders and readied myself for the next ball. The machine chucked it at me with all the intensity of a nuclear missile launch.

My eyes narrowed, and the leather surface burst into flames. The ball streaked through the air like a meteorite, dissolving into ash just before it reached me. As the charred remains pattered to the ground with a whiff of smoke, I braced myself for a matching singe across my skin, but none came. Thank buttery boom sticks. For once, my trainer couldn't complain.

"Better," Omen said. "You *can* pull it off—now you just have to keep doing that."

"Thanks for the excellent coaching, boss. Where would I be without your sage wisdom?"

The corner of his mouth curved slightly upward. "Searing yourself to a crisp, I've gathered."

Before I could come up with an acceptable retort, Thorn emerged from the shadows, back from a quick patrol of the area. We must have been safe from marauding hunters and actual missile launchers, because his expression was... if not *happy*, because Thorn rarely managed to look anything other than serious, then at least semi-relaxed.

"Maybe our mortal has put in enough work for the day," he suggested mildly. "No one can focus well once they're worn out."

I dragged in a breath and found my muscles were starting to get a bit trembly from the effort I'd been exerting for the last few hours. "You have a point. I want to be sharp for this meeting, too." I glanced at Omen with a quirk of my eyebrow. "Unless you have any objections, dog breath?"

The shifter smiled thinly at me, but his gaze wasn't anywhere near as icy as it'd been when he'd first attempted to train me weeks ago. It might even have been a tiny bit warm. "Have a break then, Disaster. But don't expect me to cut the human side of you any slack."

He stalked back to the Everymobile. I rolled my shoulders, walking in a circuit of the arena to stretch my legs at the same time. When I came around to my original spot, Thorn had lingered there, waiting for me.

"These recent events—they're weighing on you," he said.

The gentle concern that came through his low voice sent a flutter through my chest. There was nothing quite like the reminder that one of my greatest marvels had been melting this warrior's stern demeanor.

"It's a lot," I said. "Especially when all I've got now is more questions. If it'd turned out my parents had a shadowkind work magic on me or whatever, that would have been a little easier to wrap my head around. And everything with the Fund…" I rubbed my arms and let out a little laugh. "I guess I really did burn those bridges right to the ground. Maybe it's a *good* thing I'm making tonight's appeal to people who barely know me."

Thorn let out a rumbling sound. "I don't think your behavior necessarily dictated how your former colleagues responded to your request for help, m'lady."

"No? They sure acted like it had."

"I've observed—there's a way all beings tend toward—" He paused, glancing around. The other shadowkind had left as far as I could tell, but either someone had stuck around in the shadows or Thorn felt we were too close to our home base for comfort. He motioned for me to follow him.

We meandered around the rusting fence surrounding the rundown facility and on toward the river, much farther down than we'd been parked before. I scooped up a pebble from the sidewalk and tossed it at the water, accomplishing a whole one skip before it sank with a ring of ripples.

Thorn gazed solemnly toward the opposite bank with its concrete barrier. "I saw it often during the wars," he said. His expression and his tone told me he had to be talking about the vicious battles fought several centuries ago, in which the wingéd had divided to support opposing factions of humans and battled each other. "We were always trying to stir up other shadowkind to our cause, as I suppose our brethren who opposed us must have as well, but rarely did they join in even if they voiced agreement."

"To be fair, there were quite a bit more people *dying* in that conflict than have in our 'war' against the Company so far," I had to point out.

"Perhaps. But one truth I have seen across my time is that beings will almost always retreat from a fight unless they are dragged into it by a motivation much deeper than a plea to their generosity. I fought because I couldn't turn away from my brethren when they called on me, because at least for some time I thought that if I fought well enough, fewer of us would die..."

When he lapsed into silence, I tucked my hand around his powerful arm. I'd heard the warrior voice regrets that he hadn't been there for his comrades enough, but never with the hint of doubt that had come into his tone now.

"Are you thinking you might have been wrong about that?" I asked.

Thorn's jaw worked. "The things I've seen and learned over the past few weeks have made me question many things, including my own judgments of the past. I'm starting to wonder if perhaps we would all have been better off if we hadn't been so quick to leap to each other's aid at arms but instead had stopped to discuss just how necessary the warring was to begin with."

I leaned into him, pressing a quick peck to his shoulder. "You're turning into a pacifist on me. I'm shocked."

"I wouldn't go *quite* that far." He eased his arm right around me and traced a line of heat up and down my side with the stroke of his fingers. "I will defend you and the rest of our companions by whatever means necessary as long as breath remains in this body. But do you know... I never was even certain of what we were fighting *for*, or why our brothers who rose up against us were so convinced they needed to strike out at us. How many of us leapt into the fray so ignorantly? What if most of those deaths could have been avoided?" He shook himself. "But we're getting away from your concerns of the present."

"That's okay. I get to be concerned about you too. And it sounds like it's a good thing you're questioning the past. Better now than never. I still think the Fund doesn't have anywhere near as much an excuse for staying out of our battles. Their whole purpose is supposed to be helping the shadowkind—and they've heard plenty about why we're fighting the Company."

"Well, there are other, less honorable reasons one might avoid conflict too." Thorn's hand stilled against me. "When I first heard that the Company's presence extends into Europe, I must confess that something in me balked. To return to the lands where I fought before, or at least close to them—But it isn't as if much remains of that time anyway. It's only in my mind that the uneasiness dwells. The few of us remaining wingéd scattered far and wide after the slaughter. We're closer now to one of my former companions than I might ever be across the ocean."

I raised my head. "There's another wingéd around here? Where've you been hiding them away?"

Thorn chuckled grimly. "With so few of us remaining, we're attuned to each other's presence. I couldn't tell you how many exist in the entire world, but a few hours before arriving in this city, I could tell there was another of my kind some distance to the west. Perhaps even in San Francisco."

I was about to point out how that could potentially come in handy when Ruse hollered from the direction of the distant RV. "Oh, Sorsha! You've got a gentleman caller."

Thorn frowned. I gave his arm a tug. "Come on, let's see what he's going on about."

It didn't take long to figure out. When we reached the Everymobile, the rest of our group was standing on the pavement outside it, in a loose ring around a lanky figure with floppy black hair and pointed ears. Gloam the elf had come to visit.

If it hadn't been for the hair and the ears, I might not have recognized him. The evening was settling in around us, but Gloam was glancing around with far more pep than I would have imagined he could exude. His hair no longer drooped but swished with the movement of his head. He rubbed his hands together and shot a wide grin my way.

Maybe I was hallucinating? But Omen, Ruse, and the others were all staring at the elf with equal amounts of bemusement.

"I've come to join your quest," Gloam said with a playful bow.

"You mentioned that you were looking for more shadowkind to help you tackle these enemies of all of us. How can I hide away when adventure calls?"

I just barely held myself back from gaping at him. Antic bounded around him, jerking at his clothes and poking him here and there, her mouth twisting at a puzzled angle.

"What's the big deal?" she demanded. "You got two beings in the same body or something?"

"Just the one." He smiled at her too as if oblivious to her prodding.

She turned to the rest of us and jabbed her thumb at him. "No way is this the same guy we met in the sewers. Maybe toxic waste mutated a twin!"

"Oh!" Gloam said with a lilting laugh. "I see the confusion. I apologize for how downcast you must have found me yesterday. You see, I'm a *night* elf. When the stars and moon are out, I'm rejuvenated. During the daylight hours, I haven't much energy to put on a good face."

Understatement of the year. But having now met the perky version of Gloam, I could believe Luna had been best buds with him.

"I don't suppose you bring any special combat skills or potent magic to the table?" Omen asked.

Gloam shrugged with the same buoyant grin. "I can cast my own darkness."

"In more ways than one," Ruse remarked, smirking.

"We're glad to have you on board," I said, half afraid the others' skepticism would send him back into his previously depressed state. "You made it just in time. We're going to be heading out any minute now."

Antic was still eyeing the elf suspiciously, but she snapped her fingers and darted toward the RV. "Come on. I'll show you where *you* can make a spot for yourself. Just remember, any pranks or tricks, I call the shots."

Omen caught my eye as the rest of us moved to follow them. His voice came out cool, but he couldn't totally flatten the amusement in it. "How is it that you manage to conscript the most useless beings to our cause, Disaster?"

I held up my hands, matching his tone. "Don't blame this on me, boss man. *You're* the one who mentioned our grand crusade to him."

Omen's expression twitched as he must have realized I was right. "I didn't *invite* him," he said. "But I suppose I can't blame you if he invited himself. Other than your optimism might have influenced me into mentioning it at all."

I swatted him. "Sure, I'll take the blame, as long as I also get the credit when he ends up foiling the Company on our behalf."

"Rather than waiting on the chance of that, you'd better keep practicing that self-control. A little of me has to rub off on *you* eventually."

"Hey, my amazing abilities are thanks to me alone."

"And aren't we all grateful for that," Omen muttered, climbing the steps, but I thought I caught a flicker of a smile.

He hadn't needed to practice with me today. He hadn't needed to dedicate himself to helping me control my powers at all. I wouldn't have expected it to necessarily matter to him if one human—well, half-human—burnt herself up as long as I burned down the baddies in the process. But apparently he did, and that softened any snappy retorts I might have tossed at him.

However much he'd come to value my contributions, it didn't stop Omen from tossing out a little more snark when Ruse parked down the street from the gaming store. "Make your plea and be back here in ten, or maybe we'll leave you with these bozos."

"You'd better leave me Darlene, then, since you won't be needing her without my mortal ass around," I informed him on my way out.

I'd texted Monica to give her a heads up that I'd be stopping by. Apparently the Austin branch of the Fund was particularly cautious about people infiltrating their secret lair: the password had already changed, to "Yoshitaka." I gave it to the same dude behind the counter and strolled on in to the evening meeting.

A couple more people had shown up for this one: a slight, middle-aged woman with a Tinkerbell pixie cut and a young man whose not-entirely-successful attempt at growing a moustache looked like tufts of grass poking up from a desert plain. Klaus was standing at the foot of the table, waving his arms emphatically as he made some point about, "…might be the only real chance we get."

Everyone looked over when I came in, and a smile leapt to Klaus's face. "I think we're all decided," he said before turning back to the others. "Are we?"

Monica nodded slowly, the Man in Black and the scraggly moustache dude more emphatically. Klaus beamed, the rosiness in his rounded cheeks making him look even more like Saint Nick.

"That's great," I said. "Er… What are you decided about?"

"You made it clear there's a menace lurking that's a threat to both the shadowkind and those of us trying to help them. We can't look the other way. Let us know where you need us and what we can do, and we'll pitch in however we can."

I'd expected to have a debate on my hands, but apparently it'd already happened without me, spearheaded by Father Christmas himself. And it wasn't anywhere near December 25th. I'd still take this gift, thank you very much.

I grinned back at him. "Okay, I take back my 'great' and raise it to 'awesome.' We're definitely going to need all the help we can get. I can't stay very long because we're about to head out, but we'll be regrouping in San Francisco. If any of you are willing to make the trip and help us on the ground, maybe even just coordinating with the Fund branch there, that'd be huge. But even doing some information gathering or similar from afar would be useful."

Klaus rubbed his hands together. "I haven't been out to the west coast in years. A vacation and a campaign of righteousness in one—sounds good to me. I'll just have to check the flights." He glanced around at his companions. "Who's with me? You've got to figure out your own way there, but I can cover an AirBNB big enough for all of us."

"I've got the time off already," the Man in Black said. "Count me in."

The pixie woman raised her hand. "I think I can make it work. I'll just have to make a couple of calls."

"Same here," Monica said, and inclined her head to me. "Keep me in the loop with what's going on and what else you discover. If you could email me a full run-down of how you've tackled these people so far so we can start our own strategizing, that would be great."

I wasn't sure I really wanted them knowing that our strategy so far had involved a lot of torn-off heads, disemboweled torsos, and charbroiled corpses. As the memories darted through my head, a wavering heat shot over my arms—and a flame shot up over the knuckles of my right hand.

It was barely a flash of light, there and then gone as I jerked my hand against my side. I bit my tongue at the stinging sensation but held in my yelp. Still, spontaneously catching on fire is the sort of thing it's difficult to keep on the down-low. When I looked up, several of the eyes watching me had widened.

Time to divert and refocus! "Of course," I said quickly, clasping my hands in front of me as if nothing at all unusual had sparked from them. "It'll be a bit of a novel, but I can give you the gist with all the important stuff."

"Excellent." Monica smiled, which I hoped meant everything was still a-okay. I had the feeling apologizing for my near-combustion would only make things worse.

"I'll get started on that then. And reach out once we're in San Francisco so we can meet up. Don't you lose my number." I wagged a finger at the group at large and hightailed it out of there before my prickling nerves could let loose any further supernatural special effects.

TWENTY-ONE

Sorsha

When I came out in the morning to grab breakfast, Gloam was drooping over the table like a plant that had wilted with too much sun. The downcast nature that consumed him by day made it hard to believe he'd been gleefully discussing favorite mortal desserts with Snap yesterday night.

Antic perched on the counter across from him, holding the new map book Ruse had picked up for her. A vibrant pink sticky note poked from the top of the cover announcing *This Way Up*. I wasn't sure trusting her to give directions even with that safeguard was the best idea.

She looked up from the book to stick out her tongue at the night elf. Her skinny legs swung against the cabinets. "I keep telling him he should take that sour face into the shadows where at least we won't have to look at it."

Gloam sighed. "I know it isn't pleasant to observe my dejection. I can remove myself if that's what you'd all prefer."

I shot a warning look at Antic and sat down across from him with the muffin I'd picked up. "Don't be silly. You are the way you are, and if you'd rather stay in physical form, that's up to you. Anyone who doesn't like looking at you can just point their eyes in another direction."

The imp huffed and hopped down from the counter to stand closer to Ruse, who was back on driving duty. "In another, I'd say, ten miles we're taking an exit south." She turned the book sideways and then her head sideways to match, which didn't exactly add to my confidence.

Even with shadowkind drivers who had no need for sleep, we weren't going to make it to the Golden Gate City until tonight. At least we had our lovely home on wheels to enjoy for the journey. And we hadn't even stolen it or conned it out of anyone—legitimate rides for the win!

As I bit into the doughy sweetness of my muffin, Gloam raised his head enough to peer at me from beneath his thin eyebrows. "There's so much more Luna was hiding from me than I ever could have guessed. *You* came from a human and an ifrit…" He stopped there, just staring, as if the impossibility of it had rendered him mute.

"Hey, no one's more surprised than me," I said. "She raised me for thirteen years and never made a peep about me potentially having voodoo skills or anything like that." Really, a warning would have been nice. What if I'd accidentally set one of my high school teachers up in flames for disparaging my essay-writing attempts or what have you? Not that I was thinking of anyone in particular who might have deserved it…

"I never thought such a thing could have happened. I suppose that just shows how little I truly understand this world."

I had to restrain myself from rolling my eyes at his insistence in making the insanity of *my* existence all about *his* failings. "I'm sure it wasn't easy. Omen has been around for, like, a thousand years or something and he's never heard of anyone managing it."

Somehow my reassurance only turned Gloam gloomier. He looked down at his hands. "They must have wanted you an incredible amount to try so hard to bring you into being. I can't imagine anyone will ever care that much about *my* being."

No wonder Luna had only hung out with this guy during the night. I was starting to rethink my rebuke to Antic. But his comment stirred up a trickle of warmth too, one that spread through my chest as I soaked it in. For the first time since Ellen had texted to say she and the rest of that part of the Fund were out, my nerves completely settled.

"They did," I said. "Love me a lot. I remember…" My recollections of my parents were vague, but every impression I had of my mother's face framed by her ruddy hair was beaming with affection. In the note they'd left for me, they'd called me their "treasure." And Luna had believed in their commitment to each other and to having a child enough to not only help them with their search for a solution but to devote her life to me for more than a decade after their deaths.

So what if I was an impossibility? Yeah, I was a freak of nature who still had a lot of work to do when it came to controlling her hocus pocus. But I'd also been born out of the most immense love I could ever have imagined.

My parents and Luna had believed I deserved to be brought into this world—that I'd make things here better rather than worse. I had to believe in myself at least as much in their honor.

The Everymobile swayed as Ruse changed lanes, to no honks just this once. "We're officially halfway there!" he called back to us.

"Woohoo!" I raised my arm in a fist-pump. A moment like that called for a song. "We're as spry as a tiger; we're as chill as a kite, rising up to the challenge on arrival!" I belted out.

Gloam blinked at me with a bewildered expression, but Antic giggled and did a little jig with the map book.

Omen materialized next to the table with his arms folded over his chest. "If you want to actually 'rise' to that 'challenge' without barbequing yourself any more than you already have, I'm thinking another training session might be in order. If you think you can manage not to burn down Darlene around us?"

I stuffed the last of my muffin into my mouth with a quick nod. How many challenges had I already tackled and lived to tell the tale? I'd get the hang of this. If my mom and dad had managed to get their differing natures to cooperate enough to produce an entirely new being, I could talk the opposing sides of myself into getting along.

Swiping my hands together, I got up. "All right. Let's do this." I paused, considering our limited options for training space. "Maybe not right here near the driver's seat, since I can't promise a flame or two won't get a *little* out of hand. And I'd rather not make a bonfire out of my own bed, so… the master bedroom?"

"I could just stuff you into the bathroom, since no one else here needs that."

"Yeah, but there'd be no room for you to join me in there to boss me around."

I marched past him to the narrow doorway at the very back of the RV. I'd only gone in there once before, when Gisele had been curled up on the bed unconscious from her battle wounds. Apparently she'd wanted to shake that memory too by changing the surroundings—the bedspread was different, a dark blue that twinkled here and there like stars. She must have gotten Bow to scrounge up a new one for her.

"All right," I said. "What's on the menu today? Any sparkly things you'd like scorched out of existence?"

Omen cast a baleful look around at the bedroom, which had more surfaces that shimmered than not. Even the ceiling had been dabbed with patches of gold glitter like a shiny hurricane was about to descend on us.

The unicorn shifter's taste in décor was unmistakable. It really was too bad she and Luna had never gotten the chance to meet.

"I thought we'd go back to the first trick that worked." Omen brandished a handful of torn strips of paper he'd pulled from his pocket. "Simple and easy to work with in a confined space. But first—I thought back to when I originally decided I needed to temper my, ah, temper. We can try a few centering and calming techniques that might help you stay cool while you're summoning your fire."

Anything that reduced the chances of me ending up in cinders sounded good. "I'm ready. Teach away!"

Omen talked me through a couple of mental exercises involving measured breathing and visualization. I decided it was wisest not to mention that his instructions sounded an awful lot like the yoga guru meditations Vivi's mom was addicted to.

Who was I to poke fun, anyway? Picturing a serene stretch of still ocean water, I could compel its imagined cooling sensation all the way across my skin. Of course, what really mattered was whether my mental imagery would continue to hold water once very real flames came out to play.

"Do you think you've got a good enough grip on yourself now?" Omen asked. After several minutes of pacing while he lectured, he'd finally allowed himself to sit on the edge of the bed—a foot away from me, but even when I closed my eyes, the heated power of his presence tickled over my skin.

"I'd better be," I said. "Bring out the papers!"

He got up again to stand in front of me and held one pinched between his fingers about two feet from my face. The bedroom, for all its impressiveness, *was* still an RV bedroom, and we didn't have a whole lot of room to work with. He waggled the paper slip so it swayed above his grasp. "You should feel honored. I'm trusting your aim enough to put my hand in harm's way."

"Of course, what that actually means is you still don't believe I could actually incinerate you."

He really smiled then, with a cocky slant to it that abruptly made me wish I was getting a grip on *him*. "Glass half full, glass half empty —it's up to you how you see it."

He shouldn't be tempting me, or one of these days my uneasiness about the energy that sometimes rose up inside me would be outweighed by my desire to teach him a lesson about underestimating humans… or half-humans… whatever.

I focused my gaze on the paper. Imagined that serene ocean landscape spread out through my body—and a jolt of my inner heat leaping up through that, aimed only at my target. *Burn!*

The paper went up in flames. If they stung Omen's fingers, he didn't let on. Still smiling, he closed his hand around the fire to snuff it out and then brushed away the ashes that remained. "Excellent. Now we just need to do that a thousand or so more times."

I restrained a groan. "Suddenly I feel like I've become your personal shredder. I'll have lots of practice if I ever want to take a job in covering up paper trails when all this is over."

"There you go. I'm setting you up for new and exciting career opportunities too." He paused, and the wry tone left his voice. "Did it feel all right? You didn't burn yourself at all?"

"All good. Perfectly cool and oceanic." I made a beckoning gesture. "Let's get on with the rest of that practice, or we'll be in Uruguay by the time I'm done."

By taking a moment to center myself and bring up the calming imagery before each blast of flame, I managed to barbeque four more small slips of paper and then a couple of larger ones without any ill effects. Were we going to work all the way up to a complete encyclopedia set?

Of course, when I needed to extend my voodoo in the middle of a fight, I wasn't necessarily going to have time to perform a little meditation before I jumped into the action, or I might get barbequed by our attackers in the meantime. My visualizations weren't going to deflect bullets or daggers or laser whips.

As Omen prepped his next target, I dragged in a breath and let the cooling sensation wash through me again, as thoroughly as I could summon it. I needed to see how long the effect would last if I didn't keep bolstering it with every surge of power.

The hellhound shifter started mixing things up by crumpling one paper into a ball, letting another wave as he dangled it, and whatever else he could think of to vary the practice. I blasted each of them one-by-one, not letting myself hesitate to gather my emotions this time. Pretend we were in the midst of the fray, and each of those scraps was a Company asshole about to slaughter me or my shadowkind allies. *Burn. Burn. Burn it all…*

A sharper flare of heat shot through my chest, and a flame licked up across my forearm at the same instant as Omen's paper caught fire. I slapped my arm against the bedspread, an ache already spreading through my flesh. When I checked it, the skin gleamed dark pink.

"Fuck finicky flapjacks," I muttered.

Omen grabbed a bottle of aloe he'd had on hand, proving he hadn't really trusted my control all that much. "Were you concentrating?" he demanded.

"Yes, yes. But I had to pick up the pace. My powers aren't going to do us much good if I'm stopping to praise the seas while some prick is stabbing a knife into me."

"I'm sure you'll get there. You're rushing it."

I made a face at him. "Right, I have no idea why I feel any time pressure at all. It's not as if dozens, maybe even hundreds of shadowkind are being tortured as we speak, all to develop some sickness that'll kill the lot of you."

"You won't accomplish much to stop the Company if you're too busy scalding yourself."

Rather than handing the bottle to me, he squeezed a dollop onto his own fingers and sat next to me to smooth the gel over my burnt skin. At least the shadowkind part of me seemed to heal the wounds it dealt me faster than any human would have recovered.

The real cool of the aloe spread over my arm. As the pain drew back, other sensations came into more vivid awareness. Like the brush of Omen's fingers, unexpectedly gentle, as he finished his administrations. Like the not-at-all unpleasant heat emanating from him where he was now poised just inches away.

As he let my arm go, I gave in to the urge to poke one of his substantial pecs. "Who would have thought the hellhound could be so sweet?"

Omen snorted. "Yes, my preference that you remain uncharred so you can actually participate in those upcoming battles is clearly a sign of boundless devotion."

"There you go," I said, cheerfully ignoring the sarcasm dripping from his voice, and leaned back on my hands. "I knew underneath all the rancor you adored me."

The shifter's gaze skimmed over my breasts and down the rest of my body, the flicker of orange light in it kindling a very different flame all through me. Then he pushed away from the bed with a jerk, that familiar ice forming in his eyes. Any good humor flattened from his tone. "You should get back to practice. With a minimum of burnt flesh this time, if you can manage that?"

I glowered at him. "Why do you have to revert back to being Bossypants the Asshole? Is it that hard to admit that you care at least a tiny bit what happens to me beyond my usefulness to your cause? And, y'know, to act like it for more than a few seconds at a time?"

"We've talked about this. I'm not interested in being another one of your fuckbuddies. I can't see any way that won't just lead to more disaster."

"I'm going to have to point out that *you're* the one who brought up fucking. I'm not even asking you to kiss me. All I'm talking about is a little more consistency in the respect and compassion department. Or do you figure since I'm only half shadowkind, I'm only half worth caring about?"

He bared his teeth. "I certainly didn't come here to make friends with mortals."

"I'm not 'mortals'—I'm *me*. And I think I've proven that I'm nothing like the ones you hate."

"I never said you were like them."

I threw my hands in the air. "Then what's the problem? You know I'm in this to the end. I've given up pretty much everything I had before you all crashed into my life to see this mission through. Why are you still so convinced that being a little friendly will ruin *your* life somehow?"

"Who says it's my life I'm worried about ruining?" Omen said, with an edge of a snarl. "Do you really think getting more wrapped up in my business is going to turn out so hot for you?"

How could I resist an opening that good? I peered at him through my eyelashes. "Yes, actually I expect it'd be incredibly hot."

The hellhound shifter let out a strangled sound. "And of course you have to turn things around like that. I don't for one second think you'll be the one hitting the brakes if I stopped doing it."

"So what you're saying is you don't trust your own self-control, and you're blaming me for it."

"That's not— I know what you're like. I've seen how you've drawn the others in, even if there was nothing malicious about it. Don't try to pretend this is all about making friends, because I see *you*."

He said the words like an accusation, but the deeper truth of them rippled through me, dispelling most of my frustration. My fingers relaxed where they'd clenched the bedspread as we'd argued. One corner of my mouth lifted in a crooked smile.

"Yeah," I said. "You do. Not just like that. You're the only one who saw that I was more than human when even I was turning a blind eye. You see what I'm capable of, and you see when I'm struggling—and you like me at least enough to push me or bandage me up as I need it. That's why *I* like you, or at least why I'm trying to through all the hot-and-cold routines you pull."

At my change in tone, Omen's stance had gone rigid. "What are *you* trying to pull now?"

Huh, it looked like kindness pissed off the hellhound shifter even more than snark did. Because it got under his emotional armor more than he liked?

I shrugged, keeping the same calm attitude. "I'm simmering things down—which doesn't mean I'm *backing* down. I just don't see the need to keep throwing insults at each other. Call me a disaster all you want, but no one's ever believed in me as much as you do."

Another flicker of flame passed through Omen's eyes. His hands balled at his sides, and his voice came out terse. "I believe you're a fucking headache."

"Nope. I'm not doing this. The bickering has been fun, but aren't you getting tired of it? If we're going back to practicing, then it's with the understanding that I know you're doing this to help me, because it matters to you that I come out of this mess okay."

"You don't get to announce how I feel."

I gave him a wry smile. "I'll agree to that rule if we also make one that you don't get to pretend you've got no feelings at all."

"Don't go all Dr. Phil on me," Omen snapped. When I didn't respond, he took a swipe at my shoulder, knocking it just enough to make my body sway. "Where's your fight, Disaster? Aren't you always going on about all the incredible strength you're holding back?"

"I don't want to fight you. And frankly, I think it shows a lot more strength to own up to what you really want than to walk around with some tough-guy front."

"It's a hell of a lot more than a front." Omen took a jab at my other shoulder. "If you think I'm some kind of puppy dog, you're sorely mistaken. Do I need to show you just how hellish I can be?"

"Better that than the Ice-Cold Bastard," I said. "Who said I wanted a puppy dog anyway?"

"Then show you can take on the hound."

He shoved me more roughly, his eyes flaring, his hair rumpling like it always did when his temper emerged. I wasn't going to give him the satisfaction of pushing back.

I raised my arms in a gesture of surrender instead, and that enraged him to the point of blazing. His fangs came out, the magma glow and lava darkness coursing over his skin.

With a full snarl, he slammed me back on the bed. His hands

pinned my wrists to the mattress with a prick where one of his claws nicked my skin. He clamped his jaws around my throat. His fangs nicked my flesh with a sliver of pain. And all that dangerous, delicious heat flooded over me.

If he thought he could push me into giving him the fight he wanted instead of the fondness I'd been offering, he hadn't seen quite enough.

"I trust *you*," I said quietly. "Whether you want me to or not. You can't scare me enough to make me run away."

A growl reverberated up from Omen's chest, transforming into a groan as it spilled across my throat. His body hovered over mine, his muscles tensed. Then his tongue swiped across the sensitive skin he'd been threatening, drawing a rush of pleasure with it.

My breath caught with a gasp taut with desire. I dared to raise my hand to that wild tawny hair—

And he wrenched his mouth from my neck to my mouth, claiming me with a kiss of scorching breath and searing tongue.

My fingernails scratched across his scalp. His fangs were still out, his hellhound heat radiating all across his otherwise mostly human form, but damn if that didn't make the embrace that much more intoxicating.

I arched up toward him, the need to meld with that heat clanging through me like a fire alarm. Without breaking the kiss, Omen dragged me farther up the bed, his hips pushing between my thighs. The hottest part of him, long and hard, pressed between my legs, setting off a shock of bliss. I let out a very undignified whine.

There wasn't anything dignified at all about the collision of our bodies. It was all savage fury. Our mouths crashed together again and again, a metallic tang creeping across my tongue where his fangs had scraped my lip. I tore at his shirt, and he flung it the rest of the way off so violently it smacked a china figurine off the dresser to smash on the floor.

More veins of orange glow blazed across his chest. When he lowered himself again, my shirt crackled with the raging heat. As the fabric charred and fell away like soot, he might have blistered the skin beneath it, but I instinctively called up my own fire to meet him. The flames of our beings danced together between us, searing away the rest of our clothes but licking against my flesh with only the most ecstatic of burns.

Apparently I could also avoid incinerating myself in painful ways if I was in the process of being thoroughly fucked. Good to know.

My legs splayed farther apart with a need too overwhelming to deny, and Omen didn't require any further invitation. His cock rammed into me, sending pleasure sizzling through my nerves.

As he plunged deeper, he grasped my thigh as if to haul us even closer together than we were already joined. My body bucked with his of its own volition, urging him faster, harder. With each forceful thrust, ecstasy roared through me in a growing inferno.

Omen tore his mouth from mine to ravage the side of my neck and the curve of my shoulder. "*You*," he growled, but if he was pissed off about what we were doing, it wasn't enough to stop. Stopping was a concept that had burned away with our clothes and any common sense I'd still possessed. Why the fuck had we waited so long to *start*?

It might not have been the wisest act I'd ever taken part in. Leaving aside the whole fiery destruction element, there was our new discovery about shadowkind fertility—but if my parents had needed some unknown magic to perform the impossible feat of my conception, the possibility of it happening by accident felt far too distant to wrench me from this bliss.

An unexpected sensation slid across my calf, like the teasing of a finger—except Omen's fingers were currently tangled in my hair and clutching my jaw to yank my lips back to his.

An inkling crept through my pleasure-hazed mind. I groped across the sculpted planes of his blazing back to the even more tempting ass I'd admired through his slacks on more than one occasion, and found out just how much those slacks had been hiding.

He *did* have a tail even in his unshifted form—the one shadowkind feature he couldn't lose when otherwise in his full mortal guise. A tail that shivered as my hand closed around its warm, sinuous length.

My touch must have sparked something enjoyable for Omen, because one of those groaned growls pealed out of him. It reverberated into me with a fresh rush of delight. The tail's devil-pointed tip traced another giddy line up my leg and then along my side in its own caress.

Just how much control did he have over *that* part of his body—and when would I get to test that out?

I wasn't going to ask him now, both because I wasn't sure any request wouldn't knock him out of the furor of the moment and back into his frigid restraint and because I was skyrocketing toward my orgasm too swiftly now to let out more than a moan.

Omen pounded into me with all that fiery intensity, his tail flicking along my ass. With another moan bursting from my lips, I crackled apart like a firework, ecstasy singing through every part of my heat-flooded body.

I dug my fingers into Omen's back, and a ragged breath stuttered out of him. Even more heat pulsed into me as he reached his own climax.

And then it was done. I was lying there on the bed with the hellhound shifter poised over me, coming down from the high of what he'd just minutes ago sworn he never wanted to happen. Uncertainty dampened the afterglow.

Did I want to look into his eyes and see what reaction was waiting for me there?

I might have been bold to a fault, but that didn't mean I couldn't procrastinate. My gaze slid first to the bedspread beside us, and a giggle tickled up my throat.

The fabric was scorched black. When Omen eased back, withdrawing from me, the charred area disintegrated into flaky cinders.

"Well," I said, "I guess we're going to have to find the equines a new bedspread. Maybe if it's twice as twinkly, they won't mind."

I dared to glance up at Omen then. He was staring down at me, his skin returned to its normal pinkish human shade and his eyes their mortal blue. Any bits of his short-cropped hair that weren't sticking up were plastered to his forehead with sweat from that rather intensive workout with bonus flames.

His expression wasn't exactly warm, but it wasn't hostile or horrified either. He ran a finger across my collarbone and rubbed the soot he'd wiped off my skin against his thumb. "It's a mess all around. Still a disaster."

His tone was even enough that I felt comfortable trailing my hand across his pecs to smear the effects of our merging there too. "I'm pretty sure the burning was at least as much your fault as mine, demon dog. Not that I'm complaining. I don't think I'd consider what we just did a catastrophe. The world hasn't ended yet, has it?"

Omen's shoulders relaxed incrementally. "No, not yet," he said, and there was definitely a droll note in his voice now.

"I didn't intend for us to end up like this, you know."

"I know. If you had, it wouldn't have happened." He exhaled with a rough sound that pinched at my gut.

"Then I hope we can move forward without any regrets," I said.

"We'll see how I feel about it when you're attempting to yank my chain again." He gave me a sharp look. "Even if you kept up with my fire after all, that doesn't mean you're getting out of the rest of your training."

My heart swelled with relief and perhaps even affection. I bobbed up to steal a quick kiss before he decided to set himself off limits again. "Well, I think the one who can recreate his outfit in the shadows and move between rooms unseen should grab me some new clothes from the other bedroom. Then you can train away."

"I'm going to hold you to that, Disaster," he said with what might have been a smirk before he vanished into the darkness.

TWENTY-TWO

Sorsha

THE ONE THING WE DID OCCASIONALLY HAVE TO STOP FOR WAS GAS. Around noon, Ruse pulled into a station that had a pizza place next door. While he cajoled free gas out of the station staff, I grabbed my wallet to head over to the pizza place, figuring it wouldn't be a horrible thing to actually pay for what we were going to consume now and then.

"Bleeding heart," Omen said lightly as he stepped out into the midday sun behind me.

"Talk like that, and I'll order pineapple across the whole thing," I replied, anticipating his grimace. One definitive thing I had learned on our road trip so far: the hellhound shifter didn't approve of fruitiness on his cheesy pies, the poor soul.

"Heavy on the pepperoni, and maybe I'll forgive you anyway. Just—"

"Make it snappy—I know, I know."

The guy at the counter told me it'd be a fifteen-minute wait for the three pizzas I ordered—only one sprinkled with the pride of Hawaii, since I was feeling kindly—so I stepped out of the humid seating area to bask in the warm early fall breeze and the greasy scents wafting from the kitchen vent.

Apparently Gloam had felt the need to stretch his legs too, because he came trudging over in his typical daytime slouched stance.

"I doubt the pizza we get here will compare to what they offer in the city," he said with equally typical gloom.

I gave him an encouraging smile even though I knew the effort was likely in vain. "I subscribe to the idea that all pizza is good pizza."

He made a humming sound and drifted toward the alley between the pizza place and the gas station shop. A moment later, a clang of metal colliding carried through the restaurant's windows. Antic popped into view in the alley with a distinctly guilty expression.

"The chefs looked so bored, I thought I could cheer them up a little," she said. "I guess I didn't set the prank up well enough. It all just slipped..."

I raised my eyebrows at her. "As long as you didn't ruin our pizza."

"Oh, no, it was all empty pans! I was going to roll them across the floor." She made a sweeping motion with her scrawny arm to demonstrate.

Okay, so maybe I couldn't blame Omen for being skeptical about how much these two would add to our master plan. I motioned to the RV. "Why don't you go get the table set up with drinks and napkins and stuff? I'm sure you can find something fun to do with them."

A glint danced in her eyes. "Oh, yes, I can do that! You're going to love this." She darted off, blinking invisible again after her first few steps.

Our pizzas were ready at fifteen minutes on the dot. As I carted them to the RV, the spicy scent of the pepperoni set my mouth watering. The hellhound shifter had better not mind if I grabbed a slice or two of his pie.

Antic had formed a leaning tower of pop cans on the table. I laughed, and she did a jig of delight on the sofa-bench. Snap came hustling over for the food but first gave me a peck on the side of my neck as if in thank you. We all dug in, the devourer's eyes gleaming neon with pleasure, more slices vanishing as Ruse and Gloam rejoined us. The night elf didn't even complain about the slice he slowly nibbled at.

Ruse tucked his arm around me in a casually affectionate gesture, letting his fingers trail across my shoulder to enticing effect. "Thorn decided he needed to patrol, naturally," he told me. "Omen must have gone with him, probably to make sure he doesn't take the whole day at it. I suppose we should save a slice or two for them."

"That seems wise," I agreed, and reached to pet Pickle, who'd hopped up on the sofa beside me.

The little dragon flinched at the motion of my hand. As he took me in, his wings came down, but his body stayed tensed as I scratched his shoulder. Despite the deliciousness filling my stomach, a pinch of sadness ran through my gut. Was he ever going to be completely comfortable with me again?

"You feel a bit tense, Miss Blaze," the incubus said. "Let's see if we can't work that out of you."

He shifted his pose to set his thumbs against the admittedly tight muscles along my spine. A massage *while* eating pizza—could there be anything more heavenly? I wasn't sure what in blue blazes I'd done to deserve this doting, but I wasn't going to say no.

Snap watched this development with a glimmer of consternation. He stroked my knee under the table and motioned to the tower of pop cans. "Would you like something to drink? If nothing here is quite right, there was a large selection in the store."

"I'm good, thank you." I nudged his knee with mine and leaned back into Ruse's hands. "What's with the spoiling me all of a sudden?"

"You've been working hard," Ruse said in his sly voice. "Don't you deserve to be spoiled? We could make a competition out of it. See if the devourer can keep up with an incubus."

At the determined light that flared in Snap's eyes, I gave Ruse a light kick. "I'm not sure I'd survive that competition, even if it'd be a spectacular way to die. You've been doing such a good job of sharing— it'd be a shame to ruin that."

"Hmm. I suppose it would." He leaned in to press a brief but tender kiss above my ear. Apparently satisfied that his devotion wasn't being questioned, Snap returned to his meal, leaving an only slightly possessive hand on my thigh.

A matching tenderness tightened my throat. Omen might have seen more in me than anyone else, but my original shadowkind trio had been there for me in their diverse ways from the very beginning. How quickly one's romantic fortunes could change. A few months ago, I hadn't been sure I could manage to handle even a friends-with-benefits arrangement without it going sideways—and not in the way you'd hope to end up sideways as a benefit.

Now I had two gorgeously monstrous men vying for the chance to pamper me the most—and a third out there patrolling with an unshakeable determination to ensure my safety. I must have done something very, very right in a past life I couldn't remember. I tipped my head to offer Ruse a kiss over my shoulder, which he accepted with delight, and hooked my ankle around Snap's in an effort to show how much affection I held for them both in return.

As Ruse worked over my back, I offered Pickle a bit of bacon off one of the pizzas, but he wasn't inclined to fully forgive me yet. The dragon nipped it from my fingers with a squeaky snort—and promptly scuttled to the other side of the table.

Before I could ply him with more meaty delicacies, my ringtone pealed out. I swiped sauce off my fingers and groped for my phone. Ruse released me but left his hand resting on the back of my neck.

The call was from Klaus. "Sorsha, I'm glad I could reach you," he said, his normally deep but jovial voice more hesitant than usual. He didn't sound particularly glad.

The pinch in my gut turned into a knot. "What's up? Are you still planning on flying into San Francisco this afternoon?"

"Oh, yes, everything's covered there. *I'm* good to go. The trouble is… the rest of my colleagues are backing out."

The knots were now multiplying like bunnies. "What? I thought they were on board—most of them, anyway. They just had a change of heart?"

He sighed. "It seems they felt you were behaving a little oddly at the end of our last meeting… Monica reached out to your original branch of the Fund to check in about you. Apparently the things they told her left her rather disturbed."

"Oh." I swallowed thickly. Huyen—or maybe even Ellen—had given these people the idea that I was some kind of menace? Or just off my rocker? They didn't know about my fire powers… but they could have shared plenty about the destruction that had followed me across the city. "Everything that happened back home—we didn't have much choice if we wanted to take on the Company of Light. They're way too vicious to just sit down and negotiate with or something."

"I can imagine. And I'm not judging you. I've been around in this scene longer than any of the others—I've seen how horrible we mortals can be to each other and to the shadowkind." He paused with a rustling sound as if he was rubbing his beard. "I don't know what exactly you've gotten yourself into, Sorsha, but I know your father was a good man, and I think you deserve a chance. And I wouldn't be here at all if it wasn't for the shadowkind who had the kindness to stop and help when my wife and I got lost on a trip through the desert ages ago, so I figure they deserve whatever I can offer too."

"Thank you," I said around the constricting of my throat. "I appreciate it."

"I wish I could convince the others, but youth do like to dismiss their elders. You'll at least have me, and I'll do what I can. I think your Fund leaders might have reached out to the branch in San Francisco as well, so I'm not sure you can expect much help from that quarter either, but I may be able to weasel my way in there without them realizing I'm working with you. I told my people I'd cancelled my plans so they wouldn't pass on any additional warnings."

That was something. I summoned all the gratitude I could manage into my voice. "We'll make the best of it. Thanks again—I mean it."

"Of course. I'll touch base once I've touched *down* on the west coast."

My fingers clenched around the phone before I dropped it back into my purse. As I drew my hand back into my lap, a burst of sparks leapt from my palm, prickling across my thigh. I squeezed my hand into a fist to snuff any lingering ones out.

I *was* a menace, wasn't I? The Fund folks back home might not have known exactly why people should be cautious of me, but they hadn't exactly been wrong.

Omen was going to be just ecstatic when he heard this news. I could already hear the "I told you so" lilt that would creep into his voice. Damn it.

Damn Huyen and Ellen and the rest of them who hadn't even wanted to try. That was what the Company relied on, wasn't it? The fact that everyone who might have supported the shadowkind they were set on eradicating was too scared to tackle enemies as big and brutal as they'd built themselves up to be.

Snap was watching me, a half-eaten pizza slice dangling, shockingly forgotten, from his hand. "What happened?"

I opened my mouth, and Thorn materialized by the door. I braced myself for the hellhound shifter to join him, pulling together the words to reveal yet another failing of mortal kind. But Thorn strode over alone.

"Where's Omen?" I asked.

The warrior frowned. "Is he not here? He was when I left."

Ruse's forehead furrowed. "We assumed he went with you. I haven't seen him since just after we pulled in here."

"Same." I glanced at Snap and the others.

The devourer shook his head, his mouth slanting at a worried angle that looked all wrong on his beautiful face. Antic scrambled up with a sharp salute. "I can go looking for him!"

Thorn considered her with unveiled skepticism. "I think you'd better stay here and let me do the searching, little one." He glanced around at the rest of us. "I'm sure he can't have gone far. Perhaps he discovered something nearby that caught his interest."

As Thorn vanished into the shadows, an uneasy tremor ran over my skin. If my stomach had been knotted before, now it might as well have been one solid lump of limestone.

It wasn't like Omen to get distracted, and he'd been determined to make it to San Francisco as quickly as possible. Even if he'd wandered off for some bizarre reason, I'd have expected him to be back by now, if only to let the rest of us know something needed our attention.

Had the Company managed to capture him again? But it wasn't their style to stealthily scoop up just one of us if they could easily see where the whole squad was. I couldn't imagine the hellhound shifter being caught without a major fight that *one* of us would surely have noticed.

Snap set his pizza down, the first time I'd ever seen him lose his appetite. He tucked his hand around mine instead, but I was too on edge to take much comfort from the gesture or Ruse's squeeze of my shoulder.

It felt like ages before Thorn returned the second time, but the slice I was forcing myself to nibble at hadn't even gotten cold when he appeared with no ice-cold bastard beside him. He looked even graver than when he'd talked about failing to protect his boss the first time, before we'd rescued Omen.

"I can find no sign of him," he said. "I can't imagine where he would have gone."

My heart ached for the warrior even as a twisting sensation ran through my chest. The only thing I could think of that had happened recently and might have affected Omen's mood was our scorching interlude in the bedroom this morning. He'd seemed like he accepted what had happened, even if he wasn't crowing from the roof about hitting a home run with me. He'd hassled me when we'd gotten here like I'd have expected him to.

But who really knew what was going on behind those icy eyes and his carefully constructed self-control? Had he gotten angry at me for provoking him—had he gotten angry with himself for giving in to his lust? Would he really have compromised our mission just to go cool himself off?

Maybe, if he felt he was fraying enough to warrant it.

Ruse had been tapping at his phone. "I'm not getting any response the mortal way. He might be in the shadows. Phones don't work there."

"He wouldn't have *left* us," Snap said, but he looked at his companions for them to confirm that was a fact.

The incubus chuckled. "And miss out on the chance to call the shots for the grand finale of our trip? I can't imagine it." But the worried crease hadn't left his brow.

We picked at the rest of the pizza until the incubus declared a ceasefire and packed the rest of it into the RV's tiny fridge. With each passing minute, Omen's absence weighed heavier. Finally, Thorn cleared his throat.

"We know what Omen wanted us to do—to continue to San Francisco as swiftly as this vehicle can convey us. He knows if we're not here, that's where we should be heading. And he may be able to arrive there even faster than us making use of the rifts through the shadow realm. I say we move out. The longer we linger here, the more likely we'll draw the attention of the wrong people."

That was true. I nodded despite the lump in my throat, which seemed to have spawned from my stomach.

Ruse swiped his hand across his mouth. "Just watch. We'll pull up to the city limits, and he'll be standing there ready to chide us for taking so damn long."

His jaunty tone fell flat. My original trio had gone on without their leader before, but then they'd known what had happened to him and had some idea of how to get him back. Now, we didn't have a clue how to help Omen or whether he even needed help.

And after the way I'd been losing us allies left and right, I had to admit that whatever had happened to him, chances were I wasn't totally blameless.

TWENTY-THREE

Thorn

With every passing minute after we'd left our last stop behind us, Omen's disappearance gnawed at me more perniciously. I stalked the length of the RV—physically and through the shadows and then back into my solid body again—but I couldn't wear out the uneasiness winding through my nerves.

It'd been my suggestion to move on without our commander. I stood by that suggestion without a single doubt. It was what he would have wanted, regardless of what had happened to him. Whether he was with us or not, the Company of Light still needed to be demolished.

But it was so unlike him to abandon us without a word. I couldn't imagine how our enemies could have attacked and seized him without my coming across any trace of that incident in my patrols. The mystery of it loomed over me in a way that was, well, ominous.

As the incubus drove us onward to the city that was the Company's base of operations on this side of the ocean, my faint awareness of the other wingéd presence thickened too. It didn't tug or gnaw but simply spread through my chest like a pang of recognition on seeing an old friend you barely recognized.

The one who dwelled out here couldn't be any actual friend of mine, though. The brethren I'd been close enough to that I'd have considered them friends as well as comrades had all fallen in the war. This one might not even have fought on the same side as I had... not that I was certain I could have distinguished who'd belonged to one party or the other after all these centuries.

We were going to pass the spot where that one must be dwelling, though. The pang came with a vague sense of direction—northwest of our current position, shifting closer to pure north the farther we traveled along the highway. I paused to gaze out the window as if I might see a sweep of vast wings in the distance.

"You made the right call," Sorsha said to me, observing my pensiveness but not being aware of the full source. "Omen knows where we're heading. We won't be hard to find once we're in the city. Maybe this is another one of his beloved tests."

Her smile looked tight around the edges, and she didn't sound as though she were as relaxed about the situation as her words were meant to imply. She'd said very little at all since we'd pulled away from the fuel station.

What if Omen *wasn't* in the city when we arrived? What if he never returned to us at all? I had trouble conceiving of that possibility, but we needed to be prepared. I'd committed myself to this cause, and I wouldn't let it fall apart while I was still standing.

My gaze skimmed over my other companions: Ruse humming with disconcerting merriness behind the steering wheel, Snap stroking Sorsha's hair comfortingly, the imp dancing invisibly through the air with ridiculous attempts to provoke our mortal into a smile, and the downcast presence that was the night elf lurking in the shadows beneath the table.

Could we take on the highest level of the Company with just our current allies? Tackling even a less powerful leader had required one of our equine companions and more than a dozen shadowkind helpers from a local criminal syndicate—and we'd had Omen with us too.

I looked toward the window again. My kin was almost directly north of us now. Another road veered away from our highway up ahead, dust billowing behind a speeding car's tires as it raced that way.

My muscles tensed all through my body. But my own discomforts mattered far less than our mission. I meant to see us emerge victorious from this war no matter the cost to myself.

"We should make a brief diversion," I said abruptly.

The incubus glanced back at me. "Not satisfied with patrolling the vehicle, my overeager warrior? I promise you we'll be safer driving in a straight line at the highest possible speed."

"It's not to patrol. There's someone I think I might be able to persuade to join our cause. And it seems now more than ever we should attempt to gain every possible ally. Take that next right turn."

Sorsha was studying me with a glimmer of understanding in her eyes. I'd mentioned my awareness of the nearby wingéd to her. She was respectful enough of my preference for keeping my nature secret not to speak up, though. A flutter of gratitude passed through me even as I prepared to end that secrecy myself.

Ruse pulled onto the narrower, dustier road, but he wasn't as mindful of his own tongue. "And what makes you think this random potential ally will have any interest in joining our wild and crazy mission?"

"It's not random. This is one of my own kind. One of the few remaining. If anyone can make an appeal that will succeed, it'll be me."

Snap's expression turned more alert at that statement, his head cocking with curiosity. The imp ceased her endless bounding about to solidify in the middle of the table.

"Oooh," she said, placing hands on her hips. "We're going to find out what the big scary shadowkind is."

Ruse swiveled right around to look at me, leaving me thankful that the road ahead of him was so barren. "Are you actually going to put an end to the guessing game? I should have started a betting pool."

"You don't have to do this," Sorsha said softly. "If you think it's worth it, I'm all for it—but we'll manage with the help we've got."

My tenacious lover could be so tender when she wanted to be. Her acceptance of my hesitations made me all the more sure that it was time to end them. If I was going to reveal myself for any reason, it should be to ensure I'd done everything I could to make sure *she* survived the upcoming battle.

"We'll manage better with more," I said. "I'm not certain how this member of my brethren will react to being approached, though... Perhaps I should prepare you. You'll want to pull over to the shoulder, incubus, so you don't risk crashing our means of transportation."

"You think very highly of the shock value of your secret identity," Ruse teased, but he did as I'd asked.

When the vehicle was parked, he got right out of his seat and propped himself against the wall just beyond it, watching me expectantly. Antic bobbed on her toes with excitement.

Suddenly the act felt too momentous. I hadn't intended to build it into some earth-shattering announcement. What would the others make of me when they saw what I was? Sorsha had taken my full physical form in stride—but she didn't have the same awareness of the history most of the shadowkind would, and besides, she was hardly a typical example of *her* kind.

But then, none of the beings around me were quite typical, were they? They wouldn't have joined this crusade to begin with if they'd been your standard shadowkind. I had to assume any goodwill I'd garnered with my contributions over the recent months would hold out against their feelings about my kind.

I inhaled deeply and allowed the energies I usually kept tamped down within this mortal body to rise to the surface.

My limbs and torso expanded. My eyes prickled as the heated darkness came over them, not hazing my vision but sharpening it to every movement around me. My feathered wings flared up from below my shoulders, arcing as high as the Everymobile's ceiling and as wide as its windows even only partly open. This space was too confining to show my true shadowkind form in its full glory, but that might be for the best.

No snarky remarks came from the incubus. His lips had parted with the slackening of his jaw. He collected himself with a rough chuckle, but he kept staring. "Holy hell. I should have guessed. Of all the damned beings out there—" He shook his head in disbelief.

The imp had cowered back to the corner of the sofa-bench. Not the reaction I'd wanted to provoke, but an unsurprising one. She peeked at me through her fingers.

"I have no interest in hurting you," I told her, my wingéd voice resonating from my lungs.

A scrabbling sound drew my attention behind me. Sorsha's tiny dragon had emerged from the bathroom where he'd built his nest. At the sight of me, he stiffened, letting out a squeak with a flare of his nostrils. Then he flexed his wings as if to say, *I've got those things too*.

He didn't scramble away, but he didn't come any closer either. This might be the end of my amity with the little creature.

One of our number wasn't taken aback, though. The devourer smiled at me, his wide eyes offering nothing but awe. "Of course you wouldn't hurt any of us. You've been hurt *yourself* so many times to protect us. Your form is marvelous. Why didn't you show us it before?"

Ruse let out another short laugh. "You never heard about the wingéd, huh, devourer? They have an… interesting reputation."

His gaze had definitely become warier. I could accept that. It wasn't as if we'd been the closest of comrades before. He hadn't fled for the hills or hurled cutting remarks my way, which I could count as a victory.

"I'd prefer not to be judged based on events long past," I said. "We all have questionable moments in our histories, don't we?"

"Most don't have moments that involve an entire war that nearly exterminated your own race—but by all means, let us focus on the present." The incubus offered a grin that looked more like his usual playful self, and just this once, I was glad to see it. "You've stuck to smiting the right people as long as I've known you. I'll trust that you'll continue to do so."

The imp had lowered her hands. Snap glanced over his shoulder toward the window. "The shadowkind we're going to see—they're another 'wingéd' like you?"

I nodded. "The only one I've come close enough to recognize in well over a century. Let us hope time has mellowed him as it has me."

Ruse muffled what might have been a snort of disagreement with his hand, but he returned to the wheel. "Direct away, oh angelic one."

There. It was done, and the world hadn't crumbled apart around me. Relief washed through me so abruptly I had to pause to catch my breath. With a tug of my will, I pulled my features back in to leave only my mortal-appearing form on display.

"Drive onward," I said. "I'll inform you when we need to deviate from that course."

The pang in my chest grew stronger with each mile that passed beneath the wheels. When a dirt road even more desolate than the one we were on veered off to the left, I directed Ruse down it. Finally, a shack that looked as if it had been put together out of discarded, beaten-up planks of wood came into view in the midst of a plain that was otherwise all hard-baked earth and tufts of yellow grass.

No road or even pathway led from the one we were on to that building. Ruse parked, and we studied the shack through the windows.

"I think you'd all best stay here—as much as you might enjoy spectating," I said, adding the last piece when Ruse started to open his mouth with what I suspected would be a protest. "No one lives so far away from civilization because they enjoy company."

"Fair enough," the incubus said with an air of resignation. "But I'm certainly going to watch as much of the show as I can from in here." He plopped himself down at Sorsha's other side and promptly twined his fingers with hers.

I caught our mortal's gaze for a brief moment, hoping I could convey with mine my thanks for her faith in me—in this and so many other things. Then I moved through the shadows onto the barren plain and strode toward the shack.

My fellow wingéd would have been able to sense my approach as well as I'd sensed what I was approaching. A small part of me worried that I might find the place abandoned and feel the presence dashing away from this intrusion, but our kind didn't tend toward fleeing. The sense of his presence remained steady until I was only a few feet from the shack's crooked door. Then a figure formed out of the patch of shadows there.

As was to be expected, the wingéd who emerged before me matched me in stature: tall and broad with much muscle filling out his powerful frame. His knuckles were similarly hardened, but with ridges of a ruddy hue that looked more like copper than crystal. His eyes gleamed the same metallic shade beneath straggling gray hair that fell past his shoulders and shadowed his brow.

"What business do you have here?" he demanded. "I have no interest in reuniting with the remnants of our kind."

"Only one remnant at the moment," I said. "My companions are… various other sorts. And this isn't about reunification." I studied him and the shack. "You've lived a long time in this part of the mortal realm."

"So that I could remain undisturbed. In the emptiness, I can meditate on the failings that led me to continue to be in existence at all."

My companions might rib me about my severity at times, but I didn't believe I'd ever put forth attitudes quite that grim. If I had, it was a wonder none of them had shoved me back through a rift. Although I supposed my stature might have had something to do with that as well.

As somber as the disgraced warrior was being, however, I did at least understand the sentiment he was expressing. It was only a darker shade of the guilt and regret I'd recently begun to shed.

"What if I could offer you something better than that?" I asked.

He scowled at me. "That you would even think any of us deserve better—"

I held up my hand to stop him. "Not in that way. In the way that you might be able to make amends for the errors of the past by contributing to a new struggle with even greater stakes. We're in dire need of assistance."

My kin didn't stop frowning, but I thought his eyes brightened just a little. He shifted his weight and folded his bulging arms over his chest. "How can you be sure we won't simply bring about an even more horrible fate than before?"

That question had haunted me ever since Omen had first come calling. I hadn't always been confident in my answer. But here, thinking of his leadership even if he wasn't with us in the flesh, of the deeper understanding of my capabilities and flaws that Sorsha had brought out in me, and of the cause we'd all come together for, the words came to my lips without a hint of hesitation.

"One can never be sure," I said. "But I've seen enough to believe that in this conflict, I can make a difference for the good of all shadowkind. I can save far more lives than were ever lost in the wars of the past. And you could too, if you'll lend your instincts and your fists."

The other wingéd was silent for a long spell, considering me. Then he said, in a tone that ignited a flicker of hope within me, "Tell me more about this new war."

TWENTY-FOUR

Sorsha

When we came up on the San Francisco city limits, I found myself drifting to the front of the Everymobile to watch the buildings whip past us through the windshield. Their lights and the glow of the streetlamps streaked in the growing darkness. My gaze snagged on every figure we passed.

None of them were Omen. I hadn't *really* expected him to be standing waiting for us to turn up with his impatient glare and his authoritarian stance. Still, I couldn't help being a little disappointed that he wasn't. I'd have taken a heaping of criticism about our discipline and arrival time just to know where the hell he'd gone.

"I suppose we should find some cozy nook where we can settle in for the night," Ruse said in his usual flippant tone, but his expression looked a tad weary. I'd bet the incubus could last for days between the sheets without losing energy—a wager I wouldn't mind taking to the bed one of these days, just to confirm—but he wasn't made for driving mortal roads for hours on end.

"Where would Omen think to look for us?" Snap asked, coming up behind me. "We should pick a spot where it'd be easy for him to find us."

"But not likely that the Company will notice our arrival," Thorn put in.

"Yeah." I sucked my lower lip under my teeth. "We've usually had the best luck finding areas without much mortal activity around the fringes of the cities. Let's ramble through the suburbs and see what we turn up."

If that didn't work... Post an ad in the Missed Connections section of a newspaper? Put out an emergency bulletin over the public TV? Hire a plane to skywrite a message? He'd be most likely to see that last one, but then, so would every other person in the city, Company assholes included.

In the end, Ruse found a vacant lot between a couple of faded warehouses and parked the RV there in cargo van guise. Thorn stayed up to continue discussing the situation with his new wingéd friend, whose name—Flint—matched his appearance better than any shadowkind I'd met yet, and I tugged the incubus and the devourer into the bedroom with me.

They came without complaint and settled in on either side of me. I was too tangled up to want to conduct any experiments in stamina right now, but with Ruse brushing his fingers down my back in a fond caress and Snap tucking his chin over my forehead to encompass me with his fresh scent, I was able to sink into sleep faster than I'd thought.

My two lovers were still there when I woke up. As I stirred, Snap pressed a kiss to the top of my head and Ruse let his fingers skim over my waist. "Anything we can do to make this a happy morning for you, Miss Blaze?" the incubus murmured.

I tipped my head up to kiss Snap on the lips and then rolled over to offer the same to Ruse. His claiming of my mouth was so fervently tender that my pulse fluttered. I might have given in to the temptation to rediscover all the other sensations he could rouse with his touch if the absence of my most recent paramour hadn't been hanging over us.

"What would make me happy is to see the entire Company going up in flames," I said. "Then maybe we can spark a few metaphorical fires around here."

"I will happily take that rain check."

I had the urge to pass some of that loving on to Thorn too, but when we emerged into the RV, there was no sign of him. Flint sat at one end of the sofa-bench looking at a mug in front of him as if he wasn't quite sure whether to drink from it or crush it with his rock-like fist. Gloam was meandering through the hall in full droop-mode. Antic flashed into visibility at the sight of me, balancing on one hand on the edge of the counter with her spindly legs wheeling in the air.

I cracked a smile mostly so that she'd be satisfied that she'd gotten a reaction from me and quit goofing around.

"The first big dude went off to check for bad guys," she said as she flipped onto her feet, anticipating my question.

"Thorn said he would return shortly," Flint added. I'd always thought Thorn's voice was low and rumbling, but compared to Flint's thunderous tones, our original wingéd was a soprano.

I plopped down onto the sofa across from him and nodded to the coffee cooling in his mug. "Typically that stuff is better enjoyed hot."

He gave it a skeptical glance. "I have not consumed mortal provisions in many centuries. I hesitate to begin now."

Antic bobbed beside us as if debating snatching the mug for herself but seemed to decide it wasn't worth the possibility of pissing off a shadowkind of Flint's stature. She settled for pouring some out of the pot into two new mugs, splashing the brown liquid liberally on the floor and counter alike, and plunking one of those down in front of me.

"What's the plan?" she asked in an intrepid tone, taking a noisy swig from her mug.

What *was* the plan? We'd been going to figure that out once we got here, assuming Omen would have plenty to contribute. Now...

I might have suggested we wait and see if Thorn's patrol turned up the hellhound shifter, but before I could speak, the warrior emerged from the shadows, his mouth set at a pained angle. My heart sank. No luck in that respect, clearly.

We had to go forward without Omen then. If he didn't like the plans we made in his absence, then he shouldn't have fucking absented himself.

I dragged in a breath and looked around the table. All of my shadowkind companions were watching me. Somehow I'd become the substitute boss when the regular one was away. No pressure there.

My gaze caught Flint's metallic brown eyes—and a hail of impressions burst in my head.

I wasn't in the RV anymore but in the middle of a battlefield scattered with bloody bodies, more figures charging over them with blades gleaming. The stink of gore flooded my nose, and clangs and groans filled my ears. Someone hurtled right past me, knocking me to the side hard enough to make my arm throb—

And I was back on the sofa, gasping and shaking as my mind reeled.

"Sorsha!" Thorn grasped my shoulder and stared at his comrade. The other wingéd grimaced, lowering his gaze.

"My apologies, mortal," he said in that deepest of deep voices. "My particular talent is to spark visions of horror—I would generally only apply it to my enemies. I've used it so little in so long, I'm no longer as used to moderating it. I didn't intend to aim that memory toward you."

A memory. So that was one glimpse of the brutality he and Thorn had managed to survive, to their apparent disappointment. I set my hand over my warrior's, letting his touch steady me. My heart was still racing, but a sharper sense of determination rose through the dwindling panic.

That kind of brutality wasn't so different from how we'd approached our conflicts with the Company so far. Rush in, burn them to cinders or rip their heads from their necks—y'know, whatever suited our particular skill set best. But we'd found another way back in Chicago. Sure, the plan I'd suggested there had ended with a fiery skirmish anyway, but there'd been at least a little less death and destruction than before. Give me a little credit for a partial win, won't you?

I might have been part shadowkind, and I might have accepted the fact that I enjoyed laying down with monsters, but that didn't mean we had to prove the stereotypes right. We could use the same tactics as in Chicago, only on a bigger and better scale. Show all the jerks who were too scared to help us that the Company could be decimated without a single drop of blood spilled.

Okay, maybe that was a little too optimistic. We could probably manage it without more than a bucket of blood, though. That'd still be a step up from the torrents the shadowkind had unleashed when we'd stormed Victor Bane's mansion back home.

I didn't think Omen would like my continued resistance to carnage at all, but he was welcome to show up any time and tell me about that.

I leaned my elbows onto the table. "We need to figure out who here is running the North American operations of the Company, right? But destroying them isn't going to fix anything. The real leader is off in Europe somewhere. What if instead of trying to burn everything down, we figure out a way to get to that guy and use *him* to get to the man in charge overseas."

Ruse cocked his head. "Interesting. Go on."

I motioned to him. "You can work your charm over the phone. All we've got to do is convince the head guy here to put us in touch with *his* boss, and then you can bend the ear of the guy who controls everything the Company does. Imagine all the things you could convince him to do."

A smirk curved the incubus's lips. "Oh, there are many, many acts I'd like to talk him into committing. But starting with having *him* destroy the Company from the inside out sounds ideal."

Thorn frowned where he was still standing over me. "Would that work? Could you maintain enough control over him to compel him to cause that level of destruction?"

"That's the thing," I said. "The head honcho wouldn't need to destroy anything in a physical way. He must have access to all the Company data—we can get him to wipe it off the networks. We can have him call up the regional leaders and disband the branches. Maybe we'd need to force him to act in some crazy way to convince his followers that he's been wrong all along so they don't start things up again. I'm sure we can figure out the details once we have a hold on him."

Antic swung her little fists in the air. "Or we could just go across the sea and give him what-for the traditional way."

"But that might not work," Snap said, understanding lighting in his face. "We keep destroying parts of the Company, and more of these people rise up in their place. The fact that we're destroying them convinces them that they need to keep fighting us."

I snapped my fingers. "Exactly. Knock off one leader and someone else will step up to take his place. I think it's over-ambitious to assume we can eradicate the people who hate shadowkind and all the work they've done by picking them off bit by bit, and we can't tackle them all at once. But whoever's running the show—he can. And if we play this right, he can tie all the loose ends in a bow for us too."

One by one, the heads around the table nodded. Gloam was the last, caught in despondent hesitation. "It sounds very grand—I don't see how I could contribute."

An inkling about that had already started to form in my head. I made a reassuring gesture toward the night elf. "Oh, I'm nothing if not resourceful. I'll find a way for even you to pitch in; don't worry."

Flint stirred in his seat. "This plan sounds worth the attempt. How do we begin?"

I patted my purse. "The one guy who's on our side in the Fund was able to talk to some of the local members last night. Klaus couldn't find out a lot, but one of the things he did put together was a probable hunting location where the Company has been collecting shadowkind near one of the rifts. We grab one of those Company hunters, and then we can follow the trail that one gives us to another and another until we get our hands on someone who can point us to the big gun."

"Of course, we don't know how often they stake out that spot," Thorn pointed out.

I smiled at him. "So we'll just have to make a little mischief there to draw them out."

TWENTY-FIVE

Sorsha

For once, the Company of Light played right into our hands. Less than an hour after Antic had darted through the park near the rift invisibly, making chess pieces fly through the air over the stone tables and leading people on wild goose chases after hats that appeared to have taken on minds of their own, a white van with an exterminator logo pulled into the public lot. How very fitting.

Four men tramped out, their silver-and-iron protective gear hidden under thick hazmat suits, which I guessed they could pass off as being protection from the supposed wild animal they were here to contain. Any mortal not watching for the glint of metal would have missed the edges of the helmets and vests beneath.

They strode to the area near the rift where the imp had pulled off her pranks and hollered for the nearby patrons to leave for their own safety. When all witnesses had dispersed—other than my shadowkind allies watching from various patches of darkness and me in my perch hidden on the roof of a historic cottage in view of the clearing—they drew out their shiny nets and whips and stalked through the area.

Of course, we didn't need—or want—them to catch Antic, or any other shadowkind for that matter. We'd only needed them to come.

After a thorough search, a vigil while they waited to see if the shadowkind would emerge if they gave it some space, and another scouring of the area, they packed up into their van, muttering about how inconvenient this monster had been.

Little did they know that a few of said monsters were hitching a ride in the shadows attached to their vehicle.

I kept my phone at my side as I waited for the first stage of our plan to come to fruition. Half an hour of pacing later, a text from Ruse appeared on the screen.

We've got a loner. He took off the worst of the gear but is still wearing a badge. Come on by and steal it off him for us, my lovely thief?

My pleasure, I wrote back, and passed on the address he gave me to the Uber I hailed.

It was a simple enough operation. I knocked on the door of the guy's apartment like I just needed to borrow a cup of flour. The moment he opened it, Ruse leapt out of the shadows next to him. The guy startled, his head jerking around, and before he could even see me moving, I'd kicked his legs out from under him. Thorn and Flint emerged to pin his limbs to the floor while I yanked open his button-up to uncover the silver-and-iron badge he'd fixed to his undershirt.

Borrowing my tricks—tsk tsk.

As soon as I'd tossed the toxic metals aside, Ruse started talking in his cajoling tone. "Good day to you, my friend. I'm so sorry about the sudden intrusion. If you'll give me a moment, I'll get this all straightened away to attend to your best interests."

Within minutes, he had our captive laughing at his jokes and beaming eagerly when the incubus told him we desperately needed his help. "I don't know who's giving the orders," he said. "But I can tell you a few locations we've worked out of. Maybe someone at one of them can tell you more."

Ruse smiled. "Perfect. We so appreciate anything you can contribute. I'll be sure to inform your colleagues what a team player you were."

We hopped from lead to lead across the afternoon and into the evening. The first several Company dupes had no idea where the big boss might live, but they all knew someone else who was connected to the Company. Finally, our game of leapfrog led us to a woman who'd worked on our Very Important Person's security detail. After chatting with Ruse for a bit, she coughed up an address in the Financial District, as well as some other choice information.

"I never got the guy's name," she said. "Never even saw him. He lives in the penthouse, and I worked outer security, patrolling the block outside. Never had any trouble, but I guess you can't be too careful with these monsters, especially when he's helping keep the whole Company organized." She sighed. "It was an easy gig, that's for sure. But I got bored and asked to be in on more of the action. Kind of regret it now."

"We've got the building," Snap said eagerly when we were back in the RV. "Does that mean we can carry out the rest of Sorsha's plan now?"

"We've got to investigate the place first and determine our best point of access," Thorn said. "It doesn't sound as though reaching this man will be a simple matter, even knowing his location."

I shot a fond smile at the incubus, who was back behind the wheel. "We need Ruse to get a hold of one of the head honcho's current security people. That should be our ticket in."

The Financial District was a forest of skyscrapers, concrete faces and gleaming windows towering so high they looked as if they really might touch the clouds. Ruse cruised by the condo building our contact had indicated. I definitely wasn't scaling that slick face from the outside. But that didn't matter when we could charm ourselves an inside man—or woman. We'd gotten this far, hadn't we?

"Every blame you lay," I sang as we rounded the corner, "every sprite you slay, we'll be watching you."

Antic shuddered as if she thought I was anticipating some slaying going on tonight. "Don't worry," I said. "If it looks like anyone's getting slain, we'll do a lot more than watch."

"I'd like to slay *them*," she muttered. "Big bullies."

We parked several blocks from the building with a mind to how thoroughly the Company tended to guard their more prominent members. After setting the RV to look like a tour bus that had every business parking downtown, Ruse, Thorn, and Snap went to scope out the big boss's place, the three of them insisting that Flint stay back with me in case we had to deal with Company attackers after all.

I paced the narrow hall, trying not to fidget and carefully avoiding looking directly into the wingéd's eyes. Antic bounced between twisting my discarded shirts into ridiculous poses and chattering with Gloam, who'd shed his despondency with the sinking of the sun.

My trio returned with matching pensive expressions.

"We could only go so far up," Thorn reported. "The highest floor had silver and iron panels built into the walls and floor—possibly the ceiling too."

Snap nodded. "We couldn't check it very closely, because the floor underneath was totally vacant. Very bright lights all across the ceiling, making sure there were no shadows for us to travel through, and cameras watching for intruders. I didn't pick up any useful impressions from the areas we could reach."

"The main elevator doesn't go up to the penthouse," Ruse added. "The only access we could identify was through a secondary elevator on that shiny sub-penthouse floor. There aren't any guards there, although that may cause more problems than it solves. We don't know who's working 'internal' security with him. From what our recent friend told us, the external folks don't know much about getting to this guy."

I exhaled slowly. "All right. Then we wait, and we watch. Unless this guy's got all his security living with him twenty-four seven, *someone's* got to come out of there eventually. We see who it is, track them until we can get to them alone, and prep them for Ruse's charm like we did the others. We've made it this far. No rushing, or it could all fall apart."

Thorn and Snap left again, Thorn to keep watch over the brightly-lit buffer floor and Snap to test the public areas of the building for any impressions that could point us in the right direction. I touched base with Klaus, who had nothing further to report.

"If you want me getting in on anything other than information-gathering, just let me know what I can do," he said.

I grimaced at the ceiling. After everything we'd been through with the Fund, I was uneasy even with him knowing we were in San Francisco. I wasn't sure I wanted to tip him off to our exact location. What if he had his own change of heart?

"We're covered for now," I said. "The best thing you can do is keep an eye on the local Fund and let us know if they seem to be on the lookout for us."

Night fell with no sightings of the head honcho's inside men. Finally, I curled up on my bed to get some sleep. I wasn't going to be much use to my companions if I was zombified with exhaustion by the time they needed me.

It was Thorn who woke me, but not in the way I'd have liked one of my lovers to come to my bed in the wee hours of the morning. He cleared his throat, and that yanked me out of sleep with a jolt through my nerves. When I looked up at him, it was still dark, only a little artificial light filtering through the small window to catch on his white-blond hair.

"We have our guard," he said. "I believe now may be an excellent opportunity to prepare him."

"Right, right." I shoved myself out from under the covers, finger-combed my hair back into a messy ponytail, and allowed myself the small indulgence of tapping the warrior's impressive chest. "Next time you wake me up, I expect it to come with benefits, not work."

His dark eyes gleamed. "We might have a moment for a brief benefit if it would raise your spirits to the task."

"Perfect way of looking at it." I gripped his tunic and rose up on my toes to kiss him. Thorn returned the gesture, his mouth so hard and hot it left no doubt that there would be *plenty* of benefits to come when the time was right.

Ruse had driven the Everymobile to new digs while I'd slept. I stepped out into the quiet of a residential street, bungalows and two-storey houses set behind small, neat lawns. The incubus emerged from the shadows by one of the smaller places down the block and beckoned me over silently.

When I reached him, he tipped his head toward the house, his voice dropping to a whisper. "We were hoping you could keep your beauty sleep, but he wears his damned helmet to *bed*. The boss man must have made these lackeys awfully paranoid."

"Yep," I said. "Clearly they have no reason at all to worry about shadowkind descending on them in the middle of the night."

"Well, not before now. You want to put those thieving skills to further use?"

I didn't have my lock picks with me, but I didn't need them. The guard's security wasn't quite that tight. I crept through the backyards to make a discreet approach, and Ruse slipped into the shadows around the back door to unlock it from the inside. When he eased it open, I slunk in past him. He pointed me to the door that led to our target's bedroom.

As I stepped inside, I almost started feeling bad for the dude. He must have had a softer side in him somewhere: his walls were adorned with posters of cartoon ponies frolicking with their magical friends. He even had a plastic figurine of a purple one watching over him from the bedside table.

That said, he was still a shadowkind-hating prick. And now he'd get to experience a truly magical friendship.

Ruse hadn't lied—the guy had his silver-and-iron helmet pulled tight over his head, covering it from his forehead down his temples to just above his ears. It looked as if he'd added some padding to it, but it still couldn't be all that comfortable. He was either very dedicated or very exhausted.

He had a badge pinned to his nightshirt as well, I saw—it poked just above the sheet that slanted across his chest. That would be easy enough to deal with, thank holy hand grenades.

I padded across the floor, breathing silent and shallow. With cautious fingers, I peeled the sheet down far enough that I could grasp the badge. This maneuver called for delicacy rather than speed. Just my luck that I was familiar with both.

A few twists of my fingers detached the clasp. I set the badge on the bedside table and motioned to where I assumed Ruse was watching from the doorway, not risking taking my eyes off our target. As I reached for his helmet, the guy made a muttering sound and rolled over.

Fine, I'd just have to lean farther over the bed. As soon as I had it off, Ruse could work his voodoo. We could forget delicacy now.

I set my hands against the cool metal surface, readied myself, and heaved as hard as I could.

The dude yelped and flailed. I darted backward, carrying the helmet with me, and Ruse swept in, his smooth, chocolatey voice already lilting from his lips.

"Hello there, my friend! Nothing to be disturbed about. This is the moment you've been waiting for all this time."

He must have read something in the guard's emotions to suggest a solid angle for his charm. As he talked on, I shoved the helmet into the closet, made an apologetic gesture to the poster ponies staring at me wide-eyed, and stepped back to join Thorn, Snap, and Flint, who'd emerged from the shadows.

Ruse could always tell when he had his subject eating out of his hand. It wasn't long before the incubus offered a simpering smile and said, "All we need to know is when we can expect your boss to leave his fine abode."

"Oh." The lackey's face fell with obvious distress. "I don't think I can help you there."

After all this, we still hadn't found someone with answers? I restrained a groan.

"Why not?" the incubus asked.

"Well, he just… never leaves. We come and go in shifts during the day, but in the year I've worked there, I've only seen him leave maybe three times. He had an essential appointment a few weeks back, so I doubt there'll be anything else for months unless something special comes up. Anything he needs, he has delivered."

"If I could even talk to him on the phone—"

The guy shook his head. "He's on his phone a lot, that's for sure, but I don't have the number for it. If I was ever going to be late for or miss a shift, I'm supposed to tell the head of the team, and they just send someone else."

My stomach sank. It wasn't that this guy didn't have answers—it was that the answers he had sucked donkey balls. If we couldn't lure his boss out of his apartment with its shell of toxic metals to somewhere Ruse could get his ear, the incubus wouldn't be able to charm the man we most needed to reach.

I stepped closer again. "Can't you think of *anything* he'd be willing to leave for?"

"I'm sorry. I wish I could do more."

I paused, feeling the weight of my companions' attention on me. This had been my plan, and now I had to salvage it before all our efforts had to be chucked in the trash.

A glimmer of inspiration lit in my head. It might not work—but it was worth a shot. Story of my life.

With a thin smile, I propped myself against the dresser. "Actually, I think there is one more thing you could do to prove your loyalty to the cause. Listen carefully."

TWENTY-SIX

Omen

THERE WERE TIMES WHEN THE FREQUENT SUNLIGHT OF THE MORTAL WORLD became wearying, and I missed the constant dim of the shadow realm. The cycle of days and nights did have its benefits, though. For example, if I'd had more than this constant dimness during my long wait for the Highest to offer their attention, I might have some idea how long that wait had been.

It felt like an eternity or so at this point. Apparently the most ancient of shadowkind had decided to give the DMV a run for their money. Or maybe it only seemed like days on end because I didn't have much to think about besides what trouble my crew might be getting into in my absence.

I hoped that they'd at least had the sense to keep moving and scope out the situation in San Francisco so we could jump right into action when I returned. And also that their scoping out hadn't involved too much action on its own. Maybe it was too much to wish for both rather than one or the other, especially with our fiery not-quite-mortal in the mix.

My mind veered in that direction now and then of its own accord. To her scarlet hair and the defiance in her bright eyes… to the heated taste of her on my tongue and the feel of her matching my heat flame for flame…

I had no physical presence here, but the memory managed to stir a flare of lust all the same.

I hadn't meant to give in to that temptation—but possibly it was all right. The world *hadn't* ended because we'd fucked. I'd enjoyed it, and so had she, and she'd still been the same mouthy but frustratingly appealing nuisance afterward as she'd been before. It hadn't been a vow or a nuptial. Releasing all that pent-up desire had eased the tensions inside me in a way I could actually appreciate.

It might not even be such a bad thing if we did it again. In moderation.

That was, if I could sort out whether I was more unsettled or gratified by the realization that no matter how much I'd insisted that I'd seen *her*, I now couldn't shake the sense of how much she saw *me*. More of me than I'd have wanted anyone in all the realms to see. She'd struck straight through all my best intentions with the tenderness in her voice and those knowing eyes…

I should have been furious. I *had* been furious. But at the same time, the memory of her proclamation that I couldn't scare her sent an odd twinge of longing through me.

Of course, none of that would matter if the Highest decided to keep me on hold until the end of time.

I shifted my awareness, searching for the lackey that had instructed me to wait here. If I bit that being's head off, would the Highest decide it was time to turn their attention my way? The lackey didn't appear to have lingered, though, and neither had the fiercer beings who'd caught me by the gas station and insisted I return with them to the nearest rift at once.

I could have taken down even the four of them if they'd been sent by anyone else. Damn the Highest and their fucking deals.

The call finally came, wordless but insistent, with a constricting tug around my neck. I sprang forward, wanting to shed that sensation as quickly as possible. The less I was reminded of my ties to these bastards, the better.

The deep, dark hollow roiled with an uneasy energy I hadn't felt there before. The Highest loomed as monumental as always, but the sharpness of their attention now that they had deigned to lower it to me prickled through to my soul.

"Hellhound," one intoned. "There you are." As if I hadn't been waiting on their doorstep for the last decade or so.

"Here I am," I agreed. "What do you want, oh ancient ones?"

The thicker thrum that echoed through the air suggested the edge that had crept into my tone hadn't gone unnoticed. The Highest let it slide, though, which should have been all the warning I needed right there.

"We've heard reports from your travels," another said, her voice reverberating through every particle of my being. "More than one shadowkind have claimed you are working with a human woman who can work shadowkind powers."

Fucking hell, not that complaint again. I'd known as soon as Rex's crew got a glimpse of Sorsha in action, word would start to get out. The Highest would just *love* the idea that I might be collaborating with a sorcerer. Those mortal miscreants were little better than the hunters and collectors, the way they used our kind.

It seemed simpler to circumvent the complicated full story and stick to a half-truth. I shook my head, as much as I had one in this space, in feigned exasperation. "You bought into that story? I'd sooner disembowel myself than ally with a sorcerer. No, all of my comrades are shadowkind. One of them made a joke to a few rather dim-witted beings about being human—the humor must have gone over their heads."

They studied me with more of that prickling intensity. "You've had no associations with any humans or being at times presenting themselves as human?"

What was that second bit supposed to mean?

"Not at all," I said. "Plenty of our own kind to call on as I need to." Not that many of them had responded to that call, but the Highest didn't give a rat's ass how my mission was going, as they'd made very clear during my last visit.

The tug at my throat came again, along with a jab of pain. I didn't give them the satisfaction of a wince. They could yank my chain all they wanted, but their hold over me couldn't stop me from lying as seemed necessary. I had at least that much freedom left.

"The reports were somewhat disjointed," one of the Highest allowed after a moment. "The less experienced shadowkind are not always as astute as would be ideal. No matter. We have another subject to discuss with you."

Joy of all joys. "Let me have it." Then I could get back to my crew and leave these giant bastards behind.

"Seeing as you are spending so much time mortal-side as it is, and given your familiarity with that world and your earlier interest, we have decided on the final favor you will carry out for us."

My spirits leapt with a wash of exhilaration I couldn't have contained if I'd wanted to.

They could call it a favor all they wanted, but what it really amounted to was slave labor. Ten tasks, anything they demanded, was what I'd agreed to carry out for them in exchange for not ending up a savaged corpse like Tempest. The most generous favor my former partner-in-crime had ever offered *me* was the lesson of just how badly things could go once the Highest's wrath came down on you if you didn't think quickly enough.

Ten tasks, and I'd jumped at the snap of their fingers nine times already—the last more than a century ago. They'd taken a good long while deciding how they could best use me this final time.

As soon as the terms of my deal with them were fulfilled, I was slipping this leash and running free, and they could forget it if they thought they'd ever get a reason to have me kowtowing to them again.

"I'm at your service," I said. It might disrupt our plans to take on the Company in the moment, but that would be worth it to shake off my shackles. "What is it you need?"

"We would like you to find the being named Ruby and inform us of her location."

Ah. Well, that was good news in that I'd have liked to find that being too, but less so in that I'd already given it a pretty good go and had little to no luck so far. No one seemed to even know Ruby had ever existed except the Highest themselves and the shadowkind they'd informed of the fact. Were they setting me up on an impossible task so they could keep me chained to their will forever?

I resisted the urge to produce my fangs and dipped my head in acknowledgement instead. "I'd be happy to do so. I'll be able to accomplish that task faster if you could let me know her last known location and any other details you have about her appearance and behavior."

The Highest made a grumbling sound between them as if they were offended by my request, but they obviously wanted this Ruby more than they cared about any impudence they thought I was expressing.

"She slipped through our fingers many years ago, shortly after we first became aware of her existence. We've had no further information since. That is your responsibility. As for the rest, you must be aware that she is highly dangerous, although she may not appear to be at first. Avoid direct contact at all costs. As soon as you have identified her, come straight to us."

Oh ye of so little faith. I sighed. "That's really not much to go on. Presumably if this shadowkind is so adept at hiding herself, she won't be going by the name you've been asking after her by anymore. What type of being is she? What mortal appearance does she take? What are these horribly dangerous secret powers of hers?"

There was more grumbling as the Highest appeared to confer with one another. Had they really thought they could send me off on this ridiculous quest without giving me a single hint about who I was looking for?

Probably, yes.

Finally, someone else spoke up from their immense huddle. "We can tell you more, but if we discover that you have spoken of this matter to any other being, our deal will be forfeit and you will be at our mercy."

Oh, for fuck's sake. "Yes, yes," I said. "That's fine. Just tell me." It wasn't as if I hadn't kept plenty of other secrets—like the fact that the Highest had any sort of grip on me at all—from my companions.

"Very well. The one named Ruby may not appear to be a shadowkind at all. That is part of what makes her so treacherous. When a shadowkind abases themselves to a mortal level, it is in rare circumstances possible for them to bear a child with a mortal. As few beings would lower themselves in such a way to begin with, we are aware of only three such unions in all existence. The first two we were able to deal with promptly. With this third, we have been foiled so far."

A nauseous chill started to unfurl in my gut. "And this Ruby... is the shadowkind who produced that child?"

A harsh sort of chuckle echoed through the space. "No. That one and her mortal partner met the fates they deserved. But some accomplice of theirs escaped with the child. That is Ruby—the name they gave her. As if she were a jewel and not a menace to all existence."

I tried to find the words, but for a moment I could barely think, let alone speak. They couldn't really mean—Sorsha had never given me the impression she thought she'd had another name. That was the sort of thing that would have come up while searching out her history. And from what I'd seen, she was more a danger to her own existence than to anyone else's.

Had we gotten the wrong information somewhere in our search? Mixed wires that had crossed her history with this shadowkind-human hybrid? But she *did* have powers no full human should have been able to possess.

"I hope you'll forgive my confusion," I managed, gathering myself. "But wouldn't a creature born of shadowkind nature mingled with humanity be *weaker* than a pure shadowkind, not stronger?"

"One would wish it was so, but that is not the case. Do *not* approach and especially do not provoke this being when you come across her. The unnatural bond in her natures creates a connection to both realms. She can inflict all the damage her powers allow on both without bringing any harm to herself from either side. If we could have snuffed out that alchemy when she was a mere infant... Now it will have had time to grow within her. All it will take is a little fuel, and she will set our realm and theirs alight in the most searing flames."

The Highest had been wrong about a lot of things in their time. Their understanding of the mortal realm was utterly second-hand, and they'd admitted themselves that the only other two hybrid beings they were aware of, they'd slaughtered in infancy. But their words brought back the momentary terror I'd seen in Sorsha's expression now and then when we'd fought. Her warnings that she might be able to hurt me more than I could imagine.

She'd sensed something in herself, something more than I'd been able to see. Maybe I shouldn't have dismissed her fears so quickly.

But still—how could I wrap my head around the idea that the sassy thief who liked nothing more than to tease the beast out of me and sing songs to her own lyrics was some kind of destructive force on a global scale?

I couldn't, not yet. Maybe when I saw her again, knowing what the Highest had told me—

And then what? They'd called in their last favor. I would never be free until I fulfilled it. They would never believe I'd fulfilled it until they were sure "Ruby" was dead. Even speaking of what I'd learned today might mean I met the same fate as Tempest after all this time despite everything I'd sacrificed.

I reined in that inner turmoil. I couldn't make the decision now in front of these ancient goliaths—that much I was sure of.

"I understand," I said, even though there was a hell of a lot I still didn't, and then another thought struck me, slicing straight through the core of me. I gathered myself and forced out one more question. "If this hybrid mortal-shadowkind has had time to mature… might she not have created children of her own?"

Could the fiery union I'd remembered fondly be an even bigger disaster waiting to happen?

"We are unsure if this monstrosity would even be fertile. If she has mated with another human, perhaps it is possible, but their offspring would not have the same balance of powers that gives her such potency. You could destroy those without threat to yourself."

"And if she's mated with another shadowkind?"

The Highest who'd spoken let out a sound like a huff. "That would require the same ceremony of abasement as that of her mother. We expect that to be exceedingly unlikely—and even if so, the balance would again be skewed. Ruby herself should be your primary concern."

And so she was. I had to assume this ceremony was more than simply allowing oneself to mash genitals with a mortal, or there'd be a hell of a lot more hybrids running around just of my stock, not to mention the many incubi and succubi of all existence. I was safe from hellhound pups for the time being, apparently. That hardly solved my larger problem.

I made a gesture of deference. "Any trace I discover of her, I'll pass on to you as soon as I hear of it."

"We will be waiting," another of the Highest said in a tone that sounded more like a threat than a promise, and I felt their dismissal with a lightening of the constriction around my neck.

As I made my way through the shadows, my thoughts whirled, but I didn't try to pin down any one thread. An insistent pull drew me onward—not to one of the rifts that would have spilled me out into the San Francisco area, but one that would return me to Austin.

I tore through the boundary between shadow and mortal realms with the quivering electricity the transition always provoked. Roaming from shadow to shadow, I made my way to the office that held the city's records. The one where Sorsha had tried and failed to find evidence of her birth.

If I couldn't find anything either, it wouldn't mean much. Her parents might never have registered her, given their situation. But if I did…

The office was closed for the night. I slipped beneath the door and found a computer that booted up without any special commands.

We'd celebrated her birthday only a little more than a week ago. I knew what date it was supposed to be.

The names rippled by, none of them familiar. Then a tickle of sensation passed over my eyes. I paused, studying the screen.

A fae glamour was embedded in the data, just as it'd been in Sorsha's memories.

With my stomach clenching, I willed a bolt of my power at the illusion. The magic crackled and fell away. And there, glowing before my eyes, were the damning words.

Twenty-eight years ago on September 4th, Philip Woodsen had registered the birth of his daughter, Ruby.

TWENTY-SEVEN

Sorsha

THE SPOILS OUR GUARD HANDED OVER AFTER HIS SHIFT IN THE PENTHOUSE didn't look like much of a bounty. He'd gathered them in a shopping bag so that his body wouldn't tarnish the impressions on the objects with his own thoughts and feelings, and it held only a crumpled, ketchup-stained paper napkin, a dried-up pen that was slightly gnawed at the end, and the severed plastic packaging from a… Tibetan singing bowl set?

I guessed we could hope the big boss had been meditating on his sins.

"Sorry," the charmed young man said. "That was all he had in the garbage can by the end of my shift. I had to knock over his wine carafe just to fill up the bin so I'd have an excuse to take out the trash."

"That's okay," I said, deftly picking out a few spare shards of glass that clung to the packaging. We'd specifically instructed him to stick to the garbage so that there'd be no thefts to alert his boss to our scheme. "If we can't get anything out of this, we'll just try again. He didn't seem at all suspicious about the accident?"

The guard shook his head. "He really had left the carafe too close to the edge of the counter. I made sure he was watching so he'd see all I did was walk by it."

Ruse patted him on the shoulder. "You've done excellent work. I'll see that you're properly rewarded when all this is over."

Snap was waiting for us back in the RV. He sat up straighter on the sofa at the sight of the bag. "Those are the head man's things?"

The incubus tossed the bag onto the table. "Yep. Ripe for the tasting. See what you can slurp out of them."

As Snap eased open the bag, our other companions emerged from the shadows to observe more directly. The Everymobile's living area was becoming a tight fit, especially with the second hulking wingéd in the mix... even without Omen here.

That thought twisted my stomach. Shoving down my uneasiness about our own boss's continued absence, I squeezed over to the sofa and sat down there. Pickle scuttled beneath the table, hopped up beside me—and for the first time in days, scrambled right onto my lap. A little of my apprehension melted as I tickled his chin.

If my dragon could get over my failings and come back to me, then surely everything else could turn out all right too.

"The pen might provide the most information," Thorn suggested, peering at the small collection of items. "The other objects would have been used much more temporarily, would they not?"

Antic bobbed on her feet, only able to make out the surface of the table when her heels left the ground. "Yes! The pen first." With her last bounce, she sprang right onto the edge of the table but kept swaying there, adrift on waves of excitement.

Snap took the pen in his slender hands and brought it to his face. His forked tongue flicked out, skimming through the air just above its surface.

I'd seen him work his subtler devourer magic plenty of times, but the distance that came into his expression as he sorted through the impressions he'd gleaned from the past still sent a tiny shiver up my spine. To be able to know so much about a person just by testing something they'd touched... Say whatever you wanted about the whole soul-devouring thing, *this* was damned amazing.

His tongue flicked out a few more times, but the pen didn't have much surface area to test. As his eyes refocused on us, his mouth settled into a frown. "I'm not sure anything I sensed will give us a strategy to encourage the boss out of his home. The main impression I get from his use of the pen is boredom. He used it for writing numbers into boxes in some sort of game? And also words in other boxes in a different game. Nothing he felt very strongly about."

Yeah, I didn't think Sudoku or crossword puzzles were going to be our ticket to luring the boss man away from his protective walls so Ruse could work his voodoo. "That's okay. What about those?" I tipped my head toward the other two items without a huge amount of hope. Maybe we were waiting to launch our grand plan until our charmed guard could take out another haul of trash.

Snap picked up the ketchup-y napkin gingerly and tested all around it. A hint of a smile curled his lips, but not for the reasons we'd have wanted.

"He had a very delicious meal," the devourer reported. "One of those burgers of ham, very juicy with seeds on the bun." He paused. "And he became frustrated because of a call that interrupted his meal. But he put the napkin down when he answered. I don't know what it was about."

At least Snap had gotten some second-hand deliciousness out of that one. I restrained a sigh as he picked up the torn packaging.

It was the largest of the items, so it took several minutes before the devourer had checked it over thoroughly. He lingered on one spot, his tongue flicking here and there around a seam in the plastic. A glint of neon flashed in his eyes.

I straightened my posture, watching him. *Something* had caught his interest, and in a different way from the burger.

"It was a long time ago," Snap said, slowly and softly. "But he remembers it sometimes at odd moments. He didn't realize how much this set would look like the one she showed him…"

"Who showed him what?" Antic demanded, practically tap dancing across the table in her eager impatience.

I waved her silent. Snap took another taste of the impressions attached to the packaging. "A young woman he cared about a lot. He had asked her to connect her life with his—he gave her a ring." He glanced at me.

"Humans exchange rings when they get engaged to be married," I said. "It's basically the highest form of commitment any person offers anyone else."

The devourer hummed to himself. "Yes. That. But there is much sadness when he thinks about her. I think it must have been a very long time ago, years and years, but it still hurts him a lot. And—there is anger too. Something dark and large with vicious teeth… Blood…" His forehead furrowed. "I think perhaps she was killed by a shadowkind. That could be why he would want to kill us, couldn't it?"

"Not that I think one murder excuses attempted genocide, but yeah, that could do it." I rubbed my mouth. If this guy still thought so much about his long-lost fiancé, she might help us prevent that genocide. "Did you see anything else about her? What she looked like, her name…?"

"Yes. Yes, there was—" His tongue flicked. "Carmen. That was her name. Her voice is very soft in his memories… She called him 'Isaac'."

The pieces were starting to interlock in my head to form a rather impressive picture, if I did say so myself. Ruse leaned in and tugged on my ponytail. "I like that sly look on you, Miss Blaze."

Snap peered at me hopefully. "You can use that?"

"It might be perfect," I said. "The ring you saw… Was the impression clear enough that if you went to a store with lots of rings, you could recognize which one was the most like it?"

The gleam came back into Snap's eyes. "I think so."

"Is there anything else you'd require, m'lady?" Thorn asked.

"A wig," I said. "Since he's probably been warned about a redhead running with the monsters by now. With that and a ring—we can make this happen tonight."

The wig wasn't the most comfortable thing I'd ever worn. My shadowkind companions—who were becoming as adept as thieves as I was, with the additional benefit of being able to sneak into just about any building without any need for tools—had found me a good quality one, thick black waves that looked natural once my real hair was all tucked underneath. But the edges still itched at my skin. I didn't want to fix it on completely until it was actually time to head out.

I took one last look at my transformed self in the mirror and then tugged the wig off. The plan was to move out in a little more than an hour. We wanted to be sure the business day had begun in Europe before we grabbed the boss here, because we couldn't count on keeping our hands on him for all that long once we had him. Get in there, pull him and then *his* boss under Ruse's spell, and end the Company for good—as fast as we could manage it.

All our running and fighting might be over tonight. It was too bad Omen wasn't here to see it. Of course, maybe he'd have argued every detail of my scheme.

I'd found a part for each of us to play. Antic had brought in our first Company lackey; Snap had found the ticket to the boss. The rest of us would tackle that boss tonight. Our combined if very different skills were going to bring this all together… as long as I hadn't miscalculated in any way.

As long as all those pieces lined up just right when it mattered most. And as long as the powers lurking inside me didn't act up at the wrong moment in the wrong way.

I inhaled slowly, reminding myself of the inner cooling techniques Omen had talked me through, and someone knocked on the bedroom door. I could tell it was Ruse from the jaunty rhythm of it before he even spoke. "I hope that black monstrosity hasn't swallowed you whole, Miss Blaze."

I opened the door. "I wouldn't call it a monstrosity. It's actually not a bad look. Maybe I'll have to keep it when all this is done."

Ruse made a scoffing sound and curled a stray red strand around his fingers, his chuckles caressing my jaw. "You can't be Miss Blaze without this."

"The actual fire that can pour out of my body isn't enough to justify the nickname?"

"I suppose I might make a temporary exception." He stroked the side of my face again, a whiff of his bittersweet scent reaching my nose. The gentleness of the gesture woke up a flutter in my chest alongside the heat that always came with his touch. "Shouldn't you be getting a little more sleep before the big play?"

I grimaced. "I tried—and I managed a little. I don't think I'll be able to totally relax until this is over."

"It should be simple enough, shouldn't it? You coax the Man In Charge onto that elevator, and the second you're out on the floor below, we pop out to distract him while you yank off any protections he brought with him. Then I'll get him eating out of my hand." The incubus smirked. "Possibly literally, if we have time for that."

"Right. Piece of cake." But I'd thought that plenty of times in the past, and ever since these shadowkind had entered my life, my ability to judge hadn't been quite as sharp as it'd used to be. Too much chaos in the mix.

Leaning into his caress, I rested my hand on his chest just below the collar of his sleek button-up shirt. "The plan does put a lot of the burden on you."

"Do you hear me complaining?" The incubus slid his fingertips along my jaw to tilt up my chin, his warm hazel eyes holding mine. "I never expected to be the cornerstone of any operation we carried out here, Sorsha. I figured I'd be a convenient tool to smooth along the larger plans. Turns out I'm good for more than that after all—and I'm flattered that you believed that before it ever occurred to me."

I couldn't help smiling back at him with a playful tug of his collar. "I do have a talent for spotting valuable objects. Very handy in my usual line of work." My good humor faded as I considered the point of uncertainty our entire plan rested on. "We don't know what kind of personal protections he might be wearing, though. It won't necessarily be as simple as luring him out and snapping off a badge. If you all jump out at him too early..."

"Then we decide on a signal for you to give us as our cue."

"That won't work if I need you to spring out the second the elevator opens. And even if I don't, anything odd I say or do might tip him off. He'll already be on edge."

Frowning, I dropped my gaze. If we could have used radio gear, I might have been able to make a subtler signal that way, but electronics wouldn't function in the shadows. If only there was some way I could have passed on the message essentially invisibly—

I hesitated, my hand stilling against Ruse. There *was* a way, wasn't there? The thought sent a momentary flicker of panic through me, but it petered out as quickly as it had risen up. I gazed up into the incubus's face again, and the answer came to me clear as anything.

I'd seen who he was. I trusted him. This monstrous man had stood by me and stood up for me in so many ways, and I didn't have a particle of fear left that he'd ever intend to harm me.

"Yes?" Ruse said, meeting my gaze with one eyebrow arched.

"I know how we can time it perfectly without the Company boss having a clue." I reached to unclasp the silver-and-iron badge of my own and set it on the dresser with a clink. Lately I'd been wearing it more from habit than any real sense that I needed it. "As soon as we're out of his apartment, you'll be able to look inside my head and sense how I'm feeling—whether I'm confident and ready to go or still scrambling to work out the best approach. Go by that, and we're golden."

Ruse stared at me, the nonchalance I was so used to in his roguish face broken by shock. "Just to be clear, you're giving me permission—"

"I'm *asking* you to read my emotions," I said. "It's the best possible option. And—when I made the rules before, I didn't really know you. I do now. And I know you'd never use this opening against me. I don't just believe in your skills. I believe in *you*."

The incubus blinked at me once more, and then he was pulling me to him, branding my mouth with a kiss so hot and giddying that I nearly melted on the spot. I barely had time to kiss him back before he'd eased away just an inch, his breath tingling over the lips he'd left tender with his embrace.

"I love you," he said in a voice both stiff with tension and ringing with sincerity. "I realize—from an incubus, it may not be—and of course I couldn't expect—"

My heart swelled with an ache of affection so great that I lost my breath. I touched his cheek, swallowing the lump that had risen in my throat. I wouldn't have been able to let him in as much as I was offering if this hadn't been true. It was easier saying it the second time.

"I love you too."

Ruse let out a rough sound and yanked my mouth back to his. This time the kiss stretched on and on, sending tingles all through my body and setting my skin alight. Without breaking it, he slid his hands down my sides and grasped my hips to lift me onto the edge of the dresser. More heat flooded me as our bodies aligned even more tightly.

He drew his lips from mine only to mark a scorching path along my jaw and down my neck. "I want to toss you onto that bed and ravish you until you've come a million times," he murmured against my skin, each brush of his lips sparking new pleasures. "But we have a kingpin to topple, so that'll have to wait. But I'll be damned if I'm not going to have you at least once right now. It's been too long since I was last inside you."

No arguments here. I tucked my legs around his thighs, urging him even closer. "You have me. Let's see what you can do with me, lover boy."

He laughed, the sound thick with promise, and reclaimed my mouth. As he drew every ounce of pleasure from my lips, he worked my blouse free from my skirt. With what seemed like magical speed, he whipped it off over my head, unhooked my bra, and cupped my breasts.

His deft thumbs rolled over both nipples simultaneously, and the surge of bliss made me whimper against his mouth. He smiled into our next kiss, working me over with skillful strokes until I was dying with need.

My teeth nicked his lip as I kissed him harder. I arched into him, burning for more.

"Give me the incubus," I said, knowing he'd understand what I meant.

Ruse grinned, no protests about my ability to handle him in his full shadowkind form now. And apparently while he'd been teaching Snap a few tricks, he'd picked up one from the devourer. As he closed his eyes, his clothes blinked away, giving me an instant view of his transformation.

The golden sheen glowed from his skin. His horns curled farther out of his hair. And down below, his already rigid cock curved upward at that angle I knew could send me soaring in a matter of seconds, his pubic bone jutting just far enough to stimulate my clit as well.

In every sense, he was made for fucking—and making a fucking miracle out of that intimate act.

When his eyes caught mine again, they gleamed as gold as the rest of him. He captured my mouth with an even headier kiss, and his hands skimmed up my thighs.

Never had I been so glad to be wearing a skirt. I'd chosen it for the Company boss's benefit, figuring a feminine look would work in my favor, but it was definitely benefiting *me* right now. Ruse yanked the fabric up to my hips in one smooth gesture and divested me of my panties with another. Then his glorious erection was pressing right up against my sex.

I managed to keep my senses enough to remember the caution that had come over me with Snap—and just how much I did *not* want to add a baby to this mix any time soon. "Condom," I gasped out, groping for my purse, expecting Ruse to laugh.

But no doubt the incubus had gotten the same request from an awful lot of his conquests in recent decades. He delved inside my purse to produce one as if it'd never have occurred to him not to.

The second he drove into me, as if his cock were meant to be nowhere else, all thought of the ridiculousness of safe sex with an incubus flew out of my mind with the rush of bliss. I matched Ruse's thrusts, the dresser rattling beneath me. His glow seeped through every pore in my body. Everywhere it touched, more desire flared.

The head of his cock pulsed against the sweet spot inside me. He hit it again and again, grazing my clit at the same time, his mouth on my lips and then my neck and then my shoulder, his hands seemingly everywhere. I wrapped one arm around him for balance and let the other tease up into his hair to grasp one of his horns.

Ruse groaned and plunged into me even harder. Pleasure crackled through me, whiting out my vision. I came, gasping and moaning and deeply glad that his incubus sound-proofing magic would keep my cries of ecstasy from alerting the entire Everymobile to what we'd gotten up to.

"I love you," I mumbled again, wanting to say it unprompted, and those three words tipped Ruse over the edge after me. He came with a heave of his hips and a guttural sound that rang through me with a burst of afterglow.

I clung to him as his rhythm slowed and his body came to rest against me, soaking in every bit of that glow that I could.

I might have lost one of my lovers, but I still had the three who'd dedicated themselves to me from the very beginning. Yeah, okay, you could call them monsters, but they'd looked out for me and stood by me more than any human in my life had ever managed to. They'd accepted both my mortality and my own monstrousness without hesitation.

If they believed in *me*, who the hell would I be not to?

TWENTY-EIGHT

Sorsha

I approached the Big Bad Boss the same way our charmed guard had said delivery people did—and you might say I *was* delivering something to his doorstep. Chaos? Hocus pocus? Retribution? A little of all three, really.

Of course, I'd imagine his typical deliveries didn't arrive at five in the morning, but that might have worked in my favor. When I brandished the courier envelope I'd slapped several *Priority* stickers on for emphasis, the lobby security dude gave me a slightly glazed look before waving me on to the elevators. Then it was simply a matter of punching the button for the top floor the main elevator let out onto.

As the elevator car hurtled upward, I stuffed the empty envelope into my purse and palmed the ring Snap had procured—round setting, 1-carat diamond, white gold. With something that simple, I could hope the big boss's own memory wouldn't be so exact as to notice any tiny differences. Sweet summer sandwiches, let him not have gotten the original one engraved.

The wig didn't itch now that I'd fixed it on properly, but I couldn't shake my awareness of its weight on my head. I resisted the urge to tug at it and rocked on my feet instead, singing a little tune to keep my energy pumped up. "If I blow there will be rubble; if I slay there will be double. So come on my little foe."

The elevator dinged, letting me out on the sub-penthouse floor. The blaze of light from the glaring panels set all across the ceiling made my eyes water. Strips of more fluorescent light beamed along the baseboards, and the seamless floor was polished like a mirror to reflect all of it. What the hell did a regular delivery person make of this funhouse hall?

It was a good thing we'd been prepared for this in advance. My shadowkind allies who'd snuck with me onto the elevator unseen would have been shit out of luck for darkness to conceal themselves in out here—if it wasn't for the skill our night elf possessed that Omen had scoffed at.

Gloam could produce his own darkness. As I walked down the hall to the private elevator at the far end, a streak of shadow trailed along the edge of the floor, long enough to accommodate all my allies but so thin I could barely see it unless I looked hard. Here was hoping that meant it wouldn't show up on the security cams mounted at intervals along the ceiling.

One of those cameras was pointed at the spot directly in front of the private elevator that only moved between this floor and the penthouse above. Our new friend had told us that one of the two guards always on duty would be keeping an eye on that feed at all times.

To catch that dude's attention, I gestured wildly, setting my face in a fraught expression. Then, as if frantic to get my message across, I snatched a paper out of my purse and pretended to scrawl a message I'd actually written ahead of time. I held it up to the camera with both hands and a pleading gaze.

I MUST SPEAK TO ISAAC. IT'S ABOUT CARMEN. PLEASE!!!!!

Very important to add the multiple exclamation marks. Each one could serve as a little jab of guilt over my apparent desperation.

I held my breath. If the strangeness of my arrival and the message wasn't enough to prompt the guard to wake up his boss and ask for guidance, and instead the guy came down to chase me off without checking in, the situation would become ten times more complicated.

But our charmed guard had said that his boss didn't like them taking their own initiative, and this time that worked against the head honcho rather than for him.

I waited there, holding up the sign and waggling it now and then, for long enough that my shoulders started to twinge from keeping them in position. Mr. Big Bad would have plenty to think about, faced with my message. How had anyone connected his real first name to the condo where he didn't even let his direct employees identify him as anything other than "boss"? How had I found out about his long-ago fiancé? What could I possibly know about her that would bring me to his doorstep?

He might be wary, but we were counting on the questions eating at him too deeply for him to dismiss. He had no reason to suspect that this intrusion could have anything to do with the gore-and-fire-happy monsters who'd ransacked various laboratory facilities belonging to the Company in cities far away.

Finally, a thrumming sound carried through the wall. I lowered the sign, my body tensing.

The door opened to reveal not the silver-buzzcut, square-jawed guy our charmed guard had described as his boss, but a muscle-bound woman who looked only a little older than me. She pointed a gun at me, her other hand at a whip hanging in a coil from her belt, and jerked her head toward the shiny elevator car she was standing in.

"Get on. The boss will see you. No funny stuff—hands to yourself, avoid sudden movements. Understood?"

I nodded meekly. We'd expected the process of roping in the boss man to go something like this. I might have piqued his curiosity, but he'd want to indulge that curiosity in the comfort of his well-shielded home. The *real* trick was going to be convincing him I had a legitimate enough cause to get him out of that home and vulnerable enough for us to make our move.

Leaving my shadowkind allies behind, I stepped into the elevator. They couldn't follow me up into that realm of silver and iron without it shattering their disguises and their strength. However much monster I had in me, I was still that much human.

As the door slid closed, the guard patted me over from shoulders to feet. She rifled through my purse too, but I'd emptied that of anything unusual. Finally, she motioned for me to open my mouth and peered into it. Satisfied I wasn't carrying weapons anywhere accessible on my person, she wiped her hands together and pressed the control button.

A faint vibration ran through the polished floor as the elevator whisked us upward. Its doors whispered apart, and I found myself face-to-face with Isaac, last name unknown, grandmaster over the North American Company of Light.

From the guard's description, I'd expected his jaw to be a little squarer, his buzzcut a little more severe. The man of fifty-something years who was staring at me somewhat blearily could have passed for a college professor easier than the military general I'd pictured him as. The clearly hastily-thrown-on button-up and slacks, rumpled where he'd stuffed the former into the waist of the latter, didn't help.

But then, as he looked me up and down with a tightening of that jaw, I caught a steely vibe that removed any doubts about this guy's claim to authority.

One of the most important things he'd have been watching for was how I reacted to entering his condo. The sheets of silver and iron I knew were built into his walls didn't affect me at all, as he could no doubt observe.

I hugged myself as if nervous for totally normal human reasons, still clutching my sign. Isaac's gaze dropped to it, and his shoulders went even more rigid. He'd worked very hard to keep so much of himself private from his employees. That worked in our favor now too. What did he want to protect more: his identity and the details of his past, or his current presence from whatever threat he thought some shivering stranger might pose.

"You checked her over?" Isaac asked the guard standing next to me. Another, a middle-aged man, stood behind his boss in the entry hall.

The woman gave a brisk nod. "I wouldn't have let her up if I found anything to be concerned about."

"All right. Retire to the surveillance room—both of you. If she comes any closer to me or I move to leave the hall without first giving you the okay signal, intervene. Otherwise, leave us be."

The man looked startled. "Sir?"

"You heard me. This is a matter I need to handle on my own." A hint of a sneer curled his lips as he looked me over again. "And I think I should have no trouble handling her at all."

Was that so? He was lucky he wasn't meeting my cat burglar, pyromaniac self just yet.

The guards left without another word. Obedient sorts, obviously. No doubt he'd picked them with that criteria in mind. One more choice that would no longer work in his favor.

I'd gotten the hook down his gullet. All that was left was to reel him in.

The boss man waited several seconds after his lackeys had vanished to give them time to get out of earshot. Then he said, low and curt, "Who are you?"

"A friend of Carmen's," I said.

A muscle in his cheek twitched. "That's impossible."

I let the words spill out as if in an anxious rush. "You thought she was dead. They wanted you to think that, the horrible creatures. Some of them can cast illusions—you know that, don't you? Ones that can fool all sorts of people for ages. That's all it was."

"And how would you know this? How did you know to come here? What is it you *want*?"

I gazed at him from beneath my fake black waves with widened eyes. "They had me too. She told me everything. How much she wished she could find her way back to you. The bond she still felt must have mingled with their magic somehow—she started having visions; she saw this building. We managed to break free and come here, but she's ill. I'm afraid to try and move her, so I told her I'd come get you."

"Then she's here? She's waiting—" He shook himself, and his tone hardened again. "No. It can't be. I *buried* her."

"You buried an illusion. I swear it. She *needs* you, now." I held out my hand, showing him the ring. "She gave me this so you'd know it was her."

Isaac froze. Then he reached out and took the ring from me, holding it up to the light. His throat bobbed. "She really... She managed to hold on to this all this time?"

"Nothing meant more to her," I said softly.

"And those monsters—" His voice shook with more fury than it could hold.

An answering anger flared inside me. What about all the monsters he'd ordered tortured and slaughtered who'd never harmed a single mortal? Did none of their lives count while he acted out his revenge for the savage one that had ripped his fiancé from him?

Heat prickled through my chest—and I yanked it back with a hitch of breath I couldn't quite hide. Cool waves, a salty breeze, the rhythmic hiss of the ocean. Focus on that. Focus on that and keep my fire in, or so many more monsters would die under this man's orders because I'd screwed up our one chance to stop him.

My emotions settled with an ache around my heart. I could do this. I could stay in control. At least as long as I didn't *need* to fling any fire around and could keep all of it inside.

The big boss was watching me again. "Are you all right?" he said carefully.

"I'm not totally well either," I said as if embarrassed to admit it. "But it's Carmen who kept me going all this time—I had to do this for her. Will you come to her? She's nearby—it won't take five minutes. I don't want to leave her too long. If she sees anyone but you, I think she might run."

So don't call up someone else to handle this. You don't really want to anyway, not when it shows so much of the life you've tried to keep away from all your colleagues' eyes.

Resolve flashed in his eyes. Something I'd said or done had gotten through. He spun on his heel and hollered to his guards. "Is there anyone at all in the lower hall or any report of trouble from the lobby?"

An intercom crackled. "No, sir," the woman replied. "It's been totally quiet all night except your guest."

He wavered but only for a second this time. Then he gave a brisk nod, made a gesture toward the camera, and strode off. He returned moments later pulling on a suit jacket that he stuffed a phone into the pocket of. Something about the way it hung on him pinged understanding in my brain.

"That's a good one," I said, eyeing the jacket with feigned approval. "It's got strips of silver and iron sewn right into it? I knew a lady who had a dress made like that." I patted the lapel, just a brush of my fingertips to prove to him that I didn't shy away from those metals. And to get a feel for the fabric. Sooner rather than later, I was going to have to wrench this thing off him.

"I believe in taking every precaution," he said. "Let's go. You and Carmen will be safe from the fiends in here. I can bring in doctors and whatever else you need."

He opened the door to the elevator, leaving his guards behind. Leaving them watching the surveillance feeds. Fresh tension wound through my body as I followed him in.

We'd thought he might bring his lackeys with him, so that Thorn and Flint would need to bash their helmeted heads right off their bodies when we emerged into the hall. It looked like we wouldn't be able to stage our ambush there after all. If we attacked just him, the guards would see and come running to the rescue.

The others would have to wait until we were out of the hall below. Actually, better that we weren't even in the building, since I knew for sure he had his phone. We couldn't rely on this going so smoothly that the building's own security wouldn't notice and interfere.

Ruse would be relying on his read on my emotions to tell him all of that. I concentrated on the worry of them acting too soon, my longing to be somewhere out of the cameras' view. *Not yet. Not yet.* And woven through all that was my hope that he'd understand.

The elevator door slid open on the brilliant hall of light. No shadowkind leapt from their constructed patch of darkness. And how terrible it would be if they did just yet. I let that horror fill me all the way to the second elevator, even as I studied Isaac from the corner of my eye. To get the jacket off him as quickly as possible, I'd need to stand—yeah, just like that would be fine.

No one had used the main elevator since I'd gotten off. The door opened the second he pushed the button. We stepped on, and I kept the same anxiety racing through my veins. Oh, to be out in the open air, away from *any* potential prying eyes.

We descended without interruption. I hurried through the lobby a step ahead of the big boss, both to maintain my story that I was worried about the supposed Carmen and to get on with the part of the plan that didn't rest entirely on me.

"This way," I said on the sidewalk, hustling a few buildings over and then ducking away from the streetlamps down a driveway currently closed off with a thick chain. A tarry smell drifted in the darkened air.

When I paused, Isaac came up beside me. His head swiveled. "Is this where she was? We have to—"

As he spoke, I placed myself at his right flank, braced myself, and let relief and urgency wash through me. *We're in the clear. Let's do this!*

My feelings must have pealed through loud and clear. Ruse, Snap, Thorn, and Flint sprang into being around us.

The boss man startled with a fearful cry, and I grasped his suit jacket by the collar. With one sharp yank, I'd pulled it to his elbows—but then he connected one of those elbows with my forehead.

The impact radiated through my skull, sending my thoughts reeling. I clung on, but he was twisting around to strike another blow, and while he had the jacket on him my allies could barely touch him—

I could use my fire. I could control it enough to have it do my bidding down to the letter. I *could*.

Through a hasty swell of ocean imagery, I coaxed my flames from my hands and into the fabric of Isaac's jacket.

He let out a hiss of shock. The wool melted into cinders, the sagging strips of metal pattered to the pavement—and there he was, naked of protections, the fabric of his dress shirt only faintly singed.

The emotion that hit me then was nothing less than elation. I could have hugged the dude I'd just traumatized for staying uncrispified if he wouldn't have tried to punch my nose in again.

Ruse shot me the swiftest of winks, already talking with the full force of his power thrumming through his voice. "We're so glad you could join us, my friend. We have the answers to destroying the monsters you wish to exterminate. Unfortunately, you've been helping them rather than hindering them. Because of you, so many more young women like your fiancé have fallen."

The big boss pressed his hands to his head. "What are you talking about? I've—that can't be true."

"Oh, but it is. We've been watching, and we've seen. What you don't know, what your bosses don't know, is that the entire Company of Light is a trick dreamed up by the monsters themselves. They set this whole thing in motion, made the first crusaders feel they had to come together to fight back. But the truth is that they *need* your anger and fear to continue passing into this world. Every bit of evidence about them you take down in your computers, every order anyone gives to capture or kill them, it allows the pathways between the realms to remain strong."

"I can show you," Flint said with that voice like a roll of thunder. He fixed his gaze on Isaac's. An eerie light flickered into being in the depths of his eyes, and the color drained from our target's face.

We hadn't been sure if even Ruse's charm could win the boss man over convincingly enough. But Flint—Flint could show him the supposed horrors the Company of Light was enabling in vivid reality, as if he were standing in the midst of the worst of it. We'd determined that his ability could work across great distances as long as he could look into the other person's eyes. As soon as we got the biggest boss of all on the phone, Ruse was going to cajole him into a video call.

By the time the vision the second wingéd stirred up had faded away, Isaac was trembling. He swiped his hand across his mouth, looking as though he might vomit. "I never realized—I had no idea…"

"None of you did," Ruse said with false sympathy. "The worst of it is, you're the only ones left who even understand that the monsters exist. If *you* stopped all your activities around them, wiped clean all the data you've collected on them—their pathways to this world would close up, and they'd never threaten another mortal again."

The key, Ruse had said once, was to give the person you were charming what they'd wanted in the first place. Those ideas took hold like nothing else. And what Isaac wanted more than anything in existence was to rid this realm of monsters.

"My God," he said. "We have to—I'll do whatever I can, but I don't have control over everything. I'll start reaching out—"

"First," Ruse said smoothly, "we should talk to the man who gives you *your* orders. Otherwise he may not understand and might even stand in your way while you try to set this right. You have the means to contact him, don't you?"

The boss man dragged in a breath. "Yes. I have a way to indicate to him that I need him to call me. He'll want to know immediately."

As he fumbled for his phone, Ruse caught my gaze over Isaac's shoulder. The corner of his mouth quirked with the start of a smirk, his eyes glowing with triumph. I couldn't help grinning back at him.

We had the Company by the throat, and in just a few minutes, we were going to snap its neck so hard not one piece of it would ever rise again.

TWENTY-NINE

Sorsha

If you've never partied with shadowkind, I've got to say I highly recommend finding an opportunity to do so.

I was running on about three hours of sleep, but the rush of our victory and the energy humming through the air inside the RV from the beings who didn't need sleep to begin with pepped me up no problem. Ruse and Snap had "liberated" a large amount of snack food and some very nice champagne from a couple of stores downtown. Now we were all full of frothy alcohol and bubbling over with laughter and jubilant remarks.

Ruse had managed to find an '80s station on the RV's radio, sending bouncy notes careening through the narrow space. He spun me around and sent me flying into Snap's arms, who stole a kiss while he danced with his usual sinuous grace. Thorn and Flint toasted each other—a little carefully after their earlier attempts had resulted in several cracked glasses. Pickle darted around on the table with energetic little hops, managing to stir a smile even from Gloam after he'd sunk into his usual daytime despondency.

"The look on that mortal's face when I showed him a vision of the destruction his Company would bring about," Flint said, his thunderous voice sounding almost jovial, and let out a chuckle that vibrated through the room.

Ruse smirked. "He couldn't demolish his own work fast enough. And we accomplished all that from thousands of miles away. I do enjoy modern mortal technology."

"There will still be the independent hunters and collectors," Thorn pointed out, even though he was smiling too.

I dismissed that concern with a wave. "We can deal with them like we always have. No big deal. And with those last tidbits Ruse planted in the big bosses' heads, they'll have the Company cracking down on *anyone* who's doing business around the shadowkind from now on. After all, who else will they have to blame when the shadowkind don't vanish completely after the Company is disbanded?"

I paused to take another swig of champagne—and two figures popped from the shadows so abruptly I almost choked.

Antic's arrival wasn't a surprise. She'd insisted on being the one to go off and collect some more refreshments, restless after standing back so long after her initial contribution to our plan. But standing next to her, in all his tight-jawed, icy-eyed glory, was our missing hellhound shifter.

With a sputtered cough, I set down my glass, my mouth already stretching into a welcoming grin. My heart had skipped a beat both startled and ecstatic. But as I took in the stern set of Omen's mouth and the way he was looking at me, as if I'd created some new catastrophe even worse than the ones he'd accused me of before, my pulse hitched again in a much less pleasant way. I found myself glancing around to confirm that I hadn't somehow burned the Everymobile to the ground without noticing.

Everyone else had fallen momentarily silent. Ruse found his tongue first. "Omen! Very convenient of you to skip out while we did all the work and only return for the victory party."

The hellhound shifter's gaze slid from me to the incubus. "The imp told me about your scheme—and that, miracle of all miracles, you pulled it off. So, you managed to topple the Company without me. Not a bad day's work."

I folded my arms over my chest. "You don't sound all that happy about it." Was he upset that we hadn't waited for him to show up before taking action, even though we'd accomplished more than he could have even been hoping?

"Oh, I'm very glad to know that particular thorn is no longer in our side. Ecstatic, even. It just hasn't had time to sink in. And I've had more pressing concerns on my mind."

"More pressing than bringing down a massive organization dedicated to exterminating all shadowkind?"

"They could have been ignored for a few days without total disaster. This might not." He glanced around, noting the second wingéd in our midst with only the barest flicker of surprise. "Out. All of you except the mortal. *Now.*"

Antic squeaked and darted into the shadows. Gloam's mouth dropped open, but a second later he followed her.

Flint stood, his solemn face reaching new levels of stony grimness that Thorn could only have aspired to. "If there is some concern with—"

"I'm not *concerned*," the hellhound shifter growled. "I just want you all out. I assume you know how to follow orders?"

The warrior winced and vanished. Omen swiveled to consider the three remaining shadowkind, who'd drawn closer around me rather than departing.

"What's going on, Omen?" Ruse asked.

Thorn inclined his head. "I would prefer to remain and hear the news you've brought, given the option."

Omen glared at them. "I wasn't giving options. When I said 'all of you except the mortal,' I meant the three of you as well. Get going."

"Hey," I broke in. "You should know by now that *I* don't jump just because you say so. If you make them take off, I'm leaving too. Whatever's going on, they deserve to know." And I wanted them here, especially when Omen was looking at me like that.

His cool eyes pierced mine and held there. I stared right back at him, all my celebratory elation fading away behind my defiance.

"Fine," he muttered. "They'll end up finding out soon enough anyway." He made a curt gesture. "Disaster, you've mentioned a note your parents wrote to you. Would you let me have a look at that?"

Snap peered at him wide-eyed. "Are you going to tell us where you've been first?"

"The Highest called me in for a talk I couldn't refuse," Omen said flatly. "They weren't very prompt about their invitation." He raised his eyebrows at me. "Well?"

"Yeah, of course, I can get it." I swiveled, slightly dizzy from both the champagne and the sudden change in atmosphere, and hurried over to the bedroom to grab the pearly trinket box.

Had he found out something else about my parents—from the Highest shadowkind or somewhere else on his way back? What could be so urgent about people who were *dead*? And why wouldn't he have wanted the other shadowkind hearing about it?

When I returned with the box, Ruse and Snap had sat down on the sofa-bench. Omen was leaning against the table, his face the same stern mask it'd been since he'd arrived. Thorn stepped to flank me as I approached, as if to guard me. I'd have felt better about that if I'd had any idea what he might be guarding me from. I didn't think even *he* knew that yet.

Omen snapped open the box's lid and withdrew the folded notepaper. His mouth twisted into a crooked smile. "As I thought."

"What?" I demanded, leaning closer and ignoring the heat that rose up between our bodies with our arms nearly touching.

The note looked the same to me as it always had with its few lines about how much my parents had loved me and how sorry they were not to be with me now. But Omen flicked his fingers toward my name scrawled at the top of the page.

"What about that?" I started to ask—and the ink shifted before my eyes. The letters wavered and reformed. My back stiffened, and any other words I might have said died in my throat.

There'd been a glamour on the letter, just like whatever ones Luna had fixed in my memories. She'd altered this piece of my past too. Now Omen had broken it, and the name I'd thought was mine had vanished.

In its place, the curving lines of ink formed a new one I couldn't wrap my head around: *Ruby*.

My mouth opened and closed and opened again. "I—But—The note wasn't for me?"

Omen gave me a penetrating look. "Of course it's for you. Your parents didn't name you Sorsha. *You* are Ruby. I'd imagine your fae guardian must have worked some awfully complex glamour repressing all memory of that name from your mind, woven into your thoughts so thoroughly so long ago I couldn't have picked up on the magic."

Thorn shifted his weight behind me. "How can this be? Not even Sorsha was aware of her powers until recently. She was a small child the last time she was in Austin. How could she have done something to cause such a hunt from the Highest?"

Very good questions, and I was glad he'd asked, since I was still having trouble formulating full sentences.

Omen grimaced. "The Highest didn't want people to know what exactly they were looking for or why. Ruby hadn't done anything except come into existence—and escape their attempt to end that existence."

He paused and met my eyes again. There might have been something a little sad behind the ice now. "It wasn't hunters who killed your parents. It was shadowkind. The Highest sent their warrior minions to slaughter the three of you. The fae woman got you out of there and was clever enough to ensure they never caught wind of your location again."

My parents… had been killed by *shadowkind*? Shadowkind who'd meant to kill three-year-old me as well? Just when I thought I was starting to get a grip on his revelations, another one threw me for a loop.

I curled my fingers around the edge of the table to hold myself steady. "Why? I mean, I know a mortal and a shadowkind managing to have a kid is pretty much unheard of, but—is it really such a horrible thing, enough that they'd want us all dead?"

"As far as I could tell, it's about the most horrible thing the Highest can conceive of."

"Why should it be?" Snap spoke up, unusually fierce. "If that was what Sorsha's parents wanted—no harm came out of it—"

"That's where you might be wrong," Omen said. His voice had gone taut. "The Highest believe that a union between a mortal and a shadowkind would create a being of incredibly destructive power—enough power to ruin both this world and ours." He studied me.

"You've felt it. I didn't believe you when you told me, but it seems you might have been right to be wary of what lurks inside you."

The fire I'd managed to control so well just hours ago? It flared in my chest now, prickling hot and jittering, but I willed it down, swallowing hard. "I just—I just need to practice more, to get a total handle on it, like *you've* always said. I haven't done anything that awful with it."

"Not yet. They think you will if you're allowed to live long enough." He tucked the notepaper back into the trinket box and set the box down on the table. "Whatever exactly you are, the most ancient and powerful beings among all the shadowkind are absolutely terrified of you."

The absurdity of that statement left me lost for words again. Pickle crept over and nuzzled my hand, but I couldn't take a whole lot of comfort from his gesture of solidarity in the face of this discovery. All of the celebratory joy had drained out of me.

The Highest shadowkind wanted me dead. I might contain some kind of world-shattering power. How was I supposed to respond to that? What were we going to *do* about it?

I might have asked one or both of those things, except before I could recover my voice, Omen's phone rang.

His head jerked down, and he frowned at his pocket for a second before reaching to answer it. Obviously he hadn't been expecting a call. Did shadowkind have to deal with spammy telemarketers just like the rest of us? This one couldn't have had worse timing.

Omen's frown deepened as he took in the screen. I was standing close enough to him to see no number or name was showing up on the display, not even a note of *Unknown Caller*—it was totally blank. But his ringtone sounded again.

Cautiously, he hit the answer button and lifted the phone. "Hello? Who is this?"

A sharp laugh pealed from the speaker, so loudly that the hellhound shifter yanked the phone away from his ear. "Omen," an equally sharp female voice said, as clearly as if he'd put her on speakerphone. "I knew I'd get you."

Omen's posture went rigid. He stared at the phone as if he'd suddenly realized he was holding a viper. "Who is this?" he asked again, but with a slight hesitation that suggested he was bracing for an answer he already expected.

"My goodness. I recognize *your* voice after all this time. Do you really not know your favorite associate in all things havoc-raising? I'm wounded."

A chill shot down my spine, my own troubles briefly forgotten. What was the name of that formidable shadowkind Omen had said he'd harassed mortals with ages ago?

He offered it up hoarsely, his knuckles whitening where he was gripping the phone. "Tempest. You—I watched a squad of wingéd *murder* you."

"You watched them *attempt* to murder me. I must have put on a very convincing show of being murdered. It was necessary, you know, to get those stuffy windbags that call themselves the Highest off my back, and once I had the freedom of being supposedly dead, I didn't really want to give it up. I'm sorry if you've grieved for me across all these years."

From the set of Omen's mouth, I suspected he was more likely to be grieving her return. "You had to do what you had to do," he said, evening out his tone with his usual strict composure. "Why are you honoring me with the secret now?"

The sphinx tsked. "It seems you've been making mischief for the wrong side. Nearly putting all my diligent work to waste. Thankfully I caught on and knocked the delusions out of my good friend's head before he blew up the entire Company of Light."

I wouldn't have thought I could get any more stunned, but that comment smacked me right through speechless and out the other end. "*You're* working with the Company of Light?"

"One of your new friends, Omen? She catches on quick. Although I'm not so much working for them as *they're* working for me. Tempest the sphinx bows to no one."

"If I could interject," Ruse said, looking as discombobulated as I felt. "I don't know who you are, but you're obviously shadowkind. Why in blue blazes are you running a 'company' set on destroying the lot of us?"

"Oh, you haven't told the stories of our glory days, Omen?" Tempest sighed with exaggerated dramatics. "No matter. I can assure you the mortals won't manage to wipe us out no matter what they do —at least, not those of us smart enough to deserve this life. If you'd like to discuss the matter further, I won't make it hard to find me. You remember that architectural dream of mine? I got to make it come true."

Omen froze and then gave a disbelieving chuckle. "You didn't—"

"Oh, I did. The king was only too happy to oblige when I nudged him in all the right directions. I suppose I'll see you there shortly. I'd appreciate it if you'd leave my sycophants alone until then. You've already caused me enough of a headache."

The connection cut off as abruptly as her voice had first blared out. For several seconds, we all just gaped at Omen, who was trying valiantly not to gape at his phone and not entirely succeeding.

A fresh wave of heat swelled inside me. "A *shadowkind* is convincing people to torture and slay the rest of you?" We'd made that claim to the big bosses just hours ago—but nothing I'd actually heard from any of my companions would have indicated it was true. And the damage the Company had done to untold numbers of shadowkind certainly wasn't make-believe.

"She always did care more about sowing chaos for her own satisfaction than anything or anyone else," Omen said in a shell-shocked tone.

A flame broke out across my forearm before I could suppress a surge of anger and betrayal. I slapped it against my side, but the hellhound shifter's gaze snapped to it.

He shook himself as if shedding all the bewilderment of the last few minutes and pushed himself away from the table. When his eyes met mine, something in them made the bottom drop out of my stomach.

"Dealing with her will have to wait until later. First we have to deal with you. I'm sorry."

My heart lurched. "Omen—"

He didn't give me a chance to plead or protest. As his name slipped from my lips, he lunged at me, his arm swinging faster than I could track.

With the slam of his fist into my temple, my mind spiraled into darkness.

DUSK AVENGER - BONUS SCENE

What happened to Snap after he went to appeal to the Company of Light, and how did he end up losing his memories? This bonus scene from his point of view fills in that blank in the story.

Snap

It took some time to find the people my recent Company of Light victim must have been working with. I slipped through the shadows for hours, watching for sights that matched the fragmented memories I'd gleaned from him, tasting various surfaces and objects for the impressions left behind by those who'd come nearby.

Here and there, I caught wisps of the same righteous determination and defiance that had flowed through so many of the man's thoughts. And as I drew closer to the place I realized was my ultimate destination, the uncomfortable prickling sensation from large amounts of silver and iron nearby started to affect my other senses as well.

I hadn't known any mortals other than the Company of Light and other groups of the humans who hunted and captured shadowkind to use those two metals together to that extent. Not that I had all that much experience with the wide variety of humans out there, but following the metals felt like a good starting point.

I studied the building I'd come up on, which looked like a lump of concrete, though I could feel the quivers of the toxic metals embedded in its frame. A shiver ran through my being even in my shadow form.

The glow of dawn was only just starting to seep along the edges of the horizon. It seemed that like we shadowkind, the Company of Light was most active during the dark hours, despite their name. Maybe because they were looking for us? In any case, I watched several figures head out through the front door to a waiting truck, all of them wearing the kinds of protective clothing we'd seen on them before. I spotted the emblem of the Company on one of their chests.

This was definitely the right place. I lingered in the shadows a little longer, debating the best way to approach them. Apprehension coiled around me.

I wanted them to cut the monstrousness out of me. I wanted to know I'd be safe for Sorsha always. They should want that too, shouldn't they? If I couldn't devour any more souls, then they had no reason to fear me or to want to eliminate the rest of me.

We had the same goals in this one instance. It shouldn't be difficult. I just didn't know what to say.

Sorsha would have strode right up to them and announced her intentions, wouldn't she? She wouldn't have cowered in the dark afraid of facing the necessary fate. I had to be brave for her. She deserved a mate who was bold—a mate who'd never consider harming her.

I could give her that. I *would*.

I darted through the slowly shrinking patches of shadow until I reached the door to the building. Should I take on my physical form here or slink right inside?

I debated for a moment and decided on knocking. I'd seen enough of human behavior by now to know that they typically announced themselves at new buildings that way. I should make every effort to show that I could display proper manners.

As I pulled my being into the sharper focus of a physical presence, the cool early morning air closed around my newly formed skin, the scent of car smoke tickling my nose. My muscles twitched with the vibrations emanating off all the unpleasant metals embedded in the walls in front of me, but I held myself steady. I raised my hand to knock and then quickly glanced down to confirm I'd remembered to compose all appropriate clothing. All good there.

My knuckles rapped against the steel door. I held myself still and calm, doing my best to look unthreatening. I had the urge to taste the door to find out what impressions it might hold but restrained myself. Somehow that behavior seemed impolite.

With a faint squeak of the hinges, the door swung open. A man and a woman peered out at me, the man's forehead creasing and the woman's mouth set in a slight frown.

"Yes?" the man said.

I dipped my head in acknowledgment and then thought maybe I should wave in greeting as well. And offer a handshake? No, they probably wouldn't want to touch a shadowkind while I still had my murderous abilities.

"Hello," I said. "You're part of the Company of Light, aren't you?"

"Who's asking?" the man said gruffly, but the woman gripped his arm with a flash of panic across her face. She yanked out a weapon at the same time—one of those beaming whips I didn't like at all.

"It's one of them," she hissed. "One of the beasts."

I blinked, momentarily confused about how she'd figured that out so quickly, and then realized she must have noticed my forked tongue. The man's hand leapt to a device attached to his belt.

I smiled at the two of them with as much friendliness as I could convey and held up my hands in what I believed was a peaceful gesture. "Yes, I'm a shadowkind. I promise I'm not here to hurt you, though. I'm just hoping—I heard that there's a way that you can take out the monstrous parts of beings like me—I'd like you to do that. To me. I don't want my powers."

The statements didn't come out as coherently as I'd intended to express myself, but having the two mortals look so disturbed by my presence had rattled me. Had I gotten my intentions across clearly enough to reassure them?

It was difficult to tell. The woman continued clutching the whip, but she didn't extend its condensed blaze from the handle. "Stay right where you are," she said. "We're not falling for any tricks."

The man seemed more open-minded. "You can talk to us from there," he said, his posture stiff. "Tell us exactly what it is that you want."

I thought I'd already done that, but obviously I hadn't laid the situation out thoroughly enough. I groped for the right words to explain without mentioning the fact that I'd shredded one of their colleague's souls into agonizing pieces last night. They weren't likely to feel at all friendly if they found out about that.

"I don't want to hurt *anyone*," I said. "Whatever you do to… 'hollow the danger out' or however you'd put it, I'd like you to do that for me. Then I'll be safe and you won't have to worry about anything I'll do afterward, and we'll all be happy."

I beamed brighter, but neither of the mortals looked convinced.

What else could I say? Wasn't it enough that I'd come here alone, willing to put myself at their mercy so they could do their work? I searched my mind for something that might persuade them of my intentions.

Maybe I should mention my motivations, and they'd see it was all out of love.

"There's a woman," I said. "A mortal I adore very much. I want any harmful tendencies taken out of me so I never have to worry that I might hurt her by accident. It's the least I can do for her. I don't mind if it hurts *me*, having those parts taken out. She's worth it. And when you're done, there'll be no reason you can't let me—"

I didn't get to finish my suggestion. The man's expression tensed just slightly, and I paused with the sense that something was wrong—but I didn't figure it out quickly enough. The next thing I knew, a heap of material flew over my head from behind and collapsed on me with a far-too-familiar burning sensation.

It was one of their nets, all twined with silver and iron—the kind the hunters had used to capture Thorn, Ruse, and me before we'd ended up in those cages that Sorsha had freed us from. Someone had crept up behind me while I was talking.

I cried out as the pain jabbed all through my limbs and chest, hazing the thoughts in my head. My arms flailed out instinctively, but the searing fibers were already pressing too close, penning me in so tightly I couldn't transform, couldn't escape into shadow, couldn't do anything but grit my teeth and stiffen my body against the agony.

Voices reached my ears, blurred and distant through the pain echoing in my head.

"Quick, haul him in. He's a powerful one."

"What's the strongest cage we have—or should we use one of the booths?"

"Don't loosen up your grip for a second! He was trying to pull something over on us."

"Someone go check the perimeter. He might not have come alone."

But I did, I said silently in my mind, because I couldn't will my jaw to move. *It's just me, and I just wanted to let you do your work. We don't have to fight. It doesn't have to be like this.*

But apparently in the eyes of the members of the Company of Light, it did. My awareness of the world beyond the net dwindled more and more as they hauled me through the building, but I felt the thump of my physical body hitting the metal floor of cell that might have been like the one we'd found Omen in. I wasn't in a state where I could make many clear observations. The pain somehow dulled and expanded at the same time, as if it were gnawing at every particle of my body instead of jabbing at just the most vital bits.

No. No. This isn't what I meant. Can't you please just listen? You don't have to be afraid of me. You don't have to treat me like this.

None of the protests made it past my lips. I didn't think anyone was near enough to hear them anyway. The door had closed. I was alone, surrounded by reflective metal surfaces that bounced the glaring light around to hit me from all sides.

When I'd recovered from the net's grasp enough, I pulled into my shadow form as much as I could. It was more comfortable than maintaining my physical presence, less draining, even though the metals around me and the constant light still scraped at my awareness like... like... like that material we'd found in a furniture workshop we'd searched that Ruse had told me was called "sandpaper."

It'd felt almost pleasant to rub the pad of my thumb against the stuff, but having it grating all across my being was not enjoyable at all.

Sometime later, after time had blurred together beyond any ability I had to follow hours or days, I found out that there were worse things than the sandpaper sensation. A panel in the ceiling clicked open to drop another net on me, one that jerked me back into the physical plane against my will. Hands dragged me out of the cell and onto a hard table where various tools sliced and stabbed me.

Everything was pain. Dull and sharp, burning and throbbing. There was nothing else.

I tried to think of Sorsha, to wrap my love of her around me like a shield. But when I pictured her face, the image that sprang into my mind was the shock and horror that'd been etched there when she'd seen me devour that man's soul. It brought a deeper pain into the core of me, down in the corners even my tormenters hadn't been able to touch with their instruments of torture.

You deserve this, a little voice started to murmur in the back of my mind. *You tore mortal souls apart, and now you're being torn apart too. It's perfect justice. Did you really think you deserved better?*

You wanted to devour her. *How could you think you could be with her again after that? How could you think you really love her when you almost—*

I wrenched my thoughts away, but there wasn't anything outside my body that I could shift my attention to. So I pulled in, retreating from them. Renouncing the me that had felt those urges. Deep, deep, deeper, as far as I could go.

If I swallowed myself all the way down, devoured every shred of my own soul, there'd be no one left to feel this revulsion or this pain. I wouldn't exist at all. I wouldn't *be*.

Bit by bit—rip, slash, gulp it down. There was no Snap. I wasn't here.

I was gone, gone, gone where they couldn't touch me... and I could never touch another soul. Especially hers.

DARK CHAMPION

FLIRTING WITH MONSTERS #4

ONE

Sorsha

You wouldn't think anything could be worse than the most ancient supernatural beings in existence wanting to murder you before you ended the world. Tough luck—it could.

For starters, you could wake up in a room so dark you couldn't determine a hint of what it held other than dank, stuffy air and a lumpy mattress that was poking your backside, with no idea where you were or how you'd gotten there. Or how many people might be lurking in that darkness preparing to murder you at this very moment. Then you could sit up and discover one of your wrists was chained with a heavy metal cuff to some fixture that refused to budge, making the possibility of lurking murderers even more likely.

And to be clear, by "you," I mean me.

The frame that held the mattress squeaked with my movement. I tested the cuff with a jerk of my arm. The chain clinked, holding firm—and light washed through the space. A fairly dim light, really, cast by an electric lantern, but the darkness before had been so complete I was left blinking the glare from my eyes.

The room around me appeared to be some kind of underground bunker. Rough rock walls, floor, and ceiling surrounded me. The metal cot had a dappling of rust on the frame and squatted next to a matching metal cabinet that I guessed held some kind of supplies. The whole space couldn't have been more than ten feet both long and wide, and standing in the middle of that space, gripping the lantern, was the most powerful supernatural being I'd had the irritation—and, okay, sometimes enjoyment—of actually meeting.

The wan artificial light turned the angles of Omen's narrow face sharper. His icy blue gaze fixed on me, as piercing as ever. His tawny hair lay flat, slicked back over his head, which meant he had his temper in check for now. I supposed I should be glad his hellhound fangs and claws weren't out.

He didn't look like he was planning on murdering me *quite* yet.

I couldn't take a whole lot of comfort from that fact, though, or even from knowing that up until now this monstrous man had been fighting whole-heartedly on the same side as me. Wherever this room was and however we'd reached it, this dude had dragged me here. The last thing I remembered was him clocking me hard enough to knock me right out.

My temple ached dully where his fist had rammed into it. No doubt I was sporting a pretty spectacular bruise. Thank furtive fiddlesticks I didn't feel any signs of a full-out concussion.

Hey, might as well count my blessings, meager though they were.

Omen hadn't turned me straight over to the Highest, at least. If he had, I'd probably already be dead. As long as I was still alive, I had a slim chance of staying that way.

Why the hell had he brought me to this wretched place?

My mouth, as it so often did, started moving without consulting the rest of me. "What a coincidence, running into you. Come here often?"

Omen's voice came out as little more than a growl. "Sorsha..."

I raised my cuffed wrist, which I could now see was attached to one of the legs of the cot—which was in turn bolted to the stone floor; fat chance of wrenching that up by hand. The metal chain clinked again as I waggled it. "You wanted to dive right in with the kinky stuff, huh? Next time, you could just ask."

We *had* actually hooked up once before, chains not included but with plenty of fire. The hellhound shifter didn't appear to appreciate the reminder. A few tufts of his hair rippled upward. He bared his teeth, which were already looking pointier than they had a moment ago. "Do you *ever* stop joking?"

I leaned back on my hands and gave him a tight smile. "Nope. It's called a coping mechanism. Look it up, dog-breath."

All right, so insulting one's captor, especially when that captor is a highly dangerous shadowkind, was probably in the What NOT To Do column of advice for kidnapping victims. I couldn't claim to be a paragon of wisdom.

But despite my attempt at keeping my spirits up, when Omen took another step toward me, both fear and anger jittered through my nerves. The jolt of adrenaline set off a flare of heat in my chest that tingled all the way up to my skin—and sent fire licking across both the collar of Omen's shirt and my bare forearms.

As Omen slapped at his shirt, I smacked my arms against my sides as quickly as I could to snuff out the flames. They vanished, but they left my skin pink and prickling with a fresher pain.

Omen took one last swipe at the singed fabric around his neck and held the lantern out—to check my arms, I realized. To see how much damage I'd done to myself. He wouldn't have bothered with that if he was sure I'd be kaput within the next few hours anyway, right?

"Look," he said, his tone oddly less growly than before I'd set him on fire, "I'm not happy about this either. But you've just proven exactly why I can't completely ignore the Highest's warnings."

"So you decided to haul me off to some desolate cave?"

"I need time to think and decide what to do without your fan club interfering."

He meant the trio of shadowkind men he'd brought into this realm to help with his mission, who'd ended up more entwined in my life than I'd expected to let anyone get these days, let alone a bunch of monsters. But sweet Snap with his eerie demonic powers, sly Ruse with his incubus passion, and stoic Thorn with the haunted weight of his warrior angel past had made me feel like I was getting the better end of the bargain.

What did they make of all this? We'd barely had time to process Omen's announcement that I was the supposedly fearsome being named Ruby that the Highest had spent decades searching for—and that it'd been their shadowkind lackeys and not vengeful mortal hunters who'd killed my parents and sent my fae guardian on the run with me—before Omen had grabbed me.

My trio had been obsessive about ensuring my safety even when I wasn't doing anything riskier than walking down a street. Left without any idea where their boss had taken me or what might be happening to me there, they'd be frantic.

Unless they decided that if the Highest of the shadowkind were terrified of me, they were better off free of me too.

I wet my lips, my fingers curling into the coarse sheet that covered the mattress. My first urge was to keep snarking at the hellhound shifter, but that hadn't been what had gotten through to him before. The time he'd let down his guard the most—the time he'd let himself indulge in that act of searing intimacy with me after swearing it would never happen—it'd been after I let go of the fight and simply been open and honest with him.

Back then, I'd told him I wasn't scared of him. I'd told him I knew he cared about me. Maybe we knew things now we hadn't back then, but I could summon some of that faith again.

Inhaling slowly, I forced my own temper to settle. "Do you really think I'm some huge threat to all existence?" I asked, holding Omen's gaze. "That I'd destroy all the beings I've been risking my neck trying to save? That I *could* cause mass destruction on the scale the Highest are talking about?"

"I don't know." He considered me. "You warned me before. The fire inside you frightened you. Are *you* sure you couldn't burn the realms down?"

At that question, I couldn't help thinking back to the moments when we'd squabbled and the raging inferno had surged in my chest. Just remembering it called up a waft of that blaze. I didn't like being trapped here—I didn't like being betrayed by someone I'd been starting to care about. Somewhere in the depths of my being, a little prickling voice whispered, *Burn. Burn it all. Burn the fuckers to the ground.*

My lungs constricted. I willed that desire away, but the heady heat lingered, nibbling at the edges of my chest.

Was I totally confident that I could control it? No. Let's be real—just a few minutes ago, I'd scalded myself with that power without meaning to.

Could I say it definitely wasn't as big and bad as the Highest claimed? I didn't want to think it was. But there'd been moments when I'd been able to picture leveling entire cities. Just how fiercely could those flames fly if I gave them free rein, if I let them build and build—?

The nibbling turned into a scorching gnawing. I dragged in another breath, dampening the inner fire as well as I could.

Omen was still studying me. The taut slant of his mouth suggested he'd been able to read a fair bit of my inner struggle. The fact that I hadn't answered yet was probably answer enough.

"I don't *want* to destroy anything," I said. "Well, other than the Company assholes… and I suppose that former co-conspirator of yours who's apparently supporting them?"

His revelations about my past had been interrupted by a much more current shocker: our plan to demolish the Company of Light, an organization dedicated to ridding all realms of the creatures they considered monsters, had been foiled by a powerful shadowkind Omen had once associated with. He'd believed this sphinx named Tempest was dead, killed centuries ago on the orders of the Highest for the havoc she'd wreaked among mortals.

Why any shadowkind would want to help mortals torment and destroy her own kind was beyond me, and Omen hadn't appeared to have any idea either.

Now, he grimaced at me. "No changing the subject. I'll deal with Tempest when the time comes. The problem you pose is more pressing."

"Why? Can't we just assume I'll get my superpowers under control with a little more practice, like you've always said? I've managed to go twenty-eight years without decimating the entire planet—how urgent can it be?"

"You hadn't really activated your powers until a few weeks ago. In that time, I've watched them grow swiftly. I don't think you'd be able to make much of a case with the Highest based on that argument."

My stomach was starting to sink, but there'd never been a situation where a little spin on an '80s song couldn't brighten at least a little. I raised my eyebrows at him and let a lyric slip out. "I'm starting with the man even nearer. I'm asking, rearrange this day-a-ay."

There came the fangs again. "Do you really think buffoonery is the answer to—"

"Fine, fine. I'm trying to stay in glass-half-full territory. I can be a model of seriousness that'd make even Thorn proud." I put on my best somber expression, definitely channeling the stalwart wingéd. "Why do you care what the Highest want anyway? They hardly bother with this world unless some shadowkind is causing a total catastrophe, right? I'm assuming you didn't *tell* them you've been hanging out with the horrifying human-shadowkind hybrid they've been searching for. Couldn't we get back to crushing the Company, and if my powers start heading in a direr direction, then you can make a decision?"

"It's not that simple," Omen said, and paused, as if he was debating whether he could get away with leaving it at that. I cleared my throat as a prompt to continue, and he glared at me. "The rest isn't your concern."

Oh, yeah? I drew on whatever reserves of calm I still possessed and managed to ask the question in a quiet, earnest tone rather than the acidic one that I'd wanted to toss at him. "Considering what happens here is a matter of life or death for me, I think it's more my concern than it could be anyone else's. If there's something else going on, don't I deserve to know?"

Omen's jaw worked. "It isn't about what you deserve."

"What is it about, then?" When he continued to balk, I peered up at him, wishing I had Ruse's skill for cajoling. "Hell, maybe if you explain it to me, I'll see some loophole you haven't noticed. I'm very good with getting out of tight situations, as you may have observed."

He let out a rough chuckle. "I think this is beyond even your thieving talents, Disaster."

"I've proven you wrong before." I sucked in a breath. "Please. I just want to understand. I thought—I thought we'd gotten to a place where we *did* understand each other pretty well. If you're going to lead me to the slaughter, I'd just like to know why."

Something in my voice must have gotten through to him. Omen turned away with a muttered curse. He paced the width of the room, his hands clenched at his sides, and then turned back to me.

"The Highest didn't just tell me what you are and what they'd like to see happen to you," he said. "They outright ordered me to inform them of where 'Ruby' is as soon as I found that out."

"From what I've seen, you don't generally follow orders just because someone gave them to you," I felt the need to point out.

"Yes, well, this is a special case." He fell silent, and for a moment I thought he might clam up again. But then he spoke, low and terse. "I didn't see the error of my infernal ways soon enough. Before I ended my vicious games with the mortals, the Highest caught wind of them and of my past schemes with Tempest. They would have ended me the way they did her if I hadn't managed to convince them it was worth their while to strike a deal instead."

A chill rippled down my spine. "What kind of deal?"

"I carry out ten tasks of their choosing, and then we're even as long as I keep my nose clean. Until then, they've got a magical choke chain around my neck that they can tug on whenever they please. They made finding Ruby my last task."

"Oh." Even though I was sitting still, my balance wavered on the mattress. "So until you deliver on that…"

"I remain in their grasp," he said grimly.

"And what would happen if they found out you know where I am but didn't turn me over right away?"

"I'd imagine they'd decide I've reneged on our deal and that it's fair play to eviscerate me after all."

I swallowed hard. All he had to do was point the Highest my way, and he'd have his freedom back. I had plenty of experience with the hellhound shifter's pride—I couldn't imagine how much it'd chafed at him having that leash around his neck all this time. By even thinking it over, he was risking his entire continued existence.

It was a miracle he hadn't pointed a blinking neon sign my way the second they'd made their demand.

An unfamiliar emotion rolled over me, suffocatingly heavy. Hopelessness—that was the word for it. I wasn't just backed into a corner but down the bottom of a deep, dark pit without a single avenue out.

"Well," I said, and for once in my life I didn't have any words to follow that with.

"Yes." Omen sounded more resigned than anything. "You're welcome to put your sticky situation skills to that."

I met his eyes again, searching them for some kind of answer there. "Why haven't you thrown me to them already?"

The narrowest of smiles curled his lips. "You've made an impression." He set the lantern down, produced a plastic bag that he tossed onto the mattress beside me, and tipped his head toward the floor beneath the cot. "Something to eat, and there's a bucket if you need to take care of other bodily needs. I'll leave you to it while I contemplate my options."

With that, he vanished into the shadows, leaving me wondering if there were any options at all that didn't end with me flayed and gutted.

TWO

Snap

The gash on my arm was already closing up, but it still stung beneath the gauze Thorn had wrapped around it. The way I'd gotten that gash stung far more, though. First Omen had lunged at Sorsha, and then he'd attacked the rest of us when we'd started to intervene. During that skirmish, one of his hellhound claws had sliced through the flesh just below my shoulder almost all the way to the bone.

If we hadn't been so shocked by everything we'd just found out and by his sudden hostility, surely between the three of us, we could have stopped him? But I hadn't been prepared to tackle our leader as an enemy. When he'd hit my beloved, my first reaction had been confusion. All those precious seconds I'd lost while I realized I wasn't mistaken, he really *did* intend to carry her away from the rest of us, perhaps to the Highest who wanted her dead…

Our failure clearly weighed heavily on Thorn too. He strode back and forth in the narrow hall of the Everymobile, his expression the grimmest I'd ever seen it, and he wasn't a being who spent much time smiling even on good days.

When Omen had charged off with Sorsha's limp body, we'd chased after him, but in his hellhound form he'd outpaced us in minutes.

After he'd vanished into the sparse wilderness where we'd parked outside San Francisco, we'd retreated to regroup, but looking at the gouge marks on the glittery cupboards and the crack now running through the table, I only felt more scattered.

Could Omen really mean to turn Sorsha over to beings who'd kill her? The thought of losing her caused the most stabbing pain of all, so sharp I could barely breathe.

It was hard to imagine him taking that step. While, yes, he'd been annoyed with her now and then, they'd seemed to be getting along well enough in the past couple of weeks. She'd done so much for us. How could he think she'd ever turn around and harm us, let alone all the other beings in both realms?

The little dragon our mortal had looked after appeared to be equally bewildered. Pickle darted here and there through the broken shards of plates and wine glasses that littered the floor, letting out harsh little squeaks at no one in particular. I tried holding out my hand and clucking my tongue at him the way I'd seen Sorsha do, but he just snorted louder and snapped at the table leg as if it were responsible for her disappearance.

Thorn opened and closed his massive fists at his sides, still pacing. His low voice boomed through the room. "If he's already harmed her—he'll face a reckoning, I can say that much."

The other wingéd among us, an equally massive shadowkind man named Flint who'd joined our party only a few days ago, glanced up where he was sitting across from me at the table. "If he saw something in her that made him feel she was that much of a threat—"

The warrior rounded on him. "You don't know anything about her! *He* would still be in the Company's clutches, enduring their torture, if she hadn't helped us free him. She is the kindest and most compassionate being I've ever had the honor of standing beside. I've never seen her hurt any who didn't deserve as much ten times over."

Flint set his jaw as if it were made of the same stone as his name, apparently deciding it was better not to speak at all. Omen had wanted to keep the full secret of Sorsha's identity secret from the newer shadowkind in our group, so we hadn't shared the entire story with them, but it'd been impossible for them *not* to notice him tearing off with her. I supposed we'd have to tell them some version of the truth, just not all of it.

Ruse swiped his hands over his face, which had turned pallid in the time since Omen's betrayal, and looked up at us from where he was leaning against the wall near the driver's seat. "All that is true, and Omen could still be doing whatever the hell he wants with her. How can we stop him? It could already be done."

"He might not have completed that betrayal yet. He knows how valuable she is to his cause, and he wouldn't want to jeopardize that. I *know* he's dedicated to ending the Company's plans." Thorn swung around again, a dark crimson gleam flashing in his near-black eyes. "I might not have anticipated this, but I have known him a long time. If he's still in the mortal realm, I may be able to locate him."

My heart leapt, and I sprang to my feet with that sensation. "What are we waiting for, then? Let's find Sorsha."

The incubus straightened up too, but Thorn shook his head at both of us. "I'll move much faster on my own with no need for explanations, and I'm the only one of us who has any chance of matching him if it comes to a fight. I'll return as soon as I'm able."

"Thorn!" Ruse protested, but the warrior didn't respond. He vanished into the shadows and had raced off beyond the range of my awareness before I'd so much as blinked.

"Big bad angel taking off without the rest of us," Antic muttered in a sing-song voice, crunching broken shards under her feet in time with the rhythm. The imp took a couple of jabs at the kitchen counter, which was about the same height as her head. "I'd give that hellhound what-for."

"Yes, and a few seconds after that, you'd be cinders," Ruse said dryly, but I could tell his heart wasn't in the attempt at humor. He grimaced at the floor. "I should have realized as soon as he started talking about—all of it. I should have… I don't know. Fuck."

He cast about as if looking for something to hold onto, and a glimmer of an idea quivered through my head.

"Did he touch anything?" I asked, glancing around.

Ruse paused and stared at me. "What? Who?"

"Omen. When he was in here."

"I don't see what that matters after—"

I didn't normally interrupt my companions. Normally I listened carefully to whatever they were saying, since all of them had much more experience than I did in either realm and especially this mortal one. But the sting of Omen's violent departure and my wrenching worries for Sorsha sent a surge of determination rushing through me.

I had a purpose here. There was a reason Omen had brought me onto this mission—there were things I could *do*.

"Of course it matters," I cut in with a voice louder and more forceful than felt totally comfortable. A twinge ran through my chest at the stricken expression that crossed the incubus's face, but maybe it was time he listened to *me* for once. Sorsha was mine, and I was hers, and if there was a way to save her, I would find it.

I squared my shoulders and went on. "If Omen touched anything with his bare hands—or any other bare skin—he might have left an impression that could tell me where he was thinking of going. Do you remember whether he touched any spot on the walls or the table or wherever while he was talking to us?"

After he'd grabbed Sorsha, he'd had his hands full with her. The wreckage on the floor had mostly been caused by us colliding with objects around the room as he'd shoved us away. He hadn't transformed into his hellhound shape until he'd been loping across the ground outside, my beloved slung across his back—

An even stronger jolt of hope rushed through me. I motioned vaguely to the others, including the night elf who'd remained huddled in the shadows since Omen's violent frenzy. "Take a moment to think about it. I'll have a better chance outside anyway."

Out in the humid air that had collected under the thick clouds overhead, I hesitated for a moment. The ground was dry and covered with patches of yellowed grass and weeds—and a jumble of faint footprints, the soles of human shoes. Had Omen's hellhound paws left a mark anywhere? He'd run off in this direction…

I hurried between the trees. He'd definitely shifted by the time he'd reached this spot.

There—scratches in the dirt where his claws had scraped the ground. I bent down and flicked my tongue through the air over them, tasting the impressions he'd left behind.

Images even more fragmented than usual flashed through my

awareness. The feel of Sorsha's slack weight on his back, the hellish heat coursing over his skin, the effort of his swift strides—and a tangle of resolve and regret. He hadn't been happy about lashing out at us. That didn't reassure me much. He'd done it anyway, so who knew what other awful things he might do next?

I couldn't pick up any sense that he'd known where he was going. He'd simply wanted to be as far as he could get from us, far from the possibility that we might stop him. What if he hadn't decided yet?

I shoved that thought away and prowled onward, stopping here and there to test other patches of disrupted earth that appeared to be caused by animal rather than human-like feet. The impressions I gleaned tasted mostly the same as that first one. No clear sense of direction other than to keep moving as quickly as he could. He hadn't been heading for a rift yet, as far as I could tell. That was one small relief.

When I pushed myself upright after the tenth or so testing, uncertain whether there was any point in continuing as the trail got vaguer, Ruse stepped through the trees to join me. His hopeful look faded at the sight of me. "Nothing?"

My frustration at that fact prickled through me. "Nothing that would tell us where he's gone. But… I don't think he was heading straight to the Highest. He felt the weight of some responsibility toward them, but he was resisting it."

"I suppose if she's still in this realm and alive, Thorn does have the best shot of tracking the two of them down."

A fierceness that surprised even myself erupted out of me. "He should have given us the chance to help. If he'd waited just a few minutes, I might have been able to tell him something that would narrow down his search." I spun on my heel, unable to stop myself from glaring at the trees. "*Omen* should have given us a chance. We know her better than he does—he should have listened to what we had to say, not followed what the Highest told him. They've never met her at all!"

Ruse raised his eyebrows at my outburst, but when he clapped his hand to my shoulder, the gesture was gentle. "I agree with you, devourer. Unfortunately, I think Omen was also aware that the three of us have become awfully invested in our mortal's happiness. If we'd had more of a chance to rally against him, he might not have gotten past—well, Thorn, anyway."

"Then he should have realized we have good reason for that devotion."

The prickling frustration was expanding, rising through my ribs and up to the base of my throat. Sorsha had saved me not once but twice. She'd woken up a whole world inside me I'd had no idea even existed. I *had* to protect her.

I marched onward, searching for more signs of Omen's passing, but I was reaching the area where he'd outpaced us. I wasn't sure exactly which direction he might have veered in from here. We were getting close to the road, where a whiff of a cloying chemical smell lingered from the occasional cars passing this way.

I pushed past another tree—and found myself faced with a portly mortal man who was strolling along the side of that road. He paused, blinking at me, and the prickling sensation dug into me like the rows of splintery teeth that could spring up within my mouth.

Everything I cared about had gone wrong, and *someone* needed to pay. I could rip his soul to shreds and devour it down—

My body was moving before I'd even finished that thought, propelled by the all-encompassing hunger of my nature. The man's eyes widened, his round cheeks paling.

"Snap!" Ruse hissed, but I was already yanking myself backward. I clenched my jaw before it could extend any farther and propelled myself away from the mortal and the tempting thrum of his life's energy.

I was better than that. I was a monster, and I would bring out my fangs if it helped us—but not just to distract from my frustrations. Savaging that man wouldn't bring Sorsha back.

If only I had a better idea what would.

When the RV came into sight, I stopped with a ragged exhalation. Ruse halted beside me.

"I don't know what to do," I said to him. The urge to rend and tear was still clanging through me. Just for an instant, a small part of me was glad Sorsha wasn't here to see how my control had frayed.

Ruse gave me a crooked smile that looked rather painful. "You've already managed more than I've been able to contribute. Fat lot of good my charm can do for us or Sorsha right now." He sighed. "I think I found a few places in the Everymobile that Omen touched—or rather, slashed or smacked. Do you want to come give them a taste?"

If our leader hadn't been sure of his destination while he'd dashed away out here, I didn't imagine he'd been clearer on it before he'd even made it out of the vehicle. But confirming that would do us more good than murdering random passers-by.

I raised my chin. "All right. And then we find something else to try. We keep trying, no matter how ridiculous it seems, until Sorsha's back with us."

I wouldn't let myself consider yet what I'd do if she was lost to us forever.

THREE

Sorsha

If Omen had wanted to keep the location of his hidden bunker a secret from me, he hadn't done a very good job of it. In with the pre-wrapped chicken sandwich and bottle of orange juice in the bag he'd tossed me, I found a rumpled napkin with the logo for the Grand Canyon Visitor Center.

I'd always wanted to take a gander at the Grand Canyon. Of course, I'd have preferred to be looking at it from the rim rather than this incredibly inside view of the rock it was made of. Omen really didn't have the tour-guide instinct.

I had to assume he'd picked this cave as a stash spot because it was nowhere near anyplace mortals generally went in the canyon. I wouldn't be surprised if the door at the other end of the room led out to a nearly sheer several-hundred-foot drop, and the bastard hadn't brought along my grappling hook. No doubt I was about as far from human civilization as you could get in the entire country.

Maybe he'd *wanted* me to see that napkin to dissuade me from attempting to slip my bonds.

After I'd wolfed down the sandwich and chugged the juice—because my chances of survival were hardly going to get better if I starved myself—I examined the cuff around my wrist and the chain that attached me to the cot's frame. I'd melted metal with my fiery powers before. The first time just a pop can, sure, but I'd also wrenched through the bars of cages in one of the Company's facilities.

Even those bars had been significantly thinner than the links on this chain, though. I'd have given it a go anyway, but a twist of uncertainty in my gut held me back.

Fraught emotions always seemed to set my flames veering in unpredictable and sometimes undesirable ways, and I wasn't feeling all that fine and fancy-free at the moment. I'd say there was a not insignificant chance that if I tried to exude enough fire to reduce those rings of steel into a puddle, I'd become a pile of ashes in the process. I didn't have anyone around to toss a bucket of water at me if I turned the mattress or, y'know, *myself* into an inferno.

No, as long as I suspected I wouldn't be able to escape the prison even if I got loose from the chains, I wasn't going to risk it. I might laugh in the face of danger, but only when I was reasonably certain I could dance around it at the same time.

It didn't take long before I started wishing I'd been a little less hasty with my meal. At least eating had been something to do. Being essentially a prison cell, there wasn't a whole lot to occupy myself with other than counting the ripples in the beige rock walls or mulling over exactly how painfully the Highest would have me killed as revenge for evading their grasp for so long.

After a while, I flopped down on the bed and grimaced at the ceiling. At this rate, my actual cause of death would either be boredom or stomach ulcer.

To try to pass the time somewhat constructively, I considered what new arguments I might make to persuade Omen that I wasn't anywhere near a big enough threat for him to worry his houndish head about. I mean, I didn't *want* to blow up both the realms—or even any substantial portion of either of them. I might have fried a few things I hadn't meant to here and there, but I'd always been able to rein those over-zealous flames in before I did serious damage. If I got really concerned about my self-control, I could just not use my powers in the first place, right?

But even as I thought all that, the heat in my chest continued churning so furiously that *I* wasn't totally convinced. Fuck a flipping flounder. Had my parents gone into this hybrid baby-making scheme with any idea just how much hassle they were inflicting on me as a theoretically impossible being?

They'd loved me enough to pull out all the stops to bring me into this world, but I wasn't sure they'd thought the whole plan through all that well. No offense to Mom and Dad, may they rest in peace.

It might have been one very long hour or a dozen short ones when the shadows around the door wavered. Omen formed in pretty much the same spot I'd last seen him, standing next to the lantern. He had another plastic bag that appeared to contain food. Apparently it'd been long enough for me to get hungry again without realizing it, because my stomach gurgled at the sight.

Well, I had to assume he wouldn't be feeding me just to lead me to the slaughter. I held out my free hand, and he threw the bag to me.

He'd ventured farther abroad this time to bring me something more dinner-like: a fast-food hamburger and a carton of fries, as well as a bottle of water. The fries had gotten a little droopy during his journey through the shadows, but I wasn't going to pick a fight about that or the fact that he hadn't brought any ketchup to go with them, as grave an offense as that was.

I popped a fry into my mouth, the salty greasy flavor buoying my spirits a little, and waggled another in his direction. "How did all that brainstorming go? Have you figured out the meaning of life while you're at it? Inside tip: I hear the number forty-two is involved somehow."

The hellhound shifter glowered at me. "You still don't seem to be taking this situation anywhere near as seriously as it warrants."

"Would you rather I was slumped on the bed groaning like I need my appendix out?"

"No. Just—" He cut himself off with a huff, maybe not sure what exactly he would have liked to see.

My life was still in his hands. And until today's events, I had actually been starting to like and even trust this guy. How could I remind him of the woman *he'd* been starting to care about before this whole Ruby problem had exploded in our faces? He needed to see me as a real person and not just a walking disaster.

I lowered the fry and tamped down on my urge to shoot my mouth off, speaking more honestly instead. "I understand I'm in an incredibly serious situation. If I let myself dwell on it too much, I'll end up rocking in the corner like I belong in a mental institution, and I don't think that's going to help either of us. But I definitely don't think it's a laughing matter either." I spread my arms with a clink of the chain. "You've got me at your disposal. What can I tell you to help you make up your mind? Ask away."

Omen gave me a narrow look, as if he suspected me of setting him up for some kind of prank, but he leaned himself against the wall opposite me as if he was settling in for a longer conversation. "Well, since you're offering... Why don't you tell me some more about what it was like growing up with that fae woman who helped your parents? Now that you know the whole story, is there anything that stands out? She must have known the Highest and their minions were after you."

I sucked my lower lip under my teeth, thinking back. "I don't know what other bits of memory Luna might have glamoured over—but maybe you'll notice if there's a gap I don't realize while I'm talking." He'd been able to break one glamour in my memories already.

"Start talking then."

Lord knew when I'd ever get another invitation like that from him. I drew my legs up on the cot. "Honestly, it was pretty predictable considering I was an essentially mortal kid being raised by a shadowkind. Luna would find us an apartment in one city or another —I'm not totally sure how she even paid for them, but maybe her glamours did the job there too—I'd go to school and all the usual human things, and then every year or so she'd get nervous that the people who'd killed my parents might find us and we'd move to a pretty similar apartment in a different city."

"She never said anything to indicate she was watching to see if you'd show any powers, or that she was worried you might hurt someone?" Omen asked.

I shook my head. "No. I would definitely remember that. Maybe she didn't realize that's what the Highest expected to happen. She was pretty carefree about most things other than avoiding getting murdered."

Even though it'd been twelve years since the Company's hunters had killed her, a pang shot through me at the loss. I could picture so clearly how she used to sashay around the apartment to whatever '80s band she was currently particularly obsessed with, her sparkly hair swishing in its scrunchie-d ponytail, her wings showing in glittery glimpses here and there when she completely let loose. The way she'd always find the perfect joke to make in her melodic voice to reassure me if some asshole kid at school had picked on me. The joy she took in dressing me up in frills and sequins, and her playful grousing when I'd developed enough of my own taste to start chucking those clothes in the back of the closet in favor of darker hues and simpler designs.

I couldn't think of any moment when she'd seriously criticized me, let alone made me feel there might be something terribly wrong with me. Maybe she hadn't been built to fill a parental role, and maybe a fae couldn't produce the same sort of maternal love a human could, but she'd cherished me beyond all reason. She was the only person in my life that I could really remember who'd never been anything but fully devoted to me.

"The time when I guess my powers had the most reason to come out—but didn't—was when I was a kid and this shadowkind jerk thought it'd be fun to work his mind control voodoo on me to use me like a puppet." I'd told Ruse about that incident before, but talking about it out loud made my skin itch. I resisted the urge to hug myself. "Luna told him off and brought me home. She didn't ask anything about how I was feeling. I mean, it must have been pretty obvious how shaken up I was with the way I was crying, but she didn't seem concerned that I might lash out. She just grabbed my favorite ice cream for us to eat right out of the carton and put on my favorite movie, even though it bugged her that I liked something modern rather than her 'classics,' and sat there with her arm around me petting my hair."

In spite of the awfulness of my present, a smile crossed my lips at the memory. Auntie Luna might have learned her cues about human behavior from all that '80s media she'd consumed, but she'd been able to put them to practice pretty damn well.

Omen was watching me intently. "She was important to you."

"Of course she was," I said. "She was my whole world. I didn't exactly have much time to make friends when we were constantly moving... After a while, it seemed like there was so little point in getting to know people better that I stopped putting in an effort. If I wasn't doing the essential stuff, I was hanging out with her. She knew how to make even mundane things like buying groceries or dealing with a scraped knee fun. It was a little lonely sometimes, but she did her best by me. I've managed to pass for reasonably normal, as humans go."

A dry chuckle fell from Omen's mouth. "Only to someone who doesn't know shadowkind enough to pick up on the influence." He paused. "I didn't get any sense of glamoured bits from what you'd said, but I'm not sure I'd pick up on them from general thoughts. And I don't think we have time for you to recite your entire history if there aren't any particular incidents that seem connected to your powers."

"She probably figured it wasn't any big deal, and if I started showing some, she'd deal with it then. She wasn't much of a planner either." I rubbed my mouth, the pang of mourning combining with all the tensions I'd already been feeling in an indigestion stew. Was any of this making Omen more kindly disposed toward me? Maybe I'd be better off reminding him of *his* past—and the responsibilities that came with it—instead.

"It sounds like this Tempest gal is the total opposite of that," I went on, picking at my fries. "How long ago was it you thought the Highest had killed her—several centuries, or something like that? All that time, she's been playing some kind of long game, keeping it all under wraps… Did she ever turn against other shadowkind back when you two hung out together?"

The downward twitch of Omen's lips told me he didn't like the change of subject. "Tempest's main goal was sowing chaos. She mainly did it among the mortals, but she wasn't above ensnaring weaker shadowkind to add to her amusement. I wouldn't have expected a scheme on this scale, but…"

"But?"

He was silent for a moment. "I once watched her spend the better part of a week plucking the claws off little beasts like your dragon so that she could then jab them one by one into a mortal who'd offended her until he resembled a pin cushion. A bloody one. If she's found some way to turn the Company's operations around on mortals in an epic fashion, it's not difficult to imagine her going to even more epic lengths at the rest of our expense to get there."

Ah. So we were dealing with a total psychopath. Not that I'd had much doubt about that after hearing her taunt Omen over the phone, but that little story solidified the impression.

"And you don't think stopping that kind of epic crazy is a little more important than the slim chance that I'm somehow going to explode like a hundred nuclear bombs in the next few days?" I couldn't help saying.

"I think I don't know how slim that chance actually is."

I couldn't argue that point very easily. Time to shift the focus back to him. "Why did you go around with a shadowkind like that anyway? Were *you* that bad back then?" He'd told me that he'd played pranks on mortals—convincing them he was the devil himself had been a favorite—but I hadn't imagined him that sadistic, especially to other creatures of the shadows.

Something in Omen's expression shuttered. "I can't say I was at all considerate of the mortals in my vicinity, but I never harmed any of my own kind purposefully."

"You just stood by while someone else did it."

"If you think I never had arguments with Tempest, or that there was any chance she'd change simply because I said—" He shook his head. "It doesn't matter. I looked the other way too often when it was convenient to my purposes, and I've learned to do better than that. I won't make those same mistakes again. Which is exactly why I'm being much more careful in my associations now."

The pointed look he gave me made me bristle despite my best intentions. "I'm nothing like *her*."

"No, I don't think you are. The problem is, if the Highest are right, you might be even worse."

He straightened up, and then he was vanishing into the shadows without another word. I stared at the spot where he'd stood, but he didn't return.

Had all that talk gotten me anywhere with him, or had I only screwed myself over even more?

FOUR

Sorsha

When I got tired enough that I figured I should try to get some rest, I turned off the electric lantern. I jolted awake sometime later to a room that was as pitch black as my first experience of it. But before Omen even spoke, I could tell from some shift in the air and the prickle of his scorching aura over my skin that I wasn't alone. Probably his arrival was what had jarred my nerves.

"You managed to sleep," he said. The lantern flared on to illuminate his well-built form.

I shoved back the sheet and sat up, rubbing the bleariness from my eyes. I hadn't slept for half as long as it felt as if my body had needed. "It *is* a physical necessity for some of us."

Not that I really wanted him thinking about my mortal side. It might be my shadowkind powers that were causing the biggest issue, but I'd bet he'd be much more inclined to believe that I could control those if it weren't for the weaknesses that came with the human part of me. Although I'd still argue that I didn't have half as many weaknesses as he liked to claim.

His lips had curled with a familiar hint of disdain, but his pale eyes looked only solemn. My pulse hitched. Had he made up his mind about my fate? If so, I didn't think I was going to like the outcome.

The words spilled out of their own accord. "We've come a long way from when we first met, haven't we? I know you're more than an ice-cold bastard. You know I can handle anything you throw at me. We pulled off some pretty amazing missions when we put our heads together."

He raised his hand to stop me before I could keep babbling. His expression hadn't turned any less somber. I closed my eyes, groping for any shred of inner calm I could find. Whatever happened, I was *not* going to die flailing in panic. I had a smidge more dignity than that.

One last mangled '80s song to do Luna proud and offer a final plea? "Hate from the start," I sang at a murmur. "Tell me we can take it all apart…"

"Sorsha." His voice sounded strained. "I don't like that I've had to do any of this."

I could believe that. But he was going to do it anyway. Because why wouldn't he? How could I possibly be worth more to him than finally getting his freedom back after eons under the thumb of these pompous ancients? I was sick of them already, and I hadn't even met them yet.

Delay. Delay, and there was a chance, however miniscule, that I'd figure out another option.

"Can we talk a little more? I can go through some of my strongest memories of Luna in case there's anything she did glamour over, and—"

Omen jerked around abruptly, as if he'd heard a noise beyond the door that I hadn't. His posture tensed. He moved like he was about to spring into the shadows around that door—but at the same moment, an even larger and more muscular figure materialized beside him.

Thorn's brawny bulk made the room feel twice as small, but I'd never been more relieved to see anyone in my life. I'd have leapt to him with a kiss designed to get across every particle of that gratitude if it hadn't been for the damned chain fixing me to the cot.

The wingéd warrior took in my pose and the cuff around my wrist, his expression darkening with horror. He swiveled to face Omen. "What is the matter with you? You've chained her up like an animal!"

"The split-second before you noticed that, weren't you simply pleased I've left her alive?" Omen retorted, his tone now dry. "You know how difficult it is to keep this one anyplace she doesn't want to be."

"You shouldn't have dragged her off to begin with. She isn't going to destroy the realms, and we're not handing her over to the Highest."

The warrior stepped toward me, but Omen sprang in front of him, holding up his hands. "Hold on. It's not as simple as that."

"Of course it is," Thorn bellowed, the reverb of his shadowkind voice creeping into his words. I caught a dark flicker around his shoulders as if his wings had threatened to burst into sight. "Sorsha is the most compassionate being I've ever known—she'd never harm anyone who hadn't brought it on themselves. She's shown multitudes more dedication to us and our cause than any of our shadowkind brethren."

The hellhound shifter arched his eyebrows. "You have to admit you might be a *tad* biased when it comes to assessing her worthiness. You're not exactly an impartial party after how closely you've been getting to know her."

"Whatever desire I've felt hasn't clouded my mind. She's proven herself time and time again. Get out of my way, hound."

He loomed on Omen threateningly, a good half a foot taller and nearly twice as broad. The hard crystalline ridges that covered his knuckles glinted in the thin light.

My pulse skipped a beat. I'd never heard the wingéd speak to his boss like that before—hell, I'd never heard him talk to Omen with anything less than total respect and deference. The fact that he'd gotten this riled up on my behalf sent a flutter of affection through me, but also a jab of fear.

I'd had multiple occasions to witness Thorn's preferred strategy when people he cared about were threatened. It tended to involve heads wrenched from necks and guts spilling on floors. I would've thought he cared enough about Omen as a colleague that it would at least mostly balance out his determination to help me, but maybe I'd underestimated his devotion. It wouldn't have been the first time.

Omen's natural shadowkind coloring, a dark gray tint lined with glowing magma-line rivulets, broke out over his skin. His hellhound claws formed at the tips of his still—for now—humanoid fingers. He let out a snarl that told me his fangs had come forth too.

"Back down, old friend," he snapped. "This is my responsibility, my call, and I will *not* let you rush or override my decision."

It kind of sounded like he might not have come to a definite decision yet after all. Maybe he would have taken me up on the suggestion to talk more. Maybe he'd only stopped by to ask how I wanted my morning coffee, and I'd started shooting my mouth off before he had the chance.

A hasty remark or two getting me into trouble? It wouldn't be the first time for that either.

Thorn's loyalty was too ingrained for him to push this stand-off straight to a battle without at least trying to reason with the other shadowkind. "What does it matter what the Highest say? They know nothing of who Sorsha is, and we owe them nothing. Only the four of us are aware of what we discovered about her, and Snap and Ruse would never think of sharing that information. If they did, they'd be dealing with a wingéd's rage." The muscles in his arms flexed to impressive effect.

"You don't know what you're talking about," Omen growled, and it struck me how true that was. Thorn clearly had no idea how much Omen *did* owe the Highest or the dire consequences he'd face if he failed to carry out their orders. No wonder the warrior was so furious. He assumed the hellhound shifter had carted me off on the basis of a little hearsay.

Omen didn't appear to be inclined to fill the warrior in on his situation, though. "I'll tell you again," he added through gritted teeth. "Stand *down*."

I felt the inexplicable need to speak up on my captor's behalf. "Thorn, Omen has to—"

The hellhound shifter wheeled on me, a blaze lighting in his eyes. "Shut up, or I'll sock the mouth right off of you."

"Don't you lay another hand on her," Thorn roared, and shoved Omen away from me. He reached to smash the chain, but Omen spun around and lunged at the warrior.

Hellhound claws seared slashes through Thorn's shoulder. The smoke that shadowkind contained instead of blood billowed up from the wound.

Thorn threw a punch I suspected would have been solid enough to send Omen crashing straight through the door, but the shifter dodged the worst of it, taking only a gash as the warrior's knuckles grazed the side of his arm. He transformed into the massive beast of his hellhound form before my eyes. With a howl, he bounded off one of the walls and crashed into Thorn, his fangs gnashing and his underworldly glow hazing the room with an orange tint.

The warrior stumbled but pummeled Omen in the face at the same time. More smoke flooded the small space from so many more new wounds. It clogged in my throat and stung my eyes.

I scrambled back on the bed just before the fight brought Thorn slamming into the side of the cot. My lungs had constricted. "Stop it!" I hollered at them. "Just take a breath and *talk* about it."

My appeal went unheeded. The way the two powerful shadowkind were going at each other, I wasn't sure if Thorn would even hear me if I revealed Omen's secret—if it would have made a difference at this point anyway.

At this rate, they were going to kill each other. Over me. I valued my life pretty highly, but no part of me wanted to see either of my monstrous lovers end their existence while vying to decide my fate. How much destruction was I going to cause right here without even using my supernatural sparks?

Just thinking that in the midst of the chaos brought a stinging surge of my flames licking up over my chest. As I smacked at them, willing down the fire, Thorn hurled the hellhound against the wall. One of Omen's paws hit the rough stone with a crunch that turned my stomach, but he flung himself back at the warrior with his fangs flashing.

More heat churned up from the bonfire inside me. This wasn't how I wanted this catastrophe to end. *I* was responsible—for myself, for what my powers might do, and for what I allowed to happen here if I stood silent and let these two men tear each other apart.

I'd accomplished a lot of supposedly impossible things in the past month. Maybe it was time to try one more if that meant I didn't have to watch anyone else die in an attempt to protect me.

"Stop!" I shouted, louder than before, and hopped onto my feet. I stood as tall as I could manage given the length of the chain and waved my free arm frantically. "*Stop!* I'll go. I'll go to the Highest."

The two shadowkind careened past me in their fight without giving any sign of acknowledgment, so I did what might have been the most foolhardy act of my life so far—which if you've been following along, you'll know is saying a lot. I hurled myself right into the middle of that smoky clash of fists and claws.

Of course, thanks to my close friend Chain, I only made it a couple of feet from the bed, but that was enough to propel my arm between the two fighters.

Thorn heaved himself backward with a startled grunt and wild eyes. Omen, for all he'd threatened to rearrange my face a few minutes ago, recoiled in the opposite direction with just as much force. They both stared at me, Omen panting as he shifted back into human form, Thorn checking me over for damage as if he wasn't standing there pouring his life essence into the room.

"I'll go to the Highest," I said again, now that I was sure I had their attention. The words caught in my throat, but I forced myself to keep going anyway. "You don't need to fight about it or make any decisions. I'm deciding. They want me, so I'll go."

Thorn's tan face grayed. "M'lady—they mean to *destroy* you."

"I know." I swallowed thickly. "But they haven't met me yet. I've stolen a lot of things in my life—possibly I can manage to steal a little goodwill too."

When I shifted my gaze to Omen, he looked equally stunned. The fire had gone out of his eyes, and the blue that remained looked more pained than icy. "What are you playing at, Disaster?" he said, but without any of his typical rancor. He sounded almost *worried*.

About my sanity, possibly. I was questioning that too. But I'd made my decision, and I wasn't going to go all wishy-washy now.

"You can tell the Highest where I am and fulfill their orders," I said. "I'm just asking that you also tell them how much good I've done trying to help the shadowkind and how much I want the chance to keep doing that. Tell them I've been trying to *stop* the extermination of your kind, and the last thing I want to do is devastate the realms myself. See if there's any way they'd consider making some kind of deal with me rather than going straight to murder. Please."

He blinked, his expression still frozen in its state of shock.

"Sorsha," Thorn rumbled. "You don't have to do this."

"Yes, I do. Because I like the alternatives even less."

Omen drew himself up straighter abruptly. I didn't know how to read the brooding look he gave me. Then he motioned to the warrior with a jerk of his hand.

"You heard her. She doesn't want to be rescued. Let's go, before you insist on doing it anyway. You can weigh in on where I take things from here—outside, in the fresh air, like comrades."

Thorn shot me an imploring glance that wrenched at my heart. I nodded encouragingly. "It'll be okay," I said, with no idea at all how that could turn out to be true. "Go with him and give him some pointers on how to present my better qualities in a good light."

The warrior grimaced, but at another beckoning gesture from Omen, his bulky form vanished into the shadows. As Omen dove after him without a backward glance, it occurred to me with a lurch of my gut that this might be the last time I'd ever see them before I faced the direst possible fate I'd ever imagined I might meet.

FIVE

Omen

I nudged Thorn down the dark passage beyond the door of my canyon safe house, out to the narrow ledge of yellow-brown rock where the morning sun shone. He went without protest but with tension still ringing through his presence.

We could have talked in the shadows, but the blurred awareness of the outer world made my thoughts feel muddled. And they'd been muddled enough already after Sorsha had made her offer and her plea just now.

I waited at the mouth of the passage long enough for the cool shade to knit the wounds from our fight to the point that I wasn't worried about how much smoky essence I was leaking, and then I emerged into the sunlight.

Thorn followed me into physical form but stayed in the passage. There wasn't really room for him to join me on the ledge, considering it only jutted about a foot from the entrance and a few feet across. Getting to and from this place while carrying Sorsha had required a precarious scramble down the uneven rock face above, which held nothing wide enough to be considered an actual path. No human could have made it here alone without a host of rock-climbing gear.

We were about halfway down the canyon wall. Rocky cliffs stretched out all around us, towering over a valley flecked with green vegetation on either side of its shimmering river. The wind whistled through the crags, dry and fresh with no hint of human occupation.

The grandeur of the landscape before me might have been the closest any place in the mortal world came to matching the sublime if oppressive enormity of the Highest and their vast hollow in the shadow realm. Looking out over it in the flood of warm light from above, it was hard to imagine that Sorsha had volunteered to trade her existence here for the complete and infinite darkness of the death the Highest wished on her. Even harder to imagine that only minutes ago, I'd been wavering on the edge of consigning her to that darkness.

And the first point was exactly why I was now feeling so unsettled about the second.

Thorn had wrapped a strip of cloth around the worst of the slashes my claws had dealt. With another uncomfortable pang, I watched him secure it. I hadn't enjoyed fighting him any more than I'd enjoyed the idea of subjecting Sorsha to the Highest's potentially irrational brutality.

"You can't listen to her," he said, fixing the full depth of his dark eyes on me. "She was only trying to stop us from hurting each other. She doesn't *want* to die. And you know the Highest won't be moved by any overtures on her behalf. If they'd been willing to believe she might not be such a terrible threat, the twenty-five years in which she failed to incinerate the world while they searched for her should have made them rethink their position."

"Agreed." He hadn't even heard how the Highest spoke about her. I had no doubts at all about how quickly they'd dismiss any appeals I made.

Had Sorsha wanted to save both of us from each other, or only to protect Thorn in case I savaged him beyond repair? I hadn't been aiming for that, had only wanted to force him to surrender, but in the heat of battle, one's intentions didn't always carry through. She could have taken the gamble, hoping that he'd best me, free her, and convey her to safety…

But whatever chance she'd seen of escape, she'd decided it was worth less than the chance of losing Thorn. Possibly even of losing me to *his* blows, though darkness only knew why she'd care about that after the way I'd treated her over the past two days.

The past two days? That was the least of it. What about the past *month*?

I'd cut her only the tiny portion of slack my unexpected respect for her had demanded, and I'd reproached myself for every bit of that, thinking it was emotional weakness. But perhaps she'd been right that day when my frustration had boiled over into passion—when she'd told me there was more strength in owning one's emotions than burying them.

Over and over, I'd told myself that I shouldn't allow myself to be impressed by her or desire her. That no matter what I saw, her mortal frailty would come through and screw us over when it mattered most. And here I was with her words still ringing in my ears, hearing her take a greater stand and making a greater sacrifice than I'd ever been willing to do with all the amends I'd tried to make to my kind.

Who the hell was *I* to judge a woman willing to lay down her life to spare our pain?

Yes, she'd risked her life plenty of times in her capers to free captive shadowkind and during our missions. Somehow I'd managed to dismiss all that as adventure-seeking rather than generosity. But there was no adventure to be had in lying down at the mercy of the most inhumane—and inhuman—of all shadowkind. That was pure, selfless sacrifice.

I couldn't shake the sense that at least some small part of it was for *my* benefit. I might be adept at pretending away my own emotions, but I couldn't deny the compassion I'd seen cross her eyes when I'd spoken of my ties to the Highest and the consequences that would come from defying them.

Did I really think a woman with that much valor and forgiveness in her would allow herself to cause some global act of destruction? By the looks of things, she'd sooner throw herself on my claws than let herself spiral anywhere near that far out of control.

"Omen," Thorn started again, but I stopped him with a gesture.

"Stop fretting. I'm not turning her over to the Highest."

He paused, his stern face so befuddled in that moment it was almost amusing. "But she— You were adamant— What in the worlds were we fighting over if you had no intention—"

"I did intend," I said tersely. "Then she proved how far she'll go just to spare the two of us from pain. It's a little hard to continue believing she could possibly exterminate us all after that, don't you think?"

Thorn scowled. "I don't fully understand why she made that offer either. I would have subdued you and freed her, given enough time…" He glowered at me as if daring me to argue about his combat prowess.

I patted one of his massive arms. "Don't be a grouch about it. You're getting the outcome you wanted, and it didn't even require any near-fatal wounds—for either of us, which I'm especially glad of."

"She should have seen I wouldn't have come all this way or forced the issue with you if her survival hadn't been more important than a few battle wounds."

The furrows on the wingéd's forehead deepened. No doubt he still couldn't understand why I'd considered turning Sorsha over in the first place. What *could* he attribute it to other than the frequent clashes between us? I might have made demands of her that, I'd admit, looked petty in retrospect, but I'd never been anywhere near *that* vindictive toward her—or anyone, in ages.

But explaining my reasoning would mean revealing the leash I'd allowed the Highest to fix around my neck, the way I'd abased myself to save my life, and the thought of doing that sent a far deeper jab of revulsion through me than the possibility that the wingéd might see me as overly callous. It'd been hard enough admitting it to Sorsha. Thorn would have a far clearer understanding of just what my deal had required of me.

Thorn wasn't the type to dwell on minor conflicts anyway, not when he'd had such a huge transgression of his own weighing on him for so long. After a moment, he shook his head. "You're right. If we're agreed to protect her from the Highest's plans, that's all that matters. Then we'd better go—"

The peal of my phone interrupted him. Maybe remembering what had gone down the last time that ringtone had split the air, Thorn cut himself off into an uneasy silence.

I hadn't been expecting a call… just like I hadn't been last time.

Tempest didn't enjoy being ignored. As I pulled the phone out of my pocket, I braced myself, anticipating the blank screen and all that would follow.

The thought of hearing her needling voice carrying from the speaker again made me want to hurl the phone into the depths of the canyon. But I knew better than anyone that my former co-conspirator wasn't a problem you could expect to just go away. Even when a horde of immensely powerful beings went to extreme lengths to ensure she was battered out of existence, somehow she was still here, playing out another of her gleefully malicious schemes.

I hit the answer button and held the phone a good foot away from me, remembering how loudly she'd projected her remarks through it two days ago. "For someone who hid her existence from me for the better part of six centuries, you seem awfully eager to chat all of a sudden, Tempest."

Her voice slithered out in a languid tone I knew better than to believe. "I simply wanted to confirm you hadn't met some sudden calamity after we last spoke. Have you become a much slower traveler in your old age?"

"I haven't started traveling yet," I said. "Funny thing—when you drop out of the blue into someone's life, they often have prior affairs they need to take care of first."

"And here I thought meddling with the Company of Light was your largest concern at the moment. I have all the answers you need on that subject."

"Yes, well, for all your sphinxly wisdom, you never did manage to know everything. How many guesses did it take you to get my phone number right, hmm?"

She would have managed to hit on the right one with a guess—plucking the correct answer to anything remotely like a riddle out of thin air was as much a talent of hers as coming up with riddles designed to confound was. It wasn't an exact science, though. I'd be willing to stake my tail that she'd gotten at least ten wrong numbers before she'd heard my voice on the other end of the line.

That suspicion was born out by the irritation that crept into her tone while she dodged that question. "You sound displeased with me.

No rejoicing at the chance for us to join forces again? Have you forgotten what a good run of it we had long ago?"

I hadn't at all, and that was the problem. The question sent a slimy sensation down my spine as if she'd trailed decaying seaweed over my back. Sorsha might call me a bastard now, but what a bastard I'd truly been back then—not ice-cold but searingly sadistic, as selfish when it came to indulging my disdain for mortals as that mortal woman had proven herself the opposite moments ago.

And Tempest had gleefully egged on that side of me. She'd stoked my flames and my contempt, and nothing had made her applaud louder than seeing our mortal targets twisted into agony. If she'd been around when the hunters had burst in on the innocent creatures I'd inadvertently led them to, she'd have laughed at their mistake and found some way to amplify it without a second's regret for the deaths of the lesser beasts.

And maybe I'd have done the same if she'd still been standing with me in all her sly, vicious glory.

But I was better than that now, even if she didn't understand. I was better than that... and was there perhaps a better way through this mess than had occurred to me before?

Tempest might hold a different sort of answer. She might even delight in providing it, if I played the game right. I had known her awfully well, and she didn't appear to have changed much.

"It has been a long time," I said, bringing out all the inner cool I'd worked so hard to cultivate. "But of course I haven't forgotten. I know exactly where I'll find you when I have the chance to make my way in your direction. Since you're so enthusiastic for that reunion, I'll see if I can't make it there in a day or so."

"If you're going to dillydally about it, be prepared that you might find yourself stranded on your lonesome for a good while before *I* get around to stopping by," Tempest retorted, but I doubted she'd leave me hanging all that long. If nothing else, she had to be *dying* to brag about this bizarre, immense scheme of hers to someone with the discernment to fully appreciate it.

I smiled thinly. "I'll see you sooner or later, then."

Before she could respond, I hung up. Let her stew over that rather than think she had me wrapped around her finger.

I turned to Thorn. "We're taking a little trip. It'll be useful to have back-up. Assemble whichever of our allies is inclined to stick with us and meet me in Barstow with the RV—that should make a suitable halfway point. I'll see to Sorsha."

Thorn frowned as if he wasn't entirely sure he should trust me with that responsibility. "We're continuing our campaign against the Company as before?"

"Not exactly as before. I need to determine what precisely Tempest is using those mortals for. But you can be sure I intend to see the lot of them crushed—and for *our* mortal to be right there alongside us making that happen. Now get on with it. Or are you still in an insubordinate mood?"

Thorn's jaw tightened at the memory of just how far he'd pushed against my orders less than a half hour ago. His gaze lingered for a moment on the few wounds his fists had dealt that were still seeping trickles of smoke, and then he dipped his head in acknowledgment.

As he stepped into the shadows, I drew in a heavy breath and headed back down the passage to confront my most recent crimes.

When I slipped through the shadows around the door, I found Sorsha sitting in the same spot on the bed, tensed as if she expected the next being to emerge in the room to be arriving to lead her to her death —or perhaps to kill her on the spot. A reasonable enough assumption, considering what I'd put her through.

At the sight of me, her stance went even more rigid, but a familiar determination lit in her eyes. While she'd agreed to willingly surrender herself to the Highest, she hadn't surrendered her spirit. If I'd been coming to haul her off, no doubt she'd have gone with plenty of choice remarks.

The worst shame of it was how much her defiance made me want her—and how much her surrender had crumbled my defenses against admitting that. Even with her hair rumpled and her clothes wrinkled, her face drawn from lack of sleep, she was breathtaking.

And that damned joke about the chain had wormed its way inside my head. For a moment, I couldn't help picturing chaining both her wrists to the bedframe and then working over her body so thoroughly she'd lose both her own breath and all those snarky remarks, until we both reached an even more ecstatic release than the last time.

I wasn't going to kid myself that she'd be quite so forgiving as to go for that proposition, though. And we did have a maniacal, nearly immortal evil genius of a shadowkind to contend with on top of all the problems we'd been up against before.

I stalked over and unlocked the cuff at Sorsha's wrist, doing my best to tune out the heat that coursed over my body when I stood so near her.

She swallowed audibly. "How are we doing this? Are you taking me to a rift?"

"No. I have a better idea. One that, if it works, will ensure the Highest never think about having their minions brutalize you again."

She blinked at me. "What? I thought you figured they might be right to want me dead."

"I changed my mind. Even shadowkind are allowed to do that, you know."

"But—*why*?"

I grasped her forearm, careful to avoid the reddened marks where the cuff had rubbed her wrist, and tugged her onto her feet. "Don't look a gift hound in the mouth, Disaster." And then, because the nickname had brought a tightness of regret into my throat as it'd rolled off my tongue, "You wouldn't have told me to hand you over if protecting shadowkind didn't matter more to you than your own existence. That's enough for me. It just won't be enough for the Highest."

Sorsha stretched, limbering up now that she had her full range of movement. Her gaze stayed wary. "And what do you think will be enough?"

I smiled again, even narrower than before. "We're going to set it up so it appears you've destroyed someone who's foiled them far more than 'Ruby' ever did. Tempest might even agree to help us with the ploy for the extra chaos it'll cause. If you accomplish more on their behalf than even their most loyal subjects ever did before, how can they possibly accuse you of meaning them harm?"

At least, I hoped that was the case. And if it wasn't, well, then I'd have a battle with their minions on my hands. If Sorsha died at the Highest's command, it'd only be over my dead body as well.

SIX

Sorsha

I'd never been to any sort of reunion—family, class, or otherwise—but I doubted there'd ever been one as joyful as when Omen ushered me across the cracked pavement of an otherwise vacant lot to the waiting RV.

I was still ten feet from the door when it burst open. Snap sprang out first and dashed to me with his usual serpentine grace.

He wrapped his arms around me and tucked my head under his chin with a sigh as if my arrival had put every wrong thing in the world right. I hugged him back just as eagerly. Didn't I wish our problems could be solved that easily.

Pickle scampered after the devourer with excited little squeaks, Thorn chasing behind the little dragon with a worried glance over his shoulder to make sure no mortals were close enough to the parking lot to see. My foster creature twined around my ankles, still chirping away.

Ruse sauntered over to join us at a more languid pace, but his smile beamed with far more affection than his typical smirk. Heedless of the hold Snap had on me, the incubus leaned in to claim a kiss so intent it left every part of me tingling, in part because I knew just how enjoyable it could be to be adored by both these men at the same time.

Thorn made a sound of consternation but looked as though it was more that he wished he'd thought of making the same gesture than that he objected to the incubus's forwardness. He seemed to decide Pickle wasn't causing any real trouble as long as the tiny creature stuck close to my legs and left off that chase. When Ruse released me, the warrior squeezed my shoulder, not quite smiling himself but with a thrum of pleased energy emanating from his brawny frame.

"It's good to have you back where you belong," he said, which from the wingéd was practically a standing ovation.

"Then I expect an even more enthusiastic welcome than that," I informed him. I bobbed up on my toes with the devourer's arms still around me, and a hint of a real smile crossed Thorn's lips. He brought them to mine, giving me a taste of the passion that resided beneath his stoic front.

The other wingéd man who'd joined us more recently, Flint, hung back but appeared to at least be not upset to see me. Antic bounded around our cluster with actual applause and bursts of gleeful giggling.

"She's back, she's back; the Highest didn't eat her!" she crowed.

Yes, I was rejoicing that fact too, even if I wasn't totally clear on what had won Omen over. Just for that moment, I didn't feel any need to dwell on that. I was back where I belonged, a monstrous human among monstrous shadowkind, and I couldn't imagine wanting any company more. Not even the bitter tang of asphalt baking in the warm autumn air could cut through my relief.

Omen gave Snap a sharp look. "How much do our new recruits know now?"

The imp's chant appeared to have stirred something in my devourer. He lifted his head just enough to fix his moss-green eyes on Omen. I felt his body bristle against me with a trickle of aggressive energy as if he might be about to rise into full devourer form, both wondrous and horrifying.

"Enough to realize how awfully you treated Sorsha. How could you have even *thought* about giving her to them?" His clear, sweet voice came in a more forceful tone than I'd ever heard it take before. "You didn't even talk to her—or us. You *hurt* her." He touched his gentle fingertips to the bruise Omen's blow had left on my temple, careful not to provoke any further pain. His other arm tightened around me as if he thought the hellhound shifter might change his mind and attempt to charge off with me again.

Huh. Apparently it wasn't just the warrior wingéd who was prepared to do battle to keep me safe. I'd never thought of Snap as much of a fighter, but *I* wouldn't have wanted to go up against him at his fiercest.

I glanced over in time to see Omen practically gaping at the devourer, obviously startled by the chiding. His jaw worked, and his face returned to the same tense, unshakeable mask it'd been since he'd hauled me out of the cave. He took in the rest of our companions assembled around me, all of them now watching him in silence. Possibly wondering whether he was going to attempt to take off Snap's head for insubordination.

I shifted my weight, preparing to do some defending of my own if the hellhound laid into the devourer, but I didn't need to. Omen ducked his head, just slightly, and said, "I acted too hastily. It won't happen again."

He was admitting he'd made a mistake? My eyebrows shot up. "It's the end of the world as we know it," I couldn't help saying.

Omen's eyes narrowed as they returned to me, and I tensed all over again. I had the feeling my release wasn't so much a free pass as a conditional reprieve. And Omen hadn't bothered to tell me what the conditions of my remaining free were. Probably he'd be noting every slip *I* made for any excuse to proclaim me a real disaster after all.

"It had better not happen again," Snap said to the hellhound shifter. "If you try, it might be the end of *you*."

I wasn't sure how easily he could make good on the threat, but given that he had Thorn for back-up, it wasn't impossible.

Omen appeared to take it seriously enough. His voice turned curt, a few tufts of his hair rising with his temper. "If I say something, I mean it. She's back, isn't she?"

Snap made a discontented sound as if to say he wasn't excusing the matter that easily, but he let it drop for now.

Omen scanned the lot again. "Did we lose the night elf?"

Ruse waved his hand dismissively. "Gloam felt 'uncomfortable' with the 'hostile energies' and took off."

My heart sank a little. We were just getting started against an even more powerful enemy than we were anticipating, and we were already shedding allies like a cat shed hair.

The incubus folded his arms over his chest. There was something wary in his expression as he considered his boss. "So, where are we taking things from here?" he asked, a little too purposefully casual to be casual at all. "Off to tackle your good friend who's mixed herself up with the Company?"

"Tempest is not my 'friend'," Omen muttered, and drew himself up a little straighter. He wasn't the tallest of our bunch by a longshot, but the power and authority he exuded simply standing there gave him a stature that couldn't be ignored. "But I do know her well, and I think we may be able to use her to our own ends—both to dismantle the Company and to convince the Highest they can lay off on Sorsha. But first we need to get over there."

Thorn frowned. "Over where?"

"From what she's said, I assume she's set up shop in Versailles. She always used to talk about this dream of convincing some royal figure to build a palace so lavish it outdid all others. She finds mortal extravagance both incredibly amusing and appealing. I thought the Sun King's tastes in that area aligned awfully close to hers—if I'd known she was still alive, I'd have recognized her influence in it immediately."

Omen squinted past the warrior toward the Everymobile. "Do you think you and your wingéd brethren could handle heaving Darlene through the nearest rift—and bringing her out one of the Paris-area openings?"

"I might even be able to manage it on my own," Thorn said without hesitation. "I'm not sure how well the mortal vehicle will adapt to the journey, though."

I'd never heard of any shadowkind taking a mortal-side object that large through the shadow realm before. I'd never been taken into the shadow realm before myself. A chill rippled over my skin despite Snap's embrace. "Are we sure that *I'll* adapt to the journey?"

Omen gave me another of those unreadable looks he kept a

collection of. "I'd imagine you're shadowkind enough to survive the trip, but I wasn't planning on making an experiment of it just yet. There may be something about your hybrid energies that would alert the Highest if you ventured into their realm. I was thinking you'd fly over the traditional way, with the incubus to smooth over matters of tickets and passports, and we'll meet up on that side. That way we'll have our living space and transport wherever we have to go rather than starting over from scratch."

That made sense. Before the unicorn shifter and centaur who owned the Everymobile had lent it to us, we'd been going through vehicles like a squirrel went through nuts. Although generally those nuts didn't get blown up. It was awfully handy having a place to crash —if you needed to sleep, like I did—and to hold meetings in and so on that could be on the road at the same time.

And I wasn't in any hurry to make my first foray, however brief, into the world of shadows.

"I approve of that plan," I said, and nudged Ruse. "Can you hook us up with first-class seats?"

He grinned. "Hooking up *is* my specialty."

Even though that sounded delightful all around, Thorn's frown had deepened. "Perhaps I should also accompany Sorsha, to ensure..." He trailed off with unusual reluctance.

"I'll be fine," I said, and hugged Snap to me once more before easing away from him, since I knew the devourer was even more likely to worry about letting me out of his sight. "They'll need you to toss the Everymobile through the rift. It's not as if the Company of Light will be searching every airplane to Paris for me. Omen's friend isn't going to expect his people to be traveling the human way."

"Again," Omen started. "She isn't—"

I waved him off. "I know, I know, she's not your friend. Po-tay-to, po-tah-to." But Thorn didn't appear to be at all reassured. I cocked my head. "Is something else bothering you? You know I look after myself pretty well."

Who would have thought his frown could get even deeper? For a second, he looked adorably awkward—at least, as adorable as a musclebound giant of a man *could* look. "It's no matter, m'lady," he said, starting to turn away.

Oh, no, he wasn't getting away with that non-answer. Thankfully, I'd been around Thorn enough to know exactly how to break through his stoicism. I marched over to him and tucked my hand around his elbow. "A word with you in private, my good sir?"

Even though I was teasing him a little, he couldn't resist the formal politeness of the request. "As the lady wishes," he said, and for once strode off with me to the edge of the parking lot without glancing at Omen to confirm the boss was all right with the delay. Interesting. Maybe their skirmish back in my prison room had left more fault lines in our alliance than I'd realized. I didn't think that was necessarily a good thing.

When we were far enough from the others that they wouldn't overhear us, I turned to Thorn. "All right. What's the matter? And don't tell me nothing—I can tell something's eating at you."

He grimaced and looked at the ground. "It doesn't need to concern you."

"Sure it doesn't, but I'm concerned anyway. And I'm not letting it go until you spill the beans, so you might as well speed things along by getting right to that part."

He gave me a glower that was as fond as it was exasperated. Then any trace of humor in his face faded. "In the canyon. You forced an end to our fight—you gave yourself up."

"Well, seeing as it was either that or watching you two tear each other to pieces…"

His jaw clenched. "I would have managed to get you free. I struck out at the one I swore to serve to ensure it. But you… you were willing to stay caged? To let the Highest do with you what they will?"

Ah. I could see how that idea might not sit well with him.

I rested my hand on his arm. "I didn't *like* the idea of facing the Highest. I just liked the idea of you or Omen—or both of you—dying instead because neither of you would back down even less. They're not going to stop looking for me, and I've made myself a hell of a lot more visible in the last few weeks, so chances are I'm going to have to face them eventually anyway. But if no one else's lives are on the line, I'll make sure that 'eventually' is as far away as possible."

"I *would* fight to the death if it meant saving you from some awful fate," Thorn began, and I gripped his forearm harder.

"Think about how you feel when you picture the Highest sending their minions to kill me. I felt at least that awful watching you and Omen bashing each other around. If you're allowed to save me, I'm allowed to save you too, remember?"

He opened his mouth and then closed it again. "I see," he said finally. "When you put it that way... It was not giving up. It was simply a different maneuver in your own battle."

"That's one way of putting it." I shot him a smile. "You should know I'm not in the habit of giving up."

"That was precisely why the possibility was so disconcerting."

"Well, you don't have to worry about it. Now I'm totally focused on kicking some sphinx butt the old-fashioned way. Come on. You've got an RV to schlep all the way through another dimension."

When we returned to the others, Snap tugged me to him for a lingering kiss. "If you *should* need anyone else to come with you on the plane..."

I could just imagine how many stares his heavenly beauty would draw. "I think we'll be lower profile if it's just the two of us. But I'll aim to be back with you as soon as humanly possible. And I promise when we don't have murdering psychos to deal with anymore, we'll take all kinds of plane rides until you're bored with them."

He beamed at me and stole one more kiss. Then he shot Ruse a stern look, as if to say the incubus had better take good care of me, before following the others onto the RV.

Only Ruse and Omen remained. The hellhound shifter considered me so intently the hairs rose on my arms under his scrutiny.

"I promise not to crash the plane," I said tartly.

The corner of his mouth twitched upward. "Do hold to that promise, Disaster. And be careful in general. We don't know what minions the Highest might still have on the prowl. If you can manage not to cause any kind of spectacle, that would probably be for the best."

Was he worried I might get myself caught before he could wriggle his way out of his deal? Well, I wouldn't like the outcome of that either. "I'll do my best to remain unchained."

His lips twitched in the other direction at that remark. For a second, I thought he was going to add something, but then he shook his head with a jerk and stalked onto the Everymobile without another word in farewell.

Ruse went all out on the plane ride. As far as I could tell, he'd decided it was his job to pamper me into forgetting the dingy digs I'd been stuck in for the two days prior.

Along with charming a sales rep at the L.A. airport into giving us a couple of snazzy first-class seats, he somehow managed to get us served an extra posh—as airplane food went—three-course meal complete with fine wine.

"Would you prefer caviar or filet mignon?" he asked me while he held the attendant in his thrall.

I blinked at him. "Is that a joke?"

"There are very few things I won't joke about, but one of those is good food."

Well, if he was offering… "I'll take a slab of beef over fish eggs any day, thank you."

After we'd eaten, he insisted that I pick the movie we watched together on the little screens, and didn't make a peep of complaint when I went with a slapstick comedy with about as much nuance as a steamroller. He massaged my shoulders and my feet until I got dozy. Then he tucked me in with a cashmere blanket on my reclined seat. I'd swear I heard him crooning some operatic French lullaby as I drifted off to sleep.

I woke up with the crackle of an announcement that the plane was about to begin its descent and opened my eyes to find the incubus gazing down at me with an almost fraught expression. It was only there for an instant, and then he was jerking his gaze away before returning his attention to me with a more typical sly smile and possibly the faintest of blushes coloring his pale cheeks. "Rise and shine, Miss Blaze."

Ruse had told me he loved me for the first time less than an hour before our last mission. It'd obviously been difficult for him to reveal that emotion, even though I'd returned the sentiment. We hadn't had time to settle into any kind of new normal afterward—maybe he was feeling a bit awkward about that still.

I squirmed upright with the swing of the seat back and reached over to grab his hand. "You've been awfully sweet the whole flight. Trying to give Snap a run for his money now that he's honing in on *your* usual territory?"

Something flickered through the incubus's expression and vanished just as quickly. He shrugged, a familiar twinkle lighting in his warm hazel eyes. "It's the least I can do."

"Well, your efforts have not gone unnoticed… nor will they go unrewarded." I winked at him and walked my fingers along his jaw to draw him into a kiss, wishing I could slip them right under his cap to grasp his horns the way he liked without exposing them for all the regular mortals around us to see.

With the seatbelt lights already on, I couldn't make that reward a membership to the mile-high club, but maybe that wasn't what Ruse would have wanted most anyway. At least one woman he'd cared about in the past had shown *she* only cared about how well he could get her off in bed. Instead, I rested my head against his shoulder, nestling closer when he put his arm around me.

It was hard to feel all that sour about the bounty on my head when this whole mess had also brought the most fascinating, thrilling, and delectable men I could have imagined into my life.

Once we'd departed the plane, a few texts with Omen directed us to a quiet spot off the road between Paris and Versailles where he and the others had parked the Everymobile to wait for us. As we got out of the cab across the road from the RV, I couldn't stop a startled laugh from spilling from my lips.

"What in sweet Satan's name happened here?"

Maybe to someone who'd never seen it before, the Everymobile in its current state wouldn't have looked that odd. But the trip through the shadow realm had definitely made an impact.

In its current tour bus form, bright purple polka dots spotted the lower edge of the vehicle's otherwise dark walls with their sweeping yellow—made-up—logo. A crooked antenna I'd never seen before protruded at an angle over the windshield. And toward the rear end, a propeller I couldn't figure out the function of was spinning wildly as if in a brisk wind, although the cool evening air around us barely moved.

The door opened, and Omen beckoned. "Stop gawking and get your asses on here."

I reeled my jaw back in, but I stayed where I was. "What did you do to Darlene?" I said, intending to rankle him by using the name he'd given the vehicle despite it not really being his.

He let out a short huff of breath. "The transition through the shadow realm may have had a few side effects. She still runs just fine. Are you coming or did you fly all this way just to park yourselves here?"

I rolled my eyes at him with a teasing smile. "Excuse me for asking."

We tramped on board. In the dining area, Snap promptly pulled me onto his lap where he was sitting on the sofa-bench and planted a possessive kiss on my mouth. The engine started up with a sputter and... a sound like distant bells ringing?

"Keep any commentary to yourself," Omen grumbled from behind the wheel.

"All I have to say is, you definitely can't blame *this* vehicular mishap on me." I made a flourish with my hand toward the road ahead. "Next stop, Versailles!"

SEVEN

Sorsha

I'D PROWLED AROUND QUITE A FEW OPULENT MANSIONS IN MY TIME, mostly to separate shadowkind collectors from their cages of lesser beasties, but none of those sights had prepared me for the Palace of Versailles. "Palace" was definitely the word for it, to the power of one million.

Staring up at the three stories of sprawling, ornately carved and gilded walls, my jaw went slack for a few seconds before I managed to recall it and myself.

"I see what you mean about extravagance," I said to Omen as we crossed the vast, shadowy courtyard, keeping my voice low. There wouldn't have been visitors here this late in the evening anyway, and from the signs we'd passed on our way in, the sphinx had contrived some way to shut down the estate to visitors, but I couldn't quite shake my well-trained thieving instincts. We were guessing that she'd ensured an absence of security guards as well, but we hadn't confirmed that yet.

Omen matched my subdued tone. "If Tempest is anything, she's a hedonist. The trouble for most other beings, mortal or otherwise, is the things she tends to take pleasure from do the opposite for everyone else involved."

"A hedonistic sadist with no concern for consent. I can't wait to meet her."

The hellhound shifter gave me a sharp look, as if I hadn't laid on the sarcasm doubly thick. Or maybe because of the sarcasm. "I know restraint isn't your strong suit, but if you could manage to let me handle most of the negotiations, it'll work out better for all of us. She'll ask you some direct questions, so obviously answer those, but... don't give away more than you need to."

"Funnily enough, I do have some experience dealing with dangerous shadowkind." I poked him in the arm.

He bared his teeth at me, but, shocker of all shockers, it looked more like a grin than a grimace. The closest thing to a good-humored smile I'd gotten from him since he'd dragged me off and chained me up. Maybe I'd earned myself a few more points in the Keep Sorsha Alive column without realizing it.

"Considering that your main approach to 'dealing' with me is to provoke my temper in every possible way, I'm going to suggest you take a different tactic here," he said.

"Where would be the fun in that?"

"We're not here for *fun*, Disaster."

"I know, I know. I figure after you've literally had me in chains, I should be allowed to tug on yours a little to even the score."

As soon as the words fell from my lips—because, I admit it, I really did have a bit of a problem of shooting my mouth off without quite as much forethought as might be wise—a flicker of panic shot through my chest. Had I gone too far, reminding him of the actual if magical chains the Highest had him in? I hadn't meant to imply anything about the bonds that obviously rankled him more than anything in his existence, but that was the problem with not thinking before you spoke.

Omen merely rolled his eyes skyward with a wordless sound of exasperation, so I guessed I wasn't ending up back in my own chains over that affront.

Just as we reached the door, it swung open. Thorn peered at us from the other side. He and Flint had joined us for this meeting so we'd have extra muscle along in case talking didn't pan out so well, and Snap was lurking too, having refused to hang back. With my thieving past, I couldn't help envying the shadowkind ability to slip right around doors and unlock them from the inside as need be.

The hall we stepped into took my breath away all over again. In the thin light that streaked through the immense arched windows from the security lamps outside, gold glittered all across the molded walls and ceiling. Between the gleaming mouldings, richly colored paintings covered nearly every surface. Dozens of crystal chandeliers as tall as I was dangled at intervals.

If I'd been here on burglar business, right about now I'd have been thinking I should have brought a bigger bag. Possibly an entire trailer.

As Omen and I headed down the hall, Thorn vanished back into the shadows. Our feet whispered across the polished floor.

The looming grandeur made vigilance feel even more necessary. My voice dropped another octave. "Where in this place do you think we'll find Tempest? Or is she going to find us?"

"Oh, no, she'll enjoy having us come to her." Omen tipped his head to the right as we rounded a corner. "Chances are she'll have claimed the queen's bedroom as her own."

Where else? I might have appreciated the shadowkind woman's aplomb if she hadn't allied herself with an army of murderous mortals.

Omen couldn't have been here with her before, but he'd probably been in other bedrooms with her if he could make that statement so confidently. A question prickled up through me that I tried to suppress... but why? It might be useful to know to help me follow the conversation ahead.

"So, you've made it very clear that you're no longer friends with Tempest. Were you ever *more* than friendly?"

Omen's mouth flattened. "If you're asking if we ever fucked, then yes, a handful of times when we couldn't find more exciting activities to pass the time with. It wasn't any kind of love affair. It meant nothing more than momentary physical satisfaction to either of us."

Was that all our passionate tumble into bed had meant to him too? I didn't know if I wanted it to have meant more. The encounter had certainly been off the scales in the physical satisfaction department. And now I was remembering the sear of his kiss and the literal flames that had flowed between us, which wasn't exactly helping my focus, so maybe I shouldn't have brought up the subject after all.

"Well, it's good that you should know your way around her in a bedroom," I said in a breezy tone, and Omen shot me a look so scorching it made me want to feel his kiss again for real.

Whoa there, hormones. I had three other monstrous lovers who weren't watching my every move for signs that I was going to incinerate all life in both realms. No need to be greedy. Or stupid.

We walked through a few more of the ornate rooms that smelled faintly of jasmine. Omen slowed coming up on the next doorway.

A voice rang out from the room beyond in the same sharp, droll tone I'd heard rising up from Omen's phone at the start of this recent mess, the effect amplified when it only had to travel through air. "Here you are at last, Omen. Come on then. Don't tell me you've gone shy."

"Only perhaps a little more cautious," he said, sauntering in.

I followed him into a room so full of splendor it took everything I had in me not to start gaping again.

Two lamps lit the space, catching on the masses of gold that coated the walls and ceiling. There was enough of it around us to buy one of those collectors' mansions back home, gilded across delicate filigree-etched borders and painted in with the pinks, blues, and greens of intricate floral patterns. Between two more crystal chandeliers, a massive gold canopy rippling with sculpted leaves protruded from the wall, flowery curtains falling from its edges to frame an immense bed. The jasmine smell had thickened, adding to the opulent atmosphere.

If this was how royalty lived, sign me up to start a dynasty of my own.

Somehow, the figure lounging on the silk covers of the bed managed to top her surroundings in extravagance. Tempest would have been a difficult figure to miss even without any special trappings: she had to be at least six feet tall and built like an Amazon, both muscular and buxom. Her bronze-brown hair gleamed as brilliantly as the gold around her, twisted into waving locks that lifted and swayed around her face as if they had minds of their own. Like some kind of Medusa—Omen had said she liked to take on different roles.

True to the lion-ish aspects of her nature, her shining eyes held cat-slit pupils, and there was something feline about her prominent cheekbones and flared nose as well. Definitely not a face you'd easily forget. The fabric draped across her voluptuous figure had the cut of a bathrobe, but hardly the kind you'd pick up at Target—this was a bathrobe fit for a queen, scarlet and violet satin strung through with gold embroidery.

Over that magnificent bathrobe, she'd draped so many golden bangles heavy with emeralds and sapphires that I wasn't sure she *could* sit up straight under it all even if she'd wanted to. Good luck walking under all that weight of riches. Although she looked perfectly happy sprawled as she was.

What made the biggest impression, though, and not one I could poke fun at even in passing, was the sense of power that wafted off of her like the wind off a stormy ocean, chilly and razor-edged. Omen might have cultivated his ice-cold bastardom to a T, but the energy that thrummed off him still held his natural heat. Tempest was a bastard down to her bones.

Annoyingly, in the midst of the awe and uneasiness I was already trying my best to tamp down, a jab of jealousy pricked at me too. The hellhound shifter had been so close to this woman, even if he disdained to call her so much as a friend now, even if he said their "fucking" hadn't mattered at all. She knew him in ways I likely never would, considering he now saw me as only slightly better than a ticking time bomb.

Yeah, I really shouldn't have ever asked him about their past liaisons.

I shoved the jealousy aside along with the rest and held myself steady. We came to a stop a few feet from the gilded barrier that ran through the room in an attempt to keep tourists away from the most valuable furniture.

Tempest's gaze slid over Omen to rest on me. "Well," she said in the same tone, which managed to sound like she was making both a threat and a joke, "what have we here?"

"Just a lowly mortal," I replied, attempting to match that tone. That seemed safe enough to say before we knew exactly how and how much we might be able to work her into our plans.

"Hmm." Her cat-like eyes flicked toward the shadows along the edges of the room. "Let's see your whole troop, Omen. All the indomitable beings who worked so hard to disrupt my plans."

Of course she'd be able to sense the shadowkind who'd stayed in the darkness. Omen had expected that. He made a casual gesture, and our three companions materialized around us.

Omen had said it'd been a force of wingéd who'd attempted to destroy Tempest on the Highest's orders. If the sphinx could identify Thorn and Flint as beings of the same kind, considering she had pretty direct experience with their kin, she showed no sign that their presence bothered her at all. She cocked her head, the locks of her hair continuing their sinuous dance around her face. "This isn't all of them. You had an incubus."

"He's attending to other business tonight," Omen said, which was sort of true. Ruse had offered to stay back and ensure that Antic didn't follow us to insist on contributing her impish version of "help." "Not much my talents can offer against a sphinx," he'd said in a flippant way that had felt a little forced to me.

The hellhound shifter made a point of looking around the room, his stance casual but poised. "You've hardly brought all your allies to this parley. Of course, it appears you've gotten yourself a whole host of them, more than perhaps could fit in this palace. All of them mortals, oddly enough. What grand scheme have you concocted this time, Tempest?"

"Oh, you know me. To some extent I simply play it by ear." The sphinx gave a smile that didn't quite manage to be demure and trailed her fingers across the bed covers. "It's provided immense amusement having a horde of mortals at my beck and call, hating shadowkind with all their being while in service of one."

"They're *hurting* shadowkind," Snap spoke up with some of the new boldness he'd shown since I'd returned. He should know more about that hurt than anyone here other than Omen—they'd both spent time in the Company of Light's cages, tormented by their experiments.

Tempest lifted one shoulder in the most languid of shrugs. "Fewer incompetent beings to irritate me. The Company of Light would hardly be effective if I never let them indulge their basest desires, would they?"

"Effective at *what*?" Omen demanded, commanding but not angry.

Not one tuft of his tawny hair had risen yet, as provocative as his former conspirator was obviously trying to be. I couldn't suppress a twinge of affection that didn't have much place in this moment.

He'd used to run wild with this woman, yes, and it wasn't hard to see how tempting she could have made the prospect. He'd been savage and cruel and selfish. And somehow while she'd stayed exactly the same or perhaps gotten even worse, he'd shaped himself into something so much better than that. A leader who could be compassionate as well as harsh, who saw what people were capable of and gave them a chance even when he was skeptical.

Call him a monster all you wanted, but he was a hell of a lot more than that too. And he'd reached that point through lifetimes of effort and determination.

No wonder he'd gotten pissed off at my many attempts to poke holes in his carefully constructed cool.

I suspected Tempest would have liked to do the same, but she clearly didn't know him all that well as he was now. She chuckled slyly and gazed at him through her eyelashes. "I expect by now you've managed to uncover their ultimate plan?"

"They're attempting to create some sort of sickness that will spread through the shadowkind and kill us all," Omen replied. "I expect *you* aren't actually out to commit suicide by mass genocide?"

"Oh, I'll ensure I remain above the fray. The hardiest amongst us will be just fine. The mortals and the weaklings, not so much."

If I caught the slight stiffening of Omen's posture, she must have too. "Then what they're working to create," he said, "you really do expect it to infect and kill shadowkind."

"Oh, don't look at me like that, Omen. I'm sure *you* have nothing to worry about. Eliminate most of the feckless beings who venture out here and might cramp my style, wipe out a good chunk of humanity as well and leave the survivors wrenched with guilt over their miscalculation…" She batted her eyelashes. "It should be a smashing time all around."

My stomach had plummeted to my feet. Omen had assumed the Company's stated mission was also a front for some other scheme of Tempest's. Not so much, apparently. This went so far beyond trampling a few lesser creatures on the way to screwing over some mortals that we might as well be in a different solar system.

Chances that she'd be willing to set aside those plans to participate in a ploy where I pretended to defeat her, just to foil the Highest for a brief moment? I'd place them at about a trillion to one.

Thorn shifted on his feet, and I could feel the horror he must be reining in while he let Omen take the lead. Snap couldn't restrain a shiver. He was the youngest of my shadowkind crew—was *his* accumulated power enough to protect him from this menace and her constructed disease?

Did it even matter whether they survived when either way, scores of shadowkind—and humans—were going to die because of the path Tempest was leading the Company down?

"They're almost finished," she boasted as if she had an audience avid with enthusiasm rather than alarm. "Just another leap of inspiration or two, and we'll have it ready. You've been a thorn in my side for the past little while unintentionally… Are you ready to get in on the most epic strike of both our careers?"

My stomach twisted. I glanced at Omen, wondering if he'd play along to humor her for the time being. But his jaw had clenched even tighter, an orange sheen of hellfire glowing over the pale blue of his eyes.

"When did you move from games to outright warfare?" he asked. "This plot is so far below the Tempest I associated with that I can't believe you don't see that."

She sniffed. "I haven't sunk at all. Perhaps the problem is that you all have forgotten what you're meant to be. They call us monsters for a reason, don't they?" She narrowed her eyes at each of my shadowkind companions. "You must have leashed your hound so long you've forgotten what it is to run free, Omen. Where's the vicious fury at the pathetic arrogance of mortals that used to fuel you? And you wingéd, aren't you done sulking over your losses yet? What do you use that spectacular physique for now—squashing cockroaches? Or do you offer leniency even to them?"

"I have bashed open plenty of skulls and rib cages in *defense* of my fellow shadowkind," Thorn rumbled, unable to hold himself back any longer.

"As if they were worth the effort." Tempest gave a tinkling laugh like shattering glass that made me want to punch *her* skull in and turned her attention to Snap. "And a devourer—one of the rarest of all our kind, and yet what are you putting your talents toward other than looking pretty? You ought to be out there rending soul by mortal soul apart to become as great as you're meant to be. You could contain a multitude if these insipid sympathies didn't hold you back."

"Those souls belong to the mortals who contain them," Snap replied, but he'd shivered again at her words. The color had drained from his face, leaving him wan beneath his golden curls.

That was the moment my tongue got away from me. "You're one to talk, acting like you're some pinnacle of shadowkind when you've spent how many decades now encouraging a bunch of mortals to annihilate your own people. As far as I can tell, *you're* the one who's forgotten what you are."

The sphinx's eyebrows arched. "Brave—and ridiculous—words from the mortal who's currently standing alongside *these* shadowkind. Have you convinced yourself you'll ever be more than a groupie to their evidently deviant tastes?"

The jab rankled me more than it should have. "You have no idea—" I started, and managed to yank my temper back under control before I said something I'd regret. "You know nothing at all. And here I thought a sphinx could at least pretend a little wisdom."

Unfortunately, while I could harness my words, I wasn't quite so good with my powers. I'd barely finished speaking when the revulsion and rage churning inside me lurched with a flare of my inner fire.

The flames shot up from my elbows toward my shoulders. Thorn caught them for me with a clap of his broad hands against my arms before they could set my hair alight.

My mouth went scorchingly dry. Tempest was staring at me now with far more interest than she'd shown anything else in this conversation so far. The sweep of her gaze over me left an uncomfortable prickling in its wake.

She sat up straighter as if to look at me even more closely. I resisted the urge to back away, holding my ground and raising my chin, daring her to comment. But when she did, it wasn't in the mocking tone I'd expected.

"Not so mortal after all." She laughed again, but this time it was more breathless with awe than disdainful. "And here I thought the devourer was your greatest find, Omen. Where on earth did you acquire a phoenix?"

I should have been gratified that she was impressed, but everything about this woman told me she wasn't the sort of being I should want to awe. A phoenix? Just because I caught myself on fire along with whatever else I was aiming at?

Watching me, Tempest's lips curled into a smirk. "You didn't know, did you? Oh, I am glad I'll be around to witness this. When you burn, the whole world will burn with you."

A wave of cold flooded me at that declaration, washing away any lingering fire. My voice came out tart. "Then it's a good thing I'm not planning on burning."

"You keep telling yourself that, darling." The sphinx rose to her feet, her innumerable baubles swaying around her, and peered down at Omen from the bed. "Well? Have you come all this way just to grimace your disapproval at me, or will you remember yourself and join the revelry?"

"It's been a long time," Omen replied in a low voice. "I no longer revel in the same things you do."

"Then we have nothing left to discuss. Stay out of my business, and I'll leave you to the rest of yours. You know what you can expect if you deny that request."

"Tempest," Omen started, but she was already leaping into the shadows. At a jerk of the hellhound's hand, Thorn and Flint threw themselves after her.

My legs had taken on an uncanny resemblance to spaghetti. When they wobbled despite my best efforts, Snap was at my side in an instant, his hand on my back.

"It doesn't matter what she called you," he said. "We know who you are."

Did they? Did *I*?

Omen's hands had clenched at his sides. At the return of our wingéd warriors with no sphinx in sight, he didn't look surprised.

"We failed to detain her," Thorn said with a pained expression. "She traveled so swiftly—"

"Don't apologize. None of us quite anticipated what we'd find here." The hellhound shifter exhaled roughly.

"She's not going to help with the plan to appease the Highest about Sorsha," Snap ventured.

Omen gave a bark of a laugh. "No, I'd say not."

My own fingers curled into fists. I crossed my arms over my chest, burying the sphinx's needling comments—*the whole world will burn with you*—under the immensity of everything else she'd admitted to.

"There's one very obvious answer to that problem," I said. "We always meant to destroy the Company. Now I'll just have to add defeating her to that to-do list—for real."

EIGHT

Sorsha

No one had turned on the Everymobile's radio, but it'd decided to start blaring about ten minutes ago, switching back and forth between strident classical music and a talk show where everyone seemed to be yelling in Russian—which was particularly odd considering we were currently in Paris.

Ruse and Antic jabbed at the buttons to no avail. Finally, Thorn strode over to the dash.

"My apologies," he said solemnly to the RV, and slammed his fist into the radio controls. The noise sputtered, but it did die, as just about everything did after a punch from the warrior.

Omen grimaced at the smashed spot we'd have to find some way to explain to the equines when they reclaimed their ride, but he didn't criticize Thorn's tactics. He turned back to the rest of us from his usual post leaning against the kitchen counter. No doubt it really would signal the end of the world if he ever lowered himself—both figuratively and literally—to sitting on the leather sofa-bench with us.

"Our observations across the past few days have made it quite clear that we can't rely on our previous tactics," he said. "Whether based on Tempest's urging or their own initiative, the local Company facilities are under total lockdown. We can't charm or threaten anyone into getting us past the outer defenses if no one ever comes out in the first place."

"Do you really think all the Company workers are living inside those buildings?" Snap asked. He nestled me even closer against him as he spoke, which was quite a feat when he'd already had me practically on his lap. He seemed to have become extra possessive after our confrontation with Tempest a few days ago.

I gave him a peck on his cheek to return the affection, and he beamed at me before continuing. "The facilities we found didn't appear to be made as homes. Won't the Company people get bored spending all their time at work? Won't some of them have families they'll be separated from?"

"I'm sure the answer to both of those questions is yes," Omen said. "They're just willing to sacrifice a few freedoms to make sure they can continue screwing us over."

I drummed my fingers on the table. Days of surveillance and no real action had left me restless, especially with my resolve to defeat Tempest hanging over me. "To be fair, being bored and lonely probably beats getting beheaded or disemboweled. If they think they're in mortal danger, I could see them putting up with a lockdown for quite a while."

Thorn glanced at Omen. "The sphinx knows we'll be investigating in this city. Our prior sources have indicated that the mortal leader of the Company of Light travels across Europe. The map we saw displayed several bases of operations here. Might they be less stringent elsewhere?"

"I don't think Tempest will be cutting any corners. Even the leader himself might be cloistered somewhere until she feels we no longer present much of a threat." The hellhound shifter rubbed his jaw. "She was only able to interrupt our last plan, which came very close to working, because she intervened quickly enough. If we could find another point of access and distract her well enough at the same time —or even attempt to take her down completely before we tackle the mortals... But without that point of access, we have no way of getting at their current operations or potential weaknesses."

"I could put out feelers for another mortal with hacking skills,"

Ruse suggested. "Someone who's not already working for the Company but who might be able to dig up some data that'll give us a lead. These jackasses can't run their operations without *any* interaction with the world around them."

Omen nodded. "Good idea. Your computer person back in the US contributed quite a lot. Run with that. And while you're tracking an appropriate human down, the rest of us will head underground. Paris has a mass of tunnels and catacombs that sprawl under a significant portion of the city. We'll split up and check the areas near the Company facilities for any alternate means of entrance. It's a long shot, but we might as well try whatever we can."

"I'll test for impressions in case the Company has used those passages themselves," Snap said, brightening at the opportunity to contribute his non-lethal supernatural talent.

"Excellent. In case we run into trouble, let's have someone with plenty of combat experience in each party. Snap, you go with Flint. Thorn, see if you can wrangle the imp into some sort of usefulness. And our disaster"—he rested his icy eyes on my face—"is coming with me."

Because he didn't trust any of the others to keep a close enough eye on me? I bit back half a dozen snarky remarks I'd like to have tossed at him. After seeing the echoes of his history in our conversation with Tempest the other night, I'd made a point of not hassling him quite so much, and I'd been succeeding at that pretty well, if I did say so myself. Why ruin my winning streak just to get a tiny dig in?

"It's a date," I said instead, and was rewarded with the twitch of the hellhound shifter's jaw.

My devourer wasn't feeling quite so generous. I didn't think he'd forgiven Omen for his past transgressions yet. Snap's arm tightened around me. "I would prefer to stay with Sorsha. I can defend her if I need to."

Omen gave him a baleful look. "I promise I have no nefarious intentions. She'll be returned to you soon in approximately the same state she's in now, depending on what we find in those tunnels."

"I still think we would be a better pairing."

"And *I've* already given my orders. If you don't trust me to lead this group with all our best interests in mind anymore, you know where the door is."

Omen's tone had been mild, but Snap bristled. I squeezed his arm before he could continue the argument—or escalate it into something more. It'd been bad enough watching Omen and Thorn fighting over my fate.

"Hey," I said. "I can defend *myself* pretty well, as both of you should remember. I'll be fine. I'm sure if Omen has decided to get rid of me after all, he wouldn't bother making up a big tourist expedition around it."

Snap made a grumbling sound, but he accepted a kiss and simply hugged me extra hard before releasing me so I could join the hellhound shifter, who was now glowering at me. This date was off to a great start already.

Sad to say, if it had been a date, tramping around in Paris's underground tunnels late into the night wouldn't have been the worst I'd been on. It was definitely in the bottom ten, though. The cool, earthy-smelling air that filled the passages made me feel as if I was just shy of being buried alive. The low ceilings and general darkness didn't help with that claustrophobic impression.

Omen let the glow of his hellhound skin emerge to cast an orange haze over the walls of stone, clay, and—oooh, even better, a stack of embedded bones. I tipped my head toward those. "Really your kind of place, huh, hellhound?"

"I don't think I've slaughtered quite enough mortals in my time to make an entire catacomb out of their remains," he replied, which wasn't exactly reassuring considering there looked to be a few thousand bodies' worth just within view.

We walked on until we reached the spot Omen said was beneath a chocolate factory the Company appeared to be doing business out of—I had to take his word for it, since one dreary wall looked pretty much the same as any other down here. Squinting in the dim light, I couldn't make out any trap doors or other openings that might have given us a sneaky path up into the building.

"I could bring out some fire for a little more light," I said, with a hesitation I couldn't help even though I didn't like it. Tempest's remarks had clung to me like a nettle, with an equal amount of irritating prickling. If I was a phoenix, did that mean I was doomed to burn myself up with my power sooner or later?

And how much would I burn down with me if it came to that?

Omen considered me. He'd been surprisingly thrifty with the snark himself during our exploration. I couldn't tell whether he was sizing me up for destructive potential or self-confidence.

"She isn't always right, you know," he said, as if that answered my offer.

"What?"

"Tempest. Sphinxes might be known for their wisdom, but they also speak in riddles, and sometimes they get the two tangled up in their heads. She isn't all-knowing, and she has plenty of reasons to want to shake you up." He paused, his gaze shifting to the passage around us. "And I can see well enough to say that this spot is a wash too. We're done here. Come on." He stalked on down the tunnel.

I picked up my pace to keep up with him. "You don't think I'm actually a phoenix, then?"

"Oh, I believe that part. It's the first explanation that's really made sense, what with the whole habit of inadvertently setting yourself on fire. I just don't think that necessarily means you're going to burn up much else if you happen to go down in flames. Although I'd rather not experiment to find out." He glanced back with a flash of a tight but obvious smile in the darkness. "I'm going to guess that you're much better company uncharred."

"Well, I'm glad to hear you've revised your initial opinion of me at least that much."

He laughed. "You've remained full of surprises. Thankfully not all of them bad ones."

As recommendations went, I'd take that.

"Have you ever known a phoenix before?" I asked. What had happened to other beings like me? Tempest had indicated there weren't many of us.

Which Omen's answer confirmed. "No," he said. "And the stories I've heard have belonged more to mortals than shadowkind, so I have no faith in their accuracy. It could be that only a hybrid can become one. I highly doubt Tempest has ever met one either."

Okay, I could take a little reassurance in that. She was just spouting off half-baked fables, not speaking from any kind of inside knowledge.

Omen led us through several increasingly narrow passages, which didn't help with the suffocating sensation, and then up a set of rough stairs that ended at a span of thick wood paneling.

"The sphinx isn't the only one who knows a few tricks around this city," Omen said, and pressed a knob in the wood. One of the panels swung open to give us enough room to squeeze out into a small, dusty room stacked with chairs and boxes of tapered candles.

With a waxy scent tickling my nose, I followed Omen out the doorway at the other end and discovered that Versailles hadn't used up all my capacity for awe.

We'd come out into a cathedral—and sweet chirping cherubs, what a cathedral it was. The stone ceiling arched so high above our heads I could have believed it brushed the sky. High over the altar area, intricate stained glass windows streaked lamplight from outside in patches of color across the tiled floor. The columns that stood at intervals all along the pews were immense enough that I wasn't sure I could have wrapped my arms around one even if I'd cloned myself for extra help.

I wasn't much for religion, but if any place could have convinced me of the grandeur of a life beyond this one, this would be it.

"Notre Dame," Omen intoned beside me, gazing up at the towering stained glass windows. "I'll never claim that mortals haven't managed to make a few spectacular things in their time."

Speaking of surprises... I'd never have imagined I'd hear the hellhound shifter offer any praise to mortals as a general group.

A different sort of uneasiness rippled under my skin, stirring a flicker of fire with it. I willed the unsettled heat down, but maybe it'd be easier to deal with that if I said what'd been on my mind since our confrontation with Tempest.

I lowered my gaze to the floor, feeling unusually awkward. "You know, I'm sorry. For laying into you about your attitude so much. I mean, you deserved it at the start when you were being a real asshole to me, but even after you eased off on the tests and all that—I didn't appreciate how far you've come from who you used to be and how hard that must have been. You're nothing like Tempest. I don't know how much you used to be, but you're not now. Not when you're being the ice-cold bastard and not when you let your fire out. In case you still worry about that."

From stray comments he'd made across our conversations over the past weeks, I suspected he did.

Omen sputtered a laugh, which wasn't quite the response I'd hoped to provoke with my attempt at extending an olive branch.

"You're apologizing to *me*?" he said, turning to face me head-on. "I'm the one who had you chained up in anticipation of your possible death less than a week ago."

I folded my arms over my chest. "I'm not saying that was the highlight of my life, but with what you'd heard and the hold the Highest have over you… I get it. It means a lot that you didn't toss me straight to them—that it was a decision you couldn't have made lightly." I paused. "I'm still not totally sure why you *didn't* take the free pass I gave you."

He reached to graze his knuckles down the side of my face, a whisper of a touch that set off a wave of a much more enticing heat. His eyes pinned me in place, incredulous and maybe a little conflicted but not at all scornful. "If you would throw your life on the Highest's mercy just to save two shadowkind, one of whom hadn't given you much reason for generosity, I find it exceedingly hard to believe that you'd turn around and tear down the rest of the world on a whim."

My throat had constricted. "I don't know if I'll get much choice."

"Of course you will. There are always choices. And for all your snark and defiance… you obviously care enough to make the choices that won't result in mass destruction." Omen's gaze dropped for a second before catching mine even more intently. "I should have pieced that fact together well before you had to throw yourself between Thorn and me. You haven't really made a secret of *your* mind-set. I just didn't recognize your altruism for what it was—or maybe I didn't let myself recognize it—until it was that blatant."

I swallowed thickly. "So… you're not still waiting for me to fuck up so you'll have an excuse to haul me off to the Highest after all?"

He looked honestly startled by that question. "Is that what you thought?"

"You haven't exactly been Mr. Talkative since you unchained me, even by your standards."

He stroked his hand down my face again with a tad more pressure than before. My heart skipped a beat. Then it kept right on jitterbugging away like it was '50s prom night in my chest.

Omen's mouth had twisted. "Ah. Well. There've been things I've known I should say to you, but I hadn't quite settled on how to say them, so I may have erred too much on the side of saying nothing at all." He drew in a long breath. "I need to apologize to you. I *was* far more of an asshole to you than you deserved when we first met, and I should have let up on you sooner—to a greater extent— You've had even less say over the hand you've been dealt than I have, and it's taken you a lot less time to make something admirable out of it. You put my own efforts to shame."

The thought of the hellhound shifter apologizing to anyone, let alone me, was so bizarre that my thoughts kept spinning around his words for several seconds as they slowly sunk in. "So... being nicer to me is your attempt to pull ahead in some competition of who's the most stellar being around?"

Omen let out a huff. "I'm trying to tell you I'm sorry for not recognizing your 'stellar' qualities sooner. Do you always have to make everything as hard as possible?"

A laugh spilled out of me. I still couldn't quite wrap my head around the praise he was offering me, but I knew him well enough now to recognize the gleam of orange fire in his eyes and to note that his hand had lingered against the crook of my jaw as if he wasn't ready to stop touching me yet. I might not know how to respond to kindness from Omen, but I knew what to do with that heat.

I trailed my fingers down the front of his shirt, stopping just an inch above the fly of his slacks. "I can think of one or two things we both enjoy my making harder."

Omen let out a growl, but it was all hunger. Then he was tugging my mouth to his, his lips descending on me with a kiss so blazing it branded me all the way down to my toes.

I gripped his shirt, kissing him back with everything I had in me. No matter how much we'd squabbled, no matter how much we might both have to apologize for, there was nothing but rightness in the way our bodies sparked against each other.

Omen's tongue swept into my mouth. He pulled me tighter against him, one hand on my ass, the other sliding up my side to cup my breast. He was plenty hard already, and the feel of that solid length pressing against me through our clothes sent a shock of heat straight to my sex.

A famous cathedral wasn't where I'd have pictured getting it on with any of my lovers, least of all the most hellish of them, but not a single particle in me had any interest in pausing this encounter to move elsewhere.

Omen pushed me up against one of the columns. A flicker of his fiery power raced between us—and my inner flames rose up to meet it like they had before. Pleasure burned across every inch of my skin.

The hellhound shifter dropped his mouth to the side of my neck, and I tangled my fingers in the short tufts of his hair, sprung wild in his abandon. The slick of his tongue beneath my chin drew a whimper from my throat.

"Tell me what you want," Omen said, his voice thick with desire and portent.

Oh, there were a hell of a lot of things I wanted, but right now only one seemed to matter. "Fuck me. Fuck me as hard as you can."

A scorching chuckle fell from his lips and spilled hot across my skin. "Just this once, I'll happily submit to your command."

Last time, he'd burned the clothes right off me. Or maybe I'd burned them off myself—it'd been kind of difficult to tell with all the flames dancing around. This time, maybe in recognition that I didn't have an easy change of clothes waiting one room away, he yanked my shirt off the mortal way and tossed it aside instead. There might have been supernatural power in the speed with which he unlatched my bra, though.

A split-second later, he'd sucked my nipple between his teeth with a spike of bliss so sharp I gasped. I held onto his hair and tugged at his shirt with my other hand. His hellish light flared all across his body, and *that* piece of clothing disintegrated into ash. Along with every other piece of clothing he'd been wearing. Lucky me.

I traced my fingers over the taut muscles of his torso, and his devilish tail, newly freed, teased across my forearm. I couldn't resist wrapping my fingers around its warmth, lithe length. It twitched against my palm, the tip tracing a giddy line along my thigh. Then Omen was tipping me down onto the tiled floor, wrenching the rest of my clothes off as we went.

It shouldn't have been a comfortable surface to sprawl on. But before any chill from the smooth stone could penetrate my skin, a wash of Omen's fire coursed around and beneath me. It cushioned me like the fieriest of duvets.

Omen's mouth branded mine with even more heat, his body poised just above mine. "I will fuck you until you're screaming with the pleasure of it," he promised, so confidently I'd have soaked my panties if I were still wearing any. "But I'm going to take my time enjoying you so I can remember every bit. That first time was something of a blur—a blur of good things, but still."

He grazed his fangs over my collarbone, and I inhaled with a pleased hum. "No arguments here." But maybe one tiny speck of concern, now that we were taking our carnal collision a little more slowly.

As he teased those houndish teeth over my breast, I almost lost my words, but they tumbled out with my next hitch of breath. "We should probably make sure—I'd rather not end up with hell-puppies out of this."

The shifter let out a snort that somehow managed to be as sexy as everything else about him and flicked my nipple with the tip of his tongue. "Not going to happen without the same shadowkind ceremony your mother used. And seeing as only three shadowkind have ever managed that in the history of existence, I think it's doubtful I've undergone it unknowingly."

That did sound like a fair assumption. Especially considering I suspected he'd sear right through anything resembling a condom, not that I had any lying around anyway, and I *really* didn't want to put an end to this fucking before we'd even gotten started.

Omen caught my other nipple in his lips and dipped his hand between my thighs at the same time. The deeper jolt of pleasure wiped away anything else I might have said. I released a growl of my own, my hips arching to meet him. His fingers curled right inside me, hot as every other part of him and setting off fresh flames, but it wasn't half as much as I was hungry for.

"I'm going to take you apart and put you back together again, and you'll be begging for more," Omen murmured. He eased lower down my body with a kiss to my belly.

The sound that slipped from my lips in response wasn't particularly articulate, but I meant it to say something along the lines of, *Sounds fantastic to me, get on with it!* I didn't need to express that sentiment any more clearly, though, because the next second the hellhound shifter had pressed that scorching mouth of his to my core.

Oh, let the angels sing. The force of his lips and the slick of his tongue sent waves of pleasure pulsing through me. All I could do was moan and gaze up at the vast ceiling overhead, the ecstasy building so fast I might as well have been soaring up to meet it.

But Omen made good on his promise to savor the moment. Every time I started soaring toward my release, he eased up just slightly, slowing the flicks of his tongue, teasing with his fingers rather than stroking me to completion. A knot of need built in my core, expanding with each glimpse of a climax.

I clutched the short tufts of his hair, my fingers scraping his scalp. Finally, the words he must have been waiting for spilled out of me in a growl of my own. "Please, damn it. *Please.*"

I felt the curl of Omen's lips against me as he grinned. At a sharp suck on my clit and a deeper plunge of his fingers, I really might have screamed with delight. My vision whited out with a ringing in my ears as I spiraled over the edge into an explosion of bliss.

The flames I lay on rippled beneath my back as if urging my orgasm to greater heights. I'd barely caught my breath, the afterglow pealing through me, before Omen rose up over me. He hefted my hips right off the floor to meet him.

His mouth crashed into mine, smoky with both our flavors, and his rigid cock drove inside me. I wrapped my legs around him and bucked to match his rhythm, wanting more and more as the pleasure swelled through me again. Our flames crackled between us with a stinging that was all joy, no pain.

I wouldn't have thought the shifter could wring even more ecstasy out of my body, but I hadn't counted on all his special features. As our bodies rocked together at an increasingly furious pace, something glided across my ass. The devilish tip of his tail traced gleeful patterns across my skin—and slipped between the cheeks to stroke my other opening.

Another bolt of pleasure raced to join the sensations already surging through me. A gasping cry broke from my mouth.

Omen kissed me as if to drink down that sound. His cock rammed into me to the hilt, his tail teased a giddying trail from behind, and I did break—into a thousand shimmering, scorching pieces, lit up from the inside out.

As I shuddered and sank my fingernails into Omen's back and ass, he groaned. With a few increasingly erratic thrusts, he threw himself after me with what might as well have been a spurt of liquid fire.

As his muscles relaxed, the hellhound shifter lowered us both to the ground, letting some of his weight rest against me. I didn't hesitate to look into his eyes this time. The orange flare mingled with the icy blue in perfect contrast.

He gave me a sardonic smile, as if he couldn't quite bring himself to look totally satisfied even after the vulnerabilities and admiration he'd already admitted to. That diffidence was so perfectly Omen that a flutter of fondness passed through my chest.

A bittersweet pang followed it. Suddenly I was remembering how he'd talked in the palace about his time with Tempest.

I felt the need to clarify the situation, for both our sakes. "This means more than just fucking. To me, anyway. *You* mean more to me than that." I wasn't totally sure what or how much yet, but I knew what I'd said was true.

Omen's smile softened just slightly around the edges. "I don't think anything with you is ever going to be 'just', Disaster." He dropped his head, his lips grazing my cheek, answering a question I hadn't even formed yet. "You're a finer being than Tempest ever was or could be. As many regrets as I may have collected over the years, you won't be one of them. Even if it damns us both."

An unexpected lump filled my throat. He might be giving up not just his freedom but his life if the Highest found out how he'd betrayed their orders.

I tucked my arm around his neck, and he met me for another kiss, sweeter but no less searing. As he urged my lips apart with his tongue, a lightbulb blinked on in my head. I kissed him even harder and then pulled back.

"What?" Omen asked, looking amused as he took in my expression.

I grinned up at him. "I know how we can get at the Company pricks even if they never set one foot outside."

NINE

Ruse

AFTER STOPPING FOR GAS JUST BEFORE WE REACHED THE ITALIAN BORDER, Omen took over the driver's seat in the Everymobile. I appreciated the release from that duty, especially since the RV had taken to randomly flashing its blinkers in time with the bells that were dinging through the rumble of the engine. Sinking into the smooth leather padding of the sofa, I got out my phone.

Sorsha sashayed over a moment later with a grin. "Any more dirt from our new hacker associate?" she asked, hopping up to sit on the table with her legs dangling.

She'd had a more buoyant energy to her since she'd come back from the search of Paris's tunnels with her latest brilliant idea. I liked seeing her lit up like this, but at times it seemed almost frenetic, as if she were racing along to stay a step or two ahead of some deeper anxiety.

I also hadn't been able to help noticing that when she'd returned all energized, the smoky smell clinging to her skin hadn't been just her natural fiery scent but a tang of brimstone that belonged to the hellhound shifter as well. How much was she buoyed by her new brainstorm, and how much by whatever the two of them had gotten up to after they must have made their peace?

It was bad enough being an incubus in love without getting jealous about my lover's other partners. Darkness forbid she ever asked for a count of how many women I'd gotten it on with over the centuries. But somehow knowing she'd been hooking up with Omen—and was clearly happy about how that had gone down—rubbed up against other anxieties of my own that had been gnawing at me.

"He hasn't come up with much in the past few hours, but being mortal, he does need to sleep occasionally," I said. "Now that we've determined there's significantly more Company activity happening in Rome than anywhere else on this side of the ocean, he'll be checking for more distinctive patterns there. We'll narrow in on family and friends soon enough."

Sorsha sighed, the swing of her legs slowing. "Of course, it'll only work if the Company employees have been allowed at least a little contact with the people they care about outside. Their boss—the mortal one or Tempest—might have them under a total communications lockdown too."

I gave her thigh a light squeeze. "Then you'll come up with some other brilliant plan. You've been pulling out the inspiration as fast as your flames."

The Everymobile chose that moment to hiccup, a little lurch vibrating through the entire frame. Sorsha had to grip the edge of the table to keep her balance. Then, like actual hiccups, the RV hitched again. Up at the front, Omen let out a growl of frustration.

"I'm starting to think taking 'Darlene' through a rift wasn't such a great idea," I said, just loud enough to make sure he'd hear me.

Sorsha laughed, broken by another tiny lurch. "She isn't quite the same as she used to be, that's for sure. How do you figure we cure vehicular hiccups? Give her a glass of water? Jump out in front of her to scare her out of it?"

"Well, we did just fill her up with her liquid of choice, so I'm guessing that won't do it." I chuckled along with her for a moment until the fact that I honestly had no idea what to do about our transportation issues or much of anything else clouded over my good humor.

I tried to keep my smirk from faltering, but Sorsha quieted too, her gaze lingering on my face. She slipped off the table, caught my hand, and tugged me toward her bedroom. "Come here a moment."

Ready for more action, was she? My own desires woke up as I followed her down the hall. But even the familiar sensation of lust—and the less-so sensation of a sweeter affection—didn't offer much of a balm to my restless thoughts.

In bits and pieces, the others had laid out their encounter with Tempest for me. All the sphinx's haughty remarks and dismissals of their concerns—and her accusation that they'd forgotten their monstrous natures. She hadn't levied that charge at me, but merely because I hadn't been there, I had to assume. The moment Snap had mentioned it with a pained twist of his mouth, I'd felt it like a jab to the gut.

Had I really fallen for Sorsha in defiance of my promiscuous inclinations? Or... had some subtler aspect of my powers simply recognized what a blessing it'd be to have an easy source of nourishment at my side for all time?

She'd been the first mortal—or semi-mortal, at least—to accept me for all I was. I could sate my hunger for pleasure night after night without needing the slightest supernatural seduction. In many ways, it was incredibly *convenient* that I'd found myself longing for a relationship of more commitment with her.

Did I love her, or was convincing myself that I did the biggest con I'd ever pulled yet, this time on myself?

I didn't want to look all that closely at that question. And showing Sorsha a good time of the intimate variety was the one thing I absolutely could do beyond a doubt. So if she wanted that from me, I'd damn well deliver it.

"I hope you know I'd intend to make this last for more than a *moment*," I teased as she shut the bedroom door behind us. "I do have a reputation to uphold."

She poked me in the chest. "I didn't bring you in here for a ravishing, although I won't necessarily say no to that once we're done talking. What's up with you? You've seemed a little out of sorts since we started this trip."

My lover was far too perceptive. I gave a quick laugh and

attempted to turn the conversation around. "Have I not been attentive enough, Miss Blaze?"

Sorsha poked me again with an expression that brooked no arguments or foolishness. "You've been perfectly adoring, as I think you know. But we've spent enough time together that I can tell when you're not your usual carefree self, Mr. Charm. I've opened every part of me up to you. Don't you know by now that I'm not going to judge whatever it is that's bothering you?"

A particularly unfamiliar pang of guilt struck me with that question. Our mortal *had* opened herself up—had given me permission to read her mental state even though she'd had a terrible experience with another shadowkind manipulating her mind as a child. She'd said she loved me, and she didn't have any supernatural hunger to give her an ulterior motive.

She'd believed in me, and I'd better get into the habit of believing in her, or I'd lose her regardless of my own motivations.

I tugged her into my arms and ducked my head next to hers. She smelled only like herself now, fiercely sweet. Whatever else might be going on inside me, there was no denying that the feel of her against me released some of the tension in my chest.

"Ruse," she prodded, but her tone had gentled. I could bring that out in her too—the tenderness that complemented her fire so well.

"Omen dragged you off," I said. "He might have thrown you to the Highest to be killed. And there was nothing at all I could do to stop him or to help you. Thorn and Snap got right on the case—hell, even the *imp* might have contributed something, whether it worked out or not."

"You've helped with plenty of other things. Not everyone's talents are going to fit every problem."

"You're the most important thing I've had in my life since… since ever." As I found the words, the truth of that statement cut through me, sharply poignant. Maybe I should have been reassured to put one doubt to rest, but the certainty that my feelings were real only brought my failure into harsher relief. "If I can't do a thing to protect you when your entire existence is on the line, how in the realms could I possibly deserve you?"

Sorsha made a strangled sound and turned in my arms to meet my gaze. She touched my face, her thumb stroking over my cheek, and thanks to this miraculous love I'd found myself capable of, that touch sparked more warmth than I'd ever found in clinching genitals with those untold numbers of other women.

"You know I don't blame you for not throwing yourself in front of the hellhound's jaws, right?" she said. "There wasn't a single moment when Omen had me locked up that I thought to myself, 'Gosh, where is that incubus? He should have rescued me by now.'"

"That doesn't mean you *shouldn't* have been thinking it," I muttered.

"Well, I wouldn't want to be looking at it that way. I don't think love is supposed to be some kind of transaction where you earn enough points to 'deserve' someone. If it was... how the hell would *I* deserve any of you? For all we know, I'm going to explode in a ball of flame at any moment and take you all down with me."

She spoke flippantly, but I caught enough strain in her voice to know that wasn't a totally imaginary fear. Tempest had stirred up doubts in her too. She was worried she might hurt us.

I kissed her temple. "*I* know that's not going to happen. So does everyone else, including Omen, despite his momentary lapse in judgment. If a tiny bit of fire scalds us now and then, we're a pretty resilient lot. And some types of burning are very enjoyable."

Sorsha hummed as if she didn't quite accept my argument but didn't feel like pushing the matter. "That's not the point. I've decided *you* deserve me. I want you in my life for all the wonderful things you do bring into it. And you'd better not be telling me I don't get to make my own decisions."

The corner of my lips quirked up before I could stop it. Our mortal did have her own knack for persuasion. "Woe betide anyone who attempts that." Maybe her proclamation didn't ease my guilt completely, but maybe I should never have been letting that guilt interfere with what we had in the first place. If what I could offer was enough for her, then whether it was enough for me was only a problem between me and myself.

"I suppose I'll be forever wondering how I managed to con you into making that decision," I added, lightly enough to show it was a joke.

Sorsha rolled her eyes at me and did a little shimmy against me with a lilt of her mixed-up lyrics. "Oh, I, I just glide to your charm, all right? It must have clean gone to my head."

I caught her jaw and drew her so close my nose brushed hers. "I'll show you a lot more than charm," I said, one promise I knew I could make good on, and captured her lips.

Why shouldn't this be enough? Making her laugh, making her sigh with pleasure... I *did* have talents none of our other companions possessed.

I kissed her harder and lowered her onto the bed. Her fingers slid down my chest while the other hand hooked around one of my horns in that way that sent an electric thrill over my skin. I was just easing up her shirt when a tiny scaly body wriggled its way between us as if attempting to join what he saw as a cuddle fest.

"Pickle!" Sorsha protested with a snicker, scooping her hand around the little dragon. Her shadowkind pet let out an indignant chirp. "Have I been neglecting you? I promise you'll have my full attention after I finish this... conversation with Ruse." As she got up to see him out the door, she shot me an amused look. "Sorry. I didn't realize he was in here."

"So much competition for your affection these days," I teased.

"Good thing I have so much to go around." She nudged me back down on the bed, leaning over me, and then paused. "There are different ways of saving someone, you know. Maybe duels to the death aren't your forte, but so many times you've bolstered my spirits when that was what I really needed. I know I can always count on you."

"Sorsha," I said, filled with more emotion than I was prepared to navigate. Getting back to kissing seemed like the simplest way to show her. But before I could bring her mouth to mine, we were interrupted again, this time by the chime of her phone.

Sorsha groaned, but she grabbed her purse. So few people called her that it was likely to be important. Her stance stiffened at the sight of the call display.

"It's Vivi. I've already put her off twice in the last few days."

The hesitation in her voice pricked at me. The woman she was avoiding had once been her best friend—I recalled the fondness her voice used to hold when talking about or to Vivi. But the longer she'd spent with us, the more she'd withdrawn. Was there anyone from her life before meeting us that she hadn't pulled away from?

If she was worried about hurting *us* in our semi-immortal state, how scared must she be when it came to people like Vivi? Did she think putting distance between her and them was the only way *she* could save them… from herself?

It wasn't right for her fears to separate her from the people she'd cared about and who'd cared about her before all this had come to light. Our mortal might be more shadowkind than she'd ever suspected, but that shouldn't mean she didn't deserve human friendship. Perhaps she needed a reminder of that to calm those fears—a chance to talk to someone who could speak to her non-monstrous side for once.

I sat up next to her and kissed her cheek. "Answer it. I can wait, and you know I can share."

Sorsha drew in a breath and nodded. She hit the answer button. "Hey, Vivi! I know, I know. Things have been crazy, but—I'm sorry."

I propped myself against her pillow, watching the tentative smile cross her lips at her best friend's banter. A deeper contentment than I'd felt in days settled over me.

I'd done at least one thing right here. Perhaps I should remember what she'd said about there being different ways of saving. The ways I could protect Sorsha didn't look anything like Thorn's warrior strength, but that didn't have to mean they mattered so much less, as long as I spotted those opportunities when they came.

TEN

Sorsha

I peered up at the stucco apartment building, its thin face looming several stories above the street. Patches of orangey-brown and a paler cream color mottled the stucco, and rust speckled the hinges on the antique-looking front door.

"This is the place?"

"Unless our stalwart hacker connected the phone number he traced to the wrong address." Ruse cocked his head and then motioned for me to stand back from the door. "Wait here. I'll take the lay of the land from the shadows first. If we're lucky, we won't even need your thieving skills. The fellow up there is engaged to his Company lady, but they're not living together yet. As far as we know, he's not involved in the Company himself. There's no reason for him to be particularly protected."

Because the Company had no reason to believe the man up there knew anything that could help their enemies—a.k.a., us. But if his fiancée hadn't let anything useful slip during their phone conversations, Ruse would simply charm the dude into forgetting we'd ever stopped by like he would anyway, and we'd see what other connections his new hacker ally could dig up from back in Paris. Thank all that was wired and wild for the internet.

Ruse stepped into the shadows of the narrow alley between that apartment building and the next—so narrow it'd have been a tight fit for me to walk down it—and vanished. While I waited for his report, I pulled out my phone to give the impression I was occupied with more than just loitering here. The three other members of my shadowkind quartet had come along, but they were staying in the darkness until we knew what we were looking for.

Too bad I couldn't text with them while they were in their shadow forms. My lips quirked at the thought of what enthusiastic observations and dour cautions Snap and Thorn would pass on.

Omen? Who knew what the hellhound shifter would think it worth saying to me. But although he hadn't exactly gotten less enigmatic, I'd felt more comfortable in whatever uncertainties he stirred up since our interlude in the cathedral.

He intended to ensure I made it through this alive, Tempest and the Highest be damned. That much I was convinced of now. And if we had the chance to steal another heated moment or two along the way... I didn't think either of us would turn it down.

Ruse reformed out of the shadows looking pleased with himself. "Not a bit of iron or silver around, at least not enough to be of any concern."

I tucked my phone back into my purse, feeling abruptly adrift. This had been my plan, but it working well meant I didn't have any part to play in it. "I guess I should head back to the Everymobile then."

"Not at all! Come on." He nudged me toward the doorway. "I've already chatted with our host enough to ensure he's open to visitors. You can't come all the way to Rome without doing a little sightseeing. And I promise you, you'll get quite the sight from up there."

As usual, his playful cajoling was irresistible, even without him turning any of his supernaturally-powered charm on me. I tramped after him into a cramped corridor that led to a rickety lift so small I was practically snuggling with the incubus inside its car. Good thing the rest of our companions could shrink to a much smaller size when they traveled through the shadows.

The lift whirred upward with only an occasional wobble. Naturally,

Ruse couldn't resist the excuse of the tight space to give my ass a squeeze. I swatted his in return as he got off ahead of me, and he laughed.

I wasn't sure he'd completely dropped the whole "I should have protected you better" idea he'd expressed to me on the drive here, but at least his usual carefree flirtiness was back in full force.

"The rest of you can come out too," he announced to the landing at large as he knocked on a door that had clearly seen better days. Just as the worn surface with its flaking white paint swung open to admit us, Thorn and Snap materialized behind me.

"Omen wanted to survey this and the surrounding buildings more closely," Thorn informed us in an undertone as we headed inside. His mouth was set at a displeased slant, his near-black eyes scanning the room we stepped into even more warily than usual.

Our charmed Italian host waved us on into a small living room with threadbare chairs, a scratched up coffee table, and a window so big the warrior could have stepped through it with arms outstretched without brushing the frame. It looked out across sprawling parkland toward the grandiose ruins of the Colosseum.

"Wow," I said, needing to catch my breath. Ruse hadn't been lying about the sights. I walked right up to the glass as if drawn by a magnetic pull, taking in the full view up close.

Snap joined me, looping his arms around my waist and pressing a kiss to a sensitive spot just behind my ear that sent a welcome tingle through me. Even the impressive view couldn't distract him from offering the public display of affection, although afterward he leaned his head next to mine, his chin brushing my temple, and considered it with widened eyes.

"That building—it's very old even by mortal standards. Thorn says he was young when he saw it newly built. I don't believe I had come into existence yet."

Shadowkind, not being the type to celebrate birthdays seeing as they weren't quite *born* and, y'know, the whole lack of concept of time in their own realm thing, didn't tend to keep very close track of their age. Snap might have been only a little older than me or decades more. But in the mortal world, he was still pretty much a newbie.

"Lots of battles fought in that place," I told him, trailing my fingertips over his knuckles. Was his embrace even more insistent than usual? Maybe seeing Ruse grope me on the elevator had woken up his possessive instinct with a fiercer edge. "Mostly for fun, though—for the people watching, anyway. Like those soccer games you saw on my TV, back when I had a TV."

And an apartment to house that TV in. I couldn't even blame my shadowkind companions for that loss when I was the one who'd set the place on fire. Of course, they'd been the ones who'd brought the Company to my doorstep attempting to kidnap and possibly kill me. But who was keeping score?

Thorn came up at my other side. "Mortals do have strange priorities at times."

I raised my eyebrows at him. "Says the wingéd who fought in some immense war for reasons he can't even remember?"

He let out a grunt as if accepting my point, but his frown made me wonder if I'd gone too far with my teasing. Or maybe something else was bothering him. He'd looked a little more serious than usual since he'd appeared, which for the warrior was pretty dire.

I shifted in Snap's embrace, and the devourer let me go with only a faint noise of discontent. I stepped closer to the wingéd and tucked my arm around his muscular one. Sometimes it was easy to forget how passionate a heart lay under all this bulk and brawn, but in some ways, my warrior lover was the most deeply affected out of all of them.

I twined my fingers with his. "Is everything okay? Did Omen notice something that made him think we could be in trouble here?"

Thorn shook his head. "Not that I'm aware of. I believe he simply meant to confirm there were no signs of Tempest's presence, as he's best equipped to identify that." He let his hand come to rest on my hip with an affectionate stroke of his thumb, but his gaze shifted to the horizon beyond the Colosseum. "There is at least one other nearby who might remember what we fought for."

Another wingéd? Thorn could sense when any of the few remaining members of his kind were nearby—that was how we'd found Flint. It made sense that he'd be encountering more of them as we jetted all across the world. He didn't seem all that happy about it, even though he'd already revealed his nature to the rest of us.

I squeezed his hand. "Maybe they'd join in, like Flint did. You persuaded him easily enough."

"Perhaps. But to have lingered mortal-side in much closer vicinity to the terrain of our shame… I'm not certain what their mindset might be."

"It can't hurt to ask, can it?" Snap said brightly, turning from the view. "Bringing more shadowkind on board has only helped us, as Sorsha expected it would." He leaned in to give me another peck, this time on the temple.

"But those that do not come on board have the potential to cause trouble," Thorn muttered.

Did he think this wingéd might outright work against us? It was hard to imagine a being with a similar solemn nature to his and Flint's taking a stance like Tempest's, but then, there were a lot of ways a powerful warrior could be destructive if he—or she—got the idea to be.

Behind us, Ruse's dupe let out a loud burst of laughter. I swiveled to watch the incubus's "interrogation." The wingéd left off his brooding enough to turn with me at my tug.

Our host chattered away in eager Italian, so fast I didn't catch a single word I even partly recognized, although my local vocabulary was admittedly mostly limited to "spaghetti" and "fettuccine." The man's hands swept through the air with each exclamation. Ruse nodded and retorted something in the same language with a perfectly authentic accent. Apparently languages came to the incubus naturally too.

Watching the mortal guy's gesticulations, I tried to guess what they might be talking about. The apartment building was growing yet another floor? Pineapple was the best ever pizza topping? We should all hop on a Ferris wheel for a ride?

Ruse's voice dropped, his demeanor turning more serious. He made several statements with some dramatic gestures of his own. I was pretty sure the jerk of his hand was the shutting—or opening?—of a door. A flap of his hands like wings—indicating some sort of shadowkind creature? From his tone, he was getting down to business.

His dupe's smile faded too, but he responded with as much emotion as before, just sounding upset instead of excited now. He mimed something that I was going to assume was *not* icing flowers on a cake, however much it might look that way, and then what might have been an explosion. That didn't give me the impression of good news. If it'd been an explosion of joy, surely he'd have looked happier about it.

As the incubus and our charmed host continued their urgent discussion, Omen slipped out of the shadows by the bathroom doorway and ambled over to us. He caught Ruse's eye but didn't say anything. The incubus acknowledged him with a quick tip of his head.

"Do you understand what they're saying?" Snap asked him, nuzzling my hair.

"I can pick up a little, but I haven't spent much time in this country in centuries, and the language has, you might say, evolved."

"Indeed," Thorn rumbled. "And not for the better."

I nudged him gently with my elbow. "Kids these days and their crazy slang, huh?"

The warrior shot me a wounded glance, but the effect was diminished by the hint of amusement that glinted in his eyes. "I seem to manage to keep up with you, m'lady."

"So you do. In so many wonderful ways."

Omen cleared his throat in what I took as a shockingly polite way to say, *Shut up*, but I'd have shut my mouth anyway at the tense expression on Ruse's face as he rejoined us. His new friend was sitting on one of the chairs, head bowed and shaking in some sort of denial.

"His fiancée hadn't told him very much," the incubus said, his voice uncharacteristically grim. "But I was able to draw out a decent amount of information from piecing together what he has heard and seen and unconscious impressions from his mind. The Company definitely has major operations happening here. They're particularly focused on this disease they hope to spread to the shadowkind. And his woman on the inside has been talking as if they're just days away from releasing it."

ELEVEN

Sorsha

Getting into the Colosseum wasn't a cakewalk, but I'd slinked through tighter situations before. With an only mildly scraped elbow from one particularly rough bit of stone I'd had to scramble over, I slipped away from the towering walls of the former stands to where Omen was standing in the moonlight on the stretch of smooth flooring at one end of the massive arena.

He had his arms folded over his chest as if he'd been waiting there for a while, but not all of us could dart invisibly through shadows to avoid all security measures. I spread my arms to say, *Here I am*, and glanced around at the space he'd decided we should use for my next training session.

The span of even terrain ended several feet away at a pit full of deteriorating stone walls and arches that rose nearly to ground level. Strange to imagine that some two thousand years ago, gladiators and beasts had battled their way across this stage… and now here I was, about to enter a different sort of battle. Whether it'd be more with the hellhound shifter in front of me or my inner demons, I'd find out soon enough.

"All right," I said. "What's the big idea? Or did you just want a place with as much room as possible in case my powers explode?"

Omen gave me a narrow look. "If you're going to play a significant role in taking Tempest out of commission, you'll need to develop that focus of yours even more than I anticipated. Since you have a lot more practice with physical rather than mental gymnastics, I figured we'd start with that." He tipped his head toward the broken ground ahead of us. "Let's see you make a circuit of the arena. No falls."

Yeah, I didn't think falling that far would have been a good idea even if he hadn't made it one of the rules. I dragged in a breath of the cool night air, a dry mossy scent filling my lungs, and made a running start of it.

I vaulted over the little metal fence meant to stop tourists who didn't have a death wish from tumbling into the depths and landed on the top of the nearest arch with only a slight sway. *This* part was a piece of cake. I'd scrambled along ledges higher and narrower than this dozens of times.

Making my way around the arena was like a combination of a tightrope walk and an obstacle course, one that mostly involved leaps and bounds. Any part of it might not have been the most difficult feat I'd had to pull off, but I'd never had to play quite such an extended game of hopscotch. By the time I'd circled back around toward the platform, sweat was trickling down my neck beneath my ponytail and my calf muscles had a few things to say about my chosen nighttime activity, none of them pleasant.

I did make it back to Omen with nothing worse than a little fatigue and a tiny ache in my heel where I'd landed on an especially obnoxious lump on one of the crumbling walls. As per usual, the hellhound shifter kept any overt signs of approval to himself.

"Good," he said in his terse voice. "We know you can survive the journey. Let's make it challenging now."

He vanished into the shadows and reappeared only as flickers here and there along the course I'd followed—where pale squares of what I quickly deduced was paper blinked into being on top of the aged stone protrusions. Omen had planted at least twenty of them before he returned to the platform, swiping his hands together with a hint of satisfaction with his work.

"You want me to light them all up?" I asked before he had to give the order.

The corner of his mouth curled upward just slightly, but that ghost of a smile was enough to bring back the memories of our interlude in the cathedral. I didn't think the heat that washed through me at that thought was the sort he'd wanted to inspire, but it *was* a lot less likely to literally burn me.

Maybe we could enjoy an impassioned work break in here too? Make this a grand tour of fucking across the landmarks of Europe?

The flash of orange in his cool eyes suggested he might have guessed at my thoughts—or had similar thoughts of his own. But Omen was sadly very good at keeping it in his pants. He motioned to the path he'd laid. "You know how this works. Get to it. Extra points if you can light them all up on your first time around without having to stop."

"And without lighting myself up in the process."

"Yes, I assumed that went without saying."

"I don't know. Sometimes you like it when I bring out the fire up close and personal," I teased, and sprang over the fence before he could grouse about me not taking the training seriously enough.

I couldn't say I'd ever been an avid student, but I'd take this version of training over most of Omen's past methods, which had included speeding toward me in a camper van and nearly torching Pickle in an attempt to terrify me. The majestic sprawl of the arena and the haze of the night sky overhead made it easy to leave any worries that'd been niggling at me behind and give myself over to the moment.

No matter what anyone said, the fire inside me was *mine*. I was going to figure out how to work with it or die trying… and we'd just ignore the fact that the latter possibility had sometimes seemed way too likely for comfort.

I narrowed my awareness down to the little white squares that caught the moonlight, the momentum of my body soaring from perch to perch, and the flames that rose in my chest at my beckoning. Out, out, out, just a little at a time, enough of a jolt of heat to set that slip of paper and the next one curling and blackening under a bright flare.

I didn't quite manage a perfect run. My balance wobbled after one particularly long leap, and I had to stop and gather myself before I could incinerate the paper there and dash onward. But Omen was fully smiling by the time I reached him.

"You always do rise to the challenge, don't you, Disaster?" he said in a tone warm enough that I had to restrain the urge to grab him by the shirt and see what else I could make rise.

"Maybe one of these days you'll have to stop calling me a disaster," I retorted instead.

He chuckled. "Don't take it as commentary on your present skill-set. It reminds me of where we started."

"And how far we've come?"

"That too." He tapped my chin. "Tempest isn't going to know what hit her when we unleash your powers for real." Then he stepped back and sprang into the shadows again to reset his course, laying out more papers this time—because no matter how much he might like me now, I knew better than to expect he'd ever cut me any slack.

As I readied myself to race through the course again, a trickle of heat, maybe at the thought of Tempest and her sneer, prickled across my back. I smacked at it as well as I could over my shoulder. The little flames that had emerged nipped my fingers before they settled down.

Shit on a soda cracker. How was I supposed to stop the self-scorching side of my powers from emerging when half the time it seemed to come out of nowhere? If the trick was never feeling annoyed about anyone anywhere, I was screwed.

My frustration must have shown on my face when Omen reappeared. He looked me over with a particularly searching expression. "Are you good to go again?"

Asking rather than ordering—that was an improvement. I rolled my shoulders and dragged in a breath. I hadn't *really* hurt myself, now or any time before. My shadowkind powers healed me up faster than a regular human would have, almost as easily as they burned me in the first place. If a few blisters here and there came with the territory, I could handle that, as long as it meant I was taking down the baddies at the same time.

"No problemo," I said. "You can't start a fire without a spark."

"As you would know better than most. Get on with it, then."

Even with the extra targets, I made it through that round and the next without faltering and with all the papers at least singed if not turned to ashes. I'd also scalded a couple more spots down my spine and the backs of my arms, but ignoring the stinging was working out okay. If I could hide it well enough that Omen wasn't noticing, then that was some kind of improvement.

When I'd finished the last lap, I paused to lean against the railing. A yawn stretched my jaw before I could catch it. At least part of the reason I hadn't outright burst into flames was the sweat now sticking my damp shirt to my skin.

"All right," Omen said. "That's enough obstacle-course running for one night. You've come a long way. There's one more thing I think we should work on."

"Sure. What's that?" I shook the fatigue out of my limbs as well as I could, doing my best to tune out the tender spots my shirt rubbed against.

They'd heal. No big deal. I wasn't letting nerves stop me from stopping that psychotic sphinx.

"We can't forget what makes you such a formidable foe—what you bring to the table that none of the rest of us can." Omen stepped into the darker recesses of the building and pulled a sack from a shadowy nook. I thought I saw him suppress a wince, though from the heft of it, the bag couldn't be that heavy.

Then he upended the bag in the middle of the platform, and I understood. He'd brought several metal items, some silver and some iron.

I studied his face. "You hauled all this in here? You could have asked—"

He waved me off. "I can survive being in close proximity for a little time here and there. I just can't manipulate it well enough to effectively use it. But if *you* can bind Tempest with silver and iron, she won't be able to escape into the shadows like she did the last time. You can force her to hold her physical form, and then we'll have a real chance of taking her down."

"Right. So what exactly am I doing with this right now?"

"I'm having a chain manufactured that'll combine both metals and be long enough to wrap around her, but it won't be ready until tomorrow. For the moment, I'd imagine it'd be most useful for you to practice melting this stuff. Get used to how much fire you need to summon to heat the metal to that point. You'll want to meld the chain right around Tempest to be sure she can't simply shake it off."

I'd melted the silver-and-iron bars of Company cages before. This wasn't so different. I sifted through the collection of items, raising an eyebrow at a few of them. The ornate silver sugar bowl looked like it'd been stolen from Versailles itself, and the cast iron frying pan would have been very satisfying whacking into the sphinx's head all on its own. A little tricky to keep hidden until the right moment, though.

I focused on the smaller pieces first, letting the floodgates inside me ease open until the searing sensation rose to my throat. A burst of flames reduced a silver necklace to a shimmering puddle. A sharper spurt of fire liquified an iron bar the size of my thumb. The burns I'd given myself earlier prickled, but no fresh ones broke out on my skin. Two victories in one.

The frying pan proved the most difficult. I glared at it for a full minute before the flames I'd called up brought the edges and handle sagging down.

My frustration sparked an answering flare across my hip. I swiped at it, hoping Omen was too distracted by the metal spectacle to notice.

"You won't have to work with anything that dense when we face Tempest," he said. "Good to know you could if we needed you to."

I let out a hoarse guffaw, twice as weary as before even though I'd barely moved in the past half hour. "As long as whoever I'm trying to melt that pan at doesn't mind waiting around while I work up to it."

"Hey." Omen touched my shoulder, thankfully not on any spot where I'd barbequed myself. His tone turned unusually gentle. "You've got this. She thinks she knows all, and that's her biggest downfall. She's got no idea what she's in for when you really step up to the plate."

"She doesn't really know you anymore either," I reminded him, and couldn't resist the opportunity to lean in and claim a kiss. If it was as much to reassure myself that he was still invested in this—and in me—as to satisfy a pang of desire, I didn't see how anyone could blame me.

Omen kissed me back, his hand sliding up to tease over my hair, but it seemed a world tour of landmark sex spots wasn't in the cards tonight. When he drew back, despite the hellish heat glinting in his eyes, he looked intent in his typical all-business way.

Maybe even more serious than usual. He didn't speak as we crossed the platform to the Colosseum's looming walls, or after our separate trips through the shadows, when I caught up with him on the street a block away. A pensive furrow had formed in his brow.

We'd left the Everymobile—and the rest of our crew—parked in a lot nearby that had cleared out for the night. The city bus guise still functioned decently well. It had even adapted to the city. I just hoped no one wondered why this particular city bus featured a whirling satellite dish on its roof.

The second I stepped inside, Snap hustled to my side to escort me to the table and tuck his arm around me there. Ruse had picked up pizza to indulge in, and they'd left a few slices for the one member of the party who actually *needed* that kind of food.

After I'd downed one of those, I didn't feel half as exhausted. I leaned back in Snap's arms, letting my other hand come to rest on Thorn's thigh where he'd sat down beside me, bolstered by the presence of all four of my lovers and the other allies who'd followed us this far as well.

"From what Tempest said when we met up with her and what Ruse got from the guy here, we should make our move soon," I said, looking at Omen. "She survived an onslaught of wingéd in the past. How are *we* even going to get close enough to attack her?"

"With extreme difficulty. But it's occurred to me that we may have already hit on the perfect strategy. One that doesn't involve our own wingéd, at least not right away." He glanced from Thorn to Flint with a slightly apologetic tip of his head. "No criticism meant to present company, but the wingéd aren't exactly known for subtlety or slyness. I'm not sure we'll ever get her in a position where we could attempt that kind of onslaught again, let alone succeed in it."

"Unfortunately, I suspect I can't charm her into going along with our requests," Ruse said.

"No. But another aspect of our mortal's recent plans may point us in the right direction." Omen let out a sharp breath. "There isn't much Tempest cares about other than her own satisfaction—but she did value the association she and I had enough to reach out to me rather than simply rebuffing us. She offered us the chance to join her based on that association. I think we may be able to work with that."

The thought of cozying up to Tempest in any way made my skin crawl, but I nodded. "In what way?"

"I can put out word that I've reconsidered and I'd like to join forces with her. She'll be wary, but she'll believe it enough to meet up again. Her ego is too big for her to dismiss the possibility entirely. You and I will go alone. I'll present you as a weapon we can use for her cause, as if you're under my control. When her guard is down, you'll strike—hard enough to at least give me an opening to finish this."

"And by 'finish', you mean...?"

Antic did a little dance between the table while dramatically dragging her finger across her neck. Omen grimaced at her, but he didn't object to the gist of her suggestion.

"She should have left this world centuries ago. It's time that reprieve came to an end. As long as she remains living, she's proven herself an immense threat to mortals and shadowkind alike." He paused, his gaze settling on me. "And the Highest will be much more likely to grant *you* a reprieve if we have irrefutable proof that you dispatched her."

He was willing to kill one of his former friends—but after what I'd seen of her, I couldn't summon much discomfort at the thought. I'd burned up dozens of mortal Company lackeys so far. If they'd deserved it, then Tempest did a thousandfold more for urging them on.

Thorn stirred next to me. "I believe I should speak to the other wingéd nearby in case we require more manpower after all, concerns about our capacity for subterfuge aside."

"It never hurts to have a backup plan. Tell them what they need to hear." For the first time ever, Omen sank onto the sofa-bench across from me. He rested his forearms against the edge of the table. "Sorsha and I will need some time to go over our opponent's weaknesses. One thing I can say without a doubt—we're only going to get one chance at this trick. And if we miss the mark, Tempest *will* make us pay."

TWELVE

Thorn

Standing in the vast courtyard, looking up at the peaked dome topping the majestic building ahead of us, an uncomfortable tightness spread over my limbs. The columns framing the courtyard and the weathered stone of their construction brought back far too many echoes of the archaic times before the war that had nearly ended the entirety of the wingéd race. The fact that Flint and I were on the verge of addressing two more survivors of that catastrophe didn't do anything to alleviate my uneasy spirits.

As we crossed the courtyard through the shadows of the buildings and passing tourists, my companion gave off an equally discomforted vibe alongside his usual dour energy. When we'd found Flint, he'd been living alone in a hut in the middle of the desert, flagellating himself mentally—and perhaps physically, not that I was inclined to check for the scars—for remaining while so many of our kind had died. That had been mere weeks ago.

I was only just coming to terms with the idea that my survival might have been the result of keen thinking on my part rather than a failing of valor. But Sorsha had been right when she'd pointed out that I scarcely recalled what we'd even been fighting about. More and more

I was coming to believe that if I'd heeded my doubts back then *more* rather than less, the outcome for all my brethren might have been better.

There was no telling what we might encounter with the two wingéd I could sense in this place the mortals called the Vatican, though. For them to have chosen to linger on the rooftop in such a place did not bode well for them having moved beyond wallowing in our history. As one who might have wallowed now and then myself, I was well-equipped to recognize the signs.

But they were here, and every wingéd had a warrior's instincts and power. We needed allies now more than ever. And I would like to contribute something to our current cause beyond nearly battering our commander into a senseless pulp.

That was all the mortal woman who'd earned my heart had seen from me in recent days. How could I stake any claim on her affections in days to come, let alone as large a claim as I'd have liked to make, if all I could offer her was brutality and gore?

I'd brought Flint into our band. I could do the same with these two. Act the diplomat rather than the barbarian.

"I do not like the echoes of this place," Flint muttered as we drew close to the main building. "Why do so many mortals flock to it?"

"They weren't alive to experience the past these structures harken back to," I said. "The echoes are more fanciful than real for them."

He replied with only a grunt. Without needing to discuss our approach, we rose up through the shadows around the columns that framed the doorway, aiming for the rooftop where our brethren's presence rang out most strongly.

They'd set up their sort-of camp around the back of the intricate dome. High above the surrounding buildings, I allowed myself to step from the patches of darkness into physical form to meet them in a presentation more suited to this realm. If they wouldn't even detach themselves from the shadows, they wouldn't be much use to us in our conflict.

The warmth of the morning sunlight steadied me. "My brethren," I said, low but loud enough to carry around the pale stone. "We come to pay our respects in a time of great need."

The dual impressions shifted, coming around to the side of the dome one right behind the other. Something about their form in the darkness sent a skittering sensation through my nerves. Then they materialized onto the dingy concrete, and I understood why.

Both of the figures, one male and one female, had the same stature and might Flint and I could boast. They were also both damaged beyond the abilities of their shadowkind powers to heal.

The man stood lopsided, one of his arms missing and little more than a hollow where his right shoulder had been, the flesh there twisted into thick, knobby scars. The woman had lost her left leg from the knee down, a worn wooden post fixed in its place, but more striking was her face, where half of her jaw had been carved away.

We could form our physical features and dissolve them again as we leapt from and back into the shadows, but those features were set in our essence… and if they were damaged beyond repair, they remained so, just as a shadowkind who died mortal-side remained dead. By all appearances, these two had only narrowly escaped the latter fate.

A different sort of uneasiness rippled through my chest. Even with the mangling of her face, the sight of the woman wingéd struck me with an unexpected sense of familiarity.

One she evidently shared. Her gaze skimmed over us and settled on me. Her voice came out warbled around the remains of her jaw, but no less weighty for it. "If it isn't Thorn. Back after all these years to finally attend to the wreckage you left behind, are you?"

My lungs constricted. I drew myself up to the full extent my considerable frame would allow. "What do you speak of?"

"Oh, do you not even remember those you fought alongside? You once stood shoulder to shoulder with one I might have called my brother, we came into being so near together and so similar in nature."

That was what I recognized. In her violet eyes, in her silvery hair, there were echoes of another aspect of the past. My own voice came out quieter than before. "You speak of Haze."

He'd been one of my closest comrades. I couldn't count the times we'd fought together shoulder to shoulder. How many times I must have deflected a lethal blow before it could land on him and the same from him for me. Until that last battle when I'd abandoned my post and failed to return in time.

The woman who'd considered him even more than a comrade

simply stared at me with her stormy eyes. More words slipped from my mouth unbidden. "I searched for him. If there'd been anything I could have done—"

"You could have remained with us and fought as you were meant to," she spat out. "Instead you took a coward's way."

Not long ago, I might have accepted that judgment without argument. It would only have been how I'd already judged myself. But now, a protest rose up. "I didn't leave for cowardice. I left because I saw how many of us had already fallen, and it seemed wrong to me that we tore into each other so violently over matters none of us truly understood. I meant to prevent the battle altogether if I could."

The man guffawed. "Prevent the battle? Are you wingéd or weakling? It was our duty to stand with our brethren and respond to the call to war. That we linger at all is our own shame, but *you*—those minor scars show how little you paid."

The comment summoned the sphinx's harsh remarks from days ago—her accusation that I'd forgotten what I was. From her the suggestion had rankled; hearing the same from one of my own drove it deeper. The stabbing of guilt, my constant companion of many centuries, lanced through my gut as I'd thought it never would again. *Had* I strayed too far from what I was meant to be?

I swallowed thickly. "What is done is done. I believed it was for the best for us all—including you, including Haze. There is no glory or benefit in dwelling in the shame. We have other wars in which we are needed, where we might see a better outcome for all our kind if we respond to the call."

What remained of the woman's lips curled into an undeniable sneer. "Is that what you're here for? To call us into some new fray—what, so that you can see us cut down even more while you stand back and simply watch?"

She might have summoned up old guilts, but I hadn't lost my sense of honor. "I have already spilled more blood and protected more of my kind in these past weeks than I'd imagine you have in centuries."

At her wince, a deeper pang of guilt struck me. That statement had been a blow in itself, one that should have been beneath me. I coughed and fumbled for the right recovery.

"I do not mean to criticize. You have borne a terrible burden, one greater than my own ever was. I respect that. It is simply that we face a far greater threat to all shadowkind than we ever encountered in the ages long past. There has never been a greater cause. I wouldn't step back from this one even for a moment, knowing how much hangs in the balance."

"It is our chance to win where we lost before," Flint spoke up in his hollow of a voice. "An opportunity to make something of the shame of our continued existence, to make it more than a matter of shame."

There, he could speak their grim language better than I could now. But our two brethren looked unconvinced. The woman worked her fractured jaw from side to side in a nauseating motion. "You betray us all that time ago and now you seek our help? Ha!"

Was clinging to her sense of righteousness more important to her than doing what was needed in this moment, regardless of who was delivering the message?

Perhaps, knowing my kind, that was a foolish question. Of course it was.

I ignored the sting of the word "betray" and focused on the now. "The existence of *all* life in both realms may be at stake. This isn't a matter of my own wants but of the greater good."

"So you say," the man remarked. "We have no one's word for it but yours and this one you've already deluded."

Frustration prickled up from beneath the guilt. "If you'll come with me, you can speak to others who can assure you the impending disaster is far too real. It would merely—"

"No," the woman interrupted. "You will not appear out of nowhere and demand an even greater sacrifice from us, you who sacrificed so little. If you truly wish to atone for the offenses of centuries ago, you will honor those fallen, including Haze, now."

Some part of me wrenched at the thought that there might be something I could do for those who'd met their deaths in my stead, as difficult as I found it to imagine what that might be. "How would you have me honor them?" I asked.

"We had a box..." She looked down at her hands. "Of mortal make, but as fine as anything you ever saw. It held what fragments we could gather of those who fell completely, including my greatest brother at arms. But a pack of griffins sensed the power lingering in those remains and flew off with it. In our deficient state, we haven't the power to challenge them and win it back."

A pack of griffins. The creatures with their mix of eagle and lion features could be formidable foes, but no match for an uninjured wingéd unless in immense numbers. "I could see to that. Where has this pack absconded to?"

"We know not," the man replied. "It was some years ago, and we weren't able to continue pursuing them. They are territorial creatures, though. No doubt they are still somewhere in this region."

By region he might have meant all of Italy or even the Mediterranean. "Years ago," I repeated, my heart sinking.

The woman let out a sharp huff. "Far less time than you've spent skulking around offering nothing in recompense. Are you only willing to lend your strength when it's *easy*?"

The words gnawed at me even though I knew they weren't true. But—what *had* I offered to make up for the losses my brethren had suffered in my absence?

"The matter we are currently engaged with is urgent," I said, groping for a middle-ground. "If you would see that through with us, as soon as we are sure of the security of the realms, I would gladly—"

"Ha!" the woman said again. "I see how it is. No, you go back to your playing at honor while we remember how the world truly is. Do you think our own matters have no urgency? The griffins tear at the remains and devour them scrap by scrap... I can feel even from a distance Haze's last fragments of energy fading away..."

Her face twisted with such agony that my stomach twisted alongside it. How long could it take to track down a roving gaggle of griffins for the sake of my old comrades? To show I hadn't abandoned all concern for them as I'd abandoned our battle?

But what might happen to Sorsha and the others if I left *their* sides for long enough to see to address this issue?

Flint was watching me with obvious uncertainty. I took in the ruin of my brethren's bodies again—the ruin I'd been able to escape by shirking my duty, regardless of the purity of my motives—and an oath tumbled out before I could rethink it.

"I swear I will help you in the best way I can, as I owe and have always owed those who fought and fell."

THIRTEEN

Sorsha

Omen had been right about one thing: Tempest cared about him enough to agree to another meeting. It'd have been nice if she hadn't insisted on holding that meeting a three-hour drive away, but hey, why shouldn't we get in some more sightseeing now that we'd come this far from home?

We parked the Everymobile and our restless companions a couple of miles from the site she'd chosen, because Omen had promised he'd "deliver" me to her on his own, and the sphinx would sense any other shadowkind who ventured nearby. As we got out, the hellhound shifter caught Thorn's eye and pointed toward the night sky.

"You and Flint can hover in the darkness up there where you have a decent view of the tower area. As soon as any flames come out, get your asses to us as quickly as possible." He cast his gaze toward the others. "The rest of you, stay put and out of trouble."

Snap frowned and tugged me to him for a quick but demanding kiss, as if to remind me why I'd better come back. Ruse didn't look all that pleased to be left behind either, but his contribution in charming the Company woman's fiancé seemed to have eased some of his doubts about his worthiness.

"Give her hell for us," he said to both me and Omen.

Antic hopped from foot to foot in a frenetic dance around the two of us, looking like a little kid who desperately needed to pee. "Are you sure I can't do anything—cause a distraction? Get her guard down with a laugh? I haven't even seen this crazy lady yet!"

"Believe me, you're better off that way," Omen said dryly.

I had a vision of Tempest pouncing on the imp like a lion on a wobbly baby gazelle. "We can produce some laughs," I assured her. "The two of us are practically a comedy act."

She looked at me skeptically while Omen let out a resigned huff. Even if this was the most important scheme we pulled off in his entire crusade, he didn't expect me to take it with Thorn-level solemnity, did he?

At least we didn't have a two-mile trudge ahead of us. After we'd walked a few blocks, Omen hailed one of the few taxis cruising the city late into the night. As I sat down in the back seat, my purse clinked faintly.

The cab took off, and Omen glanced over at me. "Are you ready for this?"

I nodded, even though "ready" wasn't exactly the word I'd have used. I was ready to accept that there was no way I'd ever feel more prepared to face off against a shadowkind psychotic genius than I did right now, so we might as well get it over with. We'd trained more throughout the day. I knew the movements I wanted to make by heart. But neither of us could predict exactly how Tempest would behave once we had her in front of us.

Would the silver-and-iron chain in my purse be enough to restrain her voodoo? Would I manage to meld the ends into place around her in time? How much of myself would I scorch while burning her eyes blind?

All very good questions I'd soon have the answer to, whether I liked them or not.

It wasn't hard to tell when we were coming up on our destination. The Leaning Tower of Pisa caught the light from the streetlamps on its pale, slanted surface, looking for all the world like a several-tiered wedding cake a few seconds from toppling over. Here was hoping our little duel didn't give it the final shove. I'd already destroyed one city landmark in the course of this crusade.

Tempest wasn't visible when we first stepped out, but a couple of young men were standing near the base of the tower. I hesitated, not sure how we could go through with this meeting when we had mortal spectators, but the sphinx materialized out of the darkness a moment later in between the two guys without showing any concern at all. Actually, she patted one of them on the shoulder with the air of someone petting a dog.

She'd dressed differently but no less lavishly for this occasion. Tonight's robe looked like a toga, I guessed to fit the Italian theme, but not your standard white sheet. No, when Tempest wore a toga, naturally it had to be rich crimson silk adorned with an ornate golden clasp and stitched with glinting gemstone beads. While we were in view of the public—though quiet—streets, the thick locks of her bronze hair lay peacefully around her head, but as I watched, a couple of them twitched as if jonesing for the chance to fly free.

I couldn't get close to her just yet. Judging by his own sensitivity, Omen had estimated that she wasn't likely to notice the chain of noxious metals I was carrying as long as I kept at least ten feet away, ideally more just to be safe. I stopped on the grassy lawn that filled much of the yard around the tower and curled my fingers around my purse strap, resisting the urge to check yet again that I'd left the top open so I could dip my hand inside in an instant.

Omen ambled forward with an unusually casual air—but then, he *was* supposed to be convincing Tempest that he was here to make friends. He tipped his head toward the sphinx's mortal lackeys. "You brought company. I thought we were meeting alone."

"You have your semi-human toy, so I figured I was allowed two that are fully human." Tempest gave her mortal underlings a disdainfully amused glance. "Not that they serve much use here, but it does delight me to have them assist what they hate so much."

Did they know what she was, then? How could any member of the Company of Light tolerate being ordered around by a shadowkind?

The same way we'd managed it in the past, no doubt. "You've got them under some kind of spell," I couldn't help saying, even though I'd been meant to keep my mouth shut. Omen should know by now to allow a little leeway whenever that rule was part of a plan that involved me.

Tempest let out a lilting chuckle. "Oh, hardly. I asked a riddle, and they couldn't answer it, and that bound them to protect me until the effect wears off, unless they die serving that purpose in the meantime." She gazed through her eyelashes at the man she'd patted. "If it wasn't for that, you'd want to murder me just like you do all shadowkind, wouldn't you?"

"You're a monster," the guy said stiffly. "All our work goes toward ridding this world of you and those like you. As soon as I'm out from under this magic—"

Tempest waved her hand in a bored gesture to stop him. "Yes, yes. We'll see about that." Her gaze slid back to me. "Does it bother you, semi-mortal that you are, to hear how viciously your own kind hates the monstrous side you've uncovered?"

I managed to speak with an impressive amount of calm. "Not as much now that I know they've all had someone magically pulling the strings behind the scenes."

The broken-glass laugh I remembered from Versailles tinkled out of her. "Do you think I conjured their hatred? I only gave them a purpose to put it toward, one they leapt to pursue oh so easily. I have no supernatural power that allows me to change the contents of men's minds or produce motivation where there is none—Omen can attest to that."

The hellhound shifter's expression was all the confirmation I needed. "I'd imagine you talked a good game leading them down the garden path, though," he said lightly. "You are a master of words."

"Hmm," Tempest purred. "To some extent. They certainly have no idea everything they're in for, but that's only in regards to how their goal will affect them, not us." She nudged the man beside her. "Why do you want to slaughter all shadowkind?"

"Why call them that?" he said immediately, with a disgusted curl of his mouth as he glared at her. "We all know they're monsters, like you are. They lurk in the shadows and steal from us, stalk us—we'll never be safe until they're gone from this world."

"And who told you all that about these monsters?"

"No one needed to tell me. The first Company hunter I worked under showed me. The one we trapped would have slashed us all to pieces if we hadn't acted quickly enough."

The sphinx arched her eyebrows. "And what makes you so sure we're all like that?"

"Look at what you're doing to us right now," the man shot back. "Forcing us to be here against our will, to help you, over a stupid question I couldn't answer. As soon as that magic wears off, I'm going to—"

"You know what, I can see now that bringing two of you may have been overkill. I won't force you to endure this apparent misery any longer." Tempest swung back her hand, flicked a row of knife-like claws from her fingers, and drove them straight into the side of the guy's head.

I bit back a cry, biting my tongue at the same time. The metallic flavor of blood seeped through my mouth as the same liquid seeped across the young man's head.

His eyes rolled up, and he collapsed to the ground the second the sphinx retracted her claws. She wiped her hand nonchalantly on the other man's shirt, ignoring his flinch. "There. Am I not merciful?"

They weren't wrong to call *her* a monster, in every meaning of that word. But at the same time, she'd made their human monstrousness all too clear. As much as I'd have liked to believe that I could blame the horrors of the Company of Light on this one shadowkind being, I'd met too many independent hunters and collectors over the years. That depth of hatred and revulsion could absolutely dwell in mortal hearts without any coaxing necessary. Hell, we mortals slaughtered other groups of *humans* often enough with less justification.

My own emotions flared inside me, anger and disgust at both this woman and the mortals working beneath her—and more than a little fear at the powers she *could* wield. I clamped down on a burst of flame just before it shot to the surface of my skin. It seared across my muscles all the same, and I clenched my jaw tighter against the pain.

I was supposed to be here willingly—I was supposed to be letting Omen hand me over to Tempest for her purposes.

"No less than he deserved," I made myself say.

Tempest's eyes gleamed approvingly. "Precisely." She turned her attention to her former lover and co-conspirator. "So, you've come around to seeing the 'light', have you, my dear friend?"

I could only guess how he winced inwardly at that label. "It's as the phoenix says," he replied. "They deserve whatever hell you're going to rain down on them. And who better to help you than a hellhound? I'd rather be by your side than scrambling around attempting to protect the pathetic creatures of our kind who can't take care of themselves."

To someone who'd heard Omen speak so emphatically about what he owed the lesser shadowkind and his shame over having brought harm their way in the past, those remarks held no ring of truth. But they must have been the sort of thing he might have said to appease the sphinx back then, and they were what she wanted to hear, what she thought he *should* feel. She had no idea what he'd been through in the centuries since they'd last schemed together.

Tempest smiled and inclined her head. "I knew you'd come around. Such good timing. We're nearly ready for the grand finale."

As she'd hinted before and Ruse's questioning had appeared to confirm. Omen smiled lazily back, but his gaze had turned more intent. "Your disease is perfected?"

"Only another tweak or two. I doubt we're more than a week away from making good on all these years of work." She rubbed her hands together and studied me again. "And for whatever other havoc we wish to wreak, you've brought me this lovely gift. How have you convinced *her* to turn against her own kind?"

"They're not my kind," I said automatically, as we'd rehearsed.

Omen nodded approvingly. "The human side of her has its weaknesses. My incubus was able to charm her into following my will. Whatever I tell her to do, she'll do."

He wished. I resisted the urge to give him my most saccharine grin and a cloying, "Yes, Master." Go too over the top and the jig would be up.

"Wonderful. You'll have to expand that influence to include me."

"Sorsha," Omen said with a hint of a sardonic drawl, "do as Tempest says."

"Of course." I smiled brightly at her, and another flare of fire crackled up through my chest. Thankfully, my purse hid the balling of my hand as I willed it down.

Keep it under control. Keep my cool until I needed to blaze. I could handle this.

"Better under your sway than following her irrational mortal compulsions." Tempest curled a finger to beckon me over. "Let's look at you up close and see what you're capable of, firebird."

Oh, she was about to experience my capabilities, all right. This was the moment Omen and I had planned for. As I walked toward her, I inhaled deeply, every muscle coiling for the perfect launch of my powers. Two more steps, one—

I shoved one hand into my purse and whipped the other toward the sphinx at the same moment. While my fingers closed around the chain and yanked it out, fire streaked through the air from my extended palm.

It didn't go the way it had when we'd practiced, though. My emotions were churning too fast and furious—the fire's warble blared behind my ears. Flames sizzled around my neck and down my spine, and the blast I'd intended to hurl straight into Tempest's eyes like the stab of a scorching dagger instead flickered apart into a whirlwind of sparks.

No. I flung the chain, aiming a heft of heat with it to guide its course and soften its metals, but my initial slip had given Tempest just enough warning for her to dodge. The chain smacked into the side of her robe but didn't quite whip all the way around her.

Omen lunged at her, shifting into hellhound form in midair, but the sphinx was already diving into the shadows. I'd swear I heard a snarl of harsh laughter echo from the darkness around the tower.

Omen vanished too. I was left with a blob of melted metal, Tempest's other trapped mortal, and the singed grass that marked my failure.

Fuck a donkey's dingus.

A burnt smell lingered in the air, and my scalded skin stung with the movement of the breeze. Fresh heat was already roaring up inside me. I strode back and forth across the grass, gulping air and tamping the fire down as well as I could. The stinging sensation spread all the way down to the small of my back.

When Omen reappeared, the two wingéd had joined him. All of them looked both weary and pained.

I stated the obvious. "She escaped again."

Of course she had. Omen had known we didn't stand a real chance without tricks up our sleeves—and I'd bungled the damn trick. My fury with myself seared even hotter than the rest of my anger, blistering the bottom of my tongue.

We wouldn't get another chance like this. She'd never trust Omen again. And in a week or less, she'd have the Company unleashing their hell on this entire realm.

Somehow, the fact that Omen didn't point out my failure made the guilt slice deeper. "We'll find another way," he said. "There'll be other options."

But this had been our best one. I'd just gotten so fucking pissed off...

"If all those shithead mortals who joined up with the Company weren't so excited to murder every being they don't understand," I started, and the blistering heat spread through my gums.

"She's collected the worst of them," Omen said. "They feed off each other's hate. They hardly represent all of your kind."

He couldn't quite make that reassurance sound convincing. I knew how he felt about mortals. In his mind, *I* was the exception, and mainly because of the shadowkind side of me. He only cared about shadowkind hurting humans because it brought more rage back down on his own people.

I couldn't stop moving, my feet carrying me to the base of the tower and back again. If I stopped, if I so much as slowed *down*, the flames surging through me might spring farther ahead—right out of me.

Thorn took a step toward me, his expression fraught. "Sorsha."

I shook my head before he could go on. "One fight lost. There'll be plenty more. There always are, right? I just need to cool off. You all go ahead, fly back to the Everymobile or whatever. I'll walk it. That should be enough."

My companions hesitated. "Something makes me think you could use a chaperone," Omen said, managing to keep his tone mild.

I glared at him, reining in the fire so well for just a moment that the searing dwindled away. "I know what I need better than you do. And what I need is a good long walk without anyone judging my every move. We all know I fucked up here. Please don't rub it in. I promise Darlene will be perfectly safe from me by the time I get there."

He paused, his face tensing, but he didn't snap back. When he replied, it was in the same mild voice. "I know you gave it everything you had, and I can't judge you badly for that. You need space to work out your judgments of yourself? It's yours. If you lose your way, call us and we'll come get you."

Not a chance I'd humiliate myself like that. I nodded curtly.

Thorn frowned. "Are you sure? I could give you space but still stay within sight, in case you should have need of me."

My loyal warrior with his determination to protect me. The worst part was, his insistence only made the fire inside me prickle more fiercely.

"Did you see any other shadowkind around, or people who might be working with Tempest?" I asked.

"No," he admitted.

"Then I shouldn't 'have need.' Give me a chance to breathe, all right?"

Thorn still looked reluctant, but he followed Omen and Flint into the shadows at his boss's gesture.

Tempest's dupe kept standing there, but I felt more like burning him to a crisp than doing anything to help him. I spun on my heel and stalked away from the tower.

With every block I covered, the fire inside me blazed hotter. My fingernails dug into my palms within my fists. I passed rows of stucco buildings, restaurant patios abandoned for the night, shadowed doorways and winding alleys. All the windows were dark, any inhabitants sleeping behind them.

Sleeping and blissfully unaware of the terrors being committed around them. Would they care even if they knew? The Company tortured and murdered shadowkind, but the whole rest of the human race happily told their ghost stories and made their monster movies and fueled that hatred, and maybe they'd have all joined in if they'd realized how real those creatures actually were.

Pricks and bastards, all of them. And I was too, wasn't I, wanting even for that brief moment to blame Tempest for their crimes? The real monsters were right here, all around us, laughing and living their mindless lives—

A wave of heat so huge it qualified as a tsunami rolled through me—and out of me. Flames crashed and caught all across the face of the buildings along the street ahead of me. More lashed down the backs of my arms and legs.

I dropped to the ground, smacking my limbs against the pavement to put out the fire. That did nothing for the inferno already swallowing up the entire block of shops I'd been approaching.

The fire roared, smoke billowing up. Glass shattered as the flames whipped higher. Cries rose to join it as people in the apartment building across the street woke to the blaze. They were lucky my flames hadn't headed in that direction, burning up them instead of store merchandise.

My gut twisted into one huge knot. *I* was lucky.

The heat that washed over me on the night wind woke up a renewed throbbing across all the spots I'd been burned myself. I froze, staring—at a fruit and vegetable market where all the delicacies my devourer would have swooned over had already blackened. At a musical instrument vendor where piano strings were twanging as they snapped. At a watch store where the melting glass faces in the shattered window showed I'd literally made time fry.

I'd done that. Dozens of people's livelihoods were being incinerated before my eyes because of the fury I'd let loose. And there wasn't a single thing I could do to calm those flames. Every part of me ached with the suspicion that if I reached with my power to try to control the fire, I'd only end up hurling out more.

So I followed the strategy that had served me so well in my career as a thief—I ran as fast as my feet would take me.

The crackling roar of the fire and then the swell of sirens dogged me long after I'd left the scene behind. As I dragged in each breath, a smoky smell congealed in my lungs. I pushed myself onward toward the spot where the RV was waiting, a heavier sensation welling up inside me, drowning the last of my inner fire.

I was a menace. How much more was I going to destroy before this battle was over? What if the Highest were right? What if I was a greater threat to both mortals and shadowkind than Tempest had ever been?

I should march right into the Everymobile and tell Omen to take me to the Highest to meet the fate I'd escaped so long.

I paused and shut my eyes. The hopelessness squeezed around my ribs, suffocating. But through it, the image of Tempest's gleaming slit-pupil eyes, of her broken-glass laugh, returned to me.

She'd provoked me. She'd figured out the best buttons to push and jammed on them like a six-year-old pulling an elevator prank. She'd *wanted* me to explode, probably way more than I actually had, so she could snicker about it afterward.

I hadn't wanted to hurt anyone. And if I gave up, I'd only be stepping out of Tempest's way. She'd like that, wouldn't she?

I'd been our best chance of stopping her, and maybe I'd get another chance.

I knew better what to expect from her now. The others were counting on me. I had to stick with this at least long enough to save the rest of the world from the brutal chaos she intended to inflict on it.

And after that… then maybe I'd feel I needed to be put down. But not yet. Too much was riding on me. Too many lives hung in the balance.

I raised my chin and started walking again. The air that filled my lungs tasted cleaner now. The sirens had faded away.

I intended to see this mission through to the end, and heaven help anyone who got in my way.

FOURTEEN

Sorsha

As he smoothed another dab of aloe gel over the burns on my back, Snap's hands couldn't have been gentler, but my skin was so raw that I winced anyway. He made a fierce hissing sound through his teeth.

"I'd devour the sphinx without any regrets whatsoever," he declared.

Of the many things I could have pointed the finger at Tempest for, flambéing my body wasn't one of them. This had definitely been a self-barbequing. But I couldn't quite bring myself to correct my lover, any more than I wanted to ask if anyone had heard anything about a sudden blaze in downtown Pisa last night. Denial might be a river in Egypt, but I could transport it to Italy if I wanted to, thank you very much.

None of my companions had mentioned the flashfire, but then, we'd driven right back to Rome, and they weren't exactly avid watchers of the news. And maybe they wouldn't have thought much of it anyway. A block of shops and all their contents incinerated? Just the dangers of mortal living.

I wished I could dismiss it that easily—and at the same time the thought of ever overcoming the guilt twisting through my gut horrified me.

"If that would be enough to end her, we'd toss her right to you," Omen said from the doorway, although he'd know even better than I did that Tempest wasn't likely to let anyone toss her anywhere in the first place.

I shifted where I was lying chest-down on my bed so I could pull my hair out of the way. Snap smeared more of the aloe—my second coating since I'd returned last night—across the back of my neck. "How *are* we going to come at her next, now that she won't be accepting any friendship bracelets from you?"

"I've been thinking about that while you've been sleeping," the hellhound shifter said, as if my repose had been pure laziness and not a physical necessity. "With our best option for stealth out the window, we may need to return to your old strategy of strength in numbers. Perhaps we can round up a shadowkind or two with some ability that proves to be a game-changer."

"I think our hacker friend can come up with a few more people with Company connections for me to sweet-talk in the meantime," Ruse said, sauntering past Omen into the bedroom and propping himself against the small dresser. "Might as well wring everything we can out of them."

Thorn formed out of the shadows at the base of the bed so he could get in on the conversation too. "I could attempt to speak to my wingéd brethren once more. They were hesitant to become involved, but if I could quickly see to their concerns… It might be a simple matter." He sounded doubtful, though.

"I will aid you in whatever their demands require," Flint put in, peering over Omen's shoulder.

A second later, Antic bounded in, her kindergartener-sized body jittering with excitement. "I know! You all haven't been thinking big enough. You've only been looking mortal-side. Why don't I go through a rift and see if I can round up some real help from the shadow realm?"

Omen folded his arms over his chest. "We don't need a horde of gnomes and pixies."

"Hey, a horde can get plenty done! And I can convince beings bigger than me! One of my best friends was a sea dragon, I'll have you know."

Between the lot of them, there was barely space to move in here anymore. I made a grumbling sound and reached toward the stack of clothes beside my bed. "Whose idea was it to have a strategy meeting in my bedroom—and while I'm shirtless? Let her go through the rift. There are a hell of a lot more of you on that side than here. I'm sure she'll find someone."

"Off with you, then," Omen told the imp. "We'll see how long it takes for you to find that someone."

"Aye, aye, captain!" She saluted him and scampered back out, which didn't exactly open up a whole lot more space. I tugged on my shirt, careful of the sensitive patches of healing skin on my neck, back, and arms.

Snap rested a protective hand on my hip. "You and I could go looking for shadowkind together, Peach," he said. "I can spot the ones in the shadows—but you're better at explaining how much we need their help."

Omen gave a definitive clap. "Perfect. I'll search around the city as well, Ruse will do his charming, and Thorn and Flint can barter with their not-so-angelic acquaintances. Let's attempt to meet back here by midnight. Tempest will be rushing her plans along even faster than before now that she's seen how far we're willing to go to stop her."

Thorn's mouth twisted at his orders, even though he'd suggested the plan of action. As everyone moved to leave, I caught his hand. "Give me a sec," I told Snap.

When we were alone, the massive warrior peered down at me. "Is there more I can do for you before I go, Sorsha?" His brawn had already tensed as if ready to spring to my aid.

"I was just wondering if there's anything I can do for *you*," I said, squeezing one of those impressive biceps. "From what you said before, your 'brethren' out at the Vatican gave you kind of a hard time."

The tightening of Thorn's jaw suggested he hadn't even told us the half of it. "I'm accountable for whatever tensions remain between us, and I will resolve them," he said. "It is the least I owe them."

"I don't think you owe them anything at all. It's been centuries. You didn't even do anything wrong to begin with."

"There are varying opinions on that matter. And the past is more present in its impact on them than it is for me." He sighed and lowered his head to brush his lips to mine, his voice dropping too. "Believe me, if I could simply stay by your side at all times, I'd much rather be here."

"Well, hurry back then," I said, giving him a peck in return, and headed out after him to where Snap was waiting near the door.

Normally, I couldn't have asked for a better companion for exploring a city than the devourer. He devoured new sights and experiences as avidly as he did his favorite fruits—and human souls.

For the first hour or so, that expectation held true. Snap peered with wide eyes at the looming ruins of antiquity in the Forum, listened in with eager little hums as a tour guide described the ancient activities that had taken place there, and sampled the energies around the structures with his forked tongue when no other tourists were near enough to see.

But we didn't find any shadowkind to beg to lend a hand—the couple that Snap sensed in the shadows darted off as soon as he paid any attention to them. As we passed a gaggle of college-age sightseers who jostled against me without so much as a glance back, let alone an apology, the devourer's usual bright demeanor started to dim.

"The shadowkind are nervous of all the mortals around," he said. "Humans haven't been all that kind to this place, even though it's their own history. I can't taste anything from the times when all this was whole and celebrated… Too many impressions of people chipping away at it, bumping against it without watching, carving words that make them laugh into it to show how *little* they think of it… Why would they do that?"

The fraught confusion in his voice brought a lump into my throat. "We don't always appreciate our history," I said. "It's harder when we don't live anywhere near as long as shadowkind do, you know. For the people seeing this now, the society who used this place was gone before any of our great-great-great-however many times grandparents were born. It doesn't feel totally real."

"I didn't exist that long ago, and I still find it fascinating."

I bumped my arm against his playfully. "Well, that's part of what makes you so special."

The compliment lit him up again, but only for a little while. We failed to gain any supporters from the creatures lurking near the Pantheon and the grand museums. Clouds clotted in the sky as we approached Trevi Fountain, and Snap shivered with the fading of the sunlight.

"Someone carved that whole sculpture without any magic at all," I said over the burbling of the water. "Pretty amazing."

"It is," Snap agreed, but the brightness of his voice diminished too. "They built so many things… and so many of them wish no being like me ever got to see them. They would be upset that I enjoy all the fruits and the honey and…" His brow knit. "*Most* humans would want us dead if they knew of us, wouldn't they? That's why we keep our existence secret."

"Well, maybe not *dead*," I started, but I didn't really know how to follow that up. Because, yeah, it was possible the majority of humans *would* wish to see beings like my monstrous lovers slaughtered if they found out shadowkind existed. I didn't want to lie to him. But the hurt in his eyes and the gloom creeping into his words made my heart ache.

The Company hadn't killed Snap while they'd held him captive, but how much was he really *Snap* if they destroyed his sense of wonder?

A spurt of flame lanced through my insides. I coughed and barely managed to swallow it down so it seared nothing but my stomach. For my devourer's sake and my own, I groped for a lyric to spin this conversation in a lighter direction.

"Come on. We've still got to find some shadowkind to make our appeal to." I tugged on Snap's elbow and sang, "And if I only could, I'd make an eel maraud, and I'd bet him with all our aces."

"I don't think an eel would be very helpful against Tempest," Snap said, but it was with a smile to show he hadn't really taken me seriously. Good. Between two wingéd with maybe a couple more on their way, Omen dealing with a very solid specter from his awful past, and me burning innocents left and right, we had enough sombreness hanging over our group already.

Perking Snap up didn't help us find any new allies, though. We returned to the Everymobile just shy of midnight. Omen emerged from the shadows before we'd quite reached the doorway and motioned

Snap inside. "I need to speak with our mortal," he said, without even bothering to ask how our quest had gone. I guessed our failure was obvious enough.

Snap bristled with a brief flare of neon green in his eyes, but his loyalty to the shadowkind who'd called him to this cause was clearly at war with his devotion to me. He paused and then said, in a careful but firm voice, "What do you want with her now?"

Omen sighed. "I'm just going to talk to her, honestly. If anyone's going to haul her off to some dire end, it won't be me. Aren't you convinced of that yet?"

The devourer looked chagrined, but only slightly. "I didn't think you'd do it in the first place," he informed the hellhound shifter, but after one more caress of my arm, he vanished into the RV.

The early autumn night was warm enough, but Omen's solemn expression sent an icy quiver through my gut. "What's the big secret?"

He guided me off to the side of the RV. Not all of Rome was so scenic—the rundown suburb where we were hiding out smelled like tar rather than gelato, and a loose door somewhere in the distance was creaking on its hinges in the breeze. The Everymobile added to the atmosphere with the rotating hubcaps it'd recently produced, which rattled like hamster wheels as they spun endlessly on.

"It's not a secret," Omen said. "I just thought I should tell you first so there's no time for misunderstandings. I've decided I'm going to approach the Highest again."

Even after what he'd just said to Snap and everything he'd said to me in the past few days, my pulse stuttered. Before I could say anything, he held up his hands. "I won't even mention you. I'm going to tell them what I've found out about Tempest and see if they'll change my final order to taking her down rather than finding 'Ruby'. And whether they will or not, they might lend some brawn to our cause. They did want to destroy her enough to sic a whole bunch of their lackeys on her before."

It made sense—enough sense that Omen obviously hadn't been able to talk himself out of doing it, as much as I could tell he disliked the idea of chatting with the beings that had put him in their leash.

"That would certainly be helpful," I said. "It's about time they pitched in rather than pitching fits."

The corner of Omen's mouth quirked upward. "We'll see. In any case, nothing ventured, nothing gained. They should have no way of discerning that I've had contact with the mortal-shadowkind hybrid they've been searching for. I didn't want you spending any time worrying about that, even if it was only the time it took to answer half a dozen questions from our companions."

I set my hands on my hips. "Me, worry?" I teased. "Do you know me at all?" But the truth was, he did know me. Enough that I had to add, "Thank you. For worrying about whether I'd worry."

He made a dismissive sound, but then he ran his fingers along my jaw to draw me to him. He kissed me hard, the intensity of it sparking all kinds of flames beneath my skin, but only the pleasant kind.

Why couldn't my inner fire always feel this delicious?

When he let me go, another ache formed in my chest to join the one Snap's disillusionment had provoked. I couldn't help curling my fingers around Omen's before he could drop his hand. "Make sure you come back."

He gave me a full smile then. "No one's managed to crush me yet, as many as have wanted to. You're not getting rid of me that easily, Disaster."

I laughed and followed him into the Everymobile so he could tell the others where he was going, but underneath my good humored response, the ache remained.

How had I gotten to the point with this man where the thought of *anyone* getting rid of him made me want to rain fire from the sky?

FIFTEEN

Omen

It said something about how eager the Highest were for any news of the mission they'd sent me on that the slathering goblin who stopped me at the edge of their vast hollow came barreling back mere minutes later with an urgent rasp that rippled through the clotted darkness around us. "They'll see you now. Come on!"

That welcome was a far cry from my last visit, when they'd left me waiting for what had turned out to be more than a day. And that time *they'd* summoned me. I'd just have to hope they'd be too distracted by the news I'd brought to sulk over the news I hadn't.

As far as I was concerned, I had no idea where a hybrid being named Ruby might live. The only human-shadowkind mishmash of a being I knew was named Sorsha, and the Highest hadn't asked me about anything to do with *her*.

Besides, Tempest had ruined about a realm's worth of lives already. You couldn't find a threat much clearer than that.

The goblin followed me all the way into the yawning cavern, where the potent if ponderous energies of the Highest beings washed over me with an itch through my shadow-side body and a twinge around my neck. They never quite let me forget the hold they had over me. I'd have preferred not to have their slathering lackey witness it, but it wasn't my place to send him off. Or to take a good chomp out of his throat, which would have accomplished nearly the same thing with much more satisfaction.

Shadowkind couldn't die in our shadow forms, but we could certainly be maimed to the point that we might as well be dead.

The Highest's penetrating attention weighed down on me even more heavily than before. The goblin dipped into a sort of groveling bow as if looking for praise for managing the incredible task of walking me the short distance from the entrance. Self-respect was not a quality the behemoths looked for in their minions.

The Highest ignored him. "What word have you brought, hellhound?" one of them demanded, her hollow bellow of a voice echoing through every particle of my being.

Oh, I had a whole lot of words for them, but I'd better choose which ones I actually said carefully. I gathered myself. "I have not encountered a being that goes by the name Ruby, but my search has turned up an even graver danger to both realms. The shadowkind you believed you dispatched ages ago, the one whose vicious tricks I admit I sometimes assisted with, has survived after all. Tempest the sphinx lives, and she has a plot more immense than ever before underway."

I couldn't make much of the muttering that passed between the pompous leviathans. "It cannot be so," another said. "Our warriors tore her to shreds. They reported as much—they would not have lied."

"I doubt they knew they were lying," I said. "I'd imagine she performed one of her tricks on them too, to make them think she'd died or that they had her at all. But whatever they tore up, it either survived despite their ravaging or it wasn't her. I've spoken to her face to face. And if anyone should recognize that menace, it's me."

One of the massive beings loomed closer with a thicker, harsher surge of energy. "How can we know this isn't *you* playing tricks on us?"

For all my own power, it took the tensing of every muscle in my body for me to resist the urge to cringe. As easily as I could have ripped the goblin—who was still watching all this, gaping dopily, the dimwit—into a pulp so mangled it would have taken centuries for it to reassemble into his proper being, the Highest could flay me to shreds even faster. The only reason they hadn't in the first place, all those years ago when we'd made our deal, was that they'd believed I was of more use to them in one piece. I had to make sure they continued to believe that.

"What possible reason could I have for making this up?" I asked, holding my ground. "I'm on the verge of completing my deal with you. No good could come from reminding you of my old association with the sphinx if she didn't pose a real threat now."

The rumbling that followed sounded at least slightly agreeable. My hackles came down, but I stayed braced where I was.

"What is this plot the sphinx is carrying out?" the first speaker demanded. "How much danger could she pose when no word of her has reached us all this time until now?"

"That's probably what she wants you to think. She wanted to lull you into complacency." A prod to their dignity couldn't hurt. "And this scheme is so dangerous precisely *because* she's spent so much time putting the pieces in place. She intends to see as many mortals dead as she can—and knowing her and her methods, it could be more than remain alive in the entire mortal realm after she's through—and to sicken and kill nearly every shadowkind who's ventured mortal-side as well."

Another of the Highest spoke up. "You've mentioned this sickness before. You said there were mortals creating such a thing."

"Apparently Tempest has been directing those mortals—and ensuring it'll come around to bite them in the ass," I said. "But she made it clear to me that shadowkind will die too, and she doesn't care how many. I'd imagine if she can find a way to have the sickness spread all the way to *your* doorstep, she'll do her best to make that happen. She's carrying a bit of a grudge after the whole nearly-slaughtered-by-wingéd incident."

The gawking goblin gave a shudder. Really he should have been more worried about himself. Somehow I suspected his constitution wasn't up to resisting Tempest's manufactured disease.

The grandiose goliaths muttered to each other some more. It'd been a thin line between offending them by suggesting they were vulnerable and driving home the threat Tempest posed as hard as I could. They sounded as if they were taking my report at least somewhat seriously.

"You have been in much communication with the sphinx," one said finally. "We presume you convey this information to us with some concept of how she might be brought down."

For once, they'd played right into my hands. I smiled as well as I could in my hazy state and bowed my head. "Of course. It would be an honor to not only present the problem but solve it for you as well. I do think, though, that combating a being of such experience and proven power goes well beyond a typical walk in the park. I thought perhaps you might want to adjust your orders to account for that."

"In what way?"

They were going to make me spell it out, were they? Typical. "Your original instruction was for me to notify you of Ruby's location—but this Ruby hasn't caused any noticeable trouble that anyone's been aware of in decades. Tempest, on the other hand, is days away from unleashing the worst catastrophe any shadowkind has wrought on the realms. If you would rather I pursue her, I would happily take responsibility for—"

A booming laugh cut me off—and reverberated down to my bones, turning what shadowy gut I had into water. What in darkness's name was *funny* about my proposition? The question rose up with a rankling irritation, but at the same time I hesitated to ask.

I didn't need to. The same being who'd laughed turned a waft of attention onto me that fell even thicker and darker than before. "Of course you would be happy to do so. This has been your scheme all along, hasn't it? You had to invent the sphinx's resurrection so we would take your crusade more seriously. Did you really think we would fail to see through such a deception?"

Well, I probably wouldn't have if it'd actually been a deception. Now that he put it that way, it was difficult to avoid seeing how it'd appear to be a trick of my own to someone who hadn't stood face to face with Tempest in the recent days.

"No," I said, working to keep as much irritation as possible out of my voice. "Which is why I wouldn't have attempted it as a deception. She really is alive and pulling the strings behind the Company of Light. I'd be happy to take a few of your minions to meet her to confirm, although I can't promise she won't chew them up and spit them out much worse off than they were when they arrived."

"I see no reason why that should be necessary," another of the Highest intoned. "Your intentions are transparent enough. You will resume following your original directive, and you will return to the mortal realm to see about carrying it out *now*. We have waited long enough."

They might have waited decades to find "Ruby", but they'd only asked *me* to take up the search a couple of weeks ago. I guessed I didn't get any benefit of their patience.

I wasn't the type to back down without some sort of fight. "If something isn't done to stop Tempest, then there might not be anything left in the realms that's worth saving from whatever you think this Ruby is going to do. Do you really want to leave me in the position to be able to say I told you so?"

The murmur that passed between them sounded unsettled, but not concerned enough. "If the sphinx truly poses such a threat, then attend to her as you see fit. We have seen no evidence of it."

They hadn't seen any evidence that Sorsha was a threat either, other than what they'd made up in their own heads about human-shadowkind hybrids. I bit my tongue against flinging that point at them, though. It wouldn't be good for her or me to appear too invested in her.

The damned puffed-up giants. What could I say that would get through their incredibly dense skulls?

The simpering goblin was already darting to my side. "I can see the hellhound away from you so he won't bother you any further, your greatnesses," he said.

"Back off," I snapped, far less worried about what *he* thought of me, and advanced a little closer to the Highest. "Do you want to be known as the ones who prevented a catastrophe of immense proportions or the ones who stood by and let it happen? I'm giving you the chance to be the former. And believe me, if Tempest rains down all her rage on the rest of us, I'm not going to stay quiet about your complacency."

That was a threat in itself, and a gamble I nearly regretted. A wallop of chilling fury hit me, tossing me backward like a tidal wave, head over feet. I shook myself, regaining my bearings and confirming I'd kept possession of all my limbs, and the blustering fools shoved me again. The impression of a choke collar around my throat yanked painfully tight.

Several of their echoing voices rang out together. "Begone, hellhound, and we will hear no more of this ridiculousness from you."

There was a thing or three I could have said about who was being ridiculous here, but I wasn't saving anyone if I ended up in tiny pieces scattered across the entire shadow realm. I spoke through gritted teeth. "As you command, oh Highest ones."

I loped off with only one thing I hadn't possessed before this visit: the certainty that in this war, no matter what else came of it, my companions and I were utterly alone.

SIXTEEN

Sorsha

"I mean, it's really no surprise, right?" I said when Omen had finished filling us in on his conversation with the Highest. "We already knew they're obnoxious and overly obsessed with me."

"Yes, silly of me to think they might be concerned by news about the re-emergence of a being they'd already decided was so dangerous they put her to death centuries ago." Omen rolled his eyes toward the Everymobile's ceiling, but despite the dryness of his tone, I could tell how frustrated he was with the ancient shadowkind that held him in their sway.

"We've taken on the Company of Light without any help from the Highest before," Snap said, stroking my hair where he was sitting next to me on the sofa-bench. "They don't seem to know much of anything anyway."

At his other side, Ruse made a vaguely obscene gesture in the general direction of the shadowy overlords. "Hard for them to have much awareness of a realm they've never bothered to venture into."

"Right." As Pickle curled up tighter on my lap, I scratched his belly with careful fingers, putting on my best impression of being totally okay with all this. The thought of those overbearing beings ignoring

Omen's totally valid warnings—of them declaring me a much more urgent threat than a centuries-old genocidal maniac who'd already been responsible for innumerable deaths of humans and shadow creatures alike—definitely wasn't stoking the angry fire inside me to uncomfortable heights. And if I decided that fire wasn't there, then it definitely couldn't justify their insistence that I be exterminated.

If pretending away reality worked for the Highest, why shouldn't it work for me?

But heat I couldn't totally will out of my consciousness prickled under my skin. I jerked my hand from Pickle's side as a particularly sharp flare seared across my palm. I'd already scorched the little dragon once, and it'd taken days for him to forgive me. If even *he* wasn't safe around me...

He was. I had it under control. With a few deep breaths and an image of the ocean I summoned into my head, the flames were retreating.

"No one's heard from Thorn yet?" I asked.

Omen shook his head. "I've yet to convince our wingéd companion of the wonders of cell phones. He did say he might need to lend his former comrades a hand before they'd agree to help us. I suppose we'll see whether it was worth the bargain when they show up."

He couldn't disguise his skepticism, but it was hard to mind when I was pretty skeptical myself. The warrior could take a physical beating without a wince, but from the way he'd looked after his first talk with those two lingering wingéd, they'd mauled something in his spirit. He'd felt so guilty about not being there for the final battle, about not *dying* there... How much would they shake his faith in himself this time?

"Once he's back, my hacker back in Paris did turn up an interesting lead we might want to pursue," Ruse said. "He's found an interesting pattern of—"

Cutting the incubus off, a swell of triumphant trombones blared through the RV with a multicolored flash of the overhead lights. As the electric panels blinked from pink to orange to green as if we were in a very cramped dance club, they caught on three figures who'd just appeared by the front door.

Antic hopped up and down with a guffaw at the unexpected

welcome. Behind her, Gisele and Bow stared around them, the delicate unicorn shifter and the burly centaur looking equally bewildered.

Uh oh. As much use as we'd been putting the Everymobile to, it actually belonged to the two equines, who'd generously lent it to us to continue our quest. *When* they'd lent it to us, it hadn't been sprouting odd instruments from its roof or producing music at random moments. It seemed the vehicle was happy to have them back, but I wasn't sure how happy they'd be about the way it was expressing that joy.

Omen dashed past them to jab at the buttons on the dashboard, with a deeper grimace when he took in the smashed spot where Thorn had "disabled" the radio not long ago. Gisele's doe-eyed gaze followed him, her rainbow-streaked hair swishing over her shoulder.

"What did you do to the Everymobile?" she said, her melodic tinkle of a voice rising over the cacophony. "I thought you were going to take it for a road trip, not renovate it."

Omen managed to shut up the trumpets, but the lights kept flashing strobe-like over us. The hellhound shifter had expressed plenty of disdain for the equines when they'd first joined us, but since then they'd proven themselves capable fighters and generous allies. Worthy of guilty tensing of his expression as he groped for an explanation.

I managed to suppress a smile at seeing him put in his place by shadowkind he'd once sneered at, but I couldn't help tossing a remark of my own his way. "Yeah, Omen, why don't you tell them all about what you've put *Darlene* through?"

Bow ran a hand through his thick mohawk mane of chestnut hair, still staring befuddled at his former mortal-side home. "Who's Darlene?"

Omen shot a glare at me. Served him right for naming things that didn't belong to him. I leaned back in Snap's embrace to watch as the hellhound shifter straightened his posture.

"Never mind that." He waved to the RV's interior. "We didn't do this on purpose. We could hardly drive her across the ocean, and… she didn't come through the rifts quite the same as when she went in."

"I think the word you're looking for is, 'Sorry'," Ruse supplied helpfully.

Omen glowered at him too, but a hint of sheepishness had come into his expression that looked odd but unaccountably adorable on the powerful shifter's face. He turned back to the equines. "My apologies. I had no idea what effect the shadow realm would have on your vehicle. It's a little more... unique than it was before, but I can at least say that it seems to function just as well as it always did."

"I guess that's the important thing." Gisele peered up at the lights, which had finally faded back to their typical white glow. "Maybe some of the changes are even an improvement. I could get into the dance club vibe."

As if on cue, her partner grasped her hand and spun her around. The unicorn shifter giggled as she twirled, and some of the tension in my chest loosened. I'd forgotten the mood these two set with their easy-going presence—and there was a relief in seeing Gisele fully recovered from the injuries the Company's soldiers had dealt to her. You'd never have known that the last time we'd seen her, weeks ago, she hadn't been able to stand up without Bow's help.

"How'd you manage to track these two down?" I asked Antic. The imp had never met the equines, having joined our merry band after they'd headed back to the shadow realm to speed up Gisele's recovery.

Antic leapt up to sit on the edge of the table and grinned over her shoulder at me. "It was easy-peasy. I was ping-pong balling all over the place, talking up the cause, and they tracked *me* down. I figured there couldn't be any better allies to bring back than ones you already knew."

Bow popped open one of the cupboards. "We've still got our grass and our *grass*! I wonder what the trip to the shadow realm did to that stuff."

Omen cleared his throat. "Maybe not the best time to find out just yet."

"There are fresh strawberries in the fridge," Snap offered generously. "They're very good."

Bow retrieved the delicacies, and a moment later we were all chowing down tart berry sweetness—except Omen, who watched the whole to-do with his mouth set in a crooked line. The centaur gave Snap a thumbs up while he chewed. "Excellent pickings. Man, did I miss mortal food."

A bright smile crossed the devourer's face. He popped another strawberry into his mouth and watched avidly as the equines recounted one of their early battles with the Company soldiers for Antic's benefit, complete with physical re-enactments of key moments. Snap glanced at me and then Ruse. "It's good to have them back, isn't it?"

"The imp did well," Ruse said with amusement, and gave Snap a nudge to the shoulder. "It's good to see *you* looking this cheerful, my friend. Have we not been enough fun lately to keep your spirits as shiny as usual?"

Snap blinked at him with a hint of chagrin. "I didn't expect this mission to be 'fun'. Have I done something that bothered you?"

"No, no, not at all. I just remember the good old days when all I had to do was mix up some bubbles in the sink to get that kind of smile out of you."

The devourer beamed. "I do still like the bubbles. You stopped making them."

The incubus chuckled and gave the other man's shoulder another squeeze. "All right, something to add to my to-do list."

It *was* good seeing Snap more his sunny self again—and to see Ruse enjoying it too. The incubus might have worried about how much he could pitch in compared to the others, but he'd always felt like an essential part of this group. Maybe he was settling back into that sense of belonging after his moment of doubt.

I enjoyed the comradery next to me for a few seconds longer before the equines brought the conversation back around to our present situation.

"We'd have brought Cori too," Gisele said, "but after all that time in his cage, he was hesitant to make another trip mortal-side. As soon as we've wiped the floor with the Company, we'll tell him the coast is clear."

Omen straightened up from where he'd propped himself against the wall. "It may be more difficult than a simple wiping. We've uncovered some unfortunate information about the powers behind the Company."

The unicorn shifter's eyebrows shot up. "In what way?"

I could tell Omen was reluctant to get into that subject, but it wasn't as if we could bring our returned allies on board without giving them the full picture. He dragged in a rough breath. "There's a former associate of mine, a shadowkind of great strength, who's been pulling their strings behind the scenes. We *almost* had them beaten, but she intervened in their defense. It seems she cares very little what shadowkind get hurt along the way."

The fiery fury that had risen inside me when he'd talked about the Highest's dismissal stirred again. As he went on with his report of everything we'd heard from and experienced with Tempest, the flames danced higher despite my best efforts.

A searing sensation spread across the small of my back. Was that a whiff of burnt leather?

I couldn't let the sphinx get the better of me—especially when she wasn't even in the goddamned vicinity. I set my teeth, but every time I managed to settle my inner fire, Omen mentioned some other detail that set it sparking violently again.

He hadn't mentioned anything about my difficulties with my powers or what I was to the equines. Presumably he was going to keep the most damning aspects on the down low like he had with Antic and Flint. I'd rather not make a vivid demonstration of my habit of setting myself on fire. It wasn't as if I needed to hear this rundown anyway, considering I'd been there for most of it.

I gave Snap a kiss on the cheek so he wouldn't worry and got up. The bedroom I'd claimed as my own felt like the safest spot right now. If I moved to leave the RV completely, that would inevitably raise questions.

I might have singed the covers a tad when I flopped down on them, but without Omen's voice and Tempest's name in my ears, the heat inside me started to dwindle. It wasn't much more than glowing embers when a knock sounded on the door.

Ruse's voice carried through, lightly cajoling. "Miss Blaze?"

I weighed my options and decided I was better off inviting him in than turning him away. For all his carefree airs, the incubus had proven he could worry plenty too, given the right provocation.

"What's up?" I asked, pushing myself into a sitting position.

He slipped right in through the shadows without further prompting, as I'd figured he would. Shadowkind and their very lax concept of privacy. Snap wouldn't even have knocked.

When he saw me on the bed, empty-handed, Ruse paused. "Were you resting? I didn't mean to wake you up. I got the sense you might have left because something had irked you. Not because I looked inside your head," he added quickly, with a flash of a smile. "I *have* gotten to know you rather well in many other ways."

I had to smile back at that remark. A surge of affection filled my chest, drowning out the last of the prickling flames. The incubus did take certain requests for privacy very seriously, knowing how important they were to me, even now that I'd already given him permission to read my mental state once.

He'd wanted so badly to be there for me, to protect me. I didn't know if it was possible for any of my shadowkind lovers to really do the latter, but maybe I should give him the chance to do the former.

I motioned for him to sit beside me. "Not irked. Well, okay, Tempest as a whole is pretty irksome. But I'm totally okay with feeling that way about her. It's just, when I think about what she's doing—all the awfulness she's caused and still wants to—my powers get pretty, ah, heated up."

Ruse brushed a few strands of hair back from my cheek, offering so much tenderness in that simple gesture. "I'd have thought that was a good thing. Plenty of fire to rain down on her when the time comes."

"Well, yeah, but the time isn't now, and—" Something in me balked at admitting the rest. Sweet simpering sycamores, when had I become a *coward* of all things?

I forced the words out. "The Highest think I might end up destroying even more than Tempest will. I know Omen's decided it won't happen—I know none of you want to believe I could be capable of it—but when all that fire builds up inside me, sometimes I'm not sure they're wrong. I'm *not* in control, not completely."

"Hmm. I'd make a comment about how much I enjoy you letting loose, but I don't think that's what you're looking to hear."

I elbowed Ruse, and he chuckled. Then he slipped his arm around me and tugged me to him, dipping his head so his lips brushed my temple as he spoke.

"You've accomplished a lot of impossible things in the last few months, Miss Blaze. You've conjured love in an incubus, desire in a devourer, gentleness in a wingéd warrior, and mercy—along with a few other things, it's becoming clear—in a hellhound. Proving a riddling sphinx and some stuffy Highest bastards wrong will be the least of your accomplishments when you're through."

He spoke so confidently and with such affection that I almost believed him. Enough that even if he hadn't melted my doubts, I could shove them far enough aside to tease my hand into his hair. "Suddenly I can think of a few things I'd like to accomplish right now."

As if to punctuate that statement, a panel popped open on the ceiling above us, a plastic birdie on a spring swinging out. "Cuckoo!" it said cheerfully, like a demented clock. "Cuckoo!"

Poor Darlene. Ruse and I exchanged a glance and burst into laughter. With weirdly buoyed spirits, I drew him down with me on the bed, pulling his mouth to mine.

Here was hoping that if I soaked up all of his faith in me, I could make that certainty my own.

SEVENTEEN

Sorsha

Ruse had only gotten in a few—incredibly delicious—kisses when Bow's voice carried through the bedroom door. "Thorn! Good to see you again too."

The incubus let out a stifled groan, teasing his lips from my jaw down my neck before raising his head. "Interrupted again. I look forward to the day when sphinx and Company alike have been tossed out with the trash so I can enjoy you at my leisure, but for now I think we'd better find out what the lunk has come back with."

Every part of me except the heat pooled between my thighs agreed. I stole one more kiss for good measure, and then paused. "You know, if you ever *need* to feed, all you have to do is—"

Ruse held up his hand to stop me. His mouth flattened at an odd angle for a second before he recovered his usual smirk. "I have no problem speaking up. Trust me, you've kept me quite satisfied, my lovely thief."

But would I always? A strange sensation ran through my chest, twinges of concern and jealousy clashing. I swallowed down the latter. Ruse was what he was, and I accepted that. I wouldn't ask this man to starve just to indulge my human notions of fidelity. And really, who was I to fuss about fidelity in the first place, when I'd been canoodling with three other men right here in this RV?

"If I ever don't—I mean, if you need more than one woman's energies to keep you sated—I understand. Cubi kind have got to cubi and all that."

Maybe I hadn't shoved that jealousy down quite far enough. Despite my attempt at nonchalance, Ruse's warm eyes softened as he took me in. He trailed his fingers down my cheek and drew me into a kiss so deep it took my breath away.

"I appreciate the sentiment," he murmured against my lips afterward. "But you don't ever have to worry about that."

Because I really was enough or because he'd be discreet enough that I'd never know? I guessed it didn't make much difference either way.

"Good," I said, and twined my fingers with his on our way out into the Everymobile's main room.

I stepped out expecting to see both of our stalwart wingéd looming in the hallway, but it was only Thorn's considerable bulk filling the space, no sign of Flint. While Thorn's expression was often grim enough to send lesser creatures fleeing in terror, now his chiseled features held shades of pain and shame as well. My stomach twisted at the sight.

"—decided to stay with them and continue the search," he was just saying to Omen. "But my first responsibility is to you—I wouldn't be mortal-side at all if not for your mission."

A crackle of flame rippled through me. I managed to hold it in as I marched over, but I couldn't keep the searing sting out of my tone. "Those asshole wingéd tried to make you think you owed *them* more?"

Thorn's head drooped like I'd only seen once before—after we'd first gotten Omen out of the Company prison, when the shifter had laid into him for not orchestrating that jailbreak sooner. Oh, my dearest warrior. Tearing heads off was more his style than mine, but right then I wouldn't have minded dropkicking a few wingéd skulls into the stratosphere. I loved his loyalty and his sense of honor, but sometimes they didn't serve him well.

"The remains of one of my closest comrades were stolen by a pack of griffins," he said. "I attempted to locate it on the request of my brethren. I came upon several griffins and did battle, but I could not discover the object I was looking for in their midst. It remains adrift."

No doubt he had fresh scars to add to those that mottled his face and body from that battling. My hands clenched. "They should be grateful you did even that much for them. How is it *your* fault that they didn't take good enough care of this dude's ashes or whatever? Why don't they go fight a horde of griffins if it means so much to them?"

Even more strain crept into Thorn's voice. "As I related before, the wars of long ago dealt permanent damage to their forms."

Omen let out a dismissive growl. "That doesn't give them carte blanche to appropriate the one wingéd I actually like. I hope you told them to shove it."

The tensing of Thorn's stance told me he hadn't stated his refusal in terms quite that blatant. "I informed them that my duty required I return to you and discuss the situation."

And then possibly leave to go back to them? The emotion that shot through me at that thought wasn't just anger but a jab of cold-edged refusal. I didn't want to go into the battles *we* faced ahead without our warrior by my side.

"If those pompous asses think they have any claim—" the shifter started, clearly building up to a full-on rant complete with houndish snarls, but his tone had already made Thorn turn even more rigid. Lambasting Thorn's people wasn't the way to reassure him—it'd only make him feel he was betraying them even more if he stayed.

I strode right up to the wingéd, nudging Omen to the side with my elbow to cut off his spiel before he could get any more of it out. "Take a walk with me?" I said to Thorn. "I think you've had enough people telling you what to do today. I'd like to listen to what *you're* thinking."

Omen muttered something disparaging under his breath but didn't outright protest. Thorn hesitated and then offered me a smile that was small and tight but at least *there*. "Perhaps that would help me sort out my thoughts, m'lady. I would be glad of having your ear."

I followed him out of the Everymobile. We meandered into a

stretch of parkland, patchy with weeds and holding a playground no one could actually use thanks to the broken ladder on the slide, the swing tossed over its support beam, and a teeter totter that had toppled right over. Tonight was cooler than past nights, the stars and moon clouded over. I walked close to Thorn to soak up the warmth his brawny frame exuded.

"It may be that I was right in questioning our wars of the past," the warrior said after a stretch of silence. "But that doesn't absolve me of all responsibility for my actions. I *did* leave at a time when others ended up falling in battle or meeting similarly harsh fates... My doubts meant leaving them to suffer."

"They might have met the exact same fates even if you'd been there," I pointed out. "You can't know how much of a difference you would have made. They were all just as strong and fierce as you can be, right? Maybe it'd have happened the exact same except you wouldn't be here to feel guilty about it either."

"That is possible. I won't deny it." The breeze hissed tauntingly through the leaves of a nearby tree, and he frowned at it. "I cannot say how much of a difference I'm making to Omen's cause either, though, can I? Why should he deserve my aid more than my brethren of old?"

"It's not just for him, is it? What good does it do chasing after the remains of someone who's already *dead*? Tackling Tempest could mean saving millions more lives than were lost way back when."

"But if I take the time to make up for past failures now, perhaps I can bring new allies to that cause as well."

"Okay, when you put it that way, I can see it's not an easy dilemma." I stopped in a clearing between the scattered trees and glanced up at Thorn. In the faint light that traveled this far from distant street lamps, his white-blond hair looked closer to silver, his tan skin duskier, his dark eyes utterly black. A furrow had creased his forehead. An ache squeezed my heart, watching him struggle.

He gazed down at me. "I have other reasons for wishing to stay, of course. Reasons that are much more selfish."

When he took on that low, impassioned tone, my pulse fluttered with giddiness despite my concern for him. "And I have plenty of selfishness too. But I wouldn't want you to stay because I put the screws to you and then have you feeling guilty about it."

"So you aren't going to make an argument on your own behalf?"

I inhaled sharply. "I want you with us. I want you with *me*. But I'll muddle through this either way. What I'd really like is for you to figure out what you think is the right course of action for *you*. Not what will make anyone else happy. What you'll be able to look back on that will let you know right in here that you made the best decision you could." I gave him a gentle poke to the middle of his chest.

Thorn caught my hand and curled his fingers around it. His touch and the intentness of his gaze sent heat coursing over my skin. "I suppose I haven't considered that factor often in the past. What *I* think is best. What orders I would give myself, if it were up to me."

"It is up to you, you know. You're always the boss of yourself in the end, as much as I'm sure Omen—or those other wingéd—would like you to think otherwise."

"But how does one untangle one's sense of responsibility to others from one's own judgment?"

"Now you're getting into the hard questions," I teased, and lifted my other hand to caress his square jaw. "I can think of a few ways you seem to be different from the average wingéd. Maybe getting in touch with the more selfish side of yourself will help you figure things out?"

Thorn hummed as if in agreement and leaned in to kiss me. The passion of his lips claiming mine reverberated through my body. I gripped the collar of his tunic, pushing myself up on my toes to meet him with all the enthusiasm I could offer in return.

He drew back just an inch, his breath washing over me with his musky scent. "If you asked me to stay for you, I would, you know. You have proven yourself the most loyal comrade I could ask for, and so much more than that as well… I don't think I could bring myself to deny you, no matter what else was at stake."

I swallowed hard, the vehemence in his words ringing through me and waking up an answering devotion. "And if you told me you had to leave to believe you've fulfilled your purpose, I *wouldn't* ask you, as much as I might want to. I'd rather have you at peace somewhere else than torn up by guilt right next to me. Obviously if I can have both the peace *and* the proximity…"

He chuckled and kissed me again. Then he murmured, "I want to show you something, m'lady."

Before I could ask what, his body shifted against mine. His chest expanded, his body enlarging to even greater heights of brawn. A ruddy glow like embers still smoldering in a fireplace lit in his eyes. His great black wings unfurled from his back, their feathers warbling in the breeze.

He captured my mouth again with a smoky edge beneath his musky flavor, and at the same time he caught me in his arms, one solid mass of corded muscle across my shoulder blades and the other around my ass, lifting me against him. With a majestic flap of his wings, his feet left the ground too.

Between the kiss and the sensation of soaring upward, dizziness washed through me, but I was more than happy to embrace it. As the wind licked sharper over us, I kissed Thorn hard through the stutter of my heartbeat.

He hefted me higher against him, and my legs came up instinctively to wrap around his waist. A firm bulge there was no mistaking came to rest against my sex. I dragged in a breath shaky with desire, gripped the thick strands of his hair, and let my tongue slip from my mouth to tangle with his.

Our bodies rocked together with each sweep of his wings, creating a torturous friction that brought a gasp to my lips. Looping my arms around Thorn's neck, I dared to glance down. The view knocked all the air from my lungs.

Holy mother of meteors, we were really flying. The city sprawled below me in a vast spread of twinkling lights, some of them coursing along roadways and others blinking off even as I watched as people turned in for the night.

Who needed stars when you could have a vision like this *below* you?

My life had never been more literally in Thorn's hands. If I'd slipped from his grasp, no spurt of fiery power could have stopped me from making an excellent impression of a pancake, splat on the ground below. But even as my pulse beat faster while I took in the scene we were soaring over, not a hint of that adrenaline was panic. I had a hell of a lot more faith in the warrior's strength than in my hocus pocus.

"It's spectacular." I brought my gaze back to my lover, to the smoldering wingéd visage that was even more awe-inspiring to me than the sights beneath us, and my throat constricted.

I didn't want him to leave us, for however long he might feel he needed to—now or ever. This brutal, valiant monster was like no one I'd ever met or would again. And despite the turmoil he'd been going through, he'd offered up this moment just for me.

I touched his face, tracing my thumb over his lips before meeting his eyes again. I wasn't trying to sway his choice, but he deserved to know exactly what he was choosing between, didn't he?

"I love you," I said.

The words came out so quietly I was afraid they'd be lost in the wind. But the flare of the glow in Thorn's eyes left no doubt that he'd heard them. Even with the unearthly reverb that came into his voice, his response came out ragged with emotion. "And I you, Sorsha."

He kissed me so hard my head spun—or maybe it was that we really were spinning with another flap of his wings, spiraling even higher into the sky. A waft of chilly air licked across my neck, but it only created a perfect contrast with the heat coursing between us.

Thorn's lips traveled from my mouth to my jaw and down the side of my neck, sparking pleasure everywhere they touched. His resonant voice sent giddy tremors over my skin. "You would not hate me instead if I left?"

I shook my head against him, soaking in everything I could of the being that held me. "The fact that you wouldn't let love stop you from fulfilling your responsibilities is part of what makes you who you are. It's an honor to mean so much to you that I'd factor in at all."

He made a rumbling sound low in his throat and managed to maneuver his hand to stroke over my breast. Bliss quivered through my chest with the swivel of his palm against my nipple. "How could my absence not wound you? It's hard enough for me to think of it."

"It would hurt, but that's okay." I thought of that moment in Omen's cave when I'd jumped between him and Thorn and thrown my life on the line to save them both. "Sometimes the right thing hurts. It's just that the wrong thing would hurt more. And whatever you do, I know it's a measure of what you need to be the man you believe you should be, not how much you care about me. You've proven all you need to about that already."

I pressed a kiss to the edge of his jaw with a little smile and sang, "Because I've had the climb of my life, no, I'd never melt this way and more."

Thorn let out a huff that sounded more amused than anything. "You and your ridiculous songs," he rumbled, and then he was kissing me again, pulling me flush against his muscle-packed body at the same time. His thickly corded erection rubbed against me through the layers of our clothes, and it was a miracle I didn't spontaneously combust from that.

If I ever went down in flames, that'd be the way to do it.

A needy whimper slipped from my lips, and my warrior knew how to answer it. Without hesitation, he wrenched at my jeans with a rasp of tearing fabric. I fumbled between us to undo the lacing on his trousers. Fuck the cool night air against my suddenly bare ass or any concern about where we'd find a new pair of pants to prevent a very revealing walk of shame back onto the RV—I wanted my lover inside me, filling me with all the power his body could offer.

Thorn whirled us in the air again and settled me over him with incredible steadiness that clashed with the storm of hunger in his eyes. As I sank onto him, we groaned together.

His cock was even more massive in his shadowkind form, but the burn of it stretching me felt so fucking good, like he was both splitting me in two and the only force in the universe holding me together. Every particle in me quivered with desire for more.

Our mouths crashed together, no room for tenderness left in our hunger for each other. I swayed against the warrior, slowly as my body adjusted to his girth and then faster as I could handle more.

Each burst of friction sent a rush of pleasure roaring through my body, along with noises wilder than I'd known I had in me. Thorn gripped my ass and the back of my head, moving with me, his strength radiating through every facet of our joining.

He plunged deeper still, and a moan spilled from my mouth into his. His wings sent us careening higher. I'd never felt anything like this, racing toward my peak inside while my body hurtled upward in unison.

The tingling of ecstasy washed through me from my core out to the tips of my fingers and toes, swelling sharper and harder. With one final thrust, it exploded inside me with such force that all I could do was cling to Thorn and shudder.

Thorn came too, with a ringing bellow that wrapped around me in its passion. His arms squeezed tighter, as if he never meant to let me go. I did melt into him then, flying high and yet perfectly grounded by this monstrous man who was still mine for at least one more moment.

EIGHTEEN

Sorsha

"Souvlaki and moussaka, here we come!" Ruse announced as we roared away from the border crossing between Albania and Greece. Just a few cajoling words with the border patrol, and they'd been waving us through with broad smiles.

The incubus glanced back from the wheel to shoot a grin Snap's way. "Just wait until you see how many edible delicacies there are to discover here."

The devourer's forked tongue flicked across his lips. He leaned past the driver's seat to check the dash. "Perhaps we should be stopping for more gas soon? And Sorsha will need more to eat before much longer." He caught my eye with a playful glint in his.

"Yes, all for our mortal's benefit, I'm sure," Ruse teased, but I thought I could still hear a hint of tension in his voice that had been there ever since he'd informed the rest of us yesterday that his charmed hacker had found a promising lead that pointed us to Crete. Something about this venture bothered him.

The traces of phone calls and emails the hacker had dug up suggested there might be someone out on the ancient island who'd been working very closely with Tempest, though, so whatever the problem was, he'd obviously decided it wasn't worth mentioning. The next time I got him alone, I'd have to prod him about it.

I was starting to see how the ability to simply peek inside people's heads could be awfully tempting.

"Straight flush!" Antic declared, slapping her playing cards down on the table where I'd agreed to a few rounds of poker with her and the equines just to pass the time. Snap had briefly joined in until we'd switched to bidding with pennies rather than strawberries—which was really his own fault for eating them all.

Maybe that was for the best, though, because the imp was proving to be a menace. She chortled to herself as she scooped up more copper to add to her already considerable heap, and Bow let out a snort of frustration.

Omen emerged from the shadows in the hall and gave us a baleful look, but he managed not to remark again about how much faster we could have gotten to Crete if he'd stuck me on a plane and then hopped the RV through a couple of rifts. Gisele's usually sparkly temperament had become more like the glint of a sharpened scalpel the last time he'd brought it up.

"Haven't you already put her through enough?" she'd said with a jerk of her hand toward the sink, which at that point had been sputtering alternating dribbles of pineapple juice and sour milk, and the hellhound shifter had been wise enough to shut his mouth.

I had to say the pineapple juice was actually kind of enjoyable. Hey, don't judge. The warm iced tea that had been spewing from the showerhead for a few hours this morning? Not so much.

"We *will* need to fill up the gas again before we reach our destination," Omen said to Ruse. "Pick the stop at your discretion."

"Letting me play the boss? That could be dangerous." Ruse motioned Snap closer. "Grab my phone and let's look up our options for delicious satisfaction."

Omen must have made a gesture of his own, because Thorn materialized a moment later and dipped his head before making a report. "No sign of concerning activity in the area. I don't believe we're being followed."

The warrior had decided to stay the course for this potentially crucial stage of our mission, but I knew he still felt uneasy about the debt his fellow wingéd had suggested he owed them. His gaze slid to the landscape passing by the window, his face set in a pensive expression.

I passed my cards over to Gisele so she could shuffle and looked up at Omen. "If this is some kind of trap Tempest set up, she wouldn't need to have anyone following us—she'll be waiting for us there."

He grimaced. "I wouldn't put it past her to employ multiple tactics so she can keep an eye on us. We've already surprised her once."

"I know you and Thorn enjoy worrying," Ruse called back, "but I wouldn't have suggested we embark on this voyage if it looked anything like a trap. The bits and pieces connecting the Company to this guy are mostly from months or even years back. We didn't uncover any communication between them and him since he was sent off to Crete last month. Tempest didn't even know we'd be looking for her back then."

"I wouldn't have agreed to your suggestion if I thought it was likely to be a trap either," Omen muttered. "I just know that when it comes to the sphinx, more care is a much better strategy than not enough."

Antic bounced on the sofa. "Too much doom and gloom around here. Are we playing another hand or what?"

I happily indulged in another round of that distraction, even though it cost me the last of my pennies and several nickels to boot. The imp was just crowing over her winnings when the RV slowed.

Ruse pulled off at a faded gas station with only two antique-looking pumps and a similarly scruffy café next door. I couldn't read the lettering on the grimy sign over the door. The mock columns that ran along the front of the building on either side of it, designed to look like a Greek temple if those temples had been painted with red and blue stripes over the whitewashing, had gone dingy with time, and not in a way that gave them historic grandeur.

"Ignore appearances," the incubus said as he led the way out. "This place is supposed to have the best dolmades in a hundred-mile radius."

Rather than salivating, Snap was peering at the restaurant front with a faint frown. He'd jarred to a stop a few feet from the RV. When I touched his arm, he shook his head as if to clear it and aimed one of his brilliant smiles at me. "Should we discover what these dole mad Es are?"

Ruse took it upon himself to do all the ordering, but I trusted the incubus's affinity for carnal pleasures. As he, Snap, and I schlepped the bulging bags to the RV, where the equines were basking in the sun, a man so skinny he could have passed for a signpost seemed to shimmer out of the shadow cast by an actual signpost and stalked over to Omen. I stopped in my tracks.

"What is the meaning of this excursion?" the unfamiliar shadowkind demanded in a haughty, nasal voice.

Omen reined in a bristle with visible effort. "Who the hell wants to know?"

The skinny guy, whatever sort of being he was, folded his arms over his chest. "The Highest expect you to be taking your commitment to them much more seriously. While Ruby is on the loose, this isn't the time for taking vacations."

Shit a slimy slug, they were following Omen to nag at him now? And to nag at him specifically about the being he was supposed to be reporting on... who was, er, standing right here carrying a load of dips and pitas. My pulse skipped a beat.

The hellhound shifter rolled his eyes with a long-suffering expression, but he managed to flick his glance my way with the swiftest of warning glances in the process. Trying not to look suspicious about it, I hustled onto the Everymobile.

Omen's voice followed us. "It just so happens that I'm coming this way on a very promising lead. The Highest managed to maintain some patience over how many years already? But if they'd rather that *you* take over the search, by all means. I'll just head back to—"

"Certainly not!" the lackey said in a tone of both horror and deep offense, as if he couldn't imagine taking on such a huge responsibility and simultaneously found it demeaning that Omen would try to pass it off on to him. Then the door clicked shut, muffling their conversation.

Thorn appeared for just long enough to reassure me, "It's just the one skulking around here," and then vanished, presumably to make sure that continued to be the case. My appetite had vanished too.

Ruse set his bag down on the table, his mouth slanted at an

awkward angle. "If they knew," he murmured, "they wouldn't be showing up just to pester Omen about his promptness."

"That doesn't mean they couldn't find out," I said, keeping my voice similarly low. I resisted the urge to go up to the window and watch the rest of the conversation play out.

Snap stared out at Omen and the walking signpost with an anxious flick of his tongue. His shoulders came up. "If this being tries to come after you..."

"I'm sure it'll be fine," I said, with much more breeziness than I actually felt, and flopped down on the sofa.

Pickle scrambled onto my lap. I ran my fingers absently over his back between his wings. How closely were the Highest's minions watching us? What if they happened to stop by right when I was fucking up my powers again?

Heat sizzled from my fingers, and the little dragon yelped.

"Pickle!" I cried, forcing my voice into a whisper. "Pickle, I'm sorry."

He darted away to the bedroom with his wings pressed flat to his sides. My stomach knotted. Thinking about worst case scenarios had practically made me create one.

"I'll go out and see if Omen needs a little help talking his way out of this," Ruse volunteered, "seeing as making friends with strangers isn't typically on his to-do list. You stay put, Miss Blaze." He couldn't quite hide the worry in his gaze before he slipped into the shadows.

Snap sat down next to me and examined my hands. My palms had only turned mildly pink. He hurried to get the aloe anyway, despite my protest that I'd probably heal in an hour or two anyway.

"I'm looking after you in every way I can," he said, and shot another glance toward the window with an uneasy air that I didn't think was just about our unexpected visitor. "No matter what I have to do."

Something in that phrasing gave me a clue. I tugged him down beside me. "I don't think you'll be called on to devour that lackey. *Can* you even use that power on shadowkind? Anyway, if he needs offing, I'd imagine between Omen and Thorn, every vital part of his body will be 'off' in about five seconds flat."

Snap only managed a glimmer of a smile at my joke. He sighed and tucked my head under his chin in his favorite pose. "I've never tried on a shadowkind. But I would, for you. If it's to defend my beloved, there's nothing monstrous about that."

I pulled back to peer up at him. "Are you worrying about that again? You haven't done anything wrong. You are what you are, and you've used your nature when you've needed to."

"Not only then." He let out a breath like a shudder and hugged me tighter. "That place—the colors and those columns all in a row—it looks a little like the place where I took my first devouring."

Ah, that explained a few things. I rested my arm over his and stroked the back of his hand from knuckles to wrist. "That time was an accident, wasn't it?"

"Does that make it less horrible or more? It was the first time I'd ventured through a rift into the mortal realm—I didn't know what to expect. There was a man in an alley yelling and smashing bottles. It bothered and confused me. Unsettled me. I didn't know why he would do that, and I wanted him to stop, and before I even realized what I was doing, I was already swallowing his soul. Feeling all the agony that I was putting him through. Wanting more."

"And then you punished yourself for that mistake by hiding away in the shadow realm for ages to make sure you never did it again. It's not like you just brushed it off."

"I know. But..." He tipped his head close to mine again. "The sphinx may do evil things, but she's wise about a lot too. She said we were only pretending not to be monsters, that we can't just ignore what we are forever. I wish I could. I wish I hadn't liked it. I wish I didn't still feel pinches of the hunger now and then. I'd like to just be your beloved and one who can taste impressions to help with our mission, and that's all. Even if you can accept how I am, I don't know if *I* can."

Was that why he'd been even cuddlier than usual the last few days? I turned in his arms to offer him a kiss. He kissed me back with such sweet tenderness that it was impossible to picture this man as some kind of savage beast.

"I just burned my one-hundred-percent innocent dragon because I still haven't gotten a handle on my powers," I said. "If you can forgive me for that, then I hope you can forgive yourself for not having full control over every impulse. You're doing a much better job keeping your urges in check than I am."

Snap let out a huff. "You've had much less time to get used to them."

"But much more practice *using* them. And I'm still fucking up. We just... We do our best, right? No one goes through life never wanting anything that could hurt someone else. You decide what's most important, and act on that as well as you can, and that shows who you really are." I kissed him again. "And I think you're pretty damned fantastic."

He hummed and nestled me against him, his gaze returning to the windows warily. The voices had fallen silent. I hoped that meant Omen had sent the skinny lackey off—with or without assistance from our companions—and not that the prick was investigating to make sure the hellhound shifter had been true to his word.

Fuck the Highest for hassling Omen when they wouldn't help him with the actual catastrophe we were facing. Fuck Tempest for messing with all of my shadowkind lovers' minds.

The anger nibbled at my nerves, but Snap's adoring warmth around me stopped it from flaring into a real fire.

The equines tramped on board first with a defiant air, followed by a skipping Antic, then Thorn and Ruse, and finally a scowling but no longer impeded Omen.

"He's gone," the hellhound shifter said before I had to ask. "But I can tell they'll be sending more. Bloated self-important jackasses. I don't know how much warning we'll have."

I forced a smile. "I'll work extra hard at keeping my flambéing tendencies tamped down."

As Omen took over at the wheel, the atmosphere stayed subdued. Gisele and Bow retreated to the master bedroom with a joint of their "other kind of" grass. Antic tried to coax Pickle out of my room and sulked when he didn't respond. The rest of us eyed the bulging bags that held our lunch, but none of us moved to open them.

Ruse had pulled out his phone. He tapped at it, swiped through some pages, and tapped some more, his expression getting noticeably stiffer with each passing minute.

"Have you realized that place actually only had the *second*-best dolmades in this half of the country?" I said after a while, just to prod a response out of him.

The incubus chuckled without much humor and shoved his phone in his pocket. His gaze shifted to the window, but the haziness in his eyes suggested he was thinking about something far beyond the view outside.

"I told you once about a particular mortal woman I occupied myself with back in the mists of time," he said, painfully droll. "It happens that she lived not far from Athens. As do rather a lot of her descendants now."

A prickle ran down my spine. He meant the first mortal woman he'd thought he'd fallen in love with—the one who'd rejected him. "Are you planning on doing anything about that?" I couldn't help asking.

A bittersweet smile played with his lips. "I was thinking if the timing works out, I might make a brief detour to pay a call on her granddaughter."

NINETEEN

Ruse

As he hefted his motorcycle—or as he liked to call it, "Charlotte"—off the back of the RV, Omen couldn't quite restrain a frown. He set it on the darkened road where we'd parked on the outskirts of Athens and gave me an evaluating look, as if he thought I might break his treasured vehicle just by standing next to it.

"Don't spend too long on this side trip," he said in a terse but even tone.

I offered him a jaunty tip of the cap that hid my horns. "By the time you've found yourself a ship, I'll be right there to talk us onto it."

"I'm going to hold you to that."

He got back into the RV, but Sorsha wasn't in quite so much of a hurry to see me off. My mortal love trailed her fingers over one of the motorcycle's handlebars and then turned her unusually pensive gaze on me. "Are you sure you need to do this? Are you sure you *want* to?"

She'd so generously given me her blessing to fulfill my appetites freely, but I thought I caught a whiff of possessiveness or perhaps a more general uneasiness in her demeanor, potent enough that I didn't need to extend my supernatural abilities to pick up on it. But then, we couldn't help our emotions, could we?

I touched her cheek, reveling for perhaps the hundredth time as I hoped to hundreds more in the way her bright copper eyes lit up at that simple caress. "There's nothing this woman could stir in me that you don't a thousandfold more."

"You don't know that yet. You haven't really had the chance to compare before." Sorsha let out a rush of breath. "It's not really that anyway. I just— I know how much she hurt you. Well, the woman this woman will remind you of. No matter what happens, no matter what you see or what she says if you talk to her, it doesn't change anything about who you are."

"Maybe it does," I said.

The gleam in her eyes flared, and I felt a waft of heat she must have suppressed before her anger condensed all the way into flames. "She barely knew you. She didn't bother to. And her granddaughter has no idea at all what—"

"I know. That's not what I meant." I teased my thumb over Sorsha's chin just below those tempting lips. "What happened back then has stuck with me, though. You've seen that, or you wouldn't be rising to my defense—very admirable of you, of course. That fragment of my history has held like a splinter under the skin of my soul, as much as I have a soul, and I think confronting it might be necessary to finally pulling it out. I'd like to be who I am without it."

Sorsha made a face at me, but her tone was light. "Well, fine, give a perfectly understandable reason so I can't grumble about it anymore." She leaned in to steal a kiss as deftly as she'd stolen so many other things in her career, not least of all my heart. I let my mouth linger against hers, absorbing one last bit of love and courage to carry with me.

As she left me, I swung my leg over the bike. It wasn't the first time I'd borrowed Omen's ride, and my body settled into place on the seat easily enough. But despite my reassurances to Sorsha, my spirit was not at all settled as I revved the engine and took off through the crisply warm Mediterranean dusk.

Sorsha's emotions weren't the only impressions that had snagged on my incubus senses. From all around, more and more with each passing day, faint ripples of anticipation skipped across my skin from indistinct directions. Ripples with a vicious edge.

I couldn't say for sure what they were. Possibly it was merely a global epidemic of emotional indigestion. I suspected, though, that I was picking up the violent hopes of those who knew about the Company's goals and weren't currently shuttered behind steel and silver. Those who knew that Tempest was only days from reaching that goal.

It wasn't just Sorsha who needed me. It was the companions I'd promised to help in this mission and all the shadowkind who'd wither away if the sphinx got what she wanted. Maybe I wasn't all that fond of every one of those shadowkind, but I wasn't the type to wish them dead either. I vastly preferred it if they stayed alive and at a distance where they wouldn't weigh on my limited conscience.

And if I was going to make sure of that, I'd damn well better be at my best. No niggling splinters of shame and doubt, no nagging memories I should have put to rest before Sorsha had ever come into my life.

Danae had lived in a hilltop villa with a view of the distant sea—the sort of home I'd now have said looked more believable as a movie set than in reality. But it was still here, the pale stucco walls of the house rising amid the bushes no longer in bloom. A few cracks and patches of repaired plaster showed here and there that hadn't existed before, but the place was in much better condition than Danae herself would be these days, wherever they'd laid her old bones to rest.

I left Charlotte at a safe distance and traveled around the matching garden walls through the darkness. The gnarled old olive tree I'd once playfully called to my one-time lover from had gone as kaput as she had, but I found a rocky protrusion a few feet from the wall that allowed me nearly as good a glimpse into the yard. As I clambered onto it, my chest tightened.

If my memories of Danae were a splinter, then that shard of noxious wood was digging into my gut right now, prodding out trickles of embarrassment and shame. The way she'd looked at me when I'd made the proposition that we take our relationship beyond mere physical pleasures—the way she'd *laughed*...

What should it matter now? I was here, and she wasn't. My capacity for love had endured after all, despite my nature, despite her dismissal of it. Still, I braced myself as I peered into the garden, preparing for a more wrenching wave of pain.

The current owners had changed the landscaping quite a bit. The only feature I recognized was the marble fountain dribbling water in the center of the space. The poor cupid poised over the pool had lost his head, which gave the whole piece a much more macabre look.

A newer wrought-iron bench stood nearby beneath the shade of a lemon tree, and the bushes stood scattered across the terrain in abandon rather than their former neat order. The varying shades of green in their leaves made for a delight of color even without their flowers. An herbal scent carried on the breeze thickly enough that I could taste it even from the shadows.

The sky had deepened into the indigo of night, but a few windows on the villa still gleamed with light. I was about to slip over the wall to spy through the glass when the woman I'd come to see saved me the trouble by strolling out.

It had to be the granddaughter—Demi, the miraculous internet had informed me. She was a tad taller and a shade slimmer than her grandmother had been, but her hair shone the same honey-brown, loose across her shoulders. Here and there the light caught a strand of gray—she was a decade or so older than Danae had been during our… acquaintance. But that only meant there were a few more lines around her graceful features, which held an echo of the woman who'd come before her. I could have believed I was seeing Danae herself in her middle age.

I took all that in—and my pulse beat evenly onward. The shame had faded away into the tranquility of the night. No jab of loss or regret ran through me. I couldn't even say I felt a twinge of anger at the reminder of the woman who'd seen me as little more than a very animated, multi-featured dildo.

No, mostly what I felt was a mild curiosity. How far had the apple fallen from the tree?

Not all that far in some respects, if the book she held was anything to go by. She lifted the canvas-covered volume, the frayed ribbon placeholder dangling, and spoke in a low, sweet voice. Reciting the lines to a play—one of Aristophanes', if my sketchy recollection served.

She must have picked up that hobby from her grandmother. That was how I'd fallen for Danae—watching her stride around her garden, making impassioned speeches and cracking the best of ancient Grecian jokes. She hadn't wanted to act professionally, just to live out those scenes at her leisure, enjoying the poetry and the drama. Finding more depth in them than she'd ever been willing to see in me.

Should watching a woman so like her go through the same motions have rankled me? It didn't. Instead, a strange, serene certainty washed over me.

Demi *was* merely going through the motions, just as her grandmother had been. Neither of them had ever really passionately declared a challenge to combat or plotted the demise of unspeakable enemies or bantered with scurrilous rogues. I'd fallen for the roles Danae had admired, but she'd only been playing at them.

Sorsha was every bit the fierce and unshakeable woman contained in those roles—and more. The love that had grown in me in her presence ran right down to my core, as true as anything. She was as tangled in my being now as the roots of that lemon tree were with the earth.

And I wouldn't have had it any other way.

Whatever splinter had remained from the follies of times past, it crumbled away with that understanding. I drew back from the wall without a moment's hesitation and returned to the motorcycle.

It wasn't hard to find my companions, even though they'd driven right through Athens down to the harbor. When I reached that area, I opened my supernatural senses to the energy I'd recognize as Sorsha's—not pushing hard enough to get more than a taste, just enough to direct me.

Long ago, I'd let the scraps of desire I'd read in one woman's mind convince me that if I only told her how much more I'd wanted, she'd find the same longing in herself. Now I didn't need to scour my love's soul for an answering emotion. I had a woman who offered up her affection with every word and gesture she directed my way.

The Everymobile was parked outside a closed fish shop. Its tour bus guise was thrown off a little by the tinsel it'd decided to sprout along the edges of the roof, which wavered up and down even without a breeze to carry it. It was definitely for the best that we hadn't braved another trip to the rifts. It might have come out decked with a full set of holiday lights.

I left the motorcycle around back and traveled in through the shadows, only stepping out by Sorsha's door. I could tell she was inside the bedroom, but it gave me an inexplicable pleasure to honor her privacy with the small gesture of knocking. "I've returned with all my parts intact, Miss Blaze."

"I should hope so," she said dryly, but when I slipped inside, I found her smiling. She looked me up and down as if confirming that claim for herself and gave my hair a fond ruffle. Her hand lingered over one of my horns in a way that never failed to send a thrill through me before it dropped to her side. "You look happy. Was she everything you expected?"

"She was exactly what she should have been, which was nothing I have any interest in anymore. I'd have had an awfully dull time of it if she'd been open to my full range of charms after all."

I winked at Sorsha, and she laughed, but maybe the remark rubbed up against that thread of jealousy a little too closely. Just for an instant, flames coursed up over her hands, nearly translucent but hazy with heat. They vanished so quickly, with no change in her expression, that I wasn't sure she'd even noticed her power had snuck out.

I took hold of the hem of her shirt and tugged her to me, tilting my face so my forehead rested against hers. Our mortal exuded so much strength and fire it was easy to forget she had her own vulnerabilities. She hadn't asked me this, and she shouldn't need to. It was a pleasure and an honor to say it for its own sake.

"In case I wasn't clear enough earlier, there's no one I need or want other than you."

The corners of her lips curled upward again, and she met my kiss with that smile. But I knew even as I enjoyed the moment that it wasn't enough. She had worries far beyond my part in her life.

She needed more than *me*... Maybe more than all four of us, despite all we could offer. She was a being of two worlds and uncertain abilities with possible apocalyptic potential.

All we could speak from was the shadowkind side. I could see that she got whatever other perspective she might need too, couldn't I? The sort of help she never would have allowed herself to ask for.

Whatever Tempest was going to throw at us in the next few days, Sorsha had to be at her best to meet it too.

When I left her, I stepped outside and pulled out my phone, but it wasn't to do any more digging into my own past. It was to bring up the number of the most vital presence from Sorsha's.

"Hello?" said the voice that answered, energetic and cautious at the same time.

I leaned against the RV's side, tipping back my head to watch the tinsel waving in its manufactured breeze. "Hello, Vivi. It's your best friend's favorite incubus. How would you feel about embarking on a little trip?"

TWENTY

Sorsha

I BRACED MY LEGS TO KEEP MY BALANCE ON THE SWAYING DOCK AND EYED the seafaring vessel Omen had pointed to. "*This* is the ship you got us?"

The boat was big enough—that wasn't the problem. But more of the hull's white paint had been scratched or worn off than was left on, which made me wonder just how intact the wood was beneath that. Aged beams jutted every which way around the small cabin, making the ship look like a mutated narwhal.

"She's an old fishing boat," Omen said, aiming a pleased glance at his find. "Outfitted with a modern motor, but still with all the other trappings. I thought we should make use of the time we'll be at sea to get in some more training, and props are always useful for that. Unless you've got something better to do?"

I dragged damp, salty air into my lungs. I guessed if there was anywhere I could safely practice my fiery skills, out in the middle of an immense body of water would make the top of the list. "I suppose you've already named her?"

His lips curved upward, and he waved down the length of the boat. "I didn't need to."

Curling lines of blue swept through the patchy white paint, the letters spelling out *Penelope*. I had to admit it was an Omen-esque name if I'd ever heard one. I cocked my head at him. "Now I see the real reason you bought her."

He waved off my remark and motioned me on board in one smooth movement. "Let's get going, Disaster, while you've still left the harbor in one piece."

I stuck my tongue out at him and darted across the plank that led onto the ship. Not wanting to draw attention in case Tempest's lackeys or some other member of the Company asked around, the other three shadowkind in our crew had leapt on board out of sight in the shadows.

We were back to our original quartet, leaving the equines and Antic back in Athens with the Everymobile. If we hadn't returned from Crete within three days, they were meant to launch a rescue mission. I'd expected Antic to complain about being left out, but she'd danced around with so much joy at the thought of being a potential rescuer that she might even have been hoping we were heading into a trap.

It was going to be a long voyage, but Omen had vetoed any talk of planes for this final part of the journey. "Too many records, too tight a space." As if we had a whole lot of places to flee to out in the middle of the sea. I definitely couldn't have gotten in any training on a flight, though, and maybe the rhythm and hiss of the waves would settle my nerves more before the confrontation ahead.

Omen cast off, and I gamely raised my hand in greeting to the other boaters we passed to show we were perfectly normal people off on a pleasure cruise, if on a somewhat unusual ship for that job.

When the harbor had dwindled into blobs in the distance, Ruse, Snap, and Thorn materialized on the deck. Snap leaned over the metal railing that was mounted along most of the starboard side and drank in the sea scents with a blissful expression. Thorn immediately clambered up to the top of the tallest post with its bedraggled sail still wrapped around it, where he'd get the widest view for surveillance.

Ruse flopped into one of the deck chairs, his face slightly greenish and his hand resting on his stomach. "Never been a huge fan of water travel," he admitted.

I sat down next to him, tipping back my head to soak up the

Mediterranean sun. "You could stick to the shadows. Plenty of them around."

"That actually makes it worse. Which is a pretty mean feat considering I barely have a stomach in that state."

"I suppose that means this picnic lunch is all for me, then."

As I rifled through the large bag of edible supplies we'd brought for a bottle of lemonade, Snap hustled over with a sound of mock consternation. *"I'll* take Ruse's portion."

The incubus felt well enough to laugh. "That's no surprise."

The devourer gave me the sly look he was starting to perfect, turned adorable by his beaming grin. "You'd make yourself sick too if you tried to eat all of it, Peach. I'm simply keeping your best interests in mind."

"Of course you are," I said with a playful swat. "But it's hardly lunchtime yet. We just had breakfast."

The next sound Snap made wasn't so joking in its consternation, but he settled for only plucking a plum out of the bag. He perched on the railing, long legs dangling over the water, and hummed happily as he bit into the fruit. *"I* like the sea."

"You're welcome to it," Ruse muttered, but after a stretch of calm waters and the soothing rumble of the motor, he'd come back more to his usual color.

For the first few hours, Omen focused on sailing, which apparently he had some experience with, and left the rest of us to lounge—or, in Thorn's case, to broodingly eye the horizon. I knew that reprieve wouldn't last. Not long after we'd dug into our picnic lunch, the hellhound shifter emerged from the cabin, considered the vast sprawl of endless blue all around us, and snapped his fingers at me.

"All right, Disaster. Let's see what we can do to mitigate that catastrophic nature of yours."

I licked the last few flecks of icing sugar from my custard bougatsa dessert off my fingers. "I'm not the canine here, dog-breath. How about a 'please'?"

He glowered at me and dipped into a little bow. "Would Her Highness kindly allow me to continue teaching her how she might avoid incinerating herself?"

"That's more like it." I got up, stretching my arms and then cracking my knuckles—and trying not to notice that three other gazes had focused on me with varying levels of concern.

Snap sprang from the arm of the deck chair where he'd been cozying up to me. "If there's any way I can help—"

"I've got this," Omen said dryly. "She isn't going to leave your sight, so you can ensure I leave her in one piece."

Was the devourer worried about what Omen might do to me or what I might do to myself? At this point, it was hard to say which of us was a larger threat to my well-being. Ruse might have even straightened up a tad as if preparing for some kind of intervention, and Thorn was peering at me instead of the horizon now.

I folded my arms over my chest. Okay, so I'd let loose a few more flames than usual in the last couple of days, but we did have a psychopathic, immensely powerful shadowkind who might be launching a double-genocide any moment now, so who could blame me for being a smidge wound up?

How immense a genocide would we be facing if I *didn't* get those powers completely under control?

I shoved that question aside and nodded to Omen. "Got some more bits of paper for me to charbroil?"

"I thought we'd try something different for a change. We're just going to spar. And by 'just', I mean fists and feet only. No supernatural powers. You let your fire out, you automatically lose, no matter how pissed off I made you. Oh, and to add a little challenge…" He leapt up onto one of the railings with a nimbleness I wouldn't have expected from his well-built frame. "Touch the deck with both feet, and you also lose. Should we make it the most wins out of five, or do you need more chances than that to get warmed up?"

As I climbed onto a wooden beam that crossed the stern, I raised my eyebrows at him. "You're assuming I'll even need five. I'm the one who spent most of the past few years scrambling across rooftops and through windows."

Omen smiled at me with a gleam of his teeth. "I suppose we'll see."

He didn't give me any more warning than that. The next thing I knew, he'd launched his muscular frame right at me.

I dashed down the pole protruding from the stern, swayed, and hurled myself upward to grab one of the salt-gritted ropes so I could swing over the hellhound's head. Ruse let out a whoop of appreciation, but all I'd done was flee, not land any blows. I spun around, ducked the fist speeding toward me, and managed to jab my heel into Omen's calf before he dodged.

I stalked after him along the pole, both of us over the open water now. "What's the rule about wet dogs? Does that count as a loss too?"

"I guess it'd better," Omen said, and threw himself at me.

I nearly did perform a spectacular belly flop then. It was only by a hair's breadth that my fingers snagged on a ridge on the upper hull, giving me just enough leverage to toss my leg back over the railing.

As I scrambled back up, the hellhound was already barreling toward me. I dashed along the railing and hefted myself onto a rope near the bow.

My foot skimmed Omen's face, just shy of a strike—and he caught my ankle. With a yank, he sent me tumbling onto the deck. I hit the worn wooden boards ass-first.

Sprawling on my back, I waggled my legs in the air. "Technically my feet didn't touch it."

Omen snorted. "And here I thought the spirit of the rules was clear. But if you're determined to be a cheater as well as a thief…"

The words should have rolled right off me. It wasn't as if I hadn't been called worse—hell, *he'd* called me worse several times over. But something about that accusation struck a spark inside me, and I had to clench my hands to will back the flare of heat before it burst from my skin.

All the more reason to play along with this training. That inner fire had damn well better learn to stay tamped down until I called on it with a purpose.

"Fine," I said. "I'll just have to whoop your ass the other four times."

Omen's icy eyes glinted. "Come and try me."

I had to say I didn't think the rules were exactly fair. Omen might not have been bringing out his own hellish fire, but his speed and dexterity were several cuts above mortal standards. Not that I was going to complain that I couldn't keep up with him to his face. A gal's got to have some self-respect.

I'd just have to be more tricksy.

We exchanged more feints and parries around the edge of the boat until I saw my opportunity. I dropped low, hooked my arm around the railing, and heaved both of my feet into the side of Omen's legs.

He groped for balance, but not fast enough. This time the smack of flesh meeting wood wasn't my own. I pushed myself up straight, grinning down at him, as he dusted himself off.

"We're just getting started," he promised. "You need to be able to hold yourself in check and bend those flames to your will when you're face to face with Tempest, and she isn't going to be half this easy on you."

"Bring it on," I shot back, but something—maybe the mention of Tempest—sent another jolt of heat through me. This time it coursed up through my ribs and into my shirt before I quite got a grip on it. With a hitch of my pulse, I slapped my arms against my sides to smother it.

Omen didn't comment, but a flicker of tension passed through his face, his mouth tightening into a brief frown. Before I could do more than take a breath, he sprang at me again.

The momentary loss of control must have rattled me. Omen threw his swipes and punches with brutal fury, and each time his knuckles clipped my body, another spurt of anger threatened to break the surface of my composure.

Stop it! I thought at the fire searing from my gut up to my chest. *He wants to rile you up. He's not really a threat. Chill out already.*

My mental commands didn't have much effect. I banged my knee against a board while dodging a roundhouse, and a sputter of flames licked over my hand, blistering my fingers.

Omen didn't see—my hunched torso had hidden the lapse from view. *Not again. Stay the fuck* inside *me,* I ordered the roiling energies.

Both to distract myself and to annoy my opponent, I danced backward with a little musical accompaniment. "And if you only scold and spite, we'll be holding on forever. But we'll only be faking a fight—"

Omen growled and charged at me, cutting me off as I had to fling myself at the ropes to escape. My feet skimmed the deck by mere inches, but I wrenched myself up and around fast enough to clock him in the back of the head.

He teetered but caught himself and whirled around to leap after me. The singing hadn't boosted my spirits as much as I'd hoped—or really at all. Gritting my teeth against another waft of flame, I scrambled across the netting. I kicked Omen in the shoulder, let out a hiss when he hauled on my leg so hard he almost dislocated my hip, and finally made it within jumping distance of the opposite railing.

"Come on, Disaster," the hellhound shifter said, hurtling after me. His voice was taut, his face set in an expression that looked as uneasy as it did fierce. "Is this how you're going to fight all those Company bastards and the sphinx who's egging them on—by running away? Didn't they *kill* your guardian? How many more are you going to let them murder?"

"I'm not running away," I snapped, and reversed course to throw an uppercut he neatly avoided. My sneakers squeaked on the metal bar. "Isn't it called fighting smart?"

"Doesn't look so smart to me. We don't have time for pussyfooting around the problem now, do we?"

"I know that." Holy humping harpies, was he pissing me off. Even more fire crackled through me. Every muscle in my body went rigid, holding it in. "I'll be ready."

"Are you sure? You've got to tackle it head on, before we come right down to the wire. Maybe I shouldn't expect any better from a being who's only half—"

Before he could even finish that sentence, the fire blazed up so sharp and sudden my vision hazed. All I could see was the glare of the flames; all I could feel was every inch of my skin sizzling and charring. The pain shocked the air from my lungs.

A solid force slammed into me. I crashed into the placid ocean head first, salty water bubbling to a boil around me for an instant before it doused the flames.

I came up sputtering—and feeling the prickle of raw patches all across my skin. My ponytail drifted over my shoulder into view, its tip burnt black. Nausea pooled in my stomach.

Omen had tossed himself into the water along with me. He shook the moisture from his hair in a gesture that was undeniably dog-like and glanced over me with a gaze that was all man, lit with his own orange heat. His mouth twisted.

"That was a low blow," he said. "It should have been beneath me."

It took me a second to process that he was apologizing and another to realize the apology was for the comment that had provoked my inferno, not for the unexpected swim. I glanced up at the boat, taking in the scorch marks streaking across the mottled paint, and my stomach lurched again.

I'd almost burnt up our sole mode of transportation with no land in sight, and Omen was apologizing to *me*.

My tongue turned leaden in my mouth. I'd failed. I'd been a fucking disaster.

But what was the point in talking about that when Omen knew it just as well as I did?

After a fumble for words, what fell from my mouth was, "Well, now we're both beneath the boat. Maybe we should fix that?"

Thorn had flown down from the mast. As he leaned over the railing, the smoldering darkness cleared from his eyes and his wings vanished. A moment later, Ruse and Snap joined him, looking equally worried. Now we had a whole party celebrating my ineptitude. Wonderful.

Omen swam closer to me. The damp darkened his eyelashes, making his gaze even more piercing, but it wasn't chilly right now. Treading water, he examined one of my forearms and then the other.

The red patches were already fading back into their usual pink. "Your healing abilities are heightening as quickly as your fire is," he remarked.

"Oh, joy. More time to burn alive if there's no convenient ocean to throw me into."

His eyes met mine, stormy with an emotion I couldn't read. "Maybe I've been going about this wrong."

"What do you mean?" What fresh hell did he have in store for me now?

But he brushed his fingertips over my soaked hair, sparking a much more welcome heat, and it occurred to me that *he* might be worried about me too, however much trouble he had showing it.

"I've been trying to push you to the brink," he said. "Get you used to the sensation so you can control it. But maybe this power isn't something you can control that way. Maybe the answer isn't suppressing your anger but making sure it's focused on the right target."

I arched an eyebrow at him. "Trying to keep it off of you, hmm?"

This once, he didn't rise to the bait. "No," he said, all seriousness. "I'm trying to keep it off of *you*. Whatever the Highest or Tempest or anyone says, there's nothing wrong with you. You don't deserve the shit they're trying to put you through, so you sure as hell shouldn't be putting yourself through even more. You're incredible."

"I'll second that motion," Ruse called from the deck.

"Fantastic," Snap murmured in eager agreement.

A smile stretched Thorn's lips. "I couldn't have expressed it more eloquently."

In the face of that deluge of admiration—prompted by the being who'd once been my biggest critic, no less—I didn't know what to do with myself. My mouth opened and closed and opened again only to sputter sea water back out. One thing I definitely had to keep doing: treading this damn water. No matter how distractingly tender my hellhound shifter had unexpectedly become.

Omen glanced up at our audience and then back at me, his hand lingering against my jaw. "I'm not sure just saying that is quite enough. It could be that you don't avoid destruction by ignoring everything that's against you—you do it by remembering everyone who's for you. So how about instead of tossing you around, we try grounding you instead?"

I blinked at him, and a snarky response fell out before I could catch it. "That might be a little difficult considering there's literally no solid land in sight."

One side of Omen's mouth quirked up. "Then it's a good thing I had a more metaphorical 'grounding' in mind." He motioned overhead. "Thorn, could you toss a net down—one that's fixed well to the ship. And then the rest of you can toss yourselves in. Our mortal deserves a group effort."

Was that the first time he'd ever referred to me as *theirs*?

I didn't have much time to puzzle over his unexpected compliments or his intentions before the warrior had heaved a heavy length of net over the side of the boat. As Omen drew me through the cool water over to it, the others leapt in after us. No big deal for them if they left their clothes on—they could rematerialize them from the shadows dry the second they got out. Although from my glance at Snap, it appeared *he'd* decided to simply chuck off all garments right from the get-go.

Omen tugged my attention away from the pale gleam of Snap's naked body with an insistent press of his fingers beneath my chin. He looped one arm through the net. "To make sure Penelope doesn't go astray," he said with that same crooked smile, and guided my mouth the rest of the way to his.

I felt all kinds of naked with my body coming to rest against the hellhound shifter's in the water, our clothes plastered to our skin, his lips branding mine. The traces of sea salt that lingered on those lips gave the kiss an extra tang—and so did the knowledge that this was the first time he'd ever made a public display of his affection in front of his companions.

Ruse let out a low chuckle. Three other bodies drifted around mine, their warmth encircling me in the cool water. Omen released my mouth, keeping his head tipped close to mine. "You're ours. We won't let you lose yourself, Phoenix."

Ours. The word tingled through me, too sweet for me to bother with protests about whether I belonged to anyone at all. I knew him well enough by now to be sure he didn't mean it that way. I belonged *with* them, and I had no arguments about that at all.

And they were all here with me—the men I loved.

Naturally, the incubus took the initiative to move things along first. As Omen brought his mouth to the crook of my neck, Ruse leaned in to capture my lips. The shifter eased to the side to give him more room.

Thorn's massive form had come up behind me. He circled my waist with his hands and trailed one up to cup my breast. His fingers flicked over my nipple one by one, drawing it to a stiffened peak through the wet fabric with quiver after quiver of pleasure.

Another hand, slender and lithe, traced the curve of my thigh. Snap pressed his mouth to my shoulder, with a little nip to shift my shirt collar so he had access to more skin.

I didn't know if this would ground me the way Omen had hoped, if it would do anything at all to calm my inner flames when I needed them under control, but I couldn't have imagined a more enjoyable strategy. All of my lovers had joined together to share and adore me. The fire coursing through me now held only bliss.

They stayed clustered around me, their mouths marking my skin with their own heat, their fingers teasing every inch of my skin with giddy waves that echoed the rocking of the sea. Thorn wrenched off my shirt and bra and flung them over the hull onto the deck; Snap pulled me higher in the water to slick his forked tongue over my breast. As Omen sucked my other nipple between his lips, Ruse's hand glided between my legs to stoke the sharpest blaze my body was capable of when they had me like this.

My hips swayed with his caress, pleasure pulsing through me. Omen swallowed my gasp with another kiss. Thorn ran his fingers down my spine and nibbled my shoulder blade with startling delicacy.

I fumbled with Ruse's shirt with one hand, refamiliarizing myself with Snap's lean chest at the same time. The incubus paused just for an instant, and his clothes vanished as the devourer's had. When he flicked open my fly, Omen helped him peel off my pants.

Too much desire was flowing through me and around me to leave room for patience. I hooked my legs around Ruse's to pull him closer. As he teased the tip of his cock over my clit and farther downward, a needy whimper slipped from my mouth. Snap caught me in a kiss, and the incubus plunged right into me with a rush of the headiest delight.

Thorn was fondling my breasts again from behind, holding me in place to meet Ruse's thrusts. Omen grazed the sensitive skin of my throat with the tips of his houndish fangs. I reached down his body, now nude too, and wrapped my hand around his erection. The shifter groaned against my neck.

My hips bucked with Ruse's, my mind glazed with the pleasure—so much of it—they were conjuring across my entire being. As the incubus hit the perfect spot inside me, Snap dipped his hand between us. His fingers found my clit. The devourer kissed me again, circling that nub of nerves in time with the delicious pounding of the incubus's cock.

Thorn pinched my nipples. My fingers squeezed tighter around Omen's cock, jerking it faster as I careened into the breathless surge of my orgasm. A cry broke from my throat with the force of the release, which crackled through me with a brilliance no flames could match.

The hellhound shifter thrust into my hand, his own breath stuttering. Ruse spilled himself into me with a groan. I was still floating on the bliss of that first release when he withdrew and Snap pushed in front of me with all his possessive determination.

"My peach?" he murmured in a tone that left no doubt about what he was asking.

I squeezed his shoulder. "Please."

He penetrated me so swiftly and deeply that a fresh gasp propelled from my lips. A gust of heat against my wrist and the crush of Omen's mouth on mine told me another of my lovers had reached his own peak. I groped behind me, and Ruse guided my hand through the water to Thorn's groin with a knowing hum.

"Sorsha," Thorn rumbled as I clutched his rigid thickness. His mouth seared against my cheek. I twisted my head so I could receive his kiss where I wanted it most.

No, I didn't feel grounded at all. I was soaring as much as I had that night with the wingéd, buoyed now by all of the four monstrous men who offered up their fondness in such different but delectable ways. My body arched and rocked between them with the shifting currents, Snap drove deeper still with a hungry panting, Omen's tail flicked across my ass, and I was coming again, ricocheting up to the clear blue sky.

Snap buried his face in my neck and shuddered with his own release. Thorn followed with a groan moments later. We drifted there, twined and sated, our own circle of ecstasy in what might as well have been an otherwise empty world.

Would this extraordinary encounter tame my fire? I didn't know, but right then the bonds between us felt too potent for any sphinx or murderous mortal to tear them apart.

It was evening by the time we docked the boat and started up the rocky terrain to the location Ruse's hacker had pinpointed. By the time Ruse pointed out the shabby cabin from which Tempest's mortal lackey had been doing his work, night had fully set in.

"From what we've gathered," the incubus whispered as we crept toward the building, "she's had this fellow investigating ruins that were constructed with protections to repel shadowkind. Looking to see what secrets the ancients might have wanted to keep from monstrous eyes."

I studied the thin glow that seeped from the cabin's one dingy window. "She must think whatever he could find will be important to completing her plan, or she wouldn't have him still poking around out here rather than behind Company building walls."

Thorn reappeared next to us, back from a quick scouting. "There are plates of silver and iron in the walls of that place, but it's fragile enough that I should be able to smash it with only minor discomfort."

"Not exactly subtle," Ruse said.

"We don't have time for subtle—and if this mortal is as wrapped up in Tempest's affairs as it seems, he might contact her at any sign of interference before we have a chance to carry out a longer plan." Omen wiped his hands together. "So, let's see some crashing."

Thorn gave us a grim smile, squared his massive shoulders, and hurtled toward the cabin. I'd seen him smash through concrete walls, so this wasn't a surprising feat. Adrenaline hummed through my veins all the same.

The warrior rammed into the side of the cabin fists first. The weathered wood creaked and crumpled. Jaw clenched against the toxic effects of the metals around him, Thorn grabbed the startled middle-aged man standing inside and wrenched him out from under the teetering roof.

The rest of us were already hustling over the hillside to meet them. I spotted the gleam of a thin silver-and-iron-twined band on the man's index finger and pushed myself faster. As soon as I reached him, I snatched his hand and tore the ring off.

The man flinched with an oddly faint cry. A second later, Ruse was at his side. The incubus fell into his cajoling tone. "Hello, friend. We're here to help you escape the fiend who's held you in her sway."

The usual glaze didn't come over the man's gray eyes. He attempted to shove away, but Thorn still gripped his shoulders firmly.

A momentary frown crossed Ruse's face, but he soldiered on. "We only want what's best for you. We'll sort this all out—you don't have to worry about a thing."

The man thrashed in Thorn's hands again, totally unaffected. Then he made a desperate gesture at Snap, as if assuming the sweetest looking figure among us was most likely to be on his side.

Something about the movement of his hands struck a pang of recognition. Understanding clicked in my head.

A rough chuckle fell from my lips. "Tempest didn't bother to hide him for a reason. She knew no shadowkind could charm him with a little sweet-talking."

Omen shot me a sharp look. "What are you talking about?"

I motioned to the man. "I'm pretty sure that gesture he just made was sign language. He can't hear a thing Ruse is saying—he's deaf."

TWENTY-ONE

Snap

"Look at it," Ruse said, waggling his phone in the mortal man's face. The glow of its screen showed a message the incubus had typed. "Doesn't it make you want to follow my every command?"

The man who worked for Tempest jerked his head to the side, unable to move any farther than that thanks to Thorn's strong hands holding him in place.

We'd gone inside the partly smashed cabin, taking spots around a rough wooden table now scattered with splinters from the wall the warrior had bashed through. Thorn had the man planted in a chair while he loomed from behind. Ruse sat across the table from him. Sorsha and I stood on either side of the incubus, watching the proceedings, while Omen paced the small space by the cabin's kitchen. Without even looking at him, I could tell the hellhound shifter was just as unhappy with the situation as our captive looked.

"Would it work even if you *could* make him read it?" I asked.

Ruse grimaced. "I don't know. I've never tried to charm through visuals before. Persuading with my voice is what comes naturally. It'd be easier to tell if we could force him to read in the first place. Even if our stalwart lunk here holds this asshole's eyelids open, we can't make him focus on the words."

"Try this." Omen tossed a piece of paper and a pen onto the table. "Your handwriting might contain more power than words typed on some mortal device."

"If he'll read *that*." Sorsha leaned over the incubus's shoulder. "Write the letters really big so he can't help seeing them."

Ruse chuckled to himself. "Like I'm trying to teach a child how to read." But he scrawled across the sheet of paper in as broad strokes as it would fit. KEEP READING WHAT I WRITE. "Might as well cover that hurdle first."

Thorn gripped the man's head to turn it toward the table, and Ruse brandished his message like a flag. The man appeared to glance at it, but all he did was screw up his face into an expression so sour it made my tongue curl up. He whipped his hands through the air in more of those gestures that were his own way of speaking. I didn't understand the physical language, but I got the distinct impression he'd told Ruse to shove his paper—and possibly other things—up his anus.

If the incubus's charm was having any effect, it definitely wasn't making the man any friendlier. I bent over the table, flicking out my tongue to capture more definite impressions. Perhaps we didn't need this fellow's help. I might be able to glean something useful about his investigations for Tempest without him offering any cooperation at all.

The man didn't seem to have used the table for his work. I caught wisps of fingers closing around a hot mug with a whiff of coffee smell, laying out a knife and fork for a simple meal of grilled meat, and resting a book against it as he contemplated a story of men on horseback shooting at each other while wearing large hats.

Moving away from the table, I tested the cupboard beside it, the narrow bed with its scratchy blanket, and finally circled around Omen to check the kitchen. With each flicker of sensation that rose up, the fragments I'd gathered formed a patchy picture of the man's life here—not vivid or comprehensive, but something.

"He's been here for a while," I reported, taking a taste of the walls between comments. "Long enough that he's gotten bored with it. He imagines a woman who lives in some other place—she smiles a lot, and he thinks she is very pretty. He gets annoyed when he sees her with a man that puts his arm around her."

I frowned, sorting through the emotions I'd picked up from our captive's reminiscing. "I think maybe she is mates with someone else, but he wants her to be his. He keeps working because somehow he believes the sphinx will help that happen."

Sorsha wrinkled her nose and aimed a glare at the man. "He's helping Tempest so he can force some woman to hook up with him? What a catch. And the Company calls you all 'monsters'."

Those impressions left me uncomfortable too. They didn't help us defeat Tempest, though. "I can't get much sense of his work. He leaves early and comes back late, tired. Walking a lot, and digging. Maybe he's been looking for something?"

I knelt by a wicker basket in the corner where a rumpled shirt slumped over the rim. My tongue darted through the air above it, and a tingle of past excitement raced through me, spurring my own. "He found it. I can't tell what it was, but he was eager to tell Tempest about it so he could finally leave."

Omen's head jerked around. "Has he already told her?"

"I think he's told her some things, but he still had to go back and uncover more of whatever it was." I tipped my head to the side as if that would knock the jumbled impressions into a more coherent story. It didn't work.

At the table, Ruse had flipped the paper over and pushed it and the pen toward the man. He gestured to them emphatically. The man's lip curled. He snatched the paper up, crumpled it with a few twists of his fingers, and hurled it at the incubus's face.

"All right," Ruse said, standing up. "I think we've determined that my charm doesn't extend to the written word or pantomiming. What now?"

Perhaps if I tried the clothes the man was wearing right now? I edged over beside Thorn and bent my head. A ripple of the deeper, chilling hunger nibbled at my gut. I closed my mind to it and inhaled more impressions.

"It's too present," I said with a jab of regret. The blare of emotions the man was experiencing right now drowned out any subtler information. "He's angry and frustrated—and a little scared. But that's when he thinks of the sphinx discovering we've found him, not so much of what we'll do."

Omen growled under his breath. "We haven't got any leverage. There's clearly nothing he cares about in this place other than his own life, and you can be sure he knows Tempest would slaughter him in epically painful fashion if he betrayed her, so *us* threatening to kill him won't do much."

Sorsha's mouth twisted. "He's got to know something useful if he's been working so much for Tempest. Whatever he uncovered here might be what's allowing her to finally unleash the sickness the Company created."

Omen's gaze veered to me and then away again. He hesitated, which was so unlike our leader that I turned to study him.

"There is one way," he started, measuring out his words.

All at once, our captive jerked forward. With our attention on the hellhound shifter, Thorn's grasp on our captive must have loosened just slightly. The man's knees banged the underside of the table, and he swung up a small gun that must have been fixed there.

The warrior slammed him toward the ground. The gun went off with a *boom* that shattered the quiet of the night and clipped the ragged edge of the wall behind Sorsha.

He'd almost killed her. That bullet would have hit her in the forehead if it'd flown a few inches to the right. Without thinking, without *feeling* other than the swell of vengeful horror, I threw myself between my beloved and her attacker.

As I loomed over the slumped man, my rage simmered down to a duller anger within moments. He couldn't stage any further attack while he was pinned firmly under Thorn's bulk.

Omen kicked the gun off into the night, none too gently. He glared down at the man. "No, you don't value your life all that much, do you?"

Even with the initial jolt of my protective instincts fading, a ball of hunger remained at the base of my throat, gnawing rather than merely nibbling now. My jaw itched to let loose the needle-like teeth that could pierce this man's skull and siphon away his soul shred by shred.

I sucked in a ragged breath, and Omen glanced at me. Something in his expression sent a shock of comprehension through me.

He didn't want me to subdue my hunger. When he'd said there was a way, he'd been going to suggest that I use my power. That I flay our captive's being down to the barest essence, for all the torment it would put him through, to see everything he'd been and done.

If the man refused to communicate with us and Ruse couldn't wheedle him into doing so, devouring him was the obvious answer. It would tell us more in a matter of minutes than we might get out of him or his home... ever. And what this lackey knew might make the difference between saving hundreds of millions of other beings, mortal and otherwise, untold amounts of pain.

Still, my body balked. My tongue quivered over my lips, and the hunger rose up my gullet. How could I know whether I was making this decision out of justice or monstrousness?

My voice came out in a croak. "Tell him. Make him understand that he'll die if he doesn't agree to share what he knows. He should have a choice." Even if we were already sure of which one he'd make.

"Snap?" Sorsha said softly. Her hand slipped around my forearm, a gentle warmth. So much gentleness my beloved could offer despite all the fire and strength in her as well.

She wasn't concerned about herself. She'd shown she loved me regardless of whether I turned to this power. It was only my own well-being she was worried about—how I felt about going through with this act.

"I'm not going to order you," Omen said. "It's *your* choice too. I'll just point out that there's a lot on the line. Sometimes there isn't any answer that isn't at least a little monstrous."

The truth of those words settled in my chest. Sorsha squeezed my arm, and the resistance inside me started to melt.

Yes. Avoiding devouring this man would likely sentence all those other beings to their own horrifying deaths. Would letting that devastation happen be somehow more humane of me simply because I hadn't carried out the destruction through my own jaws?

This was what my beloved and my friends saw in me: not a monster giving in to viciousness, but a shadowkind with an ability that could reverse an immense catastrophe. I could do this. I was *meant* to do this. And I found I could think that without cringing for the first time since that night long ago when I'd sunk my teeth into my first meal's skull unknowingly.

Why had I joined Omen's cause at all if I wasn't going to give this mission everything I had?

While I'd grappled with myself, Ruse and Thorn had conveyed the situation to our captive as well as they could with motions and scribbled words. He shook his head against the floor with a defiant scowl. Inhaling slowly, I crouched beside him.

"You are helping to hurt many people who've done nothing wrong," I told him, in case some of my meaning might travel into him even if he couldn't hear my voice. "I must hurt you to make sure those horrors end. It's what I was made for—I won't deny it. Sometimes it takes a monster to fight monsters."

I knew in that moment through my entire body that as long as I cared about this realm and mine and all the beings in them, I wouldn't ever let my monstrousness overwhelm me.

Greenish light glittered across my vision. I gave myself over to the change into my full devourer form. The stretch of my limbs and sprouting of sharper teeth came over me as though I were breaking free of a blanket that had been wrapped around me suffocatingly tight. A burn that was almost pleasant spread through my muscles.

Part of me would enjoy this act, as horrifying as it was. That was all right too. The enjoyment could belong to the good I knew I was doing even as I mourned the agony that came with it.

My jaw gaped open. Pulled by a mix of determination, justness, and the swelling hunger, I clamped my teeth shut around the man's head.

I'd forgotten how intense the rush of images could be. Sights and sounds and, oh, the *tastes* surged through me, so vivid they might have swept away my sense of purpose if I hadn't held on tight.

Yes, the rush of a young boy racing across a field to an ice cream truck—and the creamy sweetness flooding his mouth afterward—was meant to be savored. Yes, I could allow a moment's satisfaction from his internal scream as I scoured through the memory of his teenage self smashing someone else's prized violin into the smallest pieces his heels could produce. But farther, deeper, there would be the answers we needed.

There would be a sphinx and awful promises and mysteries unraveled. And I could devour until I found them.

The moments I'd been searching for hit me unexpectedly: a flash of amber eyes, graceful movements of bejeweled hands that I couldn't follow, a caustic sense of agreement racing through the man in response. Tall towers, deep caverns, dry heat and damp darkness, chambers lit by an artificial glow. Glints of the metals he could pass but his master couldn't tolerate. Writing, carved or painted, that he snapped photos of or copied with painstaking precision.

Spurts of triumph. Maybe this time would be enough. Maybe this time.

I lingered over every morsel as long as I could, inhaling every detail and marking in my own memory. The man's silent wail of agony wound through the images brittler and harsher, until—*snap!*

My hunger severed the last thread. Nothing remained inside his husk of a body.

I heaved myself backward, falling into my regular mortal body as I did. Emotions still churned through me, some of them mine and some of them my victim's, but the strongest sensation that expanded in my chest was relief.

The words spilled out of me. "He found writings—stories about shadowkind weaknesses. Rumors of poisons and other toxins. It wasn't enough. She wanted more. There were claims of mortals sickening shadowkind and sickening themselves in turn. Ways to protect against that too. He saw just a day or two ago— *To shield against the weaknesses one or the other possesses, you must contain both their strengths.* I don't know what that means, but Tempest was pleased when he told her. And… something about a place with many large rocks. He found a painting of it. Energies could resonate from it. I think she decided to unleash her disease from there."

"Large rocks?" Sorsha repeated. "A mountain?"

I reached back into my mind's eye. "No. One rock here and one there, many of them, standing in a circle. A large circle, with a smaller ring inside it. Some of them were stacked on each other like… tables."

Ruse's eyebrows leapt up. He tapped at his phone and held it toward me with a photograph on the screen. "Like this?"

My breath caught. "Yes. That's the pattern."

"Stonehenge," Omen murmured. "If that's where she plans to launch her catastrophe from, she must be working out the final details close to there. We'll just have to—"

With a *boom* that rang through my ears, the roof over our heads exploded in a shower of shingles.

Thorn bellowed and leapt up from the limp corpse. Orange light flared across Omen's body. Shouts volleyed all around us—a glittering net heaved through the air—laser-like whips streaked across the darkness.

The wingéd warrior ducked, dodged, and bashed his fists into the faces of two of the attackers who appeared to be careening down the hillside in a wave. I spun around, grasping for some sort of weapon—

But we hadn't been their main target after all—not the four of us shadowkind. Two figures were lunging at Sorsha from behind. One of them jabbed something into the base of her neck with a crackle of electricity that made her body spasm before she could land her first punch.

I leapt at them, not caring that all I had to defend her were my bare hands, which weren't half as suited to the job as Thorn's. The brutes were already propelling her sagging body out onto the rocky terrain. I shoved one of them aside, but it was too late. As I reached for my beloved, a feline creature swooped down on vast wings to snatch Sorsha up in her paws.

A whip lashed across my shoulder. Ruse knocked the helmet off my attacker with the clang of a cooking pot. Omen tore past us all, his hellhound claws gouging the man's stomach open as he sprang.

She was already gone. Bodies lay broken and bleeding around us. A few figures who'd seen the turn of the tide fled into the night. And the sphinx had soared off into the blackness of the sky, not a hint of her or her precious cargo in sight.

She'd taken Sorsha. My fingers curled into my palms as every particle of my body cried out in horror. What did Tempest mean to do with her?

I'd devour every member of the Company if that was what it took to save her.

TWENTY-TWO

Sorsha

I WOKE UP CURLED INTO A BALL, MY KNEES PRESSED TO MY FOREHEAD, every muscle still tensed with the memory of the electric shock that had knocked me out, as if it had happened only seconds ago. Even my hands had clenched tight to my chest. And, nestled against my palm—

Footsteps tapped toward me. I jerked my hand up to swipe it over my mouth and tentatively raised my head.

I was locked up in a cage like the ones I'd seen in Company facilities before: a solid metal floor rigid against my shoulder and hip, bars gleaming all around me in the stark light. But they mustn't have been silver or iron, which wouldn't have affected me anyway, because Tempest was now resting her hands against those bars as she peered between them at me with her catlike eyes.

With her that close, the razor-edged chill of her innate power walloped me harder than it had in our meetings before. My pulse hiccupped, a tickle of my inner heat flaring in response.

I directed that first jolt of flames into my cheek. The sensitive skin stung, but the sphinx didn't give any sign that she'd noticed anything amiss. Her plump lips had curved into a smirk.

I didn't have much room to straighten out my posture. The roof of the cage stood only a foot above my prone body, and I couldn't have stretched my legs toward the walls without banging my feet on the bars. Tempest and her Company lackeys must have had quite the time squeezing me in here.

More fire stirred in my chest. If she thought I was simply going to lie here quietly—

"Throw your power around if you must," the leonine woman said. "It won't get you anywhere. I'd vanish into the shadows before I got more than a sunburn, and nothing else in here will smolder."

My gaze slipped beyond her to the wider room. Sweet twinkly trash cans, she wasn't kidding. The entire space looked as if it were constructed out of steel, from ceiling to floor and every piece of furniture in the place. There wasn't much of that anyway—a lab table behind Tempest and a smaller table laid with similarly glinting instruments next to it.

I *really* didn't like the look of those.

The flames in my cheek had smoothed the lump there into a thinner mass that tucked against my gums. I flexed my jaw and decided it was safe to speak. "Where'd you get this place—from the set of some low-budget alien horror flick? I'll skip the probing, if it's all the same to you. With the way you treat your guests, it's a wonder you're not more popular."

Tempest chuckled at my sarcasm, her languid voice turning the sound sultry. "You could have been a proper guest if you hadn't attempted to incinerate me on our second meeting. But look at all I've done for you regardless! I had this entire space constructed just for you, my darling phoenix."

Well, that was certainly some level of obsession. I shifted my weight, my arms already starting to ache from the awkward position I was lying in. "Any particular reason I'm getting this star treatment? I'm assuming it wasn't just so you could taunt me."

If she'd wanted me dead, I'd already be kaput. She'd had me helpless while I was knocked out. Instead I was here, so clearly she needed something from me… How exactly did she think she was going to get it?

Hopefully not with that spread of torture tools, but knowing how her Company tended to operate, I suspected those hopes were worth about as much as the ashes I'd like to leave this place in. It wasn't so much a matter of whether I'd face a version of those extra-terrestrial bodily excavations as how soon.

"You met one of my instruments," the sphinx said. "I suppose you didn't learn enough from him to connect the dots. That's quite all right. The less you know, the easier it'll be to take it from you." Her smile somehow turned even sharper.

Psychotic bitch. A fresh flare of anger erupted within my ribs, and flames crackled across my back. I gritted my teeth, biting back a hiss and yanking the fire inside me as well as I could.

Tempest cocked her head with a twinkle in her eyes as if she found my erratic powers highly amusing. "Just FYI, in case you get any ideas of martyrdom: if you start letting off too much smoke, your cage is rigged to douse you with rather a lot of water. You're not getting away from me by that avenue either."

I had no hope at all of getting through to this maniac in my current state, but I couldn't help prodding at her non-existent conscience anyway. "Does it really not bother you even a little that you're *helping* people who hate you and every other being like you? How are you winning when getting what you want depends on years of giving them what they want?"

"Ah, but once I have this, so many more mortals will sicken and fall than ever enjoyed carrying out my business. This realm will never recover. Forever is worth quite a lot."

"So then what? You get to sashay around, gloating about how horrible things are for eternity?"

Her eyes glittered piercingly. "I'm sure I'll find plenty of ways to occupy myself."

More frustration was trawling through me, dredging up flames with it. "They think you're all monsters, and you're proving them right."

"Who says they're wrong? I'm a monster. I'll own that. And no one is going to stop me from being just as monstrous as I please."

She stepped back with a sway of her hips. The dress suit she wore today wasn't quite as extravagant as her robes from our previous meetings, but she'd still managed to find or manufacture one with diamonds stitched in patterns across the collar of the jacket and the hem of the skirt. They sparkled against the deep violet silk. She waved a hand that was just as sparkly with all the rings it was laden with.

"It's time for you to give me the last piece I need to make this scheme come together. Isn't it lovely that *you're* the one making my apocalypse possible? I'll leave my lackeys to it. Oh, and before you get any ideas about them, I should mention that it's not only your cage fitted with water pipes."

She vanished into the shadows under the larger table just as at least a dozen sprayers clicked on overhead. In an instant, a deluge filled the room, as if a thunderstorm had broken over it. The heavy drops rattled across the tables and gurgled down a drain I hadn't noticed in the far corner of the floor.

The angle of the spray meant plenty of it leapt between the bars to splatter my skin and clothes, but getting soaked was the least of my worries. The door opened just long enough to admit five figures wearing plastic visors to protect their eyes from the worst of the spray. In seconds, the downpour drenched the rest of them, from their hair to their tan uniforms.

The burliest three of the bunch advanced on my cage. I braced myself, ignoring the growing throbbing in my cramped muscles. The moment one of them unlocked the front of the cage, I whipped my legs forward—and discovered my ankles were bound together with just half a foot of chain between them.

I still landed a kick, but it didn't hit quite as hard as I'd meant it to. One of the other burly dudes grabbed my legs before I could haul them back. I punched and thrashed, not really expecting to prevent whatever they were going to do but intending to extract every bit of discomfort I could for the indignity and the pain they were no doubt about to inflict on me.

My inner fire wasn't any help. As the thugs manhandled me over to the waiting table, water rained down on me. All the furious heat that wanted to leap from my body instead sizzled against my skin, scalding me briefly before more spray washed the boiling liquid away. Maybe a few flecks gave my captors a blister or two, but nothing that made them so much as wince.

They shoved me down on the table on my back, wrenching my arms into place at my sides. Steel cuffs snapped over my wrists, ankles, waist, and finally my neck. The edge of that last one dug into the tender skin at the top of my throat, an ache forming there when I swallowed.

The deluge was still pounding down on me, blurring my vision and filling my ears. I let my lips part just slightly to drink a little down in sips. I wasn't going to be able to fight anyone if I let myself get dehydrated as well as imprisoned. Lord only knew when Tempest might decide to feed me.

The two figures without quite as much beef on them stepped up on either side of the table, rivulets slicking down their visors. One held a scalpel from the smaller table, the other a syringe. "Preparing to take samples while subject is conscious," the first one said, her voice warbling through the falling water. "Bags labeled A."

As she pressed the scalpel to my forearm, I bit back a yelp. A stinging sensation rippled over my skin. It felt as if she dug out a sliver of my flesh—she dropped a solid scrap of red into a baggie. Then she tugged up my shirt to slice into the muscles over my ribs.

My heart thumped harder. She dug the blade right between two of those ribs, and the pain splintered right through my chest. I couldn't quite hold back a strained whine.

I hadn't been able to shake Tempest's resolve, but these people—they weren't ancient monsters with no concept of morality. They were my fellow fucking human beings.

I tipped my head so I wouldn't drown by fully opening my mouth and spat out the words. "I'm a person just like you are. I think and feel just like you do. I'm not some mindless beast that goes around ripping apart innocent people. How can you think it's okay to torture me like this?"

The lab techs kept working without so much as a blink. You'd have thought they were deaf like the man in Crete if they hadn't been talking to each other.

"Shin bone," the man reminded his colleague, and she reached to pull up my pant leg. My ankle jarred against the cuff with the instinctive urge to wrench away. An even deeper pain radiated up through my leg.

"I was born in Austin, Texas," I said into the rush of artificial rain. "When I was a little kid, I loved ice cream and watching the bats fly over the bridge. I went to school—I learned all the presidents' names, how to write an essay, and that we're supposed to treat each other with respect even if we have personal differences. I've fallen in love. I've had my heart broken. I'm *human*, for fuck's sake. You're carving up a person."

Not that it was any more okay when they did crap like this to a shadowkind. But my captors clearly didn't give a shit how much like them I was. They'd happily destroy me just as they'd destroyed so many other creatures—even their own people, when they'd thought their opponents were getting too close to the truth—just for the chance to exterminate a whole realm of beings, most of whom hadn't done any more damage than the average human.

How could they hold so much hate? How could they let it burn out every bit of compassion in them?

Or maybe human beings weren't all that compassionate to begin with. I wasn't fully one myself, was I? Were all mortals capable of turning this sociopathic if given a nudge in the right direction?

"Listen to me!" I shouted, my voice breaking with a cry as the scalpel slashed the tip off my baby toe. Rage whipped up inside me and surged from my body—only to meet the falling water with a hiss of dissipating steam. My tormenters stepped back just for a second as the scalding droplets cleared, but for all the notice they gave me, I might as well have been a malfunctioning radiator rather than a living, thinking being.

Thinking for now. As they closed in on me again, the man raised his syringe. "Now to take the unconscious samples. Bags labeled B."

"No!" I said, managing to choke back a sob.

He jabbed the needle into my neck just below the cuff. Darkness unfurled over my mind. My awareness narrowed and spiraled down, down, into cool blackness—but not quite so fast that I missed one last remark the woman made, with a sigh as if slicing and dicing me was cramping her style.

"This had better be enough to get that cure."

TWENTY-THREE

Thorn

The imp eyed us as we moved out of the shadows into the interior of the Everymobile. "That was a fast trip." She had the impudence to curl her lip in the slightest pout, as if she were actually *put out* that we hadn't fallen into enemy hands.

That was, most of us hadn't. My jaw clenched in the wake of yet another wave of rage and loss.

"We returned through a rift," Omen said curtly. "Seeing as we needed to move quickly—for the same reason as we were able to make use of a rift without worrying about the Highest."

Gisele's gaze had already traveled over the four of us. She leapt up, the ferocity that appeared incongruous with her petite frame sparking in her eyes. "What happened to Sorsha?"

Those words brought the little dragon scuttling out of the bathroom. Pickle peered at us, his wings trembling at half-mast, and let out a snort that sounded of both consternation and anxiety.

"Tempest took her," Snap said, his usually bright voice turned dagger-sharp. Impassioned fury had been radiating off the devourer from the moment we'd regrouped. "The sphinx was too swift—we were overwhelmed by the Company attackers—we have to get her back before they hurt her!"

I didn't want to see what state it would bring him to if I acknowledged that the sphinx and her murderous Company had likely already harmed our mortal in some way. My hopes centered around recovering her *alive*.

They'd held Omen for months when they'd captured him, conducting their torturous experiments. But that had been while they were still determining the shape of their plans. Tempest had indicated she expected to see those plans through in mere days now. Had she even wanted Sorsha for some use or simply to deprive us of all our mortal offered?

My hands balled into fists of their own accord. If Tempest had been following the second reasoning, she'd have been motivated to end my lady's life the moment she could. If she had—if she'd taken Sorsha from us in the most irrevocable possible way... I would see the pieces of that venomous being's body torn apart bit by bit and scattered to the ends of the earth before I was through. I would rend the wings from her back and stuff them down her throat. I would—

Our commander spoke up again. "We can't be completely sure of where Tempest will have taken her, but from what Snap gleaned from the man in Crete, it sounds as though the sphinx intends to be near Stonehenge in the near future. If she thinks our mortal is going to play some part in her scheme, it seems most likely she'll be in southern England." Omen grimaced. "Which hardly narrows our search down."

Ruse's fingers were flying over his phone, which he'd pulled out the moment we'd emerged. "Better than scouring all of Europe. I've already gotten my hacker on the job, pulling more details on the suspicious activity he's already dug up in that region. He should be able to help us get a more specific location."

Snap shifted on his feet, the neon green of his shadowkind form whirling in his eyes. "We can't just stay here waiting. We've got to start our own search as quickly as we can."

Bow got up too. "We'll be right there with you." The centaur glanced at Gisele. "Do you think it'll be safe to leave the Everymobile here for however long we're gone?"

Mortals did have a habit of getting finicky about any vehicle sitting in the same spot for what they deemed was an inappropriate length of time, which from what I'd gathered often wasn't very long at all.

Gisele frowned and then tossed back her hair. "Let's not risk it. We might need a good getaway vehicle once we're there anyway. And it'll be nice to give Sorsha a familiar place to recover in as soon as we've rescued her. The Everymobile survived one trip through the shadow realm—I'm sure she can handle one more, when it's this important."

Omen's lips twitched with a hint of strained amusement. "We'll do our best to keep the trip short for minimal side effects. Perhaps all her new features will revert back to normal on the second time through." He motioned to the driver's seat. "Would one of you prefer to do the honors? The nearest rift isn't far."

Gisele hopped up behind the wheel. With a look of utter determination, she hit the gas and turned the RV in the direction he indicated.

The portal between the mortal realm and our natural home was invisible to human senses, but I assumed all of us could sense the faint vibration rippling through our bodies that heightened the nearer we came. This one lay over open waters just beyond the shore, around a peninsula from the harbor. The quiet of the night allowed us to veer down a darkened side-road and heave the vehicle out of the physical world into the shadows, all of us gripping its walls to speed the transition.

We propelled it toward the rift, the thrum of the opening pulling us in like a vacuum. We'd just shot through into the amorphous world on the other side, a thick chill condensing around my being, when a familiar voice carried through the churning darkness.

"Thorn! I was just coming in search of you."

It was Flint's deeply melancholy tone. We all stopped, and I turned to face my fellow warrior. His presence loomed large and weighty in the murky atmosphere.

"What is it?" I asked with a flicker of hope. Had he decided to rejoin us? Was it possible the other wingéd from Rome might aid us in this battle after all?

But as he drew nearer, my hopes were extinguished with the impression I got that he was bracing himself. He wasn't pleased with what he was about to say.

"Our brethren wish for you to attend to them. They have great need of your attendance."

Irritation prickled through me before I could catch it. I shouldn't resent those who had given so much of themselves while I'd escaped our past essentially unscathed. And yet—if I accepted this delay, how scathed might my lady be by the time I reached her?

Omen made the decision for me before I had to grapple with my conflicting responsibilities. "Go. See if you can stir them into getting off their asses and pitching in before Tempest sends the whole world to hell. It'll take us some time to find out where Sorsha's being held anyway. You can smash your way through to her when you get back."

Yes. I could meet both responsibilities—and perhaps turn one into part of the solution to the other. I nodded to Omen and set off in a different direction from my companions.

It would have been difficult for me to explain to a mortal how exactly we ascertained which rift led where and how we reached those rifts in our own realm. The portals floated here and there with hints of the sensations that waited on the other side. One could spring through any at random for a trip of unexpectedness or focus on the place one most wanted to experience—and somehow or other, arrive at the appropriate portal without any great passing of time.

Flint already had a clear course in mind, having just come from what was now our destination. As we barreled through the murk, I felt his attention settle on me. "Your mortal—or somewhat mortal—companion. Something untoward has happened to her?"

"She has been stolen by our greatest enemy, the one who means to end most mortal and shadowkind existence if she has her way," I said. "It is possible that our lady's capture may even help bring that catastrophe about. By every indication, the destruction the sphinx intends to inflict on both worlds is imminent."

The other wingéd asked nothing more, but his presence beside me gave off a more palpable uneasiness.

"What is this urgent matter our brethren have sent you to me about?" I asked.

"I think it would be better for them to explain. They didn't share all the details with me, only said it was your trial to bear."

That phrasing didn't sound particularly promising. I managed to hold in an ethereal sigh. Those who had fought valiantly deserved better than my disdain, regardless of my impatience.

We emerged over a roadway only a mile or so from the palace the mortals considered holy where my brethren had made their home. As if they wished to think of themselves as some sort of "angels." That idea rankled me as we hustled on through the shadows that were starting to split with the brightening dawn.

The two with their mangled bodies were poised on the rooftop as if they'd been standing there awaiting my return since the moment I'd left. Both of their expressions looked even more grim than I recalled. And here I'd found Flint overwrought. With every one of my kind I encountered, I discovered new depths of dourness.

"You took so long in your rambling adventures I started to doubt you still had any sense of duty at all," Viscera said in her wheezing voice before I could even greet them.

My hackles rose at the attack on my honor. I held my temper in check. "I had urgent matters to attend to, as we discussed. It was hardly for my enjoyment. And an even more critical matter faces us now."

"Faces *you*," Lance said. "Do not include us in your foolishness."

"It isn't foolishness. All our fates may depend on the outcome of the next few days." I dragged in a breath and squared my shoulders. "What is it you need from me? I'll help you however I am able."

Viscera raised her broken chin. "We believe one of the griffins flew by here and dropped the box they stole, allowing what little of its contents remained to scatter. I can sense the fragments of my brother's being all around. But we dare not venture into view in our physical forms to collect them. The mortals would flee in horror."

A shudder ran through me at the thought of my former comrade's remains abandoned in that way, but I couldn't restrain the question that rose up. "Could not Flint—"

"*You* fought beside my brother. You will recognize the bits of his essence. The rest we can worry about later. You will go forth into the city and collect all you can of him."

I glanced down at the courtyard below with its framing of bleached columns. "Where exactly do those fragments lie? I will gather them immediately."

"The wind has blown them through the streets far and wide. It may take some doing, but we will bring what still exists back together."

They expected me to hunt all across one of the largest cities in the world for the tiny particles of our long-dead comrade's essence, all while a vicious menace of a shadowkind brought about a near-Armageddon?

I peered at my kin, suddenly wondering if any of this story were even true. To lie to a fellow wingéd would be shameful... but she'd already proven how little she thought of me. How could it be that these griffins had happened to pass by at exactly this time?

"Well, what delays you?" she demanded.

The thinning thread of loyalty that had brought me here fractured with an ache that shot straight through my chest. As I drew myself to the fullest my height could reach, the memory of Sorsha's arms around me came back to me—her warm voice in my ears, telling me I could leave her if I truly felt that was right, if it would satisfy my conscience.

That was how devoted brethren ought to treat each other. Trusting their judgment of their own needs. Giving them room to make choices. Not scolding them like some sort of *child* for mistakes made centuries ago that might not even be mistakes.

"I fought as hard as I could with your brother all those ages ago," I said. "And I left the battle for his and the rest of your sake as much as my own. There was no betrayal or shame in it, and I will claim none now. My first duty is to the beings alive who stand to suffer and die if I don't act, and that includes both of you and so many others—and it isn't finding scraps of one long snuffed out that will save any of you."

Both of them were gaping at me now. Lance tried to puff himself up in some image of righteousness that now only looked ridiculous to me. "Then you forsake all your—"

I cut him off with a glower. "I forsake *nothing*. I go now to fight for so many more than died even then, and if *you* had any honor, you would be doing the same. It's up to you whether you show what wingéd are meant to be or wallow here in the pain of the past. I've made my decision."

I waited with a thudding of my heart in my chest. They hesitated and then shrank back into their wounded stances, and I knew it was hopeless.

They were hopeless. I could see that now. They weren't the final bastions of our kind but a pale shade of what we used to be, what we'd always striven to be, and it had nothing to do with the ruined bits of their bodies but of the lapses they'd allowed in their souls. I intended to do better than that.

"Fine. You've distracted me enough with your demands." I swiveled on my heel and caught Flint's gaze. His stern face had blanched in shock. "Are you staying to wallow with them, or will you stand by me and the rest of our kind when it matters most?"

The other wingéd wavered too, but only for an instant. The duck of his head hid a wince of humiliation. "I should have stayed with that fight to begin with. You're right, as you were right before. We must do what we can for all the other beings who now face so much danger. I apologize—"

"It doesn't matter," I said. "You chose what you thought was right, and then you changed your mind. It's an asset all thinking creatures possess… even those two."

I shot one last glance over my shoulder, but the ragged wingéd hadn't budged. So be it. With a nod to Flint, I hurtled into the shadows.

Long ago, I hadn't found a way to be what my companions then needed. This time, I refused to let them down—not Sorsha nor Omen, nor any of the others I meant to save.

TWENTY-FOUR

Sorsha

The next time when I woke up, I was still clamped to the lab table. Aches ran all through my back and limbs from the awkward position I'd been lying in, sharper in the spots where the experimenters' tools had cut into my body. The lights had dimmed, giving the room a hazy, dream-like feel.

The deluge from the sprinklers had stopped, although the clothes still clinging damply to my body were proof that I hadn't imagined it. The experimenters were gone. Had they noticed—? With a stutter of my pulse, I probed the base of my gums with my tongue and relaxed slightly. Thank hamstrung hippos for that smallest of small mercies.

Had they left me on the table because they weren't quite finished carving me up? At least that would mean Tempest hadn't gotten what she'd wanted yet. I'd sooner cuddle up with a cockatrice than make this quest of hers one bit easier for her.

The last words I'd heard from the Company scientists tickled through my head. *To get that cure.* I wouldn't have understood why the sphinx thought I had anything to do with curing anything if it hadn't been for Snap's devouring of her lackey in Crete. What was it exactly that he'd said the dude had found…?

A warbling sound broke through my reminiscing: a voice, not much more than a whine that sounded more animal than human, wavering from the direction of the door. Then a gasp of pain and a hoarse plea: "You don't have to— I came here because I—"

That was Snap's voice, its usual brightness tarnished. My limbs jerked against the restraints automatically—and the steel cuff around my left hand popped open.

I started at it for the space of a few heartbeats, barely believing it. How could Tempest's people have been anything less than perfectly careful? But they were mortal, and as I'd imagine she'd have grumbled hundreds of times, mortals were infinitely fallible.

Lucky for me, shadowkind were far from perfect too.

I lifted my arm with a wince and fumbled with the cuff around my neck. It only took a matter of seconds for my groping fingers to snag on the latch and wrench it open. A moment later, I'd released the cuff around my other wrist and then my waist as well.

I shoved myself upright so fast my head spun, both with dizziness in the aftermath of whatever sedative my tormenters had injected me with and the lance of pain that shot up my spine. My breath caught just shy of a sob. I gritted my teeth and snatched at the cuffs around my ankles.

Snap's voice was getting more distant but no happier. Had the others come to break me out and been trapped? Damn it. But maybe I could turn the tables on these Company assholes one more time.

I swung around and lowered my feet to the ground. As I eased my weight onto them, my legs wobbled and then held with the stiffening of my calf and thigh muscles. My gaze fell on the smaller table, but its spread of torture instruments had been cleared off.

Oh well. Slicing and dicing wasn't my typical style anyway. It was barbequing time.

My hand was just coming to rest on the door handle when the fading whimper rose to a scream. I flinched, the hairs on my arms standing on end. The shriek carried on, quavering and hitching. It didn't sound as if they were simply tormenting my devourer. It sounded like they were *killing* him.

My throat constricted. I yanked at the door handle, but it didn't budge. Of course they'd have locked that.

I closed my eyes, groping for calm despite the rattle of my frantic pulse in my ears. I knew my way around a lock. If I just melted the right bits—if the sprinklers overhead didn't trigger from the concentrated heat—

An even more piercing cry sent another shock of urgency through me. I pressed my hand over the lock area and let anger mingle with my panic. How *dare* they hurt my lover. They would pay—all of the assholes here would pay in every way I could make them.

Heat flared across my collarbone, sharp enough to sear, but my fiery voodoo surged toward my intended target as well. I thrust more in that direction, wanting to reduce every mechanism in there to goop.

The shrieking had faded into a sputtering gurgle. Would I even make it to him in time?

I gritted my teeth and hauled at the door. It flung open to reveal two drenched scientists standing right on the other side.

My stomach lurched, but I didn't have time to move so much as an inch. One of the experimenters was already slashing a scalpel across my forearm; the other slammed a container over the cut. A container that caught the rush of smoke that streamed up from the wound in my adrenaline-spiked state.

Fury clanged through me alongside the jolt of understanding. My inner fire whipped out in a blaze—but before it had done more than sizzle across the moisture flecking my attackers' faces, a fresh downpour burst from the sprinklers both in the room behind me and in the hall, this time icy cold.

My breath rasped at the sudden smack of frigid water. The scientists were already fleeing with their ill-gotten plunder, and the burly guards from before barged in to replace them. I only managed to land two blows before I found myself tangled up so tightly in one of those glittering nets that I could barely wiggle my pinkie. I couldn't even congratulate myself for the blood trickling from the one nose it appeared I'd broken.

Snap's voice had vanished. But it had never really been him, had it? Or at least not him now. As the guards rolled me out of the net back into my cage, the remaining pieces clicked together.

The Company had captured my devourer before. The bits I'd heard of him actually speaking, they must have recorded while they had him in their facility. The screams and shrieks might have been from then too or simply been sound effects they'd picked to reasonably match his tone. It wasn't as if I could have identified anyone accurately from that cacophony of agony.

They'd set me up. Tempest must have decided she needed the shadowkind essence I only bled when I was particularly worked up to manufacture her cure. Had she known for sure it would come out when I was frantic, or only been experimenting after I'd bled like a mortal during the initial torture? Maybe one of the Company assholes had noticed me leaking smoke during one of our battles. Shit.

It still might not be enough. She obviously hadn't figured out how to transform what she was getting from me into whatever exactly she wanted.

The cure...

Maybe Tempest wasn't quite as impervious as she wanted us to think.

For what felt like a millennium or two, I sprawled there in my cage. When I attempted the same melting trick on the lock at its base, the sprinklers went off in an instant, and all I got for my trouble was another freezing shower. After that, I pulled my knees up to my chest for warmth and willed my teeth not to chatter.

If Tempest *had* gotten what she wanted from me this time, what did that mean for my chances of surviving the next day? Or even the next hour?

She couldn't be sure of her "cure" when she'd never made it before —or unleashed this disease before—right? I didn't think she'd take the chance of offing me until she was one hundred percent convinced she had no further use for me. Of course, if that meant living out the rest of my days in this cramped box, death didn't sound all that bad. Especially if Tempest went down with me.

My chilly reflections halted at the shimmering of a figure into sight just beyond the bars. The sphinx herself had returned. To gloat, it appeared, judging from the coy tilt of her head and the smirk curling her lips. I willed a small spurt of flame along my gums, ignoring the burning sensation of the flesh there.

"You really thought I'd give you a chance to escape," she said, her voice languid with amusement.

I wasn't in any mood to go easy on her ego. "Hard as it might be to believe, you don't actually come across as all that smart."

Tempest shrugged, but the twitch of her eyelid suggested I'd irritated her at least a little. Not the greatest victory ever, but give me a break. At this point I couldn't be much of a chooser.

Unfortunately, she knew just how to needle me in return. "How does it feel knowing you've provided the final step in the plans you've been trying so hard to interrupt?"

"Pretty crappy," I said breezily. "How do you feel knowing that you weren't quite stealthy enough to stop me from figuring out what's going on here? *To shield against the weakness one or the other possesses, you must contain both their strengths.* You're trying to find some part of my essence to protect you from your own disease, because *you're* not strong enough on your own."

A spark flashed in her eyes. She managed to keep her tone even. "Not *trying*. I've succeeded. There's nothing left that stands in our way. My people are ready to let loose our sickness tomorrow, and I'll get to watch and laugh while both they and the ones they wanted so badly to destroy crumple in its throes."

Using my smoky essence had worked, then? Or was she just trying to fake me out to set me up for some new trick?

"You seem to take a lot of pride in being a traitorous butcher," I remarked. "And here I thought you were all about brains and brilliant schemes, not random slaughter." I let my voice lilt into a skewed lyric. "Shows your lies, living so grand, darling. Do you mean to start cheating? Is your plunder planned?"

Another victory: warping songs appeared to annoy Tempest just as much as it had Omen. "Shut up," she said with a wave of her hand that was clearly meant to be casual. The momentary narrowing of her eyes showed the truth. "I can't imagine how Omen and his lot put up with you for as long as they did. I'd expect they'll be pleased to find out you're no longer their burden to carry."

If she thought I was going to believe that after everything I'd been through with my shadowkind men, she was even more off her rocker than I'd figured. I rolled my eyes at her. "I think you'll find it's the opposite. But why don't you invite them over to see who's right? I'd like to watch that visit go down."

She chuckled. "Perhaps you will. When I hold the only protection against this sickness, I hold all the power. Do you think I won't have them bowing to me if their survival hangs in the balance?"

Of course. If even *she* couldn't withstand the disease on her own, no other shadowkind would either.

Would my lovers compromise their principles to save their own lives? I wouldn't blame them for appeasing Tempest for long enough to guarantee their immunity if they eviscerated her afterward. But I already knew that Snap would never willingly back down, not once this woman had become my murderer, and I couldn't imagine Thorn putting his survival over his sense of justice. He'd already spent centuries beating himself up for remaining alive after the last war he'd waged.

She'd destroy not just me but possibly all of the beings I loved as well. A larger surge of fire shot through the nonchalance I'd been trying to convey. I clenched my jaw, but heat crackled just under my skin with a stinging wave of pain.

"You see," the sphinx said, her voice dripping with vicious sweetness. "You really could have been something, my phoenix, but that mortal side of you hasn't got the power to aim those talents properly. Such a shame."

"Or maybe the only shame will be how quickly we'll snuff *you* out," I retorted. "You can't see everything. We've already screwed up your plans at least a dozen times."

"And yet not badly enough that it stopped me from getting to where we are now." Her smile came back, thinner now. She motioned to her broad forehead. "It's not just these two mortal-esque eyes that I see with, but my inner eye as well. And a sphinx always glimpses the answers one way or another."

My gaze locked onto that smooth plane of skin beneath the fall of her gleaming bronze hair. That was where her supernatural wisdom came from—a third eye within her mind?

A jitter of excitement quivered through me. Tempest turned with a swish of her dress and vanished, leaving me alone again—but with a resolve I hadn't found until just now.

Omen had told me to fight her by blinding her. I could still do that. I had the tools right here, and now I knew which eye she truly relied on.

The only question was whether I'd get a chance to make use of that knowledge before she brought both realms to their knees.

TWENTY-FIVE

Omen

THE RUMBLE OF A DEPARTING JUMBO JET GRATED AGAINST MY NERVES. I shot a narrow look at Ruse where he was watching the stream of arriving travelers pouring out of the airport's security area. "Remind me again why you thought this diversion was a good idea? How is having a mortal tagging along going to help us extricate Sorsha any faster?"

The incubus tsked at my impatience, but I could tell from the tension in his jaw that he wasn't impervious to the same worries. "I told her she should join us. Maybe she won't be much help getting Sorsha out of the facility, but whatever *our* mortal has been through, having additional moral support can't be a bad thing."

"You don't think the four of us are enough for her?"

Ruse met my gaze, abruptly more serious than I could ever remember seeing him. "She's been struggling. I know you've seen it too. That's what our little escapade on the boat was about, wasn't it? I'm sure she'd say she's perfectly satisfied with all the wonders we shadowkind can provide… but she *is* half mortal too. There are things she thinks and feels that we can't wrap our heads around—as much as I'd like to become her be-all and end-all."

He put that desire into words so effortlessly, as if there was nothing at all embarrassing about an incubus—or any shadowkind—wanting to devote themselves to a mortal. Which I supposed there wasn't. But I couldn't imagine the same sentiment ever falling from my mouth quite that easily.

After all, I still wasn't entirely sure that my presence in Sorsha's life wouldn't be what brought about her ruin rather than what raised her above it. It was *my* former colleague who might have already ripped into her in who knew how many ways.

I just hoped I still knew Tempest well enough to have made an accurate guess of where she was working from, given the data Ruse's computer expert had looked up—and of the likelihood that she'd kept Sorsha alive. Surely she wouldn't have bothered knocking Sorsha out and dragging her off if all she needed was a corpse?

But who knew with the sphinx, now or ever?

I inhaled slowly and squared my shoulders, keeping a tight grip on the composure I'd spent so long cultivating. We weren't really squandering time. The others were investigating the facility we'd set our sights on—a supposed coat factory on the outskirts of West London, less than two hours from the standing stones—while we picked up our mortal's best friend from Heathrow, just a few miles away.

And I definitely wasn't letting myself dread finding out what this woman was going to have to say when she came face to face with the beings who'd lost her once-close companion.

Ruse perked up. A moment later, I spotted a figure with a recognizable burst of black curls atop a sleek white blouse and slacks. She actually *smiled* at the incubus when her gaze caught on him. She hustled over, dragging her carry-on—and slowed at the sight of me.

I'd barely exchanged five words with this mortal woman during our single meeting, but apparently that and whatever Sorsha had reported about me had made an impression. And not a good one.

She kept coming, though, and stopped in front of us with a determined expression that gave me some hint as to what she and Sorsha had in common. "Is this all I get for a welcoming party?" she said, cocking her head. "Where's the rest of the crew?"

"Attempting to confirm Sorsha's location to make sure that when we go charging in to rescue her, she's actually there for us to rescue," I said.

"Hmm. Or, if you're lucky, she'll rescue herself before you all get around to it."

Knowing my recent lover as well as I now did, I had to admit that was a possibility, as daunting an opponent as the sphinx could be.

"We'll see." I eyed Vivi carefully. She might be Sorsha's best friend, but she was still a mortal with all the potential weaknesses that could entail. My voice dropped. "You do understand the full situation, don't you? That Sorsha is as much shadowkind as she is human?"

If that news had frightened the woman when she'd first heard it, she gave no indication of fear now. All she did was shrug, aiming a glower at me that dared me to challenge her. "I just wish she'd felt she could open up to me about it on her own. Hopefully after this..." Her chin came up defiantly. "Maybe I didn't know exactly that the whole time, but I've always believed she's something special. Why do you think I came all this way? Human, monster, polka-dot potato bug—she's still *Sorsha*, and I'm here for her, whatever I can do."

Her vehemence convinced me that this one matter, at least, wouldn't be a problem. I motioned for her to follow us. "Come on, then. We can go meet up with the others and see what they have to say."

When we reached Darlene in her current state, Vivi raised her eyebrows but was polite enough not to remark on the RV's appearance. I had the feeling one more trip through the shadow realm would render the vehicle completely useless as a disguise.

Her tour bus form now looked more like a touring vehicle for rock stars... Rock stars who'd revamped it while on acid. Neon yellow streamers fluttered around all the windows—we'd tried trimming them off and they'd just grown back—and the exhaust pipe had expanded to the size and shape of a trombone. Unfortunately, it also *sounded* like a trombone when the engine started up.

The inside had gone through a similar makeover. The formerly white leather sofa was now decked out with stripes of gold shag—an update the equines had actually approved of. The faucet emitted no liquid at all but only a screeching electric guitar sound. And the fridge was now baking anything put inside it like an oven.

Basically, we were shit out of luck if we wanted a cold beverage anywhere around here.

Pickle scampered over at the sound of our arrival and snorted indignantly when his master didn't appear alongside us. Vivi stared at the little dragon and then shook her head. "Okay. That's not even the weirdest thing I've seen in the last couple of weeks. Is it part of the crew too?"

"He's Sorsha's pet." Ruse snapped his fingers at Pickle, beckoning him, but the creature lobbed a puff of smoke at him and turned tail. "I think she figured you'd disapprove."

"Of keeping a shadowkind beastie like a cat? That is... a little unusual. But I'm sure she had her reasons." The mortal woman flopped down on the sofa, her fingers curling into the patch of shag next to her. "What exactly is this shadowkind that's captured her now?"

Since the incubus was the one who'd insisted on bringing the mortal on, I left it to him to make all the necessary explanations and slid onto the driver's seat. There was a certain reassurance in maneuvering the massive vehicle with the power of my hands on the wheel. That was, until I noticed my new hangers-on were still, well, hanging on.

The skinny goblin who'd hassled me at the gas station in Greece was propped against a lamp post, ogling Darlene as we cruised by. Up ahead, I spotted a gargoyle on the top of a building that had shifted position just slightly to keep us in view.

Did the Highest really think that I'd deliver Ruby to them faster if they simply irritated me enough? Maybe we could enjoy some goblin shish kabob after we were done crushing Tempest and her schemes.

If I lived long enough after that to have a final meal. With the way these pricks were tailing me, chances were they'd figure out what Sorsha was during that battle and report my transgressions back to the Highest in a blink. And darkness only knew what kind of army they'd send after *her* while they were annihilating me.

I pulled up behind a dreary-looking business hotel where we'd agreed to meet and tried to tune out Ruse regaling Vivi with his extravagant tales of our adventures—the more intimate bits edited out. The incubus had some small sense of propriety. I wasn't sure Sorsha would appreciate him filling in her best friend with even that much detail, but she could take that up with him when we got her back.

When, not if. Even if it *was* over my dead body.

It was less than an hour before our companions emerged from the shadows around the furniture. Antic kicked things off with a squeal, leaping onto the table in front of Vivi.

"The other human is here! I love your hair. Does it grow all twisty like that naturally?"

The woman looked a tad taken aback before she found her voice with a laugh. "The braided parts, no, but this?" She fluffed the poof at the back of her head. "That's what God gave me."

"It is good to have you joining us," Thorn said, with a frown at the imp that suggested he didn't approve of her frivolous questions, and turned to me. "Everything we observed fits the information Ruse's contact conveyed to us. The building has been recently outfitted with iron and silver protections all through the outer walls—so much that we couldn't get close enough to touch them while in the shadows. Snap was able to pick up impressions from the gate and from a few pieces of litter."

The devourer nodded. "I also caught an impression of one of the workers talking about their boss bringing in a monster who could create fire. That's got to be Sorsha."

Between that and the extensive sprinkler systems we knew had also been ordered for installation in the building, I was inclined to agree with his assessment. I steepled my fingers in front of me. "All right. So, how do we get in? Are there employees guarding the place or coming and going that Ruse can con?"

Bow shook his head. "We didn't see anyone go in or out while we were watching. There was a delivery that looked like food, but it was placed in a storage box embedded in the wall. We figure there's got to be an opening on the inside for them to bring the supplies in."

I grimaced. "And I assume that's got those noxious metals all around it."

"Naturally." Gisele tapped her lips. "Do you think the sphinx is giving all the orders from the outside? How could she handle being surrounded by all that silver and iron?"

"It's a big building. If it's only the outer walls, she may be able to work in the center of the space with only mild discomfort. There might be an entrance on the roof or underground that allows her access without passing too closely to the protections." I glanced at Thorn. "I assume you couldn't examine the roof because you couldn't get close enough to use the shadows on the way up."

"And I could hardly fly up there visibly," the warrior acknowledged. "But we could assume there's a less protected spot up there and build our plans around that."

"No. I don't like counting on an assumption. She may not be using the roof at all—it would please her to pick the option that suits her form less well just to confuse us. And no doubt whatever entrance she uses will be heavily guarded regardless, with those on the inside having all the advantage. You've smashed through reinforced walls before. I don't suppose—"

Thorn was shaking his head before I'd finished the question. "I considered that myself, but I don't think I could summon enough strength to break all the way through so much of those metals with their weakening effect, not to mention the steel reinforcing the walls as well. An army of warriors could batter their way through, no doubt, but even with you and Flint and Bow… I don't think brute force will be the answer with our current numbers."

"That's fine," I said quickly, not wanting him beating himself up any more than he already had for failing to convince the other two wingéd to come on board with our mission. We'd gotten by without brute force before. Our mortal herself had come up with all those pacifistic plans—well, pacifistic by our typical standards.

But there were no employees for Ruse to charm, and even if we had the time to ferret out a loved one or two beyond the factory walls, what could they possibly tell us that would present us with a way in?

An army, Thorn had said. The words resonated through my thoughts and clicked into place. My mouth opened automatically with a rush of inspiration and an almost furious delight. "What if we—"

I cut myself off with a clenching of my teeth. *No.* That was the kind of viciously daring plan I'd have taken the same delight in centuries ago—the kind that had stirred rages in my victims and brought down suffering on innocents' heads. I'd been done with that past version of myself for so long. What the fuck was I thinking, nearly giving over to it on a moment's whim.

The others were watching me now. I should have kept my mouth shut.

Vivi crossed her arms over her chest. "Whatever idea you have, spit it out. It's got to be better than the nothing cherry on a nada sundae you all have come up with so far. And I didn't come all this way to watch you *not* get my bestie away from this maniac."

"I'd prefer we stick to plans that don't stand an equal chance of sealing Sorsha's doom."

"It looks like her 'doom' is guaranteed if you don't do anything, so fifty-fifty odds sound good to me."

I restrained myself from baring my teeth at her, feeling my hair ruffle with a current of frustration. "Maybe those who won't be involved in the actual rescue attempt shouldn't be spouting opinions about it."

"Maybe you shouldn't have invited me here if you didn't want to hear my opinions," Vivi shot back. "Do you actually care about Sorsha or only about making sure you don't look bad if your plan has a few hitches?"

A *few hitches*? She had no idea what she was talking about. But even with that knowledge, something about her words cut straight through me.

Even after everything we'd been through, some part of me wanted to deny that I cared about our mortal. Not because she didn't deserve that caring, but because when *I* cared... that was when all the hellish inclinations in me came out to play, and the outcome wasn't generally pretty. The way I got by, the way I made sure I didn't lead anyone into a shitstorm of my own making, was by tamping down on every emotion I had in me and focusing on pure cold strategy.

It hit me then in a way it hadn't before that Tempest had been wrong about me. I'd never forgotten I was a monster. I'd spent the last few centuries with that fact at the forefront of my mind and doing whatever I could to chain the beast inside.

But Sorsha hadn't seen my beast as a monster—or if she had, it'd been one she'd embraced as much as she had Snap's cruel hunger and Thorn's brutal strength. She'd lain beneath me on a bed less than ten feet from where I currently stood with my jaws clamped around her throat and told me she wasn't afraid of me. How many times had she asked to see me fierce and passionate rather than the "Ice-Cold Bastard," as she liked to put it?

I'd changed so much about myself since my days with Tempest, but somehow I hadn't managed to alter that one most basic thing: the belief that whatever I did and whoever I was with, if I gave in one inch to my baser nature, everything would go to hell, and most likely sooner rather than later.

Somehow I had the feeling I knew exactly how Sorsha would respond to that. *Who's to say a little hell is a bad thing?*

I did care about her, and the reserves of rage and power I'd held in check were beyond even Tempest's imagining. Wasn't it time to put all that hellishness to good use, for the sake of the woman I—

Yes.

I spun on my heel. "I have to bait the hook. Wait here. The rest of you, do whatever you need to so you're ready to storm that factory the second we get our opening. I doubt it'll take very long."

"Omen?" Snap said, his eyes widening, but I didn't stick around to answer questions. If I was going to do this, I was going to do it now, before the Ice-Cold Bastard's judgment reined me back in.

Bringing in new allies. It was exactly the kind of plan Sorsha would have loved. One I could admit I might never have thought of if she hadn't wriggled her way so far into my mind.

My lips curled into a wry smile. I doubted she'd ever have expected me to pull off quite this spectacular a magic trick, though.

I loped through the shadows a short ways and then emerged to amble down the street, scanning the buildings around me. Stop and smell the flowers. Buy myself a chocolate bar. Give every appearance of not having a care in the world except indulging myself at my leisure. Yeah, that would rile them up quickly enough.

Footsteps tapped along the sidewalk to catch up with me. A banshee fell into step at my side, her chin raised at a haughty angle. "This is not what the Highest ordered you to do. Get on with your quest."

I waved the candy bar at her. "What makes you think my quest doesn't require plenty of chocolate?"

When she glared at me, I took the final bite, allowed myself a few seconds to enjoy the sticky sweetness, and tossed the wrapper into a nearby trash bin. "Actually, I was hoping to get your attention. I figured it'd be faster than heading to the nearest rift. I've found out where Ruby is, but it won't be easy getting to her. Tell the Highest they'd better send their best—and lots of them."

The minion sucked in a startled breath. "Where? I must inform them at once."

"A coat factory not far from here. It's heavily fortified, though. You can check it out for yourself before you make your full report." I rattled off the address, gesturing in the general direction.

The banshee dove into the shadows and raced off like a bullet. I watched her go, a strange flavor creeping through my mouth—a metallic tang that was both terror and exhilaration.

Time to burn it all to the ground and see who was left standing. And if this didn't work out the way I hoped, I suspected Sorsha would applaud the effort even as she fell.

TWENTY-SIX

Sorsha

It started with a distant crashing. My ears perked up, and I raised my head from where it'd been resting against my tucked arms.

A thud reached me next, still muffled but not as faint as before—then a shout and a grunt like someone taking a punch to the gut.

I pushed myself as upright as I could get in my cage, eyeing the door to my room. Was this another trick to get a reaction out of me? But it wasn't as if I could do much with the cage properly locked this time. I'd checked the latches before I'd laid my head down, and I rattled them now just in case. They didn't budge so much as a fraction of an inch.

More thumps and booms filtered through the walls. A cry, thin and fraught with pain, pierced my eardrums. My body tensed.

This racket could mean good things for me—it could be my allies breaking in—but it could also mean a whole lot of bad. Maybe some other shadowkind had found out about Tempest's plans and meant to inflict their vengeance on everyone in the building. Maybe her own allies had figured out she was double-crossing them and were wreaking havoc out there. Who knew what other enemies she might have accumulated over the centuries who wouldn't have any reason to spare me?

Instinctively, I ran my tongue along the seam of my gums, restraining a wince at the scalded flesh there. I might not have much in this ridiculous horror show of a lab room, but I'd kept the tools I'd come in here with. Sweet chomping chimps, let me get the chance to use them.

A clang reverberated down the hall, followed by a snarl I wanted to think sounded familiar. Before that could amount to anything, the last familiar face I'd have wanted to see wavered out of the shadows into the dim light.

Tempest's gleaming locks were writhing about her head in an agitated state. As she unfastened the door to my cage, her leonine face remained in a rigid mask of resolve. I braced myself—but I couldn't make my move here. I needed my fire to finish things off, and I had no guarantee anyone had disabled the sprinklers.

"What's going on?" I asked as she gripped the door. "Not having such a good day after all?"

She grinned at me fiercely, showing catlike fangs. "There's still been plenty good about it, and I don't intend to lose that now." She yanked open the door and flicked a pair of handcuffs around my wrists so quickly I didn't have time to dodge them.

My ankles were already chained again. I put up the best fight I could, attempted to knee her in the shoulder or elbow her in the face, but physical combat with all my limbs restrained and aching stiffly wasn't exactly a piece of cake.

Tempest hauled me out of the cage to tumble to the floor. As I squirmed around so I had some chance of defending myself, she loomed over me, her shadowkind form taking over.

Her face still looked almost the same, just even more feline with a broadening of her cheeks. Her body expanded into that of a massive lion. Tawny wings burst from her back with a hiss of their long feathers. She clamped her muscular forelegs around my chest and stomped on the floor just beside the lab table.

With a whirring sound, a panel in the tiles pulled back. Letting out a breathy chuckle, the sphinx dragged me into the darkness beneath.

I only caught a glimpse of the passage we dropped into: just a few feet wide and high with packed dirt walls, the length of it falling into total darkness ahead of us. Then the panel snapped shut again, blotting out all light. The earth smell that filled my nose wasn't remotely pleasant: pungent clay with a rotting note that turned my stomach.

Tempest managed to bound through the darkness while still holding me pressed to her thickly furred chest with one foreleg. When I tried to thrash free, her claws dug into my side deeply enough for the jolt of pain to shatter my breath.

"I'm not sure what use you think I'm going to be when you're abandoning everything else you've been working on," I said, fighting to keep an agonized rasp from my voice.

"If you'd rather I tore out your throat and was done with you, that can be arranged."

"Somehow I don't think you'd be getting this cuddly if you were willing to throw me away that easily."

"Perhaps, but I'm willing to be convinced." Her eyes flashed in the darkness. A more cloying rotten-meat scent spilled with her breath over my face. "You must know by now that I don't put all my stock in any one person—or place. I might be a sphinx, but I can play hydra too. No matter how many facilities the fools destroy, there'll be more popping up in their place. I'm *everywhere*."

The vehemence in her voice turned my blood to ice. She really believed there was no way she and the horrors she'd set in motion could be stopped. Had she already unleashed her sickness on the world, and all she was doing now was protecting the source of her cure in case she needed more?

If she'd already hurt my lovers—

I clamped down on the flare of heat that thought provoked before it could sizzle from my skin. This wasn't the place to play my last gambit either—I had no idea what protections she might have built into this tunnel. But as soon as I got my opening, she was going to regret every bit of the pain she'd inflicted and urged others to inflict, no matter how eagerly those mortals had leapt to the task.

Heat seared across my tongue. I swallowed hard, gritting my teeth, and aimed it along my gum. I'd *better* be ready.

All at once, Tempest heaved upward. A large circle of metal swung up and over to bang against asphalt. Still clutching me tightly, the sphinx clambered out into the cool night air that drifted through a vacant parking lot. A ratty shopping bag coasted by us.

It wasn't the most glamorous escape route. I guessed I was cramping poor Tempest's style.

Not for long, it seemed. With a sweep of her wings, we lifted off the ground. Yells and a metallic crunching sound careened from somewhere down the street. I'd better figure out exactly what mess we were leaving behind before I took my shot at destroying the woman who'd set it all in motion.

Twisting my head, I made out a big brick building with lights flashing in some of the windows. Immense, monstrous silhouettes charged in and out of view. One wall was crumpled in across most of the left side. A few human figures scrambled through the rubble. As I watched, a shadowkind of some sort sprang at one and slashed through his neck. Several more creatures tore from the darkness in pursuit of the others.

I hadn't seen any being I recognized yet. Maybe this really didn't have anything to do with my crew. Where in Pete's name would Omen and the others have found themselves this many new allies so fast—if the hellhound shifter would even have considered sticking out his neck to ask without me badgering him about it?

Tempest wrapped her other foreleg around me again now that her wings were doing most of the work. As she soared higher into the air, the pressure squeezed my ribs against my lungs. My voice came out more strained than I liked. "Pissed off a whole lot of beings this time, did you?"

"They don't even know what they're intruding on," Tempest muttered. "Nitwits, the whole horde of them. Bashing their way in, yammering about some ruby they were looking for. If I'd had the time, I'd have directed them to a fucking jewelry store and introduced a diamond cutter to their vital organs."

I just barely bit back a startled laugh. Ruby—that horde of shadowkind was looking for me.

And who knew of me as Ruby other than my closest companions... and the minions of the Highest, who wanted me dead to the point that they'd spent twenty-five years scouring the mortal realm for me?

Omen had stuck his neck out, all right. I never would have expected him to go this far. Technically, he'd stuck *my* neck out too, but it wasn't as if my life hadn't been under plenty of threat as it was. He'd used the Highest's forces as his own tool to crash Tempest's party.

I *had* kept telling him that getting his fellow shadowkind in on the cause was our best bet of coming out on top. Nice that he'd finally embraced my approach whole-heartedly.

Of course, all his efforts would amount to jack shit if I let this psychotic sphinx carry me off to conduct her nefarious schemes elsewhere.

Tempest must have sensed the readying of my muscles. She glared down at me. "Throw one whiff of flame at me and we'll find out whether you can survive a trip into the shadows, phoenix."

What would happen if I didn't? Would I die as she wrenched me into the darkness, or would she find herself losing her grip on me?

We were swaying with the beating of her wings at least thirty feet above the ground now. The odds of surviving a fall weren't in my favor. But at this point, all that mattered to me was that my captor *didn't* survive.

Even with all the rage scorching my insides, I might not be able to completely destroy her on my own. If Omen could use the Highest's minions, there was nothing stopping me from borrowing his strategy in turn.

"You think you know everything, but you have no idea," I told Tempest, and sang another mangled lyric at her. "Not very smart, and you're insane, you can shove your mad game."

"Big talk from a little birdie in the clutches of a cat."

"We'll see how long that lasts." I tipped back my head and bellowed at the top of my lungs, propelling a jet of fiery power alongside the words. "Hey, you beastly bastards! The Ruby you want is right here!"

My voice rang through the air, and the spurt of flames blazed across the night sky to mark our spot like a signal flare. As I blinked the after-glare away, a mass of shadowy figures surged from the ruined brick building toward us.

Tempest spat out several words that sounded deeply profane in a language I didn't know and dug her claws into my sides again. A warble of her frigid energy penetrated my skin as she made good on her promise to try to yank me into the shadows with her.

Even if I survived the trip, in the shadows I couldn't hurt her. I had to keep her here. I had to pin her to the fabric of this physical world. And luckily I'd shaped myself just the means to do that.

"Hey, Tempest, there's something else you should know," I shouted, and dug my tongue along my gums, where trickles of my supernatural fire had masked any noxious vibes the tiny instrument might have given off.

She swung her head down, her eyes glittering viciously. "What?"

"Your lackey in Crete had a very nice ring."

A ring I'd melted into a tiny silver-and-iron spear. I flicked the miniature weapon between my lips, clamped my teeth on it to hold it steady, and slammed my mouth into the sphinx's forehead with all the force I could muster.

As my jaw jarred against the bridge of her nose, the dull end of the needle scraped my tongue, but the sharpened point drove home.

A screech tore from Tempest's throat. She flailed her head from side to side as if trying to shake the sliver of toxic metals free, but it held in place, smack in the middle of her treasured third eye. Blood welled around the puncture point.

My makeshift weapon prevented her from shedding her physical form, but it didn't make that form any less deadly. With an ear-splitting howl, she raked her claws down my side and raised a paw as if she meant to slash my face right off.

A glimmer of hellish orange was streaking toward us through the darkness below. I sent up a silent prayer to the universe that the owner of that glimmer would reach us in time and yanked back the barriers that'd been tamping down my inner fire.

The flames erupted from my body like I'd been drenched in gasoline and torched. They flooded every inch of me, stinging and scalding—and they roared across Tempest too. Ignoring the pain as well as I could, I focused every bit of energy I had on hurling more and more heat across and into her leonine body.

The claws on her extended paw drooped and melted with the intensity of the heat as her foreleg fell. The shriek that rattled from the sphinx's throat then was nothing but agony, no room left for rage. Her other foreleg moved as if to wrench away from me, but I flung my arms around her charred, furry body and squeezed as tight as I could.

The sickly smell of burnt flesh—not all of it hers—filled my nose. Her wings flapped weakly, trailing flames taller than she was, and then we plummeted.

As we dropped, the fire streamed over us like the tail of a meteor. Then the heat glazed my vision so thickly I couldn't see anything but the flickering light. I choked back a sob at the throbbing digging down to my bones and propelled even more of the raging inferno at my captor.

This was for egging on the mortals' hate. *This* was for Luna's death. *This* was for the torments Tempest had encouraged her lackeys to inflict on so many shadowkind, including my devourer and my hellhound. *This* was for the new horrors she'd meant to enact on them and so many mortals too.

Let her burn. Let her burn until there was nothing left of that sadistically cavalier fiend than the barest scraps of ashes—and let them blow down into the foulest sewer in existence for good measure.

Her body started to disintegrate in my hands. Cinders sloughed off into the sizzling wind. She tumbled from my arms just as I collided with someone else's.

I smacked into a broad chest, a familiar smoky scent with a hint of sulfur washing through the blaze. Arms glowing with a magma-bright light embraced me and eased me the rest of the way to the ground, but their fiery heat didn't scorch me further. Instead, they absorbed the flames that had been ravaging my body.

The pain snuffed out along with the fire. As I looked up into my protector's face, only a dull prickling sensation continued to ripple over my skin.

Omen smiled at me, the charcoal gray and glowing orange fading from his skin. "You defeated her. That was spectacular. And here I thought I'd get to come charging to your rescue for once."

I beamed back at him, feeling slightly delirious. The sharpest flames might have dwindled, but the fire inside me was raging on, its heat crackling through me. "Don't sell yourself short. Your brigade gave me the opening I needed."

I turned on shaky legs to stare at the blackened corpse that had fallen beside me. Tempest's wings had smashed into crisp chunks when she'd hit the ground; one of her hips had fractured, blackened all the way through. The silver needle had melted into a gleaming blob in the blackened mass that had once been her head.

She'd defied death before. I wasn't taking any chances, thank you very much. I nudged the sphinx's side with the toe of my sneakers—and her entire charred rib cage crumpled in.

Triumph flared inside me next to my still-smoldering anger. I aimed a kick at her head and watched it burst into burnt dust.

Omen stepped up behind me and took one of my hands, raising it over my head. When I lifted my gaze, my pulse stuttered. A swarm of shadowkind had surrounded us—the horde Tempest had ranted about. The Highest's minions.

Omen pitched his voice to carry. "The phoenix Ruby has destroyed our true enemy! You saw what the sphinx was preparing in that building. You witnessed how the mortals she conspired with attacked every shadowkind they met. This being has ended all of that. Ruby is our *hero*!"

Holy glittering guacamole, was that gambit actually going to work?

Plenty of the gazes that had fixed on me shone with hostility. But they hesitated, many of them turning to look at the largest beings among them, who started murmuring amongst themselves in harsh voices.

Omen tugged me back toward him. He twined his fingers with mine, his other hand rising to my cheek. The pale blue eyes that met mine were anything but cold.

"So, you took my advice for once," I couldn't stop myself from saying.

The corner of his mouth crooked upward. His thumb traced the line of my cheekbone. "There's a first time for everything. You're not *always* wrong."

I made a face at him. "If they're not convinced, they'll kill you."

"It'll be worth it."

He said it without a hint of hesitation, and a strange flutter passed through my chest. Naturally, rather than figure out what to make of that, I kept shooting off my mouth. "Oh, yeah? Because I seem to remember plenty of times not at all long ago when you were doing your darndest to get me *out* of your—"

"Shut up just this once in your life, Disaster," Omen murmured, tipping his head closer, and I didn't think anyone had ever said those words more sweetly. "They'll have to rip me to shreds before they get one piece of you. I'd put my entire existence on the line for you all over again in a heartbeat. I told you that you've made an impression—in more ways than one." He did hesitate then, his fingers going still against my skin. "I love you."

I'd never anticipated hearing those three words fall from the hellhound shifter's mouth. A giddy warmth spread from around my heart, swallowing up the fiery rage as it came. Still, one last question tumbled out. "Even though I'm partly human?"

Omen chuckled. "*Because* you're partly human, it seems. Don't let it go to your head."

"I know better than that." My fingers curled into his shirt just below his collar. "I love you too."

He answered me with a kiss, so fierce and demanding it made my knees wobble. What our spectators made of that, I had no idea, but I couldn't say I cared. This indomitable, passionate man was *mine*, the missing piece in the quartet I hadn't known I needed, and I'd never felt more at home than in his arms in that dismal parking lot.

When he drew back, I grinned up at him for a moment longer. Then I glanced toward the crowd to search for the rest of my shadowkind lovers. It wasn't a matter of *whether* they'd be here but only where. My gaze skimmed over the mass of figures—

And with a whine that rang through my ears, a gleaming bolt of metal pierced the darkness and rammed into Omen's back.

TWENTY-SEVEN

Sorsha

The metal projectile stabbed right through Omen's heart, the pointed tip tearing through his shirt as it burst from the middle of his chest. A plume of smoke so thick it hid his face gushed up from the wound. His body sagged into me.

A cry wrenched from my throat. "Omen? *Omen!*"

My frantic appeal did nothing to stop his legs from crumpling. I clutched at him, but my attempts to steady him only sent the rest of him falling to sprawl on the dirty asphalt. The smack of his back hitting the ground drove the stake through farther.

A fucking *stake*, made of silver and iron, like some kind of three-in-one multipurpose monster-murdering device for mortals who couldn't tell the difference between vamps, werewolves, and fae.

I dropped to my knees beside my lover, searching his slack features, but the concentration of those metals ripping through his most vital physical organ was enough to murder even a hellhound.

Omen's head lolled to the side, his eyelids twitching. The faintest wheeze whistled from his lungs—and then every part of him went limp, oblivious to my shouts and my shaking of his shoulders.

More smoke billowed up in a congealing cloud. The color had

already drained from his lifeless face. He looked more like a wax figure than a man—a man who'd once contained so much snark and power—a man *I'd* have put my own existence on the line for if there'd been the slightest chance—

Fury surged through me, scorching hot. It blotted out every thought except one question burning through my mind: Who did this?

My head jerked up. Fire blazed from my body in every direction, but most of it downward. The rush of searing flames propelling me up into the air—up over the swarm of shadowkind gathered around us, up into the night sky, glaring in the direction from which the stake had flown.

A woman was crouched on the rooftop of the low building that stood between the parking lot and the taller brick structure that had been Tempest's hideout. She was decked out in the standard Company armor, shoving another gleaming bolt into a crossbow.

My hands clenched at my sides, my fingers branding my palms with their scorching heat. *Die.*

Before she could end another shadowkind life, a surge of flame shot up from beneath the woman's feet. In seconds, it had swallowed her completely, even her shriek of pain. Her body crumpled much like Omen's had, the fire still eating away at it, but watching her form shrivel and blacken didn't tame the rage coursing through me one bit.

A thumping of footsteps reached my ears through the roar of the flames that held me. A mass of Company lackeys were running toward the crowd of shadowkind. One of them was fumbling with a plastic box, yanking it open and drawing out one of several laboratory vials—

Tempest's disease. Of course her death wouldn't stop the asshole mortals who had no idea that her creation would end them as quickly as the shadowkind it infected. Of course their first thought while their colleagues lay dying and their building in shambles was to unleash that horror on the world.

Not today, motherfuckers.

Burn. Burn them all to the fucking ground.

More fury flared through me, and flames erupted all through the swarm of would-be exterminators. I squeezed my fists tighter. The glass of the vials melted, fusing together and snuffing out the deadly microbes that floated within.

That wasn't enough either. Who knew how much more of the Company's vile invention was still stockpiled in that building—or in other facilities across the world? How many sites and people held the information to recreate it?

They all had to go. Every last one of the pricks who'd dreamed of ridding the world of shadowkind, who'd tortured and slaughtered for their own satisfaction, and the empire they'd built could damn well die with them.

My flames raced along the sidewalk to the smashed-open building. The roar beneath me propelled me higher still. More fire burst from my back with a stinging sensation that was offset by the rush of satisfaction as crackling flames swept through the air on either side of me to form wings.

They'd messed with a fucking phoenix, and every last one of them was going to burn.

I poured my rage toward the brick structure, and an inferno as sizzling as the bonfire inside me engulfed it. The taint of all those vicious intentions crawled over my skin. Without questioning it, I simply knew that I could follow that trail.

My awareness expanded through the darkened sprawl of the world below. An apartment here. A warehouse there. A blast of flames, and they were nothing but charcoal.

My rage spilled out along lines of communication and connection that shone clearer to my heightened senses with every passing second. It burned through the fraying threads of self-control I'd been holding onto so tightly, but what the hell did I care?

None of these pricks had cared one bit about who *they* were hurting.

My hellhound shifter, lying dead on the ground below me. Luna, shattering herself apart to avoid their capture. All the scalpel incisions and needle injections, all the slashing knives and suffocating nets, all the crashed cars and battered bodies.

But that was what humans did. One monster did them wrong, scared them, or screwed them over, and they thought that gave them the right to commit genocide on every being remotely like it.

A laboratory in Berlin. A processing office in Madrid. My attention sizzled across the ocean all the way to the shores I'd left behind, the hot spots lighting up like the pins on the map we'd seen in the shoe museum in Chicago.

The fire was gushing out of me in waves now, and I could see it all in my mind's eye: Good-bye, a few dozen Company employee houses in San Francisco. Sayonara, an entire condo building in Queens.

My reach was infinite, my fire inexhaustible, and every one of them was going to pay.

Burn. Burn. Burn it all down, until there's nothing left but ashes.

Glaring light dotted my vision. The stench of bubbling tar and frying varnish filled my lungs. Whatever grip I'd had on myself had gone up in smoke. There was nothing in me or around me but my fiery fury, like it was always meant to be.

My skin crackled and blackened; my stomach steamed. That was fine. If I had to burn myself up to take every douchebag who deserved it down with me, so be it.

More and more buildings succumbed to my flames. More and more bodies crumbled into cinders. My soul screamed in vengeful triumph. More, more, *burn it all…*

The trails I'd traced petered out. Every person who'd contributed to the Company's horrors, every place where they'd conducted their cruel business, every device that had contained their secrets had been swallowed up in the fire of my fury—but it still wasn't enough.

An ache consumed me from throat to gut, rage churning through it, roaring to be set free.

Why should the Company be the only ones to take the blame? How about all the other mortals out there who would have attacked the shadowkind if they'd known about them—which was pretty much all humans, wasn't it?

What about the shadowkind themselves who'd only hurled themselves into the fray not to protect their fellow beings but to destroy *me*? Who'd slaughtered my parents—ripped my father's head off and thrown it out a fucking window—for the sole crime of creating me?

Hell, what about the damned Highest who'd send their minions on that wretched quest? Did they think they were so invulnerable, lurking in the depths of the shadow realm?

Ha. With the prickling of the fire through and around me, I could taste how easily I could reach through the rifts and rain my searing fury across the darkness until it barbequed their ancient souls.

They thought I was a force to be extinguished? I'd show them who'd get eviscerated.

The flames were already leaping higher—from the smashed brick building to those neighboring it, across the parking lot below me to smack into one brutal being and another. I sucked in a scalding breath.

I really could do it. I could burn both the realms down and myself with them, and when I emerged from the ashes, maybe it would all be reborn into something better. Seriously, how hard could it be to do better than the shitshow we had now?

I gathered the fire swelling ever wider inside me, ready to spew it as far as I could cast it—and a voice penetrated the warbled blare in my ears. A bright, sweet voice ragged with an emotion that made my chest clench up.

"Sorsha! Sorsha, please, can you hear me?"

Then another voice: a chocolatey baritone that'd turned strained. "You're not in this alone, Miss Blaze."

And another: a deep ragged rumble. "We'll fight whatever battles need fighting, m'lady. Just tell us what you need."

The flames around me faltered slightly. I sank a few feet with a lurch of my stomach, and made out three figures hovering in the air in front of me, their forms lit by wavering orange light.

The light of my fire. Of my vast, violent blaze.

Thorn's massive wings swept through the air, holding himself and the two men he was supporting aloft. Ruse had his arm stretched out to me, a desperation in his roguish face I'd never seen before. Snap's eyes flashed brilliant green, wide and frantic.

"My peach," the devourer said when I met his gaze. "Don't go. I promised you I wouldn't leave, no matter how upset I got—don't you leave me."

I wasn't leaving. I was here, and I would still be here when the fire ravaged me to the bones and spewed me back into being. It was everything else, everyone else—couldn't they see how rotten our worlds had become?

Omen's voice echoed up from my memories. *Remember everyone who's for you.*

Those words choked me up and provoked a fresh wave of anger at the same time. As the flames around me leapt and dipped again, another winged figure soared into sight.

It was Flint, but he wasn't alone. He was holding... Vivi. My best friend, clinging tight to the warrior's bulging arms, her face turned ashy and soot staining her typical white outfit. My pulse hitched.

She gave me a bright smile that was all too familiar. "Sorsha, you don't need to do any more. You knocked those assholes flat. If there are any left, we'll take them out, however many we need to, like shooting rats in a barrel of dynamite. But first let's cool off and figure out where we stand. Please come down?"

Down. Down. Down to the place where my most recent lover's corpse lay slumped; down to where the Highest's horde stood waiting to lay judgment on me. My teeth gritted. Flames lashed around me.

But I couldn't drag my eyes from the figures in front of me. As I stared at them, more images rose in my mind.

It was also the world where my devourer delighted in everything from extravagant hotels to a simple banana; where we'd discovered his capacity for desire together. The world where my incubus had offered every pleasure he could imagine to leave me satisfied, not just bodily but in mind and heart as well. The world where I'd fought side by side with my wingéd warrior while he let his strength buoy mine rather than supress it.

The world where my bestie and I had passed cartons of Thai food back and forth on her couch in front of our favorite cheesy movies, where we'd laughed and danced together and made plans for grand adventures we hadn't yet seen through.

Could I burn down the realms and spare the few who held a piece of my heart? Could we even hold onto any of the happiness that had brought us together in the wreckage my raging fire would leave behind?

All those people out there, all the beings drifting through the rifts—so many of them had laughed and delighted, fought and loved too. There were so many other parents, other guardians, other lovers and other friends who'd be mourned.

Maybe some of them were monsters. Maybe we were all monsters. But that didn't mean there was nothing good in us.

Scalding tears pricked at my eyes. I didn't want this. I didn't want to spread nothing but pain through the realms. Who would I have to be furious with then except myself?

I could make Omen right about one last thing. I wasn't like Tempest, not at all.

As the rush of heat beneath me dwindled, my fiery wings did as well. I glided to the ground, my body seeming to contract in on itself.

My clothes hung in singed scraps, my skin equally charred. When I shuddered in the sudden cool of the night air, the blackened bits fluttered off me like moulting feathers, revealing unmarred flesh beneath.

Even in the dim light from distant streetlamps, I could see that I'd scorched the parking lot around me to an even darker shade than the pavement had been before. Tempest's ashes had dispersed in the inferno. As my companions drifted down to join me, my gaze came to rest on Omen's slumped form, which had somehow held its shape.

His body lay on a streak of silver and iron. The heat of my flames had melted the crossbow bolt so thoroughly that the liquid metals had rippled across the lot to pool in a nearby pothole. His clothes, burnt into a solid mass, hid the wound on his chest, but I knew exactly where the fatal stake had struck him. I knew—

His chest moved.

It rose and fell with a shallow breath, and my heart just about leapt up my throat to do a dance number on the asphalt.

"Omen?" I threw myself to his side. His body shuddered, and the carbonized layer coating his form cracked and began flaking off like mine had.

My fire hadn't burned him. Of course not. It never had before—he was a being that thrived on fire. The flames I'd poured down had melted the toxic metals from his body and absorbed right into the gap of his wound. Had—had they—

My hand shot to that spot in the middle of his chest. The remains of his shirt disintegrated, and my palm rested against a solid plane of hellhound-shifter flesh, only a white blotch of a scar showing where he'd taken the wound.

Naturally, that was when he opened his eyes.

For a second, Omen blinked at me as if he needed to clear his vision. A faint furrow creased his forehead. Then a thin smile crossed his lips. "Can't resist the opportunity to cop a feel even in the middle of an apocalypse, huh, Disaster?"

"You fucking bastard!" I said, which wasn't really fair, since I doubted he'd *wanted* to get himself killed. But he probably figured out I didn't really mean the insult from the enthusiasm with which I threw my arms around him right afterward.

Omen let out a hoarse chuckle, lifting one arm to return the embrace. Another hand squeezed my shoulder. A third rested on my back, and a fourth brushed over my hair. My other three lovers knelt around us, welcoming me and their commander back.

"Are you all right?" Snap asked, a question that might have been for either of us or most likely both.

For my reply, I lifted my head from Omen's shoulder to pull my devourer into a kiss. Then Thorn's broad arms were tugging me to my feet as the hellhound shifter heaved onto his. Vivi leapt to my side, looping her arm around mine, and I hugged her just as hard as I had my lovers.

"You came a long way to watch me burn down the world," I said.

A startled laugh spilled out of her. "It was an epic performance, but I don't think I want any repeat showings."

"Good, because neither do I." The fire inside me felt subdued in a brand-new way, like the vast calm of the ocean after a monster of a storm.

I *had* been going to end the world... but I hadn't. And now that I'd walked up to the brink and taken a good hard look at it before stepping back, I couldn't imagine ever allowing myself to be pushed even close to over it. That vast calm was *mine* now. I was a phoenix reborn as something better, even if it hadn't worked quite the way anyone had predicted.

"I'm just glad you're okay," Vivi said.

I hugged her even tighter. "Me too. Thank you for helping talk me down."

"Any time, bestie. All you've got to do is say the word."

It seemed that was true. I'd been awfully worried about how she'd react if she found out what I was, but she'd seen the worst of me tonight, and she was still here. Maybe it was time to stop worrying.

About Vivi, anyway. Omen's gaze slid past us to the crowd of shadowkind, slightly thinned by my recent torching but still a whole lot larger than our little cluster. Larger and taking some tentatively threatening steps toward us now that the torching was over.

"I'm getting better by the moment," the hellhound shifter said to Snap, "but I'm not sure how long this lot will allow that to last, though. I don't suppose our equines and imp came through with their part in the plan?"

"We haven't seen—" Ruse started.

"Ruby!" one of the larger minions bellowed, raising an axe, and just then a clatter of racing hoofbeats echoed down the road.

Gisele and Bow led the charge, Gisele gone full unicorn and Bow showing off his centaur form. Antic perched on Gisele's gleaming back, brandishing her tiny fist in the air.

And with them came dozens more shadowkind, rippling out of the shadows into the physical world and careening toward us in a wave.

They rushed through the crowd of minions, most of them small enough to skirt between the beefy legs, the equines jostling to make room as need be. Before the Highest's lackeys could raise much protest, one familiar figure in the oncoming swarm stepped in front of me and swiveled to take in our audience.

It was the equines' friend Cori. "This woman rescued me from the clutches of mortals who'd tormented me," he shouted over the growing clamor. "She risked her life to break open our cages and usher us all to freedom."

"She broke me out of a laboratory where I was being held," another being piped up. "I would have died if the mortals had their way."

More voices rose, one after the other.

"She fought through silver and iron to break us out and let us return home."

"She burned the place where the mortals caged us so they couldn't torture any more beings."

"I thought I'd never reach the shadows again until she came for us."

The lesser beings in the crowd of new arrivals chittered and barked in their own versions of language with what sounded like a cacophony of agreement.

A lump filled my throat. It didn't seem possible that the equines could have rounded up every being I'd ever saved, and yet there were also dozens more here than I'd realized I'd rescued. All the collectors whose homes I'd slunk into, all the Company facilities we'd razed to the ground...

I guessed it had added up.

As the barrage of testimonials faded, Thorn cleared his throat. "And she took down the shadowkind responsible for encouraging the worst group of mortals in their horrific dealings—the sphinx called Tempest, which the Highest failed to subdue centuries ago."

Omen took my hand and held it up as he had when he'd first reached me. "The phoenix has burned, and it is Sorsha, not Ruby, that remains. You can tell the Highest how badly they screwed up... or you can tell them, truthfully, that Omen the hellhound dealt with Ruby and no further threat from her remains."

Another round of muttering commenced, but at least no one was waving an axe in my direction for the moment. Some of the minions pointed toward the ruined building, others toward the sky where I'd dealt out my flaming vengeance. Antic darted among them, tossing out interjections here and there as she saw fit. As we waited for the verdict, my fingers clamped tight around Omen's.

Finally, a figure that must have been some sort of giant stepped to the fore of the crowd and raised his hand for silence. His voice carried through the lot.

"It is settled. We have witnessed that this being, whatever she is, destroyed those that threatened us. We witness that her fire has abated as the hellhound stands beside her. We will report to the Highest that he has fulfilled his duty and the danger is past."

Then, as elation welled up behind my ribs, he caught my gaze and dipped his head in a slight but unmistakable bow.

The horde vanished into the shadows in a wavering surge. I stared, half afraid to move in case my legs failed to hold me.

"It's over?" I said to Omen. "No more bounty on my head?" I lowered my voice. "No more deal hanging over yours?"

The hellhound shifter laughed. "It would appear that way. Let's wait and see if the Highest send their minions charging back after all. But I think you may just have pulled off the greatest heist of your career, thief." He offered a quiet smile that was just for me. "You stole back both our freedoms from the most powerful beings in existence."

Ruse clapped his hands, a smirk curling his lips. "And I'd say this calls for a celebration. Come on, Miss Blaze. Wait until you see what we've done with the Everymobile now!"

"Sweet scintillating seahorses, do I even want to ask?" I shook my head with a disbelieving chuckle, pulled my best friend and my lovers close, and set off to see what the road ahead would hold.

TWENTY-EIGHT

Not quite one year later

Sorsha

It was never a bad idea to blow off some steam before a heist. You wanted to go into the operation with a clear head and absolute focus. And, lucky me, I now had four sexy shadowkind to contribute to the blowing and the steaming—generally by indulging in all the fun and thrilling ways our bodies could come together.

I'd never get tired of the way Omen's breath broke when I slicked my tongue around his cock, I guarantee. The hellhound shifter's brimstone scent laced his nether regions with a sharper smoky tang that was nearly as delicious as hearing him come apart under my attentions.

More delicious still? The tingling pulses of pleasure that shot through me with each stroke of *Thorn's* tongue over my clit, alongside Snap driving into me from behind, hitting the perfect spot of bliss every time.

Thorn lapped harder, and I gasped over Omen's erection, a quiver running through my body. The hellhound shifter growled at the loss of contact, his fingers tightening in my hair. I smiled and pressed my lips around his length again, and he thanked me with a groan and the teasing of his tail across one already stiffened nipple.

Snap dipped his head to flick his forked tongue against my spine. Thorn squeezed my ass with a scrape of his hardened knuckles that I'd discovered sparked their own bonus thrill, and at the devourer's next thrust, the final wave of ecstasy sent me soaring.

I sucked Omen down, determined to bring him with me. A groan reverberated out of him as he gushed smoky heat into my mouth. I swallowed gleefully and clutched on to him as Snap sped up. The devourer finished with a swift plunge that sent me cartwheeling over the edge all over again.

As we sagged together into a sated tangle of bodies, I glanced up at Ruse, who'd chosen to stick to watching this time. He met my questioning gaze with a smirk and a heated glint in his eyes.

"That was quite the show," he said.

I grinned back at him. "As long as you don't feel left out."

"It isn't as if I haven't gotten plenty of mine before. And I'm calling dibs on the bed tonight."

"*My* peach," Snap murmured in protest, slinging his slim arm around one of my legs.

If he could have, the devourer would have cuddled up with me every night, but as impressive as the Everymobile was, this bed was barely big enough for two bodies to sleep next to each other. When one of those bodies was Thorn's, it was barely big enough for one. My lovers had come up with some sort of schedule of fairness in which they switched off who got snuggle benefits, other than the occasional night when I wanted my space and kicked out the whole bunch of them.

Omen chuckled, his tail still tracing lazy lines over my ribs. "The next time we have an opportunity to barter for some magical renovations, we should see about having this room—and its furniture—expanded."

I wouldn't have thought *he* would ever be one to complain about missed opportunities to cozy up to me, but the hellhound shifter had proven unexpectedly cuddle-happy—possibly even to his own surprise. The nights he spent with me, he always started out on the far side of the bed, only a hand resting against my shoulder or curled around my wrist. Then I'd wake up to find myself tucked against him from head to toe, wrapped in his limbs and our matching fiery heat.

The first time it'd happened was the only time I'd swear I saw him actually blush, but the sheet-scorching sex we'd had afterward seemed to have reassured him that what his body got up to when he let it sleep wasn't so bad.

"Sounds good to me," I said, and squirmed around to get up. Thorn grasped my elbow to help, and I leaned over to give him a quick kiss.

"Are you sure you want to charge ahead with this mission tonight?" Ruse asked. "It *is* your birthday. The creatures can survive in their cages another day."

I wagged a finger at him. "How selfish would I be to leave them to another day of torment at this collector's hands when I can celebrate just as easily tomorrow? We're here now. You can carry out whatever grand plans you've been putting together once we've taught this asshole a lesson."

"Well spoken, m'lady," Thorn said with one of his rare smiles that it still made me giddy to see on his stern face.

"Thank you." I grabbed a robe to maintain a little modesty around our RV-mates. "That doesn't mean I'm going to skip my shower. I'll be a clean cat burglar."

"A little dip into the shadows would accomplish the same thing," Omen reminded me with a teasing note in his voice.

Technically he was right. With some trial and error, we'd determined that I could meld with darkness like a full shadowkind, although I still didn't enjoy the clammy sensation that came with it, and I hadn't quite gotten the hang of jumping from one patch to another yet. Still, my answer was the same as always. "Some things are better enjoyed in a physical body—as I'm sure you know." I let my gaze trail down his naked form in all its muscular glory.

"And thank all things dark for that," Ruse said.

As I reached for the door, Snap made a soft noise in his throat. "We should still—on her real birthday—"

When I glanced back, he was shooting a meaningful glance around at the other men. Thorn had set his face into an expression that seemed designed to indicate he had no idea what the devourer was talking about, but so obviously it had the opposite effect. Ruse's smirk widened.

Omen rolled his eyes and prodded Snap in the ribs with his heel. "Let her take her shower first. There'll be time."

Time for some kind of shadowkind surprise? Intriguing. I'd better make this shower a fast one.

Of course, that was easier said than done in our current accommodations. The sylph who'd conducted our initial renovations in gratitude for getting her out of the Company's clutches had possessed an aptitude for airiness but not for plumbing, and the beings who'd attempted to pitch in since then had only partly solved the Everymobile's quirks. Any time I turned on the shower, I had a fifty-percent chance of first getting pelted with hot cocoa, sesame oil, or a rainbow of tiny gumdrops. And every now and then, even after I got the water to start, it turned into a dust shower partway through.

Today I received a gulp of coffee *and* a mouthful of gumdrops—both caught in the mug I kept on hand for such occasions, because why not make the best of it?—before the showerhead resigned itself to a spray of standard water.

I washed quickly, keeping an ear out for the faint hissing sound that usually warned of impending dust, and then pulled on my standard burglar gear. My tastes hadn't changed in that department: all black all over, though I wasn't bothering with my hat yet. And I didn't need a scorch-knife anymore now that I could melt metal by force of will alone.

As I stepped into the hall, giving my hair one last rub of the towel, Vivi emerged from the RV's new upstairs, which was the main result of the sylph's help. The Everymobile didn't look any taller from the outside, but inside, a narrow spiral staircase beside the bathroom now led to a loft bedroom.

Vivi's eyebrows leapt up, an eager gleam coming into her eyes. "Is it time to get started already?"

I poked her in the arm playfully. "It's only just getting dark. We go by cover of night, remember?"

She bobbed on her feet in a gesture so like Antic I reminded myself

I shouldn't be surprised she and the imp got along well. "Right, right. I still get so pumped up even though I'm not the one going out there!"

The destruction of the Company of Light hadn't rid the world of independent hunters and collectors. When my quartet of shadowkind and I had decided to take the Everymobile on tour as a sort of traveling Shadowkind Defense Fund, I'd known I had to invite my bestie.

It was hard to put any stake in the doubts I'd once had about whether Vivi would accept my less-than-legal hobbies after the way she'd pitched in against the Company—and all the other things she'd accepted about me. So, we'd arranged an extra bedroom for her, and she was getting the adventure she'd always dreamed of, coordinating with our various contacts, monitoring security systems, and doing reconnaissance whenever we needed someone who could pull off "normal" better than the rest of us.

She was clearly having the time of her life. I was sure it didn't hurt that she and Cori had started getting awfully chummy during his regular visits mortal-side.

Antic herself dashed past us then, giggling as she sprinted after Pickle in a game of hall tag. The little dragon appeared to have prompted it by stealing one of the jelly bracelets the imp had stolen from a tween fashion stall in a mall several cities ago. Pickle waved it at me from his jaws with a puff of smoke and dove past us into one of the kitchen cupboards.

Vivi laughed. "Always an exciting time around here."

I nudged her with my elbow. "I'll let you know when it's about to get even more exciting."

I stepped back into my bedroom to find all four of my lovers crammed along the edge of the bed, back in their clothes, with an air of anticipation that made my skin twitch. Were they nervous or just eager about whatever they were up to—or maybe a little of both?

Snap jumped up, beaming bright, apparently the ringleader of this particular venture. "We have something for you," he announced, and held out his hand to take mine.

It'd never been easy for me to deny the devourer, and I had no interest in doing so now. I reached for him, but rather than twining his fingers through mine, he gently folded them all toward my palm except my index finger. In his other hand, he produced a glinting band that he slid down my finger to the root.

The ring was delicate, so light I could barely feel its weight, rose and white gold woven together in a vine-like pattern. "It's beautiful," I said, meaning it even if I didn't totally understand what had sparked this fervor for jewelry.

Ruse had gotten up too. He took my hand from Snap and eased a ring of his own down my middle finger, equally light but this one with a pattern that looked like merging waves. I stared down at the two rings side by side, a fizzy feeling collecting in my stomach.

Before I could say anything, Thorn loomed over me. His broad fingers clasped mine less deftly but with just as much affection as the other two. The band he fit onto my ring finger shone with the same contrasting metals in an intricate spiral.

As Omen stood, the fizzing sensation welled into my chest. The hellhound shifter lifted my hand and guided a final ring over my pinkie. The strands of rose and white gold merged together like flames.

Snap touched my shoulder, leaning in to nuzzle my hair. "You told me before that humans give each other rings to show their highest form of commitment. When they want to be with only that person and no one else, always."

"Not that we haven't made our devotion to you awfully clear, Miss Blaze," Ruse added. "But our devourer here felt a concrete token was in order, and the rest of us could see his point."

Thorn rested his hand on my back and ran his thumb up and down with a stroke of warmth. "Obviously we wouldn't require that you wear them, especially when they might interfere with your endeavours. I must say it's pleasing to see them all together like this on your lovely hand, though."

I raised my eyes to meet Omen's. Maybe there wasn't any literal magic in this gesture, but it was a symbolic binding, one I could feel in the fizzing sensation that had now spread through my whole body. It'd been less than a year since the hellhound shifter had sensed the official severing of his deal with the Highest—no acknowledgment from them, just a sudden falling away of their hold that had made him jump up with a joyfully relieved cry he hadn't been able to restrain.

Less than a year since he'd won the freedom he'd lost for centuries.

"And you're ready to commit too, are you?" I said.

All it would have taken was for him to shrug it off or make some disparaging remark, and he could have shattered any meaning the ring contained. Instead, he gazed right back at me, a hint of a smile playing with his lips. "I'm afraid you're stuck with me, Disaster. Be glad I went subtle—I could have pulled out the chains again."

Any tension to the giddiness inside me broke with that joke. I knuckled his chest, unable to contain a huge smile of my own. "Hey, chains have their place. Just as long as you don't mind that you ended up with the little finger."

Omen tapped Thorn and Snap on either side of him, both of them standing half a foot taller than the shifter's well-built frame. "I think I've amply proven that smaller isn't necessarily lesser."

"Hey!" Snap said.

The wingéd let out a rumbling chuckle, and a second later we were all laughing. I closed my hand, admiring my rings shimmering next to each other and reveling in the warmth from the larger circle formed by my lovers around me.

"Thank you. You picked them well. I don't think they'll get in the way under my gloves." I tugged my lovers one by one into a kiss. "That's to hold you over until I can return the gesture, which you'd better believe I will. Here's to some good thieving tonight!"

"Scouting complete!" Gisele hollered from where she must have just emerged in the RV's main room, her melodic voice carrying through the wall. "Who's ready to take this prick down?"

As the equines and Flint shared their observations and we discussed our final strategy, I gathered all my gear. Tonight's target was a prick supreme—not just a collector but a hunter as well, keeping the rarest of his catches while selling the others. I was looking forward to sending that mansion of his up in flames. And the trinkets I pilfered would let us enjoy all our other indulgences while paying those who deserved it.

When the street was fully dark beyond the windows, we set off with a wave good-bye and a "Ditto!" to Vivi. I slunk through the night, melding with the shadows nearly as well as my companions did.

They might be invisible, but I felt their presence all around me, their goals and their love entwined with mine like the metals on the rings they'd chosen. Tomorrow, we'd celebrate the start of the next year in my life. Tonight, we were meting out justice for those who couldn't claim it on their own.

Just call me the Robin Hood of monster emancipation. And now that I had my band of merry men, our future together would be both legendary and endless.

DARK CHAMPION - BONUS SCENE

What led to Omen's change of heart during his skirmish with Sorsha on the boat in Chapter 20? Read those events from his perspective to find out...

Omen

Seeing Sorsha sitting with my colleagues on the boat's deck, chattering and laughing over the picnic lunch I'd abstained from, shouldn't have bothered me. It wasn't as if I hadn't witnessed her companionable vibe with them before. It wasn't as if there was anything in particular they should have been doing instead. Really, I should be glad she was eating, since that would help her stamina and focus. And possibly the amusement she got out of the others' company bolstered her strength in some way too.

But the niggling sensation didn't go away. Part of me wanted to march out of the cabin and hurl the other three shadowkind overboard, as if it were a crime that they'd brought that delighted smile to her face. What in the realms was the matter with me?

Maybe it wasn't anything to do with the company she kept or how she expressed her affections, but with my sense of the impending doom Tempest and her human dupes were bringing about. Also the doom the Highest felt our not-so-mortal woman would cause.

There was a lot of doom to go around. The most I'd ever faced in my very extended lifetime. Anyone would be on edge.

There *was* actually one thing we could do in an attempt to stave off some of it. When I could tell the bunch on the deck had eaten their fill and were mostly just relaxing, I marched out to put an end to their leisure. Or Sorsha's, anyway.

I snapped my fingers. "All right, Disaster," I said, the nickname coming out a little sharper than I'd been using it lately, maybe because of the edge in my nerves. "Let's see what we can do to mitigate that catastrophic nature of yours."

The woman licked her fingers with a show of tongue that was practically obscene, and I had to will back a rush of heat at the thought of that tongue wrapping around certain parts of me. I hadn't gotten to indulge in that particular activity with her yet, but I could sense from the way my colleagues' gazes snapped to her mouth at the same time that at least a couple of them had.

The additional burn that prickled up inside me was definitely not jealousy, only irritation that she was taking her time answering me.

She lowered her hand and returned the provocative tongue to her mouth. "I'm not the canine here, dog-breath. How about a 'please'?"

Okay, now I was definitely irritated. I was trying to make sure she didn't end all existence, and she wanted to harp on politeness?

With a glower, I dipped forward in a bow I intended to radiate as much sarcasm as my tone did. "Would Her Highness kindly allow me to continue teaching her how she might avoid incinerating herself?"

"That's more like it." She got to her feet with a flex of her arms and a crack of her knuckles.

I didn't like the flash of concern I saw cross all three of my colleagues' faces. The devourer, with that damn near obsessive devotion of his, leapt up too. "If there's any way I can help—"

I redirected my glower at him. It wasn't as if I'd *damaged* her in any way the one time I had dragged her off, and I'd played fair since then. "I've got this. She isn't going to leave your sight, so you can ensure I leave her in one piece."

Sorsha glanced around at her fan club, and an emotion I didn't like the look of flickered in her eyes. They could be worried about her all they wanted, but I needed *her* to be fully confident and focused. If she didn't believe she could control her powers, there was no way in hell she'd rein them in when the going got tough. Even a shred of uncertainty could mean the difference between survival and total global annihilation.

She buried the hint of doubt quickly, though, and folded her arms over her chest. "Got some more bits of paper for me to charbroil?"

Did she really believe that was the best I could come up with when I'd had hours on this boat to do nothing but think?

"I thought we'd try something different for a change," I said. "We're just going to spar. And by 'just,' I mean fists and feet only. No supernatural powers. You let your fire out, you automatically lose, no matter how pissed off I made you. Oh, and to add a little challenge…" I sprang onto one of the railings that protruded across the ship. "Touch the deck with both feet, and you also lose. Should we make it the most wins out of five, or do you need more chances than that to get warmed up?"

Sorsha clambered onto a nearby beam and raised her eyebrows at me. "You're assuming I'll even need five. I'm the one who spent most of the past few years scrambling across rooftops and through windows."

There was the self-assurance I'd wanted. I grinned at her, letting my lips curl enough to show my teeth. "I suppose we'll see."

Show me everything you've got. Prove that you're the one in control.

Even as that benediction passed through my mind, I was hurling myself forward. Sorsha dodged out of the way just in time to escape my lunge, stumbling off her beam but catching hold of the hull and swinging herself onboard again.

I didn't give her a chance to recover. As she shoved herself to her feet, I charged at her, forcing her to flee along the railing she'd landed on.

I was about to make a cutting remark about how this wasn't much of a sparring match if all she did was run away when she snatched at a rope overhead and whipped around, nearly smacking me in the face with her foot. I jerked to the side and yanked on her ankle. With a grunt, she tumbled onto the deck on her ass.

But even in theoretical defeat, this woman had to make a mockery of the situation. She waved her legs in the air and smirked at me. "Technically my feet didn't touch it."

I couldn't restrain a snort. "And here I thought the spirit of the rules was clear. But if you're determined to be a cheater as well as a thief…"

I'd said far worse things to her before, but her expression tightened for an instant as if this jab had hit home in a way others hadn't. I didn't like that either. But my apprehension fell away as she pushed herself upright.

"Fine. I'll just have to whoop your ass the other four times."

I bared my teeth even more. "Come and try me."

There was less fleeing the second time around. Sorsha really had gotten warmed up, and thankfully not in the world-frying sort of way. We exchanged blows and darted around each other all across the ship until she pulled a swift maneuver that slammed both her feet into my calf, hard enough that I lost my balance. I gritted my teeth as I crashed to the deck.

I picked myself up, ignoring her triumphant grin. Confidence was good. Cockiness could get us killed just as easily as self-doubt.

"We're just getting started," I warned her. "You need to be able to hold yourself in check and bend those flames to your will when you're face to face with Tempest, and she isn't going to be half this easy on you."

"Bring it on," Sorsha retorted in a typically sassy tone, but at the same moment, a fiery light wavered along the sides of her chest. She smacked her arms close to her ribs, and the little flames vanished, but my stomach sank.

She had so much farther to go. She needed to be so much stronger. How the hell was I going to get her there in time?

By pushing her right to her limit as many times as she needed. I launched myself at her, battering her with my fists, striking her with the full extent of my own shadowkind strength.

I couldn't go easy on her. I needed her to be prepared.

I swept out my leg in a kick that had her ducking close to the boards. She swiveled around and darted away, bringing out one of her ridiculous songs of all things. "And if you only scold and spite, we'll be holding on forever. But we'll only be faking a fight—"

For fuck's sake, did this woman take *nothing* seriously? I rushed at her, my fangs prickling at my gums, and she jumped at another rope to dodge me, just barely avoiding the deck. She managed to whip around and land a blow to the back of my head, but it only threw me off for a second.

I sprang after her, and she fumbled across the netting. Her next kick connected with my shoulder, but it gave me the opportunity to grab her ankle again. I heaved on her leg so hard she hissed through her teeth, but she jerked free and flung herself onto the opposite railing.

I raced after her, a roughness coming into my throat. This wasn't enough; she had to give me more.

"Come on, Disaster," I taunted. "Is this how you're going to fight all those Company bastards and the sphinx who's egging them on—by running away? Didn't they *kill* your guardian? How many more are you going to let them murder?"

"I'm not running away," Sorsha snapped, and hurled a punch at me that I dodged without missing a beat. "Isn't it called fighting smart?"

Did she really think she could heckle her way out of getting a handle on her powers? I prowled closer. "Doesn't look so smart to me. We don't have time for pussyfooting around the problem now, do we?"

"I know that," she insisted, her body tensing. "I'll be ready."

"Are you sure?" I demanded, my frustration at this entire situation spilling over. "You've got to tackle it head on, before we come right down to the wire. Maybe I shouldn't expect any better from a being who's only half—"

The words felt too venomous even as they tumbled out of me, but I still wasn't expecting the reaction I got. With a sudden roar, Sorsha's entire body erupted into flames. Her startled gasp was all pain.

I didn't think, only reacted. This woman, the woman who'd fought so hard for the rest of us, the woman who didn't deserve the awful mess she'd found herself in the middle of, was burning alive. I pounced on her and tugged her fire-drenched body with me into the ocean.

The water bubbled with the heat for a moment before the flames vanished beneath the water. I let go of Sorsha so she could right herself, and she surfaced with a sputter. Patches of raw pink stood out against the skin of her cheeks, neck, and arms. The tip of her ponytail was charred. My gut lurched.

I'd done that. With my caustic remark after my constant needling—*I'd* brought her to the point of nearly incinerating herself.

That hadn't been what I'd meant to happen, not at all.

"That was a low blow," I said when she met my eyes. "It should have been beneath me." I couldn't even say that I took issue with her human side, not after all we'd been through before now. It'd certainly allowed her to help us in many ways the rest of us couldn't accomplish.

Sorsha blinked at me with obvious confusion. Then she glanced up at the boat. When she winced, my gaze followed hers. Unsurprisingly, burnt streaks marred the side of the hull where she'd gone up in flames.

When I lowered my gaze to her again, the expression on her face made me want to incinerate *myself* with shame. She looked utterly defeated, so despairing it wrenched at my heart.

I'd made that happen too. I'd told myself my strategy would hone her skills, but all I'd managed to do was beat her down and crack her resilient spirit.

How had that approach ever made sense to me? Why would insulting and mocking this woman make her *better* equipped to face the challenges ahead? Her fire came out when she got upset… and I'd been directing all the hostility in the atmosphere at her.

The shame washed over me thicker than before, in tandem with the soft waves lapping at my shoulders.

As Thorn flapped down from the mast with a sweep of his wings, Sorsha drew up her chin, though she hesitated before she spoke. "Well, now we're both beneath the boat. Maybe we should fix that?"

Still putting on a strong front despite how shaken I could tell she was. How much *I'd* shaken her.

Swallowing thickly, I swam over and checked her arms. To my relief, the burnt spots were already fading away. "Your healing abilities are heightening as quickly as your fire is," I noted.

Sorsha let out a raw laugh. "Oh, joy. More time to burn alive if there's no convenient ocean to throw me into."

I caught her gaze, groping for the words to convey the understanding that was only just creeping over me. She deserved more than an apology.

I'd opened the fault lines in her resolve. Those might not heal on their own. So I'd better give mending them my best shot.

"Maybe I've been going about this wrong," I began.

Her brow knit. "What do you mean?"

I hesitated for a second and then brushed my fingers over her hair, forcing myself to be gentle. Forcing myself to notice how good the gentleness could feel. Sorsha's eyes darkened in a way that stirred my own inner heat, but not with anything like anger.

I repeated the gesture, hoping the tenderness I'd managed to bring to it would add weight to my words. "I've been trying to push you to the brink. Get you used to the sensation so you can control it. But maybe this power isn't something you can control that way. Maybe the answer isn't suppressing your anger but making sure it's focused on the right target."

Her eyebrows rose in those perfect arches. "Trying to keep it off of you, hmm?" she teased.

I didn't let the joke rankle me in the slightest. It was just her trying to cover up how I'd wounded her.

"No," I said firmly. "I'm trying to keep it off of *you*. Whatever the Highest or Tempest or anyone says, there's nothing wrong with you. You don't deserve any of the shit they're trying to put you through, so you sure as hell shouldn't be putting yourself through even more. You're incredible."

She was, wasn't she? No idea she was anything other than human until a matter of weeks ago, growing up without any guidance in her powers, now burdened with the knowledge that she was expected to destroy both our worlds... and she could still joke. She could still smile and laugh and bring the looks on contentment I'd seen to my colleagues' faces.

She was the strongest of us all.

Speaking of my colleagues, all three of them were now peering down at us. "I second that motion," the incubus called.

"Fantastic," the devourer murmured.

And the wingéd actually smiled. "I couldn't have expressed it more eloquently."

Somehow the outpouring of praise left our phoenix at a loss for words for the second time since we'd taken this plunge. She nearly took a gulp of seawater as her mouth opened and closed soundlessly. With her red hair turned dark with the damp and slicked against her head, her eyes standing out starkly against her pale skin, she was nothing short of gorgeous even in her uncertainty.

She was always that too, as much as I'd sometimes hated to admit it.

I considered my colleagues again, my own resolve growing, if with a certain sense of resignation. She *was* "our" phoenix. Our woman. She'd woken up something in all of us, something that was nothing short of a magic in its own right, and now we were all in this together with her.

And that was okay. That was *good*. I couldn't let it gnaw at me that the others got to enjoy her when I knew how satisfying that connection was.

Shouldn't she experience the full heights our collaborative interest could bring *her* to?

Before I could second-guess the impulse, I teased my fingers along her jaw. "I'm not sure just saying that is quite enough. It could be that you don't avoid destruction by ignoring everything that's against you—you do it by remembering everyone who's for you. So how about instead of tossing you around, we try grounding you instead?"

She gaped at me briefly again. "That might be a little difficult considering there's literally no solid land in sight."

My mouth twitched with a crooked smile. "Then it's a good thing I had a more metaphorical 'grounding' in mind." I motioned to our audience. "Thorn, could you toss a net down—one that's fixed well to the ship. And then the rest of you can toss yourselves in. Our mortal deserves a group effort."

The wingéd heaved a net over the side, and I tugged Sorsha over to it. I might be willing to share, to do so openly now instead of stealing a moment here and there just for myself, but I'd be damned if I wasn't going to claim the first bit of bliss now that I'd set this interlude in motion.

I hooked my arm through a gap in the net. "To make sure Penelope doesn't go astray," I informed her, and then pulled her mouth to mine as her other paramours gathered around us in the water.

Oh, her lips were sweet, her breath spilling hot over them despite the coolness of the water. Just like that, I realized I didn't care about the others watching, drawing closer around her to envelop her in a joint embrace.

She was mine and she was theirs, and both of those things were perfectly right.

I drew back just enough to speak, my forehead still grazing hers as I put all the determination and admiration I could into my promise.

"You're ours. We won't let you lose yourself, Phoenix."

A HOME FOR SHADOWS
A FLIRTING WITH MONSTERS BONUS EPILOGUE

Sorsha

A WHISTLING NOISE PENETRATED MY SLEEP. IT WASN'T A TOTALLY unexpected sound—the Everymobile had chilled out quite a bit over the years since we'd last taken it through a rift, but various parts still liked to announce their existence to the world in various audible ways at unexpected moments. There wasn't really much to do about it except ignore it. Whatever it was always shut up soon enough.

But getting back to sleep after the RV had so rudely interrupted it wasn't as easy. I mumbled discontentedly into my pillow and rolled onto my side, my arm brushing up against the body resting next to mine.

There was room to roll and brush up against all sorts of bodies thanks to a very welcome magical enhancement my shadowkind men had finally managed to arrange just in time for my thirtieth birthday a few years back. Technically, the bedroom we were in was only about six feet wide. But thanks to the work of some skillful fae, it'd been expanded to twice that size... somehow without taking up any more room in the frame of the RV.

I didn't understand how the magic worked. All that mattered was it did. And we'd filled most of the extra space with a massive bed that could hold both me and all four of my men in relative comfort, when we were so inclined.

The man I'd bumped into had obviously already been awake and inclined toward all sorts of things. Ruse slipped his arm around my waist beneath the blanket and leaned close. His breath sent a wash of heat down my neck along with his chocolatey whisper. "How about I make that rude awakening much more pleasant for you, Miss Blaze?"

I suspected he didn't have anything particularly *polite* in mind, which was fine by me, other than I was still half-asleep and grouchy about that stupid whistling. I let out an inarticulate grumble that amounted to, *Fine, if you really think you can make up for this grave offense.*

The incubus chuckled and ducked down under the covers. His talented hands skimmed over my sparse sleep garments, sliding the loose tank top up so he could cup my breasts unencumbered. As he lapped his tongue around one nipple and sucked it between his lips forcefully enough to bring a gasp to my throat, he tugged down my boxer shorts.

The moment his mouth closed over my clit, the rush of pleasure drowned out any lingering animosity toward the whistling thing. My breath broke with eager panting, my fingers stroking over Ruse's hair and gripping his curved horns the way I knew he liked. He hummed approvingly, the reverberation of the sound carrying through my nether regions to delightful effect, and plundered my goods even more thoroughly.

Our activities didn't go unnoticed by the rest of our bed companions. It was hard to be very stealthy when shadowkind never slept all that deeply, considering they didn't need to sleep at all.

"My peach," Snap murmured in his typically possessive way, though there wasn't a trace of actual jealousy in his tone. He scooted over from where he'd been lying beyond the incubus and claimed my mouth while Ruse continued to work his own against my sex. The flick of the devourer's forked tongue along the seam of my lips had me gasping all over again.

Then a larger form pressed against me from behind. "Would our lady care to be even more satisfied?" Thorn asked in a low rumble.

I growled encouragingly and reached back to urge him on with a squeeze of his massive bicep. As Snap's tongue continued to tangle with mine, the wingéd warrior massaged my breasts. I arched my ass back against the massive bulge of his cock, and he released a groan before bringing his mouth to the crook of my neck.

Ruse shifted under the blanket, giving my slit one last swipe of his tongue. "I can make room," he purred, and focused his attentions on the sensitive nub above that he could spark such incredible sensations in.

I yanked at Thorn's undershorts, and they vanished beneath my fingers. All of my men had picked up Snap's habit of swiftly banishing their clothes when the situation called for it. The wingéd eased my legs farther apart and pressed his thick cock between them, and a full-out moan reverberated from my lungs.

I'd had lots of practice at taking in all my supernatural men could offer, but sweet sugary salutations, having them attending to me together never failed to get my motor running from zero to a hundred in no time at all. I panted and whimpered against Snap's mouth, bucking in between Ruse's lips suckling my clit and Thorn's shaft impaling me, and it was almost shameful how quickly I was a goner.

Only almost, because there's absolutely nothing shameful about the kind of orgasm that whites out your vision and makes fireworks sizzle from the top of your head down to your toes. Don't ever let anyone tell you differently.

Thorn followed me a few thrusts later with a spurt of warmth inside me. He hugged me close, Snap nuzzled my cheek, and Ruse rose up to tuck his head against my belly. As the rush of my release faded, I eased more upright so I could peer over the not-quite-slumbering giant toward the fourth of my lovers—and sort-of husbands, if we were going to count the rings that adorned my fingers that way.

Omen was sitting cross-legged against the headboard in a casual pose, the tip of his tail swaying lightly where it rested on the sheets near his knee. When I caught his gaze, the hellhound shifter arched an eyebrow. "Still haven't gotten your fill?"

His tone was sardonic, but then, it almost always was. A flicker of orange heat danced in his cool blue eyes. I *had* been perfectly sated, thank you, but the sight of his desire roused my own all over again.

It wouldn't do to leave him on the sidelines, now, would it?

I was just about to reach for him to yank him into our tangle of limbs when my phone's ringtone started pealing. That specific ringtone jarred me into action.

"It's Gisele," I said, swinging in the other direction in a search for my phone, which I'd discarded sometime last night in a bit of a haze of fatigue. "She and Bow were supposed to be taking the week off. If she's interrupting that, it's got to be important."

After seeing how well we'd adapted their former ride to our purposes, the equines had ended up letting us keep it permanently. With the savings we'd gradually accumulated from our jobs disrupting the activities of hunters and collectors alike, we'd bought them a new RV for them to re-glitter-fy. Their friend Cori and my bestie Vivi, who'd become increasingly joined at the hip, had gone off adventuring with them.

They'd been driving around the Americas in what they'd dubbed the "Altermobile" since then, giving us a heads up whenever they stumbled on nefarious activities that threatened the shadowkind. Antic and Flint did the same now that they'd gone off roaming on their own too. But last I'd heard, the equines' bunch had been planning on baking their hides for several days on a Miami beach.

Pickle let out a fierce squeak from where he'd been napping under the bed, sounding like he was about to do battle with the pealing device. Snap peeked over the side and snatched the ringing phone from the floor with a triumphant grin.

When he passed it to me, I hit the answer button and yanked it to my ear. "Gisele—hey. What's going on? Is everything okay?"

The unicorn shifter's normally sparkly voice was unusually subdued. *"We're* okay—Bow and me and Cori and Vivi. But there's been an… incident. We're lucky we heard chatter about it before any mortals caught on. I think you should take a look—we can manage to stop anyone from stumbling on the scene for a little while. How soon can you get to Florida?"

We were currently just outside of Charlotte, North Carolina, and our other improvements to the Everymobile had included the engine and other accompaniments to travel way faster than any road vehicle had the right to—plus invisibility so we didn't get noticed by the regular vehicles on the road as we careened around them… or over them, as the case sometimes needed to be.

"Three hours, four tops depending on how the Everymobile cooperates," I said, my heart thumping. "Send us the exact address. We'll leave now."

When I hung up, all four of my men were watching me.

"What has disturbed the equines?" Thorn asked.

I swiped my hand over my face. "I don't know, but Gisele was definitely disturbed—like I've never heard her before. We'd better get down to Florida stat."

The coordinates Gisele sent led us not to Miami proper but to an isolated homestead beyond the outskirts of Palm Beach Gardens, on the edge of some sort of wildlife preserve. We parked the Everymobile next to a tree hung with Spanish moss and stepped out into the humid air to the buzz of a million insects.

I could see how whatever had happened here could have avoided immediate discovery even without the equines using their magical means to divert potential intruders. We hadn't seen another building for at least fifteen minutes before reaching the driveway. Pickle had taken one look at the property from a window and promptly scampered off to burrow into his nest of torn-up towels, which didn't bode well.

The house in front of us looked like a cross between a log cabin and a posh spa resort. Its single story sprawled across a half an acre of land, some of the walls wooden and some smooth stucco. The face next to what appeared to be the front door held several floor-to-ceiling windows, but the farther reaches appeared to have only small panes set deep in their thick frames.

A small, stucco-sided garage stood on the other side of the narrow yard. It was the first outward indication that something was very wrong here. The roof had been crumpled in, the door bowed to the side, and both of the vehicles I could see beyond the threshold had been smashed into the ground.

I stared for a moment, trying to reconcile the sight with my ideas of what was physically possible. From the damage, you'd have thought a five-ton redwood had crashed into the garage and mashed the vehicles as easily as a toddler squishes a banana. But there was no redwood or any other object lying in the wreckage.

Whatever had crushed them had... left.

A shiver ran up my spine. The only being I'd met who might be able to pummel a building like that was Thorn, and I wasn't even sure his immense strength could have battered it quite that thoroughly in one blow, the way it appeared.

Ruse let out a low whistle. "I'm glad we missed this party."

Thorn flexed his brawny arms. "I can meet any threat that comes at us."

Leaves rustled nearby, and I jerked around, alarm clanging through my nerves. But it wasn't an enemy we faced, only two graceful hooved forms trotting toward us.

"Hello," Bow said with a tight smile unlike his usual buoyant energy, contracting his centaur parts to look fully human as he reached us. "You made it here even faster than we thought."

"It sounded urgent," I said, and my pulse hiccupped. "Where are Vivi and Cori? Gisele said they were okay."

Gisele shed her uniform form next to her partner and brushed a few strands of her rainbow-dyed hair away from her doe-ish eyes. "We thought it was safer to park away from here and come back to meet you on foot. They stayed in the Altermobile."

"Safe from what, exactly?" Omen demanded. Even after several years, he didn't have much patience for the equines, who he still considered tourists—if somewhat useful ones at times.

Gisele glanced toward the house. "Whoever did this didn't care about leaving the signs of their presence behind. They're past worrying about mortals realizing something inexplicable happened here. And they're obviously out for blood. It doesn't look like they have any kindness for their fellow shadowkind. They definitely wouldn't give a crap about Vivi."

I swallowed thickly. "Thank you for looking out for her. Why don't you show us what you found?"

Bow beckoned us toward the front of the house. Compared to the garage, it looked strangely untouched. But then, a shadowkind wouldn't *need* to bash up a building to get in. They could slip through the smallest of dark crevices.

They'd destroyed the garage to ensure the people living in this place couldn't use their vehicles to escape.

Someone had already unlocked the door. Bow reached it first, shooting a concerned glance at his partner, but Gisele pranced inside with her chin high, though her jaw was tensed.

As we followed, a rancid scent filled my nose. I stopped, gathering myself before going on, since vomiting all over the place wasn't how I wanted to kick off this investigation.

"From what we understand, it happened just last night," Gisele said quietly. "But you know, the way mortal bodies are, and the heat…" She grimaced.

The humidity clung to my skin as we emerged from the front hall—and found ourselves staring at bodies that weren't mortal at all.

Well, they were mortal in the sense that their life had been severed from them. Shadowkind might be difficult to kill, but it was possibly while they were in physical form. I couldn't even tell what kind these had been from the strewn remains that covered the living room floor, a faint haze of smoke-like blood still steaming off of them.

There'd probably been more to see before. The torn parts were disintegrating into the shadow that'd formed them. I couldn't tell how many beings those pieces had belonged to. This might be the remains of one incredibly large creature or a whole bunch of middling sized ones.

My stomach started to churn.

Snap's eyes widened. "Why would anyone just… break them apart like this?" he said. "The hunters usually catch shadowkind—the collectors just lock them up—even the Company of Light didn't chop beings right up. We haven't seen anyone who treated us like this before." His gaze darted to Gisele. "You said it was other shadowkind who killed them."

"This is a sorcerer's home," Omen said before she could answer. His nostrils flared as he took in more scents than my mostly-human nose could decipher. "They conducted a lot of rituals here." He considered the ravaged body parts with a disgusted curl of his lips. "They must have had a lot of power. They summoned all those pitiful creatures and bound them to their will—bound them to defend the house."

Apparently he could tell it'd been several shadowkind who'd contributed to the mess in the living room. I studied the décor with more care, but there was nothing in sight that would have tipped me off that the inhabitants were sorcerers—other than the presence of several deceased shadowkind who wouldn't have been there otherwise, of course.

Gisele nodded. "Word from the local shadowkind is that it's a long-established family. They've been building up their talents across many generations."

I'd heard about that—the theory that the rituals sorcerers used to control shadowkind affected the conductors of those rituals all the way down to the genetic level, so that they could pass on an inherent ability to their children. And if they kept having children with other sorcerers, each generation would have even more natural talent.

Seeing the carnage before us, I could believe it. I'd rarely heard of sorcerers commanding more than one shadowkind at a time. For this family to have commanded a whole horde of guards—on top of whatever other uses they put additional creatures to…

Ruse grimaced. "This is a bad business. They overstepped, summoned some beastie they couldn't keep a handle on, and it slaughtered them for their trouble. It probably leapt right back through the nearest rift, and they got what they deserved. I'm sorry for the creatures who got caught in the middle of it, but I'm not sure why we'd get involved."

"It's not as simple as that," Gisele said. "It wasn't just one—it was an ambush from several powerful higher shadowkind. The locals sensed them in the area shortly before they struck. And they… they didn't just *slaughter* the sorcerers."

She motioned us onward with a flick of her hand. We picked our way around the disintegrating shadowkind remains through the living room, past a dining room and kitchen, and around a bend into a hall where we stalled in our tracks.

The sorcerers had tried to stage some kind of defense here. A half-drawn chalk circle marked the carpet, a few stray sigils marked around it. Their attempt to either control the shadowkind attacking them or summon reinforcements to protect them had come too late, though.

The broken piece of chalk lay next to an outstretched, blood-drenched hand, which belonged to a body that'd been wrenched open from throat to public bone. The raggedness of that wound and others on the corpse were clearly made by fangs and claws, not any human blade.

Unsurprisingly, the rancid smell was thicker here. I held my arm to my nose, taking in the scene with as much objective distance as I could manage while my heart beat out a frantic rhythm that sounded like a getaway song. I hadn't had the nervous urge to mangle lyrics in ages, not since I'd felt fully in control of my phoenix powers, but now the impulse tickled at the back of my throat. I restrained myself, searching for clues.

There were three bodies in the hall. The one closest to us who'd held the chalk was a woman, her gray hair streaked red with her blood. From that and what I could see of her face, which hadn't taken too much of the beating, I figured she'd been in her fifties.

The man lying near her was noticeably younger, not yet out of his twenties—not that he'd have the chance to get any farther along in his years now. Maybe a son?

The last of the three was a man with hair gone nearly white other than the blood-splattered parts, who I'd guess was her husband and the younger man's father.

The two men had their entire torsos ripped open just like the woman. And Thorn's keen combat-honed eyes spotted something that I hadn't amid all the general gore.

"The attackers tore out their vital organs," he remarked with a business-like air. He must have seen far worse during the epic, savage battles he'd taken part in centuries ago. Although maybe not anything quite along these lines. He frowned. "Lungs, heart, liver, intestines…"

A snarl seeped from Omen's mouth. "This *is* a bad business, twice over. I'm not going to mourn for sorcerers, but the shadowkind who came for them might be no better."

"What do you mean?" I asked.

He sighed. "There's a rumor that's been around since the earliest days of my existence that if you consume the essential bits of a sorcerer, you can absorb some of their powers—the ability to manipulate shadowkind to your bidding." He tipped his head toward Ruse. "You know that whatever persuasive powers we have typically don't work on our fellow shadow beings, only on mortals. It looks like someone's trying to get a leg up on whoever they see as their competition."

"Is it true?" Snap asked with a shudder. "Does it work?"

"I don't know," Omen admitted. "I never met any being who managed to take down more than one or two sorcerers, and not very powerful ones at that. The powerful ones tend to be difficult to destroy, and the less-powerful ones tend to get killed by some beast they summon that doesn't have any designs other than getting free. Bad enough that anyone wants to do it, though."

Thorn turned to Gisele. "The local beings you spoke to—do they have any idea who or what the attackers were?"

She shook her head. "No one got very close. They were too nervous, and I don't blame them. They weren't beings anyone around here was familiar with."

"Hmm." Omen motioned to the doorways beyond the bodies. "Let's hope their delusions of grandeur *are* only delusions, but we may as well look through the entire place in case there's anything else important to see here. Snap, taste what you can and let us know what you find."

Easing around the corpses and puddles of blood was significantly trickier than the shredded shadowkind obstacle course in the living room. The devourer moved even slower than the rest of us, his forked tongue flicking across the walls and the bodies themselves. He shuddered a few more times, his expression tightening.

"I can't tell if they were any kinds of beings I've encountered before," he said apologetically. "At least not the ones who did the killing. But there are a lot I haven't had the chance to meet. They feel very wild and fierce, not much sense of planning. There's a lot of angry feelings, and happiness that they succeeded... It's all kind of muddled with the wildness." He was starting to look a bit green around the gills.

"Maybe not all that thoughtful about it one way or another, then," Omen muttered. "This is the first incident like this we've heard about, right? Maybe it *was* just one offended summoned shadowkind, powerful but not all that bright, and a bunch of friends he got together, and they chowed down on the organs for extra offense."

Snap took another sampling of the older man's essence and cocked his head. "Most of the impressions from the humans are overwhelmed by the attack, but I get the sense... They hid something. Something precious to them that they didn't want the 'monsters' to find. It's... under the floor."

"Intriguing," Ruse drawled.

We poked our heads into each of the rooms in turn, finding a master bedroom, another bedroom that could easily have belonged to the twenty-something guy, a large study that appeared to double as a main ritual room, and a smaller bedroom that looked like it'd have belonged to a young child. The twin bed had several stuffed animals poised on it, and the bookcase held all slim chapter books and easy readers.

"You haven't seen a kid anywhere, have you?" I asked Gisele and Bow.

They shook their heads.

I treaded all across the carpeted floor, but it felt perfectly solid to me. I even peered under the bed. Then a huff of breath from Omen brought me to the last of the rooms that branched off from the hall.

This one was also bedroom-sized, but there was no bed in it. In front of a thick rug, a mahogany table had been set up like a shrine. Candles stood around a collection of items: a bronzed shoe, a teddy bear, a small trophy from a spelling bee, a bracelet of porcelain beads, a framed photograph of a blond girl who looked around ten, and another that showed an entire family of four.

"I guess the other bedroom was hers," I said, motioning to the photograph. "They must have left it the way it was when she was alive."

Thorn had picked up another picture frame from the floor. The glass pane was shattered, the frame empty. "I wonder what was in here?"

Snap leaned down to taste the shards of glass on the floor and must have gotten a different impression. He gave a little cry of victory and yanked at the rug. It slid aside to reveal a slight variation in the floorboards, one of them with a faint notch.

"Here," he said breathlessly. "The thing they hid is here."

Omen pushed in front of me and bent to grasp the board. Not just it but an entire concealed panel lifted up. He flipped it over, and a little squeak emitted from below.

A girl stared up at us. Not the same girl from the picture—this one couldn't have been more than five or six, with dark brown hair framing her wan face. She took us all in from her huddle.

"Are they gone?" she whispered. "Did you come to help us? Are... are Mom and Dad okay?"

My heart sank. The sorcerers had obviously sent her down here hoping the shadowkind who'd attacked wouldn't discover her. Which had worked, but what a horror she was returning to.

My throat constricted, but Thorn dipped his head with all the gravity the moment required. His voice came out steady but gentle.

"I'm afraid they fought fiercely to protect you and lost their lives in the process," he said. "They must have cared a great deal for you. We will do our best to restore you to those who'll continue to look after you."

The girl blinked at him, and then her expression shattered. A sob shook her entire slim frame as tears poured from her eyes.

Before I realized what I was doing, I'd slipped down into the hidey hole with her and wrapped my arms around her. Even though she had no idea who I was, she needed comfort badly enough that she clung to me all the same. As her tears soaked my shirt, my mind tripped back to another little girl who'd been sent away from danger by parents who'd cared more about saving her than themselves.

At least I'd still had Luna. And she'd used her fae magic to ease the worst of my suffering by dimming those horrible memories. My chest still ached with the deepest possible understanding of the emotions that must be gripping this kid right now.

I ran my fingers over her head and conjured the most soothing tone I could manage. "It's horrible. It's okay to be upset. You'll probably be upset for a long time. But for now, we should get you to someone who can help you with that. Do you have grandparents or aunts and uncles—"

She shook her head against me before I could finish the question. "It was just us. Just us—together. We were supposed to stick together." Another sob burst from her throat.

A sinking sensation filled my gut. This girl had just had her entire life torn apart as viciously as the beasts had literally carved open her parents. She had no one to turn to.

She cried for a long while. I suspected my shadowkind companions might have been getting impatient, but I couldn't bear to hurry along in her first bout of grieving. She was owed it.

Finally, her sobs faded into sniffles and her tears ebbed. I helped her out of the hidey hole, Thorn offering a hand for leverage. She stood next to me with one arm tucked around my back, her fingers clutching my shirt. Her gaze roamed over the shadowkind around us and halted on the broken picture frame Thorn had put back on the floor.

"Oh!" she said. "They—They ruined Amalie's thank you letter."

"Amalie?" I said.

The girl pointed to the altar. "My sister. Sort of. She died a few years before Mom and Dad adopted me, so I didn't actually know her. But she saved another girl's life when it happened, and we got a letter thanking Amalie for what she did." Her brow furrowed, and fresh tears gleamed in her eyes. "Why would anyone wreck *that*?"

"I don't know," I admitted. "Look, we should get out of here. We don't know how safe it is. Then we'll figure out what... what to do next. If we go to your room, can you pick out what you want to bring with you? I don't know when you'll be able to come back here."

At least she could collect some of her belongings. I'd never had that chance when the shadowkind sent by the Highest had murdered my parents.

"Okay," the girl said in a small voice.

"Close your eyes and hold your breath," I ordered her, not wanting her to see or smell the full carnage in the hall. She did as I'd told her, and I carried her easily to her own room.

We found a child's suitcase and a backpack in the closet, and the girl filled both of those with clothes, toys, and books between shorter bouts of weeping. I did finally get out of her that her name was Ashley. When she'd grabbed everything she wanted, Thorn hefted both bags and I conveyed her out of the house as quickly as I could.

Outside, Ashley blinked in the sunlight, flinching at the sight of the smashed garage. Then her attention focused on Thorn's crystalline knuckles for the first time, glinting now in the bright afternoon sunlight. She blanched and drew back a step, cringing close to me.

"He—he's a monster," she said in a wobbly voice. Her head jerked around. Her eyes narrowed at Ruse, presumably noticing his horns poking from his dark hair. "And so's he! We have to get away from them. They'll hurt us."

Omen scowled but thankfully refrained from growling. Groping for the right words, I bent down and tugged Ashley around so her gaze came to rest on me instead.

She'd been raised by sorcerers. Of course she thought any shadowkind not under their control was a monster and a threat. And some of them clearly had been. But it was obviously about time she learned that a lot of what her parents had taught her was wrong.

"They're actually called 'shadowkind,'" I told her carefully. "Because they can slip in and out of the shadows. And some of them are mean, just like some people are mean. Some of them are nice too, just like people. I only hang out with the nice ones. They want to help you just like I do, I promise."

I felt it was better not to mention right now that technically I was a shadowkind too. My hybrid nature gave me the benefit of a totally human appearance, no telltale monstrous features.

Ashley's eyebrows drew together. "Mom and Dad said that *all* those beasts want to hurt us. That's why we need to learn how to make them do what we want. They might trick you, but they're still looking for a chance to attack you later."

"I could ease her mind," Ruse suggested, but with a hint of hesitation. I looked up at him, knowing why he hadn't made the suggestion with confidence.

Did I really want him to persuade her to trust us through supernatural means? The idea reminded me of the shadowkind who'd bent my will and made me scamper around at his bidding when I'd been around the same age Ashley was.

Every bone in my body resisted the idea. No. She needed to come to that understanding naturally, because she really understood, not because we'd forced her into it.

"I don't think that'll be necessary," I said, and patted Ashley's shoulder. "But here, let me get you something that might help you feel safer. Come with me."

She stuck close by as I led her over to the Everymobile. We'd attached a compartment at the back to hold my tools that would have disturbed my shadowkind companions if they'd been closer at hand. I opened it up and got out a badge and a little knife.

"Your parents probably told you that shadowkind are weakened by certain metals, right?" I said, and Ashley nodded. "These are made of silver and iron worked together. That way you know you're safe."

I fixed the badge to her shirt where I'd used to wear one regularly and let her curl her fingers around the knife. She studied it and then looked back at the waiting figures. "*You're* not scared of them?"

"Not at all," I said, and bent down so I could speak at a whisper. "Let me tell you a secret: these ones are all big softies underneath. Anything I tell them to do, they'll do. Just try it out. What orders should I give?"

She bit her lip, but a glimmer of mischief lit in her eyes just for a second before her sadness swallowed it up again. "Can you make them bounce around like bunnies?"

"Sure thing." I straightened up and snapped my fingers at my men and the equines. "All right, folks. I want to see your best hopping bunny rabbit impressions."

Omen gave me an incredulous look and Ruse guffawed, but even they recognized that getting the girl's trust mattered more than keeping their dignity around her. They joined the others in hopping around in circles in the yard, Gisele getting into the role with little twitches of her nose and Snap holding up his arms by his head like ears.

A brief giggle burst out of Ashley. It faded with another teary hitch of her breath, but it was a minor victory.

"What do you say?" I asked. "Not so scary, right? Will you come with us and let us find someplace that's safe for you now?"

She sucked in a breath, hesitated, and then gave a quick jerk of her head in acceptance. More tension than I'd realized I was holding in rushed out of me. Smiling down at her with a grateful warmth filling my chest, I took her hand and led her onto the RV.

\#

It was the middle of the afternoon when we pulled up at the edge of a strip mall outside Miami, having parted ways with the equines so they could reunite with Vivi and Cori and continue their beach vacation. We'd only had a hasty breakfast—I figured we should get some food into both us and the kid before we decided what to do with her.

I'd set Ashley up in the second-floor bedroom that used to be Vivi's so she could have some space from the monstrous presences below. On my way up, the cranky step snapped at my toes and another made a farting sound. I glowered at them, abruptly exhausted by the chaos the Everymobile was constantly throwing our way.

I'd been going to ask Ashley what she wanted to eat, but I found her curled up on the bed, her head cradled by her skinny arms, fast asleep. *She* must have been exhausted—I doubted she'd gotten any rest at all while she crouched down in the hidey hole with no idea what had happened to the rest of her family.

For a moment, I just stood there and watched her. She looked so fragile—and really, she was. I'd always had shadowkind resiliency bolstering my human body even when I hadn't known about it. Ashley could count on nothing but her regular human self.

I must have ended up lingering for longer than I'd realized, because Ruse materialized out of the shadows next to me. He caught sight of Ashley's sleeping form and spoke in a low voice. "We can pick out something for her for when she wakes up. I doubt the kid is that picky."

"Yeah," I said, but I couldn't quite convince my legs to move.

The incubus's gaze slid to me. He considered me in silence.

"It's hard for you," he said. "Not knowing what to do for her, how to help her."

I raised my eyebrows at him. "I hope you haven't gone poking around in my head."

The statement had no edge to it—I knew he wouldn't have. He smirked and nudged me with his elbow. "I don't need to. I'm adept at reading body language and expressions too, you know, and I know *you* very well by now." He paused, his expression turning contemplative again. "Or maybe the problem is that you *do* know how you want to help her."

I frowned at him. "What do you mean?" But at the same time, the warmth from before started tickling up through my chest.

Ruse reached to graze his fingers over my cheek. "I think you already know my standard advice. What do you desire? Figure it out and go for it the way you always do. It's all right to find yourself wanting different things than you have before."

The warmth wrapped right around my lungs. Holy mother of mystics, maybe he'd gotten right to the core of it—to the core of me. And not in the usual incubus way.

For a second, I struggled to breathe through a rush of nervous exhilaration. "I don't know… I don't know what's best for her, or me, or any of us."

"Well, I'm with you whatever happens, Miss Blaze. Life never stays the same. I've seen plenty of change over the centuries—that's what keeps our extended existence exciting."

He leaned in to steal a kiss and then tugged me toward the stairs.

I turned over his remarks and the feelings bubbling up inside me as we walked to the cramped living-dining area of the RV. I passed the shower that still spat sand at me on the regular and listened to the chirping of the stove element that'd decided it was actually a bird. The image of the little girl sleeping upstairs stayed in the back of my mind, and the warmth inside me condensed into something solid and sure.

The other men were already gathered around the table—Snap sitting on the bench and Thorn and Omen standing, ready to go off and grab our belated lunch. I was going to delay us a little longer, but I didn't think I could wait to have this discussion.

I scooted onto the bench next to Snap. Pickle promptly jumped onto my lap, with an indignant snort that was probably in response to my refusing to let him go upstairs and make friendly with our new arrival.

I scratched his scaly back and looked around at my men. "I think… I think I want to keep her."

Omen's expression froze in an emotionless mask. Thorn's brow furrowed. Ruse simply smiled in his knowing way while Snap clapped his hands together, beaming at me.

"Really?" the devourer said. "I've always thought—I'm sure you would be good with children—and since we can't really have our own…"

"Would it not put her in more danger than is wise, having her with us in the Everymobile on our missions?" Thorn put in.

I inhaled deeply. "That's—that's the other part. I don't know about all of you. Maybe it's just me. But… we've been traveling around in this thing for more than six years now. And before that, I was moving around regularly too, ever since I was younger than Ashley is. I've never gotten to really ground myself in a place I could confidently call home. I want that. I want to settle down somewhere, to have a home base—in between missions, because of course we're not going to *ignore* the assholes out there."

"There is also the small issue of the girl thinking we're all slavering monsters eager to snack on her," Omen said in an unreadable tone. He didn't often bring out the Ice Cold Bastard these days, and I couldn't even call him exactly *icy* right now, but he was definitely doing an excellent impression of a hunk of marble.

I folded my arms in front of me. "She's *six*. She's hardly had a chance to learn anything. We can teach her not to hate shadowkind, show her that the situation is much more complex than her family said—make her into something better than her parents would have turned her into. Or not, because ultimately it's up to her. But we can at least try."

"Lots of other families could try."

"Yes, but—" I rubbed my mouth, feeling abruptly awkward, and went back to petting Pickle. "I don't want a home only for me. I—Luna saved me when I was younger than that girl is. *She* was my home, enough of one that I turned out reasonably okay. If I can do the same thing for Ashley, make up in even a tiny way for what she's lost… It feels right."

"Yes," Snap said. "How would we find anyone else to take her in who could understand the things she already knows?"

Well, there were the various Shadowkind Defense Fund members I was still in periodic contact with who I could have reached out to, but I didn't have any interest in arguing with Snap. I did tuck my hand around his under the table and shot him a teasingly questioning glance. "You're not going to mind having even more competition for my attention?"

He snorted as if the suggestion were absurd. "I love how much you care about so many people, my peach. It doesn't change that I'll always be your devourer."

A smile stretched across my lips. "Yes, you will be."

"It will still be dangerous, even having her with us in more stable accommodations," Thorn pointed out, but I could tell from the set of his mouth that he was wavering. He was probably more concerned about confirming that this really was the right thing than about anything to do with his own comfort anyway. Very little directly fazed him, after all.

"We've gotten by just fine for years," I said. "If someone comes at us, we can protect her. There's all kinds of danger she could face in any other situation out in the world. At least with us, she's got five powerful protectors on hand."

"That is true." He nodded slowly. "I think this could be a reasonable plan." His expression softened as he held my gaze. "And you do look happier just talking about it, m'lady. I wouldn't want to stand in the way of anything that pleases you so much."

That left just one vote, since I already knew where Ruse stood on the matter.

As I focused on Omen again, I let go of Snap to run my fingers over the four rings the men had given me to signify our commitment to each other. I never doubted that Omen had meant his promise wholeheartedly when he'd offered it and that he'd stick out his commitment through thick and thin… but I couldn't help wondering if that meant he'd simply stew in silence rather than veto something the rest of us were already on board with.

"Well, we can afford it," he said. "My accounts alone would cover any house in the country. Pick out one you like, and it's yours."

I still couldn't tell how he felt about any of this. "Really?" I said. "No further questions or concerns? Not even a snarky remark?"

He glowered at me. "Do you *want* an argument, Phoenix? Because I don't particularly. We can do this. I'm agreeing. Take it."

I definitely didn't want to get into an argument about whether we should argue or not. That would take us nowhere fast. The hellhound had his free will. If he decided to speak up later, he was welcome to.

"All right," I said, grinning around at the others. "Let's get something to eat and then find ourselves a new abode."

Two months later

Vivi stopped on the lawn and swiveled in a slow circle, taking in the entire grounds around the house. "Wow," she said with an awed laugh. "It really is something. Who'd have thought back when we were having teenage sleepovers that you'd end up with digs like this?"

I matched her laughter. "I sure as hell wouldn't have."

It was quite a big lawn, surrounded by thick forest on all sides except where the drive wound through the trees. We'd wanted a place with plenty of privacy so Thorn could stretch his wings and Omen could go for houndish runs without the wrong mortal eyes noticing them.

The house itself wasn't overly extravagant, but it felt perfect for me and my odd assortment of lovers. The three-story Victorian had a bedroom for each of us including Ashley, modestly sized other than the master, which held an immense bed that more often than not I shared—and not always with my men. The poor kid still had nightmares of her parents shoving her into hiding and the sounds of the attack she'd made out afterwards.

The fact that cuddling up next to me kept her fears at bay gave me an unexpected sense of accomplishment.

Other than that, the house had a standard-sized living room, dining room, and kitchen, plus a basement apartment that served as guest quarters. Which was a good thing, because we did have quite a few friends who liked to drop in on us. Vivi and Cori were only the latest to stop by in the month since the house had become officially ours. The lovebirds were enjoying some couple time while the equines touched base with their pals in the shadow realm.

Ashley bounded past us across the grass with Pickle scampering at her heels, flashing us a smile before making a beeline for Snap, who was waiting for her on one of the lawn chairs. She'd come up with a game she never seemed to tire of, handing him an object she'd focused some thought or memory on and then seeing if he could taste what she'd tried to convey.

He flicked his tongue across the bowl she offered now and smiled at her. "Yes, I think chocolate cookies are delicious too."

Ashley clapped her hands together with a squeal of delight. A smile curled my own lips, seeing it. She'd come such a long way from the scared, weeping child we'd found in the hidey hole.

Yes, she still had nightmares. Yes, there was a sadness that still haunted her. But she had plenty of moments of joy now too. Because of us. Because we'd been here for her.

There was a school nearby with a bus service that would pick her up at the end of the drive. For now, we were home schooling her the way her family had until she'd had more time to adjust. I handled most of that task, coaching her in reading, basic math, and the arts, but Ruse pitched in with historical tales he could relate first or at least second-hand, Thorn saw that she kept physically active, and Omen conveyed his knowledge of geography from having spent millennia roaming around the world. Snap had discovered an intense interest in simple scientific experiments that allowed him and our charge to delve into the mysteries of the mortal world together.

"She doesn't seem at all worried about Snap now," Vivi remarked. This visit was the first time she'd met Ashley, but I'd kept her up to date via our regular text and phone conversations.

"Thank all that's wise and whimsical." I let out a light chuckle. "It didn't actually take long for her to shrug off the toxic ideas about all shadowkind being evil. I mean, how could you be around him 24-7 and believe that." I motioned toward the devourer, who was now beaming bright enough to rival the sun.

"And you're happy staying here instead of being on the go?"

"Yeah," I said, with a rush of an exhale. "It's been kind of nice having the chance to just get comfortable somewhere again. We wanted to give her plenty of time to get her bearings before we go anywhere, but I'm sure soon enough we'll be getting called to do our usual duty."

"Well, you know I'm good for babysitting whenever duty does call," Vivi said, bumping her shoulder against mine.

Thorn strode into view, returning from his twice daily patrols of the perimeter. At the sight of him, Ashley leapt up and dashed over. Her voice carried across the lawn.

"Thorn! Thorn! Would you give me one of those flying piggyback rides, *please*?"

The wingéd warrior looked down at the little girl with apparent consternation, but she wasn't fazed by his grim expression anymore. The fact that she'd become at ease enough with him that she wasn't frightened by his wingéd form—or at least, that she appreciated the benefits of his wings enough to disregard the rest—was another sort of victory.

As he fell into negotiations about exactly how long the flying piggyback ride would be, I caught sight of Omen prowling through the shadows beyond the edge of the forest. A small twinge of uneasiness tainted my happiness.

I touched Vivi's arm. "I'll be back in a few minutes. Continue making yourself at home!"

She grinned at me. "Oh, I will."

I hurried across the grass and slipped between the trees. I'd thought I'd need to hustle to catch up with Omen, but he stopped and waited for me to approach. The shadows turned his tawny hair a brown nearly as dark as Ruse's.

"Restless?" I asked him. I still couldn't tell how pleased or not he actually was with our new arrangement. He'd continually refused to respond to my subtle attempts at prodding him.

He shrugged, turning toward the lawn where Thorn was just unfurling his wings. "I do like to stretch my legs now and then."

Maybe it was time for me to kick subtlety to the curb.

I elbowed him in the side. "It isn't so bad, is it? You've seen how well it's worked out. And we've only been off the job for a couple of months. We'll find a new swing of things now that we're settled in."

He glanced at me sideways. "Why do you feel the need to state the obvious, Disaster? Is there some impending catastrophe you're buttering me up in advance of?"

I switched to swatting him. "No. You've just been skulking around being your frequently uncommunicative self, so I got the impression you weren't exactly jumping for joy about our change in lifestyle."

Omen opened his mouth and closed it again, looking briefly annoyed. When he finally spoke, I realized that annoyance was directed more at himself than at me.

"That's not the impression I was trying to give. I…" His gaze shifted to the house again. "I've actually enjoyed this. More than I even expected to. When you first brought up the idea, something in me… I don't know. Maybe there's been some part of me that's felt I don't deserve a real home or this kind of peace."

A lump rose in my throat. I knew how difficult it was for the hellhound shifter to admit to any vulnerability.

I grasped his hand, squeezing his fingers until he turned back to me. "Don't be like that. I know what it's like having you come down hard on me, and it's definitely not fun, so I'd rather you didn't come down on yourself like that either."

The corner of his mouth twitched. "I think I'm starting to get over it."

"Good." The knot in my stomach relaxed. A little playfulness came back into my tone. "It's a change of pace, even if it's a peaceful pace. That's got to stop it from being too boring after all our wild adventures."

Omen let out a huff. The next thing I knew, he was nudging me up against a tree, his solid frame pinning me in place with its houndish heat. His eyes flared as he held my gaze. "There are always plenty of thrills when you're around. And as I've told you, you're stuck with me now."

"Just as long as *you* don't feel stuck," I said, my pulse kicking up a notch in a very enjoyable way.

"Never," he murmured. "There's nowhere in the realms I'd rather be than right here with you." Then he kissed me, hot enough that I felt it all the way down to my toes.

I might have gotten to enjoy a whole lot more of his heat if my phone hadn't rung. Omen drew back with a growl. As I answered, I gave him an apologetic grimace and a smack of his ass that promised more fun later.

Antic's squeaky voice carried through the line. "Sorsha! How are you?"

"I'm good, Antic," I said dryly. "What's up?" The imp didn't tend to get straight to the point unless you aimed her at it.

"Oh, there's something you'll want to check out here in Omaha when you're ready. I found a whole ring of hunters working together! I dodged them no problem, but they've been scooping up a lot of other shadowkind. Real meanies. When do you think you can come lay down the law?"

"I'll have to see," I said, glancing toward the lawn where Thorn had brought Ashley back to earth after a quick ride. The joy beaming from her face unwound even more of the tension inside me. "It could be soon. Send me all the details."

"You bet!"

Omen studied me as I hung up. "New job?"

"A hunter syndicate in Omaha," I said. Anticipation tingled under my skin. I definitely wasn't ready to become a total homebody. I tugged him with me toward the house. "They're going to find out how far from domesticated we are."

Ruse had come out to chat with Vivi. I shot him a smile and tapped my bestie on the shoulder. "You know, I might need to take you up on that babysitting offer sooner rather than later."

Ashley came jogging over, her face flushed. "What? Are you going somewhere?"

The wobble in her voice choked me up all over again. I knelt down and beckoned her over.

"Not until you're ready," I promised. "There are some bad people like I told you about before who we need to stop, but it doesn't have to be right away. When we do go, it'll only be for a few days, and Aunt Vivi will hang out with you and make sure everything's fine here. But it's up to you when you're all right with that."

"Okay," Ashley said. "Not *right* now, but... that might be kind of fun soon. As long as you come back."

"We'll always come back," I said firmly.

Without warning, she threw her arms around me. I hugged her back, leaning into her childish embrace. When I closed my eyes, I could feel an echo of Luna's presence rippling through me, as if she were hugging Ashley alongside me like she'd hugged *me* so many times when I'd needed it.

This was what I hadn't known I needed. The squeeze of Ashley's skinny arms made this place completely home.

ABOUT THE AUTHOR

Eva Chase lives in Canada with her family. She loves stories both swoony and supernatural, and strong women and the men who appreciate them. Along with the Flirting with Monsters series, she is the author of the Gang of Ghouls series, the Bound to the Fae series, the Cursed Studies trilogy, the Royals of Villain Academy series, the Moriarty's Men series, the Looking Glass Curse trilogy, the Their Dark Valkyrie series, the Witch's Consorts series, the Dragon Shifter's Mates series, the Demons of Fame Romance series, the Legends Reborn trilogy, and the Alpha Project Psychic Romance series.

Connect with Eva online:
www.evachase.com
eva@evachase.com

Milton Keynes UK
Ingram Content Group UK Ltd.
UKHW010609110724
445144UK00020B/76/J

9 781990 338458